Also by Ann Beattie

ANN BEATTIE

THE
NEW
YORKER
STORIES

Scribner

New York London Toronto Sydney

Scribner
A Division of Simon & Schuster, Inc.
1230 Avenue of the Americas
New York, NY 10020

First Scribner hardcover edition November 2010

SCRIBNER and design are registered trademarks of The Gale Group, Inc., used
under license by Simon & Schuster, Inc., the publisher of this work.

For information about special discounts for bulk purchases, please contact
Simon & Schuster Special Sales at 1-866-506-1949 or business@simonandschuster.com.

The Simon & Schuster Speakers Bureau can bring authors to your live event.
For more information or to book an event contact the Simon & Schuster Speakers Bureau
at 1-866-248-3049 or visit our website at www.simonspeakers.com.

Manufactured in the United States of America

1   3   5   7   9   10   8   6   4   2

Library of Congress Control Number: 2010032933

ISBN 978-1-4391-6874-5
ISBN 978-1-4391-6876-9 (ebook)

For Lincoln

Contents

CONTENTS ◆ ix

THE
NEW
YORKER
STORIES

A Platonic Relationship

When Ellen was told that she would be hired as a music teacher at the high school, she decided that it did not mean that she would have to look like the other people on the faculty. She would tuck her hair neatly behind her ears, instead of letting it fall free, schoolgirlishly. She had met some of the teachers when she went for her interview, and they all seemed to look like what she was trying to get away from—suburbanites at a shopping center. Casual and airy, the fashion magazines would call it. At least, that's what they would have called it back when she still read them, when she lived in Chevy Chase and wore her hair long, falling free, the way it had fallen in her high-school graduation picture. "Your lovely face," her mother used to say, "and all covered by hair." Her graduation picture was still on display in her parents' house, next to a picture of her on her first birthday.

It didn't matter how Ellen looked now; the students laughed at her behind her back. They laughed behind all the teachers' backs. They don't like me, Ellen thought, and she didn't want to go to school. She forced herself to go, because she needed the job. She had worked hard to get away from her lawyer husband and almost-paid-for house. She had doggedly taken night classes at Georgetown University for two years, leaving the dishes after dinner and always expecting a fight. Her husband loaded them into the dishwasher—no fight. Finally, when she was ready to leave, she had to start the fight herself. There is a better world, she told him. "Teaching at the high school?" he asked. In the end, though, he had helped her find a place to live—an older house, on a side street off Florida Avenue, with splintery floors that had to be covered with rugs, and walls that needed to be repapered but that she never repapered. He hadn't made trouble for her. Instead, he made her look silly. He made her say that teaching high school was a better world.

She saw the foolishness of her statement, however, and after she left him she began to read great numbers of newspapers and magazines, and then more and more radical newspapers and magazines. She had dinner with her husband several months after she had left him, at their old house. During dinner, she stated several ideas of importance, without citing her source. He listened carefully, crossing his knees and nodding attentively—the pose he always assumed with his clients. The only time during the evening she had thought he might start a fight was when she told him she was living with a man—a student, twelve years younger than she. An odd expression came across his face. In retrospect, she realized that he must have been truly puzzled. She quickly told him that the relationship was platonic.

What Ellen told him was the truth. The man, Sam, was a junior at George Washington University. He had been rooming with her sister and brother-in-law, but friction had developed between the two men. Her sister must have expected it. Her sister's husband was very athletic, a pro-football fan who wore a Redskins T-shirt to bed instead of a pajama top, and who had a football autographed by Billy Kilmer on their mantel. Sam was not frail, but one sensed at once that he would always be gentle. He had long brown hair and brown eyes—nothing that would set him apart from a lot of other people. It was his calmness that did that. She invited him to move in after her sister explained the situation; he could help a bit with her rent. Also, although she did not want her husband to know it, she had discovered that she was a little afraid of being alone at night.

When Sam moved in in September, she almost sympathized with her brother-in-law. Sam wasn't obnoxious, but he was strange. She had to pay attention to him, whether she wanted to or not. He was so quiet that she was always conscious of his presence; he never went out, so she felt obliged to offer him coffee or dinner, although he almost always refused. He was also eccentric. Her husband had been eccentric. Often in the evenings he had polished the brass snaps of his briefcase, rubbing them to a high shine, then triumphantly opening and closing them, and then rubbing a little more to remove his thumbprints. Then he would drop the filthy cloth on the sofa, which was upholstered with pale French linen that he himself had selected.

Sam's strange ways were different. Once, he got up in the night to investigate a noise, and Ellen, lying in her room, suddenly realized that he was walking all over the house in the dark, without turning on any lights. It was just mice, he finally announced outside her door, saying it so matter-of-factly that she wasn't even upset by the news. He kept cases of beer in his room. He bought more cases than he drank—more than most people would ever consider drinking over quite a long period. When he did have a beer, he would take one bottle from the case and put it in the refrigerator and wait for it to get cold, and then drink it. If he wanted more, he would go and get another bottle, put it in the refrigerator, wait another hour, and then drink that. One night, Sam asked her if she would like a beer. To be polite, she said yes. He went to his room and took out a bottle and put it in the refrigerator. "It will be cold in a while," he said quietly. Then he sat in a chair across from her and drank his beer and read a magazine. She felt obliged to wait there in the living room until the beer was cold.

One night, her husband came to the house to talk about their divorce— or so he said. Sam was there and offered him a beer. "It will be cold in a while," he said as he put it in the refrigerator. Sam made no move to leave the living room. Her husband seemed incapacitated by Sam's silent presence. Sam acted as if they were his guests, as if he owned the house. He wasn't authoritarian—in fact, he usually didn't speak unless he was spoken to—but he was more comfortable than they were, and that night his offer of cigarettes and beer seemed calculated to put them at ease. As soon as her husband found out that Sam planned to become a lawyer, he seemed to take an interest in him. She liked Sam because she had convinced herself that his ways were more tolerable than her husband's. It became a pleasant evening. Sam brought cashews from his room to go with the beer. They discussed politics. She and her husband told Sam that they were going to get divorced. Sam nodded. Her husband had her to dinner once more before the divorce was final, and he invited Sam, too. Sam came along. They had a pleasant evening.

Things began to go smoothly at her house because of Sam. By Christmas, they were good friends. Sometimes she thought back to the early days of her marriage and remembered how disillusioned she had felt. Her husband had thrown his socks on the bedroom floor at night, and left his pajamas on the bathroom floor in the morning. Sam was like that sometimes. She found clothes scattered on the floor when she cleaned his room—socks and shirts, usually. She noticed that he did not sleep in pajamas. Things bother you less as you get older, she thought.

Ellen cleaned Sam's room because she knew he was studying hard to get into law school; he didn't have time to be fussy. She hadn't intended to pick up after a man again, but it was different this time. Sam was very appreciative when she cleaned. The first time she did it, he brought her flowers the next day, and he thanked her several times, saying that she didn't have to do it. That was it—she knew she didn't have to. But when he thanked her she became more enthusiastic about it, and after a while she began to wax his room as well as dust it; she Windexed the windows, and picked up the little pieces of lint the vacuum had missed. And, in spite of being so busy, Sam did nice things for her. On her birthday, he surprised her with a blue bathrobe. When she was depressed, he cheered her up by saying that any student would like a teacher as pretty as she. She was flattered that he thought her pretty. She began to lighten her hair a little.

He helped her organize her school programs. He had a good ear and he seemed to care about music. Before the Christmas concert for the parents, he suggested that the Hallelujah Chorus be followed by Dunstable's "Sancta Maria." The Christmas program was a triumph; Sam was there, third row center, and he applauded loudly. He believed she could do anything. After the concert, there was a picture in the newspaper of her conducting the singers. She was wearing a long dress that Sam had told her was particularly becoming to her. Sam cut out the picture and tucked it in his mirror. She carefully removed it whenever she cleaned the glass, and then replaced it in the same spot.

As time went on, Sam began to put a six-pack of beer in the refrigerator instead of a bottle at a time. They stayed up late at night on the weekends, talking. He wore the pajamas she had given him; she wore her blue bathrobe. He told her that her hair looked more becoming around her face; she should let it fall free. She protested; she was too old. "How old are you?" he asked, and she told him she was thirty-two. She rearranged her hair. She bought him a sweater-vest to keep him warm. But the colors were too wild, he said, laughing, when he opened the box. No, she insisted—he looked good in bright colors, and anyway the predominant color was navy blue. He wore the sweater-vest so long that finally she had to remind him that it needed to be dry-cleaned. She took it with her one morning when she dropped off her clothes.

Then they began talking almost every night, until very late. She got up in the mornings without enough rest, and rubbed one finger across the dark, puffy circles under her eyes. She asked him how his studies were coming; she was worried that he was not paying enough attention to his schoolwork. He told her everything was all right. "I'm way ahead of the game," he said. But she knew something was wrong. She offered to have his professor to dinner—the one who would write him a recommendation to law school—but Sam refused. It wouldn't be any trouble, she told him. No, he didn't want to impose on her. When she said again that she wanted to do it, he told her to forget it; he didn't care about law school anymore. That night, they stayed up even later. The next day, when she tried to lead the Junior Chorus, she could hardly get out more than a few phrases of "The Impossible Dream" without yawning. The class laughed, and because she hadn't had enough sleep she became angry with them. That night, she told Sam how embarrassed she was about losing her temper, and he reassured her. They drank several beers. She expected Sam to go into his room and get another six-pack, but he didn't rise. "I'm not happy," Sam said to her. She said that he had been working too hard. He waved the thought away. Then perhaps the textbooks were at fault, or his professors weren't communicating their enthusiasm to the class. He shook his head. He told her he hadn't looked at a book for weeks. She became upset. Didn't he want to become a lawyer? Didn't he want to help people? He reminded her that most of the newspapers and magazines she subscribed to pointed out that the country was so messed up that no one could help. They were right, he said. It was useless. The important thing was to know when to give up.

Ellen was restless that night and slept very little. When she left in the morning, she saw that his door was closed. He was not even going through the pretense of going to classes. She would have to do something to help him. He should stay in school. Why should he quit now? Ellen had trouble concentrating that day. Everything the students did irritated her—even the usual requests for pop favorites. She kept control of herself, though. It was not right to yell at them. She let one of the students in Junior Chorus—a girl named Alison, who was taking piano lessons—play the piano, while she sat on her stool, looking out over the blur of faces, joining without enthusiasm in the singing of "Swanee River." Teaching had become meaningless to her. Let her husband vacuum those pastel rugs in their old house; let someone else teach these students. She knew that "Swanee River" was a trivial, silly song, and she wanted three o'clock to come as badly as the students did. When the bell finally rang, she left at once. She bought pastries at a delicatessen, selecting cherry tarts and éclairs. She planned to have a good dinner, and then a discussion in which she would be firm with Sam. She must make him care again. But when she got home Sam wasn't there. He didn't come home until ten o'clock, after she had eaten. She was very relieved when he came in.

"I was at your husband's," he said.

Was this a joke?

"No. He called when you were teaching. He wanted to ask you about some paper. We started talking about law school. He was disappointed that I'd decided not to go. He asked me to come over."

Had he been talked into going to law school?

"No. But your husband is a very nice man. He offered to write me a recommendation."

"Take it!" she said.

"No, it's not worth the hassle. It's not worth all those years of study, competing with punks. What for?"

What was there better to do?

"See the country."

"See the country!" she repeated.

"Get a motorcycle. Go out to the Coast. It's warm there. I'm sick of the cold."

There was nothing she could say. She decided that she was like a mother whose son has just told her he wants to design clothes. Couldn't he do something *serious*? Couldn't he be an architect? But she couldn't say this to him. If he had to go West, couldn't he at least buy a car? He told her it had to be a motorcycle. He wanted to feel the handlebars get warm as he got farther west. She went into the kitchen and got the box of pastries. On the way back to the living room, she clicked the thermostat up two degrees. They drank coffee and ate the éclairs and little tarts. It was a celebration; he was going to do what he was going to do. She said she would go with him on the weekend to look for a motorcycle.

On Monday he left. Just like that, he was gone. He left all his things in his room. After a few days, she realized that it would be practical to store his things in the attic and use his room for a study, but she couldn't touch anything. She continued to take care of the room, but not every day. Sometimes when she felt lonely, she would go in there and look at all his books in the bookcase. Other times, she would clean the house thoroughly at night, with a burst of energy, as if to make ready for his return. One night after she cleaned, she took some bottles of beer to put in the refrigerator, so they would be cool when she came home from work. She did not lose her temper anymore, but her programs were no longer innovative. Alison's piano playing guided the Junior Chorus through the world, sad and weary, through the winter and into the spring.

One night, her husband called (he was her ex-husband now). He was still trying to track down the safe-deposit box where his mother had placed her jewelry. Quite a lot of old pieces were there; there were a few diamonds and some good jade. His mother was old; he didn't want to disturb her, or make her think of dying, and he was embarrassed to let her know he'd misplaced her instructions. She said she would look for the paper and call him back, and he asked if he could come and look with her. She said that would be all right. He came that night, and she offered him a beer. They looked through her file and found nothing. "The paper has to be somewhere," he said, full of professional assurance. "It has to be somewhere." She gestured hopelessly at the rooms of the house; it wasn't in the bathroom or the kitchen or the living room, and it certainly wasn't in Sam's room. He asked how Sam was doing, and she told him she hadn't heard from him. Every day she expected some word from him, but none had come. She didn't tell him that—just that she hadn't heard. She drank several beers, as she did every night. They sat together in the living room, drinking beer. She asked if he would like something to eat, and fixed sandwiches. He said he would go, so she could get up in the morning. She gestured at the rooms of the house. He stayed, and slept in her bed.

In the morning, Ellen called the school and said she had a cold. "Everybody is sick," the switchboard operator told her. "It's the change in the weather." She and her husband took a drive and went to a nice restaurant for lunch. After lunch, they went to his house and hunted for the paper. They couldn't find it. He fixed her dinner, and she stayed at his house that night. In the morning, he dropped her off at school on his way to work.

A girl in Junior Chorus came up to talk to her after class. Shyly, the girl told her she played the piano. Could she also play the piano for the chorus sometime? Alison played very well, the girl said quickly; she didn't want Alison to stop playing, but could she try sometime, too? She could read music well, and she knew some classics and some Gilbert and Sullivan and a lot of popular songs, too. She mentioned some of them. Ellen watched the girl leave, blushing with nervousness at having spoken to the teacher and proud that she would be allowed to play the piano at the next meeting. She was a tall girl, with brown hair that had been cut too short; her glasses, which were harlequin-shape, looked more like something the girl's mother would wear. Ellen wondered if Sam had a girlfriend. If the girlfriend had brown hair, did it get tangled in the wind on the motorcycle? Sam would have been proud of her—the way she put the new pianist at ease, feigning interest in the girl's talent, thanking her for volunteering. The next afternoon, she thought of Sam again. He would have found it funny that the brown-haired girl also chose to play "Swanee River."

Her husband came to her house after work, and they had dinner. She had a postcard from Sam. She showed it to him—a picture of the Santa Monica Freeway, clogged with cars. The message read, "The small speck between the red and the yellow car is me, doing 110. Love, Sam." There were no specks between cars, which were themselves only specks in the picture, but Ellen looked and smiled anyway.

The next week there was another postcard—a scowling Indian—which had been mailed to her husband. Sam thanked him for the talk they had before he left. He closed with some advice: "Come West. It's warm and it's beautiful. How do you know until you try? Peace, Sam."

Later that week, while they were on their way to buy groceries, a couple on a motorcycle came out of nowhere and swerved in front of their car, going much too fast.

"Crazy son of a bitch!" her husband said, hitting the brakes.

The girl on the motorcycle looked back, probably to assure herself that they really had got through safely. The girl was smiling. Actually, the girl was too far away for Ellen to see her expression clearly, but she was certain that she saw a smile.

"Crazy son of a bitch," her husband was saying. Ellen closed her eyes and remembered being in the motorcycle shop with Sam, looking at the machines.

"I want one that will do a hundred with no sweat," Sam had said to the salesman.

"All of these will do a hundred easy," the salesman said, smiling at them.

"This one, then," Sam told him, tapping the handlebars of the one he stood by.

He paid for most of it with cash. She hadn't taken any rent money from him for a long time, so he had a lot of cash. He wrote a check to cover the rest of it. The salesman was surprised, counting the bills.

"Do you have streamers?" Sam had asked.

"Streamers?"

"Isn't that what they're called? The things kids have on their bikes?"

The salesman smiled. "We don't carry them. Guess you'd have to go to a bicycle shop."

"I guess I will," Sam said. "I've got to go in style."

Ellen looked at her husband. How can I be so unsympathetic to him, she wondered. She was angry. She should have asked Sam why she felt that way toward her husband sometimes. He would have explained it all to her, patiently, in a late-night talk. There had been no return address on the postcards. Someday he would send his address, and she could still ask him. She could tell him about the new girl who could have played anything she wanted and who selected "Swanee River." In the car, with her eyes closed, she smiled, and ahead of them—miles ahead of them now—so did the girl on the motorcycle.

Fancy Flights

Silas is afraid of the vacuum cleaner. He stands, looking out the bedroom door, growling at it. He also growls when small children are around. The dog is afraid of them, and they are afraid of him because he growls. His growling always gets him in trouble; nobody thinks he is entitled to growl. The dog is also afraid of a lot of music. "One Little Story That the Crow Told Me" by the New Lost City Ramblers raises his hackles. Bob Dylan's "Positively Fourth Street" brings bared teeth and a drooping tail. Sometimes he keeps his teeth bared even through the quiet intervals. If the dog had his way, all small children would disappear, and a lot of musicians would sound their last notes. If the dog had his way, he would get Dylan by the leg in a dark alley. Maybe they could take a trip—Michael and the dog—to a recording studio or a concert hall, wherever Dylan was playing, and wait for him to come out. Then Silas could get him. Thoughts like these ("fancy flights," his foreman called them) were responsible for Michael's no longer having a job.

He had worked in a furniture factory in Ashford, Connecticut. Sometimes when his lathe was churning and grinding, he would start laughing. Everyone was aware of his laughter, but nobody did anything about it. He smoked hash in the parking lot in back of the factory during his break. Toward the end of his shift, he often had to choke back hysteria. One night, the foreman told him a Little Moron joke that was so funny Michael almost fell down laughing. After that, several people who worked there stopped by to tell him jokes, and every time he nearly laughed himself sick. Anybody there who spoke to him made him beam, and if they told a joke, or even if they said they had "a good one," he began to laugh right away. Every day he smoked as much hash as he could stand. He wore a hairnet—everyone had to wear a hairnet, after a woman had her face yanked down to within a fraction of an inch of a blade when a machine caught her hair—and half the time he forgot to take it off after he finished work. He'd find out he was still wearing it in the morning when he woke up. He thought that was pretty funny; he might be somebody's wife, with pink curlers under the net and a cigarette dangling out of his mouth.

He had already been somebody's husband, but he and his wife were separated. He was also separated from his daughter, but she looked so much like his wife that he thought of them as one. Toward the end, he had sometimes got confused and talked baby talk to his wife and complained about his life to his four-and-a-half-year-old daughter. His wife wrote to his grandmother about the way he was acting, and the old woman sent him a hundred dollars and told him to "buy a psychiatrist," as if they were shirts. Instead, he bought his daughter a pink plastic bunny that held a bar of soap and floated in the bath. The bunny had blue eyebrows and a blue nose and an amazed look, probably because its stomach was soap. He had bought her the bunny because he was not ungenerous, and he spent the rest on Fontina cheese for his wife and hash for himself. They had a nice family gathering—his daughter nose-to-nose with the bunny, his wife eating the cheese, he smoking hash. His wife said that his smoking had killed her red-veined maranta. "How can you keep smoking something that killed a plant?" she kept asking. Actually, he was glad to see the maranta dead. It was a creepy plant. It looked as if its veins had blood in them. Smoke hadn't killed the plant, though. A curse that his friend Carlos put on it at his request did it. It died in six days: the leaves turned brown at the tips and barely unfolded in the daytime, and soon it fell over the rim of the pot, where it hung until it turned completely brown.

Plant dead, wife gone, Michael still has his dog and his grandmother, and she can be counted on for words of encouragement, mail-order delicacies, and money. Now that they are alone together, he devotes most of his time to Silas, and takes better care of him than ever before. He gives Silas Milk-Bones so that his teeth will be clean. He always has good intentions, but before he knows it he has smoked some hash and put on "One Little Story That the Crow Told Me," and there is Silas listening to the music, with his clean, white teeth bared.

Michael is living in a house that belongs to some friends named Prudence and Richard. They have gone to Manila. Michael doesn't have to pay any rent—just the heat and electricity bills. Since he never turns a light on, the bill will be small. And on nights when he smokes hash he turns the heat down to fifty-five. He does this gradually—smoke for an hour, turn it from seventy to sixty-five; smoke another hour and put it down to fifty-five. Prudence, he discovers, is interested in acupuncture. There is a picture in one of her books of a man with his face contorted with agony, with a long, thin spike in his back. No. He must be imagining that. Usually Michael doesn't look at the books that are lying around. He goes through Prudence's and Richard's bureau drawers. Richard wears size thirty-two Jockey shorts. Prudence has a little blue barrette for her hair. Michael has even unwrapped some of the food in the freezer. Fish. He thinks about defrosting it and eating it, but then he forgets. He usually eats two cans of Campbell's Vegetarian Vegetable soup for lunch and four Chunky Pecan candy bars for dinner. If he is awake in time for breakfast, he smokes hash.

One evening, the phone rings. Silas gets there first, as usual, but he can't answer it. Poor old Silas. Michael lets him out the door before he answers the phone. He notices that Ray has come calling. Ray is a female German shepherd, named by the next-door neighbor's children. Silas tries to mount Ray.

"Richard?" says the voice on the telephone.

"Yeah. Hi," Michael says.

"Is this Richard?"

"Right."

"It doesn't sound like you, Richard."

"You sound funny, too. What's new?"

"What? You really sound screwed up tonight, Richard."

"Are you in a bad mood or something?" Michael counters.

"Well, I might be surprised that we haven't talked for months, and I call and you just mutter."

"It's the connection."

"Richard, this doesn't *sound* like you."

"This is Richard's mother. I forgot to say that."

"What are you so hostile about, Richard? Are you all right?"

"Of course I am."

"O.K. This is weird. I called to find out what Prudence was going to do about California."

"She's going to go," Michael says.

"You're kidding me."

"No."

"Oh—I guess I picked the wrong time to call. Why don't I call you back tomorrow?"

"O.K.," Michael says. "Bye."

Prudence left exact directions about how to take care of her plants. Michael has it down pretty well by now, but sometimes he just splashes some water on them. These plants moderately damp, those quite damp, some every third day—what does it matter? A few have died, but a few have new leaves. Sometimes Michael feels guilty and he hovers over them, wondering what you do for a plant that is supposed to be moderately dry but is soaking wet. In addition to watering the plants, he tries to do a few other things that will be appreciated. He has rubbed some oil into Prudence's big iron frying pan and has let it sit on the stove. Once, Silas went out and rolled in cow dung and then came in and rolled on the kitchen floor, and Michael was very conscientious about washing that. The same day, he found some chalk in the kitchen cabinet and drew a hopscotch court on the floor and jumped around a little bit. Sometimes he squirts Silas with some of Prudence's Réplique, just to make Silas mad. Silas is the kind of dog who would be offended if a homosexual approached him. Michael thinks of the dog as a displaced person. He is aware that he and the dog get into a lot of clichéd situations—man with dog curled at his side, sitting by fire; dog accepts food from man's hand, licks hand when food is gone. Prudence was reluctant to let the big dog stay in the house. Silas won her over, though. Making fine use of another cliché at the time, Silas curled around her feet and beat his tail on the rug.

"Where's Richard?" Sam asks.

"Richard and Prudence went to Manila."

"Manila? Who are you?"

"I lost my job. I'm watching the house for them."

"Lost your job—"

"Yeah. I don't mind. Who wants to spend his life watching out that his machine doesn't get him?"

"Where were you working?"

"Factory."

Sam doesn't have anything else to say. He was the man on the telephone, and he would like to know why Michael pretended to be Richard on the phone, but he sort of likes Michael and sees that it was a joke.

"That was pretty funny when we talked on the phone," he says. "At least I'm glad to hear she's not in California."

"It's not a bad place," Michael says.

"She has a husband in California. She's better off with Richard."

"I see."

"What do you do here?" Sam asks. "Just watch out for burglars?"

"Water the plants. Stuff like that."

"You really got me good on the phone," Sam says.

"Yeah. Not many people have called."

"You have anything to drink here?" Sam asks.

"I drank all their liquor."

"Like to go out for a beer?" Sam asks.

"Sure."

Sam and Michael go to a bar Michael knows called Happy Jack's. It's a strange place, with "Heat Wave" on the jukebox, along with Tammy Wynette's "Too Far Gone."

"I wouldn't mind passing an evening in the sweet arms of Tammy Wynette, even if she is a redneck," Sam says.

The barmaid puts their empty beer bottles on her tray and walks away.

"She's got big legs," Michael says.

"But she's got nice soft arms," Sam says. "Like Tammy Wynette."

As they talk, Tammy is singing about love and barrooms.

"What do you do?" Michael asks Sam.

"I'm a shoe salesman."

"That doesn't sound like much fun."

"You didn't ask me what I did for fun. You asked me what my job was."

"What do you do for fun?" Michael asks.

"Listen to Tammy Wynette records," Sam says.

"You think about Tammy Wynette a lot."

"I once went out with a girl who looked like Tammy Wynette," Sam says. "She wore a nice low-cut blouse, with white ruffles, and black high-heel shoes."

Michael rubs his hand across his mouth.

"She had downy arms. You know what I mean. They weren't really hairy," Sam says.

"Excuse me," Michael says.

In the bathroom, Michael hopes that Happy Jack isn't drunk anywhere in the bar. When he gets drunk he likes to go into the bathroom and start fights. After a customer has had his face bashed in by Happy Jack, his partners usually explain to the customer that he is crazy. Today, nobody is in the bathroom except an old guy at the washbasin, who isn't washing, though. He is standing there looking in the mirror. Then he sighs deeply.

Michael returns to their table. "What do you say we go back to the house?" he says to Sam.

"Have they got any Tammy Wynette records?"

"I don't know. They might," Michael says.

"O.K.," Sam says.

"How come you wanted to be a shoe salesman?" Michael asks him in the car.

"Are you out of your mind?" Sam says. "I didn't want to be a shoe sales-man."

Michael calls his wife—a mistake. Mary Anne is having trouble in the day-care center. The child wants to quit and stay home and watch television. Since Michael isn't doing anything, his wife says, maybe he could stay home while she works and let Mary Anne have her way, since her maladjustment is obviously caused by Michael's walking out on them when he *knew* the child adored him.

"You just want me to move back," Michael says. "You still like me."

"I don't like you at all. I never make any attempt to get in touch with you, but if you call you'll have to hear what I have to say."

"I just called to say hello, and you started in."

"Well, what did you call for, Michael?"

"I was lonesome."

"I see. You walk out on your wife and daughter, then call because you're lonesome."

"Silas ran away."

"I certainly hope he comes back, since he means so much to you."

"He does," Michael says. "I really love that dog."

"What about Mary Anne?"

"I don't know. I'd like to care, but what you just said didn't make any impression on me."

"Are you in some sensitivity group, or something?"

"No."

"Well, before you hang up, could you think about the situation for a minute and advise me about how to handle it? If I leave her at the day-care center, she has a fit and I have to leave work and get her."

"If I had a car I could go get her."

"That isn't very practical, is it? You don't have a car."

"You wouldn't have one if your father hadn't given it to you."

"That seems a bit off the subject."

"I wouldn't drive a car if I had one. I'm through with machines."

"Michael, I guess I really don't feel like talking to you tonight."

"One thing you could do would be to give her calcium. It's a natural tranquilizer."

"O.K. Thanks very much for the advice. I hope it didn't tax you too much."

"You're very sarcastic to me. How do you expect me to be understanding when all I get is sarcasm?"

"I don't really *expect* it."

"You punch words when you talk."

"Are you stoned, Michael?"

"No, I'm just lonesome. Just sitting around."

"Where are you living?"

"In a house."

"How can you afford that? Your grandmother?"

"I don't want to talk about how I live. Can we change the subject?"

"Can we hang up instead, Michael?"

"Sure," Michael says. "Good night, baby."

Sam and Carlos are visiting Michael. Carlos's father owns a plastics plant in Bridgeport. Carlos can roll a joint in fifteen seconds, which is admirable to Michael's way of thinking. But Carlos can be a drag, too. Right now he is talking to Michael about a job Michael could have in his father's plant.

"No more factories, Carlos," Michael says. "If everybody stopped working, the machines would stop, too."

"I don't see what's so bad about it," Carlos says. "You work the machines for a few hours, then you leave with your money."

"If I ask my grandmother for money she sends it."

"But will she *keep* sending money?" Sam asks.

"You think I'm going to ask her?"

"I'll bet you wouldn't mind working someplace in the South, where the women look like Tammy Wynette."

"North, South—what's the difference?"

"What do you mean, 'What's the difference?' Women in the South must look something like Tammy Wynette, and women up North look like mill rats."

Carlos always has very powerful grass, which Michael enjoys. Carlos claims that he puts a spell on the grass to make it stronger.

"Why don't you put a curse on your father's machines?" Michael says now.

"What for?" Carlos asks.

"Why don't you change all the machines into Tammy Wynettes?" Sam asks. "Everybody would wake up in the morning and there would be a hundred Tammy Wynettes."

Sam realizes that he has smoked too much. The next step, he thinks now, is to stop smoking.

"What do you do?" Carlos asks Sam.

"I sell shoes." Sam notices that he has answered very sanely. "Before that, I was a math major at Antioch."

"Put a curse on that factory, Carlos," Michael says.

Carlos sighs. Everybody smokes his grass and pays no attention to what he says and then they want him to put curses on things all the time.

"What if I put a curse on you?" Carlos asks.

"I'm already cursed," Michael says. "That's what my grandmother says in her letters—that I was such a blessing to the family, but I myself am cursed with ill luck."

"Change me into George Jones," Sam says.

Carlos stares at them as he rolls a joint. He isn't putting a curse on them, but he is considering it. He firmly believes that he is responsible for his god-father's getting intestinal cancer. But he isn't really a magician. He would like his curses to be reliable and perfect, like a machine.

Michael's grandmother has sent him a present—five pounds of shelled pecans. A booklet included with the package says that they are "Burstin' with wholesome Southern goodness." They're the first thing he has eaten for a day and a half, so he eats a lot of them. He thinks that he is eating in too much of a hurry, and he smokes some hash to calm down. Then he eats some more pecans. He listens to Albinoni. He picks out a seed from a pouch of grass that is lying under the couch and buries it in one of Prudence's plants. He will have to remember to have Carlos say a few words over it; Carlos is just humble when he says he can't bless things. He rummages through the grass and finds another seed, plants it in another pot. They'll never grow, he thinks sadly. Albinoni always depresses him. He turns the record off and then is depressed that there is no music playing. He looks over the records, trying to decide. It is hard to decide. He lights his pipe again. Finally, he decides—not on a record but what to eat: Chunky Pecans. He has no Chunky Pecans, but he can just walk down the road to the store and buy some. He counts his change: eighty cents, including the dime he found in Prudence's underwear drawer. He can buy five Chunky Pecans for that. He feels better when he realizes he can have the Chunky Pecans and he relaxes, lighting his pipe. All his clothes are dirty, so he has begun wearing things that Richard left behind. Today he has on a black shirt that is too tight for him, with a rhinestone-studded peacock on the front. He looks at his sparkling chest and dozes off. When he awakens, he decides to go look for Silas. He sprays deodorant under his arms without taking off the shirt and walks outside, carrying his pipe. A big mistake. If the police stopped to question him and found him with that. . . . He goes back to the house, puts the pipe on a table, and goes out again. Thinking about Silas being lost makes him very sad. He knows it's not a good idea to go marching around town in a peacock shirt weeping, but he can't help it. He sees an old lady walking her dog.

"Hello, little dog," he says, stopping to stroke it.

"It's female," the old woman says. The old woman has on an incredible amount of makeup; her eyes are circled with blue—bright blue under the eyes, as well as on top.

"Hello, girl," he says, stroking the dog. "She's thirteen," the old woman says. "The vet says she won't live to see fourteen."

Michael thinks of Silas, who is four.

"He's right, I know," the old woman says.

Michael walks back around the corner and sees Silas on the front lawn. Silas charges him, jumps all over him, barking and running in circles. "Where have you been?" Michael asks the dog. Silas barks. "Hello, Silas. Where have you *been*?" Michael asks. Silas squirms on his back, panting. When Michael stoops to pat him, Silas lunges, pawing the rhinestone-studded shirt and breaking the threads. Rhinestones fall all over the lawn.

Inside, Silas sniffs the rug, runs in and out of rooms. "You old dog," Michael says. He feeds Silas a pecan. Panting, Silas curls up at his feet. Michael pulls the pouch of grass out from under the couch and stuffs a big wad in his pipe. "Good old Silas," Michael says, lighting his pipe. He gets happier and happier as he smokes, but at the height of his happiness he falls asleep. He sleeps until Silas's barking awakens him. Someone is at the door. His wife is standing there.

"Hello, Elsa," he says. She can't possibly hear him above Silas's barking. Michael leads the barking dog into the bedroom and closes the door. He walks back to the door. Elsa has come into the house and shut the door behind her.

"Hi, Elsa," he says.

"Hi. I've come for you."

"What do you mean?"

"May I come in? Is this your house? This can't be your house. Where did you get all the furniture?"

"I'm staying here while some friends are out of town."

"Did you break into somebody's house?"

"I'm watching the place for my friends."

"What's the matter with you? You look horrible."

"I'm not too clean. I forgot to take a shower."

"I don't mean that. I mean your face. What's wrong with you?"

"How did you find me?"

"Carlos."

"Carlos wouldn't talk."

"He did, Michael. But let's argue at home. I've come to get you and make you come home and share the responsibility for Mary Anne."

"I don't want to come home."

"I don't care. If you don't come home, we'll move in here."

"Silas will kill you."

"I know the dog doesn't like me, but he certainly won't kill me."

"I'm supposed to watch these people's house."

"You can come back and check on it."

"I don't want to come with you."

"You look sick, Michael. Have you been sick?"

"I'm not leaving with you, Elsa."

"O.K. We'll come back."

"What do you want me back for?"

"To help me take care of that child. She drives me crazy. Get the dog and come on."

Michael lets Silas out of the bedroom. He picks up his bag of grass and his pipe and what's left of the bag of pecans, and follows Elsa to the door.

"Pecans?" Elsa asks.

"My grandmother sent them to me."

"Isn't that nice. You don't look well, Michael. Do you have a job?"

"No. I don't have a job."

"Carlos can get you a job, you know."

"I'm not working in any factory."

"I'm not asking you to work right away. I just want you in the house during the day with Mary Anne."

"I don't want to hang around with her."

"Well, you can fake it. She's your daughter."

"I know. That doesn't make any impression on me."

"I realize that."

"Maybe she isn't mine," Michael says.

"Do you want to drive, or shall I?" Elsa asks.

Elsa drives. She turns on the radio.

"If you don't love me, why do you want me back?" Michael asks.

"Why do you keep talking about love? I explained to you that I couldn't take care of that child alone anymore."

"You want me back because you love me. Mary Anne isn't that much trouble to you."

"I don't care what you think as long as you're there."

"I can just walk out again, you know."

"You've only walked out twice in seven years."

"The next time, I won't get in touch with Carlos."

"Carlos was trying to help."

"Carlos is evil. He goes around putting curses on things."

"Well, he's your friend, not mine."

"Then why did he talk?"

"I asked him where you were."

"I was on the verge of picking up a barmaid," Michael says.

"I don't know how I could help loving you," Elsa says.

"Where are we going, Daddy?"

"To water plants."

"Where are the plants?"

"Not far from here."

"Where's Mommy?"

"Getting her hair cut. She told you that."

"Why does she want her hair cut?"

"I can't figure her out. I don't understand your mother."

Elsa has gone with a friend to get her hair done. Michael has the car. He is tired of being cooped up watching daytime television with Mary Anne, so he's going to Prudence and Richard's even though he just watered the plants yesterday. Silas is with them, in the back seat. Michael looks at him lovingly in the rearview mirror.

"Where are we going?"

"We just started the ride. Try to enjoy it."

Mary Anne must have heard Elsa tell him not to take the car; she doesn't seem to be enjoying herself.

"What time is it?" Mary Anne asks.

"Three o'clock."

"That's what time school lets out."

"What about it?" Michael asks.

He shouldn't have snapped at her. She was just talking to talk. Since all talk is just a lot of garbage anyway, he shouldn't have discouraged her. He reaches over and pats her knee. She doesn't smile, as he hoped she would. She is sort of like her mother.

"Are you going to get a haircut, too?" she asks.

"Daddy doesn't have to get a haircut, because he isn't trying to get a job."

Mary Anne looks out the window.

"Your great-grandma sends Daddy enough money for him to stay alive. Daddy doesn't want to work."

"Mommy has a job," Mary Anne says. His wife is an apprentice book-binder.

"And you don't have to get your hair cut, either," he says.

"I want it cut."

He reaches over to pat her knee again. "Don't you want long hair, like Daddy?"

"Yes," she says.

"You just said you wanted it cut."

Mary Anne looks out the window.

"Can you see all the plants through that window?" Michael says, pulling up in front of the house.

He is surprised when he opens the door to see Richard there.

"Richard! What are you doing here?"

"I'm so sick from the plane that I can't talk, man. Sit down. Who's this?"

"Did you and Prudence have a good time?"

"Prudence is still in Manila. She wouldn't come back. I just had enough of Manila, you know? But I don't know if the flight back was worth it. The flight back was really awful. Who's this?"

"This is my daughter, Mary Anne. I'm back with my wife now. I've been coming to water the plants."

"Jesus, am I sick," Richard says. "Do you know why I'd feel sick after I've been off the plane for half a day?"

"I want to water the plants," Mary Anne says.

"Go ahead, sweetheart," Richard says. "Jesus—all those damn plants. Manila is a jungle, did you know that? That's what she wants. She wants to be in the jungle. I don't know. I'm too sick to think."

"What can I do for you?"

"Is there any coffee?"

"I drank it all. I drank all your liquor, too."

"That's all right," Richard says. "Prudence thought you'd do worse than that. She thought you'd sell the furniture or burn the place down. She's crazy, over there in that rain jungle."

"His girlfriend is in Manila," Michael says to his daughter. "That's far away."

Mary Anne walks off to sniff a philodendron leaf.

Michael is watching a soap opera. A woman is weeping to another woman that when her gallbladder was taken out Tom was her doctor, and the nurse, who loved Tom, spread *rumors*, and . . .

Mary Anne and a friend are pouring water out of a teapot into little plastic cups. They sip delicately.

"Daddy," Mary Anne says, "can't you make us real tea?"

"Your mother would get mad at me."

"She's not here."

"You'd tell her."

"No, we wouldn't."

"O.K. I'll make it if you promise not to drink it."

Michael goes into the kitchen. The girls are squealing delightedly and the woman on television is weeping hysterically. "Tom was in line for chief of surgery once Dr. Stan retired, but *Rita* said that he . . ."

The phone rings. "Hello?" Michael says.

"Hi," Carlos says. "Still mad?"

"Hi, Carlos," Michael says.

"Still mad?" Carlos asks.

"No."

"What have you been doing?"

"Nothing."

"That's what I figured. Interested in a job?"

"No."

"You mean you're just sitting around there all day?"

"At the moment, I'm giving a tea party."

"Sure," Carlos says. "Would you like to go out for a beer? I could come over after work."

"I don't care," Michael says.

"You sound pretty depressed."

"Why don't you cast a spell and make things better?" Michael says. "There goes the water. Maybe I'll see you later."

"You're not really drinking tea, are you?"

"Yes," Michael says. "Goodbye."

He takes the water into the living room and pours it into Mary Anne's teapot.

"Don't scald yourself," he says, "or we're both screwed."

"Where's the tea bag, Daddy?"

"Oh, yeah." He gets a tea bag from the kitchen and drops it into the pot. "You're young, you're supposed to use your imagination," he says. "But here it is."

"We need something to go with our tea, Daddy."

"You won't eat your dinner."

"Yes, I will."

He goes to the kitchen and gets a bag of M&Ms. "Don't eat too many of these," he says.

"I've got to get out of this town," the woman on television is saying. "You know I've got to go now, because of Tom's dependency on Rita."

Mary Anne carefully pours two tiny cups full of tea.

"We can drink this, can't we, Daddy?"

"I guess so. If it doesn't make you sick."

Michael looks at his daughter and her friend enjoying their tea party. He goes into the bathroom and takes his pipe off the window ledge, closes the door and opens the window, and lights it. He sits on the bathroom floor with his legs crossed, listening to the woman weeping on television. He notices Mary Anne's bunny. Its eyebrows are raised with amazement at him. It is ridiculous to be sitting in the bathroom getting stoned while a tea party is going on and a woman shrieks in the background. "What else can I do?" he whispers to the bunny. He envies the bunny—the way it clutches the bar of soap to its chest. When he hears Elsa come in, he leaves the bathroom and goes into the hall and puts his arms around her, thinking about the bunny and the soap. Mick Jagger sings to him: "All the dreams we held so close seemed to all go up in smoke . . ."

"Elsa," he says, "what are your dreams?"

"That your dealer will die," she says.

"He won't. He's only twenty years old."

"Maybe Carlos will put a curse on him. Carlos killed his godfather, you know."

"Be serious. Tell me one real dream," Michael says.

"I told you."

Michael lets her go and walks into the living room. He looks out the window and sees Carlos's car pull up in front of the walk. He goes out and gets into Carlos's car. He stares down the street.

"Don't feel like saying hello, I take it," Carlos says.

Michael shakes his head.

"Hell," Carlos says, "I don't know what I keep coming around for you for."

Michael's mood is contagious. Carlos starts the car angrily and roars away, throwing a curse on a boxwood at the edge of the lawn.

Wolf Dreams

When Cynthia was seventeen she married Ewell W. G. Peterson. The initials stood for William Gordon; his family called him William, her parents called him W.G. (letting him know that they thought his initials were pretentious), and Cynthia called him Pete, which is what his Army buddies called him. Now she had been divorced from Ewell W. G. Peterson for nine years, and what he had been called was a neutral thing to remember about him. She didn't hate him. Except for his name, she hardly remembered him. At Christmas, he sent her a card signed "Pete," but only for a few years after the divorce, and then they stopped. Her second husband, whom she married when she was twenty-eight, was named Lincoln Divine. They were divorced when she was twenty-nine and a half. No Christmas cards. Now she was going to marry Charlie Pinehurst. Her family hated Charlie—or perhaps just the idea of a third marriage—but what she hated was the way Charlie's name got mixed up in her head with Pete's and Lincoln's. Ewell W. G. Peterson, Lincoln Divine, Charlie Pinehurst, she kept thinking, as if she needed to memorize them. In high school her English teacher had made her memorize poems that made no sense. There was no way you could remember what came next in those poems. She got Ds all through high school, and she didn't like the job she got after she graduated, so she was happy to marry Pete when he asked her, even if it did mean leaving her friends and her family to live on an Army base. She liked it there. Her parents had told her she would never be satisfied with anything; they were surprised when it turned out that she had no complaints about living on the base. She got to know all the wives, and they had a diet club, and she lost twenty pounds, so that she got down to what she weighed when she started high school. She also worked at the local radio station, recording stories and poems—she never knew why they were recorded—and found that she didn't mind literature if she could just read it and not have to think about it. Pete hung around with the men when he had time off; they never really saw much of each other. He accused her of losing weight so she could attract "a khaki lover." "One's not enough for you?" he asked. But when he was around, he didn't want to love her; he'd work out with the barbells in the spare bedroom. Cynthia liked having two bedrooms. She liked the whole house. It was a frame row house with shutters missing downstairs, but it was larger than her parents' house inside. When they moved in, all the Army wives said the same thing—that the bedroom wouldn't be spare for long. But it stayed empty, except for the barbells and some kind of trapeze that Pete hung from the ceiling. It was nice living on the base, though. Sometimes she missed it.

With Lincoln, Cynthia lived in an apartment in Columbus, Ohio. "It's a good thing you live halfway across the country," her father wrote her, "because your mother surely does not want to see that black man, who claims his father was a Cherappy Indian." She never met Lincoln's parents, so she wasn't sure herself about the Indian thing. One of Lincoln's friends, who was always trying to be her lover, told her that Lincoln Divine wasn't even his real name—he had made it up and got his old name legally changed when he was twenty-one. "It's like believing in Santa Claus," the friend told her. "There is no Lincoln Divine."

Charlie was different from Pete and Lincoln. Neither of them paid much attention to her, but Charlie was attentive. During the years, she had regained the twenty pounds she lost when she was first married and added twenty-five more on top of that. She was going to have to get in shape before she married Charlie, even though he wanted to marry her now. "I'll take it as is," Charlie said. "Ready-made can be altered." Charlie was a tailor. He wasn't really a tailor, but his brother had a shop, and to make extra money Charlie did alterations on the weekends. Once, when they were both a little drunk, Cynthia and Charlie vowed to tell each other a dark secret. Cynthia told Charlie she had had an abortion just before she and Pete got divorced. Charlie was really shocked by that. "That's why you got so fat, I guess," he said. "Happens when they fix animals, too." She didn't know what he was talking about, and she didn't want to ask. She'd almost forgotten it herself. Charlie's secret was that he knew how to run a sewing machine. He thought it was "woman's work." She thought that was crazy; she had told him something important, and he had just said he knew how to run a sewing machine.

"We're not going to live in any apartment," Charlie said. "We're going to live in a house." And "You're not going to have to go up and down stairs. We're going to find a split-level." And "It's not going to be any neighborhood that's getting worse. Our neighborhood is going to be getting better." And "You don't have to lose weight. Why don't you marry me now, and we can get a house and start a life together?"

But she wouldn't do it. She was going to lose twenty pounds and save enough money to buy a pretty wedding dress. She had already started using more makeup and letting her hair grow, as the beauty-parlor operator had suggested, so that she could have curls that fell to her shoulders on her wedding day. She'd been reading brides' magazines, and long curls were what she thought was pretty. Charlie hated the magazines. He thought the magazines had told her to lose twenty pounds—that the magazines were responsible for keeping him waiting.

She had nightmares. A recurring nightmare was one in which she stood at the altar with Charlie, wearing a beautiful long dress, but the dress wasn't quite long enough, and everyone could see that she was standing on a scale. What did the scale say? She would wake up peering into the dark and get out of bed and go to the kitchen.

This night, as she dipped potato chips into cheddar-cheese dip, she reread a letter from her mother: "You are not a bad girl, and so I do not know why you would get married three times. Your father does not count that black man as a marriage, but I have got to, and so it is three. That's too many marriages, Cynthia. You are a good girl and know enough now to come home and settle down with your family. We are willing to look out for you, even your dad, and warn you not to make another dreadful mistake." There was no greeting, no signature. The letter had probably been dashed off by her mother when she, too, had insomnia. Cynthia would have to answer the note, but she didn't think her mother would be convinced by anything she could say. If she thought her parents would be convinced she was making the right decision by seeing Charlie, she would have asked him to meet her parents. But her parents liked people who had a lot to say, or who could make them laugh ("break the monotony," her father called it), and Charlie didn't have a lot to say. Charlie was a very serious person. He was also forty years old, and he had never been married. Her parents would want to know why that was. You couldn't please them: they hated people who were divorced and they were suspicious of single people. So she had never suggested to Charlie that he meet her parents. Finally, he suggested it himself. Cynthia thought up excuses, but Charlie saw through them. He thought it was all because he had confessed to her that he sewed. She was ashamed of him—that was the real reason she was putting off the wedding, and why she wouldn't introduce him to her parents. "No," she said. "No, Charlie. No, no, no." And because she had said it so many times, she was convinced. "Then set a date for the wedding," he told her. "You've got to say when." She promised to do that the next time she saw him, but she couldn't think right, and that was because of the notes that her mother wrote her, and because she couldn't get any sleep, and because she got depressed by taking off weight and gaining it right back by eating at night.

As long as she couldn't sleep, and there were only a few potato chips left, which she might as well finish off, she decided to level with herself the same way she and Charlie had the night they told their secrets. She asked herself why she was getting married. Part of the answer was that she didn't like her job. She was a typer—a *typist*, the other girls always said, correcting her—and also she was thirty-two, and if she didn't get married soon she might not find anybody. She and Charlie would live in a house, and she could have a flower garden, and, although they had not discussed it, if she had a baby she wouldn't have to work. It was getting late if she intended to have a baby. There was no point in asking herself more questions. Her head hurt, and she had eaten too much and felt a little sick, and no matter what she thought she knew she was still going to marry Charlie.

Cynthia would marry Charlie on February the tenth. That was what she told Charlie, because she hadn't been able to think of a date and she had to say something, and that was what she would tell her boss, Mr. Greer, when she asked if she could be given her week's vacation then.

"We would like to be married the tenth of February, and, if I could, I'd like to have the next week off."

"I'm looking for that calendar."

"What?"

"Sit down and relax, Cynthia. You can have the week off if that isn't the week when—"

"Mr. Greer, I could change the date of the wedding."

"I'm not asking you to do that. Please sit down while I—"

"Thank you. I don't mind standing."

"Cynthia, let's just say that week is fine."

"Thank you."

"If you like standing, what about having a hot dog with me down at the corner?" he said to Cynthia.

That surprised her. Having lunch with her boss! She could feel the heat of her cheeks. A crazy thought went through her head: Cynthia Greer. It got mixed up right away with Peterson, Divine, and Pinehurst.

At the hot-dog place, they stood side by side, eating hot dogs and french fries.

"It's none of my business," Mr. Greer said to her, "but you don't seem like the most excited bride-to-be. I mean, you do seem excited, but . . ."

Cynthia continued to eat.

"Well?" he asked. "I was just being polite when I said it was none of my business."

"Oh, that's all right. Yes, I'm very happy. I'm going to come back to work after I'm married, if that's what you're thinking."

Mr. Greer was staring at her. She had said something wrong.

"I'm not sure that we'll go on a honeymoon. We're going to buy a house."

"Oh? Been looking at some houses?"

"No. We might look for houses."

"You're very hard to talk to," Mr. Greer said.

"I know. I'm not thinking quickly. I make so many mistakes typing."

A mistake to have told him that. He didn't pick it up.

"February will be a nice time to have off," he said pleasantly.

"I picked February because I'm dieting, and by then I'll have lost weight."

"Oh? My wife is always dieting. She's eating fourteen grapefruit a week on this new diet she's found."

"That's the grapefruit diet."

Mr. Greer laughed.

"What did I do that was funny?"

She sees Mr. Greer is embarrassed. A mistake to have embarrassed him.

"I don't think right when I haven't had eight hours' sleep, and I haven't even had close to that. And on this diet I'm always hungry."

"Are you hungry? Would you like another hot dog?"

"That would be nice," she says.

He orders another hot dog and talks more as she eats.

"Sometimes I think it's best to forget all this dieting," he says. "If so many people are fat, there must be something to it."

"But I'll get fatter and fatter."

"And then what?" he says. "What if you did? Does your fiancé like thin women?"

"He doesn't care if I lose weight or not. He probably wouldn't care."

"Then you've got the perfect man. Eat away."

When she finishes that hot dog, he orders another for her.

"A world full of food, and she eats fourteen grapefruit a week."

"Why don't you tell her not to diet, Mr. Greer?"

"She won't listen to me. She reads those magazines, and I can't do anything."

"Charlie hates those magazines, too. Why do men hate magazines?"

"I don't hate all magazines. I don't hate *Newsweek*."

She tells Charlie that her boss took her to lunch. At first he is impressed. Then he seems let down. Probably he is disappointed that his boss didn't take him to lunch.

"What did you talk about?" Charlie asks.

"Me. He told me I could get fat—that it didn't matter."

"What else did he say?"

"He said his wife is on the grapefruit diet."

"You aren't very talkative. Is everything all right?"

"He said not to marry you."

"What did he mean by that?"

"He said to go home and eat and eat and eat but not to get married. One of the girls said that before she got married he told her the same thing."

"What's that guy up to? He's got no right to say that."

"She got divorced, too."

"What are you trying to tell me?" Charlie says.

"Nothing. I'm just telling you about the lunch. You asked about it."

"Well, I don't understand all this. I'd like to know what's behind it."

Cynthia does not feel that she has understood, either. She feels sleep coming on, and hopes that she will drop off before long. Her second husband, Lincoln, felt that she was incapable of understanding anything. He had a string of Indian beads that he wore under his shirt, and on their wedding night he removed the beads before they went to bed and held them in front of her face and shook them and said, "What's this?" It was the inside of her head, Lincoln told her. She understood that she was being insulted. But why had he married her? She had not understood Lincoln, and, like Charlie, she didn't understand what Mr. Greer was up to. "Memorize," she heard her English teacher saying. "Anyone can memorize." Cynthia began to go over past events. I married Pete and Lincoln and I will marry Charlie. Today I had lunch with Mr. Greer. Mrs. Greer eats grapefruit.

"Well, what are you laughing about?" Charlie asked. "Some private joke with you and Greer, or something?"

Cynthia saw an ad in the newspaper. "Call Crisis Center," it said. "We Care." She thinks that a crisis center is a good idea, but she isn't having a crisis. She just can't sleep. But the idea of it is very good. If I were having a crisis, what would I do? she wonders. She has to answer her mother's note. Another note came today. Now her mother wants to meet Charlie: "As God is my witness, I tried to get through to you, but perhaps I did not say that you would really be welcome at home and do not have to do this foolish thing you are doing. Your dad feels you are never going to find true happiness when you don't spend any time thinking between one husband and the next. I know that love makes us do funny things, but your dad has said to tell you that he feels you do not really love this man, and there is nothing worse than just doing something funny with not even the reason of love driving you. You probably don't want to listen to me, and so I keep these short, but if you should come home alone we would be most glad. If you bring this new man with you, we will also come to the station. Let us at least look him over before you do this thing. Your dad has said that if he had met Lincoln it never would have been."

Cynthia takes out a piece of paper. Instead of writing her mother's name at the top, though, she writes, "If you are still at that high school, I want you to know I am glad to be away from it and you and I have forgotten all those lousy poems you had me memorize for nothing. Sincerely, Cynthia Knight." On another piece of paper she writes, "Are you still in love with me? Do you want to see me again?" She gets another piece of paper and draws two parallel vertical lines with a horizontal line joining them at the bottom—Pete's trapeze. "APE MAN," she prints. She puts the first into an envelope and addresses it to her teacher at the high school. The second is for Lincoln. The next goes to Pete, care of his parents. She doesn't know Lincoln's address, so she rips up that piece of paper and throws it away. This makes her cry. Why is she crying? One of the girls at work says it's the times they are living in. The girl campaigned for George McGovern. Not only that, but she wrote letters against Nixon. Cynthia takes another piece of paper from the box and writes a message to President Nixon: "Some girls in my office won't write you because they say that's crank mail and their names will get put on a list. I don't care if I'm on some list. You're the crank. You've got prices so high I can't eat steak." Cynthia doesn't know what else to say to the President. "Tell your wife she's a stone face," she writes. She addresses the envelope and stamps it and takes the mail to the mailbox before she goes to bed. She begins to think that it's Nixon's fault—all of it. Whatever that means. She is still weeping. Damn you, Nixon, she thinks. Damn you.

Lately, throughout all of this, she hasn't been sleeping with Charlie. When he comes to her apartment, she unbuttons his shirt, rubs her hands across his chest, up and down his chest, and undoes his belt.

She writes more letters. One is to Jean Nidetch, of Weight Watchers.

"What if you got fat again, if you couldn't stop eating?" she writes. "Then you'd lose all your money! You couldn't go out in public or they'd see you! I hope you get fatter and fatter and die." The second letter (a picture, really) is to Charlie—a heart with "Cynthia" in it. That's wrong. She draws another heart and writes "Charlie" in it. The last letter is to a woman she knew when she was married to Pete. "Dear Sandy," she writes. "Sorry I haven't written in so long. I am going to get married the tenth of February. I think I told you that Lincoln and I got divorced. I really wish I had you around to encourage me to lose weight before the wedding! I hope everything is well with your family. The baby must be walking now. Everything is fine with me. Well, got to go. Love, Cynthia."

They are on the train, on the way to visit her parents before the wedding. It is late January. Charlie has spilled some beer on his jacket and has gone to the men's room twice to wash it off, even though she told him he got it all out the first time. He has a tie folded in his jacket pocket. It is a red tie with white dogs on it that she bought for him. She has been buying him presents, to make up for the way she acts toward him sometimes. She has been taking sleeping pills, and now that she's more rested she isn't nervous all the time. That's all it was—no sleep. She even takes half a sleeping pill with her lunch, and that keeps her calm during the day.

"Honey, do you want to go to the other car, where we can have a drink?" Charlie asks her.

Cynthia didn't want Charlie to know she had been taking the pills, so when she had a chance she reached into her handbag and shook out a whole one and swallowed it when he wasn't looking. Now she is pretty groggy.

"I think I'll come down later," she says. She smiles at him.

As he walks down the aisle, she looks at his back. He could be anybody. Just some man on a train. The door closes behind him.

A young man sitting across the aisle from her catches her eye. He has long hair. "Paper?" he says.

He is offering her his paper. She feels her cheeks color, and she takes it, not wanting to offend him. Some people wouldn't mind offending somebody who looks like him, she thinks self-righteously, but you are always polite.

"How far you two headed?" he asks.

"Pavo, Georgia," she says.

"Gonna eat peaches in Georgia?" he asks.

She stares at him.

"I'm just kidding," he says. "My grandparents live in Georgia."

"Do they eat peaches all day?" she asks.

He laughs. She doesn't know what she's done right.

"Why, lordy lands, they do," he says with a thick drawl.

She flips through the paper. There is a comic strip of President Nixon. The President is leaning against a wall, being frisked by a policeman. He is confessing to various sins.

"Great, huh?" the man says, smiling, and leans across the aisle.

"I wrote Nixon a letter," Cynthia says quietly. "I don't know what they'll do. I said all kinds of things."

"You did? Wow. You wrote Nixon?"

"Did you ever write him?"

"Yeah, sure, I write him all the time. Send telegrams. It'll be a while before he's really up against that wall, though."

Cynthia continues to look through the paper. There are full-page ads for records by people she has never heard of, singers she will never hear. The singers look like the young man.

"Are you a musician?" she asks.

"Me? Well, sometimes. I play electric piano. I can play classical piano. I don't do much of it."

"No time?" she says.

"Right. Too many distractions."

He takes a flask out from under his sweater. "If you don't feel like the long walk to join your friend, have a drink with me."

Cynthia accepts the flask, quickly, so no one will see. Once it is in her hands, she doesn't know what else to do but drink from it.

"Where you coming from?" he asks.

"Buffalo."

"Seen the comet?" he asks.

"No. Have you?"

"No," he says. "Some days I don't think there is any comet. Propaganda, maybe."

"If Nixon said there was a comet, then we could be sure there wasn't," she says.

The sound of her own voice is strange to her. The man is smiling. He seems to like talk about Nixon.

"Right," he says. "Beautiful. President issues bulletin comet *will* appear. Then we can all relax and know we're not missing anything."

She doesn't understand what he has said, so she takes another drink. That way, she has no expression.

"I'll drink to that, too," he says, and the flask is back with him.

Because Charlie is apparently going to be in the drinking car for a while, the man, whose name is Peter, comes and sits next to her.

"My first husband was named Pete," she says. "He was in the Army. He didn't know what he was doing."

The man nods, affirming some connection.

He nods. She must have been right.

Peter tells her that he is on his way to see his grandfather, who is recovering from a stroke. "He can't talk. They think he will, but not yet."

"I'm scared to death of getting old," Cynthia says.

"Yeah," Peter says. "But you've got a way to go."

"And then other times I don't care what happens, I just don't care what happens at all."

He nods slowly. "There's plenty happening we're not going to be able to do anything about," he says.

He holds up a little book he has been looking through. It is called *Know What Your Dreams Mean.*

"Ever read these things?" he asks.

"No. Is it good?"

"You know what it is—right? A book that interprets dreams."

"I have a dream," she says, "about being at an altar in a wedding dress, only instead of standing on the floor I'm on a scale."

He laughs and shakes his head. "There's no weird stuff in here. It's all the usual Freudian stuff."

"What do you mean?" she asks.

"Oh—you dream about your teeth crumbling; it means castration. That sort of stuff."

"But what do you think my dream means?" she asks.

"I don't even know if I half believe what I read in the book," he says, tapping it on his knee. He knows he hasn't answered her question. "Maybe the scale means you're weighing the possibilities."

"Of what?"

"Well, you're in a wedding dress, right? You could be weighing the possibilities."

"What will I do?" she says.

He laughs. "I'm no seer. Let's look it up in your horoscope. What are you?"

"Virgo."

"Virgo," he says. "That would figure. Virgos are meticulous. They'd be susceptible to a dream like the one you were talking about."

Peter reads from the book: "Be generous to friends, but don't be taken advantage of. Unexpected windfall may prove less than you expected. Loved one causes problems. Take your time."

He shrugs. He passes her the flask.

It's too vague. She can't really understand it. She sees Lincoln shaking the beads, but it's not her fault this time—it's the horoscope's fault. It doesn't say enough.

"That man I'm with wants to marry me," she confides to Peter. "What should I do?"

He shakes his head and looks out the window. "Don't ask me," he says, a little nervously.

"Do you have any more books?"

"No," he says. "All out."

They ride in silence.

"You could go to a palmist," he says after a while. "They'll tell you what's up."

"A palmist? Really?"

"Well, I don't know. If you believe half they say . . ."

"You don't believe them?"

"Well, I fool around with stuff like this, but I sort of pay attention to what I like and forget what I don't like. The horoscope told me to delay travel yesterday, and I did."

"Why don't you believe them?" Cynthia asks.

"Oh, I think most of them don't know any more than you or me."

"Then let's do it as a game," she says. "I'll ask questions, and you give the answer."

Peter laughs. "O.K.," he says. He lifts her hand from her lap and stares hard at it. He turns it over and examines the other side, frowning.

"Should I marry Charlie?" she whispers.

"I see . . ." he begins. "I see a man. I see a man . . . in the drinking car."

"But what am I going to do?" she whispers. "Should I marry him?"

Peter gazes intently at her palm, then smooths his fingers down hers. "Maybe," he says gravely when he reaches her fingertips.

Delighted with his performance, he cracks up. A woman in the seat in front of them peers over the back of her chair to see what the noise is about. She sees a hippie holding a fat woman's hand and drinking from a flask.

"Coleridge," Peter is saying. "You know—Coleridge, the poet? Well, he says that we don't, for instance, dream about a wolf and then get scared. He says it's that we're scared to begin with, see, and therefore we dream about a wolf."

Cynthia begins to understand, but then she loses it. It is the fault of the sleeping pill and many drinks. In fact, when Charlie comes back, Cynthia is asleep on Peter's shoulder. There is a scene—or as much of a scene as a quiet man like Charlie can make. Charlie is also drunk, which makes him mellow instead of really angry. Eventually, brooding, he sits down across the aisle. Late that night, when the train slows down for the Georgia station, he gazes out the window as if he noticed nothing. Peter helps Cynthia get her bag down. The train has stopped at the station, and Charlie is still sitting, staring out the window at a few lights that shine along the tracks. Without looking at him, without knowing what will happen, Cynthia walks down the aisle. She is the last one off. She is the last one off before the train pulls out, with Charlie still on it.

Her parents watch the train go down the track, looking as if they are visitors from an earlier century, amazed by such a machine. They had expected Charlie, of course, but now they have Cynthia. They were not prepared to be pleasant, and there is a strained silence as the three watch the train disappear.

That night, lying in the bed she slept in as a child, Cynthia can't sleep. She gets up, finally, and sits in the kitchen at the table. What am I trying to think about, she wonders, closing her hands over her face for deeper concentration. It is cold in the kitchen, and she is not so much hungry as empty. Not in the head, she feels like shouting to Lincoln, but in the stomach—somewhere inside. She clasps her hands in front of her, over her stomach. Her eyes are closed. A picture comes to her—a high, white mountain. She isn't on it, or in the picture at all. When she opens her eyes she is looking at the shiny surface of the table. She closes her eyes and sees the snow-covered mountain again—high and white, no trees, just mountain—and she shivers with the coldness of it.

Dwarf House

"Are you happy?" MacDonald says. "Because if you're happy I'll leave you alone."

MacDonald is sitting in a small gray chair, patterned with grayer leaves, talking to his brother, who is standing in a blue chair. MacDonald's brother is four feet, six and three-quarter inches tall, and when he stands in a chair he can look down on MacDonald. MacDonald is twenty-eight years old. His brother, James, is thirty-eight. There was a brother between them, Clem, who died of a rare disease in Panama. There was a sister also, Amy, who flew to Panama to be with her dying brother. She died in the same hospital, one month later, of the same disease. None of the family went to the funeral. Today MacDonald, at his mother's request, is visiting James to find out if he is happy. Of course James is not, but standing in the chair helps, and the twenty-dollar bill that MacDonald slipped into his tiny hand helps too.

"What do you want to live in a dwarf house for?"

"There's a giant here."

"Well, it must just depress the hell out of the giant."

"He's pretty happy."

"Are you?"

"I'm as happy as the giant."

"What do you do all day?"

"Use up the family's money."

"You know I'm not here to accuse you. I'm here to see what I can do."

"She sent you again, didn't she?"

"Yes."

"Is this your lunch hour?"

"Yes."

"Have you eaten? I've got some candy bars in my room."

"Thank you. I'm not hungry."

"Place make you lose your appetite?"

"I do feel nervous. Do you like living here?"

"I like it better than the giant does. He's lost twenty-five pounds. Nobody's supposed to know about that—the official word is fifteen—but I overheard the doctors talking. He's lost twenty-five pounds."

"Is the food bad?"

"Sure. Why else would he lose twenty-five pounds?"

"Do you mind . . . if we don't talk about the giant right now? I'd like to take back some reassurance to Mother."

"Tell her I'm as happy as she is."

"You know she's not happy."

"She knows I'm not, too. Why does she keep sending you?"

"She's concerned about you. She'd like you to live at home. She'd come herself . . ."

"I know. But she gets nervous around freaks."

"I was going to say that she hasn't been going out much. She sent me, though, to see if you wouldn't reconsider."

"I'm not coming home, MacDonald."

"Well, is there anything you'd like from home?"

"They let you have pets here. I'd like a parakeet."

"A bird? Seriously?"

"Yeah. A green parakeet."

"I've never seen a green one."

"Pet stores will dye them any color you ask for."

"Isn't that harmful to them?"

"You want to please the parakeet or me?"

"How did it go?" MacDonald's wife asks.

"That place is a zoo. Well, it's worse than a zoo—it's what it is: a dwarf house."

"Is he happy?"

"I don't know. I didn't really get an answer out of him. There's a giant there who's starving to death, and he says he's happier than the giant. Or maybe he said he was as happy. I can't remember. Have we run out of vermouth?"

"Yes. I forgot to go to the liquor store. I'm sorry."

"That's all right. I don't think a drink would have much effect anyway."

"It might. If I had remembered to go to the liquor store."

"I'm just going to call Mother and get it over with."

"What's that in your pocket?"

"Candy bars. James gave them to me. He felt sorry for me because I'd given up my lunch hour to visit him."

"Your brother is really a very nice person."

"Yeah. He's a dwarf."

"What?"

"I mean that I think of him primarily as a dwarf. I've had to take care of him all my life."

"Your mother took care of him until he moved out of the house."

"Yeah, well, it looks like he found a replacement for her. But you might need a drink before I tell you about it."

"Oh, tell me."

"He's got a little sweetie. He's in love with a woman who lives in the dwarf house. He introduced me. She's three feet eleven. She stood there smiling at my knees."

"That's wonderful that he has a friend."

"Not a friend—a fiancée. He claims that as soon as he's got enough money saved up he's going to marry this other dwarf."

"He is?"

"Isn't there some liquor store that delivers? I've seen liquor trucks in this neighborhood, I think."

His mother lives in a high-ceilinged old house on Newfield Street, in a neighborhood that is gradually being taken over by Puerto Ricans. Her phone has been busy for almost two hours, and MacDonald fears that she, too, may have been taken over by Puerto Ricans. He drives to his mother's house and knocks on the door. It is opened by a Puerto Rican woman, Mrs. Esposito.

"Is my mother all right?" he asks.

"Yes. She's okay."

"May I come in?"

"Oh, I'm sorry."

She steps aside—not that it does much good, because she's so wide that there's still not much room for passage. Mrs. Esposito is wearing a dress that looks like a jungle: tall streaks of green grass going every which way, brown stumps near the hem, flashes of red around her breasts.

"Who were you talking to?" he asks his mother.

"Carlotta was on the phone with her brother, seeing if he'll take her in. Her husband put her out again."

Mrs. Esposito, hearing her husband spoken of, rubs her hands in anguish.

"It took two hours?" MacDonald says good-naturedly, feeling sorry for her. "What was the verdict?"

"He won't," Mrs. Esposito answers.

"I told her she could stay here, but when she told him she was going to do that he went wild and said he didn't want her living just two doors down."

"I don't think he meant it," MacDonald says. "He was probably just drinking again."

"He had joined Alcoholics Anonymous," Mrs. Esposito says. "He didn't drink for two weeks, and he went to every meeting, and one night he came home and said he wanted me out."

MacDonald sits down, nodding nervously. The chair he sits in has a child's chair facing it, which is used as a footstool. When James lived with his mother it was his chair. His mother still keeps his furniture around—a tiny child's glider, a mirror in the hall that is knee-high.

"Did you see James?" his mother asks.

"Yes. He said that he's very happy."

"I know he didn't say that. If I can't rely on you I'll have to go myself, and you know how I cry for days after I see him."

"He said he was pretty happy. He said he didn't think you were."

"Of course I'm not happy. He never calls."

"He likes the place he lives in. He's got other people to talk to now."

"Dwarfs, not people," his mother says. "He's hiding from the real world."

"He didn't have anybody but you to talk to when he lived at home. He's got a new part-time job that he likes better, too, working in a billing department."

"Sending unhappiness to people in the mail," his mother says.

"How are you doing?" he asks.

"As James says, I'm not happy."

"What can I do?" MacDonald asks.

"Go to see him tomorrow and tell him to come home."

"He won't leave. He's in love with somebody there."

"Who? Who does he say he's in love with? Not another social worker?"

"Some woman. I met her. She seems very nice."

"What's her name?"

"I don't remember."

"How tall is she?"

"She's a little shorter than James."

"Shorter than James?"

"Yes. A little shorter."

"What does she want with him?"

"He said they were in love."

"I heard you. I'm asking what she wants with him."

"I don't know. I really don't know. Is that sherry in that bottle? Do you mind . . ."

"I'll get it for you," Mrs. Esposito says.

"Well, who knows what anybody wants from anybody," his mother says. "Real love comes to naught. I loved your father and we had a dwarf."

"You shouldn't blame yourself," MacDonald says. He takes the glass of sherry from Mrs. Esposito.

"I shouldn't? I have to raise a dwarf and take care of him for thirty-eight years and then in my old age he leaves me. Who should I blame for that?"

"James," MacDonald says. "But he didn't mean to offend you."

"I should blame your father," his mother says, as if he hasn't spoken. "But he's dead. Who should I blame for his early death? God?"

His mother does not believe in God. She has not believed in God for thirty-eight years.

"I had to have a dwarf. I wanted grandchildren, and I know you won't give me any because you're afraid you'll produce a dwarf. Clem is dead, and Amy is dead. Bring me some of that sherry, too, Carlotta."

At five o'clock MacDonald calls his wife. "Honey," he says, "I'm going to be tied up in this meeting until seven. I should have called you before."

"That's all right," she says. "Have you eaten?"

"No. I'm in a meeting."

"We can eat when you come home."

"I think I'll grab a sandwich, though. Okay?"

"Okay. I got the parakeet."

"Good. Thank you."

"It's awful. I'll be glad to have it out of here."

"What's so awful about a parakeet?"

"I don't know. The man at the pet store gave me a ferris wheel with it, and a bell on a chain of seeds."

"Oh yeah? Free?"

"Of course. You don't think I'd buy junk like that, do you?"

"I wonder why he gave it to you."

"Oh, who knows. I got gin and vermouth today."

"Good," he says. "Fine. Talk to you later."

MacDonald takes off his tie and puts it in his pocket. At least once a week he goes to a run-down bar across town, telling his wife that he's in a meeting, putting his tie in his pocket. And once a week his wife remarks that she doesn't understand how he can get his tie wrinkled. He takes off his shoes and puts on sneakers, and takes an old brown corduroy jacket off a coat hook behind his desk. His secretary is still in her office. Usually she leaves before five, but whenever he leaves looking like a slob she seems to be there to say good night to him.

"You wonder what's going on, don't you?" MacDonald says to his secretary.

She smiles. Her name is Betty, and she must be in her early thirties. All he really knows about his secretary is that she smiles a lot and that her name is Betty.

"Want to come along for some excitement?" he says.

"Where are you going?"

"I knew you were curious," he says.

Betty smiles.

"Want to come?" he says. "Like to see a little low life?"

"Sure," she says.

They go out to his car, a red Toyota. He hangs his jacket in the back and puts his shoes on the back seat.

"We're going to see a Japanese woman who beats people with figurines," he says.

Betty smiles. "Where are we really going?" she asks.

"You must know that businessmen are basically depraved," MacDonald says. "Don't you assume that I commit bizarre acts after hours?"

"No," Betty says.

"How old are you?" he asks.

"Thirty," she says.

"You're thirty years old and you're not a cynic yet?"

"How old are you?" she asks.

"Twenty-eight," MacDonald says.

"When you're thirty you'll be an optimist all the time," Betty says.

"What makes you optimistic?" he asks.

"I was just kidding. Actually, if I didn't take two kinds of pills, I couldn't smile every morning and evening for you. Remember the day I fell asleep at my desk? The day before I had had an abortion."

MacDonald's stomach feels strange—he wouldn't mind having a couple kinds of pills himself, to get rid of the strange feeling. Betty lights a cigarette, and the smoke doesn't help his stomach. But he had the strange feeling all day, even before Betty spoke. Maybe he has stomach cancer. Maybe he doesn't want to face James again. In the glove compartment there is a jar that Mrs. Esposito gave his mother and that his mother gave him to take to James. One of Mrs. Esposito's relatives sent it to her, at her request. It was made by a doctor in Puerto Rico. Supposedly, it can increase your height if rubbed regularly on the soles of the feet. He feels nervous, knowing that it's in the glove compartment. The way his wife must feel having the parakeet and the ferris wheel sitting around the house. The house. His wife. Betty.

They park in front of a bar with a blue neon sign in the window that says IDEAL CAFÉ. There is a larger neon sign above that that says SCHLITZ. He and Betty sit in a back booth. He orders a pitcher of beer and a double order of spiced shrimp. Tammy Wynette is singing "D-I-V-O-R-C-E" on the jukebox.

"Isn't this place awful?" he says. "But the spiced shrimp are great."

Betty smiles.

"If you don't feel like smiling, don't smile," he says.

"Then all the pills would be for nothing."

"Everything is for nothing," he says.

"If you weren't drinking you could take one of the pills," Betty says. "Then you wouldn't feel that way."

"Did you see *Esquire*?" James asks.

"No," MacDonald says. "Why?"

"Wait here," James says.

MacDonald waits. A dwarf comes into the room and looks under his chair. MacDonald raises his feet.

"Excuse me," the dwarf says. He turns cartwheels to leave the room.

"He used to be with the circus," James says, returning. "He leads us in exercises now."

MacDonald looks at *Esquire*. There has been a convention of dwarfs at the Oakland Hilton, and *Esquire* got pictures of it. Two male dwarfs are leading a delighted female dwarf down a runway. A baseball team of dwarfs. A group picture. Someone named Larry—MacDonald does not look back up at the picture to see which one he is—says, "I haven't had so much fun since I was born." MacDonald turns another page. An article on Daniel Ellsberg.

"Huh," MacDonald says.

"How come *Esquire* didn't know about our dwarf house?" James asks. "They could have come here."

"Listen," MacDonald says, "Mother asked me to bring this to you. I don't mean to insult you, but she made me promise I'd deliver it. You know she's very worried about you."

"What is it?" James asks.

MacDonald gives him the piece of paper that Mrs. Esposito wrote instructions on in English.

"Take it back," James says.

"No. Then I'll have to tell her you refused it."

"Tell her."

"No. She's miserable. I know it's crazy, but just keep it for her sake."

James turns and throws the jar. Bright yellow liquid runs down the wall.

"Tell her not to send you back here either," James says. MacDonald thinks that if James were his size he would have hit him instead of only speaking.

"Come back and hit me if you want," MacDonald hollers. "Stand on the arm of this chair and hit me in the face."

James does not come back. A dwarf in the hallway says to MacDonald, as he is leaving, "It was a good idea to be sarcastic to him."

MacDonald and his wife and mother and Mrs. Esposito stand amid a cluster of dwarfs and one giant waiting for the wedding to begin. James and his bride are being married on the lawn outside the church. They are still inside with the minister. His mother is already weeping. "I wish I had never married your father," she says, and borrows Mrs. Esposito's handkerchief to dry her eyes. Mrs. Esposito is wearing her jungle dress again. On the way over she told MacDonald's wife that her husband had locked her out of the house and that she only had one dress. "It's lucky it was such a pretty one," his wife said, and Mrs. Esposito shyly protested that it wasn't very fancy, though.

The minister and James and his bride come out of the church onto the lawn. The minister is a hippie, or something like a hippie: a tall, white-faced man with stringy blond hair and black motorcycle boots. "Friends," the minister says, "before the happy marriage of these two people, we will release this bird from its cage, symbolic of the new freedom of marriage, and of the ascension of the spirit."

The minister is holding the cage with the parakeet in it.

"MacDonald," his wife whispers, "that's the parakeet. You can't release a pet into the wild."

His mother disapproves of all this. Perhaps her tears are partly disapproval, and not all hatred of his father.

The bird is released: it flies shakily into a tree and disappears into the new spring foliage.

The dwarfs clap and cheer. The minister wraps his arms around himself and spins. In a second the wedding ceremony begins, and just a few minutes later it is over. James kisses the bride, and the dwarfs swarm around them. MacDonald thinks of a piece of Hershey bar he dropped in the woods once

on a camping trip, and how the ants were all over it before he finished lac-
ing his boot. He and his wife step forward, followed by his mother and Mrs.
Esposito. MacDonald sees that the bride is smiling beautifully—a smile no
pills could produce—and that the sun is shining on her hair so that it spar-
kles. She looks small, and bright, and so lovely that MacDonald, on his knees
to kiss her, doesn't want to get up.

Snakes' Shoes

The little girl sat between her Uncle Sam's legs. Alice and Richard, her parents, sat next to them. They were divorced, and Alice had remarried. She was holding a ten-month-old baby. It had been Sam's idea that they all get together again, and now they were sitting on a big flat rock not far out into the pond.

"Look," the little girl said.

They turned and saw a very small snake coming out of a crack between two rocks on the shore.

"It's nothing," Richard said.

"It's a snake," Alice said. "You have to be careful of them. Never touch them."

"Excuse me," Richard said. "Always be careful of everything."

That was what the little girl wanted to hear, because she didn't like the way the snake looked.

"You know what snakes do?" Sam asked her.

"What?" she said.

"They can tuck their tail into their mouth and turn into a hoop."

"Why do they do that?" she asked.

"So they can roll down hills easily."

"Why don't they just walk?"

"They don't have feet. See?" Sam said.

The snake was still; it must have sensed their presence.

"Tell her the truth now," Alice said to Sam.

The little girl looked at her uncle.

"They have feet, but they shed them in the summer," Sam said. "If you ever see tiny shoes in the woods, they belong to the snakes."

"Tell her the truth," Alice said again.

"Imagination is better than reality," Sam said to the little girl.

The little girl patted the baby. She loved all the people who were sitting on the rock. Everybody was happy, except that in the back of their minds the grown-ups thought that their being together again was bizarre. Alice's husband had gone to Germany to look after his father, who was ill. When Sam learned about this, he called Richard, who was his brother. Richard did not think that it was a good idea for the three of them to get together again. Sam called the next day, and Richard told him to stop asking about it. But when Sam called again that night, Richard said sure, what the hell.

They sat on the rock looking at the pond. Earlier in the afternoon a game warden had come by and he let the little girl look at the crows in the trees through his binoculars. She was impressed. Now she said that she wanted a crow.

"I've got a good story about crows," Sam said to her. "I know how they got their name. You see, they all used to be sparrows, and they annoyed the king, so he ordered one of his servants to kill them. The servant didn't want to kill all the sparrows, so he went outside and looked at them and prayed, 'Grow. Grow.' And miraculously they did. The king could never kill anything as big and as grand as a crow, so the king and the birds and the servant were all happy."

"But why are they called crows?" the little girl said.

"Well," Sam said, "long, long ago, a historical linguist heard the story, but he misunderstood what he was told and thought that the servant had said 'crow,' instead of 'grow.'"

"Tell her the truth," Alice said.

"That's the truth," Sam said. "A lot of our vocabulary is twisted around."

"Is that true?" the little girl asked her father.

"Don't ask me," he said.

Back when Richard and Alice were engaged, Sam had tried to talk Richard out of it. He told him that he would be tied down; he said that if Richard hadn't got used to regimentation in the Air Force he wouldn't even consider marriage at twenty-four. He was so convinced that it was a bad idea that he cornered Alice at the engagement party (there were heart-shaped boxes of heart-shaped mints wrapped in paper printed with hearts for everybody to take home) and asked her to back down. At first Alice thought this was amusing. "You make me sound like a vicious dog," she said to Sam. "It's not going to work out," Sam said. "Don't do it." He showed her the little heart he was holding. "Look at these God-damned things," he said.

"They weren't my idea. They were your mother's," Alice said. She walked away. Sam watched her go. She had on a lacy beige dress. Her shoes sparkled. She was very pretty. He wished she would not marry his brother, who had been kicked around all his life—first by their mother, then by the Air Force ("Think of me as you fly into the blue," their mother had written Richard once. Christ!)—and now would be watched over by a wife.

The summer Richard and Alice married, they invited Sam to spend his vacation with them. It was nice that Alice didn't hold grudges. She also didn't hold a grudge against her husband, who burned a hole in an armchair and who tore the mainsail on their sailboat beyond repair by going out on the lake in a storm. She was a very patient woman. Sam found that he liked her. He liked the way she worried about Richard out in a boat in the middle of the storm. After that, Sam spent part of every summer vacation with them, and went to their house every Thanksgiving. Two years ago, just when Sam was convinced that everything was perfect, Richard told him that they were getting divorced. The next day, when Sam was alone with Alice after breakfast, he asked why.

"He burns up all the furniture," she said. "He acts like a madman with that boat. He's swamped her three times this year. I've been seeing someone else."

"Who have you been seeing?"

"No one you know."

"I'm curious, Alice. I just want to know his name."

"Hans."

"Hans. Is he a German?"

"Yes."

"Are you in love with this German?"

"I'm not going to talk about it. Why are you talking to me? Why don't you go sympathize with your brother?"

"He knows about this German?"

"His name is Hans."

"That's a German name," Sam said, and he went outside to find Richard and sympathize with him.

Richard was crouching beside his daughter's flower garden. His daughter was sitting on the grass across from him, talking to her flowers.

"You haven't been bothering Alice, have you?" Richard said.

"Richard, she's seeing a God-damned German," Sam said.

"What does that have to do with anything?"

"What are you talking about?" the little girl asked.

That silenced both of them. They stared at the bright-orange flowers.

"Do you still love her?" Sam asked after his second drink.

They were in a bar, off a boardwalk. After their conversation about the

German, Richard had asked Sam to go for a drive. They had driven thirty or forty miles to this bar, which neither of them had seen before and neither of them liked, although Sam was fascinated by a conversation now taking place between two blond transvestites on the bar stools to his right. He wondered if Richard knew that they weren't really women, but he hadn't been able to think of a way to work it into the conversation, and he started talking about Alice instead.

"I don't know," Richard said. "I think you were right. The Air Force, Mother, marriage—"

"They're not real women," Sam said.

"What?"

Sam thought that Richard had been staring at the two people he had been watching. A mistake on his part; Richard had just been glancing around the bar.

"Those two blondes on the bar stools. They're men."

Richard studied them. "Are you sure?" he said.

"Of course I'm sure. I live in N.Y.C., you know."

"Maybe I'll come live with you. Can I do that?"

"You always said you'd rather die than live in New York."

"Well, are you telling me to kill myself, or is it O.K. if I move in with you?"

"If you want to," Sam said. He shrugged. "There's only one bedroom, you know."

"I've been to your apartment, Sam."

"I just wanted to remind you. You don't seem to be thinking too clearly."

"You're right," Richard said. "A God-damned German."

The barmaid picked up their empty glasses and looked at them.

"This gentleman's wife is in love with another man," Sam said to her.

"I overheard," she said.

"What do you think of that?" Sam asked her.

"Maybe German men aren't as creepy as American men," she said. "Do you want refills?"

After Richard moved in with Sam he began bringing animals into the apartment. He brought back a dog, a cat that stayed through the winter, and a blue parakeet that had been in a very small cage that Richard could not persuade the pet-store owner to replace. The bird flew around the apartment. The cat was wild for it, and Sam was relieved when the cat eventually disappeared. Once, Sam saw a mouse in the kitchen and assumed that it was another of Richard's pets, until he realized that there was no cage for it in the apartment. When Richard came home he said that the mouse was not his. Sam called the exterminator, who refused to come in and spray the apartment because the dog had growled at him. Sam told this to his brother, to make him feel guilty for his irresponsibility. Instead, Richard brought another cat in. He said that it would get the mouse, but not for a while yet—it was only a kitten. Richard fed it cat food off the tip of a spoon.

Richard's daughter came to visit. She loved all the animals—the big mutt that let her brush him, the cat that slept in her lap, the bird that she followed from room to room, talking to it, trying to get it to land on the back of her hand. For Christmas, she gave her father a rabbit. It was a fat white rabbit with one brown ear, and it was kept in a cage on the night table when neither Sam nor Richard was in the apartment to watch it and keep it away from the cat and the dog. Sam said that the only vicious thing Alice ever did was giving her daughter the rabbit to give Richard for Christmas. Eventually the rabbit died of a fever. It cost Sam one hundred and sixty dollars to treat the rabbit's illness; Richard did not have a job, and could not pay anything. Sam kept a book of I.O.U.s. In it he wrote, "Death of rabbit—$160 to vet." When Richard did get a job, he looked over the debt book. "Why couldn't you just have written down the sum?" he asked Sam. "Why did you want to remind me about the rabbit?" He was so upset that he missed the second morning of his new job. "That was inhuman," he said to Sam. " 'Death of rabbit—$160'—that was horrible. The poor rabbit. God damn you." He couldn't get control of himself.

A few weeks later, Sam and Richard's mother died. Alice wrote to Sam, saying that she was sorry. Alice had never liked their mother, but she was fascinated by the woman. She never got over her spending a hundred and twenty-five dollars on paper lanterns for the engagement party. After all these years, she was still thinking about it. "What do you think became of the lanterns after the party?" she wrote in her letter of condolence. It was an odd letter, and it didn't seem that Alice was very happy. Sam even forgave her for the rabbit. He wrote her a long letter, saying that they should all get together. He knew a motel out in the country where they could stay, perhaps for a whole weekend. She wrote back, saying that it sounded like a good idea. The only thing that upset her about it was that his secretary had typed his letter. In her letter to Sam, she pointed out several times that he could have written in longhand. Sam noticed that both Alice and Richard seemed to be raving. Maybe they would get back together.

Now they were all staying at the same motel, in different rooms. Alice and her daughter and the baby were in one room, and Richard and Sam had rooms down the hall. The little girl spent the nights with different people. When Sam bought two pounds of fudge, she said she was going to spend the night with him. The next night, Alice's son had colic, and when Sam looked out his window he saw Richard holding the baby, walking around and around the swimming pool. Alice was asleep. Sam knew this because the little girl left her mother's room when she fell asleep and came looking for him.

"Do you want to take me to the carnival?" she asked.

She was wearing a nightgown with blue bears upside down on it, headed for a crash at the hem.

"The carnival's closed," Sam said. "It's late, you know."

"Isn't anything open?"

"Maybe the doughnut shop. That's open all night. I suppose you want to go there?"

"I love doughnuts," she said.

She rode to the doughnut shop on Sam's shoulders, wrapped in his raincoat. He kept thinking, Ten years ago I would never have believed this. But he believed it now; there was a definite weight on his shoulders, and there were two legs hanging down his chest.

The next afternoon, they sat on the rock again, wrapped in towels after a swim. In the distance, two hippies and an Irish setter, all in bandannas, rowed toward shore from an island.

"I wish I had a dog," the little girl said.

"It just makes you sad when you have to go away from them," her father said.

"I wouldn't leave it."

"You're just a kid. You get dragged all over," her father said. "Did you ever think you'd be here today?"

"It's strange," Alice said.

"It was a good idea," Sam said. "I'm always right."

"You're not always right," the little girl said.

"When have I ever been wrong?"

"You tell stories," she said.

"Your uncle is *imaginative*," Sam corrected.

"Tell me another one," she said to him.

"I can't think of one right now."

"Tell the one about the snakes' shoes."

"Your uncle was kidding about the snakes, you know," Alice said.

"I know," she said. Then she said to Sam, "Are you going to tell another one?"

"I'm not telling stories to people who don't believe them," Sam said.

"Come on," she said.

Sam looked at her. She had bony knees, and her hair was brownish-blond. It didn't lighten in the sunshine like her mother's. She was not going to be as pretty as her mother. He rested his hand on the top of her head.

The clouds were rolling quickly across the sky, and when they moved a certain way it was possible for them to see the moon, full and faint in the sky. The crows were still in the treetops. A fish jumped near the rock, and someone said, "Look," and everyone did—late, but in time to see the circles widening where it had landed.

"What did you marry Hans for?" Richard asked.

"I don't know why I married either of you," Alice said.

"Where did you tell him you were going while he was away?" Richard asked.

"To see my sister."

"How is your sister?" he asked.

She laughed. "Fine, I guess."

"What's funny?" Richard asked.

"Our conversation," she said.

Sam was helping his niece off the rock. "We'll take a walk," he said to her. "I have a long story for you, but it will bore the rest of them."

The little girl's knees stuck out. Sam felt sorry for her. He lifted her on his shoulders and cupped his hands over her knees so he wouldn't have to look at them.

"What's the story?" she said.

"One time," Sam said, "I wrote a book about your mother."

"What was it about?" the little girl asked.

"It was about a little girl who met all sorts of interesting animals—a rabbit who kept showing her his pocket watch, who was very upset because he was late—"

"I know that book," she said. "You didn't write that."

"I did write it. But at the time I was very shy, and I didn't want to admit that I'd written it, so I signed another name to it."

"You're not shy," the little girl said.

Sam continued walking, ducking whenever a branch hung low.

"Do you think there are more snakes?" she asked.

"If there are, they're harmless. They won't hurt you."

"Do they ever hide in trees?"

"No snakes are going to get you," Sam said. "Where was I?"

"You were talking about *Alice in Wonderland*."

"Don't you think I did a good job with that book?" Sam asked.

"You're silly," she said.

It was evening—cool enough for them to wish they had more than two towels to wrap around themselves. The little girl was sitting between her father's legs. A minute before, he had said that she was cold and they should go, but she said that she wasn't and even managed to stop shivering. Alice's son was asleep, squinting. Small black insects clustered on the water in front of the rock. It was their last night there.

"Where will we go?" Richard said.

"How about a seafood restaurant? The motel owner said he could get a babysitter."

Richard shook his head.

"No?" Alice said, disappointed.

"Yes, that would be fine," Richard said. "I was thinking more existentially."

"What does that mean?" the little girl asked.

"It's a word your father made up," Sam said.

"Don't tease her," Alice said.

"I wish I could look through that man's glasses again," the little girl said.

"Here," Sam said, making two circles with the thumb and first finger of each hand. "Look through these."

She leaned over and looked up at the trees through Sam's fingers.

"Much clearer, huh?" Sam said.

"Yes," she said. She liked this game.

"Let me see," Richard said, leaning to look through his brother's fingers.

"Don't forget me," Alice said, and she leaned across Richard to peer through the circles. As she leaned across him, Richard kissed the back of her neck.

Vermont

Noel is in our living room shaking his head. He refused my offer and then David's offer of a drink, but he has had three glasses of water. It is absurd to wonder at such a time when he will get up to go to the bathroom, but I do. I would like to see Noel move; he seems so rigid that I forget to sympathize, forget that he is a real person. "That's not what I want," he said to David when David began sympathizing. Absurd, at such a time, to ask what he does want. I can't remember how it came about that David started bringing glasses of water.

Noel's wife, Susan, has told him that she's been seeing John Stillerman. We live on the first floor, Noel and Susan on the second, John on the eleventh. Interesting that John, on the eleventh, should steal Susan from the second floor. John proposes that they just rearrange—that Susan move up to the eleventh, into the apartment John's wife only recently left, that they just . . . John's wife had a mastectomy last fall, and in the elevator she told Susan that if she was losing what she didn't want to lose, she might as well lose what she did want to lose. She lost John—left him the way popcorn flies out of the bag on the roller coaster. She is living somewhere in the city, but John doesn't know where. John is a museum curator, and last month, after John's picture appeared in a newsmagazine, showing him standing in front of an empty space where a stolen canvas had hung, he got a one-word note from his wife: "Good." He showed the note to David in the elevator. "It was tucked in the back of his wallet—the way all my friends used to carry rubbers in high school," David told me.

"Did you guys know?" Noel asks. A difficult one; of course we didn't *know*, but naturally we guessed. Is Noel able to handle such semantics? David answers vaguely. Noel shakes his head vaguely, accepting David's vague answer. What else will he accept? The move upstairs? For now, another glass of water.

David gives Noel a sweater, hoping, no doubt, to stop his shivering. Noel pulls on the sweater over pajamas patterned with small gray fish. David brings him a raincoat, too. A long white scarf hangs from the pocket. Noel swishes it back and forth listlessly. He gets up and goes to the bathroom.

"Why did she have to tell him when he was in his pajamas?" David whispers.

Noel comes back, looks out the window. "I don't know why I didn't know. I can tell you guys knew."

Noel goes to our front door, opens it, and wanders off down the hallway.

"If he had stayed any longer, he would have said, 'Jeepers,'" David says.

David looks at his watch and sighs. Usually he opens Beth's door on his way to bed, and tiptoes in to admire her. Beth is our daughter. She is five. Some nights, David even leaves a note in her slippers, saying that he loves her. But tonight he's depressed. I follow him into the bedroom, undress, and get into bed. David looks at me sadly, lies down next to me, turns off the light. I want to say something but don't know what to say. I could say, "One of us should have gone with Noel. Do you know your socks are still on? You're going to do to me what Susan did to Noel, aren't you?"

"Did you see his poor miserable pajamas?" David whispers finally. He throws back the covers and gets up and goes back to the living room. I follow, half asleep. David sits in the chair, puts his arms on the armrests, presses his neck against the back of the chair, and moves his feet together. "Zzzz," he says, and his head falls forward.

Back in bed, I lie awake, remembering a day David and I spent in the park last August. David was sitting on the swing next to me, scraping the toes of his tennis shoes in the loose dirt.

"Don't you want to swing?" I said. We had been playing tennis. He had beaten me every game. He always beats me at everything—precision parking, three-dimensional ticktacktoe, soufflés. His soufflés rise as beautifully curved as the moon.

"I don't know how to swing," he said.

I tried to teach him, but he couldn't get his legs to move right. He stood the way I told him, with the board against his behind, gave a little jump to get on, but then he couldn't synchronize his legs. "Pump!" I called, but it didn't mean anything. I might as well have said, "Juggle dishes." I still find it hard to believe there's anything I can do that he can't do.

He got off the swing. "Why do you act like everything is a goddamn contest?" he said, and walked away.

"Because we're always having contests and you always win!" I shouted.

I was still waiting by the swings when he showed up half an hour later.

"Do you consider it a contest when we go scuba diving?" he said.

He had me. It was stupid of me last summer to say how he always snatched the best shells, even when they were closer to me. That made him laugh. He had chased me into a corner, then laughed at me.

I lie in bed now, hating him for that. But don't leave me, I think—don't do what Noel's wife did. I reach across the bed and gently take hold of a little wrinkle in his pajama top. I don't know if I want to yank his pajamas—do something violent—or smooth them. Confused, I take my hand away and turn on the light. David rolls over, throws his arm over his face, groans. I stare at him. In a second he will lower his arm and demand an explanation. Trapped again. I get up and put on my slippers.

"I'm going to get a drink of water," I whisper apologetically.

Later in the month, it happens. I'm sitting on a cushion on the floor, with newspapers spread in front of me, repotting plants. I'm just moving the purple passion plant to a larger pot when David comes in. It is late in the afternoon—late enough to be dark outside. David has been out with Beth. Before the two of them went out, Beth, confused by the sight of soil indoors, crouched down beside me to ask, "Are there ants, Mommy?" I laughed. David never approved of my laughing at her. Later, that will be something he'll mention in court, hoping to get custody: I laugh at her. And when that doesn't work, he'll tell the judge what I said about his snatching all the best seashells.

David comes in, coat still buttoned, blue silk scarf still tied (a Christmas present from Noel, with many apologies for losing the white one), sits on the floor, and says that he's decided to leave. He is speaking very reasonably and quietly. That alarms me. It crosses my mind that he's mad. And Beth isn't with him. He has killed her!

No, no, of course not. I'm mad. Beth is upstairs in her friend's apartment. He ran into Beth's friend and her mother coming into the building. He asked if Beth could stay in their apartment for a few minutes. I'm not convinced: What friend? I'm foolish to feel reassured as soon as he names one—Louisa. I feel nothing but relief. It might be more accurate to say that I feel nothing. I would have felt pain if she were dead, but David says she isn't, so I feel nothing. I reach out and begin stroking the plant's leaves. Soft leaves, sharp points. The plant I'm repotting is a cutting from Noel's big plant that hangs in a silver ice bucket in his window (a wedding gift that he and Susan had never used). I helped him put it in the ice bucket. "What are you going to do with the top?" I asked. He put it on his head and danced around.

"I had an uncle who got drunk and danced with a lampshade on his head," Noel said. "That's an old joke, but how many people have actually *seen* a man dance with a lampshade on his head? My uncle did it every New Year's Eve."

"What the hell are you smiling about?" David says. "Are you listening to me?"

I nod and start to cry. It will be a long time before I realize that David makes me sad and Noel makes me happy.

Noel sympathizes with me. He tells me that David is a fool; he is better off without Susan, and I will be better off without David. Noel calls or visits me in my new apartment almost every night. Last night he suggested that I get a babysitter for tonight, so he could take me to dinner. He tries very hard to make me happy. He brings expensive wine when we eat in my apartment and offers to buy it in restaurants when we eat out. Beth prefers it when we eat in; that way, she can have both Noel and the toy that Noel inevitably brings. Her favorite toy, so far, is a handsome red tugboat pulling three barges, attached to one another by string. Noel bends over, almost doubled in half, to move them across the rug, whistling and calling orders to the imaginary crew. He does not just bring gifts to Beth and me. He has bought himself a new car, and pretends that this is for Beth and me. ("Comfortable seats?" he asks me. "That's a nice big window back there to wave out of," he says to Beth.) It is silly to pretend that he got the car for the three of us. And if he did, why was he too cheap to have a radio installed, when he knows I love music? Not only that but he's bowlegged. I am ashamed of myself for thinking bad things about Noel. He tries so hard to keep us cheerful. He can't help the odd angle of his thighs. Feeling sorry for him, I decided that a cheap dinner was good enough for tonight. I said that I wanted to go to a Chinese restaurant.

At the restaurant I eat shrimp in black bean sauce and drink a Heineken's and think that I've never tasted anything so delicious. The waiter brings two fortune cookies. We open them; the fortunes make no sense. Noel summons the waiter for the bill. With it come more fortune cookies—four this time. They are no good, either: talk of travel and money. Noel says, "What bloody rot." He is wearing a gray vest and a white shirt. I peek around the table without his noticing and see that he's wearing gray wool slacks. Lately it has been very important for me to be able to see everything. Whenever Noel pulls the boats out of sight, into another room, I move as quickly as Beth to watch what's going on.

Standing behind Noel at the cash register, I see that it has started to rain—a mixture of rain and snow.

"You know how you can tell a Chinese restaurant from any other?" Noel asks, pushing open the door. "Even when it's raining, the cats still run for the street."

I shake my head in disgust.

Noel stretches the skin at the corners of his eyes. "Sorry for honorable joke," he says.

We run for the car. He grabs the belt of my coat, catches me, and half lifts me with one arm, running along with me dangling at his side, giggling. Our wool coats stink. He opens my car door, runs around, and pulls his open. He's done it again; he has made me laugh.

We start home.

We are in heavy traffic, and Noel drives very slowly, protecting his new car.

"How old are you?" I ask.

"Thirty-six," Noel says.

"I'm twenty-seven," I say.

"So what?" he says. He says it pleasantly.

"I just didn't know how old you were."

"Mentally, I'm neck and neck with Beth," he says.

I'm soaking wet, and I want to get home to put on dry clothes. I look at him inching through traffic, and I remember the way his face looked that night he sat in the living room with David and me.

"Rain always puts you in a bad mood, doesn't it?" he says. He turns the windshield wipers on high. Rubber squeaks against glass.

"I see myself dead in it," I say.

"You see yourself dead in it?"

Noel does not read novels. He reads *Moneysworth*, the *Wall Street Journal*, *Commentary*. I reprimand myself; there must be fitting ironies in the *Wall Street Journal*.

"Are you kidding?" Noel says. "You seemed to be enjoying yourself at dinner. It was a good dinner, wasn't it?"

"I make you nervous, don't I?" I say.

"No. You don't make me nervous."

Rain splashes under the car, drums on the roof. We ride on for blocks and blocks. It is too quiet; I wish there were a radio. The rain on the roof is monotonous, the collar of my coat is wet and cold. At last we are home. Noel parks the car and comes around to my door and opens it. I get out. Noel pulls me close, squeezes me hard. When I was a little girl, I once squeezed a doll to my chest in an antique shop, and when I took it away the eyes had popped off. An unpleasant memory. With my arms around Noel, I feel the cold rain hitting my hands and wrists.

A man running down the sidewalk with a small dog in his arms and a big black umbrella over him calls, "Your lights are on!"

It is almost a year later—Christmas—and we are visiting Noel's crazy sister, Juliette. After going with Noel for so long, I am considered one of the family. Juliette phones before every occasion, saying, "You're one of the family. Of course you don't need an invitation." I should appreciate it, but she's always drunk when she calls, and usually she starts to cry and says she wishes Christmas and Thanksgiving didn't exist. Jeanette, his other sister, is very nice, but she lives in Colorado. Juliette lives in New Jersey. Here we are in Bayonne, New Jersey, coming in through the front door—Noel holding Beth, me carrying a pumpkin pie. I tried to sniff the pie aroma on the way from Noel's apartment to his sister's house, but it had no smell. Or else I'm getting another cold. I sucked chewable vitamin C tablets in the car, and now I smell of oranges. Noel's mother is in the living room, crocheting. Better, at least, than David's mother, who was always discoursing about Andrew Wyeth. I remember with satisfaction that the last time I saw her I said, "It's a simple fact that Edward Hopper was better."

Juliette: long, whitish-blond hair tucked in back of her pink ears, spikeheel shoes that she orders from Frederick's of Hollywood, dresses that show her cleavage. Noel and I are silently wondering if her husband will be here. At Thanksgiving he showed up just as we were starting dinner, with a blackhaired woman who wore a dress with a plunging neckline. Juliette's breasts faced the black-haired woman's breasts across the table (tablecloth crocheted by Noel's mother). Noel doesn't like me to criticize Juliette. He thinks positively. His other sister is a musician. She has a husband and a Weimaraner and two rare birds that live in a birdcage built by her husband. They have a lot of money and they ski. They have adopted a Korean boy. Once, they showed us a film of the Korean boy learning to ski. Wham, wham, wham— every few seconds he was groveling in the snow again.

Juliette is such a liberal that she gives us not only the same bedroom but a bedroom with only a single bed in it. Beth sleeps on the couch.

Wedged beside Noel that night, I say, "This is ridiculous."

"She means to be nice," he says. "Where else would we sleep?"

"She could let us have her double bed and she could sleep in here. After all, he's not coming back, Noel."

"Shh."

"Wouldn't that have been better?"

"What do you care?" Noel says. "You're nuts about me, right?"

He slides up against me and hugs my back.

"I don't know how people talk anymore," he says. "I don't know any of the current lingo. What expression do people use for 'nuts about'?"

"I don't know."

"I just did it again! I said 'lingo.'"

"So what? Who do you want to sound like?"

"The way I talk sounds dated—like an old person."

"Why are you always worried about being old?"

He snuggles closer. "You didn't answer before when I said you were nuts about me. That doesn't mean that you don't like me, does it?"

"No."

"You're big on the one-word answers."

"I'm big on going to sleep."

"'Big on.' See? There must be some expression to replace that now."

I sit in the car, waiting for Beth to come out of the building where the ballet school is. She has been taking lessons, but they haven't helped. She still slouches forward and sticks out her neck when she walks. Noel suggests that this might be analyzed psychologically; she sticks her neck out, you see, not only literally but . . . Noel thinks that Beth is waiting to get it. Beth feels guilty because her mother and father have just been divorced. She thinks that she played some part in it and therefore she deserves to get it. It is worth fifty dollars a month for ballet lessons to disprove Noel's theory. If it will only work.

I spend the day in the park, thinking over Noel's suggestion that I move in with him. We would have more money . . . We are together so much anyway . . . Or he could move in with me, if those big windows in my place are really so important. I always meet reasonable men.

"But I don't love you," I said to Noel. "Don't you want to live with somebody who loves you?"

"Nobody has ever loved me and nobody ever will," Noel said. "What have I got to lose?"

I am in the park to think about what I have to lose. Nothing. So why don't I leave the park, call him at work, say that I have decided it is a very sensible plan?

A chubby little boy wanders by, wearing a short jacket and pants that are slipping down. He is holding a yellow boat. He looks so damned pleased with everything that I think about accosting him and asking, "Should I move in with Noel? Why am I reluctant to do it?" The young have such wisdom—some of the best and worst thinkers have thought so: Wordsworth, the followers of the Guru Maharaj Ji . . . "Do the meditations, or I will beat you with a stick," the Guru tells his followers. Tell me the answer, kid, or I will take away your boat.

I sink down onto a bench. Next, Noel will ask me to marry him. He is trying to trap me. Worse, he is not trying to trap me but only wants me to move in so we can save money. He doesn't care about me. Since no one has ever loved him, he can't love anybody. Is that even true?

I find a phone booth and stand in front of it, waiting for a woman with a shopping bag to get out. She mouths something I don't understand. She has lips like a fish; they are painted bright orange. I do not have any lipstick on. I have on a raincoat, pulled over my nightgown, and sandals and Noel's socks.

"Noel," I say on the phone when I reach him, "were you serious when you said that no one ever loved you?"

"Jesus, it was embarrassing enough just to admit it," he says. "Do you have to question me about it?"

"I have to know."

"Well, I've told you about every woman I ever slept with. Which one do you suspect might have loved me?"

I have ruined his day. I hang up, rest my head against the phone. "Me," I mumble. "I do." I reach in the raincoat pocket. A Kleenex, two pennies, and a pink rubber spider put there by Beth to scare me. No more dimes. I push open the door. A young woman is standing there waiting for me. "Do you have a few moments?" she says.

"Why?"

"Do you have a moment? What do you think of this?" she says. It is a small stick with the texture of salami. In her other hand she holds a clipboard and a pen.

"I don't have time," I say, and walk away. I stop and turn. "What is that, anyway?" I ask.

"Do you have a moment?" she asks.

"No. I just wanted to know what that thing was."

"A dog treat."

She is coming after me, clipboard outstretched.

"I don't have time," I say, and quickly walk away.

Something hits my back. "Take the time to stick it up your ass," she says.

I run for a block before I stop and lean on the park wall to rest. If Noel had been there, she wouldn't have done it. My protector. If I had a dime, I could call back and say, "Oh, Noel, I'll live with you always if you'll stay with me so people won't throw dog treats at me."

I finger the plastic spider. Maybe Beth put it there to cheer me up. Once, she put a picture of a young, beautiful girl in a bikini on my bedroom wall. I misunderstood, seeing the woman as all that I was not. Beth just thought it was a pretty picture. She didn't understand why I was so upset.

"Mommy's just upset because when you put things on the wall with Scotch Tape, the Scotch Tape leaves a mark when you remove it," Noel told her.

Noel is wonderful. I reach in my pocket, hoping a dime will suddenly appear.

Noel and I go to visit his friends Charles and Sol, in Vermont. Noel has taken time off from work; it is a vacation to celebrate our decision to live together. Now, on the third evening there, we are all crowded around the hearth— Noel and Beth and I, Charles and Sol and the women they live with, Lark and Margaret. We are smoking and listening to Sol's stereo. The hearth is a big one. It was laid by Sol, made out of slate he took from the side of a hill and bricks he found dumped by the side of the road. There is a mantel that was made by Charles from a section of an old carousel he picked up when a local amusement park closed down; a gargoyle's head protrudes from one side. Car keys have been draped over the beast's eyebrows. On top of the mantel there is an L. L. Bean catalogue, Margaret's hat, roaches and a roach clip, a can of peaches, and an incense burner that holds a small cone in a puddle of lavender ashes.

Noel used to work with Charles in the city. Charles quit when he heard about a big house in Vermont that needed to be fixed up. He was told that he could live in it for a hundred dollars a month, except in January and February, when skiers rented it. The skiers turned out to be nice people who didn't want to see anyone displaced. They suggested that the four stay on in the house, and they did, sleeping in a side room that Charles and Sol fixed up. Just now, the rest of the house is empty; it has been raining a lot, ruining the skiing.

Sol has put up some pictures he framed—old advertisements he found in a box in the attic (after Charles repaired the attic stairs). I study the pictures now, in the firelight. The Butter Lady—a healthy coquette with pearly skin and a mildewed bottom lip—extends a hand offering a package of butter. On the wall across from her, a man with oil-slick black hair holds a shoe that is the same color as his hair.

"When you're lost in the rain in Juarez and it's Eastertime, too," Dylan sings.

Margaret says to Beth, "Do you want to come take a bath with me?"

Beth is shy. The first night we were here, she covered her eyes when Sol walked naked from the bathroom to the bedroom.

"I don't have to take a bath while I'm here, do I?" she says to me.

"Where did you get that idea?"

"Why do I have to take a bath?"

But she decides to go with Margaret, and runs after her and grabs on to her wool sash. Margaret blows on the incense stick she has just lit, and fans it in the air, and Beth, enchanted, follows her out of the room. She already feels at ease in the house, and she likes us all and wanders off with anyone gladly, even though she's usually shy. Yesterday, Sol showed her how to punch down the bread before putting it on the baking sheet to rise once more. He let her smear butter over the loaves with her fingers and then sprinkle cornmeal on the top.

Sol teaches at the state university. He is a poet, and he has been hired to teach a course in the modern novel. "Oh, well," he is saying now. "If I weren't a queer and I'd gone into the Army, I guess they would have made me a cook. That's usually what they do, isn't it?"

"Don't ask me," Charles says. "I'm queer, too." This seems to be an old routine.

Noel is admiring the picture frames. "This is such a beautiful place," he says. "I'd love to live here for good."

"Don't be a fool," Sol says. "With a lot of fairies?"

Sol is reading a student's paper. "This student says, 'Humbert is just like a million other Americans,'" he says.

"Humbert?" Noel says.

"You know—that guy who ran against Nixon."

"Come on," Noel says. "I know it's from some novel."

"*Lolita*," Lark says, all on the intake. She passes the joint to me.

"Why don't you quit that job?" Lark says. "You hate it."

"I can't be unemployed," Sol says. "I'm a faggot and a poet. I've already got two strikes against me." He puffs twice on the roach, lets it slip out of the clip to the hearth. "And a drug abuser," he says. "I'm as good as done for."

"I'm sorry you feel that way, dear," Charles says, putting his hand gently on Sol's shoulder. Sol jumps. Charles and Noel laugh.

It is time for dinner—moussaka, and bread, and wine that Noel brought.

"What's moussaka?" Beth asks. Her skin shines, and her hair has dried in small narrow ridges where Margaret combed it.

"Made with mice," Sol says.

Beth looks at Noel. Lately, she checks things out with him. He shakes his head no. Actually, she is not a dumb child; she probably looked at Noel because she knows it makes him happy.

Beth has her own room—the smallest bedroom, with a fur rug on the floor and a quilt to sleep under. As I talk to Lark after dinner, I hear Noel reading to Beth: "*The Trout Fishing Diary of Alonso Hagen.*" Soon Beth is giggling.

I sit in Noel's lap, looking out the window at the fields, white and flat, and the mountains—a blur that I know is mountains. The radiator under the window makes the glass foggy. Noel leans forward to wipe it with a handkerchief. We are in winter now. We were going to leave Vermont after a week—then two, now three. Noel's hair is getting long. Beth has missed a month of school. What will the Board of Education do to me? "What do you think they're going to do?" Noel says. "Come after us with guns?"

Noel has just finished confiding in me another horrendous or mortifying thing he would never, never tell anyone and that I must swear not to repeat. The story is about something that happened when he was eighteen. There was a friend of his mother's whom he threatened to strangle if she didn't let him sleep with her. She let him. As soon as it was over, he was terrified that she would tell someone, and he threatened to strangle her if she did. But he realized that as soon as he left she could talk, and that he could be arrested, and he got so upset that he broke down and ran back to the bed where they had been, pulled the covers over his head, and shook and cried. Later, the woman told his mother that Noel seemed to be studying too hard at Princeton—perhaps he needed some time off. A second story was about how he tried to kill himself when his wife left him. The truth was that he couldn't give David his scarf back because it was stretched from being knotted so many times. But he had been too chicken to hang himself and he had swallowed a bottle of drugstore sleeping pills instead. Then he got frightened and went outside and hailed a cab. Another couple, huddled together in the wind, told him that they had claimed the cab first. The same couple was in the waiting room of the hospital when he came to.

"The poor guy put his card next to my hand on the stretcher," Noel says, shaking his head so hard that his beard scrapes my cheek. "He was a plumber. Eliot Raye. And his wife, Flora."

A warm afternoon. "Noel!" Beth cries, running across the soggy lawn toward him, her hand extended like a fisherman with his catch. But there's nothing in her hand—only a little spot of blood on the palm. Eventually he gets the story out of her: she fell. He will bandage it. He is squatting, his arm folding her close like some giant bird. A heron? An eagle? Will he take my child and fly away? They walk toward the house, his hand pressing Beth's head against his leg.

We are back in the city. Beth is asleep in the room that was once Noel's study. I am curled up in Noel's lap. He has just asked to hear the story of Michael again.

"Why do you want to hear that?" I ask.

Noel is fascinated by Michael, who pushed his furniture into the hall and threw his small possessions out the window into the backyard and then put up four large, connecting tents in his apartment. There was a hot plate in there, cans of Franco-American spaghetti, bottles of good wine, a flashlight for when it got dark . . .

Noel urges me to remember more details. What else was in the tent?

A rug, but that just happened to be on the floor. For some reason, he didn't throw the rug out the window. And there was a sleeping bag . . .

What else?

Comic books. I don't remember which ones. A lemon meringue pie. I remember how disgusting that was after two days, with the sugar oozing out of the meringue. A bottle of Seconal. There was a drinking glass, a container of warm juice . . . I don't remember.

We used to make love in the tent. I'd go over to see him, open the front door, and crawl in. That summer he collapsed the tents, threw them in his car, and left for Maine.

"Go on," Noel says.

I shrug. I've told this story twice before, and this is always my stopping place.

"That's it," I say to Noel.

He continues to wait expectantly, just as he did the two other times he heard the story.

One evening, we get a phone call from Lark. There is a house near them for sale—only thirty thousand dollars. What Noel can't fix, Charles and Sol can help with. There are ten acres of land, a waterfall. Noel is wild to move there. But what are we going to do for money, I ask him. He says we'll worry about that in a year or so, when we run out. But we haven't even seen the place, I point out. But this is a fabulous find, he says. We'll go see it this weekend. Noel has Beth so excited that she wants to start school in Vermont on Monday, not come back to the city at all. We will just go to the house right this minute and live there forever.

But does he know how to do the wiring? Is he sure it can be wired?

"Don't you have any faith in me?" he says. "David always thought I was a chump, didn't he?"

"I'm only asking whether you can do such complicated things."

My lack of faith in Noel has made him unhappy. He leaves the room without answering. He probably remembers—and knows that I remember—the night he asked David if he could see what was wrong with the socket of his floor lamp. David came back to our apartment laughing. "The plug had come out of the outlet," he said.

In early April, David comes to visit us in Vermont for the weekend with his girlfriend, Patty. She wears blue jeans, and has kohl around her eyes. She is twenty years old. Her clogs echo loudly on the bare floorboards. She seems to feel awkward here. David seems not to feel awkward, although he looked surprised when Beth called him David. She led him through the woods, running ahead of Noel and me, to show him the waterfall. When she got too far ahead, I called her back, afraid, for some reason, that she might die. If I lost sight of her, she might die. I suppose I had always thought that if David and I spent time together again it would be over the hospital bed of our dying daughter—something like that.

Patty has trouble walking in the woods; the clogs flop off her feet in the brush. I tried to give her a pair of my sneakers, but she wears size 8¹/₂ and I am a 7. Another thing to make her feel awkward.

David breathes in dramatically. "Quite a change from the high rise we used to live in," he says to Noel.

Calculated to make us feel rotten?

"You used to live in a high rise?" Patty asks.

He must have just met her. She pays careful attention to everything he says, watches with interest when he snaps off a twig and breaks it in little pieces. She is having trouble keeping up. David finally notices her difficulty in keeping up with us, and takes her hand. They're city people; they don't even have hiking boots.

"It seems as if that was in another life," David says. He snaps off a small branch and flicks one end of it against his thumb.

"There's somebody who says that every time we sleep we die; we come back another person, to another life," Patty says.

"Kafka as realist," Noel says.

Noel has been reading all winter. He has read Brautigan, a lot of Borges, and has gone from Dante to García Márquez to Hilma Wolitzer to Kafka. Sometimes I ask him why he is going about it this way. He had me make him a list—this writer before that one, which poems are early, which late, which famous. Well, it doesn't matter. Noel is happy in Vermont. Being in Vermont means that he can do what he wants to do. Freedom, you know. Why should I make fun of it? He loves his books, loves roaming around in the woods outside the house, and he buys more birdseed than all the birds in the North could eat. He took a Polaroid picture of our salt lick for the deer when he put it in, and admired both the salt lick ("They've been here!") and his picture. Inside the house there are Polaroids of the woods, the waterfall, some rabbits—he tacks them up with pride, the way Beth hangs up the pictures she draws in school. "You know," Noel said to me one night, "when Gatsby is talking to Nick Carraway and he says, 'In any case, it was just personal'—what does that mean?"

"When did you read *Gatsby*?" I asked.

"Last night, in the bathtub."

As we turn to walk back, Noel points out the astonishing number of squirrels in the trees around us. By David's expression, he thinks Noel is pathetic.

I look at Noel. He is taller than David but more stooped; thinner than David, but his slouch disguises it. Noel has big hands and feet and a sharp nose. His scarf is gray, with frayed edges. David's is bright red, just bought. Poor Noel. When David called to say he and Patty were coming for a visit, Noel never thought of saying no. And he asked me how he could compete with David. He thought David was coming to his house to win me away. After he reads more literature he'll realize that is too easy. There will have to be complexities. The complexities will protect him forever. Hours after David's call, he said (to himself, really—not to me) that David was bringing a woman with him. Surely that meant he wouldn't try anything.

Charles and Margaret come over just as we are finishing dinner, bringing a mattress we are borrowing for David and Patty to sleep on. They are both stoned, and are dragging the mattress on the ground, which is white with a late snow. They are too stoned to hoist it.

"Eventide," Charles says. A circular black barrette holds his hair out of his face. Margaret lost her hat to Lark some time ago and never got around to borrowing another one. Her hair is dusted with snow. "We have to go," Charles says, weighing her hair in his hands, "before the snow woman melts."

Sitting at the kitchen table late that night, I turn to David. "How are you doing?" I whisper.

"A lot of things haven't been going the way I figured," he whispers.

I nod. We are drinking white wine and eating cheddar-cheese soup. The soup is scalding. Clouds of steam rise from the bowl, and I keep my face away from it, worrying that the steam will make my eyes water, and that David will misinterpret.

"Not really things. People," David whispers, bobbing an ice cube up and down in his wineglass with his index finger.

"What people?"

"It's better not to talk about it. They're not really people you know."

That hurts, and he knew it would hurt. But climbing the stairs to go to bed I realize that, in spite of that, it's a very reasonable approach.

Tonight, as I do most nights, I sleep with long johns under my night-gown. I roll over on top of Noel for more warmth and lie there, as he has said, like a dead man, like a man in the Wild West, gunned down in the dirt. Noel jokes about this. "Pow, pow," he whispers sleepily as I lower myself on him. "Poor critter's deader 'n a doornail." I lie there warming myself. What does he want with me?

"What do you want for your birthday?" I ask.

He recites a little list of things he wants. He whispers: a bookcase, an aquarium, a blender to make milkshakes in.

"That sounds like what a ten-year-old would want," I say.

He is quiet too long; I have hurt his feelings.

"Not the bookcase," he says finally.

I am falling asleep. It's not fair to fall asleep on top of him. He doesn't have the heart to wake me and has to lie there with me sprawled on top of him until I fall off. Move, I tell myself, but I don't.

"Do you remember this afternoon, when Patty and I sat on the rock to wait for you and David and Beth?"

I remember. We were on top of the hill, Beth pulling David by his hand, David not very interested in what she was going to show him, Beth ignoring his lack of interest and pulling him along. I ran to catch up, because she was pulling him so hard, and I caught Beth's free arm and hung on, so that we formed a chain.

"I knew I'd seen that before," Noel says. "I just realized where—when the actor wakes up after the storm and sees Death leading those people winding across the hilltop in *The Seventh Seal*."

Six years ago. Seven. David and I were in the Village, in the winter, looking in a bookstore window. Tires began to squeal, and we turned around and were staring straight at a car, a ratty old blue car that had lifted a woman from the street into the air. The fall took much too long; she fell the way snow drifts—the big flakes that float down, no hurry at all. By the time she hit, though, David had pushed my face against his coat, and while everyone was screaming—it seemed as if a whole chorus had suddenly assembled to scream—he had his arms around my shoulders, pressing me so close that I could hardly breathe and saying, "If anything happened to you . . . If anything happened to you . . ."

When they leave, it is a clear, cold day. I give Patty a paper bag with half a bottle of wine, two sandwiches, and some peanuts to eat on the way back. The wine is probably not a good idea; David had three glasses of vodka and orange juice for breakfast. He began telling jokes to Noel—dogs in bars outsmarting their owners, constipated whores, talking fleas. David does not like Noel; Noel does not know what to make of David.

Now David rolls down the car window. Last-minute news. He tells me that his sister has been staying in his apartment. She aborted herself and has been very sick. "Abortions are legal," David says. "Why did she do that?" I ask how long ago it happened. A month ago, he says. His hands drum on the steering wheel. Last week, Beth got a box of wooden whistles carved in the shape of peasants from David's sister. Noel opened the kitchen window and blew softly to some birds on the feeder. They all flew away.

Patty leans across David. "There are so many animals here, even in the winter," she says. "Don't they hibernate anymore?"

She is making nervous, polite conversation. She wants to leave. Noel walks away from me to Patty's side of the car, and tells her about the deer who come right up to the house. Beth is sitting on Noel's shoulders. Not wanting to talk to David, I wave at her stupidly. She waves back.

David looks at me out the window. I must look as stiff as one of those wooden whistles, all carved out of one piece, in my old blue ski jacket and blue wool hat pulled down to my eyes and my baggy jeans.

"*Ciao*," David says. "Thanks."

"Yes," Patty says. "It was nice of you to do this." She holds up the bag.

It's a steep driveway, and rocky. David backs down cautiously—the way someone pulls a zipper after it's been caught. We wave, they disappear. That was easy.

Downhill

Walking the dog at 7:30 a.m., I sit on the wet grass by the side of the road, directly across from the beaver pond and diagonally across from the graveyard. In back of me is a grapevine that I snitch from. The grapes are bitter. The dog lifts a leg on the gravestone, rolls in dead squirrel in the road, comes to my side finally—thank God none of the commuters ran over him—and licks my wrist. The wet wrist feels awful. I rub it along his back, passing it off as a stroke. I do it several times. "Please don't leave me," I say to the dog, who cocks his head and settles in the space between my legs on the grass.

My mother writes Jon this letter:

"Oh, John, we are so happy that September marks the beginning of your last year in law school. My husband said to me Saturday (we were at the Turkish restaurant we took you and Maria to when she was recuperating—the one you both liked so much) that now when he gets mad he can say, 'I'll sue!' and mean it. It has been uphill for so long, and now it will be downhill."

Curiously, that week an old friend of Jon's sent us a toy—a small bent-kneed skier who, when placed at the top of a slanting board, would glide to the bottom. I tried to foul up the toy every which way. I even tried making it ski on sandpaper, and it still worked. I tacked the sandpaper to a board, and down it went. The friend had bought it in Switzerland, where he and his wife were vacationing. So said the note in the package that was addressed to Jon, which I tore open because of the unfamiliar handwriting, thinking it might be evidence.

Why do I think Jon is unfaithful? Because it would be logical for him to be unfaithful. Some days I don't even comb my hair. He must leave the house and see women with their hair clean and brushed back from their faces, and he must desire them and then tell them. It is only logical that if he admires the beauty of all the women with neatly arranged hair, one of them will want him to mess it up. It is only logical that she will invite him home. That smile, that suggestion from a woman would lure him as surely as a spring rain makes the earthworms twist out of the ground. It is even hard to blame him; he has a lawyer's logical mind. He remembers things. He would not forget to comb his hair. He would certainly not hack his hair off with manicuring scissors. If he cut his own hair, he would do it neatly, with the correct scissors.

"What have you done?" Jon whispered. Illogical, too, for me to have cut it in the living room—to leave the clumps of curls fallen on the rug. "What have you done?" His hands on my head, feeling my bones, the bones in my skull, looking into my eyes. "You've cut off your hair," he said. He will be such a good lawyer. He understands everything.

The dog enjoys a fire. I cook beef bones for him, and when he is tired of pawing and chewing I light a fire, throwing in several gift pinecones that send off green and blue and orange sparks, and I brush him with Jon's French hairbrush until his coat glows in the firelight. The first few nights I lit the fire and brushed him, I washed the brush afterward, so Jon wouldn't find out. The doctors would tell me that was unreasonable: Jon said he would be gone a week. A logical woman, I no longer bother with washing the brush.

I have a scotch-and-milk before bed. The fire is still roaring, so I bring my pillow to the hearth and stretch out on the bricks. My eyelids get very warm and damp—the way they always did when I cried all the time, which I don't do anymore. After all, this is the fifth night. As the doctors say, one must be adaptable. The dog tires of all the attention and chooses to sleep under the desk in the study. I have to call him twice—the second time firmly—before he comes back to settle in the living room. And when my eyes have been closed for five minutes he walks quietly away, back to the kneehole in the desk. At one time, Jon decided the desk was not big enough. He bought a door and two filing cabinets and made a new desk. The dog, a lover of small, cramped spaces, wandered unhappily from corner to corner, no longer able to settle anywhere. Jon brought the old desk back. A very kind man.

Like Columbus's crew, I begin to panic. It has been so long since I've seen Jon. Without him to check on me, I could wander alone in the house and then disappear forever—just vanish while rounding a corner, or by slipping down, down into the bathwater or up into the draft the fire creates. Couldn't that pull me with it—couldn't I go, with the cold air, up the chimney, arms outstretched, with my cupped hands making a parasol? Or while sitting in Jon's chair I might become smaller—become a speck, an ash. The dog would sniff and sniff, and then jump into the chair and settle down upon me and close his eyes.

To calm myself, I make tea. Earl Grey, an imported tea. Imported means coming to; exported means going away. I feel in my bones (my shinbones) that Jon will not come home. But perhaps I am just cold, since the fire is not yet lit. I sip the Earl Grey tea—results will be conclusive.

He said he was going to his brother's house for a week. He said that after caring for me he, also, had to recuperate. I have no hold on him. Even our marriage is common-law—if four years and four months make it common-law. He said he was going to his brother's. But how do I know where he's calling from? And why has he written no letters? In his absence, I talk to the dog. I pretend that I am Jon, that I am logical and reassuring. I tell the dog that Jon needed this rest and will soon be back. The dog grows anxious, sniffs Jon's clothes closet, and hangs close to the security of the kneehole. It *has* been a long time.

Celebrated my birthday in solitude. Took the phone off the hook so I wouldn't have to "put Jon on" when my parents called. Does the dog know that today is a special day? No day is special without beef bones, but I have forgotten to buy them to create a celebration. I go to the kneehole and stroke his neck in sorrow.

It occurs to me that this is a story of a woman whose man went away. Billie Holiday could have done a lot with it.

I put on a blue dress and go out to a job interview. I order a half cord of wood; there will be money when the man delivers it on Saturday. I splurge on canned horsemeat for the dog. "You'll never leave, will you?" I say as the dog eats, stabbing his mouth into the bowl of food. I think, giddily, that a dog is better than a hog. Hogs are only raised for slaughter; dogs are raised to love. Although I know this is true, I would be hesitant to voice this observation. The doctor (glasses sliding down nose, lower lip pressed to the upper) would say, "Might not *some* people love hogs?"

I dream that Jon has come back, that we do an exotic dance in the living room. Is it, perhaps, the tango? As he leads he tilts me back, and suddenly I can't feel the weight of his arms anymore. My body is very heavy and my neck stretches farther and farther back until my body seems to stretch out of the room, passing painlessly through the floor into blackness.

Once when the electricity went off, Jon went to the kitchen to get candles, and I crawled under the bed, loving the darkness and wanting to stay in it. The dog came and curled beside me, at the side of the bed. Jon came back quickly, his hand cupped in front of the white candle. "Maria?" he said. "Maria?" When he left the room again, I slid forward a little to peek and saw him walking down the hallway. He walked so quickly that the candle blew out. He stopped to relight it and called my name louder—so loudly that he frightened me. I stayed there, shivering, thinking him as terrible as the Gestapo, praying that the lights wouldn't come on so he wouldn't find me. Even hiding and not answering was better than that. I put my hands together and blew into them, because I wanted to scream. When the lights came back on and he found me, he pulled me out by my hands, and the scream my hands had blocked came out.

After the hot grape jelly is poured equally into a dozen glasses, the fun begins. Melted wax is dropped in to seal them. As the white wax drips, I think, If there were anything down in there but jelly it would be smothered. I had laid in no cheesecloth, so I pulled a pair of lacy white underpants over a big yellow bowl, poured the jelly mixture through that.

In the morning Jon is back. He walks through the house to see if anything is amiss. Our clothes are still in the closets; all unnecessary lights have been turned off. He goes into the kitchen and then is annoyed because I have not gone grocery shopping. He has some toast with the grape jelly. He spoons more jelly from the glass to his mouth when the bread is gone.

"Talk to me, Maria. Don't shut me out," he says, licking the jelly from his upper lip. He is like a child, but one who orders me to do and feel things.

"Feel this arm," he says. It is tight from his chopping wood at his brother's camp.

I met his brother once. Jon and his brother are twins, but very dissimilar. His brother is always tan—wide and short, with broad shoulders. Asleep, he looks like the logs that he chops. When Jon and I were first dating we went to his brother's camp, and the three of us slept in a tent because the house was not yet built. Jon's brother snored all night. "I hate it here," I whispered to Jon, shivering against him. He tried to soothe me, but he wouldn't make love to me there. "I hate your brother," I said, in a normal tone of voice, because his brother was snoring so loudly he'd never hear me. Jon put his hand over my mouth. "Sh-h-h," he said. "Please." Naturally, Jon did not invite me on this trip to see him. I explain all this to the dog now, and he is hypnotized. He closes his eyes and listens to the drone of my voice. He appreciates my hand stroking in tempo with my sentences. Jon pushes the jelly away and stares at me. "Stop talking about something that happened years ago," he says, and stalks out of the room.

The wood arrives. The firewood man has a limp; he's missing a toe. I asked, and he told me. He's a good woodman—the toe was lost canoeing. Jon helps him stack the logs in the shed. I peek in and see that there was already a lot more wood than I thought.

Jon comes into the house when the man leaves. His face is heavy and ugly.

"Why did you order more wood?" Jon says.

"To keep warm. I have to keep warm."

I fix a beef stew for dinner, but feed it to the dog. He is transfixed; the steam warns him it is too hot to eat, yet the smell is delicious. He laps tentatively at the rim of the bowl, like an epicure sucking in a single egg of caviar. Finally, he eats it all. And then there is the bone, which he carries quickly to his private place under the desk. Jon is furious; I have prepared something for the dog but not for us.

"This has got to stop," he whispers in my face, his hand tight around my wrist.

The dog and I climb to the top of the hill and watch the commuters going to work in their cars. I sit on a little canvas stool—the kind fishermen use—instead of the muddy ground. It is September—mud everywhere. The sun is setting. Wide white clouds hang in the air, seem to cluster over this very hilltop. And then Jon's face is glowing in the clouds—not a vision, the real Jon. He is on the hilltop, clouds rolling over his head, saying to me that we have reached the end. Mutiny on the Santa Maria! But I only sit and wait, staring straight ahead. How curious that this is the end. He sits in the mud, calls the dog to him. Did he really just say that to me? I repeat it: "We have reached the end."

"I know," he says.

The dog walks into the room. Jon is at the desk. The kneehole is occupied, so the dog curls in the corner. He did not always circle before lying down. Habits are acquired, however late. Like the furniture, the plants, the cats left to us by the dead, they take us in. We think we are taking them in, but they take us in, demand attention.

I demand attention from Jon, at his desk at work, his legs now up in the lotus position on his chair to offer the dog his fine resting place.

"Jon, Jon!" I say, and dance across the room. I posture and prance. What a good lawyer he will be; he shows polite interest.

"I'll set us on fire," I say.

That is going too far. He shakes his head to deny what I have said. He leads me by my wrist to bed, pulls the covers up tightly. If I were a foot lower down in the bed I would smother if he kept his hands on those covers. Like grape jelly.

"Will there be eggs and bacon, and grape jelly on toast, for breakfast?" I ask.

There will be. He cooks for us now.

I am so surprised. When he brings the breakfast tray I find out that *today* is my birthday. There are snapdragons and roses. He kisses my hands, lowers the tray gently to my lap. The tea steams. The phone rings. I have been hired for the job. His hand covers the mouthpiece. Did I go for a job? He tells them there was a mistake, and hangs up and walks away, as if from something dirty. He walks out of the room and I am left with the hot tea. Tea is boiled so it can cool. Jon leaves so he can come back. Certain of this, I call and they both come— Jon and the dog—to settle down with me. We have come to the end, yet we are safe. I move to the center of the bed to make room for Jon; tea sloshes from the cup. His hand goes out to steady it. There's no harm done—the saucer contains it. He smiles, approvingly, and as he sits down his hand slides across the sheet like a rudder through still waters.

Wanda's

When May's mother went to find her father, May was left with her Aunt Wanda. She wasn't really an aunt; she was a friend of her mother's who ran a boardinghouse. Wanda called it a boardinghouse, but she rarely accepted boarders. There was only one boarder, who had been there six years. May had stayed there twice before. The first time was when she was nine, and her mother left to find her father, Ray, who had gone to the West Coast and had vacationed too long in Laguna Beach. The second time was when her mother was hung over and had to have "a little rest," and she left May there for two days. The first time, she left her for almost two weeks, and May was so happy when her mother came back that she cried. "Where did you think Laguna Beach was?" her mother said. "A hop, skip, and a jump? Honey, Laguna Beach is practically across the world."

The only thing interesting about Wanda's is her boarder, Mrs. Wong. Mrs. Wong once gave May a little octagonal box full of pastel paper circles that spread out into flowers when they were dropped in water. Mrs. Wong let her drop them in her fishbowl. The only fish in the fishbowl is made of bright-orange plastic and is suspended in the middle of the bowl by a sinker. There are many brightly colored things in Mrs. Wong's room, and May is allowed to touch all of them. On her door Mrs. Wong has a little heart-shaped piece of paper with "Ms. Wong" printed on it.

Wanda is in the kitchen, talking to May. "Eggs don't have many calories, but if you eat eggs the cholesterol kills you," Wanda says. "If you eat sauerkraut there's not many calories, but there's a lot of sodium, and that's bad for the heart. Tuna fish is full of mercury—what's that going to do to a person? Who can live on chicken? You know enough, there's nothing for you to eat."

Wanda takes a hair clip out of her pants pocket and clips back her bangs.

She puts May's lunch in front of her—a bowl of tomato soup and a slice of lemon meringue pie. She puts a glass of milk next to the soup bowl.

"They say that after a certain age milk is no good for you—you might as well drink poison," she says. "Then you read somewhere else that Americans don't have enough milk in their diet. I don't know. You decide what you want to do about your milk, May."

Wanda sits down, lights a cigarette, and drops the match on the floor.

"Your dad really picks swell times to disappear. The hot months come, and men go mad. What do you think your dad's doing in Denver, honey?"

May shrugs, blows on her soup.

"How do you know, huh?" Wanda says. "I ask dumb questions. I'm not used to having kids around." She bends to pick up the match. The tops of her arms are very fat. There are little bumps all over them.

"I got married when I was fifteen," Wanda says. "Your mother got married when she was eighteen—she had three years on me—and what's she do but drive all around the country rounding up your dad? I was twenty-one the second time I got married, and that would have worked out fine if he hadn't died."

Wanda goes to the refrigerator and gets out the lemonade. She swirls the container. "Shaking bruises it," she says, making a joke. She pours some lemonade and tequila into a glass and takes a long drink.

"You think I talk to you too much?" Wanda says. "I listen to myself and it seems like I'm not really conversing with you—like I'm a teacher or something."

May shakes her head sideways.

"Yeah, well, you're polite. You're a nice kid. Don't get married until you're twenty-one. How old are you now?"

"Twelve," May says.

After lunch, May goes to the front porch and sits in the white rocker. She looks at her watch—a present from her father—and sees that one of the hands is straight up, the other straight down, between the Road Runner's legs. It is twelve-thirty. In four and a half hours she and Wanda will eat again. At Wanda's they eat at nine, twelve, and five. Wanda worries that May isn't getting enough to eat. Actually, she is always full. She never feels like eating. Wanda eats almost constantly. She usually eats bananas and Bit-O-Honey candy bars, which she carries in her shirt pocket. The shirt belonged to her second husband, who drowned. May found out about him a few days ago. At night, Wanda always comes into her bedroom to tuck her in. Wanda calls it tucking in, but actually she only walks around the room and then sits at the foot of the bed and talks. One of the stories she told was about her second husband, Frank. He and Wanda were on vacation, and late at night they sneaked onto a fishing pier. Wanda was looking at the lights of a boat far in the distance when she heard a splash. Frank had jumped into the water. "I'm cooling off!" Frank hollered. They had been drinking, so Wanda just stood there laughing. Then Frank started swimming. He swam out of sight, and Wanda stood there at the end of the pier waiting for him to swim back. Finally she started calling his name. She called him by his full name. "Frank Marshall!" she screamed at the top of her lungs. Wanda is sure that Frank never meant to drown. They had been very happy at dinner that night. He had bought her brandy after dinner, which he never did, because it was too expensive to drink anything but beer in restaurants.

May thinks that is very sad. She remembers the last time she saw her father. It was when her mother took the caps off her father's film containers and spit into them. He grabbed her mother's arm and pushed her out of the room. "The great artist!" her mother hollered, and her father's face went wild. He has a long, straight nose (May's is snubbed, like her mother's) and long, brown hair that he ties back with a rubber band when he rides his motorcycle. Her father is two years younger than her mother. They met in the park when he took a picture of her. He is a professional photographer.

May picks up the *National Enquirer* and begins to read an article about how Sophia Loren tried to save Richard Burton's marriage. In a picture, Sophia holds Carlo Ponti's hand and beams. Wanda subscribes to the *National Enquirer*. She cries over the stories about crippled children, and prays for them. She answers the ads offering little plants for a dollar. "I always get suckered in," she says. "I know they just die." She talks back to the articles and chastises Richard for ever leaving Liz, and Liz for ever having married Eddie, and Liz for running around with a used-car salesman, and all the doctors who think they have a cure for cancer.

After lunch, Wanda takes a nap and then a shower. Afterward, there is always bath powder all over the bathroom—even on the mirror. Then she drinks two shots of tequila in lemonade, and then she fixes dinner. Mrs. Wong comes back from the library punctually at four o'clock. May looks at Wanda's *National Enquirer*. She turns the page, and Paul Newman is swimming in water full of big chunks of ice.

Mrs. Wong's first name is Maria. Her name is written neatly on her notebooks. "Imagine having a student living under my roof!" Wanda says. Wanda went to a junior college with May's mother but dropped out after the first semester. Wanda and May's mother have often talked about Mrs. Wong. From them May learned that Mrs. Wong married a Chinese man and then left him, and she has a fifteen-year-old son. On top of that, she is studying to be a social worker. "That ought to give her an opportunity to marry a Negro," May's mother said to Wanda. "The Chinese man wasn't far out enough, I guess."

Mrs. Wong is back early today. As she comes up the sidewalk, she gives May the peace sign. May gives the peace sign, too.

"Your mama didn't write, I take it," Mrs. Wong says.

May shrugs.

"I write my son, and my husband rips up the letters," Mrs. Wong says. "At least when she does write you'll get it." Mrs. Wong sits down on the top step and takes off her sandals. She rubs her feet. "Get to the movies?" she asks.

"She always forgets."

"Remind her," Mrs. Wong says. "Honey, if you don't practice by asserting yourself with women, you'll never be able to assert yourself with men."

May wishes that Mrs. Wong were her mother. It would be nice if she could keep her father and have Mrs. Wong for a mother. But all the women he likes are thin and blond and young. That's one of the things her mother complains about. "Do you wish I strung *beads*?" her mother shouted at him once. May sometimes wishes that she could have been there when her parents first met. It was in the park, when her mother was riding a bicycle, and her father waved his arms for her to stop so he could take her picture. Her father has said that her mother was very beautiful that day—that he decided right then to marry her.

"How did you meet your husband?" May asks Mrs. Wong.

"I met him in an elevator."

"Did you go out with him for a long time before you got married?"

"For a year."

"That's a long time. My parents only went out together for two weeks."

"Time doesn't seem to be a factor," Mrs. Wong says with a sigh. She examines a blister on her big toe.

"Wanda says I shouldn't get married until I'm twenty-one."

"You shouldn't."

"I bet I'll never get married. Nobody has ever asked me out."

"They will," Mrs. Wong says. "Or you can ask them.

"Honey," Mrs. Wong says, "I wouldn't ever have a date now if I didn't ask them." She puts her sandals back on.

Wanda opens the screen door. "Would you like to have dinner with us?" she says to Mrs. Wong. "I could put in some extra chicken."

"Yes, I would. That's very nice of you, Mrs. Marshall."

"Chicken fricassee," Wanda says, and closes the door.

The tablecloth in the kitchen is covered with crumbs and cigarette ashes. The cloth is plastic, patterned with golden roosters. In the center is a large plastic hen (salt) and a plastic egg (pepper). The tequila bottle is lined up with the salt and pepper shakers.

At dinner, May watches Wanda serving the chicken. Will she put the spoon in the dish? She is waving the spoon; she looks as if she is conducting. She drops the spoon on the table.

"Ladies first," Wanda says.

Mrs. Wong takes over. She dishes up some chicken and hands the plate to May.

"Well," Wanda says, "here you are happy to be gone from your husband, and here I am miserable because my husband is gone, and May's mother is out chasing down her husband, who wants to run around the country taking pictures of hippies."

Wanda accepts a plate of chicken. She picks up her fork and puts it in her chicken. "Did I tell you, Mrs. Wong, that my husband drowned?"

"Yes, you did," Mrs. Wong says. "I'm very sorry."

"What would a social worker say if some woman was unhappy because her husband drowned?"

"I really don't know," Mrs. Wong says.

"You might just say, 'Buck up,' or something." Wanda takes a bite of the chicken. "Excuse me, Mrs. Wong," she says with her mouth full. "I want you to enjoy your dinner."

"It's very good," Mrs. Wong says. "Thank you for including me."

"Hell," Wanda says, "we're all on the same sinking ship."

"What are you thinking?" Wanda says to May when she is in bed. "You don't talk much."

"What do I think about what?"

"About your mother off after your father, and all. You don't cry in here at night, do you?"

"No," May says.

Wanda swirls the liquor in her glass. She gets up and goes to the window.

"Hello, coleus," Wanda says. "Should I pinch you back?" She stares at the plant, picks up the glass from the windowsill, and returns to the bed.

"If you were sixteen, you could get a license," Wanda says. "Then when your ma went after your father you could chase after the two of them. A regular caravan."

Wanda lights another cigarette. "What do you know about your friend Mrs. Wong? She's no more talkative than you, which isn't saying much."

"We just talk about things," May says. "She's rooting an avocado she's going to give me. It'll be a tree."

"You talk about avocados? I thought that, being a social worker, she might do you some good."

Wanda drops her match on the floor. "I wish if you had anything you wanted to talk about that you would," she says.

"How come my mother hasn't written? She's been gone a week."

Wanda shrugs. "Ask me something I can answer," she says.

In the middle of the following week a letter comes. "Dear May," it says, "I am hot as hell as I write this in a drugstore taking time out to have a Coke. Ray is nowhere to be found, so thank God you've still got me. I guess after another day of this I am going to cash it in and get back to you. Don't feel bad about this. After all, I did all the driving. Ha! Love, Mama."

Sitting on the porch after dinner, May rereads the letter. Her mother's letters are always brief. Her mother has signed "Mama" in big, block-printed letters to fill up the bottom of the page.

Mrs. Wong comes out of the house, prepared for rain. She has on jeans and a yellow rain parka. She is going back to the library to study, she says. She sits on the top step, next to May.

"See?" Mrs. Wong says. "I told you she'd write. My husband would have ripped up the letter."

"Can't you call your son?" May asks.

"He got the number changed."

"Couldn't you go over there?"

"I suppose. It depresses me. Dirty magazines all over the house. His father brings them back for them. Hamburger meat and filth."

"Do you have a picture of him?" May asks.

Mrs. Wong takes out her wallet and removes a photo in a plastic case. There is a picture of a Chinese man sitting on a boat. Next to him is a brown-haired boy, smiling. The Chinese man is also smiling. One of his eyes has been poked out of the picture.

"My husband used to jump rope in the kitchen," Mrs. Wong says. "I'm not kidding you. He said it was to tone his muscles. I'd be cooking breakfast and he'd be jumping and panting. Reverting to infancy."

May laughs.

"Wait till you get married," Mrs. Wong says.

Wanda opens the door and closes it again. She has been avoiding Mrs. Wong since their last discussion, two days ago. When Mrs. Wong was leaving for class, Wanda stood in front of the door and said, "Why go to school?

They don't have answers. What's the answer to why my husband drowned himself in the ocean after a good dinner? There aren't any answers. That's what I've got against woman's liberation. Nothing personal."

Wanda had been drinking. She held the bottle in one hand and the glass in the other.

"Why do you identify me with the women's movement, Mrs. Marshall?" Mrs. Wong had asked.

"You left a perfectly good husband and son, didn't you?"

"My husband stayed out all night, and my son didn't care if I was there or not."

"He didn't *care*? What's happening to men? They're all turning queer, from the politicians down to the delivery boy. I was ashamed to have the delivery boy in my house today. What's gone wrong?"

Wanda's conversations usually end by her asking a question and then just walking away. That was something that always annoyed May's father. Almost everything about Wanda annoyed him. May wishes she could like Wanda more, but she agrees with her father. Wanda is nice, but she isn't very exciting.

Now Wanda comes out and sits on the porch. She picks up the *National Enquirer.* "Another doctor, another cure," Wanda says, and she sighs.

May is not listening to Wanda. She is watching a black Cadillac with a white top coming up the street. The black Cadillac looks just like the one that belongs to her father's friends Gus and Sugar. There is a woman in the passenger seat. The car comes by slowly, but then speeds up. May sits forward in her rocking chair to look. The woman did not look like Sugar. May sits back.

"Men on the moon, no cure for cancer," Wanda says. "Men on the moon, and they do something to the ground beef now so it won't cook. You saw me put that meat in the pan tonight. It just wouldn't cook, would it?"

They rock in silence. In a few minutes, the car coasts by again. The window is down, and music is playing loudly. The car stops in front of Wanda's. May's father gets out. It's her father, in a pair of shorts. A camera bounces against his chest.

"What the hell is this?" Wanda hollers as May runs toward her father.

"What the hell are you doing here?" Wanda yells again.

May's father is smiling. He has a beer can in one hand, but he hugs May to him, even though he can't pick her up. Looking past his arm, May sees that the woman in the car is Sugar.

"You're not taking her *anywhere*!" Wanda says. "You've got no right to put me in this position."

"Aw, Wanda, you know the world always dumps on you," Ray says. "You know I've got the right to put you in this position."

"You're drunk," Wanda says. "What's going on? Who's that in the car?"

"It's awful, Wanda," Ray says. "Here I am, and I'm drunk, and I'm taking May away."

"Daddy—were you in Colorado?" May says. "Is that where you were?"

"Colorado? I don't have the money to go West, sweetheart. I was out at Gus and Sugar's beach place, except that Gus has split, and Sugar is here with me to pick you up."

"She's not going with you," Wanda says. Wanda looks mean.

"Oh, Wanda, are we going to have a big fight? Am I going to have to grab her and run?"

He grabs May, and before Wanda can move they are at the car. The music is louder, the door is open, and May is in the car, crushing Sugar.

"Move over, Sugar," Ray says. "Lock the door. Lock the door!"

Sugar slides over behind the wheel. The door slams shut, the windows are rolled up, and as Wanda gets to the car May's father locks the door and makes a face at her.

"Poor Wanda!" he shouts through the glass. "Isn't this awful, Wanda?"

"Let her out! Give her to me!" Wanda shouts.

"Wanda," he says, "I'll give you this." He puckers his lips and blows a kiss, and Sugar, laughing, pulls away.

"Honey," Ray says to May, turning down the radio, "I don't know why I didn't have this idea sooner. I'm really sorry. I was talking to Sugar tonight, and I realized, My God, I can just go and get her. There's nothing Wanda can do."

"What about Mom, though?" May says. "I got a letter, and she's coming back from Colorado. She went to Denver."

"She didn't!"

"She did. She went looking for you."

"But I'm here," Ray says. "I'm right here with my Sugar and my May. Honey, we've made our own peanut butter, and we're going to have peanut butter and apple butter, and a beer, too, if you want it, and go walking in the surf. We've got boots—you can have my boots—and at night we can walk through the surf."

May looks at Sugar. Sugar's face is set in a wide smile. Her hair is white. She has dyed her hair white. She is smiling.

Ray hugs May. "I want to know every single thing that's happened," he says.

"I've just been, I've just been sitting around Wanda's."

"I *figured* that's where you were. At first I assumed you were with your mother, but I remembered the other time, and then it hit me that you had to be there. I told Sugar that—didn't I, Sugar?"

Sugar nods. Her hair has blown across her face, almost obscuring her vision. The traffic light in front of them changes from yellow to red, and May falls back against her father as the car speeds up.

Sugar says that she wants to be called by her real name. Her name is Martha Joanna Leigh, but Martha is fine with her. Ray always calls her all three names, or else just Sugar. He loves to tease.

It's a little scary at Sugar's house. For one thing, the seabirds don't always see that the front wall is glass, and sometimes a bird flies right into it. Sugar's two cats creep around the house, and at night they jump onto May's bed or get into fights. May has been here for three days. She and Ray and Sugar swim every day, and at night they play Scrabble or walk on the beach or take a drive. Sugar is a vegetarian. Everything she cooks is called "three"-something. Tonight, they had three-bean loaf; the night before, they had mushrooms with three-green stuffing. Dinner is usually at ten o'clock, which is when May used to go to bed at Wanda's.

Tonight, Ray is playing Gus's zither. It sounds like the music they play in horror movies. Ray has taken a lot of photographs of Sugar, and they are tacked up all over the house—Sugar cooking, Sugar getting out of the shower, Sugar asleep, Sugar waving at the camera, Sugar angry about so many pictures being taken. "And if Gus comes back, loook out," Ray says, strumming the zither.

"What if he does come back?" Sugar says.

"Listen to this," Ray says. "I've written a song that's about something I really feel. John Lennon couldn't have been more honest. Listen, Sugar."

"Martha," Sugar says.

"Coors beer," Ray sings, "there's none here. You have to go West to drink the best—Coooors beeeer."

May and Sugar laugh. May is holding a ball of yarn that Sugar is winding into smaller balls. One of the cats, which is going to have kittens, is licking its paws, with its head against the pillow Sugar is sitting on. Sugar has a box of rags in the kitchen closet. Every day she shows the box to the cat. She has to hold the cat's head straight to make it look at the box. The cat has always had kittens on the rug in the bathroom.

"And tuh-night Johnny's guests are . . ." Ray is imitating Ed McMahon again. All day he has been announcing Johnny Carson, or talking about Johnny's guests. "Ed McMahon," he says, shaking his head. "Out there in

Burbank, California, Ed has probably got a refrigerator full of Coors beer, and I've got to make do with Schlitz." Ray runs his fingers across the strings. "The hell with you, Ed. The hell with you." Ray closes the window above his head. "Wasn't there a talking horse named Ed?" He stretches out on the floor and crosses his feet, his arms behind his head. "What do you want to do?" he says.

"I'm fine," Sugar says. "You bored?"

"Yeah. I want Gus to show up and create a little action."

"He just might," Sugar says.

"Old Gus never can get it together. He's visiting his old mama way down in Macon, Georgia. He'll just be a rockin' and a talkin' with his poor old mother, and he won't be home for days and days."

"You're not making any sense, Ray."

"I'm Ed McMahon," Ray says, sitting up. "I'm standing out there with a mike in my hand, looking out on all those faces, and suddenly it looks like they're *sliding down on me.* Help!" Ray jumps up and waves his arms. "And I say to myself, 'Ed, what are you *doing* here, Ed?'"

"Let's go for a walk," Sugar says. "Do you want to take a walk?"

"I want to watch the damned Johnny Carson show. How come you don't have a television?"

Sugar pats the last ball of wool, drops it into the knitting basket. She looks at May. "We didn't have much for dinner. How about some cashew butter on toast, or some guacamole?"

"O.K.," May says. Sugar is very nice to her. It would be nice to have Sugar for a mother.

"Fix me some of that stuff, too," Ray says. He flips through a pile of records and picks one up, carefully removes it, his thumb in the center, another finger on the edge. He puts it on the record player and slowly lowers the needle to Rod Stewart, hoarsely singing "Mandolin Wind." "The way he sings 'No, no,'" Ray says, shaking his head.

In the kitchen, May takes a piece of toast out of the toaster, then takes out the other piece and puts it on her father's plate. Sugar pours each of them a glass of cranberry juice.

"You just love me, don't you, Sugar?" Ray says, and bites into his toast. "Because living with Gus is like living with a mummy—right?"

Sugar shrugs. She is smoking a cigarillo and drinking cranberry juice.

"I'm your Marvin Gardens," Ray says. "I'm your God-damned *Park Place.*"

Sugar exhales, looks at some fixed point on the wall across from her.

"Oh, *metaphor,*" Ray says, and cups his hand, as though he can catch something. "Everything is like everything else. Ray is like Gus. Sugar's getting tired of Ray."

"What the hell are you talking about, Ray?" Sugar says.

"Your one cat is like your other cat," Ray says. "All is one. Om, om."

Sugar drains her glass. Sugar and Ray are both smiling. May smiles, to join them, but she doesn't understand them.

Ray begins his James Taylor imitation. "Ev-ery-body, have you hoid, she's gonna buy me a mockin' boid . . ." he sings.

Ray used to sing to May's mother. He called it serenading. He'd sit at the table, waiting for breakfast, singing and keeping the beat with his knife against the table. As May got older, she was a little embarrassed when she had friends over and Ray began serenading. Her father is very energetic; at home, he used to sprawl out on the floor to arm-wrestle with his friends. He told May that he had been a Marine. Later, her mother told her that that wasn't true—he wasn't even in the Army, because he had too many allergies.

"Let's take a walk," Ray says now, hitting the table so hard that the plates shake.

"Get your coat, May," Sugar says. "We're going for a walk."

Sugar puts on a tan poncho with unicorns on the front and stars on the back. May's clothes are at Wanda's, so she wears Sugar's raincoat, tied around her waist with a red Moroccan belt. "We look like we're auditioning for Fellini," Sugar says.

Ray opens the sliding door. The small patio is covered with sand. They walk down two steps to the beach. There's a quarter-moon, and the water is dark. There is a wide expanse of sand between the house and the water. Ray skips down the beach, away from them, becoming a blur in the darkness.

"Your father's in a bad mood because another publisher turned down his book of photographs," Sugar says.

"Oh," May says.

"That raincoat falling off you?" Sugar says, tugging on one shoulder. "You look like some Biblical figure."

It's windy. The wind blows the sand against May's legs. She stops to rub some of it away.

"Ray?" Sugar calls. "Hey, Ray!"

"Where is he?" May asks.

"If he didn't want to walk with us, I don't know why he asked us to come," Sugar says.

They are close to the water now. A light spray blows into May's face.

"Ray!" Sugar calls down the beach.

"Boo!" Ray screams, in back of them. Sugar and May jump. May screams.

"I was crouching. Didn't you see me?" Ray says.

"Very funny," Sugar says.

Ray hoists May onto his shoulders. She doesn't like being up there. He scared her.

"Your legs are as long as flagpoles," Ray says to May. "How old are you now?"

"Twelve."

"Twelve years old. I've been married to your mother for thirteen years."

Some rocks appear in front of them. It is where the private beach ends and the public beach begins. In the daytime they often walk here and sit on the rocks. Ray takes pictures, and Sugar and May jump over the incoming waves or just sit looking at the water. They usually have a good time. Right now, riding on Ray's shoulders, May wants to know how much longer they are going to stay at the beach house. Maybe her mother is already back. If Wanda told her mother about the Cadillac, her mother would know it was Sugar's, wouldn't she? Her mother used to say nasty things about Sugar and Gus. "*College* people," her mother called them. Sugar teaches crafts at a high school; Gus is a piano teacher. At the beach house, Sugar has taught May how to play scales on Gus's piano. It is a huge black piano that takes up almost a whole room. There is a picture on top of a Doberman, with a blue ribbon stuck to the side of the frame. Gus used to raise dogs. Three of them bit him in one month, and he quit.

"Race you back," Ray says now, lowering May. But she is too tired to race. She and Sugar just keep walking when he runs off. They walk in silence most of the way back.

"Sugar," May says, "do you know how long we're going to be here?"

Sugar slows down. "I really don't know. No. Are you worried that your mother might be back?"

"She ought to be back by now."

Sugar's hair looks like snow in the moonlight. "Go to bed when we get back and I'll talk to him," Sugar says.

When they get to the house, the light is on, so it's easier to see where they're walking. As Sugar pushes open the sliding door, May sees her father standing in front of Gus in the living room. Gus does not turn around when Sugar says, "Gus. Hello."

Everyone looks at him. "I'm tired as hell," Gus says. "Is there any beer?"

"I'll get you some," Sugar says. Almost in slow motion, she goes to the refrigerator.

Gus has been looking at Ray's pictures of Sugar, and suddenly he snatches one off the wall. "On *my* wall?" Gus says. "Who did that? Who hung them up?"

"Ray," Sugar says. She hands him the can of beer.

"Ray," Gus repeats. He shakes his head. He shakes the beer in the can lightly but doesn't drink it.

"May," Sugar says, "why don't you go upstairs and get ready for bed?"

"Go upstairs," Gus says. Gus's face is red, and he looks tired and wild.

May runs up the stairs and then sits down there and listens. No one is talking. Then she hears Gus say, "Do you intend to spend the night, Ray? Turn this into a little social occasion?"

"I would like to stay for a while to—" Ray begins.

Gus says something, but his voice is so low and angry that May can't make out the words.

Silence again.

"Gus—" Ray begins again.

"*What?*" Gus shouts. "What have you got to say to me, Ray? You don't have a damned thing to say to me. Will you get out of here now?"

Footsteps. May looks down and sees her father walk past the stairs. He does not look up. He did not see her. He has gone out the door, leaving her. In a minute she hears his motorcycle start and the noise the tires make riding through gravel. May runs downstairs to Sugar, who is picking up the pictures Gus has ripped off the walls.

"I'm going to take you home, May," Sugar says.

"I'm coming with you," Gus says. "If I let you go, you'll go after Ray."

"That's ridiculous," Sugar says.

"I'm going with you," Gus says.

"Let's go, then," Sugar says. May is the first one to the door.

Gus is barefoot. He stares at Sugar and walks as if he is drunk. He is still holding the can of beer.

Sugar gets into the driver's seat of the Cadillac. The key is in the ignition. She starts the car and then puts her head against the wheel and begins to cry.

"Get moving, will you?" Gus says. "Or move over." Gus gets out and walks around the car. "I knew you were going crazy when you dyed your hair," Gus says. "Shove over, will you?"

Sugar moves over. May is in the back seat, in one corner.

"For God's sake, stop crying," Gus says. "What am I doing to you?"

Gus drives slowly, then very fast. The radio is on, in a faint mumble. For half an hour they ride in silence, except for the sounds of the radio and Sugar blowing her nose.

"Your father's O.K.," Sugar says at last. "He was just upset, you know."

In the back seat, May nods, but Sugar does not see it.

At last the car slows, and May sits up and sees they are in the block where she lives. Ray's motorcycle is not in the driveway. All the lights are out in the house.

"It's empty," Sugar says. "Or else she's asleep in there. Do you want to knock on the door, May?"

"What do you mean, it's empty?" Gus says.

"She's in Colorado," Sugar says. "I thought she might be back."

May begins to cry. She tries to get out of the car, but she can't work the door handle.

"Come on," Gus says to her. "Come on, now. We can go back. I don't believe this."

May's legs are still sandy, and they itch. She rubs them, crying.

"You can take her back to Wanda's," Sugar says. "Is that O.K., May?"

"Wanda? Who's that?"

"Her mother's friend. It's not far from here. I'll show you."

"What am I even doing talking to you?" Gus says.

The radio drones. In another ten minutes they are at Wanda's.

"I suppose nobody's here, either," Gus says, looking at the dark house. He leans back and opens the door for May, who runs up the walk. "Please be here, Wanda," she whispers. She runs up to the door and knocks. No one answers. She knocks harder, and a light goes on in the hall. "Who is it?" Wanda calls.

"May," May says.

"May!" Wanda hollers. She fumbles with the door. The door opens. May hears the tires as Gus pulls the car away. She stands there in Sugar's raincoat, with the red belt hanging down the front.

"What did they do to you? What did they do?" Wanda says. Her eyes are swollen from sleep. Her hair has been clipped into rows of neat pin curls.

"You didn't even try to find me," May says.

"I called the house every hour!" Wanda says. "I called the police, and they wouldn't do anything—he was your father. I did too try to find you. Look, there's a letter from your mother. Tell me if you're all right. Your father is crazy. He'll never get you again after this, I know that. Are you all right, May? Talk to me." Wanda turns on the hall lamp. "Are you all right? You saw how he got you in the car. What could I do? The police told me there was nothing else I could do. Do you want your mother's letter? What have you got on?"

May takes the letter from Wanda and turns her back. She opens the enve-lope and reads: "Dear May, A last letter before I drive home. I looked up some friends of your father's here, and they asked me to stay for a couple of days to unwind, so here I am. At first I thought he might be in the closet—jump out at me for a joke! Tell Wanda that I've lost five pounds. Sweated it away, I guess. I've been thinking, honey, and when I come home I want us to get a dog. I think you should have a dog. There are some that hardly shed at all, and maybe some that just plain don't. It would be good to get a medium-size dog—maybe a terrier, or something like that. I meant to get you a dog years ago, but now I've been thinking that I should still do it. When I get back, first thing we'll go and get you a dog. Love, Mama."

It is the longest letter May has ever gotten from her mother. She stands in Wanda's hallway, amazed.

Colorado

Penelope was in Robert's apartment, sitting on the floor, with the newspaper open between her legs. Her boots were on the floor in front of her. Robert had just fixed the zipper of one of the boots. It was the third time he had repaired the boots, and this time he suggested that she buy a new pair. "Why?" she said. "You fix them fine every time." In many of their discussions they came close to arguments, but they always stopped short. Penelope simply would not argue. She thought it took too much energy. She had not even argued when Robert's friend Johnny, whom she had been living with, moved out on her, taking twenty dollars of her money. Still, she hated Johnny for it, and sometimes Robert worried that even though he and Penelope didn't argue, she might be thinking badly of him, too. So he didn't press it. Who cared whether she bought new boots or not?

Penelope came over to Robert's apartment almost every evening. He had met her more than a year before, and they had been nearly inseparable ever since. For a while he and Penelope and Johnny and another friend, Cyril, had shared a house in the country, not far from New Haven. They had all been in graduate school then. Now Johnny had gone, and the others were living in New Haven, in different apartments, and they were no longer going to school. Penelope was living with a man named Dan. Robert could not understand this, because Dan and Penelope did not communicate even well enough for her to ask him to fix her boots. She hobbled over to Robert's apartment instead. And he couldn't understand it back when she was living with Johnny, because Johnny had continued to see another girl, and had taken Penelope's money and tried to provoke arguments, even though Penelope wouldn't argue. Robert could understand Penelope's moving in with Dan at first, because she hadn't had enough money to pay her share of the house rent and Dan had an apartment in New Haven, but why had she just stayed there? Once, when he was drunk, Robert had asked her that, and she had sighed and said she wouldn't argue with him when he'd been drinking. He had not been trying to argue. He had just wanted to know what she was thinking. But she didn't like to talk about herself, and saying that he was drunk had been a convenient excuse. The closest he ever got to an explanation was when she told him once that it was important not to waste your energy jumping from one thing to another. She had run away from home when she was younger, and when she returned, things were only worse. She had flunked out of Bard and dropped out of Antioch and the University of Connecticut, and now she knew that all colleges were the same—there was no point in trying one after another. She had traded her Ford for a Toyota, and Toyotas were no better than Fords.

She was flipping through the newspaper, stretched out on her side on the floor, her long brown hair blocking his view of her face. He didn't need to look at her: he knew she was beautiful. It was nice just to have her there. Although he couldn't understand what went on in her head, he was full of factual information about her. She had grown up in Iowa. She was almost five feet nine inches tall, and she weighed a hundred and twenty-five pounds, and when she was younger, when she weighed less, she had been a model in Chicago. Now she was working as a clerk in a boutique in New Haven. She didn't want to model again, because that was no easier than being a salesperson; it was more tiring, even if it did pay better.

"Thanks for fixing my boots again," she said, rolling up her pants leg to put one on.

"Why are you leaving?" Robert said. "Dan's student won't be out of there yet."

Dan was a painter who had lost his teaching job in the South. He moved to New Haven and was giving private lessons to students three times a week.

"Marielle's going to pick me up," Penelope said. "She wants me to help her paint her bathroom."

"Why can't she paint her own bathroom? She could do the whole thing in an hour."

"I don't want to help her paint," Penelope said, sighing. "I'm just doing a favor for a friend."

"Why don't you do me a favor and stay?"

"Come on," she said. "Don't do that. You're my best friend."

"Okay," he said, knowing she wouldn't fight over it anyway. He went to the kitchen table and got her coat. "Why don't you wait till she gets here?"

"She's meeting me at the drugstore."

"You sure are nice to some of your friends," he said.

She ignored him. She did not totally ignore him; she kissed him before she left. And although she did not say that she'd see him the next day, he knew she'd be back.

When Penelope left, Robert went into the kitchen and put some water on to boil. It was his habit since moving to this apartment to have a cup of tea before bed and to look out the window into the brightly lit alley. Interesting things appeared there: Christmas trees, large broken pieces of machinery, and, once, a fireman's uniform, very nicely laid out—a fireman's hat and suit. He was an artist—or, rather, he had been an artist until he dropped out of school—and sometimes he found that he still arranged objects and landscapes, looking for a composition. He sat on the kitchen table and drank his tea. He often thought about buying a kitchen chair, but he told himself that he'd move soon and he didn't want to transport furniture. When he was a child, his parents had moved from apartment to apartment. Their furniture got more and more battered, and his mother had exploded one day, crying that the furniture was worthless and ugly, and threatening to chop it all up with an ax. Since he moved from the country Robert had not yet bought himself a bed frame or curtains or rugs. There were roaches in the apartment, and the idea of the roaches hiding—being able to hide on the underside of curtains, under the rug—disgusted him. He didn't mind them being there so much when they were out in the open.

The Yale catalogue he had gotten months before when he first came to New Haven was still on the kitchen table. He had thought about taking a course in architecture, but he hadn't. He was not quite sure what to do. He had taken a part-time job working in a picture-framing store so he could pay his rent. Actually, he had no reason for being in New Haven except to be near Penelope. When Robert lived in the house with Johnny and Cyril and Penelope, he had told himself that Penelope would leave Johnny and become his lover, but it never happened. He had tried very hard to get it to happen; they had often stayed up later than any of the others, and they talked—he had never talked so much to anybody in his life—and sometimes they fixed food before going to bed, or took walks in the snow. She tried to teach him to play the recorder, blowing softly so she wouldn't wake the others. Once in the summer they had stolen corn, and Johnny had asked her about it the next morning. "What if the neighbors find out somebody from this house stole corn?" he said. Robert defended Penelope, saying that he had suggested it. "Great," Johnny said. "The Bobbsey Twins." Robert was hurt because what Johnny said was true—there wasn't anything more between them than there was between the Bobbsey Twins.

Earlier in the week Robert had been sure that Penelope was going to make a break with Dan. He had gone to a party at their apartment, and there had been a strange assortment of guests, almost all of them Dan's friends—some Yale people, a druggist who had a Marlboro cigarette pack filled with reds that he passed around, and a neighbor woman and her six-year-old son, whom the druggist teased. The druggist showed the little boy the cigarette pack full of pills, saying, "Now, how would a person light a cigarette like this? Which end is the filter?" The boy's mother wouldn't protect him, so Penelope took him away, into the bedroom, where she let him empty Dan's piggy bank and count the pennies. Marielle was also there, with her hair neatly braided into tight corn rows and wearing glasses with lenses that darkened to blue. Cyril came late, pretty loaded. "Better late than never," he said, once to Robert and many times to Penelope. Then Robert and Cyril huddled together in a corner, saying how dreary the party was, while the druggist put pills on his tongue and rolled them sensually across the roof of his mouth. At midnight Dan got angry and tried to kick them all out—Robert and Cyril first, because they were sitting closest to him—and that made Penelope angry because she had only three friends at the party, and the noisy ones, the drunk or stoned ones, were all Dan's friends. Instead of arguing, though, she cried. Robert and Cyril left finally and went to Cyril's and had a beer, and then Robert went back to Dan's apartment, trying to get up the courage to go in and insist that Penelope leave with him. He walked up the two flights of stairs to their door. It was quiet inside. He didn't have the nerve to knock. He went downstairs and out of the building, hating himself. He walked home in the cold, and realized that he must have been a little drunk, because the fresh air really cleared his head.

Robert flipped through the Yale catalogue, thinking that maybe going back to school was the solution. Maybe all the hysterical letters his mother and father wrote were right, and he needed some order in his life. Maybe he'd meet some other girls in classes. He did not want to meet other girls. He had dated two girls since moving to New Haven, and they had bored him and he had spent more money on them than they were worth.

The phone rang; he was glad, because he was just about to get very depressed.

It was Penelope, sounding very far away, very knocked out. She had left Marielle's because Marielle's boyfriend was there, and he insisted that they all get stoned and listen to "Trout Mask Replica" and not paint the bathroom, so she left and decided to walk home, but then she realized she didn't want to go there, and she thought she'd call and ask if she could stay with him instead. And the strangest thing. When she closed the door of the phone booth just now, a little boy had appeared and tapped on the glass, fanning out a half circle of joints. "Ten dollars," the boy said to her. "Bargain City." *Imagine* that. There was a long silence while Robert imagined it. It was interrupted by Penelope, crying.

"What's the matter, Penelope?" he said. "Of course you can come over here. Get out of the phone booth and come over."

She told him that she had bought the grass, and that it was powerful stuff. It was really the wrong thing to do to smoke it, but she lost her nerve in the phone booth and didn't know whether to call or not, so she smoked a joint—very quickly, in case any cops drove by. She smoked it too quickly.

"Where are you?" he said.

"I'm near Park Street," she said.

"What do you mean? Is the phone booth on Park Street?"

"Near it," she said.

"Okay. I'll tell you what. You walk down to McHenry's and I'll get down there, okay?"

"You don't live very close," she said.

"I can walk there in a hurry. I can get a cab. You just take your time and wander down there. Sit in a booth if you can. Okay?"

"Is it true what Cyril told me at Dan's party?" she said. "That you're secretly in love with me?"

He frowned and looked sideways at the phone, as if the phone itself had betrayed him. He saw that his fingers were white from pressing so hard against the receiver.

"I'll tell you," she said. "Where I grew up, the cop cars had red lights. These green things cut right through you. I think that's why I hate this city— damn green lights."

"Is there a cop car?" he said.

"I saw one when you were talking," she said.

"Penelope. Have you got it straight about walking to McHenry's? Can you do that?"

"I've got some money," she said. "We can go to New York and get a steak dinner."

"Christ," he said. "Stay in the phone booth. Where is the phone booth?"

"I told you I'd go to McHenry's. I will. I'll wait there."

"Okay. Fine. I'm going to hang up now. Remember to sit in a booth. If there isn't one, stand by the bar. Order something. By the time you've finished it, I'll be there."

"Robert," she said.

"What?"

"Do you remember pushing me in the swing?"

He remembered. It was when they were all living in the country. She had been stoned that day, too. All of them—stoned as fools. Cyril was running around in Penelope's long white bathrobe, holding a handful of tulips. Then he got afraid they'd wilt, so he went into the kitchen and got a jar and put them in that and ran around again. Johnny had taken a few Seconals and was lying on the ground, saying that he was in a hammock, and cackling. Robert had thought that he and Penelope were the only ones straight. Her laughter sounded beautiful, even though later he realized it was wild, crazy laughter. It was the first really warm day, the first day when they were sure that winter was over. Everyone was delighted with everyone else. He remembered very well pushing her in the swing.

"Wait," he said. "I want to get down there. Can we talk about this when I get there? Will you walk to the bar?"

"I'm not really that stoned," she said, her voice changing suddenly. "I think it's that I'm sick."

"What do you mean? How do you feel?"

"I feel too light. Like I'm going to be sick."

"Look," he said. "Cyril lives right near Park. What if you give me the number of the phone booth, and I call Cyril and get him down there, and I'll call back and talk to you until he comes. Will you do that? What's the phone number?"

"I don't want to tell you."

"Why not?"

"I can't talk anymore right now," she said. "I want to get some air." She hung up.

He needed air too. He felt panicked, the way he had the day she was in the swing, when she said, "I'm going to jump!" and he knew it was going much too fast, much too high—the swing flying out over a hill that rolled steeply down to a muddy bank by the creek. He had had the sense to stop pushing, but he only stood there, waiting, shivering in the breeze the swing made.

He went out quickly. Park Street—somewhere near there. Okay, he would find her. He knew he would not. There was a cab. He was in the cab. He rolled down the window to get some air, hoping the driver would figure he was drunk.

"What place you looking for again?" the driver said.

"I'm looking for a person, actually. If you'd go slowly . . ."

The cabdriver drove down the street at ordinary speed, and stopped at a light. A family crossed in front of the cab: a young black couple, the father with a child on his shoulders. The child was wearing a Porky Pig mask.

The light changed and the car started forward. "Goddamn," the driver said. "I knew it."

Steam had begun to rise from under the hood. It was a broken water hose. The cab moved into the next lane and stopped. Robert stuffed two one-dollar bills into the driver's hand and bolted from the cab.

"Piece of junk!" he heard the driver holler, and there was the sound of metal being kicked. Robert looked over his shoulder and saw the cabdriver kicking the grille. Steam was pouring out in a huge cloud. The driver kicked the cab again.

He walked. It seemed to him as if he were walking in slow motion, but soon he was panting. He passed several telephone booths, but all of them were empty. He felt guilty about not helping the cabdriver, and he walked all the way to McHenry's. He thought—and was immediately struck with the irrationality of it—that New Haven was really quite a nice town, architecturally.

Penelope was not at McHenry's. "Am I a black dude?" a black man said to him as Robert wedged his way through the crowd at the bar. "I'm gonna ask you straight, look at me and tell me: Ain't I a black dude?" The black man laughed with real joy. He did not seem to be drunk. Robert smiled at the man and headed toward the back of the bar. Maybe she was in the bathroom. He stood around, looking all over the bar, hoping she'd come out of the bathroom. Time passed. "If I was drunk," the black man said as Robert walked toward the front door, "I might try to put some rap on you, like I'm the king of Siam. I'm not saying nothing like that. I'm asking you straight: Ain't I a black dude, though?"

"You sure are," he said and edged away.

He went out and walked to a phone booth and dialed Dan's number. "Dan," he said, "I don't want to alarm you, but Penelope got a little loaded tonight and I went out to look for her and I've lost track of her."

"Is that right?" Dan said. "She told me she was going to sleep over at Marielle's."

"I guess she was. It's a long story, but she left there and she got pretty wrecked, Dan. I was worried about her, so—"

"Listen," Dan said. "Can I call you back in fifteen minutes?"

"What do you mean? I'm at a phone booth."

"Well, doesn't it have a number? I'll be right back with you."

"She's wandering around New Haven in awful shape, Dan. You'd better get down here and—"

Dan was talking to someone, his hand covering the mouthpiece.

"To tell you the truth," Dan said, "I can't talk right now. In fifteen minutes I can talk, but a friend is here."

"What are you talking about?" Robert said. "Haven't you been listening to what I've been saying? If you've got some woman there, tell her to go to the toilet for a minute, for Christ's sake."

"That doesn't cut the mustard anymore," Dan said. "You can't shuffle women off like they're cats and dogs."

Robert slammed down the phone and went back to McHenry's. She was still not there. He left, and out on the corner the black man from the bar walked up to him and offered to sell him cocaine. He politely refused, saying he had no money. The man nodded and walked down the street. Robert watched him for a minute, then looked away. For just a few seconds he had been interested in the way the man moved, what he looked like walking down the street. When he had lived at the house with Penelope, Robert had watched her, too; he had done endless drawings of her, sketched her on napkins, on the corner of the newspaper. But paintings—when he tried to do anything formal, he hadn't been able to go through with it. Cyril told him it was because he was afraid of capturing her. At first he thought Cyril's remark was stupid, but now—standing tired and cold on the street corner—he had to admit that he'd always been a little afraid of her, too. What would he have done tonight if he'd found her? Why had her phone call upset him so much—because she was stoned? He thought about Penelope—about putting his head down on her shoulder, somewhere where it was warm. He began to walk home. It was a long walk, and he was very tired. He stopped and looked in a bookstore window, then walked past a dry cleaner's. The last time he'd looked, it had been a coffee shop. At a red light he heard Bob Dylan on a car radio, making an analogy between time and a jet plane.

She called in the morning to apologize. When she hung up on him the night before, she got straight for a minute—long enough to hail a cab—but she had a bad time in the cab again, and didn't have the money to pay for the ride . . . To make a long story short, she was with Marielle.

"Why?" Robert asked.

Well, she was going to tell the cabdriver to take her to Robert's place, but she was afraid he was mad. No—that wasn't the truth. She knew he wouldn't be mad, but she couldn't face him. She wanted to talk to him, but she was in no shape.

She agreed to meet him for lunch. They hung up. He went into the bathroom to shave. A letter his father had written him, asking why he had dropped out of graduate school, was scotch-taped to the mirror, along with other articles of interest. There was one faded clipping, which belonged to Johnny and had been hung on the refrigerator at the house, about someone called the California Superman who had frozen to death in his Superman suit, in his refrigerator. All of Robert's friends had bizarre stories displayed in their apartments. Cyril had a story about a family that had starved to death, in their car at the side of the highway. Their last meal had been watermelon. The clipping was tacked to Cyril's headboard. It made Robert feel old and disoriented when he realized that these awful newspaper articles had replaced those mindless Day-Glo pictures everybody used to have. Also, people in New Haven had begun to come up to him on the street—cops, surely; they had to be cops—swinging plastic bags full of grass in front of his nose, bringing handfuls of ups and downs out of their pockets. Also, the day before, he had got a box from his mother. She sent him a needlepoint doorstop, with a small white-and-gray Scottie dog on it, and a half-wreath of roses underneath it. It really got him down.

He began to shave. His cat walked into the bathroom and rubbed against his bare ankle, making him jerk his leg away, and he cut his cheek. He put a piece of toilet paper against the cut, and sat on the side of the tub. He was angry at the cat and angry at himself for being depressed. After all, Dan was out of the picture now. Penelope had been found. He could go get her, the way he got groceries, the way he got a book from the library. It seemed too easy. Something was wrong.

He put on his jeans—he had no clean underwear; forget about that—and a shirt and his jacket, and walked to the restaurant. Penelope was in the first booth, with her coat still on. There was a bottle of beer on the table in front of her. She was smiling sheepishly, and seeing her, he smiled back. He sat next to her and put his arm around her shoulder, hugging her to him.

"Who's the first girl you ever loved?" she said.

Leave it to her to ask something like that. He tried to feel her shoulder beneath her heavy coat, but couldn't. He tried to remember loving anyone but her. "A girl in high school," he said.

"I'll bet she had a tragic end," she said.

The waitress came and took their orders. When she went away, Penelope continued, "Isn't that what usually happens? People's first loves washing up on the beach in Mexico?"

"She didn't finish high school with me. Her parents yanked her out and put her in private school. For all I know, she did go to Mexico and wash up on the beach."

She covered her ears. "You're mad at me," she said.

"No," he said, hugging her to him. "I wasn't too happy last night, though. What did you want to talk to me about?"

"I wanted to know if I could live with you."

"Sure," he said.

"Really? You wouldn't mind?"

"No," he said.

While she was smiling at the startled look on his face, the waitress put a cheeseburger in front of him. She put an omelette in front of Penelope, and Penelope began to eat hungrily. He picked up his cheeseburger and bit into it. It was good. It was the first thing he had eaten in more than a day. Feeling sorry for himself, he took another bite.

"I just took a few drags of that stuff, and I felt like my mind was filling up with clouds," she said.

"Forget about it," he said. "You're okay now."

"I want to talk about something else, though."

He nodded.

"I slept with Cyril," she said.

"What?" he said. "When did you sleep with Cyril?"

"At the house," she said. "And at his place."

"Recently?" he said.

"A couple of days ago."

"Well," he said. "Why are you telling me?"

"Cyril told Dan," she said.

That explained it.

"What do you expect me to say?" he said.

"I don't know. I wanted to talk about it."

He took another bite of his cheeseburger. He did not want her to talk about it.

"I don't know why I should be all twisted around," she said. "And I don't even know why I'm telling you."

"I wouldn't know," he said.

"Are you jealous?"

"Yes."

"Cyril said you had a crush on me," she said.

"That makes it sound like I'm ten years old," he said.

"I was thinking about going to Colorado," she said.

"I don't know what I expected," he said, slamming his hand down on the table. "I didn't expect that you'd be talking about screwing Cyril and going to Colorado." He pushed his plate away, angry.

"I shouldn't have told you."

"Shouldn't have told me what? What am I going to do about it? What do you expect me to say?"

"I thought you felt the way I feel," she said. "I thought you felt stifled in New Haven."

He looked at her. She had a way of sometimes saying perceptive things, but always when he was expecting something else.

"I have friends in Colorado," she said. "Bea and Matthew. You met them when they stayed at the house once."

"You want me to move out to Colorado because Bea and Matthew are there?"

"They have a big house they're having trouble paying the mortgage on."

"But I don't have any money."

"You have the money your father sent you so you could take courses at Yale. And you could get back into painting in Colorado. You're not a picture framer—you're a painter. Wouldn't you like to quit your lousy job framing pictures and get out of New Haven?"

"Get out of New Haven?" he repeated, to see what it felt like. "I don't know," he said. "It doesn't seem very reasonable."

"I don't feel right about things," she said.

"About Cyril?"

"The last five years," she said.

He excused himself and went to the bathroom. Scrawled above one of the mirrors was a message: "Time will say nothing but I told you so." A very literate town, New Haven. He looked at the bathroom window, stared at the ripply white glass. He thought about crawling out the window. He was not able to deal with her. He went back to the booth.

"Come on," he said, dropping money on the table.

Outside, she began to cry. "I could have asked Cyril to go, but I didn't," she said.

He put his arm around her. "You're bats," he said.

He tried to get her to walk faster. By the time they got back to his apartment, she was smiling again, and talking about going skiing in the Rockies. He opened the door and saw a note lying on the floor, written by Dan. It was Penelope's name, written over and over, and a lot of profanity. He showed it to her. Neither of them said anything. He put it back on the table, next to an old letter from his mother that begged him to go back to graduate school.

"I want to stop smoking," she said, handing him her cigarette pack. She said it as if it were a revelation, as if everything, all day, had been carefully leading up to it.

It is a late afternoon in February, and Penelope is painting her toenails. She had meant what she said about moving in with him. She didn't even go back to Dan's apartment for her clothes. She has been borrowing Robert's shirts and sweaters, and wears his pajama bottoms under his long winter coat when she goes to the laundromat so she can wash her one pair of jeans. She has quit her job. She wants to give a farewell party before they go to Colorado.

She is sitting on the floor, and there are little balls of cotton stuck between her toes. The second toe on each foot is crooked. She wore the wrong shoes as a child. One night she turned the light on to show Robert her feet, and said that they embarrassed her. Why, then, is she painting her toenails?

"Penelope," he says, "I have no interest in any damn party. I have very little interest in going to Colorado."

Today he told his boss that he would be leaving next week. His boss laughed and said that he would send his brother around to beat him up. As usual, he could not really tell whether his boss was kidding. Before he goes to bed, he intends to stand a Coke bottle behind the front door.

"You said you wanted to see the mountains," Penelope says.

"I know we're going to Colorado," he says. "I don't want to get into another thing about that."

He sits next to her and holds her hand. Her hands are thin. They feel about an eighth of an inch thick to him. He changes his grip and gets his fingers down toward the knuckles, where her hand feels more substantial.

"I know it's going to be great in Colorado," Penelope says. "This is the first time in years I've been sure something is going to work out. It's the first time I've been sure that doing something was worth it."

"But why Colorado?" he says.

"We can go skiing. Or we could just ride the lift all day, look down on all that beautiful snow."

He does not want to pin her down or diminish her enthusiasm. What he wants to talk about is the two of them. When he asked if she was sure she loved him she said yes, but she never wants to talk about them. It's very hard to talk to her at all. The night before, he asked some questions about her childhood. She told him that her father died when she was nine, and her mother married an Italian who beat her with the lawnmower cord.

Then she was angry at him for making her remember that, and he was sorry he had asked. He is still surprised that she has moved in with him, surprised that he has agreed to leave New Haven and move to Colorado with her, into the house of a couple he vaguely remembers—nice guy, strung-out wife.

"Did you get a letter from Matthew and Bea yet?" he says.

"Oh, yes, Bea called this morning when you were at work. She said she had to call right away to say yes, she was so excited."

He remembers how excited Bea was the time she stayed with them in the country house. It seemed more like nervousness, really, not excitement. Bea said she had been studying ballet, and when Matthew told her to show them what she had learned, she danced through the house, smiling at first, then panting. She complained that she had no grace—that she was too old. Matthew tried to make her feel better by saying that she had only started to study ballet late, and she would have to build up energy. Bea became more frantic, saying that she had no energy, no poise, no future as a ballerina.

"But there's something I ought to tell you," Penelope says. "Bea and Matthew are breaking up."

"What?" he says.

"What does it matter? It's a huge state. We can find a place to stay. We've got enough money. Don't always be worried about money."

He was just about to say that they hardly had enough money to pay for motels on the way to Colorado.

"And when you start painting again—"

"Penelope, get serious," he says. "Do you think that all you have to do is produce some paintings and you'll get money for them?"

"You don't have any faith in yourself," she says.

It is the same line she gave him when he dropped out of graduate school, after she had dropped out herself. Somehow she was always the one who sounded reasonable.

"Why don't we forget Colorado for a while?" he says.

"Okay," she says. "We'll just forget it."

"Oh, we can go if you're set on it," he says quickly.

"Not if you're only doing it to placate me."

"I don't know. I don't want to stick around New Haven."

"Then what are you complaining about?" she says.

"I wasn't complaining. I was just disappointed."

"Don't be disappointed," she says, smiling at him.

He puts his forehead against hers and closes his eyes. Sometimes it is very nice to be with her. Outside he can hear the traffic, the horns blowing. He does not look forward to the long drive West.

In Nebraska they get sidetracked and drive a long way on a narrow road, with holes so big that Robert has to swerve the car to avoid them. The heater is not working well, and the defroster is not working at all. He rubs the front window clear with the side of his arm. By early evening he is exhausted from driving. They stop for dinner at Gus and Andy's Restaurant, and are served their fried-egg sandwiches by Andy, whose name is written in sequins above his shirt pocket. That night, in the motel, he feels too tired to go to sleep. The cat is scratching around in the bathroom. Penelope complains about the electricity in her hair, which she has just washed and is drying. He cannot watch television because her hair dryer makes the picture roll.

"I sort of wish we had stopped in Iowa to see Elaine," she says. Elaine is her married sister.

She drags on a joint, passes it to him.

"You were the one who didn't want to stop," he says. She can't hear him because of the hair dryer.

"We used to pretend that we were pregnant when we were little," she says. "We pulled the pillows off and stuck them under our clothes. My mother was always yelling at us not to mess up the beds."

She turns off the hair dryer. The picture comes back on. It is the news; the sportscaster is in the middle of a basketball report. On a large screen behind him, a basketball player is shown putting a basketball into a basket.

Before they left, Robert had gone over to Cyril's apartment. Cyril seemed to know already that Penelope was living with him. He was very nice, but Robert had a hard time talking to him. Cyril said that a girl he knew was coming over to make dinner, and he asked him to stay. Robert said he had to get going.

"What are you going to do in Colorado?" Cyril asked.

"Get some kind of job, I guess," he said.

Cyril nodded about ten times, the nods growing smaller.

"I don't know," he said to Cyril.

"Yeah," Cyril said.

They sat. Finally Robert made himself go by telling himself that he didn't want to see Cyril's girl.

"Well," Cyril said. "Take care."

"What about you?" he asked Cyril. "What are you going to be up to?"

"Much of the same," Cyril said.

They stood at Cyril's door.

"Seems like we were all together at that house about a million years ago," Cyril said.

"Yeah," he said.

"Maybe when the new people moved in they found dinosaur tracks," Cyril said.

In the motel that night, in his dreams Robert makes love to Penelope. When the sun comes through the drapes, he touches her shoulder and thinks about waking her. Instead, he gets out of bed and sits by the dresser and lights the stub of the joint. It's gone in three tokes, and he gets back into bed, cold and drowsy. Going to sleep, he chuckles, or thinks he hears himself chuckling. Later, when she tries to rouse him, he can't move, and it isn't until afternoon that they get rolling. He feels tired but still up from the grass. The effect seems not to have worn off with sleep at all.

They are at Bea and Matthew's house. It was cloudy and cold when they arrived, late in the afternoon, and the sides of the roads were heaped high with old snow. Robert got lost trying to find the house and finally had to stop in a gas station and telephone to ask for directions. "Take a right after the feed store at the crossroads," Matthew told him. It doesn't seem to Robert that they are really in Colorado. That evening Matthew insists that Robert sit in their one chair (a black canvas butterfly chair) because Robert must be tired from driving. Robert cannot get comfortable in the chair. There is a large photograph of Nureyev on the wall across from Robert, and there is a small table in the corner of the room. Matthew has explained that Bea got mad after one of their fights and sold the rest of the living room furniture. Penelope sits on the floor at Robert's side. They have run out of cigarettes, and Matthew and Bea have almost run out of liquor. Matthew is waiting for Bea to drive to town to buy more; Bea is waiting for Matthew to give in. They are living together, but they have filed for divorce. It is a friendly living-together, but they wait each other out, testing. Who will turn the record over? Who will buy the Scotch?

Their dog, Zero, lies on the floor listening to music and lapping apple juice. He pays no attention to the stereo speakers but loves headphones. He won't have them put on his head, but when they are on the floor he creeps up on them and settles down there. Penelope points out that one old Marianne Faithfull record seems to make Zero particularly euphoric. Bea gives him apple juice for his constipation. She and Matthew dote on the dog. That is going to be a problem.

For dinner Bea fixes beef Stroganoff, and they all sit on the floor with their plates. Bea says that there is honey in the Stroganoff. She is ignoring

Matthew, who stirs his fork in a circle through his food and puts his plate down every few minutes to drink Scotch. Earlier Bea told him to offer the bottle around, but they all said they didn't want any. A tall black candle burns in the center of their circle; it is dark outside, and the candle is the only light. When they finish eating, there is only one shot of Scotch left in the bottle and Matthew is pretty drunk. He says to Bea, "I was going to move out the night before Christmas, in the middle of the night, so that when you heard Santa Claus, it would have been me instead, carrying away Zero instead of my bag of tricks."

"Bag of *toys*," Bea says. She has on a satin robe that reminds Robert of a fighter's robe, stuffed between her legs as she sits on the floor.

"And laying a finger aside of my nose . . ." Matthew says. "No, I wouldn't have done that, Bea. I would have given the finger to you." Matthew raises his middle finger and smiles at Bea. "But I speak figuratively, of course. I will give you neither my finger nor my dog."

"I got the dog from the animal shelter, Matthew," Bea says. "Why do you call him your dog?"

Matthew stumbles off to bed, almost stepping on Penelope's plate, calling over his shoulder, "Bea, my lovely, please make sure that our guests finish that bottle of Scotch."

Bea blows out the candle and they all go to bed, with a quarter inch of Scotch still in the bottle.

"Why are they getting divorced?" Robert whispers to Penelope in bed.

They are in a twin bed, narrower than he remembers twin beds being, lying under a brown-and-white quilt.

"I'm not really sure," she says. "She said that he was getting crazier."

"They both seem crazy."

"Bea told me that he gave some of their savings to a Japanese woman who lives with a man he works with, so she can open a gift shop."

"Oh," he says.

"I wish we had another cigarette."

"Is that all he did?" he asks. "Gave money away?"

"He drinks a lot," Penelope says.

"So does she. She drinks straight from the bottle." Before dinner Bea had tipped the bottle to her lips too quickly and the liquor ran down her chin. Matthew called her disgusting.

"I think he's nastier than she is," Penelope says.

"Move over a little," he says. "This bed must be narrower than a twin bed."

"I *am* moved over," she says.

He unbends his knees, lies straight in the bed. He is too uncomfortable to sleep. His ears are still ringing from so many hours on the road.

"Here we are in Colorado," he says. "Tomorrow we'll have to drive around and see it before it's all under snow."

The next afternoon he borrows a tablet and walks around outside, looking for something to draw. There are bare patches in the snow—patches of brown grass. Bea and Matthew's house is modern, with a sundeck across the back and glass doors across the front. For some reason the house seems out of place; it looks Eastern. There are no other houses nearby. Very little land has been cleared; the lawn is narrow, and the woods come close. It is cold, and there is a wind in the trees. Through the woods, in front of the house, distant snow-covered mountains are visible. The air is very clear, and the colors are too bright, like a Maxfield Parrish painting. No one would believe the colors if he painted them. Instead he begins to draw some old fence posts, partially rotted away. But then he stops. Leave it to Andrew Wyeth. He dusts away a light layer of snow and sits on the hood of his car. He takes the pencil out of his pocket again and writes in the sketchbook: "We are at Bea and Matthew's. They sit all day. Penelope sits. She seems to be waiting. This is happening in Colorado. I want to see the state, but Bea and Matthew have already seen it, and Penelope says that she cannot face one more minute in the car. The car needs new spark plugs. I will never be a painter. I am not a writer."

Zero wanders up behind him, and he tears off the piece of sketch paper and crumples it into a ball, throws it in the air. Zero's eyes light up. They play ball with the piece of paper—he throws it high, and Zero waits for it and jumps. Finally the paper gets too soggy to handle. Zero walks away, then sits and scratches.

Behind the house is a ruined birdhouse, and some strings hang from a branch, with bits of suet tied on. The strings stir in the wind. "Push me in the swing," he remembers Penelope saying. Johnny was lying in the grass, talking to himself. Robert tried to dance with Cyril, but Cyril wouldn't. Cyril was more stoned than any of them, but showing better sense. "Push me," she said. She sat on the swing and he pushed. She weighed very little—hardly enough to drag the swing down. It took off fast and went high. She was laughing—not because she was having fun, but laughing at him. That's what he thought, but he was stoned. She was just laughing. Fortunately, the swing had slowed when she jumped. She didn't even roll down the hill. Cyril, looking at her arm, which had been cut on a rock, was almost in tears. She had landed on her side. They thought her arm was broken at first. Johnny was asleep, and he slept through the whole thing. Robert carried her into the house. Cyril, following, detoured to kick Johnny. That was the beginning of the end.

He walks to the car and opens the door and rummages through the ash-tray, looking for the joint they had started to smoke just before they found Bea and Matthew's house. He has trouble getting it out because his fingers are numb from the cold. He finally gets it and lights it, and drags on it walking back to the tree with the birdhouse in it. He leans against the tree.

Dan had called him the day before they left New Haven and said that Penelope would kill him. He asked Dan what he meant. "She'll wear you down, she'll wear you out, she'll kill you," Dan said.

He feels the tree snapping and jumps away. He looks and sees that everything is okay. The tree is still there, the strings hanging down from the branch. "I'm going to jump!" Penelope had called, laughing. Now he laughs, too—not at her, but because here he is, leaning against a tree in Colorado, blown away. He tries speaking, to hear what his speech sounds like. "Blown away," he says. He has trouble getting his mouth into position after speaking.

In a while Matthew comes out. He stands beside the tree and they watch the sunset. The sky is pale-blue, streaked with orange, which seems to be spreading through the blue sky from behind, like liquid seeping through a napkin, blood through a bandage.

"Nice," Matthew says.

"Yes," he says. He is never going to be able to talk to Matthew.

"You know what I'm in the doghouse for?" Matthew says.

"What?" he says. Too long a pause before answering. He spit the word out, instead of saying it.

"Having a Japanese girlfriend," Matthew says, and laughs.

He does not dare risk laughing with him.

"And I don't even *have* a Japanese girlfriend," Matthew says. "She lives with a guy I work with. I'm not interested in her. She needed money to go into business. Not a lot, but some. I loaned it to her. Bea changes facts around."

"Where did you go to school?" he hears himself say.

There is a long pause, and Robert gets confused. He thinks he should be answering his own question.

Finally: "Harvard."

"What class were you in?"

"Oh," Matthew says. "You're stoned, huh?"

It is too complicated to explain that he is not. He says, again, "What class?"

"1967," Matthew says, laughing. "Is that your stuff or ours? She hid our stuff."

"In my glove compartment," Robert says, gesturing.

He watches Matthew walk toward his car. Sloped shoulders. Something written across the back of his jacket, being spoken by what looks like a monster blue bird. Can't read it. In a while Matthew comes back smoking a joint, Zero trailing behind.

"They're inside, talking about what a pig I am." Matthew exhales.

"How come you don't have any interest in this Japanese woman?"

"I do," Matthew says, smoking from his cupped hand. "I don't have a chance in the world."

"I don't guess it would be the same if you got another one," he says.

"Another what?"

"If you went to Japan and got another one."

"Never mind," Matthew says. "Never mind bothering to converse."

Zero sniffs the air and walks away. He lies down on the driveway, away from them, and closes his eyes.

"I'd like some Scotch to cool my lungs," Matthew says. "And we don't have any goddamn Scotch."

"Let's go get some," he says.

"Okay," Matthew says.

They stay, watching the colors intensify. "It's too cold for me," Matthew says. He thrashes his arms across his chest, and Zero springs up, leaping excitedly, and almost topples Matthew.

They get to Matthew's car. Robert hears the door close. He notices that he is inside. Zero is in the back seat. It gets darker. Matthew hums. Outside the liquor store Robert fumbles out a ten-dollar bill. Matthew declines. He parks and rolls down the window. "I don't want to walk in there in a cloud of this stuff," he says. They wait. Waiting, Robert gets confused. He says, "What state is this?"

"Are you kidding?" Matthew asks. Matthew shakes his head. "Colorado," he says.

The Lawn Party

I said to Lorna last night, "Do you want me to tell you a story?" "No," she said. Lorna is my daughter. She is ten and a great disbeliever. But she was willing to hang around my room and talk. "Regular dry cleaning won't take that out," Lorna said when she saw the smudges on my suede jacket. "Really," she said. "You have to take it somewhere special." In her skepticism, Lorna assumes that everyone else is also skeptical.

According to the Currier & Ives calendar hanging on the back of the bedroom door, and according to my watch, and according to my memory, which would be keen without either of them, Lorna and I have been at my parents' house for three days. Today is the annual croquet game that all our relatives here in Connecticut gather for (even some from my wife's side). It's the Fourth of July, and damn hot. I have the fan going. I'm sitting in a comfortable chair (moved upstairs, on my demand, by my father and the maid), next to the window in my old bedroom. There is already a cluster of my relatives on the lawn. Most of them are wearing little American flags pinned somewhere on their shirts or blouses or hanging from their ears. A patriotic group. Beer (forgive them: Heineken's) and wine (Almaden Chablis) drinkers. My father loves this day better than his own birthday. He leans on his mallet and gives instructions to my sister Eva on the placement of the posts. Down there, he can see the American flags clearly. But if he is already too loaded to stick the posts in the ground, he probably isn't noticing the jewelry.

Lorna has come into my room twice in the last hour—once to ask me when I am coming down to join what she calls "the party," another time to say that I am making everybody feel rotten by not joining them. A statement to be dismissed with a wave of the hand, but I have none. No right arm, either. I have a left hand and a left arm, but I have stopped valuing them. It's the right one I want. In the hospital, I rejected suggestions of a plastic arm or a claw. "Well, then, what do you envision?" the doctor said. "Air," I told him. This needed amplification. "Air where my arm used to be," I said. He gave a little "Ah, so" bow of the head and left the room.

I intend to sit here at the window all day, watching the croquet game. I will drink the Heineken's Lorna has brought me, taking small sips because I am unable to wipe my mouth after good foamy sips. My left hand is there to wipe with, but who wants to set down his beer bottle to wipe his mouth?

Lorna's mother has left me. I think of her now as Lorna's mother because she has made it clear that she no longer wants to be my wife. She has moved to another apartment with Lorna. She, herself, seems to be no happier for having left me and visits me frequently. Mention is no longer made of the fact that I am her husband and she is my wife. Recently Mary (her name) took the ferry to the Statue of Liberty. She broke in on me on my second day here in the room, explaining that she would not be here for the croquet game, but with the news that she had visited New York yesterday and had taken the ferry to the Statue of Liberty. "And how was the city?" I asked. "Wonderful," she assured me. She went to the Carnegie Delicatessen and had cheesecake. When she does not visit, she writes. She has a second sense about when I have left my apartment for my parents' house. In her letters she usually tells me something about Lorna, although no mention is made of the fact that Lorna is my child. In fact, she once slyly suggested in a bitter moment that Lorna was not—but she backed down about that one.

Lorna is a great favorite with my parents, and my parents are rich. This, Mary always said jokingly, was why she married me. Actually, it was my charm. She thought I was terrific. If I had not fallen in love with her sister, everything would still be fine between us. I did it fairly; I fell in love with her sister before the wedding. I asked to have the wedding delayed. Mary got drunk and cried. Why was I doing this? How could I do it? She would leave me, but she wouldn't delay the wedding. I asked her to leave. She got drunk and cried and would not. We were married on schedule. She had nothing more to do with her sister. I, on the other hand—strange how many things one cannot say anymore—saw her whenever possible. Patricia—that was her name—went with me on business trips, met me for lunches and dinners, and was driving my car when it went off the highway.

When I came to, Mary was standing beside my hospital bed, her face distorted, looking down at me. "My sister killed herself and tried to take you with her," she said.

I waited for her to throw herself on me in pity.

"You deserved this," she said, and walked out of the room.

I was being fed intravenously in my left arm. I looked to see if my right arm was hooked up to anything. It hurt to move my head. My right arm was free—how free I didn't know at the time. I swear I saw it, but it had been amputated when I was unconscious. The doctor spoke to me at length about this later, insisting that there was no possibility that my arm was there when my wife was in the room and gone subsequently—gone when she left. No, indeed. It was amputated at once, in surgery, and when I saw my wife I was recovering from surgery. I tried to get at it another way, leaving Mary out of it. Wasn't I conscious before Mary was there? Didn't I see the arm? No, I was unconscious and didn't see anything. No, indeed. The physical therapist, the psychiatrist and the chaplain the doctor had brought with him nodded their heads in fast agreement. But soon I would have an artificial arm. I said that I did not want one. It was then that we had the discussion about air.

Last Wednesday was my birthday. I was unpleasant to all. Mrs. Bates, the cook, baked me chocolate-chip cookies with walnuts (my favorite), but I didn't eat any until she went home. My mother gave me a red velour shirt, which I hinted was unsatisfactory. "What's wrong with it?" she said. I said, "It's got one too many arms." My former student Banks visited me in the evening, not knowing that it was my birthday. He is a shy, thin, hirsute individual of twenty—a painter, a true *artiste*. I liked him so well that I had given him the phone number at my parents' house. He brought with him his most recent work, a canvas of a nude woman, for my inspection. While we were all gathered around the birthday cake, Banks answered my question about who she was by saying that she was a professional model. Later, strolling in the backyard, he told me that he had picked her up at a bus stop, after convincing her that she did not want to spend her life waiting for buses, and brought her to his apartment, where he fixed a steak dinner. The woman spent two days there, and when she left, Banks gave her forty dollars, although she did not want any money. She thought the painting he did of her was ugly, and wanted to be reassured that she wasn't really that heavy around the hips. Banks told her that it was not a representational painting; he said it was an Impressionist painting. She gave him her phone number. He called; there was no such number. He could not understand it. He went back to the bus stop, and eventually he found her again. She told him to get away or she'd call the police.

Ah, Banks. Ah, youth—to be twenty again, instead of thirty-two. In class, Banks used to listen to music on his cassette player through earphones. He would eat candy bars while he nailed frames together. Banks was always chewing food or mouthing songs. Sometimes he would forget and actually sing in class—an eerie wail, harmonizing with something none of the rest of us heard. The students who did not resent Banks's talent resented his chewing or singing or his success with women. Banks had great success with Lorna. He told her she looked like Bianca Jagger and she was thrilled. "Why don't you get some platform shoes like hers?" he said, and her eyes shriveled with pleasure. He told her a couple of interesting facts about Copernicus; she told him about the habits of gypsy moths. When he left, he kissed her hand. It did my heart good to see her so happy. I never delight her at all, as Mary keeps telling me.

They have written me from the college where I work, saying that they hope all is well and that I will be back teaching in the fall. It is not going to be easy to teach painting, with my right arm gone. Still, one remembers Matisse in his last years. Where there's a will, et cetera. My department head has sent flowers twice (mixed and tulips), and the dean himself has written a message on a get-well card. There is a bunny on the card, looking at a rainbow. Banks is the only one who really tempts me to go back to work. The others, Banks tells me, are "full of it."

Now I have a visitor. Danielle, John's wife, has come up to see me. John is my brother. She brings an opened beer and sets it on the windowsill without comment. Danielle is wearing a white dress with small porpoises on it, smiling as they leap. Across that chest, no wonder.

"Are you feeling blue today or just being rotten?" she asks.

The beginnings of many of Danielle's sentences often put me in mind of trashy, romantic songs. Surely someone has written a song called "Are You Feeling Blue?"

"Both," I say. I usually give Danielle straight answers. She tries to be nice. She has been nice to my brother for five years. He keeps promising to take her back to France, but he never does.

She sits on the rug, next to my chair. "Their rotten lawn parties," she says. Danielle is French, but her English is very good.

"Pull up a chair and watch the festivities," I say.

"I have to go back," she says, pouting. "They want you to come back with me."

Champagne glasses clinking, white tablecloth, single carnation, key of A: "They Want You Back with Me."

"Who sent you?" I ask.

"John. But I think Lorna would like it if you were there."

"Lorna doesn't like me anymore. Mary's turned her against me."

"Ten is a difficult age," Danielle says.

"I thought the teens were difficult."

"How would I know? I don't have children."

She has a drink of beer, and then puts the bottle in my hand instead of back on the windowsill.

"You have beautiful round feet," I say.

She tucks them under her. "I'm embarrassed," she says.

"Our talk is full of the commonplace today," I say, sighing.

"You're insulting me," she says. "That's why John wouldn't come up. He says he gets tired of your insults."

"I wasn't trying to be insulting. You've got beautiful feet. Raise one up here and I'll kiss it."

"Don't make fun of me," Danielle says.

"Really," I say.

Danielle moves her leg, unstraps a sandal and raises her right foot. I take it in my hand and bend over to kiss it across the toes.

"Stop it," she says, laughing. "Someone will come in."

"They won't," I say. "John isn't the only one tired of my insults."

I have been taking a little nap. Waking up, I look out the window and see Danielle below. She is sitting in one of the redwood chairs, accepting a drink from my father. One leg is crossed over the other, her beautiful foot dangling. They all know I am watching, but they refuse to look up. Eventually my mother does. She makes a violent sweep with her arm—like a coach motioning the defensive team onto the field. I wave. She turns her back and rejoins the group—Lorna, John, Danielle, my Aunt Rosie, Rosie's daughter Elizabeth, my father, and some others. Wednesday was also Elizabeth's birthday—her eighteenth. My parents called and sang to her. When Janis Joplin died Elizabeth cried for six days. "She's an emotional child," Rosie said at the time. Then, forgetting that, she asked everyone in the family why Elizabeth had gone to pieces. "Why did you feel so bad about Janis, Elizabeth?" I said. "I don't know," she said. "Did her death make you feel like killing yourself?" I said. "Are you unhappy the way she was?" Rosie now speaks to me only perfunctorily. On her get-well card to me (no visit) she wrote: "So sorry." They are all sorry. They have been told by the doctor to ignore my gloominess, so they ignore me. I ignore them because even before the accident I was not very fond of them. My brother, in particular, bores me. When we were kids, sharing a bedroom, John would talk to me at night. When I fell asleep he'd come over and shake my mattress. One night my father caught him doing it and hit him. "It's not my fault," John hollered. "He's a goddamn snob." We got separate bedrooms. I was eight and John was ten.

Danielle comes back, looking sweatier than before. Below, they are playing the first game. My father's brother Ed pretends to be a majorette and struts with his mallet, twirling it and pointing his knees.

"Nobody sent me this time," Danielle says. "Are you coming down to dinner? They're grilling steaks."

"He's so cheap he'll serve Almaden with them," I say. "You grew up in France. How can you drink that stuff?"

"I just drink one glass," she says.

"Refuse to do it," I say.

She shrugs. "You're in an awful mood," she says.

"Give back that piggy," I say.

She frowns. "I came to have a serious discussion. Why aren't you coming to dinner?"

"Not hungry."

"Come down for Lorna."

"Lorna doesn't care."

"Maybe you're mean to her."

"I'm the same way I always was with her."

"Be a little extra nice, then."

"Give back that piggy," I say, and she puts her foot up. I unbuckle her sandal with my left hand. There are strap marks on the skin. I lick down her baby toe and kiss it, at the very tip. In turn, I kiss all the others.

It's evening, and the phone is ringing. I think about answering it. Finally someone else in the house picks it up. I get up and then sit on the bed and look around. My old bedroom looks pretty much the way it looked when I left for college, except that my mother has added a few things that I never owned, which seem out of place. Two silver New Year's Eve hats rest on the bedposts, and a snapshot of my mother in front of a Mexican fruit stand (I have never been to Mexico) that my father took on their "second honeymoon" is on my bureau. I pull open a drawer and take out a pack of letters. I pull out one of the letters at random and read it. It is from an old girlfriend of mine. Her name was Alison, and she once loved me madly. In the letter she says she is giving up smoking so that when we are old she won't be repulsive to me. The year I graduated from college, she married an Indian and moved to India. Maybe now she has a little red dot in the middle of her forehead.

I try to remember loving Alison. I remember loving Mary's sister, Patricia. She is dead. That doesn't sink in. And she can't have meant to die, in spite of what Mary said. A woman who meant to die wouldn't buy a big wooden bowl and a bag of fruit, and then get in the car and drive it off the highway. It is a fact, however, that as the car started to go sideways I looked at Patricia, and she was whipping the wheel to the right. Maybe I imagined that. I remember putting my arm out to brace myself as the car started to turn over. If Patricia were alive, I'd have to be at the croquet game. But if she were alive, she and I could disappear for a few minutes, have a kiss by the barn.

I said to Lorna last night that I would tell her a story. It was going to be a fairy tale, all about Patricia and me but disguised as the prince and the princess, but she said no, she didn't want to hear it, and walked out. Just as well. If it had ended sadly it would have been an awful trick to pull on Lorna, and if it had ended happily, it would have depressed me even more. "There's nothing wrong with coming to terms with your depression," the doctor said to me. He kept urging me to see a shrink. The shrink came, and urged me to talk to him. When he left, the chaplain came in and urged me to see *him*. I checked out.

Lorna visits a third time. She asks whether I heard the phone ringing. I did. She says that—well, she finally answered it. "When you were first walking, one of your favorite things was to run for the phone," I said. I was trying to be nice to her. "Stop talking about when I was a baby," she says, and leaves. On the way out, she says, "It was your friend who came over the other night. He wants you to call him. His number is here." She comes back with a piece of paper, then leaves again.

"I got drunk," Banks says on the phone, "and I felt sorry for you."

"The hell with that, Banks," I say, and reflect that I sound like someone talking in *The Sun Also Rises*.

"Forget it, old Banks," I say, enjoying the part.

"You're not loaded too, are you?" Banks says.

"No, Banks," I say.

"Well, I wanted to talk. I wanted to ask if you wanted to go out to a bar with me. I don't have any more beer or money."

"Thanks, but there's a big rendezvous here today. Lorna's here. I'd better stick around."

"Oh," Banks says. "Listen. Could I come over and borrow five bucks?"

Banks does not think of me in my professorial capacity.

"Sure," I say.

"Thanks," he says.

"Sure, old Banks. Sure," I say, and hang up.

Lorna stands in the doorway. "Is he coming over?" she asks.

"Yes. He's coming to borrow money. He's not the man for you, Lorna."

"You don't have any money either," she says. "Grandpa does."

"I have enough money," I say defensively.

"How much do you have?"

"I make a salary, you know, Lorna. Has your mother been telling you I'm broke?"

"She doesn't talk about you."

"Then why did you ask how much money I had?"

"I wanted to know."

"I'm not going to tell you," I say.

"They told me to come talk to you," Lorna says. "I was supposed to get you to come down."

"Do you want me to come down?" I ask.

"Not if you don't want to."

"You're supposed to be devoted to your daddy," I say.

Lorna sighs. "You won't answer any of my questions, and you say silly things."

"What?"

"What you just said—about my daddy."

"I am your daddy," I say.

"I know it," she says.

There seems nowhere for the conversation to go.

"You want to hear that story now?" I ask.

"No. Don't try to tell me any stories. I'm ten."

"I'm thirty-two," I say.

My father's brother William is about to score a victory over Elizabeth. He puts his foot on the ball, which is touching hers, and knocks her ball down the hill. He pretends he has knocked it an immense distance and cups his hand over his brow to squint after it. William's wife will not play croquet; she sits on the grass and frowns. She is a dead ringer for the woman behind the cash register in Edward Hopper's *Tables for Ladies*.

"How's it going?" Danielle asks, standing in the doorway.

"Come on in," I say.

"I just came upstairs to go to the bathroom. The cook is in the one downstairs."

She comes in and looks out the window.

"Do you want me to get you anything?" she says. "Food?"

"You're just being nice to me because I kiss your piggies."

"You're horrible," she says.

"I tried to be nice to Lorna, and all she wanted to talk about was money."

"All they talk about down there is money," she says.

She leaves and then comes back with her hair combed and her mouth pink again.

"What do you think of William's wife?" I ask.

"I don't know, she doesn't say much." Danielle sits on the floor, with her chin on her knees. "Everybody always says that people who only say a few dumb things are sweet."

"What dumb things has she said?" I say.

"She said, 'Such a beautiful day,' and looked at the sky."

"You shouldn't be hanging out with these people, Danielle," I say.

"I've got to go back," she says.

Banks is here. He is sitting next to me as it gets dark. I am watching Danielle out on the lawn. She has a red shawl that she winds around her shoulders. She looks tired and elegant. My father has been drinking all afternoon. "Get the hell down here!" he hollered to me a little while ago. My mother rushed up to him to say that I had a student with me. He backed down. Lorna came up and brought us two dishes of peach ice cream (handmade by Rosie), giving the larger one to Banks. She and Banks discussed *The Hobbit* briefly. Banks kept apologizing to me for not leaving, but said he was too strung out to drive. He went into the bathroom and smoked a joint and came back and sat down and rolled his head from side to side. "You make sense," Banks says now, and I am flattered until I realize that I have not been talking for a long time.

"It's too bad it's so dark," I say. "That woman down there in the black dress looks just like somebody in an Edward Hopper painting. You'd recognize her."

"Nah," Banks says, head swaying. "Everything's basically different. I get so tired of examining things and finding out they're different. This crappy nature poem isn't at all like that crappy nature poem. That's what I mean," Banks says.

"Do you remember your accident?" he says.

"No," I say.

"Excuse me," Banks says.

"I remember thinking of *Jules and Jim*."

"Where she drove off the cliff?" Banks says, very excited.

"Umm."

"When did you think that?"

"As it was happening."

"Wow," Banks says. "I wonder if anybody else flashed on that before you?"

"I couldn't say."

Banks sips his iced gin. "What do you think of me as an artist?" he says.

"You're very good, Banks."

It begins to get cooler. A breeze blows the curtains toward us.

"I had a dream that I was a raccoon," Banks says. "I kept trying to look over my back to count the rings of my tail, but my back was too high, and I couldn't count past the first two."

Banks finishes his drink.

"Would you like me to get you another drink?" I ask.

"That's an awful imposition," Banks says, extending his glass.

I take the glass and go downstairs. A copy of *The Hobbit* is lying on the rose brocade sofa. Mrs. Bates is sitting at the kitchen table, reading *People*.

"Thank you very much for the cookies," I say.

"It's nothing," she says. Her earrings are on the table. Her feet are on a chair.

"Tell them we ran out of gin if they want more," I say. "I need this bottle."

"Okay," she says. "I think there's another bottle, anyway."

I take the bottle upstairs in my armpit, carrying a glass with fresh ice in it in my hand.

"You know," Banks says, "they say that if you face things—if you just get them through your head—you can accept them. They say you can accept anything if you can once get it through your head."

"What's this about?" I say.

"Your arm," Banks says.

"I realize that I don't have an arm," I say.

"I don't mean to offend you," Banks says, drinking.

"I know you don't."

"If you ever want me to yell at you about it, just say the word. That might help—help it sink in."

"I already realize it, Banks," I say.

"You're a swell guy," Banks says. "What kind of music do you listen to?"

"Do you want to hear music?"

"No. I just want to know what you listen to."

"Schoenberg," I say. I have not listened to Schoenberg for years.

"Ahh," Banks says.

He offers me his glass. I take a drink and hand it back.

"You know how they always have cars—car ads—you ever notice . . . I'm all screwed up," Banks says.

"Go on," I say.

"They always put the car on the beach?"

"Yeah."

"I was thinking about doing a thing with a great big car in the background and a little beach up front." Banks chuckles.

Outside, the candles have been lit. A torch flames from a metal holder—

one of the silliest things I have ever seen—and blue lanterns have been lit in the trees. Someone has turned on a radio, and Elizabeth and some man, not recognizable, dance to "Heartbreak Hotel."

"There's Schoenberg," Banks says.

"Banks," I say, "I want you to take this the right way. I like you, and I'm glad you came over. Why did you come over?"

"I wanted you to praise my paintings." Banks plays church and steeple with his hands. "But also, I just wanted to talk."

"Was there anything particularly—"

"I thought you might want to talk to me."

"Why don't you talk to me, instead?"

"I've got to be a great painter," Banks says. "I paint and then at night I smoke up or go out to some bar, and in the morning I paint . . . All night I pray until I fall asleep that I will become great. You must think I'm crazy. What do you think of me?"

"You make me feel old," I say.

The gin bottle is in Banks's crotch, the glass resting on the top of the bottle.

"I sensed that," Banks says, "before I got too wasted to sense anything."

"You want to hear a story?" I say.

"Sure."

"The woman who was driving the car I was in—the Princess . . ." I laugh, but Banks only nods, trying hard to follow. "I think the woman must have been out to commit suicide. We had been out buying things. The back seat was loaded with nice antiques, things like that, and we had had a nice afternoon, eaten ice cream, talked about how she would be starting school again in the fall—"

"Artist?" Banks asks.

"A linguistics major."

"Okay. Go on."

"What I'm saying is that all was well in the kingdom. Not exactly, because she wasn't my wife, but she should have been. But for the purpose of the story, what I'm saying is that we were in fine shape, it was a fine day—"

"Month?" Banks says.

"March," I say.

"That's right," Banks says.

"I was going to drop her off at the shopping center, where she'd left her car, and she was going to continue on to her castle and I'd go to mine . . ."

"Continue," Banks says.

"And then she tried to kill us. She did kill herself."

"I read it in the papers," Banks says.

"What do you think?" I ask.

"Banks's lesson," Banks says. "Never look back. Don't try to count your tail rings."

Danielle walks into the room. "I have come for the gin," she says. "The cook said you had it."

"Danielle, this is Banks."

"How do you do," Banks says.

Danielle reaches down and takes the bottle from Banks. "You're missing a swell old time," she says.

"Maybe a big wind will come along and blow them all away," Banks says.

Danielle is silent a moment, then laughs—a laugh that cuts through the darkness. She ducks her head down by my face and kisses my cheek, and turns in a wobbly way and walks out of the room.

"Jesus," Banks says. "Here we are sitting here and then this weird thing happens."

"Her?" I say.

"Yeah."

Lorna comes, very sleepy, carrying a napkin with cookies on it. She obviously wants to give them to Banks, but Banks has passed out, upright, in the chair next to mine. "Climb aboard," I say, offering my lap. Lorna hesitates, but then does, putting the cookies down on the floor without offering me any. She tells me that her mother has a boyfriend.

"What's his name?" I ask.

"Stanley," Lorna says.

"Maybe a big wind will come and blow Stanley away," I say.

"What's wrong with him?" she says, looking at Banks.

"Drunk," I say. "Who's drunk downstairs?"

"Rosie," she says. "And William, and, uh, Danielle."

"Don't drink," I say.

"I won't," she says. "Will he still be here in the morning?"

"I expect so," I say.

Banks has fallen asleep in an odd posture. His feet are clamped together, his arms are limp at his sides, and his chin is jutting forward. The melting ice cubes from the overturned glass have encroached on the cookies.

At the lawn party, they've found a station on the radio that plays only songs from other years. Danielle begins a slow, drunken dance. Her red shawl has fallen to the grass. I stare at her and imagine her dress disappearing, her shoes kicked off, beautiful Danielle dancing naked in the dusk. The music turns to static, but Danielle is still dancing.

Secrets and Surprises

Corinne and Lenny are sitting at the side of the driveway with their shoes off. Corinne is upset because Lenny sat in a patch of strawberries. "Get up, Lenny! Look what you've done!"

Lenny is one of my oldest friends. I went to high school with Lenny and Corinne and his first wife, Lucy, who was my best friend there. Lenny did not know Corinne then. He met her at a party many years later. Corinne remembered Lenny from high school; he did not remember her. The next year, after his divorce from Lucy became final, they married. Two years later their daughter was born, and I was a godmother. Lenny teases me by saying that his life would have been entirely different if only I had introduced him to Corinne years ago. I knew her because she was my boyfriend's sister. She was a couple of years ahead of us, and she would do things like picking us up if we got drunk at a party and buying us coffee before taking us home. Corinne once lied to my mother when she took me home that way, telling her that there was flu going around and that I had sneezed in her car all the way home.

I was ugly in high school. I wore braces, and everything seemed to me funny and inappropriate: the seasons, television personalities, the latest fashions—even music seemed silly. I played the piano, but for some reason I stopped playing Brahms or even listening to Brahms. I played only a few pieces of music myself, the same ones, over and over: a couple of Bach two-part inventions, a Chopin nocturne. I earnestly smoked cigarettes, and all one spring I harbored a secret love for Lenny. I once confessed my love for him in a note I pushed through the slats in his locker in school. Then I got scared and waited by his locker when school was over, talked to him for a while, and when he opened the locker door, grabbed the note back and ran. This was fifteen years ago.

I used to live in the city, but five years ago my husband and I moved up here to Woodbridge. My husband has gone, and now it is only my house. It is my driveway that Lenny and Corinne sit beside. The driveway badly needs to be graveled. There are holes in it that should be filled, and the drainpipe is cracked. A lot of things here need fixing. I don't like to talk to the landlord, Colonel Albright. Every month he loses the rent check I send him and then calls me from the nursing home where he lives, asking for another. The man is eighty-eight. I should consider him an amusing old character, a forgetful old man. I suspect he is persecuting me. He doesn't want a young person renting his house. Or anyone at all. When we moved in, I found some empty clothing bags hanging in the closets, with old dry-cleaning stubs stapled to the plastic: "Col. Albright, 9-8-54." I stared at the stub. I was eleven years old the day Colonel Albright picked up his clothes at the dry cleaners. I found one of his neckties wound around the base of a lamp in an upstairs closet. "Do you want these things?" I asked him on the phone. "Throw them out, I don't care," he said, "but don't ask me about them." I also do not tell him about things that need to be fixed. I close off one bathroom in the winter because the tiles are cracked and cold air comes through the floor; the heat register in my bedroom can't be set above sixty, so I set the living-room register at seventy-five to compensate. Corinne and Lenny think this is funny. Corinne says that I will not fight with the landlord because I did enough fighting with my husband about his girlfriend and now I enjoy peace; Lenny says that I am just too kind. The truth is that Colonel Albright shouts at me on the phone and I am afraid of him. He is also old and sad, and I have displaced him in his own house. Twice this summer, a friend has driven him from the nursing home back to the house, and he walked around the gardens in the front, tapping his cane through the clusters of sweet peas that are strangling out the asters and azaleas in the flower beds, and he dusted the pollen off the sundial in the back with a white handkerchief.

Almost every weekend Corinne tries to get me to leave Woodbridge and move back to New York. I am afraid of the city. In the apartment on West End Avenue I lived in with my husband when we were first married, I was always frightened. There was a bird in the apartment next to ours which shrieked, "No, no, go away!" I always mistook it for a human voice in the night, and in my sleepy confusion I thought that I was protesting an intruder in our apartment. Once a woman at the laundromat who was about to pass out from the heat took hold of my arm and pulled me to the floor with her. This could have happened anywhere. It happened in New York. I won't go back.

"Balducci's!" Corinne sometimes murmurs to me, and moves her arm through the air to suggest counters spread with delicacies. I imagine tins of anchovies, wheels of Brie, huge cashews, strange greens. But then I hear voices whispering outside my door plotting to break it down, and angry, wild music late at night that is the kind that disturbed, unhappy people listen to.

Now Corinne is holding Lenny's hand. I am lying on my side and peeking through the netting of the hammock, and they don't see me. She stoops to pick a strawberry. He scratches his crotch. They are bored here, I think. They pretend that they make the two-hour drive up here nearly every weekend because they are concerned for my well-being. Perhaps they actually think that living in the country is spookier than living in the city. "You sent your beagle to live in the country, Corinne," I said to her once. "How can you be upset that a human being wants to live where there's room to stretch?" "But what do you do here all alone?" she said.

I do plenty of things. I play Bach and Chopin on a grand piano my husband saved for a year to buy me. I grow vegetables, and I mow the lawn. When Lenny and Corinne come for the weekend, I spy on them. He's scratching his shoulder now. He calls Corinne to him. I think he is asking her to see if he just got a mosquito bite.

Last year when my husband went on vacation without me, I drove from Connecticut to D.C. to visit my parents. They live in the house where I grew up. The crocheted bedspreads have turned yellow now and the bedroom curtains are the same as ever. But in the living room there is a large black plastic chair for my father and a large brown plastic chair for my mother. My brother, Raleigh, who is retarded, lives with them. He has a friend, Ed, who is retarded, and who visits him once a week. And Raleigh visits Ed once a week. Sometimes my mother or Ed's mother takes them to the zoo. Raleigh's chatter often makes more sense than we at first suspected. For instance, he is very fond of Ling-Ling, the panda. He was not imitating the bell the Good Humor man rings when he drives around the neighborhood, as my father once insisted. My father has never been able to understand Raleigh very well. My mother laughs at him for his lack of understanding. She is a bitter woman. For the last ten years, she has made my father adhere to a diet when he is home, and he is not overweight.

When I visited, I drove Raleigh down to Hains Point, and we looked across the water at the lights. In spite of being retarded, he seems very moved by things. He rolled down the window and let the wind blow across his face. I slowed the car almost to a stop, and he put his hand on my hand, like a lover. He wanted me to stop the car entirely so he could look at the lights. I let him look for a long time. On the way home I drove across the bridge into Arlington and took him to Gifford's for ice cream. He had a banana split, and I pretended not to notice when he ate the toppings with his fingers. Then I washed his fingers with a napkin dipped in a glass of water.

One day I found him in the bathroom with Daisy, the dog, combing over her body for ticks. There were six or seven ticks in the toilet. He was concentrating so hard that he never looked up. Standing there, I realized that there was now a small bald spot at the top of his head, and that Daisy's fur was flecked with gray. I reached over him and got aspirin out of the medicine cabinet. Later, when I went back to the bathroom and found Raleigh and Daisy gone, I flushed the toilet so my parents would not be upset. Raleigh sometimes drops pieces of paper into the toilet instead of into the wastebaskets, and my mother goes wild. Sometimes socks are in the toilet. Coins. Pieces of candy.

I stayed for two weeks. On Mondays, before his friend Ed came, Raleigh left the living room until the door had been answered, and then acted surprised to see Ed and his mother. When I took him to Ed's house, Ed did the same thing. Ed held a newspaper in front of his face at first. "Oh—hello," Ed finally said. They have been friends for almost thirty years, and the visiting routine has remained the same all that time. I think that by pretending to be surprised, they are trying to enhance the quality of the experience. I play games like this with Corinne when I meet her in the city for lunch. If I get to our table first, I study the menu until she's right on me; sometimes, if I wait outside the restaurant, I deliberately look at the sidewalk, as if lost in thought, until she speaks.

I had Raleigh come live with my husband and me during the second year of our marriage. It didn't work out. My husband found his socks in the toilet; Raleigh missed my mother's constant nagging. When I took him home, he didn't seem sorry. There is something comforting about that house: the smell of camphor in the silver cabinet, my grandmother's woven rugs, Daisy's smell everywhere.

My husband wrote last week: "Do you miss wonderful me?" I wrote back saying yes. Nothing came of it.

Corinne and Lenny have always come to Woodbridge for visits. When my husband was here, they came once a month. Now they come almost every week. Sometimes we don't have much to say to each other, so we talk about the old days. Corinne teases Lenny for not noticing her back in high school. Our visits are often dull, but I still look forward to their coming because they are my surrogate family. As in all families, there are secrets. There is intrigue. Suspicion. Lenny often calls me, telling me to keep his call a secret, saying that I must call Corinne at once and arrange to have lunch because she is depressed. So I call, and then I go and sit at a table and pretend not to see her until she sits down. She has aged a lot since their daughter's death. Her name was Karen, and she died three years ago, of leukemia. After Karen died I began having lunch with Corinne, to let her talk about it away from Lenny. By the time she no longer needed to talk about it, my husband had left, and Corinne began having lunch with me to cheer me up. We have faced each other across a table for years. (Corinne, I know, tells Lenny to visit me even when she has to work on the weekend. He has come alone a few times. He gives me a few Godiva chocolates. I give him a bag of fresh peas. Sometimes he kisses me, but it goes no further than that. Corinne thinks that it does, and endures it.)

Once Corinne said that if we all lived to be fifty (she works for a state environmental-protection agency, and her expectations are modest), we should have an honesty session the way the girls did in college. Lenny asked why we had to wait until we were fifty. "Okay—what do you really think of me?" Corinne asked him. "Why, I love you. You're my wife," he said. She backed down; the game wasn't going to be much fun.

Lenny's first wife, Lucy, has twice taken the train to visit me. We sat on the grass and talked about the old days: teasing each other's hair to new heights; photo-album pictures of the two of us, each trying to look more grotesque than the other; the first time we puffed a cigarette on a double date. I like her less as time goes by, because things she remembers about that time are true but the tone of wonder in her voice makes the past seem like a lie. And then she works the conversation around to Corinne and Lenny's marriage. Is it unhappy? Both times she visited, she said she was going back to New York on the last train, and both times she got too drunk to go until the next day. She borrowed my nightgowns and drank my gin and played sad music on my piano. In our high school yearbook, Lucy was named best dancer.

I have a lover. He comes on Thursdays. He would come more frequently, but I won't allow it. Jonathan is twenty-one and I am thirty-three, and I know that eventually he will go away. He is a musician too. He comes in the morning and we sit side by side at the piano, humming and playing Bach's B-Flat-Minor Prelude, prolonging the time before we go to bed as long as possible. He drinks diet cola while I drink gin-and-tonic. He tells me about the young girls who are chasing him. He says he only wants me. He asks me each Thursday to marry him, and calls me on Friday to beg me to let him come again before the week is up. He sends me pears out of season and other things that he can't afford. He shows me letters from his parents that bother him; I am usually in sympathy with his parents. I urge him to spend more time sight-reading and playing scales and arpeggios. He allowed a rich woman who had been chasing him since Christmas to buy him a tape deck for his car, and he plays nothing but rock-'n'-roll. Sometimes I cry, but not in his presence. He is disturbed enough. He isn't sure what to do with his life, he can't communicate with his parents, too many people want things from him. One night he called and asked if he could come over to my house if he disguised himself. "No," I said. "How would you disguise yourself?" "Cut off my hair. Buy a suit. Put on an animal mask." I make few demands on him, but obviously the relationship is a strain.

After Corinne and Lenny leave, I write a second letter to my husband, pretending that there is a chance that he did not get the other one. In this letter I give him a detailed account of the weekend, and agree with what he said long ago about Corinne's talking too much and Lenny's being too humble. I tell my husband that the handle on the barbecue no longer makes the grill go up and down. I tell him that the neighbors' dog is in heat and that dogs howl all night, so I can't sleep. I reread the letter and tear it up because these things are all jumbled together in one paragraph. It looks as if a crazy person had written the letter. I try again. In one paragraph I describe Corinne and Lenny's visit. In another I tell him that his mother called to tell me that his sister has decided to major in anthropology. In the last paragraph I ask for advice about the car—whether it may not need a new carburetor. I read the letter and it still seems crazy. A letter like this will never make him come back. I throw it away and write him a short, funny postcard. I go outside to put the postcard in the mailbox. A large white dog whines and runs in front of me. I recognize the dog. It is the same one I saw last night, from my bedroom window; the dog was staring at my neighbors' house. The dog runs past me again, but won't come when I call it. I believe the neighbors once told me that the dog's name is Pierre, and that the dog does not live in Woodbridge.

When I was a child I was punished for brushing Raleigh with the dog's brush. He had asked me to do it. It was Easter, and he had on a blue suit, and he came into my bedroom with the dog's brush and got down on all fours and asked for a brushing. I brushed his back. My father saw us and banged his fist against the door. "Jesus Christ, are you *both* crazy?" he said.

Now that my husband is gone, I should bring Raleigh here to live—but what if my husband came back? I remember Raleigh's trotting through the living room, punching his fist through the air, chanting, "Ling-Ling, Ling-Ling, Ling-Ling."

I play Scriabin's Étude in C Sharp Minor. I play it badly and stop to stare at the keys. As though on cue, a car comes into the driveway. The sound of a bad muffler—my lover's car, unmistakably. He has come a day early. I wince, and wish I had washed my hair. My husband used to wince also when that car pulled into the driveway. My lover (he was not at that time my lover) was nineteen when he first started coming, to take piano lessons. He was obviously more talented than I. For a long while I resented him. Now I resent him for his impetuousness, for showing up unexpectedly, breaking my routine, catching me when I look ugly.

"This is foolish," I say to him. "I'm going into the city to have lunch."

"My car is leaking oil," he says, looking over his shoulder.

"Why have you come?" I say.

"This once-a-week stuff is ridiculous. Once you have me around a little more often you'll get used to it."

"I won't have you around more often."

"I've got a surprise for you," he says. "Two, actually."

"What are they?"

"For later. I'll tell you when you get back. Can I stay here and wait for you?"

A maroon sweater that I gave him for his birthday is tied around his waist. He sits in front of the hearth and strikes a match on the bricks. He lights a cigarette.

"Well," he says, "one of the surprises is that I'm going to be gone for three months. Starting in November."

"Where are you going?"

"Europe. You know that band I've been playing with sometimes? One of the guys has hepatitis, and I'm going to fill in for him on synthesizer. Their agent got us a gig in Denmark."

"What about school?"

"Enough school," he says, sighing.

He pitches the cigarette into the fireplace and stands up and takes off his sweater.

I no longer want to go to lunch. I am no longer sorry he came unannounced. But he hasn't jumped up to embrace me.

"I'm going to investigate that oil leak," he says.

Later, driving into New York, trying to think of what the second surprise might be (taking a woman with him?), I think about the time when my husband surprised me with a six-layer cake he had baked for my birthday. It was the first cake he ever made, and the layers were not completely cool when he stacked and frosted them. One side of the cake was much higher than the other. He had gone out and bought a little plastic figure of a skier, for the top of the cake. The skier held a toothpick with a piece of paper glued to it that said "Happy Birthday." "We're going to Switzerland!" I said, clapping my hands. He knew I had always wanted to go there. No, he explained, the skier was just a coincidence. My reaction depressed both of us. It was a coincidence, too, that a year later I was walking down the same street he was walking down and I saw that he was with a girl, holding her hand.

I'm almost in New York. Cars whiz by me on the Hutchinson River Parkway. My husband has been gone for seven months.

While waiting for Corinne, I examine my hands. My gardening has cut and bruised them. In a picture my father took when I was young, my hands are in very sharp focus but the piano keys are a blur of white streaked with black. I knew by the time I was twelve that I was going to be a concert pianist. My father and I both have copies of this picture, and we probably both have the same thoughts about it: it is a shame I have almost entirely given up music. When I lived in New York I had to play softly, so as not to disturb the neighbors. The music itself stopped sounding right. A day would pass without my practicing. My father blamed my husband for my losing interest. My husband listened to my father. We moved to Connecticut, where I wouldn't be distracted. I began to practice again, but I knew that I'd lost ground—or that I would never make it as a concert pianist if I hadn't by this time. I had Raleigh come and live with us, and I spent my days with him. My father blamed my mother for complaining to me about what a burden Raleigh was, for hinting that I take him in. My father always found excuses. I am like him. I pretended that everything was fine in my marriage, that the only problem was the girl.

"I think it's insulting, I really do," Corinne says. "It's a refusal to admit my existence. I've been married to Lenny for years, and when Lucy calls him and I answer the phone, she hangs up."

"Don't let it get to you," I say. "You know by now that Lucy's not going to be civil to you."

"And it upsets Lenny. Every time she calls to say where she's flying off to, he gets upset. He doesn't care where she's going, but you know Lenny and how he is about planes—how he gets about anyone flying."

These lunches are all the same. I discipline myself during these lunches the way I used to discipline myself about my music. I try to calm Corinne, and Corinne gets more and more upset. She only likes expensive restaurants, and she won't eat the food.

Now Corinne eats a cherry tomato from her salad and pushes the salad plate away. "Do you think we should have another child? Am I too old now?"

"I don't know," I say.

"I think the best way to get children is the way you got yours. Just have them drive up. He's probably languishing in your bed right now."

"Twenty-one isn't exactly a child."

"I'm so jealous I could die," Corinne says.

"Of Jonathan?"

"Of everything. You're three years younger than me, and you look ten years younger. Look at those thin women over there. Look at you and your music. *You* don't have to kill the day by having lunch."

Corinne takes a little gold barrette out of her hair and puts it back in. "We don't come to your house almost every weekend to look after you," she says. "We do it to restore ourselves. Although Lenny probably goes so he can pine over you."

"What are you talking about?"

"You don't sense it? You don't think that's true?"

"No," I say.

"Lucy does. She told Lenny that the last time she called. He told me that she said he was making a fool of himself hanging around you so much. When Lenny hung up, he said that Lucy never did understand the notion of friendship. Of course, he always tries to pretend that Lucy is entirely crazy."

She takes out the barrette and lets her hair fall free.

"And I'm jealous of her, going off on all her business trips, sending him postcards of sunsets on the West Coast," Corinne says. "She ran off with a dirty little furrier to Denver this time."

I look at my clean plate, and then at Corinne's plate. It looks as if a wind had blown the food around her plate, or as if a midget army had marched through it. I should not have had two drinks at lunch. I excuse myself and go to a phone and call my lover. I am relieved when he answers the phone, even though I have told him never to do that. "Come into the city," I say. "We can go to Central Park."

"Come home," he says. "You're going to get caught in the rush hour."

My husband sends me a geode. There is a brief note in the package. He says that before he left for Europe he sat at a table next to John Ehrlichman in a restaurant in New Mexico. The note goes on about how fat John Ehrlichman has become. My husband says that he bets my squash are still going strong in the garden. There is no return address. I stand by the mailbox, crying. From the edge of the lawn, the big white dog watches me.

My lover sits beside me on the piano bench. We are both naked. It is late at night, but we have lit a fire in the fireplace—five logs, a lot of heat. The lead guitarist from the band Jonathan plays with now was here for dinner. I had to fix a meatless meal. Jonathan's friend was young and dumb—much younger, it seemed, than my lover. I don't know why he wanted me to invite him. Jonathan has been here for four days straight. I gave in to him and called Lenny and said for them not to visit this weekend. Later Corinne called to say how jealous she was, thinking of me in my house in the country with my curly-haired lover.

I am playing Ravel's "Valses Nobles et Sentimentales." Suddenly my lover breaks in with "Chopsticks." He is impossible, and as immature as his friend. Why have I agreed to let him live in my house until he leaves for Denmark?

"Don't," I plead. "Be sensible."

He is playing "Somewhere Over the Rainbow" and singing.

"Stop it," I say. He kisses my throat.

Another note comes from my husband, written on stationery from the Hotel Eliseo. He got drunk and was hurt in a fight; his nose wouldn't stop bleeding, and in the end he had to have it cauterized.

In a week, my lover will leave. I am frightened at the thought that I will be here alone when he goes. Now I have gotten used to having someone around. When boards creak in the night I can ask "What is it?" and be told. When I was little, I shared a bedroom with Raleigh until I was seven. All night he'd question me about noises. "It's the monster," I'd say in disgust. I made him cry so many nights that my parents built on an addition to the house so I could have my own bedroom.

In his passport photo, my lover is smiling.

Lenny calls. He is upset because Corinne wants to have another child and he thinks they are too old. He hints that he would like me to invite them to come on Friday instead of Saturday this week. I explain that they can't come at all—my lover leaves on Monday.

"I don't mean to pry," Lenny says, but he never says what he wants to pry about.

I pick up my husband's note and take it into the bathroom and reread it. It was a street fight. He describes a church window that he saw. There is one long strand of brown hair in the bottom of the envelope. That just can't be deliberate.

Lying on my back, alone in the bedroom, I stare at the ceiling in the dark, remembering my lover's second surprise: a jar full of lightning bugs. He let them loose in the bedroom. Tiny, blinking dots of green under the ceiling, above the bed. Giggling into his shoulder: how crazy; a room full of lightning bugs.

"They only live a day," he whispered.

"That's butterflies," I said.

I always felt uncomfortable correcting him, as if I were pointing out the difference in our ages. I was sure I was right about the lightning bugs, but in the morning I was relieved when I saw that they were still alive. I found them on the curtains, against the window. I tried to recapture all of them in a jar so I could take them outdoors and set them free. I tried to remember how many points of light there had been.

Weekend

On Saturday morning Lenore is up before the others. She carries her baby into the living room and puts him in George's favorite chair, which tilts because its back legs are missing, and covers him with a blanket. Then she lights a fire in the fireplace, putting fresh logs on a few embers that are still glowing from the night before. She sits down on the floor beside the chair and checks the baby, who has already gone back to sleep—a good thing, because there are guests in the house. George, the man she lives with, is very hospitable and impetuous; he extends invitations whenever old friends call, urging them to come spend the weekend. Most of the callers are his former students—he used to be an English professor—and when they come it seems to make things much worse. It makes *him* much worse, because he falls into smoking too much and drinking and not eating, and then his ulcer bothers him. When the guests leave, when the weekend is over, she has to cook bland food: applesauce, oatmeal, puddings. And his drinking does not taper off easily anymore; in the past he would stop cold when the guests left, but lately he only tapers down from Scotch to wine, and drinks wine well into the week—a lot of wine, perhaps a whole bottle with his meal—until his stomach is much worse. He is hard to live with. Once when a former student, a woman named Ruth, visited them—a lover, she suspected—she overheard George talking to her in his study, where he had taken her to see a photograph of their house before he began repairing it. George had told Ruth that she, Lenore, stayed with him because she was simple. It hurt her badly, made her actually dizzy with surprise and shame, and since then, no matter who the guests are, she never feels quite at ease on the weekends. In the past she enjoyed some of the things she and George did with their guests, but since overhearing what he said to Ruth she feels that all their visitors have been secretly told the same thing about her. To her, though, George is usually kind. But she is sure that is the reason he has not married her, and when he recently remarked on their daughter's intelligence (she is five years old, a girl named Maria) she found that she could no longer respond with simple pride; now she feels spite as well, feels that Maria exists as proof of her own good genes. She has begun to expect perfection of the child. She knows this is wrong, and she has tried hard not to communicate her anxiety to Maria, who is already, as her kindergarten teacher says, "untypical."

At first Lenore loved George because he was untypical, although after she had moved in with him and lived with him for a while she began to see that he was not exceptional but a variation on a type. She is proud of observing that, and she harbors the discovery—her silent response to his low opinion of her. She does not know why he found her attractive—in the beginning he did—because she does not resemble the pretty, articulate young women he likes to invite, with their lovers or girlfriends, to their house for the week-end. None of these young women have husbands; when they bring a man with them at all they bring a lover, and they seem happy not to be married. Lenore, too, is happy to be single—not out of conviction that marriage is wrong but because she knows that it would be wrong to be married to George if he thinks she is simple. She thought at first to confront him with what she had overheard, to demand an explanation. But he can weasel out of any corner. At best, she can mildly fluster him, and later he will only blame it on Scotch. Of course she might ask why he has all these women come to visit, why he devotes so little time to her or the children. To that he would say that it was the quality of the time they spent together that mattered, not the quantity. He has already said that, in fact, without being asked. He says things over and over so that she will accept them as truths. And eventually she does. She does not like to think long and hard, and when there is an answer—even his answer—it is usually easier to accept it and go on with things. She goes on with what she has always done: tending the house and the children and George, when he needs her. She likes to bake and she collects art postcards. She is proud of their house, which was bought cheaply and improved by George when he was still interested in that kind of work, and she is happy to have visitors come there, even if she does not admire them or even like them.

Except for teaching a night course in photography at a junior college once a week, George has not worked since he left the university two years ago, after he was denied tenure. She cannot really tell if he is unhappy working so little, because he keeps busy in other ways. He listens to classical music in the morning, slowly sipping herbal teas, and on fair afternoons he lies outdoors in the sun, no matter how cold the day. He takes photographs, and walks alone in the woods. He does errands for her if they need to be done. Sometimes at night he goes to the library or goes to visit friends; he tells her that these people often ask her to come too, but he says she would not like them. This is true—she would not like them. Recently he has done some late-night cooking. He has always kept a journal, and he is a great letter writer. An aunt left him most of her estate, ten thousand dollars, and said in her will that he was the only one who really cared, who took the time, again and again, to write. He had not seen his aunt for five years before she died, but he wrote regularly. Sometimes Lenore finds notes that he has left for her. Once, on the refrigerator, there was a long note suggesting clever Christmas presents for her family that he had thought of while she was out. Last week he scotch-taped a slip of paper to a casserole dish that contained leftover veal stew, saying: "This was delicious." He does not compliment her verbally, but he likes to let her know that he is pleased.

A few nights ago—the same night they got a call from Julie and Sarah, saying they were coming for a visit—she told him that she wished he would talk more, that he would confide in her.

"Confide what?" he said.

"You always take that attitude," she said. "You pretend that you have no thoughts. Why does there have to be so much silence?"

"I'm not a professor anymore," he said. "I don't have to spend every minute *thinking*."

But he loves to talk to the young women. He will talk to them on the phone for as much as an hour; he walks with them through the woods for most of the day when they visit. The lovers the young women bring with them always seem to fall behind; they give up and return to the house to sit and talk to her, or to help with the preparation of the meal, or to play with the children. The young women and George come back refreshed, ready for another round of conversation at dinner.

A few weeks ago one of the young men said to her, "Why do you let it go on?" They had been talking lightly before that—about the weather, the children—and then, in the kitchen, where he was sitting shelling peas, he put his head on the table and said, barely audibly, "Why do you let it go on?" He did not raise his head, and she stared at him, thinking that she must have imagined his speaking. She was surprised—surprised to have heard it, and surprised that he said nothing after that, which made her doubt that he had spoken.

"Why do I let what go on?" she said.

There was a long silence. "Whatever this sick game is, I don't want to get involved in it," he said at last. "It was none of my business to ask. I understand that you don't want to talk about it."

"But it's really cold out there," she said. "What could happen when it's freezing out?"

He shook his head, the way George did, to indicate that she was beyond understanding. But she wasn't stupid, and she knew what might be going on. She had said the right thing, had been on the right track, but she had to say what she felt, which was that nothing very serious could be happening at that moment because they were walking in the woods. There wasn't even a barn on the property. She knew perfectly well that they were talking.

When George and the young woman had come back, he fixed hot apple juice, into which he trickled rum. Lenore was pleasant, because she was sure of what had not happened; the young man was not, because he did not think as she did. Still at the kitchen table, he ran his thumb across a pea pod as though it were a knife.

This weekend Sarah and Julie are visiting. They came on Friday evening. Sarah was one of George's students—the one who led the fight to have him rehired. She does not look like a troublemaker; she is pale and pretty, with freckles on her cheeks. She talks too much about the past, and this upsets him, disrupts the peace he has made with himself. She tells him that they fired him because he was "in touch" with everything, that they were afraid of him because he was so in touch. The more she tells him the more he remembers, and then it is necessary for Sarah to say the same things again and again; once she reminds him, he seems to need reassurance—needs to have her voice, to hear her bitterness against the members of the tenure committee. By evening they will both be drunk. Sarah will seem both agitating and consoling, Lenore and Julie and the children will be upstairs, in bed. Lenore suspects that she will not be the only one awake listening to them. She thinks that in spite of Julie's glazed look she is really very attentive. The night before, when they were all sitting around the fireplace talking, Sarah made a gesture and almost upset her wineglass, but Julie reached for it and stopped it from toppling over. George and Sarah were talking so energetically that they did not notice. Lenore's eyes met Julie's as Julie's hand shot out. Lenore feels that she is like Julie: Julie's face doesn't betray emotion, even when she is interested, even when she cares deeply. Being the same kind of person, Lenore can recognize this.

Before Sarah and Julie arrived Friday evening, Lenore asked George if Sarah was his lover.

"Don't be ridiculous," he said. "You think every student is my lover? Is Julie my lover?"

She said, "That wasn't what I said."

"Well, if you're going to be preposterous, go ahead and say that," he said. "If you think about it long enough, it would make a lot of sense, wouldn't it?"

He would not answer her question about Sarah. He kept throwing Julie's name into it. Some other woman might then think that he was protesting too strongly—that Julie really was his lover. She thought no such thing. She also stopped suspecting Sarah, because he wanted that, and it was her habit to oblige him.

He is twenty-one years older than Lenore. On his last birthday he was fifty-five. His daughter from his first marriage (his *only* marriage; she keeps reminding herself that they are not married, because it often seems that they might as well be) sent him an Irish country hat. The present made him irritable. He kept putting it on and pulling it down hard on his head. "She wants to make me a laughable old man," he said. "She wants me to put this on and go around like a fool." He wore the hat all morning, complaining about it, frightening the children. Eventually, to calm him, she said, "She intended *nothing*." She said it with finality, her tone so insistent that he listened to her. But having lost his reason for bitterness, he said, "Just because you don't think doesn't mean others don't think." Is he getting old? She does not want to think of him getting old. In spite of his ulcer, his body is hard. He is tall and handsome, with a thick mustache and a thin black goatee, and there is very little gray in his kinky black hair. He dresses in tight-fitting blue jeans and black turtleneck sweaters in the winter, and old white shirts with the sleeves rolled up in the summer. He pretends not to care about his looks, but he does. He shaves carefully, scraping slowly down each side of his goatee. He orders his soft leather shoes from a store in California. After taking one of his long walks—even if he does it twice a day—he invariably takes a shower. He always looks refreshed, and very rarely admits any insecurity. A few times, at night in bed, he has asked, "Am I still the man of your dreams?" And when she says yes he always laughs, turning it into a joke, as if he didn't care. She knows he does. He pretends to have no feeling for clothing, but actually he cares so strongly about his turtlenecks and shirts (a few are Italian silk) and shoes that he will have no others. She has noticed that the young women who visit are always vain. When Sarah arrived, she was wearing a beautiful silk scarf, pale as conch shells.

Sitting on the floor on Saturday morning, Lenore watches the fire she has just lit. The baby, tucked in George's chair, smiles in his sleep, and Lenore thinks what a good companion he would be if only he were an adult. She gets up and goes into the kitchen and tears open a package of yeast and dissolves it, with sugar and salt, in hot water, slushing her fingers through it and shivering because it is so cold in the kitchen. She will bake bread for dinner—there is always a big meal in the early evening when they have guests. But what will she do for the rest of the day? George told the girls the night before that on Saturday they would walk in the woods, but she does not really enjoy hiking, and George will be irritated because of the discussion the night before, and she does not want to aggravate him. "You are unwilling to challenge anyone," her brother wrote her in a letter that came a few days ago. He has written her for years—all the years she has been with George—asking when she is going to end the relationship. She rarely writes back because she knows that her answers sound too simple. She has a comfortable house. She cooks. She keeps busy and she loves her two children. "It seems unkind to say *but*," her brother writes, "but . . ." It is true; she likes simple things. Her brother, who is a lawyer in Cambridge, cannot understand that.

Lenore rubs her hand down the side of her face and says good morning to Julie and Sarah, who have come downstairs. Sarah does not want orange juice; she already looks refreshed and ready for the day. Lenore pours a glass for Julie. George calls from the hallway, "Ready to roll?" Lenore is surprised that he wants to leave so early. She goes into the living room. George is wearing a denim jacket, his hands in the pockets.

"Morning," he says to Lenore. "You're not up for a hike, are you?"

Lenore looks at him, but does not answer. As she stands there, Sarah walks around her and joins George in the hallway and he holds the door open for her. "Let's walk to the store and get Hershey bars to give us energy for a long hike," George says to Sarah. They are gone. Lenore finds Julie still in the kitchen, waiting for the water to boil. Julie says that she had a bad night and she is happy not to be going with George and Sarah. Lenore fixes tea for them. Maria sits next to her on the sofa, sipping orange juice. The baby likes company, but Maria is a very private child; she would rather that she and her mother were always alone. She has given up being possessive about her father. Now she gets out a cardboard box and takes out her mother's collection of postcards, which she arranges on the floor in careful groups. Whenever she looks up, Julie smiles nervously at her; Maria does not smile, and Lenore doesn't prod her. Lenore goes into the kitchen to punch down the bread, and Maria follows. Maria has recently gotten over chicken pox, and there is a small new scar in the center of her forehead. Instead of looking at Maria's blue eyes, Lenore lately has found herself focusing on the imperfection.

As Lenore is stretching the loaves onto the cornmeal-covered baking sheet, she hears the rain start. It hits hard on the garage roof.

After a few minutes Julie comes into the kitchen. "They're caught in this downpour," Julie says. "If Sarah had left the car keys, I could go get them."

"Take my car and pick them up," Lenore says, pointing with her elbow to the keys hanging on a nail near the door.

"But I don't know where the store is."

"You must have passed it driving to our house last night. Just go out of the driveway and turn right. It's along the main road."

Julie gets her purple sweater and takes the car keys. "I'll be right back," she says.

Lenore can sense that she is glad to escape from the house, that she is happy the rain began.

In the living room Lenore turns the pages of a magazine, and Maria mutters a refrain of "Blue, blue, dark blue, green blue," noticing the color every time it appears. Lenore sips her tea. She puts a Michael Hurley record on George's stereo. Michael Hurley is good rainy-day music. George has hundreds of records. His students used to love to paw through them. Cleverly, he has never made any attempt to keep up with what is currently popular. Everything is jazz or eclectic: Michael Hurley, Keith Jarrett, Ry Cooder.

Julie comes back. "I couldn't find them," she says. She looks as if she expects to be punished.

Lenore is surprised. She is about to say something like "You certainly didn't look very hard, did you?" but she catches Julie's eye. She looks young and afraid, and perhaps even a little crazy.

"Well, we tried," Lenore says.

Julie stands in front of the fire, with her back to Lenore. Lenore knows she is thinking that she is dense—that she does not recognize the implications.

"They might have walked through the woods instead of along the road," Lenore says. "That's possible."

"But they would have gone out to the road to thumb when the rain began, wouldn't they?"

Perhaps she misunderstood what Julie was thinking. Perhaps it has never occurred to Julie until now what might be going on.

"Maybe they got lost," Julie says. "Maybe something happened to them."

"Nothing happened to them," Lenore says. Julie turns around and Lenore catches that small point of light in her eye again. "Maybe they took shelter under a tree," she says. "Maybe they're screwing. How should I know?"

It is not a word Lenore often uses. She usually tries not to think about that at all, but she can sense that Julie is very upset.

"Really?" Julie says. "Don't you care, Mrs. Anderson?"

Lenore is amused. There's a switch. All the students call her husband George and her Lenore; now one of them wants to think there's a real adult here to explain all this to her.

"What am I going to do?" Lenore says. She shrugs.

Julie does not answer.

"Would you like me to pour you tea?" Lenore asks.

"Yes," Julie says. "Please."

George and Sarah return in the middle of the afternoon. George says that they decided to go on a spree to the big city—it is really a small town he is talking about, but calling it the big city gives him an opportunity to speak ironically. They sat in a restaurant bar, waiting for the rain to stop, George says, and then they thumbed a ride home. "But I'm completely sober," George says, turning for the first time to Sarah. "What about you?" He is all smiles. Sarah lets him down. She looks embarrassed. Her eyes meet Lenore's quickly, and jump to Julie. The two girls stare at each other, and Lenore, left with only George to look at, looks at the fire and then gets up to pile on another log.

Gradually it becomes clear that they are trapped together by the rain. Maria undresses her paper doll and deliberately rips a feather off its hat. Then she takes the pieces to Lenore, almost in tears. The baby cries, and Lenore takes him off the sofa, where he has been sleeping under his yellow blanket, and props him in the space between her legs as she leans back on her elbows to watch the fire. It's her fire, and she has the excuse of presiding over it.

"How's my boy?" George says. The baby looks, and looks away.

It gets dark early, because of the rain. At four-thirty George uncorks a bottle of Beaujolais and brings it into the living room, with four glasses pressed against his chest with his free arm. Julie rises nervously to extract the glasses, thanking him too profusely for the wine. She gives a glass to Sarah without looking at her.

They sit in a semicircle in front of the fire and drink the wine. Julie leafs through magazines—*New Times, National Geographic*—and Sarah holds a small white dish painted with gray-green leaves that she has taken from the coffee table; the dish contains a few shells and some acorn caps, a polished stone or two, and Sarah lets these objects run through her fingers. There are several such dishes in the house, assembled by George. He and Lenore gathered the shells long ago, the first time they went away together, at a beach in North Carolina. But the acorn caps, the shiny turquoise and amethyst stones—those are there, she knows, because George likes the effect they have on visitors; it is an expected unconventionality, really. He has also acquired a few small framed pictures, which he points out to guests who are more important than worshipful students—tiny oil paintings of fruit, prints with small details from the unicorn tapestries. He pretends to like small, elegant things. Actually, when they visit museums in New York he goes first to El Grecos and big Mark Rothko canvases. She could never get him to admit that what he said or did was sometimes false. Once, long ago, when he asked if he was still the man of her dreams, she said, "We don't get along well anymore." "Don't talk about it," he said—no denial, no protest. At best, she could say things and get away with them; she could never get him to continue such a conversation.

At the dinner table, lit with white candles burning in empty wine bottles, they eat off his grandmother's small flowery plates. Lenore looks out a window and sees, very faintly in the dark, their huge oak tree. The rain has stopped. A few stars have come out, and there are glints on the wet branches. The oak tree grows very close to the window. George loved it when her brother once suggested that some of the bushes and trees should be pruned away from the house so it would not always be so dark inside; it gave him a chance to rave about the beauty of nature, to say that he would never tamper with it. "It's like a tomb in here all day," her brother had said. Since moving here, George has learned the names of almost all the things that are growing on the land: he can point out abelia bushes, spirea, laurels. He subscribes to *National Geographic* (although she rarely sees him looking at it). He is at last in touch, he says, being in the country puts him in touch. He is saying it now to Sarah, who has put down her ivory-handled fork to listen to him. He gets up to change the record. Side two of the Telemann record begins softly.

Sarah is still very much on guard with Lenore; she makes polite conversation with her quickly when George is out of the room. "You people are so wonderful," she says. "I wish my parents could be like you."

"George would be pleased to hear that," Lenore says, lifting a small piece of pasta to her lips.

When George is seated again, Sarah, anxious to please, tells him, "If only my father could be like you."

"Your father," George says. "I won't have that analogy." He says it pleasantly, but barely disguises his dismay at the comparison.

"I mean, he cares about nothing but business," the girl stumbles on.

The music, in contrast, grows lovelier.

Lenore goes into the kitchen to get the salad and hears George say, "I simply won't let you girls leave. Nobody leaves on a Saturday."

There are polite protests, there are compliments to Lenore on the meal—there is too much talk. Lenore has trouble caring about what's going on. The food is warm and delicious. She pours more wine and lets them talk.

"Godard, yes, I know . . . panning that row of honking cars *so* slowly, that long line of cars stretching on and on."

She has picked up the end of George's conversation. His arm slowly waves out over the table, indicating the line of motionless cars in the movie.

"That's a lovely plant," Julie says to Lenore.

"It's Peruvian ivy," Lenore says. She smiles. She is supposed to smile. She will not offer to hack shoots off her plant for these girls.

Sarah asks for a Dylan record when the Telemann finishes playing. White wax drips onto the wood table. George waits for it to solidify slightly, then scrapes up the little circles and with thumb and index finger flicks them gently toward Sarah. He explains (although she asked for no particular Dylan record) that he has only Dylan before he went electric. And *Planet Waves*— "because it's so romantic. That's silly of me, but true." Sarah smiles at him. Julie smiles at Lenore. Julie is being polite, taking her cues from Sarah, really not understanding what's going on. Lenore does not smile back. She has done enough to put them at ease. She is tired now, brought down by the music, a full stomach, and again the sounds of rain outside. For dessert there is homemade vanilla ice cream, made by George, with small black vanilla-bean flecks in it. He is still drinking wine, though; another bottle has been opened. He sips wine and then taps his spoon on his ice cream, looking at Sarah. Sarah smiles, letting them all see the smile, then sucks the ice cream off her spoon. Julie is missing more and more of what's going on. Lenore watches as Julie strokes her hand absently on her napkin. She is wearing a thin silver choker and—Lenore notices for the first time—a thin silver ring on the third finger of her right hand.

"It's just terrible about Anna," George says, finishing his wine, his ice cream melting, looking at no one in particular, although Sarah was the one who brought up Anna the night before, when they had been in the house only a short time—Anna dead, hit by a car, hardly an accident at all. Anna was also a student of his. The driver of the car was drunk, but for some reason charges were not pressed. (Sarah and George have talked about this before, but Lenore blocks it out. What can she do about it? She met Anna once: a beautiful girl, with tiny, childlike hands, her hair thin and curly— wary, as beautiful people are wary.) Now the driver has been flipping out, Julie says, and calling Anna's parents, wanting to talk to them to find out why it has happened.

The baby begins to cry. Lenore goes upstairs, pulls up more covers, talks to him for a minute. He settles for this. She goes downstairs. The wine must have affected her more than she realizes; otherwise, why is she counting the number of steps?

In the candlelit dining room, Julie sits alone at the table. The girl has been left alone again; George and Sarah took the umbrellas, decided to go for a walk in the rain.

It is eight o'clock. Since helping Lenore load the dishes into the dishwasher, when she said what a beautiful house Lenore had, Julie has said very little. Lenore is tired, and does not want to make conversation. They sit in the living room and drink wine.

"Sarah is my best friend," Julie says. She seems apologetic about it. "I was so out of it when I came back to college. I was in Italy, with my husband, and suddenly I was back in the States. I couldn't make friends. But Sarah wasn't like the other people. She cared enough to be nice to me."

"How long have you been friends?"

"For two years. She's really the best friend I've ever had. We understand things—we don't always have to talk about them."

"Like her relationship with George," Lenore says.

Too direct. Too unexpected. Julie has no answer.

"You act as if you're to blame," Lenore says.

"I feel strange because you're such a nice lady."

A nice lady! What an odd way to speak. Has she been reading Henry James? Lenore has never known what to think of herself, but she certainly thinks of herself as being more complicated than a "lady."

"Why do you look that way?" Julie asks. "You *are* nice. I think you've been very nice to us. You've given up your whole weekend."

"I always give up my weekends. Weekends are the only time we socialize, really. In a way, it's good to have something to do."

"But to have it turn out like this . . ." Julie says. "I think I feel so strange because when my own marriage broke up I didn't even suspect. I mean, I couldn't act the way you do, anyway, but I—"

"For all I know, nothing's going on," Lenore says. "For all I know, your friend is flattering herself, and George is trying to make me jealous." She puts two more logs on the fire. When these are gone, she will either have to walk to the woodshed or give up and go to bed. "Is there something . . . *major* going on?" she asks.

Julie is sitting on the rug, by the fire, twirling her hair with her finger. "I didn't know it when I came out here," she says. "Sarah's put me in a very awkward position."

"But do you know how far it has gone?" Lenore asks, genuinely curious now.

"No," Julie says.

No way to know if she's telling the truth. Would Julie speak the truth to a lady? Probably not.

"Anyway," Lenore says with a shrug, "I don't want to think about it all the time."

"I'd never have the courage to live with a man and not marry," Julie says. "I mean, I wish I had, that we hadn't gotten married, but I just don't have that kind of . . . I'm not secure enough."

"You have to live somewhere," Lenore says.

Julie is looking at her as if she does not believe that she is sincere. Am I? Lenore wonders. She has lived with George for six years, and sometimes she thinks she has caught his way of playing games, along with his colds, his bad moods.

"I'll show you something," Lenore says. She gets up, and Julie follows. Lenore puts on the light in George's study, and they walk through it to a bathroom he has converted to a darkroom. Under a table, in a box behind another box, there is a stack of pictures. Lenore takes them out and hands them to Julie. They are pictures that Lenore found in his darkroom last summer; they were left out by mistake, no doubt, and she found them when she went in with some contact prints he had left in their bedroom. They are high-contrast photographs of George's face. In all of them he looks very serious and very sad; in some of them his eyes seem to be narrowed in pain. In one, his mouth is open. It is an excellent photograph of a man in agony, a man about to scream.

"What are they?" Julie whispers.

"Pictures he took of himself," Lenore says. She shrugs. "So I stay," she says.

Julie nods. Lenore nods, taking the pictures back. Lenore has not thought until this minute that this may be why she stays. In fact, it is not the only reason. It is just a very demonstrable, impressive reason. When she first saw the pictures, her own face had become as distorted as George's. She had simply not known what to do. She had been frightened and ashamed. Finally she put them in an empty box, and put the box behind another box. She did not even want him to see the horrible pictures again. She does not know if he has ever found them, pushed back against the wall in that other box. As George says, there can be too much communication between people.

Later, Sarah and George come back to the house. It is still raining. It turns out that they took a bottle of brandy with them, and they are both drenched and drunk. He holds Sarah's finger with one of his. Sarah, seeing Lenore, lets his finger go. But then he turns—they have not even said hello yet—and grabs her up, spins her around, stumbling into the living room, and says, "I am in love."

Julie and Lenore watch them in silence.

"See no evil," George says, gesturing with the empty brandy bottle to Julie. "Hear no evil," George says, pointing to Lenore. He hugs Sarah closer. "I speak no evil. I speak the truth. I am in love!"

Sarah squirms away from him, runs from the room and up the stairs in the dark.

George looks blankly after her, then sinks to the floor and smiles. He is going to pass it off as a joke. Julie looks at him in horror, and from upstairs Sarah can be heard sobbing. Her crying awakens the baby.

"Excuse me," Lenore says. She climbs the stairs and goes into her son's room, and picks him up. She talks gently to him, soothing him with lies. He is too sleepy to be alarmed for long. In a few minutes he is asleep again, and she puts him back in his crib. In the next room Sarah is crying more quietly now. Her crying is so awful that Lenore almost joins in, but instead she pats her son. She stands in the dark by the crib and then at last goes out and down the hallway to her bedroom. She takes off her clothes and gets into the cold bed. She concentrates on breathing normally. With the door closed and Sarah's door closed, she can hardly hear her. Someone taps lightly on her door.

"Mrs. Anderson," Julie whispers. "Is this your room?"

"Yes," Lenore says. She does not ask her in.

"We're going to leave. I'm going to get Sarah and leave. I didn't want to just walk out without saying anything."

Lenore just cannot think how to respond. It was really very kind of Julie to say something. She is very close to tears, so she says nothing.

"Okay," Julie says, to reassure herself. "Good night. We're going."

There is no more crying. Footsteps. Miraculously, the baby does not wake up again, and Maria has slept through all of it. She has always slept well. Lenore herself sleeps worse and worse, and she knows that George walks much of the night, most nights. She hasn't said anything about it. If he thinks she's simple, what good would her simple wisdom do him?

The oak tree scrapes against the window in the wind and rain. Here on the second floor, under the roof, the tinny tapping is very loud. If Sarah and Julie say anything to George before they leave, she doesn't hear them. She hears the car start, then die out. It starts again—she is praying for the car to go—and after conking out once more it rolls slowly away, crunching gravel.

The bed is no warmer; she shivers. She tries hard to fall asleep. The effort keeps her awake. She squints her eyes in concentration instead of closing them. The only sound in the house is the electric clock, humming by her bed. It is not even midnight.

She gets up, and without turning on the light, walks downstairs. George is still in the living room. The fire is nothing but ashes and glowing bits of wood. It is as cold there as it was in the bed.

"That damn bitch," George says. "I should have known she was a stupid little girl."

"You went too far," Lenore says. "I'm the only one you can go too far with."

"Damn it," he says, and pokes the fire. A few sparks shoot up. "Damn it," he repeats under his breath.

His sweater is still wet. His shoes are muddy and ruined. Sitting on the floor by the fire, his hair matted down on his head, he looks ugly, older, unfamiliar.

She thinks of another time, when it was warm. They were walking on the beach together, shortly after they met, gathering shells. Little waves were rolling in. The sun went behind the clouds and there was a momentary illusion that the clouds were still and the sun was racing ahead of them. "Catch me," he said, breaking away from her. They had been talking quietly, gathering shells. She was so surprised at him for breaking away that she ran with all her energy and did catch him, putting her hand out and taking hold of the band of his swimming trunks as he veered into the water. If she hadn't stopped him, would he really have run far out into the water, until she couldn't follow anymore? He turned on her, just as abruptly as he had run away, and grabbed her and hugged her hard, lifted her high. She had clung to him, held him close. He had tried the same thing when he came back from the walk with Sarah, and it hadn't worked.

"I wouldn't care if their car went off the road," he says bitterly.

"Don't say that," she says.

They sit in silence, listening to the rain. She slides over closer to him, puts her hand on his shoulder and leans her head there, as if he could protect her from the awful things he has wished into being.

Tuesday Night

Henry was supposed to bring the child home at six o'clock, but they usually did not arrive until eight or eight-thirty, with Joanna overtired and complaining that she did not want to go to bed the minute she came through the door. Henry had taught her that phrase. "The minute she comes through the door" was something I had said once, and he mocked me with it in defending her. "Let the poor child have a minute before she goes to bed. She *did* just come through the door." The poor child is, of course, crazy about Henry. He allows her to call him that, instead of "Daddy." And now he takes her to dinner at a French restaurant that she adores, which doesn't open until five-thirty. That means that she gets home close to eight. I am a beast if I refuse to let her eat her escargots. And it would be cruel to tell her that her father's support payments fluctuate wildly, while the French dining remains a constant. Forget the money—Henry has been a good father. He visits every Tuesday night, carefully twirls her crayons in the pencil sharpener, and takes her every other weekend. The only bad thing he has done to her—and even Henry agreed about that—was to introduce her to the sleepie he had living with him right after the divorce: an obnoxious woman, who taught Joanna to sing "I'm a Woman." Fortunately, she did not remember many of the words, but I thought I'd lose my mind when she went around the house singing "Doubleyou oh oh em ay en" for two weeks. Sometimes the sleepie tucked a fresh flower in Joanna's hair—like Maria Muldaur, she explained. The child had the good sense to be embarrassed.

The men I know are very friendly with one another. When Henry was at the house last week, he helped Dan, who lives with me, carry a bookcase up the steep, narrow steps to the second floor. Henry and Dan talk about nutrition—Dan's current interest. My brother Bobby, the only person I know who is seriously interested in hallucinogens at the age of twenty-six, gladly makes a fool of himself in front of Henry by bringing out his green yo-yo, which glows by the miracle of two internal batteries. Dan tells Bobby that if he's going to take drugs, he should try dosing his body with vitamins before and after. The three of them Christmas-shop for me. Last year they had dinner at an Italian restaurant downtown. I asked Dan what they ordered, and he said, "Oh, we all had manicotti."

I have been subsisting on red zinger tea and watermelon, trying to lose weight. Dan and Henry and Bobby are all thin. Joanna takes after her father in her build. She is long and graceful, with chiseled features that would shame Marisa Berenson. She is ten years old. When I was at the laundry to pick up the clothes yesterday a woman mistook me, from the back, for her cousin Addie.

In Joanna's class at school they are having a discussion of problems with the environment. She wants to take our big avocado plant in to school. I have tried patiently to explain that the plant does not have anything to do with environmental problems. She says that they are discussing nature, too. "What's the harm?" Dan says. So he goes to work and leaves it to me to fit the towering avocado into the Audi. I also get roped into baking cookies so Joanna can take them to school and pass them around to celebrate her birthday. She tells me that it is the custom to put the cookies in a box wrapped in birthday paper. We select a paper with yellow bears standing in concentric circles. Dan dumps bran into the chocolate-chip-cookie dough. He forbids me to use a dot of red food coloring in the sugar-cookie hearts.

My best friend, Dianne, comes over in the mornings and turns her nose up at my red zinger. Sometimes she takes a shower here because she loves our shower head. "How come you're not in there all the time?" she says. My brother is sweet on her. He finds her extremely attractive. He asked me if I had noticed the little droplets of water from the shower on her forehead, just at the hairline. Bobby lends her money because her husband doesn't give her enough. I know for a fact that Dianne is thinking of having an affair with him.

Dan has to work late at his office on Tuesday nights, and a while ago I decided that I wanted that one night to myself each week—a night without any of them. Dianne said, "I know what you mean," but Bobby took great offense and didn't come to visit that night, or any other night, for two weeks. Joanna was delighted that she could be picked up after school by Dianne, in Dianne's 1966 Mustang convertible, and that the two of them could visit until Henry came by Dianne's to pick her up. Dan, who keeps saying that our relationship is going sour—although it isn't—pursed his lips and nodded when I told him about Tuesday nights, but he said nothing. The first night alone I read a dirty magazine that had been lying around the house for some time. Then I took off all my clothes and looked in the hall mirror and decided to go on a diet, so I skipped dinner. I made a long-distance call to a friend in California who had just had a baby. We talked about the spidery little veins in her thighs, and I swore to her over and over again that they would go away. Then I took one of each kind of vitamin pill we have in the house.

The next week I had prepared for my spare time better. I had bought whole-wheat flour and clover honey, and I made four loaves of whole-wheat bread. I made a piecrust, putting dough in the sink and rolling it out there, which made a lot of sense but which I would never let anybody see me doing. Then I read *Vogue*. Later on I took out the yoga book I had bought that afternoon and put it in my plastic cookbook-holder and put that down on the floor and stared at it as I tried to get into the postures. I overcooked the piecrust and it burned. I got depressed and drank a Drambuie. The week after that, I ventured out. I went to a movie and bought myself a chocolate milkshake afterward. I sat at the drugstore counter and drank it. I was going to get my birth-control-pill prescription refilled while I was there, but I decided that would be depressing.

Joanna sleeps at her father's apartment now on Tuesday nights. Since he considers her too old to be read a fairy tale before bed, Henry waltzes with her. She wears a long nightgown and a pair of high-heeled shoes that some woman left there. She says that he usually plays "The Blue Danube," but sometimes he kids around and puts on "Idiot Wind" or "Forever Young" and they dip and twirl to it. She has hinted that she would like to take dancing lessons. Last week she danced through the living room at our house on her pogo stick. Dan had given it to her, saying that now she had a partner, and it would save him money not having to pay for dancing lessons. He told her that if she had any questions, she could ask him. He said she could call him "Mr. Daniel." She was disgusted with him. If she were Dan's child, I am sure he would still be reading her fairy tales.

Another Tuesday night I went out and bought plants. I used my American Express card and got seventy dollars' worth of plants and some plant hangers. The woman in the store helped me carry the boxes out to the car. I went home and drove nails into the top of the window frames and hung the plants. They did not need to be watered yet, but I held the plastic plant waterer up to them, to see what it would be like to water them. I squeezed the plastic bottle and stared at the curved plastic tube coming out of it. Later I gave myself a facial with egg whites.

There is a mouse. I first saw it in the kitchen—a small gray mouse, moseying along, taking its time in getting from under the counter to the back of the stove. I had Dan seal off the little mouse hole in the back of the stove. Then I saw the mouse again, under the chest in the living room.

"It's a mouse. It's one little mouse," Dan said. "Let it be."

"Everybody knows that if there's one mouse, there are more," I said. "We've got to get rid of them."

Dan, the humanist, was secretly glad the mouse had resurfaced—that he hadn't done any damage in sealing off its home.

"It looked like the same mouse to me," Henry said.

"They all look that way," I said. "That doesn't mean—"

"Poor thing," Dan said.

"Are either of you going to set traps, or do I have to do it?"

"You have to do it," Dan said. "I can't stand it. I don't want to kill a mouse."

"I think there's only one mouse," Henry said.

Glaring at them, I went into the kitchen and took the mousetraps out of their cellophane packages. I stared at them with tears in my eyes. I did not know how to set them. Dan and Henry had made me seem like a cold-blooded killer.

"Maybe it will just leave," Dan said.

"Don't be ridiculous, Dan," I said. "If you aren't going to help, at least don't sit around snickering with Henry."

"We're not snickering," Henry said.

"You two certainly are buddy-buddy."

"What's the matter now? You want us to hate each other?" Henry said.

"I don't know how to set a mousetrap," I said. "I can't do it myself."

"Poor Mommy," Joanna said. She was in the hallway outside the living room, listening. I almost turned on her to tell her not to be sarcastic, when I realized that she was serious. She felt sorry for me. With someone on my side, I felt new courage about going back into the kitchen and tackling the problem of the traps.

Dianne called and said she had asked her husband if he would go out one night a week so she could go out with friends or stay home by herself. He said no, but agreed to take stained-glass lessons with her.

One Tuesday it rained. I stayed home and daydreamed, and remembered the past. I thought about the boy I dated my last year in high school who used to take me out to the country on weekends, to where some cousins of his lived.

I wondered why he always went there, because we never got near the house. He would drive partway up their long driveway in the woods and then pull off onto a narrow little road that trucks sometimes used when they were logging the property. We parked on the little road and necked. Sometimes the boy would drive slowly along on the country roads looking for rabbits, and whenever he saw one, which was pretty often—sometimes even two or three rabbits at once—he floored it, trying to run the rabbit down. There was no radio in the car. He had a portable radio that got only two stations (soul music and classical) and I held it on my lap. He liked the volume turned up very loud.

Joanna comes to my bedroom and announces that Uncle Bobby is on the phone.

"I got a dog," he says.

"What kind?"

"Aren't you even surprised?"

"Yes. Where did you get the dog?"

"A guy I knew a little bit in college is going to jail, and he persuaded me to take the dog."

"What is he going to jail for?"

"Burglary."

"Joanna," I say, "don't stand there staring at me when I'm talking on the phone."

"He robbed a house," Bobby says.

"What kind of a dog is it?" I ask.

"Malamute and German shepherd. It's in heat."

"Well," I say, "you always wanted a dog."

"I call you all the time, and you never call me," Bobby says.

"I never have interesting news."

"You could call and tell me what you do on Tuesday nights."

"Nothing very interesting," I say.

"You could go to a bar and have rum drinks and weep," Bobby says. He chuckles.

"Are you stoned?" I ask.

"Sure I am. Been home from work for an hour and a half. Ate a Celeste pizza, had a little smoke."

"Do you really have a dog?" I ask.

"If you were a male dog, you wouldn't have any doubt of it."

"You're always much more clever than I am. It's hard to talk to you on the phone, Bobby."

"It's hard to be me," Bobby says. A silence. "I'm not sure the dog likes me."

"Bring it over. Joanna will love it."

"I'll be around with it Tuesday night," he says.

"Why is it so interesting to you that I have one night a week to myself?"

"Whatever you do," Bobby says, "don't rob a house."

We hang up, and I go tell Joanna the news.

"You yelled at me," she says.

"I did not. I asked you not to stand there staring at me while I was on the phone."

"You raised your voice," she says.

Soon it will be Tuesday night.

Joanna asks me suspiciously what I do on Tuesday nights.

"What does your father say I do?" I ask.

"He says he doesn't know."

"Does he seem curious?"

"It's hard to tell with him," she says.

Having got my answer, I've forgotten about her question.

"So what things do you do?" she says.

"Sometimes you like to play in your tent," I say defensively. "Well, I like some time to just do what I want to do, too, Joanna."

"That's okay," she says. She sounds like an adult placating a child.

I have to face the fact that I don't do much of anything on Tuesdays, and that one night alone each week isn't making me any less edgy or more agreeable to live with. I tell Dan this, as if it's his fault.

"I don't think you ever wanted to divorce Henry," Dan says.

"Oh, Dan, I *did*."

"You two seem to get along fine."

"But we fought. We didn't get along."

He looks at me. "Oh," he says. He is being inordinately nice to me because of the scene I threw when a mouse got caught in one of the traps. The trap didn't kill it. It just got it by the paw, and Dan had to beat it to death with a screwdriver.

"Maybe you'd rather the two of us did something regularly on Tuesday nights," he says now. "Maybe I could get the night of my meetings changed."

"Thank you," I say. "Maybe I should give it a little longer."

"That's up to you," he says. "There hasn't been enough time to judge by, I guess."

Inordinately kind. Deferential. He has been saying for a long time that our relationship is turning sour, and now it must have turned so sour for him that he doesn't even want to fight. What does he want?

"Maybe you'd like a night—" I begin.

"The hell with that," he says. "If there has to be so much time alone, I can't see the point of living together."

I hate fights. The day after this one, I get weepy and go over to Dianne's. She ends up subtly suggesting that I take stained-glass lessons. We drink some sherry and I drive home. The last thing I want is to run into her husband, who calls me "the squirrel" behind my back. Dianne says that when I call and he answers, he lets her know it's me on the phone by puffing up his cheeks to make himself look like a squirrel.

Tonight Dan and I each sit on a side of Joanna's tester bed to say good night to her. The canopy above the bed is white nylon, with small puckered stars. She is ready for sleep. As soon as she goes to sleep, Dan will be ready to talk to me. Dan has clicked off the light next to Joanna's bed. Going out of the bedroom before him, I grope for the hall light. I remember Henry saying to me, as a way of leading up to talking about divorce, that going to work one morning he had driven over a hill and had been astonished when at the top he saw a huge yellow tree, and realized for the first time that it was autumn.

Shifting

The woman's name was Natalie, and the man's name was Larry. They had been childhood sweethearts; he had first kissed her at an ice-skating party when they were ten. She had been unlacing her skates and had not expected the kiss. He had not expected to do it, either—he had some notion of getting his face out of the wind that was blowing across the iced-over lake, and he found himself ducking his head toward her. Kissing her seemed the natural thing to do. When they graduated from high school he was named "class clown" in the yearbook, but Natalie didn't think of him as being particularly funny. He spent more time than she thought he needed to studying chemistry, and he never laughed when she joked. She really did not think of him as funny. They went to the same college, in their hometown, but he left after a year to go to a larger, more impressive university. She took the train to be with him on weekends, or he took the train to see her. When he graduated, his parents gave him a car. If they had given it to him when he was still in college, it would have made things much easier. They waited to give it to him until graduation day, forcing him into attending the graduation exercises. He thought his parents were wonderful people, and Natalie liked them in a way, too, but she resented their perfect timing, their careful smiles. They were afraid that he would marry her. Eventually, he did. He had gone on to graduate school after college, and he set a date six months ahead for their wedding so that it would take place after his first-semester final exams. That way he could devote his time to studying for the chemistry exams.

When she married him, he had had the car for eight months. It still smelled like a brand-new car. There was never any clutter in the car. Even the ice scraper was kept in the glove compartment. There was not even a sweater or a lost glove in the back seat. He vacuumed the car every weekend, after washing it at the car wash. On Friday nights, on their way to some cheap restaurant and a dollar movie, he would stop at the car wash, and she would get out so he could vacuum all over the inside of the car. She would lean against the metal wall of the car wash and watch him clean it.

It was expected that she would not become pregnant. She did not. It had also been expected that she would keep their apartment clean, and keep out of the way as much as possible in such close quarters while he was studying. The apartment was messy, though, and when he was studying late at night she would interrupt him and try to talk him into going to sleep. He gave a chemistry-class lecture once a week, and she would often tell him that overpreparing was as bad as underpreparing. She did not know if she believed this, but it was a favorite line of hers. Sometimes he listened to her.

On Tuesdays, when he gave the lecture, she would drop him off at school and then drive to a supermarket to do the week's shopping. Usually she did not make a list before she went shopping, but when she got to the parking lot she would take a tablet out of her purse and write a few items on it, sitting in the car in the cold. Even having a few things written down would stop her from wandering aimlessly in the store and buying things that she would never use. Before this, she had bought several pans and cans of food that she had not used, or that she could have done without. She felt better when she had a list.

She would drop him at school again on Wednesdays, when he had two seminars that together took up all the afternoon. Sometimes she would drive out of town then, to the suburbs, and shop there if any shopping needed to be done. Otherwise, she would go to the art museum, which was not far away but hard to get to by bus. There was one piece of sculpture in there that she wanted very much to touch, but the guard was always nearby. She came so often that in time the guard began to nod hello. She wondered if she could ever persuade the man to turn his head for a few seconds—only that long—so she could stroke the sculpture. Of course she would never dare ask. After wandering through the museum and looking at least twice at the sculpture, she would go to the gift shop and buy a few postcards and then sit on one of the museum benches, padded with black vinyl, with a Calder mobile hanging overhead, and write notes to friends. (She never wrote letters.) She would tuck the postcards in her purse and mail them when she left the museum. But before she left, she often had coffee in the restaurant: she saw mothers and children struggling there, and women dressed in fancy clothes talking with their faces close together, as quietly as lovers.

On Thursdays he took the car. After his class he would drive to visit his parents and his friend Andy, who had been wounded in Vietnam. About once a month she would go with him, but she had to feel up to it. Being with Andy embarrassed her. She had told him not to go to Vietnam—told him that he could prove his patriotism in some other way—and finally, after she and Larry had made a visit together and she had seen Andy in the motorized bed in his parents' house, Larry had agreed that she need not go again. Andy had apologized to her. It embarrassed her that this man, who had been blown sky-high by a land mine and had lost a leg and lost the full use of his arms, would smile up at her ironically and say, "You were right." She also felt as though he wanted to hear what she would say now, and that now he would listen. Now she had nothing to say. Andy would pull himself up, relying on his right arm, which was the stronger, gripping the rails at the side of the bed, and sometimes he would take her hand. His arms were still weak, but the doctors said he would regain complete use of his right arm with time. She had to make an effort not to squeeze his hand when he held hers because she found herself wanting to squeeze energy back into him. She had a morbid curiosity about what it felt like to be blown from the ground—to go up, and to come crashing down. During their visit Larry put on the class-clown act for Andy, telling funny stories and laughing uproariously.

Once or twice Larry had talked Andy into getting in his wheelchair and had loaded him into the car and taken him to a bar. Larry called her once, late, pretty drunk, to say that he would not be home that night—that he would sleep at his parents' house. "My God," she said. "Are you going to drive Andy home when you're drunk?" "What the hell else can happen to him?" he said.

Larry's parents blamed her for Larry's not being happy. His mother could only be pleasant with her for a short while, and then she would veil her criticisms by putting them as questions. "I know that one thing that helps enormously is good nutrition," his mother said. "He works so hard that he probably needs quite a few vitamins as well, don't you think?" Larry's father was the sort of man who found hobbies in order to avoid his wife. His hobbies were building model boats, repairing clocks, and photography. He took pictures of himself building the boats and fixing the clocks, and gave the pictures, in cardboard frames, to Natalie and Larry for Christmas and birthday presents. Larry's mother was very anxious to stay on close terms with her son, and she knew that Natalie did not like her very much. Once she had visited them during the week, and Natalie, not knowing what to do with her, had taken her to the museum. She had pointed out the sculpture, and his mother had glanced at it and then ignored it. Natalie hated her for her bad taste. She had bad taste in the sweaters she gave Larry, too, but he wore them. They made him look collegiate. That whole world made her sick.

When Natalie's uncle died and left her his 1965 Volvo, they immediately decided to sell it and use the money for a vacation. They put an ad in the paper, and there were several callers. There were some calls on Tuesday, when Larry was in class, and Natalie found herself putting the people off. She told one woman that the car had too much mileage on it, and mentioned body rust, which it did not have; she told another caller, who was very persistent, that the car was already sold. When Larry returned from school she explained that the phone was off the hook because so many people were calling about the car and she had decided not to sell it after all. They could take a little money from their savings account and go on the trip if he wanted. But she did not want to sell the car. "It's not an automatic shift," he said. "You don't know how to drive it." She told him that she could learn. "It will cost money to insure it," he said, "and it's old and probably not even dependable." She wanted to keep the car. "I know," he said, "but it doesn't make sense. When we have more money, you can have a car. You can have a newer, better car."

The next day she went out to the car, which was parked in the driveway of an old lady next door. Her name was Mrs. Larsen and she no longer drove a car, and she told Natalie she could park their second car there. Natalie opened the car door and got behind the wheel and put her hands on it. The wheel was covered with a flaky yellow-and-black plastic cover. She eased it off. A few pieces of foam rubber stuck to the wheel. She picked them off. Underneath the cover, the wheel was a dull red. She ran her fingers around and around the circle of the wheel. Her cousin Burt had delivered the car—a young opportunist, sixteen years old, who said he would drive it the hundred miles from his house to theirs for twenty dollars and a bus ticket home. She had not even invited him to stay for dinner, and Larry had driven him to the bus station. She wondered if it was Burt's cigarette in the ashtray or her dead uncle's. She could not even remember if her uncle smoked. She was surprised that he had left her his car. The car was much more comfortable than Larry's, and it had a nice smell inside. It smelled a little the way a field smells after a spring rain. She rubbed the side of her head back and forth against the window and then got out of the car and went in to see Mrs. Larsen. The night before, she had suddenly thought of the boy who brought the old lady the evening newspaper every night; he looked old enough to drive, and he would probably know how to shift. Mrs. Larsen agreed with her—she was sure that he could teach her. "Of course, everything has its price," the old lady said.

"I know that. I meant to offer him money," Natalie said, and was surprised, listening to her voice, that she sounded old too.

She took an inventory and made a list of things in their apartment. Larry had met an insurance man one evening while playing basketball at the gym who told him that they should have a list of their possessions, in case of theft. "What's worth anything?" she said when he told her. It was their first argument in almost a year—the first time in a year, anyway, that their voices were raised. He told her that several of the pieces of furniture his grandparents gave them when they got married were antiques, and the man at the gym said that if they weren't going to get them appraised every year, at least they should take snapshots of them and keep the pictures in a safe-deposit box. Larry told her to photograph the pie safe (which she used to store linen), the piano with an inlaid mother-of-pearl decoration on the music rack (neither of them knew how to play), and the table with hand-carved wooden handles and a marble top. He bought her an Instamatic camera at the drugstore, with film and flash bulbs. "Why can't you do it?" she said, and an argument began. He said that she had no respect for his profession and no understanding of the amount of study that went into getting a master's degree in chemistry.

That night he went out to meet two friends at the gym, to shoot baskets. She put the little flashcube into the top of the camera, dropped in the film and closed the back. She went first to the piano. She leaned forward so that she was close enough to see the inlay clearly, but she found that when she was that close the whole piano wouldn't fit into the picture. She decided to take two pictures. Then she photographed the pie safe, with one door open, showing the towels and sheets stacked inside. She did not have a reason for opening the door, except that she remembered a *Perry Mason* show in which detectives photographed everything with the doors hanging open. She photographed the table, lifting the lamp off it first. There were still eight pictures left. She went to the mirror in their bedroom and held the camera above her head, pointing down at an angle, and photographed her image in the mirror. She took off her slacks and sat on the floor and leaned back, aiming the camera down at her legs. Then she stood up and took a picture of her feet, leaning over and aiming down. She put on her favorite record: Stevie Wonder singing "For Once in My Life." She found herself wondering what it would be like to be blind, to have to feel things to see them. She thought about the piece of sculpture in the museum—the two elongated mounds, intertwined, the smooth gray stone as shiny as sea pebbles. She photographed the kitchen, bathroom, bedroom and living room. There was one picture left. She put her left hand on her thigh, palm up, and with some difficulty—with the camera nestled into her neck like a violin—snapped a picture of it with her right hand. The next day would be her first driving lesson.

He came to her door at noon, as he had said he would. He had on a long maroon scarf, which made his deep-blue eyes very striking. She had only seen him from her window when he carried the paper in to the old lady. He was a little nervous. She hoped that it was just the anxiety of any teen-ager confronting an adult. She needed to have him like her. She did not learn about mechanical things easily (Larry had told her that he would have invested in a "real" camera, except that he did not have the time to teach her about it), so she wanted him to be patient. He sat on the footstool in her living room, still in coat and scarf, and told her how a stick shift operated. He moved his hand through the air. The motion he made reminded her of the salute spacemen gave to earthlings in a science-fiction picture she had recently watched on late-night television. She nodded. "How much—" she began, but he interrupted and said, "You can decide what it was worth when you've learned." She was surprised and wondered if he meant to charge a great deal. Would it be her fault and would she have to pay him if he named his price when the lessons were over? But he had an honest face. Perhaps he was just embarrassed to talk about money.

He drove for a few blocks, making her watch his hand on the stick shift. "Feel how the car is going?" he said. "Now you shift." He shifted. The car jumped a little, hummed, moved into gear. It was an old car and didn't shift too easily, he said. She had been sitting forward, so that when he shifted she rocked back hard against the seat—harder than she needed to. Almost unconsciously, she wanted to show him what a good teacher he was. When her turn came to drive, the car stalled. "Take it easy," he said. "Ease up on the clutch. Don't just raise your foot off of it like that." She tried it again. "That's it," he said. She looked at him when the car was in third. He sat in the seat, looking out the window. Snow was expected. It was Thursday. Although Larry was going to visit his parents and would not be back until late Friday afternoon, she decided she would wait until Tuesday for her next lesson. If he came home early, he would find out that she was taking lessons, and she didn't want him to know. She asked the boy, whose name was Michael, whether he thought she would forget all he had taught her in the time between lessons. "You'll remember," he said.

When they returned to the old lady's driveway, the car stalled going up the incline. She had trouble shifting. The boy put his hand over hers and kicked the heel of his hand forward. "You'll have to treat this car a little roughly, I'm afraid," he said. That afternoon, after he left, she made spaghetti sauce, chopping little pieces of pepper and onion and mushroom. When the sauce had cooked down, she called Mrs. Larsen and said that she would bring over dinner. She usually ate with the old lady once a week. The old lady often added a pinch of cinnamon to her food, saying that it brought out the flavor better than salt, and that since she was losing her sense of smell, food had to be strongly flavored for her to taste it. Once she had sprinkled cinnamon on a knockwurst. This time, as they ate, Natalie asked the old lady how much she paid the boy to bring the paper.

"I give him a dollar a week," the old lady said.

"Did he set the price, or did you?"

"He set the price. He told me he wouldn't take much because he has to walk this street to get to his apartment anyway."

"He taught me a lot about the car today," Natalie said.

"He's very handsome, isn't he?" the old lady said.

She asked Larry, "How were your parents?"

"Fine," he said. "But I spent almost all the time with Andy. It's almost his birthday, and he's depressed. We went to see Mose Allison."

"I think it stinks that hardly anyone else ever visits Andy," she said.

"He doesn't make it easy. He tells you everything that's on his mind, and there's no way you can pretend that his troubles don't amount to much. You just have to sit there and nod."

She remembered that Andy's room looked like a gymnasium. There were handgrips and weights scattered on the floor. There was even a psychedelic pink hula hoop that he was to put inside his elbow and then move his arm in circles wide enough to make the hoop spin. He couldn't do it. He would lie in bed with the hoop in back of his neck, and holding the sides, lift his neck off the pillow. His arms were barely strong enough to do that, really, but he could raise his neck with no trouble, so he just pretended that his arms pulling the loop were raising it. His parents thought that it was a special exercise that he had mastered.

"What did you do today?" Larry said now.

"I made spaghetti," she said. She had made it the day before, but she thought that since he was mysterious about the time he spent away from her ("in the lab" and "at the gym" became interchangeable), she did not owe him a straight answer. That day she had dropped off the film and then she had sat at the drugstore counter to have a cup of coffee. She bought some cigarettes, though she had not smoked since high school. She smoked one mentholated cigarette and then threw the pack away in a garbage container outside the drugstore. Her mouth still felt cool inside.

He asked if she had planned anything for the weekend.

"No," she said.

"Let's do something you'd like to do. I'm a little ahead of myself in the lab right now."

That night they ate spaghetti and made plans, and the next day they went for a ride in the country, to a factory where wooden toys were made. In the showroom he made a bear marionette shake and twist. She examined a small rocking horse, rhythmically pushing her finger up and down on the back rung of the rocker to make it rock. When they left they took with them a catalogue of toys they could order. She knew that they would never look at the catalogue again. On their way to the museum he stopped to wash the car. Because it was the weekend there were quite a few cars lined up waiting to go in. They were behind a blue Cadillac that seemed to inch forward of its own accord, without a driver. When the Cadillac moved into the washing area, a tiny man hopped out. He stood on tiptoe to reach the coin box to start the washing machine. She doubted if he was five feet tall.

"Look at that poor son of a bitch," he said.

The little man was washing his car.

"If Andy could get out more," Larry said. "If he could get rid of that feeling he has that he's the only freak . . . I wonder if it wouldn't do him good to come spend a week with us."

"Are you going to take him in the wheelchair to the lab with you?" she said. "I'm not taking care of Andy all day."

His face changed. "Just for a week was all I meant," he said.

"I'm not doing it," she said. She was thinking of the boy, and of the car. She had almost learned how to drive the car.

"Maybe in the warm weather," she said. "When we could go to the park or something."

He said nothing. The little man was rinsing his car. She sat inside when their turn came. She thought that Larry had no right to ask her to take care of Andy. Water flew out of the hose and battered the car. She thought of Andy, in the woods at night, stepping on the land mine, being blown into the air. She wondered if it threw him in an arc, so he ended up somewhere away from where he had been walking, or if it just blasted him straight up, if he went up the way an umbrella opens. Andy had been a wonderful ice skater. They all envied him his long sweeping turns, with his legs somehow neatly together and his body at the perfect angle. She never saw him have an accident on the ice. Never once. She had known Andy, and they had skated at Parker's pond, for eight years before he was drafted.

The night before, as she and Larry were finishing dinner, he had asked her if she intended to vote for Nixon or McGovern in the election. "McGovern," she said. How could he not have known that? She knew then that they were farther apart than she had thought. She hoped that on Election Day she could drive herself to the polls—not go with him and not walk. She planned not to ask the old lady if she wanted to come along because that would be one vote she could keep Nixon from getting.

At the museum she hesitated by the sculpture but did not point it out to him. He didn't look at it. He gazed to the side, above it, at a Francis Bacon painting. He could have shifted his eyes just a little and seen the sculpture, and her, standing and staring.

After three more lessons she could drive the car. The last two times, which were later in the afternoon than her first lesson, they stopped at the drugstore to get the old lady's paper, to save him from having to make the same trip back on foot. When he came out of the drugstore with the paper, after the final lesson, she asked him if he'd like to have a beer to celebrate.

"Sure," he said.

They walked down the street to a bar that was filled with college students. She wondered if Larry ever came to this bar. He had never said that he did.

She and Michael talked. She asked why he wasn't in high school. He told her that he had quit. He was living with his brother, and his brother was teaching him carpentry, which he had been interested in all along. On his napkin he drew a picture of the cabinets and bookshelves he and his brother had spent the last week constructing and installing in the house of two wealthy old sisters. He drummed the side of his thumb against the edge of the table in time with the music. They each drank beer, from heavy glass mugs.

"Mrs. Larsen said your husband was in school," the boy said. "What's he studying?"

She looked up, surprised. Michael had never mentioned her husband to her before. "Chemistry," she said.

"I liked chemistry pretty well," he said. "Some of it."

"My husband doesn't know you've been giving me lessons. I'm just going to tell him that I can drive the stick shift, and surprise him."

"Yeah?" the boy said. "What will he think about that?"

"I don't know," she said. "I don't think he'll like it."

"Why?" the boy said.

His question made her remember that he was sixteen. What she had said would never have provoked another question from an adult. The adult would have nodded or said, "I know."

She shrugged. The boy took a long drink of beer. "I thought it was funny that he didn't teach you himself, when Mrs. Larsen told me you were married," he said.

They had discussed her. She wondered why Mrs. Larsen wouldn't have told her that, because the night she ate dinner with her she had talked to Mrs. Larsen about what an extraordinarily patient teacher Michael was. Had Mrs. Larsen told him that Natalie talked about him?

On the way back to the car she remembered the photographs and went back to the drugstore and picked up the prints. As she took money out of her wallet she remembered that today was the day she would have to pay him. She looked around at him, at the front of the store, where he was flipping through magazines. He was tall and he was wearing a very old black jacket. One end of his long thick maroon scarf was hanging down his back.

"What did you take pictures of?" he said when they were back in the car.

"Furniture. My husband wanted pictures of our furniture, in case it was stolen."

"Why?" he said.

"They say if you have proof that you had valuable things, the insurance company won't hassle you about reimbursing you."

"You have a lot of valuable stuff?" he said.

"My husband thinks so," she said.

A block from the driveway she said, "What do I owe you?"

"Four dollars," he said.

"That's nowhere near enough," she said and looked over at him. He had opened the envelope with the pictures in it while she was driving. He was staring at the picture of her legs. "What's this?" he said.

She turned into the driveway and shut off the engine. She looked at the picture. She could not think what to tell him it was. Her hands and heart felt heavy.

"Wow," the boy said. He laughed. "Never mind. Sorry. I'm not looking at any more of them."

He put the pack of pictures back in the envelope and dropped it on the seat between them.

She tried to think what to say, of some way she could turn the pictures into a joke. She wanted to get out of the car and run. She wanted to stay, not to give him the money, so he would sit there with her. She reached into her purse and took out her wallet and removed four one-dollar bills.

"How many years have you been married?" he asked.

"One," she said. She held the money out to him. He said "Thank you" and leaned across the seat and put his right arm over her shoulder and kissed her. She felt his scarf bunched up against their cheeks. She was amazed at how warm his lips were in the cold car.

He moved his head away and said, "I didn't think you'd mind if I did that." She shook her head no. He unlocked the door and got out.

"I could drive you to your brother's apartment," she said. Her voice sounded hollow. She was extremely embarrassed, but she couldn't let him go.

He got back in the car. "You could drive me and come in for a drink," he said. "My brother's working."

When she got back to the car two hours later she saw a white parking ticket clamped under the windshield wiper, flapping in the wind. When she opened the car door and sank into the seat, she saw that he had left the money, neatly folded, on the floor mat on his side of the car. She did not pick up the money. In a while she started the car. She stalled it twice on the way home. When she had pulled into the driveway she looked at the money for a long time, then left it lying there. She left the car unlocked, hoping the money would be stolen. If it disappeared, she could tell herself that she had paid him. Otherwise she would not know how to deal with the situation.

When she got into the apartment, the phone rang. "I'm at the gym to play basketball," Larry said. "Be home in an hour."

"I was at the drugstore," she said. "See you then."

She examined the pictures. She sat on the sofa and laid them out, the twelve of them, in three rows on the cushion next to her. The picture of the piano was between the picture of her feet and the picture of herself that she had shot by aiming into the mirror. She picked up the four pictures of their furniture and put them on the table. She picked up the others and examined them closely. She began to understand why she had taken them. She had photographed parts of her body, fragments of it, to study the pieces. She had probably done it because she thought so much about Andy's body and the piece that was gone—the leg, below the knee, on his left side. She had had two bourbon-and-waters at the boy's apartment, and drinking always depressed her. She felt very depressed looking at the pictures, so she put them down and went into the bedroom. She undressed. She looked at her body—whole, not a bad figure—in the mirror. It was an automatic reaction with her to close the curtains when she was naked, so she turned quickly and went to the window and did that. She went back to the mirror; the room was darker now and her body looked better. She

ran her hands down her sides, wondering if the feel of her skin was anything like the way the sculpture would feel. She was sure that the sculpture would be smoother—her hands would move more quickly down the
slopes of it than she wanted—that it would be cool, and that somehow she
could feel the grayness of it. Those things seemed preferable to her hands
lingering on her body, the imperfection of her skin, the overheated apartment. If she were the piece of sculpture and if she could feel, she would like
her sense of isolation.

This was in 1972, in Philadelphia.

Distant Music

On Friday she always sat in the park, waiting for him to come. At one-thirty he came to this park bench (if someone was already sitting there, he loitered around it), and then they would sit side by side, talking quietly, like Ingrid Bergman and Cary Grant in *Notorious*. Both believed in flying saucers and health food. They shared a hatred of laundromats, guilt about not sending presents to relatives on birthdays and at Christmas, and a dog—part Weimaraner, part German shepherd—named Sam.

She was twenty, and she worked in an office; she was pretty because she took a lot of time with makeup, the way a housewife who really cared might flute the edges of a piecrust with thumb and index finger. He was twenty-four, a graduate-school dropout (theater) who collaborated on songs with his friend Gus Greeley, and he wanted, he fervently wanted, to make it big as a songwriter. His mother was Greek and French, his father American. This girl, Sharon, was not the first woman to fall in love with Jack because he was so handsome. She took the subway to get to the bench, which was in Washington Square Park; he walked from the basement apartment he lived in. Whoever had Sam that day (they kept the dog alternating weeks) brought him. They could do this because her job required her to work only from eight to one, and he worked at home. They had gotten the dog because they feared for his life. A man had come up to them on West Tenth Street carrying a cardboard box, smiling, and saying, "Does the little lady want a kitty cat?" They peered inside. "Puppies," Jack said. "Well, who gives a fuck?" the man said, putting the box down, his face dark and contorted. Sharon and Jack stared at the man; he stared belligerently back. Neither of them was quite sure how things had suddenly turned ominous. She wanted to get out of there right away, before the man took a swing at Jack, but to her surprise Jack smiled at the man and dipped into the box for a dog. He extracted the scrawny, wormy Sam. She took the dog first, because there was a veterinarian's office close to her apartment. Once the dog was cured of his worms, she gave him to Jack to begin his training. In Jack's apartment the puppy would fix his eyes on the parallelogram of sunlight that sometimes appeared on the wood floor in the late morning—sniffing it, backing up, edging up to it at the border. In her apartment, the puppy's object of fascination was a clarinet that a friend had left there when he moved. The puppy looked at it respectfully. She watched the dog for signs of maladjustment, wondering if he was too young to be shuttling back and forth, from home to home. (She herself had been raised by her mother, but she and her sister would fly to Seattle every summer to spend two months with their father.) The dog seemed happy enough.

At night, in Jack's one-room apartment, they would sometimes lie with their heads at the foot of the bed, staring at the ornately carved oak head-board and the old-fashioned light attached to it, with the little sticker still on the shade that said "From home of Lady Astor. $4.00." They had found the lamp in Ruckersville, Virginia, on the only long trip they ever took out of the city. On the bed with them there were usually sheets of music—songs that he was scoring. She would look at the pieces of paper with lyrics typed on them, and read them slowly to herself, appraisingly, as if they were poetry.

On weekends they spent the days and nights together. There was a small but deep fireplace in his apartment, and when September came they would light a fire in the late afternoon, although it was not yet cold, and sometimes light a stick of sandalwood incense, and they would lean on each other or sit side by side, listening to Vivaldi. She knew very little about such music when she first met him, and much more about it by the time their first month had passed. There was no one thing she knew a great deal about—as he did about music—so there was really nothing that she could teach him.

"Where were you in 1974?" he asked her once.

"In school. In Ann Arbor."

"What about 1975?"

"In Boston. Working at a gallery."

"Where are you now?" he said.

She looked at him and frowned. "In New York," she said.

He turned toward her and kissed her arm. "I know," he said. "But why so serious?"

She knew that she was a serious person, and she liked it that he could make her smile. Sometimes, though, she did not quite understand him, so she was smiling now not out of appreciation, but because she thought a smile would make things all right.

Carol, her closest friend, asked why she didn't move in with him. She did not want to tell Carol that it was because she had not been asked, so she said that the room he lived in was very small and that during the day he liked solitude so he could work. She was also not sure that she would move in if he did ask her. He gave her the impression sometimes that he was the serious one, not she. Perhaps "serious" was the wrong word; it was more that he seemed despondent. He would get into moods and not snap out of them; he would drink red wine and play Billie Holiday records, and shake his head and say that if he had not made it as a songwriter by now, chances were that he would never make it. She hadn't really been familiar with Billie Holiday until he began playing the records for her. He would play a song that Billie had recorded early in her career, then play another record of the same song as she had sung it later. He said that he preferred her ruined voice. Two songs in particular stuck in her mind. One was "Solitude," and the first time she heard Billie Holiday sing the first three words, "In my solitude," she felt a physical sensation, as if someone were drawing something sharp over her heart, very lightly. The other record she kept thinking of was "Gloomy Sunday." He told her that it had been banned from the radio back then, because it was said that it had been responsible for suicides.

For Christmas that year he gave her a small pearl ring that had been worn by his mother when she was a girl. The ring fitted perfectly; she only had to wiggle it slightly to get it to slide over the joint of her finger, and when it was in place it felt as if she were not wearing a ring at all. There were eight prongs holding the pearl in place. She often counted things: how many panes in a window, how many slats in a bench. Then, for her birthday, in January, he gave her a silver chain with a small sapphire stone, to be worn on the wrist. She was delighted; she wouldn't let him help her fasten the clasp.

"You like it?" he said. "That's all I've got."

She looked at him, a little startled. His mother had died the year before she met him; what he was saying was that he had given her the last of her things. There was a photograph of his mother on the bookcase—a black-and-white picture in a little silver frame of a smiling young woman whose hair was barely darker than her skin. Because he kept the picture, she assumed that he worshiped his mother. One night he corrected that impression by saying that his mother had always tried to sing in her youth, when she had no voice, which had embarrassed everyone.

He said that she was a silent person; in the end, he said, you would have to say that she had done and said very little. He told Sharon that a few days after her death he and his father had gone through her possessions together, and in one of her drawers they came upon a small wooden box shaped like a heart. Inside the box were two pieces of jewelry—the ring and the chain and sapphire. "So she kept some token, then," his father had said, staring down into the little box. "You gave them to her as presents?" he asked his father. "No," his father said apologetically. "They weren't from me." And then the two of them had stood there looking at each other, both understanding perfectly.

She said, "But what did you finally say to break the silence?"

"Something pointless, I'm sure," he said.

She thought to herself that that might explain why he had not backed down, on Tenth Street, when the man offering the puppies took a stance as though he wanted to fight. Jack was used to hearing bad things—things that took him by surprise. He had learned to react coolly. Later that winter, when she told him that she loved him, his face had stayed expressionless a split second too long, and then he smiled his slow smile and gave her a kiss.

The dog grew. He took to training quickly and walked at heel, and she was glad that they had saved him. She took him to the veterinarian to ask why he was so thin. She was told that the dog was growing fast, and that eventually he would start filling out. She did not tell Jack that she had taken the dog to the veterinarian, because he thought she doted on him too much. She wondered if he might not be a little jealous of the dog.

Slowly, things began to happen with his music. A band on the West Coast that played a song that he and Gus had written was getting a big name, and they had not dropped the song from their repertoire. In February he got a call from the band's agent, who said that they wanted more songs. He and Gus shut themselves in the basement apartment, and she went walking with Sam, the dog. She went to the park, until she ran into the crippled man too many times. He was a young man, rather handsome, who walked with two metal crutches and had a radio that hung from a strap around his neck and rested on his chest, playing loudly. The man always seemed to be walking in the direction she walked in, and she had to walk awkwardly to keep in line with him so they could talk. She really had nothing to talk to the man about, and he helped very little, and the dog was confused by the crutches and made little leaps toward the man, as though they were all three playing a game. She stayed away from the park for a while, and when she went back he was not there. One day in March the park was more crowded than usual because it was an unusually warm, springlike afternoon, and walking with Sam, half dreaming, she passed a heavily made-up woman on a bench who was wearing a polka-dot turban, with a hand-lettered sign propped against her legs announcing that she was Miss Sydney, a fortuneteller. There was a young boy sitting next to Miss Sydney, and he called out to her, "Come on!" She smiled slightly and shook her head no. The boy was Italian, she thought, but the woman was hard to place. "Miss Sydney's gonna tell you about fire and famine and early death," the boy said. He laughed, and she hurried on, thinking it was odd that the boy would know the word "famine."

She was still alone with Jack most of every weekend, but much of his talk now was about technical problems he was having with scoring, and she had trouble following him. Once, he became enraged and said that she had no interest in his career. He said it because he wanted to move to Los Angeles and she said she was staying in New York. She said it assuming at once that he would go anyhow. When he made it clear that he would not leave without her, she started to cry because she was so grateful that he was staying. He thought she was crying because he had yelled at her and said that she had no interest in his career. He took back what he had said; he told her that she was very tolerant and that she often gave good advice. She had a good ear, even if she didn't express her opinions in complex technical terms. She cried again, and this time even she did not realize at first why. Later she knew that it was because he had never said so many kind things to her at once. Actually, very few people in her life had ever gone out of their way to say something kind, and it had just been too much. She began to wonder if her nerves were getting bad. Once, she woke up in the night disoriented and sweating, having dreamed that she was out in the sun, with all her energy gone. It was stifling hot and she couldn't move. "The sun's a good thing," he said to her when she told him the dream. "Think about the bright beautiful sun in Los Angeles. Think about stretching out on a warm day with a warm breeze." Trembling, she left him and went into the kitchen for water. He did not know that if he had really set out for California, she would have followed.

In June, when the air pollution got very bad and the air carried the smell that sidewalks get when they are baked through every day, he began to complain that it was her fault that they were in New York and not in California. "But I just don't like that way of life," she said. "If I went there, I wouldn't be happy."

"What's so appealing about this uptight New York scene?" he said. "You wake up in the night in a sweat. You won't even walk through Washington Square Park anymore."

"It's because of that man with the crutches," she said. "People like that. I told you it was only because of him."

"So let's get away from all that. Let's go somewhere."

"You think there aren't people like that in California?" she said.

"It doesn't matter what I think about California if I'm not going." He clamped earphones on his head.

That same month, while she and Jack and Gus were sharing a pot of cheese fondue, she found out that Jack had a wife. They were at Gus's apartment when Gus casually said something about Myra. "Who's Myra?" she asked, and he said, "You know—Jack's wife, Myra." It seemed unreal to her—even more so because Gus's apartment was such an odd place; that night Gus had plugged a defective lamp into an outlet and blown out a fuse. Then he plugged in his only other lamp, which was a sunlamp. It glowed so brightly that he had to turn it, in its wire enclosure, to face the wall. As they sat on the floor eating, their three shadows were thrown up against the opposite wall. She had been looking at that—detached, the way you would stand back to appreciate a picture—when she tuned in on the conversation and heard them talking about someone named Myra.

"You didn't know?" Gus said to her. "Okay, I want you both out. I don't want any heavy scene in my place. I couldn't take it. Come on—I really mean it. I want you out. Please don't talk about it here."

On the street, walking beside Jack, it occurred to her that Gus's outburst was very strange, almost as strange as Jack's not telling her about his wife.

"I didn't see what would be gained by telling you," Jack said.

They crossed the street. They passed the Riviera Café. She had once counted the number of panes of glass across the Riviera's front.

"Did you ever think about us getting married?" he said. "I thought about it. I thought that if you didn't want to follow me to California, of course you wouldn't want to marry me."

"You're already married," she said. She felt that she had just said something very sensible. "Do you think it was right to—"

He started to walk ahead of her. She hurried to catch up. She wanted to call after him, "I would have gone!" She was panting.

"Listen," he said, "I'm like Gus. I don't want to hear it."

"You mean we can't even talk about this? You don't think that I'm entitled to hear about it?"

"I love you and I don't love Myra," he said.

"Where is she?" she said.

"In El Paso."

"If you don't love her, why aren't you divorced?"

"You think that everybody who doesn't love his wife gets divorced? I'm not the only one who doesn't do the logical thing, you know. You get nightmares from living in this sewer, and you won't get out of it."

"It's different," she said. What was he talking about?

"Until I met you, I didn't think about it. She was in El Paso, she was gone—period."

"Are you going to get a divorce?"

"Are you going to marry me?"

They were crossing Seventh Avenue. They both stopped still, halfway across the street, and were almost hit by a Checker cab. They hurried across, and on the other side of the street they stopped again. She looked at him, as surprised but as suddenly sure about something as he must have been the time he and his father had found the jewelry in the heart-shaped wooden box. She said no, she was not going to marry him.

It dragged on for another month. During that time, unknown to her, he wrote the song that was going to launch his career. Months after he had left the city, she heard it on her AM radio one morning, and she knew that it was his song, even though he had never mentioned it to her. She leashed the dog and went out and walked to the record shop on Sixth Avenue—walking almost the same route they had walked the night she found out about his wife—and she went in, with the dog. Her face was so strange that the man behind the cash register allowed her to break the rule about dogs in the shop because he did not want another hassle that day. She found the group's record album with the song on it, turned it over and saw his name, in small type. She stared at the title, replaced the record and went back outside, as hunched as if it were winter.

During the month before he left, though, and before she ever heard the song, the two of them had sat on the roof of his building one night, arguing. They were having a Tom Collins because a musician who had been at his place the night before had brought his own mix and then left it behind. She had never had a Tom Collins. It tasted appropriately bitter, she thought. She held out the ring and the bracelet to him. He said that if she made him take them back, he would drop them over the railing. She believed him and put them back in her pocket. He said, and she agreed, that things had not been perfect between them even before she found out about his wife. Myra could play the guitar, and she could not; Myra loved to travel, and she was afraid to leave New York City. As she listened to what he said, she counted the posts—black iron and shaped like arrows—of the fence that wound around the roof. It was almost entirely dark, and she looked up to see if there were any stars. She yearned to be in the country, where she could always see them. She said she wanted him to borrow a car before he left so that they could ride out into the woods in New Jersey. Two nights later he picked her up at her apartment in a red Volvo, with Sam panting in the back, and they wound their way through the city and to the Lincoln Tunnel. Just as they were about to go under, another song began to play on the tape deck. It was Ringo Starr singing "Octopus's Garden." Jack laughed. "That's a hell of a fine song to come on just before we enter the tunnel." Inside the tunnel, the dog flattened himself on the back seat. "You want to keep Sam, don't you?" he said. She was shocked because she had never even thought of losing Sam. "Of course I do," she said, and unconsciously edged a little away from him. He had never said whose car it was. For no reason at all, she thought that the car must belong to a woman.

"I love that syrupy chorus of 'aaaaah' Lennon and McCartney sing," he said. "They really had a fine sense of humor."

"Is that a funny song?" she said. She had never thought about it.

They were on Boulevard East, in Weehawken, and she was staring out the window at the lights across the water. He saw that she was looking, and drove slower.

"This as good as stars for you?" he said.

"It's amazing."

"All yours," he said, taking his hand off the wheel to swoop it through the air in mock graciousness.

After he left she would remember that as one of the little digs he had gotten in—one of the less than nice things he had said. That night, though, impressed by the beauty of the city, she let it go by; in fact, she would have to work on herself later to reinterpret many of the things he had said as being nasty. That made it easier to deal with his absence. She would block out the memory of his pulling over and kissing her, of the two of them getting out of the car, and with Sam between them, walking.

One of the last times she saw him, she went to his apartment on a night when five other people were there—people she had never met. His father had shipped him some 8mm home movies and a projector, and the people all sat on the floor, smoking grass and talking, laughing at the movies of children (Jack at his fourth birthday party; Jack in the Halloween parade at school; Jack at Easter, collecting eggs). One of the people on the floor said, "Hey, get that big dog out of the way," and she glared at him, hating him for not liking the dog. What if his shadow had briefly darkened the screen? She felt angry enough to scream, angry enough to say that the dog had grown up in the apartment and had the right to walk around. Looking at the home movies, she tried to concentrate on Jack's blunders: dropping an Easter egg, running down the hill after the egg, going so fast he stumbled into some blur, perhaps his mother's arms. But what she mostly thought about was what a beautiful child he was, what a happy-looking little boy. There was no sense in her staying there and getting sentimental, so she made her excuses and left early. Outside, she saw the red Volvo, gleaming as though it had been newly painted. She was sure that it belonged to an Indian woman in a blue sari who had been there, sitting close to Jack. Sharon was glad that as she was leaving, Sam had raised his hackles and growled at one of the people there. She scolded him, but out on the street she patted him, secretly glad. Jack had not asked her again to come to California with him, and she told herself that she probably would not have changed her mind if he had. Tears began to well up in her eyes, and she told herself that she was crying because a cab wouldn't stop for her when the driver saw that she had a dog. She ended up walking blocks and blocks back to her apartment that night; it made her more certain than ever that she loved the dog and that she did not love Jack.

About the time she got the first postcard from Jack, things started to get a little bad with Sam. She was afraid that he might have distemper, so she took him to the veterinarian, waited her turn and told the doctor that the dog was growling at some people and she had no idea why. He assured her that there was nothing physically wrong with the dog, and blamed it on the heat. When another month passed and it was less hot, she visited the veterinarian again. "It's the breeding," he said, and sighed. "It's a bad mix. A Weimaraner is a mean dog, and that cross isn't a good one. He's part German shepherd, isn't he?"

"Yes," she said.

"Well—that's it, I'm afraid."

"There isn't any medication?"

"It's the breeding," he said. "Believe me. I've seen it before."

"What happens?" she said.

"What happens to the dog?"

"Yes."

"Well—watch him. See how things go. He hasn't bitten anybody, has he?"

"No," she said. "Of course not."

"Well—don't say of course not. Be careful with him."

"I'm careful with him," she said. She said it indignantly. But she wanted to hear something else. She didn't want to leave.

Walking home, she thought about what she could do. Maybe she could take Sam to her sister's house in Morristown for a while. Maybe if he could run more, and keep cool, he would calm down. She put aside her knowledge that it was late September and already much cooler, and that the dog growled more, not less. He had growled at the teenage boy she had given money to to help her carry her groceries upstairs. It was the boy's extreme reaction to Sam that had made it worse, though. You had to act calm around Sam when he got like that, and the boy had panicked.

She persuaded her sister to take Sam, and her brother-in-law drove into New York on Sunday and drove them out to New Jersey. Sam was put on a chain attached to a rope her brother-in-law had strung up in the backyard, between two huge trees. To her surprise, Sam did not seem to mind it. He did not bark and strain at the chain until he saw her drive away, late that afternoon; her sister was driving, and she was in the back seat with her niece, and she looked back and saw him lunging at the chain.

The rest of it was predictable, even to her. As they drove away, she almost knew it all. The dog would bite the child. Of course, the child should not have annoyed the dog, but she did, and the dog bit her, and then there was a hysterical call from her sister and another call from her brother-in-law, saying that she must come get the dog immediately—that he would come for her so she could get him—and blaming her for bringing the dog to them in the first place. Her sister had never really liked her, and the incident with the dog was probably just what she had been waiting for to sever contact.

When Sam came back to the city, things got no better. He turned against everyone and it was difficult even to walk him because he had become so aggressive. Sometimes a day would pass without any of that, and she would tell herself that it was over now—an awful period but over—and then the next morning the dog would bare his teeth at some person they passed. There began to be little signs that the dog had it in for her, too, and when that happened she turned her bedroom over to him. She hauled her mattress to the living room and let him have his own room. She left the door cracked so he would not think he was being punished. But she knew, and Sam knew, that it was best he stay in the room. If nothing else, he was an exceptionally smart dog.

She heard from Jack for over a year—sporadically, but then sometimes two postcards in a single week. He was doing well, playing in a band as well as writing music. When she stopped hearing from him—and when it became clear that something had to be done about the dog, and something had been done—she was twenty-two. On a date with a man she liked as a friend, she suggested that they go over to Jersey and drive down Boulevard East. The man was new to New York, and when they got there he said that he was more impressed with that view of the city than with the view from the top of the RCA Building. "All ours," she said, gesturing with her arm, and he, smiling and excited by what she said, took her hand when it had finished its sweep and kissed it, and continued to stare with awe at the lights across the water. That summer, she heard another song of Jack's on the radio, which alluded, as so many of his songs did, to times in New York she remembered well. In this particular song there was a couplet about a man on the street offering kittens in a box that actually contained a dog named Sam. In the context of the song it was an amusing episode—another "you can't always get what you want" sort of thing—and she could imagine Jack in California, not knowing what had happened to Sam, and, always the one to appreciate little jokes in songs, smiling.

A Vintage Thunderbird

Nick and Karen had driven from Virginia to New York in a little under six hours. They had made good time, keeping ahead of the rain all the way, and it was only now, while they were in the restaurant, that the rain began. It had been a nice summer weekend in the country with their friends Stephanie and Sammy, but all the time he was there Nick had worried that Karen had consented to go with him only out of pity; she had been dating another man, and when Nick suggested the weekend she had been reluctant. When she said she would go, he decided that she had given in for old times' sake.

The car they drove was hers—a white Thunderbird convertible. Every time he drove the car, he admired it more. She owned many things that he admired: a squirrel coat with a black taffeta lining, a pair of carved soapstone bookends that held some books of poetry on her night table, her collection of Louis Armstrong 78s. He loved to go to her apartment and look at her things. He was excited by them, the way he had been spellbound, as a child, exploring the playrooms of schoolmates.

He had met Karen several years before, soon after he came to New York. Her brother had lived in the same building he lived in then, and the three of them met on the volleyball courts adjacent to the building. Her brother moved across town within a few months, but by then Nick knew Karen's telephone number. At her suggestion, they had started running in Central Park on Sundays. It was something he looked forward to all week. When they left the park, his elation was always mixed with a little embarrassment over his panting and his being sweaty on the street, but she had no self-consciousness. She didn't care if her shirt stuck to her body, or if she looked unattractive with her wet, matted hair. Or perhaps she knew that she never looked really unattractive; men always looked at her. One time, on Forty-second Street, during a light rain, Nick stopped to read a movie marquee, and when he turned back to Karen she was laughing and protesting that she couldn't take the umbrella that a man was offering her. It was only when Nick came to her side that the man stopped insisting—a nicely dressed man who was only offering her his big black umbrella, and not trying to pick her up. Things like this were hard for Nick to accept, but Karen was not flirtatious, and he could see that it was not her fault that men looked at her and made gestures.

It became a routine that on Sundays they jogged or went to a basketball court. One time, when she got frustrated because she hadn't been able to do a simple hook shot—hadn't made a basket that way all morning—he lifted her to his shoulders and charged the backboard so fast that she almost missed the basket from there too. After playing basketball, they would go to her apartment and she would make dinner. He would collapse, but she was full of energy and she would poke fun at him while she studied a cookbook, staring at it until she knew enough of a recipe to begin preparing the food. His two cookbooks were dog-eared and sauce-stained, but Karen's were perfectly clean. She looked at recipes, but never followed them exactly. He admired this—her creativity, her energy. It took him a long while to accept that she thought he was special, and later, when she began to date other men, it took him a long while to realize that she did not mean to shut him out of her life. The first time she went away with a man for the weekend—about a year after he first met her—she stopped by his apartment on her way to Pennsylvania and gave him the keys to her Thunderbird. She left so quickly—the man was downstairs in his car, waiting—that as he watched her go he could feel the warmth of the keys from her hand.

Just recently Nick had met the man she was dating now: a gaunt psychology professor, with a black-and-white tweed cap and a thick mustache that made him look like a sad-mouthed clown. Nick had gone to her apartment not knowing for certain that the man would be there—actually, it was Friday night, the beginning of the weekend, and he had gone on the hunch that he finally would meet him—and had drunk a vodka Collins that the man mixed for him. He remembered that the man had complained tediously that Paul McCartney had stolen words from Thomas Dekker for a song on the *Abbey Road* album, and that the man said he got hives from eating shellfish.

In the restaurant now, Nick looked across the table at Karen and said, "That man you're dating is a real bore. What is he—a scholar?"

He fumbled for a cigarette and then remembered that he no longer smoked. He had given it up a year before, when he went to visit an old girlfriend in New Haven. Things had gone badly, they had quarreled, and he had left her to go to a bar. Coming out, he was approached by a tall black round-faced teenager and told to hand over his wallet, and he had mutely reached inside his coat and pulled it out and given it to the boy. A couple of people came out of the bar, took in the situation and walked away quickly, pretending not to notice. The boy had a small penknife in his hand. "And your cigarettes," the boy said. Nick had reached inside his jacket pocket and handed over the cigarettes. The boy pocketed them. Then the boy smiled and cocked his head and held up the wallet, like a hypnotist dangling a pocket watch. Nick stared dumbly at his own wallet. Then, before he knew what was happening, the boy turned into a blur of motion: he grabbed his arm and yanked hard, like a judo wrestler, and threw him across the sidewalk. Nick fell against a car that was parked at the curb. He was so frightened that his legs buckled and he went down. The boy watched him fall. Then he nodded and walked down the sidewalk past the bar. When the boy was out of sight, Nick got up and went into the bar to tell his story. He let the bartender give him a beer and call the police. He declined the bartender's offer of a cigarette, and had never smoked since.

His thoughts were drifting, and Karen still had not answered his question. He knew that he had already angered her once that day, and that it had been a mistake to speak of the man again. Just an hour or so earlier, when they got back to the city, he had been abrupt with her friend Kirby. She kept her car in Kirby's garage, and in exchange for the privilege she moved into his brownstone whenever he went out of town and took care of his six de-clawed chocolate-point cats. Actually, Kirby's psychiatrist, a Dr. Kellogg, lived in the same house, but the doctor had made it clear he did not live there to take care of cats.

From his seat Nick could see the sign of the restaurant hanging outside the front window. "Star Thrower Café," it said, in lavender neon. He got depressed thinking that if she became more serious about the professor—he had lasted longer than any of the others—he would only be able to see her by pretending to run into her at places like the Star Thrower. He had also begun to think that he had driven the Thunderbird for the last time. She had almost refused to let him drive it again after the time, two weeks earlier, when he tapped a car in front of them on Sixth Avenue, making a dent above their left headlight. Long ago she had stopped letting him use her squirrel coat as a kind of blanket. He used to like to lie naked on the tiny balcony outside her apartment in the autumn, with the Sunday *Times* arranged under him for padding and the coat spread on top of him. Now he counted back and came up with the figure: he had known Karen for seven years.

"What are you thinking?" he said to her.

"That I'm glad I'm not thirty-eight years old, with a man putting pressure on me to have a baby." She was talking about Stephanie and Sammy.

Her hand was on the table. He cupped his hand over it just as the waiter came with the plates.

"What are *you* thinking?" she said, withdrawing her hand.

"At least Stephanie has the sense not to do it," he said. He picked up his fork and put it down. "Do you really love that man?"

"If I loved him, I suppose I'd be at my apartment, where he's been waiting for over an hour. If he waited."

When they finished she ordered espresso. He ordered it also. He had half expected her to say at some point that the trip with him was the end, and he still thought she might say that. Part of the problem was that she had money and he didn't. She had had money since she was twenty-one, when she got control of a fifty-thousand-dollar trust fund her grandfather had left her. He remembered the day she had bought the Thunderbird. It was the day after her birthday, five years ago. That night, laughing, they had driven the car through the Lincoln Tunnel and then down the back roads in Jersey, with a stream of orange crepe paper blowing from the radio antenna, until the wind ripped it off.

"Am I still going to see you?" Nick said.

"I suppose," Karen said. "Although things have changed between us."

"I've known you for seven years. You're my oldest friend."

She did not react to what he said, but much later, around midnight, she called him at his apartment. "Was what you said at the Star Thrower calculated to make me feel bad?" she said. "When you said that I was your oldest friend?"

"No," he said. "You are my oldest friend."

"You must know somebody longer than you've known me."

"You're the only person I've seen regularly for seven years."

She sighed.

"Professor go home?" he said.

"No. He's here."

"You're saying all this in front of him?"

"I don't see why there has to be any secret about this."

"You could put an announcement in the paper," Nick said. "Run a little picture of me with it."

"Why are you so sarcastic?"

"It's embarrassing. It's embarrassing that you'd say this in front of that man."

He was sitting in the dark, in a chair by the phone. He had wanted to call her ever since he got back from the restaurant. The long day of driving had finally caught up with him, and his shoulders ached. He felt the black man's hands on his shoulders, felt his own body folding up, felt himself flying backward. He had lost sixty-five dollars that night. The day she bought the Thunderbird, he had driven it through the tunnel into New Jersey. He had driven, then she had driven, and then he had driven again. Once he had pulled into the parking lot of a shopping center and told her to wait, and had come back with the orange crepe paper. Years later he had looked for the road they had been on that night, but he could never find it.

The next time Nick heard from her was almost three weeks after the trip to Virginia. Since he didn't have the courage to call her, and since he expected not to hear from her at all, he was surprised to pick up the phone and hear her voice. Petra had been in his apartment—a woman at his office whom he had always wanted to date and who had just broken off an unhappy engagement. As he held the phone clamped between his ear and shoulder, he looked admiringly at Petra's profile.

"What's up?" he said to Karen, trying to sound very casual for Petra.

"Get ready," Karen said. "Stephanie called and said that she was going to have a baby."

"What do you mean? I thought she told you in Virginia that she thought Sammy was crazy to want a kid."

"It happened by accident. She missed her period just after we left."

Petra shifted on the couch and began leafing through *Newsweek*.

"Can I call you back?" he said.

"Throw whatever woman is there out of your apartment and talk to me now," Karen said. "I'm about to go out."

He looked at Petra, who was sipping her drink. "I can't do that," he said.

"Then call me when you can. But call back tonight."

When he hung up, he took Petra's glass but found that he had run out of Scotch. He suggested that they go to a bar on West Tenth Street.

When they got to the bar, he excused himself almost immediately. Karen had sounded depressed, and he could not enjoy his evening with Petra until he made sure everything was all right. Once he heard her voice, he knew he wanted to be with her and not Petra. He told her that he was going to come to her apartment when he had finished having a drink, and she said that he should come over immediately or not at all, because she was about to go to the professor's. She was so abrupt that he wondered if she could be jealous.

He went back to the bar and sat on the stool next to Petra and picked up his Scotch and water and took a big drink. It was so cold that it made his teeth ache. Petra had on blue slacks and a white blouse. He rubbed his hand up and down her back, just below the shoulders. She was not wearing a brassiere.

"I have to leave," he said.

"You have to leave? Are you coming back?"

He started to speak, but she put up her hand. "Never mind," she said. "I don't want you to come back." She sipped her Margarita. "Whoever the woman is you just called, I hope the two of you have a splendid evening."

Petra gave him a hard look, and he knew that she really wanted him to go. He stared at her—at the little crust of salt on her bottom lip—and then she turned away from him.

He hesitated for just a second before he left the bar. He went outside and walked about ten steps, and then he was jumped. They got him from behind, and in his shock and confusion he thought that he had been hit by a car. He lost sense of where he was, and although it was a dull blow, he thought that somehow a car had hit him. Looking up from the sidewalk, he saw them—two men, younger than he was, picking at him like vultures, pushing him, rummaging through his jacket and his pockets. The crazy thing was he was on West Tenth Street; there should have been other people on the street, but there were not. His clothes were tearing. His right hand was wet with blood. They had cut his arm, the shirt was bloodstained, he saw his own blood spreading out into a little puddle. He stared at it and was afraid to move his hand out of it. Then the men were gone and he was left half sitting, propped up against a building where they had dragged him. He was able to push himself up, but the man he began telling the story to, a passer-by, kept coming into focus and fading out again. The man had on a sombrero, and he was pulling him up but pulling too hard. His legs didn't have the power to support him—something had happened to his legs—so that when the man loosened his grip he went down on his knees. He kept blinking to stay conscious. He blacked out before he could stand again.

Back in his apartment, later that night, with his arm in a cast, he felt confused and ashamed—ashamed for the way he had treated Petra, and ashamed for having been mugged. He wanted to call Karen, but he was too embarrassed. He sat in the chair by the phone, willing her to call him. At midnight the phone rang, and he picked it up at once, sure that his telepathic message had worked. The phone call was from Stephanie, at La Guardia. She had been trying to reach Karen and couldn't. She wanted to know if she could come to his apartment.

"I'm not going through with it," Stephanie said, her voice wavering. "I'm thirty-eight years old, and this was a goddamn accident."

"Calm down," he said. "We can get you an abortion."

"I don't know if I could take a human life," she said, and she began to cry.

"Stephanie?" he said. "You okay? Are you going to get a cab?"

More crying, no answer.

"Because it would be silly for me to get a cab just to come get you. You can make it here okay, can't you, Steph?"

The cabdriver who took him to La Guardia was named Arthur Shales. A small pink baby shoe was glued to the dashboard of the cab. Arthur Shales chain-smoked Picayunes. "Woman I took to Bendel's today, I'm still trying to get over it," he said. "I picked her up at Madison and Seventy-fifth. Took her to Bendel's and pulled up in front and she said, 'Oh, screw Bendel's.' I took her back to Madison and Seventy-fifth."

Going across the bridge, Nick said to Arthur Shales that the woman he was going to pick up was going to be very upset.

"Upset? What do I care? Neither of you are gonna hold a gun to my head, I can take anything. You're my last fares of the night. Take you back where you came from, then I'm heading home myself."

When they were almost at the airport exit, Arthur Shales snorted and said, "Home is a room over an Italian grocery. Guy who runs it woke me up at six this morning, yelling so loud at his supplier. 'You call these tomatoes?' he was saying. 'I could take these out and bat them on the tennis court.' Guy is always griping about tomatoes being so unripe."

Stephanie was standing on the walkway, right where she had said she would be. She looked haggard, and Nick was not sure that he could cope with her. He raised his hand to his shirt pocket for cigarettes, forgetting once again that he had given up smoking. He also forgot that he couldn't grab anything with his right hand because it was in a cast.

"You know who I had in my cab the other day?" Arthur Shales said, coasting to a stop in front of the terminal. "You're not going to believe it. Al Pacino."

For more than a week, Nick and Stephanie tried to reach Karen. Stephanie began to think that Karen was dead. And although Nick chided her for calling Karen's number so often, he began to worry too. Once he went to her apartment on his lunch hour and listened at the door. He heard nothing, but he put his mouth close to the door and asked her to please open the door, if she was there, because there was trouble with Stephanie. As he left the building he had to laugh at what it would have looked like if someone had seen him—a nicely dressed man, with his hands on either side of his mouth, leaning into a door and talking to it. And one of the hands in a cast.

For a week he came straight home from work, to keep Stephanie company. Then he asked Petra if she would have dinner with him. She said no. As he was leaving the office, he passed by her desk without looking at her. She got up and followed him down the hall and said, "I'm having a drink with somebody after work, but I could meet you for a drink around seven o'clock."

He went home to see if Stephanie was all right. She said that she had been sick in the morning, but after the card came in the mail—she held out a postcard to him—she felt much better. The card was addressed to him; it was from Karen, in Bermuda. She said she had spent the afternoon in a sailboat. No explanation. He read the message several times. He felt very relieved. He asked Stephanie if she wanted to go out for a drink with him and Petra. She said no, as he had known she would.

At seven he sat alone at a table in the Blue Bar, with the postcard in his inside pocket. There was a folded newspaper on the little round table where he sat, and his broken right wrist rested on it. He sipped a beer. At seven-thirty he opened the paper and looked through the theater section. At quarter to eight he got up and left. He walked over to Fifth Avenue and began to walk downtown. In one of the store windows there was a poster for Bermuda tourism. A woman in a turquoise-blue bathing suit was rising out of blue waves, her mouth in an unnaturally wide smile. She seemed oblivious of the little boy next to her who was tossing a ball into the sky. Standing there, looking at the poster, Nick began a mental game that he had sometimes played in college. He invented a cartoon about Bermuda. It was a split-frame drawing. Half of it showed a beautiful girl, in the arms of her lover, on the pink sandy beach of Bermuda, with the caption: "It's glorious to be here in Bermuda." The other half of the frame showed a tall tired man looking into the window of a travel agency at a picture of the lady and her lover. He would have no lines, but in a balloon above his head he would be wondering if, when he went home, it was the right time to urge an abortion to the friend who had moved into his apartment.

When he got home, Stephanie was not there. She had said that if she felt better, she would go out to eat. He sat down and took off his shoes and socks and hung forward, with his head almost touching his knees, like a droopy doll. Then he went into the bedroom, carrying the shoes and socks, and took off his clothes and put on jeans. The phone rang and he picked it up just as he heard Stephanie's key in the door.

"I'm sorry," Petra said, "I've never stood anybody up before in my life."

"Never mind," he said. "I'm not mad."

"I'm very sorry," she said.

"I drank a beer and read the paper. After what I did to you the other night, I don't blame you."

"I like you," she said. "That was why I didn't come. Because I knew I wouldn't say what I wanted to say. I got as far as Forty-eighth Street and turned around."

"What did you want to say?"

"That I like you. That I like you and that it's a mistake, because I'm always letting myself in for it, agreeing to see men who treat me badly. I wasn't very flattered the other night."

"I know. I apologize. Look, why don't you meet me at that bar now and let me not walk out on you. Okay?"

"No," she said, her voice changing. "That wasn't why I called. I called to say I was sorry, but I know I did the right thing. I have to hang up now."

He put the phone back and continued to look at the floor. He knew that Stephanie was not even pretending not to have heard. He took a step forward and ripped the phone out of the wall. It was not a very successful dramatic gesture. The phone just popped out of the jack, and he stood there, holding it in his good hand.

"Would you think it was awful if I offered to go to bed with you?" Stephanie asked.

"No," he said. "I think it would be very nice."

Two days later he left work early in the afternoon and went to Kirby's. Dr. Kellogg opened the door and then pointed toward the back of the house and said, "The man you're looking for is reading." He was wearing baggy white pants and a Japanese kimono.

Nick almost had to push through the half-open door because the psychiatrist was so intent on holding the cats back with one foot. In the kitchen Kirby was indeed reading—he was looking at a Bermuda travel brochure and listening to Karen.

She looked sheepish when she saw him. Her face was tan, and her eyes, which were always beautiful, looked startlingly blue now that her face was so dark. She had lavender-tinted sunglasses pushed on top of her head. She and Kirby seemed happy and comfortable in the elegant, air-conditioned house.

"When did you get back?" Nick said.

"A couple of days ago," she said. "The night I last talked to you, I went over to the professor's apartment, and in the morning we went to Bermuda."

Nick had come to Kirby's to get the car keys and borrow the Thunderbird—to go for a ride and be by himself for a while—and for a moment now he thought of asking her for the keys anyway. He sat down at the table.

"Stephanie is in town," he said. "I think we ought to go get a cup of coffee and talk about it."

Her key ring was on the table. If he had the keys, he could be heading for the Lincoln Tunnel. Years ago, they would be walking to the car hand in hand, in love. It would be her birthday. The car's odometer would have five miles on it.

One of Kirby's cats jumped up on the table and began to sniff at the butter dish there.

"Would you like to walk over to the Star Thrower and get a cup of coffee?" Nick said.

She got up slowly.

"Don't mind me," Kirby said.

"Would you like to come, Kirby?" she asked.

"Not me. No, no."

She patted Kirby's shoulder, and they went out.

"What happened?" she said, pointing to his hand.

"It's broken."

"How did you break it?"

"Never mind," he said. "I'll tell you when we get there."

When they got there it was not yet four o'clock, and the Star Thrower was closed.

"Well, just tell me what's happening with Stephanie," Karen said impatiently. "I don't really feel like sitting around talking because I haven't even unpacked yet."

"She's at my apartment, and she's pregnant, and she doesn't even talk about Sammy."

She shook her head sadly. "How did you break your hand?" she said.

"I was mugged. After our last pleasant conversation on the phone—the time you told me to come over immediately or not at all. I didn't make it because I was in the emergency room."

"Oh, Christ," she said. "Why didn't you call me?"

"I was embarrassed to call you."

"Why? Why didn't you call?"

"You wouldn't have been there anyway." He took her arm. "Let's find some place to go," he said.

Two young men came up to the door of the Star Thrower. "Isn't this where David had that great Armenian dinner?" one of them said.

"I *told* you it wasn't," the other said, looking at the menu posted to the right of the door.

"I didn't really think this was the place. *You* said it was on this street."

They continued to quarrel as Nick and Karen walked away.

"Why do you think Stephanie came here to the city?" Karen said.

"Because we're her friends," Nick said.

"But she has lots of friends."

"Maybe she thought we were more dependable."

"Why do you say that in that tone of voice? I don't have to tell you every move I'm making. Things went very well in Bermuda. He almost lured me to London."

"Look," he said. "Can't we go somewhere where you can call her?"

He looked at her, shocked because she didn't understand that Stephanie had come to see her, not him. He had seen for a long time that it didn't matter to her how much she meant to him, but he had never realized that she didn't know how much she meant to Stephanie. She didn't understand people. When he found out she had another man, he should have dropped out of her life. She did not deserve her good looks and her fine car and all her money. He turned to face her on the street, ready to tell her what he thought.

"You know what happened there?" she said. "I got sunburned and had a terrible time. He went on to London without me."

He took her arm again and they stood side by side and looked at some sweaters hanging in the window of Countdown.

"So going to Virginia wasn't the answer for them," she said. "Remember when Sammy and Stephanie left town, and we told each other what a stupid idea it was—that it would never work out? Do you think we jinxed them?"

They walked down the street again, saying nothing.

"It would kill me if I had to be a good conversationalist with you," she said at last. "You're the only person I can rattle on with." She stopped and leaned into him. "I had a rotten time in Bermuda," she said. "Nobody should go to a beach but a sand flea."

"You don't have to make clever conversation with me," he said.

"I know," she said. "It just happened."

Late in the afternoon of the day that Stephanie had her abortion, Nick called Sammy from a street phone near his apartment. Karen and Stephanie were in the apartment, but he had to get out for a while. Stephanie had seemed pretty cheerful, but perhaps it was just an act for his benefit. With him gone, she might talk to Karen about it. All she had told him was that it felt like she had caught an ice pick in the stomach.

"Sammy?" Nick said into the phone. "How are you? It just dawned on me that I ought to call and let you know that Stephanie is all right."

"She has called me herself, several times," Sammy said. "Collect. From your phone. But thank you for your concern, Nick." He sounded brusque.

"Oh," Nick said, taken aback. "Just so you know where she is."

"I could name you as corespondent in the divorce case, you know?"

"What would you do that for?" Nick said.

"I wouldn't. I just wanted you to know what I could do."

"Sammy—I don't get it. I didn't ask for any of this, you know."

"Poor Nick. My wife gets pregnant, leaves without a word, calls from New York with a story about how you had a broken hand and were having bad luck with women, so she went to bed with you. Two weeks later I get a phone call from you, all concern, wanting me to know where Stephanie is."

Nick waited for Sammy to hang up on him.

"You know what happened to you?" Sammy said. "You got eaten up by New York."

"What kind of dumb thing is that to say?" Nick said. "Are you trying to get even or something?"

"If I wanted to do that, I could tell you that you have bad teeth. Or that Stephanie said you were a lousy lover. What I was trying to do was tell you something important, for a change. Stephanie ran away when I tried to tell it to her, you'll probably hang up on me when I say the same thing to you: you can be happy. For instance, you can get out of New York and get away from Karen. Stephanie could have settled down with a baby."

"This doesn't sound like you, Sammy, to give advice."

He waited for Sammy's answer.

"You think I ought to leave New York?" Nick said.

"Both. Karen *and* New York. Do you know that your normal expression shows pain? Do you know how much Scotch you drank the weekend you visited?"

Nick stared through the grimy plastic window of the phone booth.

"What you just said about my hanging up on you," Nick said. "I was thinking that you were going to hang up on me. When I talk to people, they hang up on me. The conversation just ends that way."

"Why haven't you figured out that you don't know the right kind of people?"

"They're the only people I know."

"Does that seem like any reason for tolerating that sort of rudeness?"

"I guess not."

"Another thing," Sammy went on. "Have you figured out that I'm saying these things to you because when you called I was already drunk? I'm telling you all this because I think you're so numbed out by your lousy life that you probably don't even know I'm not in my right mind."

The operator came on, demanding more money. Nick clattered quarters into the phone. He realized that he was not going to hang up on Sammy, and Sammy was not going to hang up on him. He would have to think of something else to say.

"Give yourself a break," Sammy said. "Boot them out. Stephanie included. She'll see the light eventually and come back to the farm."

"Should I tell her you'll be there? I don't know if—"

"I told her I'd be here when she called. All the times she called. I just told her that I had no idea of coming to get her. I'll tell you another thing. I'll bet—I'll *bet*—that when she first turned up there she called you from the airport, and she wanted you to come for her, didn't she?"

"Sammy," Nick said, staring around him, wild to get off the phone. "I want to thank you for saying what you think. I'm going to hang up now."

"Forget it," Sammy said. "I'm not in my right mind. Goodbye."

"Goodbye," Nick said.

He hung up and started back to his apartment. He realized that he hadn't told Sammy that Stephanie had had the abortion. On the street he said hello to a little boy—one of the neighborhood children he knew.

He went up the stairs and up to his floor. Some people downstairs were listening to Beethoven. He lingered in the hallway, not wanting to go back to Stephanie and Karen. He took a deep breath and opened the door. Neither of them looked too bad. They said hello silently, each raising one hand.

It had been a hard day. Stephanie's appointment at the abortion clinic had been at eight in the morning. Karen had slept in the apartment with them the night before, on the sofa. Stephanie slept in his bed, and he slept on the floor. None of them had slept much. In the morning they all went to the abortion clinic. Nick had intended to go to work in the afternoon, but when they got back to the apartment he didn't think it was right for him to leave Stephanie. She went back to the bedroom, and he stretched out on the sofa and fell asleep. Before he slept, Karen sat on the sofa with him for a while, and he told her the story of his second mugging. When he woke up, it was four o'clock. He called his office and told them he was sick. Later they all watched the television news together. After that, he offered to go out and get some food, but nobody was hungry. That's when he went out and called Sammy.

Now Stephanie went back into the bedroom. She said she was tired and she was going to work on a crossword puzzle in bed. The phone rang. It was

Petra. She and Nick talked a little about a new apartment she was thinking of moving into. "I'm sorry for being so cold-blooded the other night," she said. "The reason I'm calling is to invite myself to your place for a drink, if that's all right with you."

"It's not all right," he said. "I'm sorry. There are some people here now."

"I get it," she said. "Okay. I won't bother you anymore."

"You don't understand," he said. He knew he had not explained things well, but the thought of adding Petra to the scene at his apartment was more than he could bear, and he had been too abrupt.

She said goodbye coldly, and he went back to his chair and fell in it, exhausted.

"A girl?" Karen said.

He nodded.

"Not a girl you wanted to hear from."

He shook his head no. He got up and pulled up the blind and looked out to the street. The boy he had said hello to was playing with a hula hoop. The hula hoop was bright blue in the twilight. The kid rotated his hips and kept the hoop spinning perfectly. Karen came to the window and stood next to him. He turned to her, wanting to say that they should go and get the Thunderbird, and as the night air cooled, drive out of the city, smell honeysuckle in the fields, feel the wind blowing.

But the Thunderbird was sold. She had told him the news while they were sitting in the waiting room of the abortion clinic. The car had needed a valve job, and a man she met in Bermuda who knew all about cars had advised her to sell it. Coincidentally, the man—a New York architect—wanted to buy it. Even as Karen told him, he knew she had been set up. If she had been more careful, they could have been in the car now, with the key in the ignition, the radio playing. He stood at the window for a long time. She had been conned, and he was more angry than he could tell her. She had no conception—she had somehow never understood—that Thunderbirds of that year, in good condition, would someday be worth a fortune. She had told him this way: "Don't be upset, because I'm sure I made the right decision. I sold the car as soon as I got back from Bermuda. I'm going to get a new car." He had moved in his chair, there in the clinic. He had had an impulse to get up and hit her. He remembered the scene in New Haven outside the bar, and he understood now that it was as simple as this: he had money that the black man wanted.

Down the street the boy picked up his hula hoop and disappeared around the corner.

"Say you were kidding about selling the car," Nick said.

"When are you going to stop making such a big thing over it?" Karen said.

"That creep cheated you. He talked you into selling it when nothing was wrong with it."

"Stop it," she said. "How come your judgments are always right and my judgments are always wrong?"

"I don't want to fight," he said. "I'm sorry I said anything."

"Okay," she said and leaned her head against him. He draped his right arm over her shoulder. The fingers sticking out of the cast rested a little above her breast.

"I just want to ask one thing," he said, "and then I'll never mention it again. Are you sure the deal is final?"

Karen pushed his hand off her shoulder and walked away. But it was his apartment, and she couldn't go slamming around in it. She sat on the sofa and picked up the newspaper. He watched her. Soon she put it down and stared across the room and into the dark bedroom, where Stephanie had turned off the light. He looked at her sadly for a long time, until she looked up at him with tears in her eyes.

"Do you think maybe we could get it back if I offered him more than he paid me for it?" she said. "You probably don't think that's a sensible suggestion, but at least that way we could get it back."

The Cinderella Waltz

Milo and Bradley are creatures of habit. For as long as I've known him, Milo has worn his moth-eaten blue scarf with the knot hanging so low on his chest that the scarf is useless. Bradley is addicted to coffee and carries a Thermos with him. Milo complains about the cold, and Bradley is always a little edgy. They come out from the city every Saturday—this is not habit but loyalty—to pick up Louise. Louise is even more unpredictable than most nine-year-olds; sometimes she waits for them on the front step, sometimes she hasn't even gotten out of bed when they arrive. One time she hid in a closet and wouldn't leave with them.

Today Louise has put together a shopping bag full of things she wants to take with her. She is taking my whisk and my blue pottery bowl, to make Sunday breakfast for Milo and Bradley; Beckett's *Happy Days*, which she has carried around for weeks, and which she looks through, smiling—but I'm not sure she's reading it; and a coleus growing out of a conch shell. Also, she has stuffed into one side of the bag the fancy Victorian-style nightgown her grandmother gave her for Christmas, and into the other she has tucked her octascope. Milo keeps a couple of dresses, a nightgown, a toothbrush, and extra sneakers and boots at his apartment for her. He got tired of rounding up her stuff to pack for her to take home, so he has brought some things for her that can be left. It annoys him that she still packs bags, because then he has to go around making sure that she has found everything before she goes home. She seems to know how to manipulate him, and after the weekend is over she calls tearfully to say that she has left this or that, which means that he must get his car out of the garage and drive all the way out to the house to bring it to her. One time, he refused to take the hour-long drive, because she had only left a copy of Tolkien's *The Two Towers*. The following weekend was the time she hid in the closet.

"I'll water your plant if you leave it here," I say now.

"I can take it," she says.

"I didn't say you couldn't take it. I just thought it might be easier to leave it, because if the shell tips over the plant might get ruined."

"O.K.," she says. "Don't water it today, though. Water it Sunday afternoon."

I reach for the shopping bag.

"I'll put it back on my windowsill," she says. She lifts the plant out and carries it as if it's made of Steuben glass. Bradley bought it for her last month, driving back to the city, when they stopped at a lawn sale. She and Bradley are both very choosy, and he likes that. He drinks French-roast coffee; she will debate with herself almost endlessly over whether to buy a coleus that is primarily pink or lavender or striped.

"Has Milo made any plans for this weekend?" I ask.

"He's having a couple of people over tonight, and I'm going to help them make crêpes for dinner. If they buy more bottles of that wine with the yellow flowers on the label, Bradley is going to soak the labels off for me."

"That's nice of him," I say. "He never minds taking a lot of time with things."

"He doesn't like to cook, though. Milo and I are going to cook. Bradley sets the table and fixes flowers in a bowl. He thinks it's frustrating to cook."

"Well," I say, "with cooking you have to have a good sense of timing. You have to coordinate everything. Bradley likes to work carefully and not be rushed."

I wonder how much she knows. Last week she told me about a conversation she'd had with her friend Sarah. Sarah was trying to persuade Louise to stay around on the weekends, but Louise said she always went to her father's. Then Sarah tried to get her to take her along, and Louise said that she couldn't. "You could take her if you wanted to," I said later. "Check with Milo and see if that isn't right. I don't think he'd mind having a friend of yours occasionally."

She shrugged. "Bradley doesn't like a lot of people around," she said.

"Bradley likes you, and if she's your friend I don't think he'd mind."

She looked at me with an expression I didn't recognize; perhaps she thought I was a little dumb, or perhaps she was just curious to see if I would go on. I didn't know how to go on. Like an adult, she gave a little shrug and changed the subject.

At ten o'clock Milo pulls into the driveway and honks his horn, which makes a noise like a bleating sheep. He knows the noise the horn makes is funny, and he means to amuse us. There was a time just after the divorce when he and Bradley would come here and get out of the car and stand around silently, waiting for her. She knew that she had to watch for them, because Milo wouldn't come to the door. We were both bitter then, but I got over it. I still don't think Milo would have come into the house again, though, if Bradley hadn't thought it was a good idea. The third time Milo came to pick her up after he'd left home, I went out to invite them in, but Milo said nothing. He was standing there with his arms at his sides like a wooden soldier, and his eyes were as dead to me as if they'd been painted on. It was Bradley whom I reasoned with. "Louise is over at Sarah's right now, and it'll make her feel more comfortable if we're all together when she comes in," I said to him, and Bradley turned to Milo and said, "Hey, that's right. Why don't we go in for a quick cup of coffee?" I looked into the back seat of the car and saw his red Thermos there; Louise had told me about it. Bradley meant that they should come in and sit down. He was giving me even more than I'd asked for.

It would be an understatement to say that I disliked Bradley at first. I was actually afraid of him, afraid even after I saw him, though he was slender, and more nervous than I, and spoke quietly. The second time I saw him, I persuaded myself that he was just a stereotype, but someone who certainly seemed harmless enough. By the third time, I had enough courage to suggest that they come into the house. It was embarrassing for all of us, sitting around the table—the same table where Milo and I had eaten our meals for the years we were married. Before he left, Milo had shouted at me that the house was a farce, that my playing the happy suburban housewife was a farce, that it was unconscionable of me to let things drag on, that I would probably kiss him and say, "How was your day, sweetheart?" and that he should bring home flowers and the evening paper. "Maybe I would!" I screamed back. "Maybe it would be nice to do that, even if we were pretending, instead of you coming home drunk and not caring what had happened to me or to Louise all day." He was holding on to the edge of the kitchen table, the way you'd hold on to the horse's reins in a runaway carriage. "I care about Louise," he said finally. That was the most horrible moment. Until then, until he said it that way, I had thought that he was going through something horrible—certainly something was terribly wrong—but that, in his way, he loved me after all. *You don't love me?* I had whispered at once. It took us both aback. It was an innocent and pathetic question, and it made him come and put his arms around me in the last hug he ever gave me. "I'm sorry for you," he said, "and I'm sorry for marrying you and causing this, but you know who I love. I told you who I love." "But you were kidding," I said. "You didn't mean it. You were kidding."

When Bradley sat at the table that first day, I tried to be polite and not look at him much. I had gotten it through my head that Milo was crazy, and I guess I was expecting Bradley to be a horrible parody—Craig Russell doing Marilyn Monroe. Bradley did not spoon sugar into Milo's coffee. He did not even sit near him. In fact, he pulled his chair a little away from us, and in spite of his uneasiness he found more things to start conversations about than Milo and I did. He told me about the ad agency where he worked; he is a designer there. He asked if he could go out on the porch to see the brook—Milo had told him about the stream in the back of our place that was as thin as a pencil but still gave us our own watercress. He went out on the porch and stayed there for at least five minutes, giving us a chance to talk. We didn't say one word until he came back. Louise came home from Sarah's house just as Bradley sat down at the table again, and she gave him a hug as well as us. I could see that she really liked him. I was amazed that I liked him, too. Bradley had won and I had lost, but he was as gentle and low-key as if none of it mattered. Later in the week, I called him and asked him to tell me if any free-lance jobs opened in his advertising agency. (I do a little free-lance artwork, whenever I can arrange it.) The week after that, he called and told me about another agency, where they were looking for outside artists. Our calls to each other are always brief and for a purpose, but lately they're not just calls about business. Before Bradley left to scout some picture locations in Mexico, he called to say that Milo had told him that when the two of us were there years ago I had seen one of those big circular bronze Aztec calendars and I had always regretted not bringing it back. He wanted to know if I would like him to buy a calendar if he saw one like the one Milo had told him about.

Today, Milo is getting out of his car, his blue scarf flapping against his chest. Louise, looking out the window, asks the same thing I am wondering: "Where's Bradley?"

Milo comes in and shakes my hand, gives Louise a one-armed hug.

"Bradley thinks he's coming down with a cold," Milo says. "The dinner is still on, Louise. We'll do the dinner. We have to stop at Gristedes when we get back to town, unless your mother happens to have a tin of anchovies and two sticks of unsalted butter."

"Let's go to Gristedes," Louise says. "I like to go there."

"Let me look in the kitchen," I say. The butter is salted, but Milo says that will do, and he takes three sticks instead of two. I have a brainstorm and cut the cellophane on a leftover Christmas present from my aunt—a wicker plate that holds nuts and foil-wrapped triangles of cheese—and, sure enough: one tin of anchovies.

"We can go to the museum instead," Milo says to Louise. "Wonderful."

But then, going out the door, carrying her bag, he changes his mind. "We can go to America Hurrah, and if we see something beautiful we can buy it," he says.

They go off in high spirits. Louise comes up to his waist, almost, and I notice again that they have the same walk. Both of them stride forward with great purpose. Last week, Bradley told me that Milo had bought a weather-vane in the shape of a horse, made around 1800, at America Hurrah, and stood it in the bedroom, and then was enraged when Bradley draped his socks over it to dry. Bradley is still learning what a perfectionist Milo is, and how little sense of humor he has. When we were first married, I used one of our pottery casserole dishes to put my jewelry in, and he nagged me until I took it out and put the dish back in the kitchen cabinet. I remember his say-ing that the dish looked silly on my dresser because it was obvious what it was and people would think we left our dishes lying around. It was one of the things that Milo wouldn't tolerate, because it was improper.

When Milo brings Louise back on Saturday night they are not in a good mood. The dinner was all right, Milo says, and Griffin and Amy and Mark were amazed at what a good hostess Louise had been, but Bradley hadn't been able to eat.

"Is he still coming down with a cold?" I ask. I was still a little shy about asking questions about Bradley.

Milo shrugs. "Louise made him take megadoses of vitamin C all week-end."

Louise says, "Bradley said that taking too much vitamin C was bad for your kidneys, though."

"It's a rotten climate," Milo says, sitting on the living-room sofa, scarf and coat still on. "The combination of cold and air pollution . . ."

Louise and I look at each other, and then back at Milo. For weeks now, he has been talking about moving to San Francisco, if he can find work there. (Milo is an architect.) This talk bores me, and it makes Louise nervous. I've asked him not to talk to her about it unless he's actually going to move, but he doesn't seem to be able to stop himself.

"O.K.," Milo says, looking at us both. "I'm not going to say anything about San Francisco."

"*California* is polluted," I say. I am unable to stop myself, either.

Milo heaves himself up from the sofa, ready for the drive back to New York. It is the same way he used to get off the sofa that last year he lived here. He would get up, dress for work, and not even go into the kitchen for breakfast—just sit, sometimes in his coat as he was sitting just now, and at the last minute he would push himself up and go out to the driveway, usually without a goodbye, and get in the car and drive off either very fast or very slowly. I liked it better when he made the tires spin in the gravel when he took off.

He stops at the doorway now, and turns to face me. "Did I take all your butter?" he says.

"No," I say. "There's another stick." I point into the kitchen.

"I could have guessed that's where it would be," he says, and smiles at me.

When Milo comes the next weekend, Bradley is still not with him. The night before, as I was putting Louise to bed, she said that she had a feeling he wouldn't be coming.

"I had that feeling a couple of days ago," I said. "Usually Bradley calls once during the week."

"He must still be sick," Louise said. She looked at me anxiously. "Do you think he is?"

"A cold isn't going to kill him," I said. "If he has a cold, he'll be O.K."

Her expression changed; she thought I was talking down to her. She lay back in bed. The last year Milo was with us, I used to tuck her in and tell her that everything was all right. What that meant was that there had not been a fight. Milo had sat listening to music on the phonograph, with a book or the newspaper in front of his face. He didn't pay very much attention to Louise, and he ignored me entirely. Instead of saying a prayer with her, the way I usually did, I would say to her that everything was all right. Then I would go downstairs and hope that Milo would say the same thing to me. What he finally did say one night was "You might as well find out from me as some other way."

"Hey, are you an old bag lady again this weekend?" Milo says now, stooping to kiss Louise's forehead.

"Because you take some things with you doesn't mean you're a bag lady," she says primly.

"Well," Milo says, "you start doing something innocently, and before you know it it can take you over."

He looks angry, and acts as though it's difficult for him to make conversation, even when the conversation is full of sarcasm and double-entendres.

"What do you say we get going?" he says to Louise.

In the shopping bag she is taking is her doll, which she has not played with for more than a year. I found it by accident when I went to tuck in a loaf of banana bread that I had baked. When I saw Baby Betsy, deep in the bag, I decided against putting the bread in.

"O.K.," Louise says to Milo. "Where's Bradley?"

"Sick," he says.

"Is he too sick to have me visit?"

"Good heavens, no. He'll be happier to see you than to see me."

"I'm rooting some of my coleus to give him," she says. "Maybe I'll give it to him like it is, in water, and he can plant it when it roots."

When she leaves the room, I go over to Milo. "Be nice to her," I say quietly.

"I'm nice to her," he says. "Why does everybody have to act like I'm going to grow fangs every time I turn around?"

"You were quite cutting when you came in."

"I was being self-deprecating." He sighs. "I don't really know why I come here and act this way," he says.

"What's the matter, Milo?"

But now he lets me know he's bored with the conversation. He walks over to the table and picks up a *Newsweek* and flips through it. Louise comes back with the coleus in a water glass.

"You know what you could do," I say. "Wet a napkin and put it around that cutting and then wrap it in foil, and put it in water when you get there. That way, you wouldn't have to hold a glass of water all the way to New York."

She shrugs. "This is O.K.," she says.

"Why don't you take your mother's suggestion," Milo says. "The water will slosh out of the glass."

"Not if you don't drive fast."

"It doesn't have anything to do with my driving fast. If we go over a bump in the road, you're going to get all wet."

"Then I can put on one of my dresses at your apartment."

"Am I being unreasonable?" Milo says to me.

"I started it," I say. "Let her take it in the glass."

"Would you, as a favor, do what your mother says?" he says to Louise.

Louise looks at the coleus, and at me.

"Hold the glass over the seat instead of over your lap, and you won't get wet," I say.

"Your first idea was the best," Milo says.

Louise gives him an exasperated look and puts the glass down on the floor, pulls on her poncho, picks up the glass again and says a sullen goodbye to me, and goes out the front door.

"Why is this my fault?" Milo says. "Have I done anything terrible? I—"

"Do something to cheer yourself up," I say, patting him on the back.

He looks as exasperated with me as Louise was with him. He nods his head yes, and goes out the door.

"Was everything all right this weekend?" I ask Louise.

"Milo was in a bad mood, and Bradley wasn't even there on Saturday," Louise says. "He came back today and took us to the Village for breakfast."

"What did you have?"

"I had sausage wrapped in little pancakes and fruit salad and a rum bun."

"Where was Bradley on Saturday?"

She shrugs. "I didn't ask him."

She almost always surprises me by being more grown-up than I give her credit for. Does she suspect, as I do, that Bradley has found another lover?

"Milo was in a bad mood when you two left here Saturday," I say.

"I told him if he didn't want me to come next weekend, just to tell me." She looks perturbed, and I suddenly realize that she can sound exactly like Milo sometimes.

"You shouldn't have said that to him, Louise," I say. "You know he wants you. He's just worried about Bradley."

"So?" she says. "I'm probably going to flunk math."

"No, you're not, honey. You got a C-plus on the last assignment."

"It still doesn't make my grade average out to a C."

"You'll get a C. It's all right to get a C."

She doesn't believe me.

"Don't be a perfectionist, like Milo," I tell her. "Even if you got a D, you wouldn't fail."

Louise is brushing her hair—thin, shoulder-length, auburn hair. She is already so pretty and so smart in everything except math that I wonder what will become of her. When I was her age, I was plain and serious and I wanted to be a tree surgeon. I went with my father to the park and held a stethoscope—a real one—to the trunks of trees, listening to their silence. Children seem older now.

"What do you think's the matter with Bradley?" Louise says. She sounds worried.

"Maybe the two of them are unhappy with each other right now."

She misses my point. "Bradley's sad, and Milo's sad that he's unhappy."

I drop Louise off at Sarah's house for supper. Sarah's mother, Martine Cooper, looks like Shelley Winters, and I have never seen her without a glass of Galliano on ice in her hand. She has a strong candy smell. Her husband has left her, and she professes not to care. She has emptied her living room of furniture and put up ballet bars on the walls, and dances in a purple leotard to records by Cher and Mac Davis. I prefer to have Sarah come to our house, but her mother is adamant that everything must be, as she puts it, "fifty-fifty." When Sarah visited us a week ago and loved the chocolate pie I had made, I sent two pieces home with her. Tonight, when I left Sarah's house, her mother gave me a bowl of Jell-O fruit salad.

The phone is ringing when I come in the door. It is Bradley.

"Bradley," I say at once, "whatever's wrong, at least you don't have a neighbor who just gave you a bowl of maraschino cherries in green Jell-O with a Reddi-Wip flower squirted on top."

"Jesus," he says. "You don't need me to depress you, do you?"

"What's wrong?" I say.

He sighs into the phone. "Guess what?" he says.

"What?"

"I've lost my job."

It wasn't at all what I was expecting to hear. I was ready to hear that he was leaving Milo, and I had even thought that that would serve Milo right. Part of me still wanted him punished for what he did. I was so out of my mind when Milo left me that I used to go over and drink Galliano with Martine Cooper. I even thought seriously about forming a ballet group with her. I would go to her house in the afternoon, and she would hold a tambourine in the air and I would hold my leg rigid and try to kick it.

"That's awful," I say to Bradley. "What happened?"

"They said it was nothing personal—they were laying off three people. Two other people are going to get the ax at the agency within the next six months. I was the first to go, and it was nothing personal. From twenty thousand bucks a year to nothing, and nothing personal, either."

"But your work is so good. Won't you be able to find something again?"

"Could I ask you a favor?" he says. "I'm calling from a phone booth. I'm not in the city. Could I come talk to you?"

"Sure," I say.

It seems perfectly logical that he should come alone to talk—perfectly logical until I actually see him coming up the walk. I can't entirely believe it. A year after my husband has left me, I am sitting with his lover—a man, a person I like quite well—and trying to cheer him up because he is out of work. ("Honey," my father would say, "listen to Daddy's heart with the stethoscope, or you can turn it toward you and listen to your own heart. You won't hear anything listening to a tree." Was my persistence willfulness, or belief in magic? Is it possible that I hugged Bradley at the door because I'm secretly glad he's down and out, the way I used to be? Or do I really want to make things better for him?)

He comes into the kitchen and thanks me for the coffee I am making, drapes his coat over the chair he always sits in.

"What am I going to do?" he asks.

"You shouldn't get so upset, Bradley," I say. "You know you're good. You won't have trouble finding another job."

"That's only half of it," he says. "Milo thinks I did this deliberately. He told me I was quitting on him. He's very angry at me. He fights with me, and then he gets mad that I don't enjoy eating dinner. My stomach's upset, and I can't eat anything."

"Maybe some juice would be better than coffee."

"If I didn't drink coffee, I'd collapse," he says.

I pour coffee into a mug for him, coffee into a mug for me.

"This is probably very awkward for you," he says. "That I come here and say all this about Milo."

"What does he mean about your quitting on him?"

"He said . . . he actually accused me of doing badly deliberately, so they'd fire me. I was so afraid to tell him the truth when I was fired that I pretended to be sick. Then I really *was* sick. He's never been angry at me this way. Is this always the way he acts? Does he get a notion in his head for no reason and then pick at a person because of it?"

I try to remember. "We didn't argue much," I say. "When he didn't want to live here, he made me look ridiculous for complaining when I knew something was wrong. He expects perfection, but what that means is that you do things his way."

"I *was*. I never wanted to sit around the apartment, the way he says I did. I even brought work home with me. He made me feel so bad all week that I went to a friend's apartment for the day on Saturday. Then he said I had walked out on the problem. He's a little paranoid. I was listening to the radio, and Carole King was singing 'It's Too Late,' and he came into the study and looked very upset, as though I had planned for the song to come on. I couldn't believe it."

"Whew," I say, shaking my head. "I don't envy you. You have to stand up to him. I didn't do that. I pretended the problem would go away."

"And now the problem sits across from you drinking coffee, and you're being nice to him."

"I know it. I was just thinking we look like two characters in some soap opera my friend Martine Cooper would watch."

He pushes his coffee cup away from him with a grimace.

"But anyway, I like you now," I say. "And you're exceptionally nice to Louise."

"I took her father," he says.

"Bradley—I hope you don't take offense, but it makes me nervous to talk about that."

"I don't take offense. But how can you be having coffee with me?"

"You invited yourself over so you could ask that?"

"Please," he says, holding up both hands. Then he runs his hands through his hair. "Don't make me feel illogical. He does that to me, you know. He doesn't understand it when everything doesn't fall right into line. If I like fixing up the place, keeping some flowers around, therefore I can't like being a working person, too, therefore I deliberately sabotage myself in my job." Bradley sips his coffee.

"I wish I could do something for him," he says in a different voice.

This is not what I expected, either. We have sounded like two wise adults, and then suddenly he has changed and sounds very tender. I realize the situation is still the same. It is two of them on one side and me on the other, even though Bradley is in my kitchen.

"Come and pick up Louise with me, Bradley," I say. "When you see Martine Cooper, you'll cheer up about your situation."

He looks up from his coffee. "You're forgetting what I'd look like to Martine Cooper," he says.

Milo is going to California. He has been offered a job with a new San Francisco architectural firm. I am not the first to know. His sister, Deanna, knows before I do, and mentions it when we're talking on the phone. "It's middle-age crisis," Deanna says sniffily. "Not that I need to tell you." Deanna would drop dead if she knew the way things are. She is scandalized every time a new display is put up in Bloomingdale's window. ("Those mannequins had eyes like an Egyptian princess, and *rags*. I swear to you, they had mops and brooms and ragged gauze dresses on, with whores' shoes—stiletto heels that prostitutes wear.")

I hang up from Deanna's call and tell Louise I'm going to drive to the gas station for cigarettes. I go there to call New York on their pay phone.

"Well, I only just knew," Milo says. "I found out for sure yesterday, and last night Deanna called and so I told her. It's not like I'm leaving tonight."

He sounds elated, in spite of being upset that I called. He's happy in the way he used to be on Christmas morning. I remember him once running into the living room in his underwear and tearing open the gifts we'd been sent by relatives. He was looking for the eight-slice toaster he was sure we'd get. We'd been given two-slice, four-slice, and six-slice toasters, but then we got no more. "Come out, my eight-slice beauty!" Milo crooned, and out came an electric clock, a blender, and an expensive electric pan.

"When are you leaving?" I ask him.

"I'm going out to look for a place to live next week."

"Are you going to tell Louise yourself this weekend?"

"Of course," he says.

"And what are you going to do about seeing Louise?"

"Why do you act as if I don't like Louise?" he says. "I will occasionally come back East, and I will arrange for her to fly to San Francisco on her vacations."

"It's going to break her heart."

"No it isn't. Why do you want to make me feel bad?"

"She's had so many things to adjust to. You don't have to go to San Francisco right now, Milo."

"It happens, if you care, that my own job here is in jeopardy. This is a real chance for me, with a young firm. They really want me. But anyway, all we need in this happy group is to have you bringing in a couple of hundred dollars a month with your graphic work and me destitute and Bradley so devastated by being fired that of course he can't even look for work."

"I'll bet he is looking for a job," I say.

"Yes. He read the want ads today and then fixed a crab quiche."

"Maybe that's the way you like things, Milo, and people respond to you. You forbade me to work when we had a baby. Do you say anything encouraging to him about finding a job, or do you just take it out on him that he was fired?"

There is a pause, and then he almost seems to lose his mind with impatience.

"I can hardly *believe*, when I am trying to find a logical solution to all our problems, that I am being subjected, by telephone, to an unflattering psychological analysis by my ex-wife." He says this all in a rush.

"All right, Milo. But don't you think that if you're leaving so soon you ought to call her, instead of waiting until Saturday?"

Milo sighs very deeply. "I have more sense than to have important conversations on the telephone," he says.

Milo calls on Friday and asks Louise whether it wouldn't be nice if both of us came in and spent the night Saturday and if we all went to brunch together Sunday. Louise is excited. I never go into town with her.

Louise and I pack a suitcase and put it in the car Saturday morning. A cutting of ivy for Bradley has taken root, and she has put it in a little green plastic pot for him. It's heartbreaking, and I hope that Milo notices and has a tough time dealing with it. I am relieved I'm going to be there when he tells her, and sad that I have to hear it at all.

In the city, I give the car to the garage attendant, who does not remember me. Milo and I lived in the apartment when we were first married, and moved when Louise was two years old. When we moved, Milo kept the apartment and sublet it—a sign that things were not going well, if I had been one to heed such a warning. What he said was that if we were ever rich enough we could have the house in Connecticut *and* the apartment in New York. When Milo moved out of the house, he went right back to the apartment. This will be the first time I have visited there in years.

Louise strides in in front of me, throwing her coat over the brass coat-rack in the entranceway—almost too casual about being there. She's the hostess at Milo's, the way I am at our house.

He has painted the walls white. There are floor-length white curtains in the living room, where my silly flowered curtains used to hang. The walls are bare, the floor has been sanded, a stereo as huge as a computer stands against one wall of the living room, and there are four speakers.

"Look around," Milo says. "Show your mother around, Louise."

I am trying to remember if I have ever told Louise that I used to live in this apartment. I must have told her, at some point, but I can't remember it.

"Hello," Bradley says, coming out of the bedroom.

"Hi, Bradley," I say. "Have you got a drink?"

Bradley looks sad. "He's got champagne," he says, and looks nervously at Milo.

"No one *has* to drink champagne," Milo says. "There's the usual assortment of liquor."

"Yes," Bradley says. "What would you like?"

"Some bourbon, please."

"Bourbon." Bradley turns to go into the kitchen. He looks different; his hair is different—more wavy—and he is dressed as though it were summer, in straight-legged white pants and black leather thongs.

"I want Perrier water with strawberry juice," Louise says, tagging along after Bradley. I have never heard her ask for such a thing before. At home, she drinks too many Cokes. I am always trying to get her to drink fruit juice.

Bradley comes back with two drinks and hands me one. "Did you want anything?" he says to Milo.

"I'm going to open the champagne in a moment," Milo says. "How have you been this week, sweetheart?"

"O.K.," Louise says. She is holding a pale-pink, bubbly drink. She sips it like a cocktail.

Bradley looks very bad. He has circles under his eyes, and he is ill at ease. A red light begins to blink on the phone-answering device next to where Bradley sits on the sofa, and Milo gets out of his chair to pick up the phone.

"Do you really want to talk on the phone right now?" Bradley asks Milo quietly.

Milo looks at him. "No, not particularly," he says, sitting down again. After a moment, the red light goes out.

"I'm going to mist your bowl garden," Louise says to Bradley, and slides off the sofa and goes to the bedroom. "Hey, a little toadstool is growing in here!" she calls back. "Did you put it there, Bradley?"

"It grew from the soil mixture, I guess," Bradley calls back. "I don't know how it got there."

"Have you heard anything about a job?" I ask Bradley.

"I haven't been looking, really," he says. "You know."

Milo frowns at him. "Your choice, Bradley," he says. "I didn't ask you to follow me to California. You can stay here."

"No," Bradley says. "You've hardly made me feel welcome."

"Should we have some champagne—all four of us—and you can get back to your bourbons later?" Milo says cheerfully.

We don't answer him, but he gets up anyway and goes to the kitchen. "Where have you hidden the tulip-shaped glasses, Bradley?" he calls out after a while.

"They should be in the cabinet on the far left," Bradley says.

"You're going with him?" I say to Bradley. "To San Francisco?"

He shrugs, and won't look at me. "I'm not quite sure I'm wanted," he says quietly.

The cork pops in the kitchen. I look at Bradley, but he won't look up. His new hairdo makes him look older. I remember that when Milo left me I went to the hairdresser the same week and had bangs cut. The next week, I went to a therapist who told me it was no good trying to hide from myself. The week after that, I did dance exercises with Martine Cooper, and the week after that the therapist told me not to dance if I wasn't interested in dancing.

"I'm not going to act like this is a funeral," Milo says, coming in with the glasses. "Louise, come in here and have champagne! We have something to have a toast about."

Louise comes into the living room suspiciously. She is so used to being refused even a sip of wine from my glass or her father's that she no longer even asks. "How come I'm in on this?" she asks.

"We're going to drink a toast to me," Milo says.

Three of the four glasses are clustered on the table in front of the sofa.

Milo's glass is raised. Louise looks at me, to see what I'm going to say. Milo raises his glass even higher. Bradley reaches for a glass. Louise picks up a glass. I lean forward and take the last one.

"This is a toast to me," Milo says, "because I am going to be going to San Francisco."

It was not a very good or informative toast. Bradley and I sip from our glasses. Louise puts her glass down hard and bursts into tears, knocking the glass over. The champagne spills onto the cover of a big art book about the unicorn tapestries. She runs into the bedroom and slams the door.

Milo looks furious. "Everybody lets me know just what my insufficiencies are, don't they?" he says. "Nobody minds expressing himself. We have it all right out in the open."

"He's criticizing me," Bradley murmurs, his head still bowed. "It's because I was offered a job here in the city and I didn't automatically refuse it."

I turn to Milo. "Go say something to Louise, Milo," I say. "Do you think that's what somebody who isn't brokenhearted sounds like?"

He glares at me and stomps into the bedroom, and I can hear him talking to Louise reassuringly. "It doesn't mean you'll *never* see me," he says. "You can fly there, I'll come here. It's not going to be that different."

"You lied!" Louise screams. "You said we were going to brunch."

"We are. We are. I can't very well take us to brunch before Sunday, can I?"

"You didn't say you were going to San Francisco. What *is* San Francisco, anyway?"

"I just said so. I bought us a bottle of champagne. You can come out as soon as I get settled. You're going to like it there."

Louise is sobbing. She has told him the truth and she knows it's futile to go on.

By the next morning, Louise acts the way I acted—as if everything were just the same. She looks calm, but her face is small and pale. She looks very young. We walk into the restaurant and sit at the table Milo has reserved. Bradley pulls out a chair for me, and Milo pulls out a chair for Louise, locking his finger with hers for a second, raising her arm above her head, as if she were about to take a twirl.

She looks very nice, really. She has a ribbon in her hair. It is cold, and she should have worn a hat, but she wanted to wear the ribbon. Milo has good taste: the dress she is wearing, which he bought for her, is a hazy purple plaid, and it sets off her hair.

"Come with me. Don't be sad," Milo suddenly says to Louise, pulling her by the hand. "Come with me for a minute. Come across the street to the park for just a second, and we'll have some space to dance, and your mother and Bradley can have a nice quiet drink."

She gets up from the table and, looking long-suffering, backs into her coat, which he is holding for her, and the two of them go out. The waitress comes to the table, and Bradley orders three Bloody Marys and a Coke, and eggs Benedict for everyone. He asks the waitress to wait awhile before she brings the food. I have hardly slept at all, and having a drink is not going to clear my head. I have to think of things to say to Louise later, on the ride home.

"He takes so many *chances*," I say. "He pushes things so far with people. I don't want her to turn against him."

"No," he says.

"Why are you going, Bradley? You've seen the way he acts. You know that when you get out there he'll pull something on you. Take the job and stay here."

Bradley is fiddling with the edge of his napkin. I study him. I don't know who his friends are, how old he is, where he grew up, whether he believes in God, or what he usually drinks. I'm shocked that I know so little, and I reach out and touch him. He looks up.

"Don't go," I say quietly.

The waitress puts the glasses down quickly and leaves, embarrassed because she thinks she's interrupted a tender moment. Bradley pats my hand on his arm. Then he says the thing that has always been between us, the thing too painful for me to envision or think about.

"I love him," Bradley whispers.

We sit quietly until Milo and Louise come into the restaurant, swinging hands. She is pretending to be a young child, almost a baby, and I wonder for an instant if Milo and Bradley and I haven't been playing house, too— pretending to be adults.

"Daddy's going to give me a first-class ticket," Louise says. "When I go to California we're going to ride in a glass elevator to the top of the Fairman Hotel."

"The Fairmont," Milo says, smiling at her.

Before Louise was born, Milo used to put his ear to my stomach and say that if the baby turned out to be a girl he would put her into glass slippers instead of bootees. Now he is the prince once again. I see them in a glass elevator, not long from now, going up and up, with the people below getting smaller and smaller, until they disappear.

The Burning House

Freddy Fox is in the kitchen with me. He has just washed and dried an avocado seed I don't want, and he is leaning against the wall, rolling a joint. In five minutes, I will not be able to count on him. However: he started late in the day, and he has already brought in wood for the fire, gone to the store down the road for matches, and set the table. "You mean you'd know this stuff was Limoges even if you didn't turn the plate over?" he called from the dining room. He pretended to be about to throw one of the plates into the kitchen, like a Frisbee. Sam, the dog, believed him and shot up, kicking the rug out behind him and skidding forward before he realized his error; it was like the Road Runner tricking Wile E. Coyote into going over the cliff for the millionth time. His jowls sank in disappointment.

"I see there's a full moon," Freddy says. "There's just nothing that can hold a candle to nature. The moon and the stars, the tides and the sunshine—and we just don't stop for long enough to wonder at it all. We're so engrossed in ourselves." He takes a very long drag on the joint. "We stand and stir the sauce in the pot instead of going to the window and gazing at the moon."

"You don't mean anything personal by that, I assume."

"I love the way you pour cream in a pan. I like to come up behind you and watch the sauce bubble."

"No, thank you," I say. "You're starting late in the day."

"My responsibilities have ended. You don't trust me to help with the cooking, and I've already brought in firewood and run an errand, and this very morning I exhausted myself by taking Mr. Sam jogging with me, down at Putnam Park. You're sure you won't?"

"No, thanks," I say. "Not now, anyway."

"I love it when you stand over the steam coming out of a pan and the hairs around your forehead curl into damp little curls."

My husband, Frank Wayne, is Freddy's half brother. Frank is an accountant. Freddy is closer to me than to Frank. Since Frank talks to Freddy more than he talks to me, however, and since Freddy is totally loyal, Freddy always knows more than I know. It pleases me that he does not know how to stir sauce; he will start talking, his mind will drift, and when next you look the sauce will be lumpy, or boiling away.

Freddy's criticism of Frank is only implied. "What a gracious gesture to entertain his friends on the weekend," he says.

"Male friends," I say.

"I didn't mean that you're the sort of lady who doesn't draw the line. I most certainly did not mean that," Freddy says. "I would even have been surprised if you had taken a toke of this deadly stuff while you were at the stove."

"O.K.," I say, and take the joint from him. Half of it is left when I take it. Half an inch is left after I've taken two drags and given it back.

"More surprised still if you'd shaken the ashes into the saucepan."

"You'd tell people I'd done it when they'd finished eating, and I'd be embarrassed. You can do it, though. I wouldn't be embarrassed if it was a story you told on yourself."

"You really understand me," Freddy says. "It's moon-madness, but I have to shake just this little bit in the sauce. I have to do it."

He does it.

Frank and Tucker are in the living room. Just a few minutes ago, Frank returned from getting Tucker at the train. Tucker loves to visit. To him, Fairfield County is as mysterious as Alaska. He brought with him from New York a crock of mustard, a jeroboam of champagne, cocktail napkins with a picture of a plane flying over a building on them, twenty egret feathers ("You cannot get them anymore—strictly illegal," Tucker whispered to me), and, under his black cowboy hat with the rhinestone-studded chin strap, a toy frog that hopped when wound. Tucker owns a gallery in SoHo, and Frank keeps his books. Tucker is now stretched out in the living room, visiting with Frank, and Freddy and I are both listening.

". . . so everything I've been told indicates that he lives a purely Jekyll-and-Hyde existence. He's twenty years old, and I can see that since he's still living at home he might not want to flaunt his gayness. When he came into the gallery, he had his hair slicked back—just with water, I got close enough to sniff—and his mother was all but holding his hand. So fresh-scrubbed.

The stories I'd heard. Anyway, when I called, his father started looking for the number where he could be reached on the Vineyard—very irritated, because I didn't know James, and if I'd just phoned James I could have found him in a flash. He's talking to himself, looking for the number, and I say, 'Oh, did he go to visit friends or—' and his father interrupts and says, 'He was going to a gay pig roast. He's been gone since Monday.' *Just like that.*"

Freddy helps me carry the food out to the table. When we are all at the table, I mention the young artist Tucker was talking about. "Frank says his paintings are really incredible," I say to Tucker.

"Makes Estes look like an Abstract Expressionist," Tucker says. "I want that boy. I really want that boy."

"You'll get him," Frank says. "You get everybody you go after."

Tucker cuts a small piece of meat. He cuts it small so that he can talk while chewing. "Do I?" he says.

Freddy is smoking at the table, gazing dazedly at the moon centered in the window. "After dinner," he says, putting the back of his hand against his forehead when he sees that I am looking at him, "we must all go to the lighthouse."

"If only *you* painted," Tucker says. "I'd want you."

"You couldn't have me," Freddy snaps. He reconsiders. "That sounded halfhearted, didn't it? Anybody who wants me can have me. This is the only place I can be on Saturday night where somebody isn't hustling me."

"Wear looser pants," Frank says to Freddy.

"This is so much better than some bar that stinks of cigarette smoke and leather. Why do I do it?" Freddy says. "Seriously—do you think I'll ever stop?"

"Let's not be serious," Tucker says.

"I keep thinking of this table as a big boat, with dishes and glasses rocking on it," Freddy says.

He takes the bone from his plate and walks out to the kitchen, dripping sauce on the floor. He walks as though he's on the deck of a wave-tossed ship. "Mr. Sam!" he calls, and the dog springs up from the living-room floor, where he had been sleeping; his toenails on the bare wood floor sound like a wheel spinning in gravel. "You don't have to beg," Freddy says. "Jesus, Sammy—I'm just giving it to you."

"I hope there's a bone involved," Tucker says, rolling his eyes to Frank. He cuts another tiny piece of meat. "I hope your brother does understand why I couldn't keep him on. He was good at what he did, but he also might say just *anything* to a customer. You have to believe me that if I hadn't been extremely embarrassed more than once I never would have let him go."

"He should have finished school," Frank says, sopping up sauce on his bread. "He'll knock around a while longer, then get tired of it and settle down to something."

"You think I died out here?" Freddy calls. "You think I can't hear you?"

"I'm not saying anything I wouldn't say to your face," Frank says.

"I'll tell you what I wouldn't say to your face," Freddy says. "You've got a swell wife and kid and dog, and you're a snob, and you take it all for granted."

Frank puts down his fork, completely exasperated. He looks at me.

"He came to work once this stoned," Tucker says. *"Comprenez-vous?"*

"You like me because you feel sorry for me," Freddy says.

He is sitting on the concrete bench outdoors, in the area that's a garden in the springtime. It is early April now—not quite spring. It's very foggy out. It rained while we were eating, and now it has turned mild. I'm leaning against a tree, across from him, glad it's so dark and misty that I can't look down and see the damage the mud is doing to my boots.

"Who's his girlfriend?" Freddy says.

"If I told you her name, you'd tell him I told you."

"Slow down. What?"

"I won't tell you, because you'll tell him that I know."

"He knows you know."

"I don't think so."

"How did you find out?"

"He talked about her. I kept hearing her name for months, and then we went to a party at Garner's, and she was there, and when I said something about her later he said, 'Natalie who?' It was much too obvious. It gave the whole thing away."

He sighs. "I just did something very optimistic," he says. "I came out here with Mr. Sam and he dug up a rock and I put the avocado seed in the hole and packed dirt on top of it. Don't say it—I know: can't grow outside, we'll still have another snow, even if it grew, the next year's frost would kill it."

"He's embarrassed," I say. "When he's home, he avoids me. But it's rotten to avoid Mark, too. Six years old, and he calls up his friend Neal to hint that he wants to go over there. He doesn't do that when we're here alone."

Freddy picks up a stick and pokes around in the mud with it. "I'll bet Tucker's after that painter personally, not because he's the hottest thing since pancakes. That expression of his—it's always the same. Maybe Nixon really loved his mother, but with that expression who could believe him? It's a curse to have a face that won't express what you mean."

"Amy!" Tucker calls. "Telephone."

Freddy waves goodbye to me with the muddy stick. "'I am not a crook,'" Freddy says. "Jesus Christ."

Sam bounds halfway toward the house with me, then turns and goes back to Freddy.

It's Marilyn, Neal's mother, on the phone.

"Hi," Marilyn says. "He's afraid to spend the night."

"Oh, no," I say. "He said he wouldn't be."

She lowers her voice. "We can try it out, but I think he'll start crying."

"I'll come get him."

"I can bring him home. You're having a dinner party, aren't you?"

I lower my voice. "Some party. Tucker's here. J.D. never showed up."

"Well," she says. "I'm sure that what you cooked was good."

"It's so foggy out, Marilyn. I'll come get Mark."

"He can stay. I'll be a martyr," she says, and hangs up before I can object.

Freddy comes into the house, tracking in mud. Sam lies in the kitchen, waiting for his paws to be cleaned. "Come on," Freddy says, hitting his hand against his thigh, having no idea what Sam is doing. Sam gets up and runs after him. They go into the small downstairs bathroom together. Sam loves to watch people urinate. Sometimes he sings, to harmonize with the sound of the urine going into the water. There are footprints and pawprints everywhere. Tucker is shrieking with laughter in the living room. ". . . he says, he says to the other one, 'Then, dearie, have you ever played *spin* the bottle?'" Frank's and Tucker's laughter drowns out the sound of Freddy peeing in the bathroom. I turn on the water in the kitchen sink, and it drowns out all the noise. I begin to scrape the dishes. Tucker is telling another story when I turn off the water: ". . . that it was Onassis in the Anvil, and nothing would talk him out of it. They told him Onassis was dead, and he thought they were trying to make him think he was crazy. There was nothing to do but go along with him, but, God—he was trying to goad this poor old fag into fighting about Stavros Niarchos. You know—Onassis's *enemy*. He thought it was *Onassis*. In the *Anvil*." There is a sound of a glass breaking. Frank or Tucker puts *John Coltrane Live in Seattle* on the stereo and turns the volume down low. The bathroom door opens. Sam runs into the kitchen and begins to lap water from his dish. Freddy takes his little silver case and his rolling papers out of his shirt pocket. He puts a piece of paper on the kitchen table and is about to sprinkle grass on it, but realizes just in time that the paper has absorbed water from a puddle. He balls it up with his thumb, flicks it to the floor, puts a piece of rolling paper where the table's dry and shakes a line of grass down it. "You smoke this," he says to me. "I'll do the dishes."

"We'll both smoke it. I'll wash and you can wipe."

"I forgot to tell them I put ashes in the sauce," he says.

"I wouldn't interrupt."

"At least he pays Frank ten times what any other accountant for an art gallery would make," Freddy says.

Tucker is beating his hand on the arm of the sofa as he talks, stomping his feet. ". . . so he's trying to feel him out, to see if this old guy with the dyed hair knew *Maria Callas*. Jesus! And he's so out of it he's trying to think what opera singers are called, and instead of coming up with '*diva*' he comes up with '*duenna*.' At this point, Larry Betwell went up to him and tried to calm him down, and he breaks into song—some aria or something that Maria Callas was famous for. Larry told him he was going to lose his *teeth* if he didn't get it together, and . . ."

"He spends a lot of time in gay hangouts, for not being gay," Freddy says.

I scream and jump back from the sink, hitting the glass I'm rinsing against the faucet, shattering green glass everywhere.

"What?" Freddy says. "Jesus Christ, what is it?"

Too late, I realize what it must have been that I saw: J.D. in a goat mask, the puckered pink plastic lips against the window by the kitchen sink.

"I'm sorry," J.D. says, coming through the door and nearly colliding with Frank, who has rushed into the kitchen. Tucker is right behind him.

"Oooh," Tucker says, feigning disappointment, "I thought Freddy smooched her."

"I'm sorry," J.D. says again. "I thought you'd know it was me."

The rain must have started again, because J.D. is soaking wet. He has turned the mask around so that the goat's head stares out from the back of his head. "I got lost," J.D. says. He has a farmhouse upstate. "I missed the turn. I went miles. I missed the whole dinner, didn't I?"

"What did you do wrong?" Frank asks.

"I didn't turn left onto 58. I don't know why I didn't realize my mistake, but I went *miles*. It was raining so hard I couldn't go over twenty-five miles an hour. Your driveway is all mud. You're going to have to push me out."

"There's some roast left over. And salad, if you want it," I say.

"Bring it in the living room," Frank says to J.D. Freddy is holding out a plate to him. J.D. reaches for the plate. Freddy pulls it back. J.D. reaches again, and Freddy is so stoned that he isn't quick enough this time—J.D. grabs it.

"I thought you'd know it was me," J.D. says. "I apologize." He dishes salad onto the plate. "You'll be rid of me for six months, in the morning."

"Where does your plane leave from?" Freddy says.

"Kennedy."

"Come in here!" Tucker calls. "I've got a story for you about Perry Dwyer down at the Anvil last week, when he thought he saw Aristotle Onassis."

"Who's Perry Dwyer?" J.D. says.

"That is not the point of the story, dear man. And when you're in Cassis, I want you to look up an American painter over there. Will you? He doesn't have a phone. Anyway—I've been tracking him, and I know where he is now, and I am *very* interested, if you would stress that with him, to do a show in June that will be *only* him. He doesn't answer my letters."

"Your hand is cut," J.D. says to me.

"Forget it," I say. "Go ahead."

"I'm sorry," he says. "Did I make you do that?"

"Yes, you did."

"Don't keep your finger under the water. Put pressure on it to stop the bleeding."

He puts the plate on the table. Freddy is leaning against the counter, staring at the blood swirling in the sink, and smoking the joint all by himself. I can feel the little curls on my forehead that Freddy was talking about. They feel heavy on my skin. I hate to see my own blood. I'm sweating. I let J.D. do what he does; he turns off the water and wraps his hand around my second finger, squeezing. Water runs down our wrists.

Freddy jumps to answer the phone when it rings, as though a siren just went off behind him. He calls me to the phone, but J.D. steps in front of me, shakes his head no, and takes the dish towel and wraps it around my hand before he lets me go.

"Well," Marilyn says. "I had the best of intentions, but my battery's dead."

J.D. is standing behind me, with his hand on my shoulder.

"I'll be right over," I say. "He's not upset now, is he?"

"No, but he's dropped enough hints that he doesn't think he can make it through the night."

"O.K.," I say. "I'm sorry about all of this."

"Six years old," Marilyn says. "Wait till he grows up and gets that feeling." I hang up.

"Let me see your hand," J.D. says.

"I don't want to look at it. Just go get me a Band-Aid, please."

He turns and goes upstairs. I unwrap the towel and look at it. It's pretty deep, but no glass is in my finger. I feel funny; the outlines of things are turning yellow. I sit in the chair by the phone. Sam comes and lies beside me, and I stare at his black-and-yellow tail, beating. I reach down with my good hand and pat him, breathing deeply in time with every second pat.

"*Rothko?*" Tucker says bitterly, in the living room. "Nothing is great that can appear on greeting cards. Wyeth is that way. Would *Christina's World* look bad on a cocktail napkin? You know it wouldn't."

I jump as the phone rings again. "Hello?" I say, wedging the phone against my shoulder with my ear, wrapping the dish towel tighter around my hand.

"Tell them it's a crank call. Tell them anything," Johnny says. "I miss you. How's Saturday night at your house?"

"All right," I say. I catch my breath.

"Everything's all right here, too. Yes indeed. Roast rack of lamb. Friend of Nicole's who's going to Key West tomorrow had too much to drink and got depressed because he thought it was raining in Key West, and I said I'd go in my study and call the National Weather Service. Hello, Weather Service. How are you?"

J.D. comes down from upstairs with two Band-Aids and stands beside me, unwrapping one. I want to say to Johnny, "I'm cut. I'm bleeding. It's no joke."

It's all right to talk in front of J.D., but I don't know who else might overhear me.

"I'd say they made the delivery about four this afternoon," I say.

"This is the church, this is the steeple. Open the door, and see all the people," Johnny says. "Take care of yourself. I'll hang up and find out if it's raining in Key West."

"Late in the afternoon," I say. "Everything is fine."

"Nothing is fine," Johnny says. "Take care of yourself."

He hangs up. I put the phone down, and realize that I'm still having trouble focusing, the sight of my cut finger made me so light-headed. I don't look at the finger again as J.D. undoes the towel and wraps the Band-Aids around my finger.

"What's going on in here?" Frank says, coming into the dining room.

"I cut my finger," I say. "It's O.K."

"You did?" he says. He looks woozy—a little drunk. "Who keeps calling?"

"Marilyn. Mark changed his mind about staying all night. She was going to bring him home, but her battery's dead. You'll have to get him. Or I will."

"Who called the second time?" he says.

"The oil company. They wanted to know if we got our delivery today."

He nods. "I'll go get him, if you want," he says. He lowers his voice. "Tucker's probably going to whirl himself into a tornado for an encore," he says, nodding toward the living room. "I'll take him with me."

"Do you want me to go get him?" J.D. says.

"I don't mind getting some air," Frank says. "Thanks, though. Why don't you go in the living room and eat your dinner?"

"You forgive me?" J.D. says.

"Sure," I say. "It wasn't your fault. Where did you get that mask?"

"I found it on top of a Goodwill box in Manchester. There was also a beautiful old birdcage—solid brass."

The phone rings again. I pick it up. "Wouldn't I love to be in Key West with you," Johnny says. He makes a sound as though he's kissing me and hangs up.

"Wrong number," I say.

Frank feels in his pants pocket for the car keys.

J.D. knows about Johnny. He introduced me, in the faculty lounge, where J.D. and I had gone to get a cup of coffee after I registered for classes. After being gone for nearly two years, J.D. still gets mail at the department—he said he had to stop by for the mail anyway, so he'd drive me to campus and point me toward the registrar's. J.D. taught English; now he does nothing. J.D. is glad that I've gone back to college to study art again, now that Mark is in school. I'm six credits away from an M.A. in art history. He wants me to think about myself, instead of thinking about Mark all the time. He talks as though I could roll Mark out on a string and let him fly off, high above me. J.D.'s wife and son died in a car crash. His son was Mark's age. "I wasn't prepared," J.D. said when we were driving over that day. He always says this when he talks about it. "How could you be prepared for such a thing?" I asked him. "I am now," he said. Then, realizing he was acting very hardboiled, made fun of himself. "Go on," he said, "punch me in the stomach. Hit me as hard as you can." We both knew he wasn't prepared for anything. When he couldn't find a parking place that day, his hands were wrapped around the wheel so tightly that his knuckles turned white.

Johnny came in as we were drinking coffee. J.D. was looking at his junk mail—publishers wanting him to order anthologies, ways to get free dictionaries.

"You are so lucky to be out of it," Johnny said, by way of greeting. "What do you do when you've spent two weeks on *Hamlet* and the student writes about Hamlet's good friend Horchow?"

He threw a blue book into J.D.'s lap. J.D. sailed it back.

"Johnny," he said, "this is Amy."

"Hi, Amy," Johnny said.

"You remember when Frank Wayne was in graduate school here? Amy's Frank's wife."

"Hi, Amy," Johnny said.

J.D. told me he knew it the instant Johnny walked into the room—he knew that second that he should introduce me as somebody's wife. He could have predicted it all from the way Johnny looked at me.

For a long time J.D. gloated that he had been prepared for what happened next—that Johnny and I were going to get together. It took me to disturb his pleasure in himself—me, crying hysterically on the phone last month, not knowing what to do, what move to make next.

"Don't do anything for a while. I guess that's my advice," J.D. said. "But you probably shouldn't listen to me. All I can do myself is run away, hide out. I'm not the learned professor. You know what I believe. I believe all that wicked fairy-tale crap: your heart will break, your house will burn."

Tonight, because he doesn't have a garage at his farm, J.D. has come to leave his car in the empty half of our two-car garage while he's in France. I look out the window and see his old Saab, glowing in the moonlight. J.D. has brought his favorite book, *A Vision*, to read on the plane. He says his suitcase contains only a spare pair of jeans, cigarettes, and underwear. He is going to buy a leather jacket in France, at a store where he almost bought a leather jacket two years ago.

In our bedroom there are about twenty small glass prisms hung with fishing line from one of the exposed beams; they catch the morning light, and we stare at them like a cat eyeing catnip held above its head. Just now, it is 2 a.m. At six-thirty, they will be filled with dazzling color. At four or five, Mark will come into the bedroom and get in bed with us. Sam will wake up, stretch, and shake, and the tags on his collar will clink, and he will yawn and shake again and go downstairs, where J.D. is asleep in his sleeping bag and Tucker is asleep on the sofa, and get a drink of water from his dish. Mark has been coming into our bedroom for about a year. He gets onto the bed by climbing up on a footstool that horrified me when I first saw it—a gift from Frank's mother: a footstool that says "Today Is the First Day of the Rest of Your Life" in needlepoint. I kept it in a closet for years, but it occurred to me that it would help Mark get up onto the bed, so he would not have to make a little leap and possibly skin his shin again. Now Mark does not disturb us when he comes into the bedroom, except that it bothers me that he has reverted to sucking his thumb. Sometimes he lies in bed with his cold feet against my leg. Sometimes, small as he is, he snores.

Somebody is playing a record downstairs. It's the Velvet Underground— Lou Reed, in a dream or swoon, singing "Sunday Morning." I can barely hear the whispering and tinkling of the record. I can only follow it because I've heard it a hundred times.

I am lying in bed, waiting for Frank to get out of the bathroom. My cut finger throbs. Things are going on in the house even though I have gone to bed; water runs, the record plays. Sam is still downstairs, so there must be some action.

I have known everybody in the house for years, and as time goes by I know them all less and less. J.D. was Frank's adviser in college. Frank was his best student, and they started to see each other outside of class. They played handball. J.D. and his family came to dinner. We went there. That summer—the summer Frank decided to go to graduate school in business instead of English—J.D.'s wife and son deserted him in a more horrible way, in that car crash. J.D. has quit his job. He has been to Las Vegas, to Colorado, New Orleans, Los Angeles, Paris twice; he tapes postcards to the walls of his living room. A lot of the time, on the weekends, he shows up at our house with his sleeping bag. Sometimes he brings a girl. Lately, not. Years ago, Tucker was in Frank's therapy group in New York, and ended up hiring Frank to work as the accountant for his gallery. Tucker was in therapy at the time because he was obsessed with foreigners. Now he is also obsessed with homosexuals. He gives fashionable parties to which he invites many foreigners and homosexuals. Before the parties he does TM and yoga, and during the parties he does Seconals and isometrics. When I first met him, he was living for the summer in his sister's house in Vermont while she was in Europe, and he called us one night, in New York, in a real panic because there were wasps all over. They were "hatching," he said—big, sleepy wasps that were everywhere. We said we'd come; we drove all through the night to get to Brattleboro. It was true: there were wasps on the undersides of plates, in the plants, in the folds of curtains. Tucker was so upset that he was out behind the house, in the cold Vermont morning, wrapped like an Indian in a blanket, with only his pajamas on underneath. He was sitting in a lawn chair, hiding behind a bush, waiting for us to come.

And Freddy—"Reddy Fox," when Frank is feeling affectionate toward him. When we first met, I taught him to iceskate and he taught me to waltz; in the summer, at Atlantic City, he'd go with me on a roller coaster that curved high over the waves. I was the one—not Frank—who would get out of bed in the middle of the night and meet him at an all-night deli and put my arm around his shoulders, the way he put his arm around my shoulders on the roller coaster, and talk quietly to him until he got over his latest anxiety attack. Now he tests me, and I retreat: this man he picked up, this man who picked him up, how it feels to have forgotten somebody's name when your hand is in the back pocket of his jeans and you're not even halfway to your apartment. Reddy Fox—admiring my new red silk blouse, stroking his fingertips down the front, and my eyes wide, because I could feel his fingers on my chest, even though I was holding the blouse in front of me on a hanger to be admired. All those moments, and all they meant was that I was fooled into thinking I knew these people because I knew the small things, the personal things.

Freddy will always be more stoned than I am, because he feels comfortable getting stoned with me, and I'll always be reminded that he's more lost. Tucker knows he can come to the house and be the center of attention; he can tell all the stories he knows, and we'll never tell the story we know about him hiding in the bushes like a frightened dog. J.D. comes back from his trips with boxes full of postcards, and I look at all of them as though they're photographs taken by him, and I know, and he knows, that what he likes about them is their flatness—the unreality of them, the unreality of what he does.

Last summer, I read *The Metamorphosis* and said to J.D., "Why did Gregor Samsa wake up a cockroach?" His answer (which he would have toyed over with his students forever) was "Because that's what people expected of him."

They make the illogical logical. I don't do anything, because I'm waiting, I'm on hold (J.D.); I stay stoned because I know it's better to be out of it (Freddy); I love art because I myself am a work of art (Tucker).

Frank is harder to understand. One night a week or so ago, I thought we were really attuned to each other, communicating by telepathic waves, and as I lay in bed about to speak I realized that the vibrations really existed: they were him, snoring.

Now he's coming into the bedroom, and I'm trying again to think what to say. Or ask. Or do.

"Be glad you're not in Key West," he says. He climbs into bed.

I raise myself up on one elbow and stare at him.

"There's a hurricane about to hit," he says.

"What?" I say. "Where did you hear that?"

"When Reddy Fox and I were putting the dishes away. We had the radio on." He doubles up his pillow, pushes it under his neck. "Boom goes everything," he says. "Bam. Crash. Poof." He looks at me. "You look shocked." He closes his eyes. Then, after a minute or two, he murmurs, "Hurricanes upset you? I'll try to think of something nice."

He is quiet for so long that I think he has fallen asleep. Then he says, "Cars that run on water. A field of flowers, none alike. A shooting star that goes slow enough for you to watch. Your life to do over again." He has been whispering in my ear, and when he takes his mouth away I shiver. He slides lower in the bed for sleep. "I'll tell you something really amazing," he says. "Tucker told me he went into a travel agency on Park Avenue last week and asked the travel agent where he should go to pan for gold, and she told him."

"Where did she tell him to go?"

"I think somewhere in Peru. The banks of some river in Peru."

"Did you decide what you're going to do after Mark's birthday?" I say.

He doesn't answer me. I touch him on the side, finally.

"It's two o'clock in the morning. Let's talk about it another time."

"You picked the house, Frank. They're your friends downstairs. I used to be what you wanted me to be."

"They're your friends, too," he says. "Don't be paranoid."

"I want to know if you're staying or going."

He takes a deep breath, lets it out, and continues to lie very still.

"Everything you've done is commendable," he says. "You did the right thing to go back to school. You tried to do the right thing by finding yourself a normal friend like Marilyn. But your whole life you've made one mistake—you've surrounded yourself with men. Let me tell you something. All men—if they're crazy, like Tucker, if they're gay as the Queen of the May, like Reddy Fox, even if they're just six years old—I'm going to tell you something about them. Men think they're Spider-Man and Buck Rogers and Superman. You know what we all feel inside that you don't feel? That we're going to the stars."

He takes my hand. "I'm looking down on all of this from space," he whispers. "I'm already gone."

Waiting

"It's beautiful," the woman says. "How did you come by this?" She wiggles her finger in the mousehole. It's a genuine mousehole: sometime in the eighteenth century a mouse gnawed its way into the cupboard, through the two inside shelves, and out the bottom.

"We bought it from an antique dealer in Virginia," I say.

"Where in Virginia?"

"Ruckersville. Outside of Charlottesville."

"That's beautiful country," she says. "I know where Ruckersville is. I had an uncle who lived in Keswick."

"Keswick was nice," I say. "The farms."

"Oh," she says. "The tax writeoffs, you mean? Those mansions with the sheep grazing out front?"

She is touching the wood, stroking lightly in case there might be a splinter. Even after so much time, everything might not have been worn down to smoothness. She lowers her eyes. "Would you take eight hundred?" she says.

"I'd like to sell it for a thousand," I say. "I paid thirteen hundred, ten years ago."

"It's beautiful," she says. "I suppose I should try to tell you it has some faults, but I've never seen one like it. Very nice. My husband wouldn't like my spending more than six hundred to begin with, but I can see that it's worth eight." She is resting her index finger on the latch. "Could I bring my husband to see it tonight?"

"All right."

"You're moving?" she says.

"Eventually," I say.

"That would be something to load around." She shakes her head. "Are you going back South?"

"I doubt it," I say.

"You probably think I'm kidding about coming back with my husband," she says suddenly. She lowers her eyes again. "Are other people interested?"

"There's just been one other call. Somebody who wanted to come out Saturday." I smile. "I guess I should pretend there's great interest."

"I'll take it," the woman says. "For a thousand. You probably could sell it for more and I could probably resell it for more. I'll tell my husband that."

She picks up her embroidered shoulder bag from the floor by the corner cabinet. She sits at the oak table by the octagonal window and rummages for her checkbook.

"I was thinking, What if I left it home? But I didn't." She takes out a checkbook in a red plastic cover. "My uncle in Keswick was one of those gentleman farmers," she says. "He lived until he was eighty-six, and enjoyed his life. He did everything in moderation, but the key was that he did *everything*." She looks appraisingly at her signature. "Some movie actress just bought a farm across from the Cobham store," she says. "A girl. I never saw her in the movies. Do you know who I'm talking about?"

"Well, Art Garfunkel used to have a place out there," I say.

"Maybe she bought his place." The woman pushes the check to the center of the table, tilts the vase full of phlox, and puts the corner of the check underneath. "Well," she says. "Thank you. We'll come with my brother's truck to get it on the weekend. What about Saturday?"

"That's fine," I say.

"You're going to have some move," she says, looking around at the other furniture. "I haven't moved in thirty years, and I wouldn't want to."

The dog walks through the room.

"What a well-mannered dog," she says.

"That's Hugo. Hugo's moved quite a few times in thirteen years. Virginia. D.C. Boston. Here."

"Poor old Hugo," she says.

Hugo, in the living room now, thumps down and sighs.

"Thank you," she says, putting out her hand. I reach out to shake it, but our hands don't meet and she clasps her hand around my wrist. "Saturday afternoon. Maybe Saturday evening. Should I be specific?"

"Any time is all right."

"Can I turn around on your grass or no?"

"Sure. Did you see the tire marks? I do it all the time."

"Well," she says. "People who back into traffic. I don't know. I honk at them all the time."

I go to the screen door and wave. She is driving a yellow Mercedes, an old one that's been repainted, with a license that says "RAVE-I." The car stalls. She re-starts it and waves. I wave again.

When she's gone, I go out the back door and walk down the driveway. A single daisy is growing out of the foot-wide crack in the concrete. Somebody has thrown a beer can into the driveway. I pick it up and marvel at how light it is. I get the mail from the box across the street and look at it as cars pass by. One of the stream of cars honks a warning to me, although I am not moving, except for flipping through the mail. There is a CL&P bill, a couple of pieces of junk mail, a postcard from Henry in Los Angeles, and a letter from my husband in—he's made it to California. Berkeley, California, mailed four days ago. Years ago, when I visited a friend in Berkeley we went to a little park and some people wandered in walking two dogs and a goat. An African pygmy goat. The woman said it was housebroken to urinate outside and as for the other she just picked up the pellets.

I go inside and watch the moving red band on the digital clock in the kitchen. Behind the clock is an old coffee tin decorated with a picture of a woman and a man in a romantic embrace; his arms are nearly rusted away, her hair is chipped, but a perfectly painted wreath of coffee beans rises in an arc above them. Probably I should have advertised the coffee tin, too, but I like to hear the metal top creak when I lift it in the morning to take the jar of coffee out. But if not the coffee tin, I should probably have put the tin breadbox up for sale.

John and I liked looking for antiques. He liked the ones almost beyond repair—the kind that you would have to buy twenty dollars' worth of books to understand how to restore. When we used to go looking, antiques were much less expensive than they are now. We bought them at a time when we had the patience to sit all day on folding chairs under a canopy at an auction. We were organized; we would come and inspect the things the day before. Then we would get there early the next day and wait. Most of the auctioneers in that part of Virginia were very good. One, named Wicked Richard, used to lace his fingers together and crack his knuckles as he called the lots. His real name was Wisted. When he did classier auctions and there was a pamphlet, his name was listed as Wisted. At most of the regular auctions, though, he introduced himself as Wicked Richard.

I cut a section of cheese and take some crackers out of a container. I put them on a plate and carry them into the dining room, feeling a little sad about parting with the big corner cupboard. Suddenly it seems older and bigger—a very large thing to be giving up.

The phone rings. A woman wants to know the size of the refrigerator that I have advertised. I tell her.

"Is it white?" she says.

The ad said it was white.

"Yes," I tell her.

"This is your refrigerator?" she says.

"One of them," I say. "I'm moving."

"Oh," she says. "You shouldn't tell people that. People read these ads to figure out who's moving and might not be around, so they can rob them. There were a lot of robberies in your neighborhood last summer."

The refrigerator is too small for her. We hang up.

The phone rings again, and I let it ring. I sit down and look at the corner cupboard. I put a piece of cheese on top of a cracker and eat it. I get up and go into the living room and offer a piece of cheese to Hugo. He sniffs and takes it lightly from my fingers. Earlier today, in the morning, I ran him in Putnam Park. I could hardly keep up with him, as usual. Thirteen isn't so old, for a dog. He scared the ducks and sent them running into the water. He growled at a beagle a man was walking, and tugged on his leash until he choked. He pulled almost as hard as he could a few summers ago. The air made his fur fluffy. Now he is happy, slowly licking his mouth, getting ready to take his afternoon nap.

John wanted to take Hugo across country, but in the end we decided that, as much as Hugo would enjoy terrorizing so many dogs along the way, it was going to be a hot July and it was better if he stayed home. We discussed this reasonably. No frenzy—nothing like the way we had been swept in at some auctions to bid on things that we didn't want, just because so many other people were mad for them. A reasonable discussion about Hugo, even if it was at the last minute: Hugo, in the car, already sticking his head out the window to bark goodbye. "It's too hot for him," I said. I was standing outside in my nightgown. "It's almost July. He'll be a hassle for you if campgrounds won't take him or if you have to park in the sun." So Hugo stood beside me, barking his high-pitched goodbye, as John backed out of the driveway. He forgot: his big battery lantern and his can opener. He remembered: his tent, the cooler filled with ice (he couldn't decide when he left whether he was going to stock up on beer or Coke), a camera, a suitcase, a fiddle, and a banjo. He forgot his driver's license, too. I never understood why he didn't keep it in his wallet, but it always seemed to get taken out for some reason and then be lost. Yesterday I found it leaning up against a bottle in the medicine cabinet.

Bobby calls. He fools me with his imitation of a man with an English accent who wants to know if I also have an avocado-colored refrigerator for sale. When I say I don't, he asks if I know somebody who paints refrigerators.

"Of course not," I tell him.

"That's the most decisive thing I've heard you say in five years," Bobby says in his real voice. "How's it going, Sally?"

"Jesus," I say. "If you'd answered this phone all morning, you wouldn't think that was funny. Where are you?"

"New York. Where do you think I am? It's my lunch hour. Going to Le Relais to get tanked up. A little *le pain et le beurre*, put down a few Scotches."

"Le Relais," I say. "Hmm."

"Don't make a bad eye on me," he says, going into his Muhammad Ali imitation. "Step on my foot and I kick you to the moon. Glad-hand me and I shake you like a loon." Bobby clears his throat. "I got the company twenty big ones today," he says. "Twenty Gs."

"Congratulations. Have a good lunch. Come out for dinner, if you feel like the drive."

"I don't have any gas and I can't face the train." He coughs again. "I gave up cigarettes," he says. "Why am I coughing?" He moves away from the phone to cough loudly.

"Are you smoking grass in the office?" I say.

"Not this time," he gasps. "I'm goddamn dying of something." A pause. "What did you do yesterday?"

"I was in town. You'd laugh at what I did."

"You went to the fireworks."

"Yeah, that's right. I wouldn't hesitate to tell you that part."

"What'd you do?" he says.

"I met Andy and Tom at the Plaza and drank champagne. They didn't. I did. Then we went to the fireworks."

"Sally at the *Plaza*?" He laughs. "What were they doing in town?"

"Tom was there on business. Andy came to see the fireworks."

"It rained, didn't it?"

"Only a little. It was O.K. They were pretty."

"The fireworks," Bobby says. "I didn't make the fireworks."

"You're going to miss lunch, Bobby," I say.

"God," he says. "I am. Bye."

I pull a record out from under the big library table, where they're kept on the wide maghogany board that connects the legs. By coincidence, the record I pull out is the Miles Davis Sextet's *Jazz at the Plaza*. At the Palm

Court on the Fourth of July, a violinist played "Play Gypsies, Dance Gypsies" and "Oklahoma!" I try to remember what else and can't.

"What do you say, Hugo?" I say to the dog. "Another piece of cheese, or would you rather go on with your siesta?"

He knows the word "cheese." He knows it as well as his name. I love the way his eyes light up and he perks his ears for certain words. Bobby tells me that you can speak gibberish to people, ninety percent of the people, as long as you throw in a little catchword now and then, and it's the same when I talk to Hugo: "Cheese." "Tag." "Out."

No reaction. Hugo is lying where he always does, on his right side, near the stereo. His nose is only a fraction of an inch away from the plant in a basket beneath the window. The branches of the plant sweep the floor. He seems very still.

"Cheese?" I whisper. "Hugo?" It is as loud as I can speak.

No reaction. I start to take a step closer, but stop myself. I put down the record and stare at him. Nothing changes. I walk out into the backyard. The sun is shining directly down from overhead, striking the dark-blue doors of the garage, washing out the color to the palest tint of blue. The peach tree by the garage, with one dead branch. The wind chimes tinkling in the peach tree. A bird hopping by the iris underneath the tree. Mosquitoes or gnats, a puff of them in the air, clustered in front of me. I sink down into the grass. I pick a blade, split it slowly with my fingernail. I count the times I breathe in and out. When I open my eyes, the sun is shining hard on the blue doors.

After a while—maybe ten minutes, maybe twenty—a truck pulls into the driveway. The man who usually delivers packages to the house hops out of the United Parcel truck. He is a nice man, about twenty-five, with long hair tucked behind his ears, and kind eyes.

Hugo did not bark when the truck pulled into the drive.

"Hi," he says. "What a beautiful day. Here you go."

He holds out a clipboard and a pen.

"Forty-two," he says, pointing to the tiny numbered block in which I am to sign my name. A mailing envelope is under his arm.

"Another book," he says. He hands me the package.

I reach up for it. There is a blue label with my name and address typed on it.

He locks his hands behind his back and raises his arms, bowing. "Did you notice that?" he says, straightening out of the yoga stretch, pointing to the envelope. "What's the joke?" he says.

The return address says "John F. Kennedy."

"Oh," I say. "A friend in publishing." I look up at him. I realize that that hasn't explained it. "We were talking on the phone last week. He was—People are still talking about where they were when he was shot, and I've known my friend for almost ten years and we'd never talked about it before."

The UPS man is wiping sweat off his forehead with a handkerchief. He stuffs the handkerchief into his pocket.

"He wasn't making fun," I say. "He admired Kennedy."

The UPS man crouches, runs his fingers across the grass. He looks in the direction of the garage. He looks at me. "Are you all right?" he says.

"Well—" I say.

He is still watching me.

"Well," I say, trying to catch my breath. "Let's see what this is."

I pull up the flap, being careful not to get cut by the staples. A large paperback called *If Mountains Die*. Color photographs. The sky above the Pueblo River gorge in the book is very blue. I show the UPS man.

"Were you all right when I pulled in?" he says. "You were sitting sort of funny."

I still am. I realize that my arms are crossed over my chest and I am leaning forward. I uncross my arms and lean back on my elbows. "Fine," I say. "Thank you."

Another car pulls into the driveway, comes around the truck, and stops on the lawn. Ray's car. Ray gets out, smiles, leans back in through the open window to turn off the tape that's still playing. Ray is my best friend. Also my husband's best friend.

"What are you doing here?" I say to Ray.

"Hi," the UPS man says to Ray. "I've got to get going. Well." He looks at me. "See you," he says.

"See you," I say. "Thanks."

"What am I doing here?" Ray says. He taps his watch. "Lunchtime. I'm on a business lunch. Big deal. Important negotiations. Want to drive down to the Redding Market and buy a couple of sandwiches, or have you already eaten?"

"You drove all the way out here for lunch?"

"Big business lunch. Difficult client. Takes time to bring some clients around. Coaxing. Takes hours." Ray shrugs.

"Don't they care?"

Ray sticks out his tongue and makes a noise, sits beside me and puts his arm around my shoulder and shakes me lightly toward him and away from him a couple of times. "Look at that sunshine," he says. "Finally. I thought the rain would never stop." He hugs my shoulder and takes his arm away. "It depresses me, too," he says. "I don't like what I sound like when I keep saying that nobody cares." Ray sighs. He reaches for a cigarette. "Nobody cares," he says. "Two-hour lunch. Four. Five."

We sit silently. He picks up the book, leafs through. "Pretty," he says. "You eat already?"

I look behind me at the screen door. Hugo is not here. No sound, either, when the car came up the driveway and the truck left.

"Yes," I say. "But there's some cheese in the house. All the usual things. Or you could go to the market."

"Maybe I will," he says. "Want anything?"

"Ray," I say, reaching my hand up. "Don't go to the market."

"What?" he says. He sits on his heels and takes my hand. He looks into my face.

"Why don't you—There's cheese in the house," I say.

He looks puzzled. Then he sees the stack of mail on the grass underneath our hands. "Oh," he says. "Letter from John." He picks it up, sees that it hasn't been opened. "O.K.," he says. "Then I'm perplexed again. Just that he wrote you? That he's already in Berkeley? Well, he had a bad winter. We all had a bad winter. It's going to be all right. He hasn't called? You don't know if he hooked up with that band?"

I shake my head no.

"I tried to call you yesterday," he says. "You weren't home."

"I went into New York."

"And?"

"I went out for drinks with some friends. We went to the fireworks."

"So did I," Ray says. "Where were you?"

"Seventy-sixth Street."

"I was at Ninety-eighth. I knew it was crazy to think I might run into you at the fireworks."

A cardinal flies into the peach tree.

"I did run into Bobby last week," he says. "Of course, it's not really running into him at one o'clock at Le Relais."

"How was Bobby?"

"You haven't heard from him, either?"

"He called today, but he didn't say how he was. I guess I didn't ask."

"He was O.K. He looked good. You can hardly see the scar above his eyebrow where they took the stitches. I imagine in a few weeks when it fades you won't notice it at all."

"You think he's done with dining in Harlem?"

"Doubt it. It could have happened anywhere, you know. People get mugged all over the place."

I hear the phone ringing and don't get up. Ray squeezes my shoulder again. "Well," he says. "I'm going to bring some food out here."

"If there's anything in there that isn't the way it ought to be, just take care of it, will you?"

"What?" he says.

"I mean—If there's anything wrong, just fix it."

He smiles. "Don't tell me. You painted a room what you thought was a nice pastel color and it came out electric pink. Or the chairs—you didn't have them reupholstered again, did you?" Ray comes back to where I'm sitting. "Oh, God," he says. "I was thinking the other night about how you'd had that horrible chintz you bought on Madison Avenue put onto the chairs and when John and I got back here you were afraid to let him into the house. God—that awful striped material. Remember John standing in back of the chair and putting his chin over the back and screaming, 'I'm innocent!' Remember him doing that?" Ray's eyes are about to water, the way they watered because he laughed so hard the day John did that. "That was about a year ago this month," he says.

I nod yes.

"Well," Ray says. "Everything's going to be all right, and I don't say that just because I want to believe in one nice thing. Bobby thinks the same thing. We agree about this. I keep talking about this, don't I? I keep coming out to the house, like you've cracked up or something. You don't want to keep hearing my sermons." Ray opens the screen door. "Anybody can take a trip," he says.

I stare at him.

"I'm getting lunch," he says. He is holding the door open with his foot. He moves his foot and goes into the house. The door slams behind him.

"Hey!" he calls out. "Want iced tea or something?"

The phone begins to ring.

"Want me to get it?" he says.

"No. Let it ring."

"Let it ring?" he hollers.

The cardinal flies out of the peach tree and onto the sweeping branch of a tall fir tree that borders the lawn—so many trees so close together that you can't see the house on the other side. The bird becomes a speck of red and disappears.

"Hey, pretty lady!" Ray calls. "Where's your mutt?"

Over the noise of the telephone, I can hear him knocking around in the kitchen. The stuck drawer opening.

"You *honestly* want me not to answer the phone?" he calls.

I look back at the house. Ray, balancing a tray, opens the door with one hand, and Hugo is beside him—not rushing out, the way he usually does to get through the door, but padding slowly, shaking himself out of sleep. He comes over and lies down next to me, blinking because his eyes are not yet accustomed to the sunlight.

Ray sits down with his plate of crackers and cheese and a beer. He looks at the tears streaming down my cheeks and shoves over close to me. He takes a big drink and puts the beer on the grass. He pushes the tray next to the beer can.

"Hey," Ray says. "Everything's cool, O.K.? No right and no wrong. People do what they do. A neutral observer, and friend to all. Same easy advice from Ray all around. Our discretion assured." He pushes my hair gently off my wet cheeks. "It's O.K.," he says softly, turning and cupping his hands over my forehead. "Just tell me what you've done."

Greenwich Time

"I'm thinking about frogs," Tom said to his secretary on the phone. "Tell them I'll be in when I've come up with a serious approach to frogs."

"I don't know what you're talking about," she said.

"Doesn't matter. I'm the idea man, you're the message taker. Lucky you."

"Lucky you," his secretary said. "I've got to have two wisdom teeth pulled this afternoon."

"That's awful," he said. "I'm sorry."

"Sorry enough to go with me?"

"I've got to think about frogs," he said. "Tell Metcalf I'm taking the day off to think about them, if he asks."

"The health plan here doesn't cover dental work," she said.

Tom worked at an ad agency on Madison Avenue. This week, he was trying to think of a way to market soap shaped like frogs—soap imported from France. He had other things on his mind. He hung up and turned to the man who was waiting behind him to use the phone.

"Did you hear that?" Tom said.

"Do what?" the man said.

"Christ," Tom said. "Frog soap."

He walked away and went out to sit across the street from his favorite pizza restaurant. He read his horoscope in the paper (neutral), looked out the window of the coffee shop, and waited for the restaurant to open. At eleven-forty-five he crossed the street and ordered a slice of Sicilian pizza, with everything. He must have had a funny look on his face when he talked to the man behind the counter, because the man laughed and said, "You sure? Everything? You even look surprised yourself."

"I started out for work this morning and never made it there," Tom said.

"After I wolf down a pizza I'm going to ask my ex-wife if my son can come back to live with me."

The man averted his eyes and pulled a tray out from under the counter. When Tom realized that he was making the man nervous, he sat down. When the pizza was ready, he went to the counter and got it, and ordered a large glass of milk. He caught the man behind the counter looking at him one more time—unfortunately, just as he gulped his milk too fast and it was running down his chin. He wiped his chin with a napkin, but even as he did so he was preoccupied, thinking about the rest of his day. He was heading for Amanda's, in Greenwich, and, as usual, he felt a mixture of relief (she had married another man, but she had given him a key to the back door) and anxiety (Shelby, her husband, was polite to him but obviously did not like to see him often).

When he left the restaurant, he meant to get his car out of the garage and drive there immediately, to tell her that he wanted Ben—that somehow, in the confusion of the situation, he had lost Ben, and now he wanted him back. Instead, he found himself wandering around New York, to calm himself so that he could make a rational appeal. After an hour or so, he realized that he was becoming as interested in the city as a tourist—in the tall buildings; the mannequins with their pelvises thrust forward, almost touching the glass of the store windows; books piled into pyramids in bookstores. He passed a pet store; its front window space was full of shredded newspaper and sawdust. As he looked in, a teenage girl reached over the gate that blocked in the window area and lowered two brown puppies, one in each hand, into the sawdust. For a second, her eye met his, and she thrust one dog toward him with a smile. For a second, the dog's eye also met his. Neither looked at him again; the dog burrowed into a pile of paper, and the girl turned and went back to work. When he and the girl caught each other's attention, a few seconds before, he had been reminded of the moment, earlier in the week, when a very attractive prostitute had approached him as he was walking past the Sheraton Centre. He had hesitated when she spoke to him, but only because her eyes were very bright—wide-set eyes, the eyebrows invisible under thick blond bangs. When he said no, she blinked and the brightness went away. He could not imagine how such a thing was physically possible; even a fish's eye wouldn't cloud over that quickly, in death. But the prostitute's eyes had gone dim in the second it took him to say no.

He detoured now to go to the movies: *Singin' in the Rain*. He left after Debbie Reynolds and Gene Kelly and Donald O'Connor danced onto the sofa and tipped it over. Still smiling about that, he went to a bar. When the bar started to fill up, he checked his watch and was surprised to see that people were getting off work. Drunk enough now to wish for rain, because rain would be fun, he walked to his apartment and took a shower, and then headed for the garage. There was a movie house next to the garage, and before he realized what he was doing he was watching *Invasion of the Body Snatchers.* He was shocked by the dog with the human head, not for the obvious reason but because it reminded him of the brown puppy he had seen earlier. It seemed an omen—a nightmare vision of what a dog would become when it was not wanted.

Six o'clock in the morning: Greenwich, Connecticut. The house is now Amanda's, ever since her mother's death. The ashes of Tom's former mother-in-law are in a tin box on top of the mantel in the dining room. The box is sealed with wax. She has been dead for a year, and in that year Amanda has moved out of their apartment in New York, gotten a quickie divorce, remarried, and moved into the house in Greenwich. She has another life, and Tom feels that he should be careful in it. He puts the key she gave him into the lock and opens the door as gently as if he were disassembling a bomb. Her cat, Rocky, appears, and looks at him. Sometimes Rocky creeps around the house with him. Now, though, he jumps on the window seat as gently, as unnoticeably, as a feather blown across sand.

Tom looks around. She has painted the living-room walls white and the downstairs bathroom crimson. The beams in the dining room have been exposed; Tom met the carpenter once—a small, nervous Italian who must have wondered why people wanted to pare their houses down to the framework. In the front hall, Amanda has hung photographs of the wings of birds.

Driving out to Amanda's, Tom smashed up his car. It was still drivable, but only because he found a tire iron in the trunk and used it to pry the bent metal of the left front fender away from the tire, so that the wheel could turn. The second he veered off the road (he must have dozed off for an instant), the thought came to him that Amanda would use the accident as a reason for not trusting him with Ben. While he worked with the tire iron, a man stopped his car and got out and gave him drunken advice. "Never buy a motorcycle," he said. "They spin out of control. You go with them—you don't have a chance." Tom nodded. "Did you know Doug's son?" the man asked. Tom said nothing. The man shook his head sadly and then went to the back of his car and opened the trunk. Tom watched him as he took flares out of his trunk and began to light them and place them in the road. The man came forward with several flares still in hand. He looked confused that he had so many. Then he lit the extras, one by one, and placed them in a semicircle around the front of the car, where Tom was working. Tom felt like some saint, in a shrine.

When the wheel was freed, he drove the car to Amanda's, cursing himself for having skidded and slamming the car into somebody's mailbox. When he got into the house, he snapped on the floodlight in the backyard, and then went into the kitchen to make some coffee before he looked at the damage again.

In the city, making a last stop before he finally got his car out of the garage, he had eaten eggs and bagels at an all-night deli. Now it seems to him that his teeth still ache from chewing. The hot coffee in his mouth feels good. The weak early sunlight, nearly out of reach of where he can move his chair and still be said to be sitting at the table, feels good where it strikes him on one shoulder. When his teeth don't ache, he begins to notice that he feels nothing in his mouth; where the sun strikes him, he can feel the wool of his sweater warming him the way a sweater is supposed to, even without sun shining on it. The sweater was a Christmas present from his son. She, of course, picked it out and wrapped it: a box enclosed in shiny white paper, crayoned on by Ben. "B E N," in big letters. Scribbles that looked like the wings of birds.

Amanda and Shelby and Ben are upstairs. Through the doorway he can see a digital clock on the mantel in the next room, on the other side from the box of ashes. At seven, the alarm will go off and Shelby will come downstairs, his gray hair, in the sharpening morning light, looking like one of those cheap abalone lights they sell at the seashore. He will stumble around, look down to make sure his fly is closed; he will drink coffee from one of Amanda's mother's bone-china cups, which he holds in the palms of his hands. His hands are so big that you have to look to see that he is cradling a cup, that he is not gulping coffee from his hands the way you would drink water from a stream.

Once, when Shelby was leaving at eight o'clock to drive into the city, Amanda looked up from the dining-room table where the three of them had been having breakfast—having a friendly, normal time, Tom had thought— and said to Shelby, "Please don't leave me alone with him." Shelby looked perplexed and embarrassed when she got up and followed him into the kitchen. "Who gave him the key, sweetheart?" Shelby whispered. Tom looked through the doorway. Shelby's hand was low on her hip—partly a joking sexual gesture, partly a possessive one. "Don't try to tell me there's anything you're afraid of," Shelby said.

Ben sleeps and sleeps. He often sleeps until ten or eleven. Up there in his bed, sunlight washing over him.

Tom looks again at the box with the ashes in it on the mantel. If there is another life, what if something goes wrong and he is reincarnated as a camel and Ben as a cloud and there is just no way for the two of them to get together? He wants Ben. He wants him now.

The alarm is ringing, so loud it sounds like a million madmen beating tin. Shelby's feet on the floor. The sunlight shining a rectangle of light through the middle of the room. Shelby will walk through that patch of light as though it were a rug rolled out down the aisle of a church. Six months ago, seven, Tom went to Amanda and Shelby's wedding.

Shelby is naked, and startled to see him. He stumbles, grabs his brown robe from his shoulder and puts it on, asking Tom what he's doing there and saying good morning at the same time. "Every goddamn clock in the house is either two minutes slow or five minutes fast," Shelby says. He hops around on the cold tile in the kitchen, putting water on to boil, pulling his robe tighter around him. "I thought this floor would warm up in summer," Shelby says, sighing. He shifts his weight from one side to the other, the way a fighter warms up, chafing his big hands.

Amanda comes down. She is wearing a pair of jeans, rolled at the ankles, black high-heeled sandals, a black silk blouse. She stumbles like Shelby. She does not look happy to see Tom. She looks, and doesn't say anything.

"I wanted to talk to you," Tom says. He sounds lame. An animal in a trap, trying to keep its eyes calm.

"I'm going into the city," she says. "Claudia's having a cyst removed. It's all a mess. I have to meet her there, at nine. I don't feel like talking now. Let's talk tonight. Come back tonight. Or stay today." Her hands through her auburn hair. She sits in a chair, accepts the coffee Shelby brings.

"More?" Shelby says to Tom. "You want something more?"

Amanda looks at Tom through the steam rising from her coffee cup. "I think that we are all dealing with this situation very well," she says. "I'm not sorry I gave you the key. Shelby and I discussed it, and we both felt that you should have access to the house. But in the back of my mind I assumed that you would use the key—I had in mind more . . . emergency situations."

"I didn't sleep well last night," Shelby says. "Now I would like it if I didn't feel that there was going to be a scene to start things off this morning."

Amanda sighs. She seems as perturbed with Shelby as she is with Tom. "And if I can say something without being jumped on," she says to Shelby, "because, yes, you *told* me not to buy a Peugeot, and now the damned thing won't run—as long as you're here, Tom, it would be nice if you gave Inez a ride to the market."

"We saw seven deer running through the woods yesterday," Shelby says.

"Oh, cut it out, Shelby," Amanda says.

"Your problems I'm trying to deal with, Amanda," Shelby says. "A little less of the rough tongue, don't you think?"

Inez has pinned a sprig of phlox in her hair, and she walks as though she feels pretty. The first time Tom saw Inez, she was working in her sister's garden—actually, standing in the garden in bare feet, with a long cotton skirt sweeping the ground. She was holding a basket heaped high with iris and daisies. She was nineteen years old and had just arrived in the United States. That year, she lived with her sister and her sister's husband, Metcalf—his friend Metcalf, the craziest man at the ad agency. Metcalf began to study photography, just to take pictures of Inez. Finally his wife got jealous and asked Inez to leave. She had trouble finding a job, and Amanda liked her and felt sorry for her, and she persuaded Tom to have her come live with them, after she had Ben. Inez came, bringing boxes of pictures of herself, one suitcase, and a pet gerbil that died her first night in the house. All the next day, Inez cried, and Amanda put her arms around her. Inez always seemed like a member of the family, from the first.

By the edge of the pond where Tom is walking with Inez, there is a black dog, panting, staring up at a Frisbee. Its master raises the Frisbee, and the dog stares as though transfixed by a beam of light from heaven. The Frisbee flies, curves, and the dog has it as it dips down.

"I'm going to ask Amanda if Ben can come live with me," Tom says to Inez.

"She'll never say yes," Inez says.

"What do you think Amanda would think if I kidnapped Ben?" Tom says.

"Ben's adjusting," she says. "That's a bad idea."

"You think I'm putting you on? I'd kidnap you with him."

"She's not a bad person," Inez says. "You think about upsetting her too much. She has problems, too."

"Since when do you defend your cheap employer?"

His son has picked up a stick. The dog, in the distance, stares. The dog's owner calls its name: "Sam!" The dog snaps his head around. He bounds through the grass, head raised, staring at the Frisbee.

"I should have gone to college," Inez says.

"College?" Tom says. The dog is running and running. "What would you have studied?"

Inez swoops down in back of Ben, picks him up and squeezes him. He struggles, as though he wants to be put down, but when Inez bends over he holds on to her. They come to where Tom parked the car, and Inez lowers Ben to the ground.

"Remember to stop at the market," Inez says. "I've got to get something for dinner."

"She'll be full of sushi and Perrier. I'll bet they don't want dinner."

"You'll want dinner," she says. "I should get something."

He drives to the market. When they pull into the parking lot, Ben goes into the store with Inez, instead of to the liquor store next door with him. Tom gets a bottle of cognac and pockets the change. The clerk raises his eyebrows and drops them several times, like Groucho Marx, as he slips a flyer into the bag, with a picture on the front showing a blue-green drink in a champagne glass.

"Inez and I have secrets," Ben says, while they are driving home. He is standing up to hug her around the neck from the back seat.

Ben is tired, and he taunts people when he is that way. Amanda does not think Ben should be condescended to: she reads him R. D. Laing, not fairy tales; she has him eat French food, and only indulges him by serving the sauce on the side. Amanda refused to send him to kindergarten. If she had, Tom believes, if he was around other children his age, he might get rid of some of his annoying mannerisms.

"For instance," Inez says, "I might get married."

"Who?" he says, so surprised that his hands feel cold on the wheel.

"A man who lives in town. You don't know him."

"You're dating someone?" he says.

He guns the car to get it up the driveway, which is slick with mud washed down by a lawn sprinkler. He steers hard, waiting for the instant when he will be able to feel that the car will make it. The car slithers a bit but then goes straight; they get to the top. He pulls onto the lawn, by the back door, leaving the way clear for Shelby and Amanda's car to pull into the garage.

"It would make sense that if I'm thinking of marrying somebody I would have been out on a date with him," Inez says.

Inez has been with them since Ben was born, five years ago, and she has gestures and expressions now like Amanda's—Amanda's patient half-smile that lets him know she is half charmed and half at a loss that he is so unsophisticated. When Amanda divorced him, he went to Kennedy to pick her up when she returned, and her arms were loaded with pineapples as she came up the ramp. When he saw her, he gave her that same patient half-smile.

At eight, they aren't back, and Inez is worried. At nine, they still aren't back. "She did say something about a play yesterday," Inez whispers to Tom. Ben is playing with a puzzle in the other room. It is his bedtime—past it—and he has the concentration of Einstein. Inez goes into the room again, and he listens while she reasons with Ben. She is quieter than Amanda; she will get what she wants. Tom reads the newspaper from the market. It comes out once a week. There are articles about deer leaping across the road, lady artists who do batik who will give demonstrations at the library. He hears Ben running up the stairs, chased by Inez.

Water is turned on. He hears Ben laughing above the water. It makes him happy that Ben is so well adjusted; when he himself was five, no woman would have been allowed in the bathroom with him. Now that he is almost forty, he would like it very much if he were in the bathtub instead of Ben—if Inez were soaping his back, her fingers sliding down his skin.

For a long time, he has been thinking about water, about traveling somewhere so that he can walk on the beach, see the ocean. Every year he spends in New York he gets more and more restless. He often wakes up at night in his apartment, hears the air-conditioners roaring and the woman in the apartment above shuffling away her insomnia in satin slippers. (She has shown them to him, to explain that her walking cannot possibly be what is keeping him awake.) On nights when he can't sleep, he opens his eyes just a crack and pretends, as he did when he was a child, that the furniture is something else. He squints the tall mahogany chest of drawers into the trunk of a palm tree; blinking his eyes quickly, he makes the night light pulse like a buoy bobbing in the water and tries to imagine that his bed is a boat, and that he is setting sail, as he and Amanda did years before, in Maine, where Perkins Cove widens into the choppy, ink-blue ocean.

Upstairs, the water is being turned off. It is silent. Silence for a long time. Inez laughs. Rocky jumps onto the stairs, and one board creaks as the cat pads upstairs. Amanda will not let him have Ben. He is sure of it. After a few minutes, he hears Inez laugh about making it snow as she holds the can of talcum powder high and lets it sift down on Ben in the tub.

Deciding that he wants at least a good night, Tom takes off his shoes and climbs the stairs; no need to disturb the quiet of the house. The door to Shelby and Amanda's bedroom is open. Ben and Inez are curled on the bed, and she has begun to read to him by the dim light. She lies next to him on the vast blue quilt spread over the bed, on her side with her back to the door, with one arm sweeping slowly through the air: "*Los soldados hicieron alto a la entrada del pueblo. . . .*"

Ben sees him, and pretends not to. Ben loves Inez more than any of them. Tom goes away, so that she will not see him and stop reading.

He goes into the room where Shelby has his study. He turns on the light. There is a dimmer switch, and the light comes on very low. He leaves it that way.

He examines a photograph of the beak of a bird. A photograph next to it of a bird's wing. He moves in close to the picture and rests his cheek against the glass. He is worried. It isn't like Amanda not to come back, when she knows he is waiting to see her. He feels the coolness from the glass spreading down his body. There is no reason to think that Amanda is dead. When Shelby drives, he creeps along like an old man.

He goes into the bathroom and splashes water on his face, dries himself on what he thinks is Amanda's towel. He goes back to the study and stretches out on the daybed, under the open window, waiting for the car. He is lying very still on an unfamiliar bed, in a house he used to visit two or three times a year when he and Amanda were married—a house always decorated with flowers for Amanda's birthday, or smelling of newly cut pine at Christmas, when there was angel hair arranged into nests on the table-tops, with tiny Christmas balls glittering inside, like miraculously colored eggs. Amanda's mother is dead. He and Amanda are divorced. Amanda is married to Shelby. These events are unreal. What is real is the past, and the Amanda of years ago—that Amanda whose image he cannot get out of his mind, the scene he keeps remembering. It had happened on a day when he had not expected to discover anything; he was going along with his life with an ease he would never have again, and, in a way, what happened was so painful that even the pain of her leaving, and her going to Shelby, would later be dulled in comparison. Amanda—in her pretty underpants, in the bedroom of their city apartment, standing by the window—had crossed her hands at the wrists, covering her breasts, and said to Ben, "It's gone now. The milk is gone." Ben, in his diapers and T-shirt, lying on the bed and looking up at her. The mug of milk waiting for him on the bedside table—he'd drink it as surely as Hamlet would drink from the goblet of poison. Ben's little hand on the mug, her breasts revealed again, her hand overlapping his hand, the mug tilted, the first swallow. That night, Tom had moved his head from his pillow to hers, slipped down in the bed until his cheek came to the top of her breast. He had known he would never sleep, he was so amazed at the offhand way she had just done such a powerful thing. "Baby—" he had said, beginning, and she had said, "I'm not your baby." Pulling away from him, from Ben. Who would have guessed that what she wanted was another man—a man with whom she would stretch into sleep on a vast ocean of blue quilted satin, a bed as wide as the ocean? The first time he came to Greenwich and saw that bed, with her watching him, he had cupped his hand to his brow and looked far across the room, as though he might see China.

The day he went to Greenwich to visit for the first time after the divorce, Ben and Shelby hadn't been there. Inez was there, though, and she had gone along on the tour of the redecorated house that Amanda had insisted on giving him. Tom knew that Inez had not wanted to walk around the house with them. She had done it because Amanda had asked her to, and she had also done it because she thought it might make it less awkward for him. In a way different from the way he loved Amanda, but still a very real way, he would always love Inez for that.

Now Inez is coming into the study, hesitating as her eyes accustom themselves to the dark. "You're awake?" she whispers. "Are you all right?" She walks to the bed slowly and sits down. His eyes are closed, and he is sure that he could sleep forever. Her hand is on his; he smiles as he begins to drift and dream. A bird extends its wing with the grace of a fan opening; *los soldados* are poised at the crest of the hill. About Inez he will always remember this: when she came to work on Monday, after the weekend when Amanda had told him about Shelby and said that she was getting a divorce, Inez whispered to him in the kitchen, "I'm still your friend." Inez had come close to him to whisper it, the way a bashful lover might move quietly forward to say "I love you." She had said that she was his friend, and he had told her that he never doubted that. Then they had stood there, still and quiet, as if the walls of the room were mountains and their words might fly against them.

Gravity

My favorite jacket was bought at L. L. Bean. It got from Maine to Atlanta, where an ex-boyfriend of mine found it at a thrift shop and bought it for my birthday. It was a little tight for him, but he was wearing it when he saw me. He said that if I had not complimented him on the jacket he would just have kept it. In the pocket I found an amyl nitrite and a Hershey's Kiss. The candy was put there deliberately.

In the eight years I've had it, I've lost all the buttons but the top one—the one I never button because nobody closes the button under the collar. Four buttons are gone, but I can only remember how the next-to-last one disappeared: I saw it dangling but thought it would hold. Later, crouched on the floor, I said, "It stands to reason that since I haven't moved off this barstool, it has to be on the floor *right here*," drunkenly staring at the floor beneath my barstool at the Café Central.

Nick, the man I'm walking with now, couldn't possibly fit into the jacket. He wishes that I didn't fit into it, either. He hates the jacket. When I told him I was thinking about buying a winter scarf, he suggested that rattails might go with the jacket nicely. He keeps stopping at store windows, offering to buy me a sweater, a coat. Nothing doing.

"I'm going crazy," Nick says to me, "and you're depressed because you've lost your buttons." We keep walking. He pokes me in the side. "Buttons might as well be marbles," he says.

"Did you ever play marbles?"

"Play marbles?" he says. "Don't you just look at them?"

"I don't think so. I think there's a game you can play with them."

"I had cigar boxes full of marbles when I was a kid. Isn't that great? I had marbles and stamps and coins and *Playboy* cutouts."

"All at the same time?"

"What do you mean?"

"The stamps didn't come before the *Playboy* pictures?"

"Same time. I used the magnifying glass with the pictures instead of the stamps."

The left side of my jacket overlaps the right, and my arms are crossed tightly in front of me, holding it closed. Nick notices and says, "It's not very cold," putting an arm around my shoulders.

He's right. It isn't. Last Friday afternoon, the doctor told me I was going to have to go to the hospital on Wednesday, the day after tomorrow, to have a test to find out if some blockage in a Fallopian tube has been causing the pain in my left side, and I'm a coward. I have never believed anything in *The Bell Jar* except Esther Greenwood's paranoid idea that when you're unconscious you feel pain and later you forget that you felt it.

He's taken his arm away. I keep tight hold on my jacket with one hand and put my other hand around his wrist so he'll take his hand out of his pocket.

"Give me the hand," I say. We walk along like that.

The other buttons fell off without seeming to be loose. They came off last winter. That was when I first fell in love with Nick, and other things seemed very unimportant. I thought then that during the summer I'd sew on new buttons. It's October now, and cold. We're walking up Fifth Avenue, just a few blocks away from the hospital where I'll have the test. When he realizes it, he'll turn down a side street.

"You're not going to die," he says.

"I know," I say, "and it would be silly to be worried about anything short of dying, wouldn't it?"

"Don't take it out on me," he says, and steers me onto Ninety-sixth Street.

There are no stars this evening, so Nick is talking about the stars. He asks if I've ever imagined the thoughts of the first astronomer turning the powerful telescope on Saturn and seeing not only the planet but rings—smoky loops. He stops to light a cigarette.

The chrysanthemums planted down the middle of Park Avenue are just a blur in the dark. I think of de Heem's flowers: move close to one of his paintings and you see a snail curled on the wood, and tiny insects coating the leaves. It happens sometimes when you bring flowers in from the garden—a snail that looks and feels like pus, climbing a stem.

Last Friday, Nick said, "You're not going to die." He got out of bed and moved me away from the vase of flowers. It was the day I had gone to the doctor, and then we went away to visit Justin for the weekend. (Ten years ago, when Nick started living with Barbara, Justin was their next-door neighbor on West Sixteenth Street.) Everything was lovely, the way it always is at Justin's house in the country. There was a vase of phlox and daisies in the bedroom, and when I went to smell the flowers I saw the snail and said that it looked like pus. I wasn't even repelled by it—just sorry it was there, curious enough to finger it.

"Justin's not going to know what you're crying about. Justin doesn't deserve this," Nick whispered.

When touched, the snail did not contract. Neither did it keep moving.

Fact: her name is Barbara. She is the Boulder Dam. She is small and beautiful, and she has a hold on him even though they never married, because she was there first. She is the Boulder Dam.

Last year we had Christmas at Justin's. Justin wants to think of us as a family—Nick and Justin and me. His real family is one aunt, in New Zealand. When he was a child she made thick cookies for him that never baked through. Justin's ideas are more romantic than mine. He thinks that Nick should forget Barbara and move, with me, into the house that is for sale next door. Justin, in his thermal slippers and knee-high striped socks under his white pajamas, in the kitchen brewing Sleepytime tea, saying to me, "Name me one thing more pathetic than a fag with a cold."

Barbara called, and we tried to ignore it. Justin and I ate cold oranges after the Christmas dinner. Justin poured champagne. Nick talked to Barbara on the phone. Justin blew out the candles, and the two of us were sitting in the dark, with Nick standing at the phone and looking over his shoulder into the suddenly darkened corner, frowning in confusion.

Standing in the kitchen later that night, Nick had said, "Justin, tell her the truth. Tell her you get depressed on Christmas and that's why you get drunk. Tell her it's not because of one short phone call from a woman you never liked."

Justin was making tea again, to sober up. His hand was over the burner, going an inch lower, half an inch more . . .

"Play chicken with him," he whispered to me. "Don't you be the one who gets burned."

A lady walks past us, wearing a blue hat with feathers that look as if they might be arrows shot into the brim by crazy Indians. She smiles sweetly. "The snakes are crawling out of Hell," she says.

In a bar, on Lexington, Nick says, "Tell me why you love me so much." Without a pause, he says, "Don't make analogies."

When he is at a loss—when he is lost—he is partly lost in her. It's as though he were walking deeper and deeper into a forest, and I risked his stopping to smell some enchanted flower or his finding a pond and being drawn to it like Narcissus. From what he has told me about Barbara, I know that she is deep and cool.

Lying on the cold white paper on the doctor's examining table, I tried to concentrate not on what he was doing but on a screw holding one of the four corners of the flat, white ceiling light.

As a child, I got lost in the woods once. I had a dandelion with me, and I used it, hopelessly, like a flashlight, the yellow center my imaginary beam. My parents, who might have saved me, were drunk at a back-yard party as I kept walking the wrong way, away from the houses I might have seen. I walked slower and slower, being afraid.

Nick makes a lot of that. He thinks I am lost in my life. "All right," I say as he nudges me to walk faster. "*Everything's* symbolic."

"How can you put me down when you make similes about everything?"

"I do not," I say. "The way you talk makes me want to put out my knuckles to be beaten. You're as critical as a teacher."

The walk is over. He's even done what I wanted: walked the thirty blocks to her apartment, instead of taking a cab, and if she's anxious and looking out the window, he's walked right up to the door with me, and she'll see it all—even the kiss.

It amazes him that at the same time variations of what happens to Barbara happen to me. She had her hair cut the same day I got mine trimmed. When I went to the dentist and he told me my gums were receding slightly, I hoped she'd outdo me by growing fangs. Instead, when my side started to hurt she got much worse pains. Now she's slowly getting better, back at the apartment after a spinal-fusion operation, and he's staying with her again.

Autumn, 1979. On the walk we saw one couple kissing, three people walking dogs, one couple arguing, and a cabdriver parked in front of a drugstore, changing from a denim jacket to black leather. He pulled on a leather cap, threw the jacket into the back seat, and drove away, making a U-turn on Park Avenue, headed downtown. One man looked at me as if he'd just found me standing behind the counter of a kissing booth, and one woman gave Nick such a come-on look that it made him laugh before she was even out of earshot.

"I can't stand it," Nick says.

He doesn't mean the craziness of New York.

He opens the outside door with his key, after the kiss, and for a minute we're squeezed together in the space between locked doors. I've called it jail. A coffin. Two astronauts, strapped in on their way to the moon. I've stood there and felt, more than once, the lightness of a person who isn't being kept in place by gravity, but my weightlessness has been from sadness and fear.

Barbara is upstairs, waiting, and Nick doesn't know what to say. I don't. Finally, to break the silence, he pulls me to him. He tells me that when I asked for his hand earlier, I called it "the hand."

His right hand is extended, fingers on the bone between my breasts. I look down for a second, the way a surgeon must have a moment of doubt, or even a moment of confidence, looking at the translucent, skin-tight rubber glove: his hand and not his hand, about to do something important or not important at all.

"*Anybody* else would have said 'your hand,'" Nick says. "When you said it that way, it made it sound as if my hand was disembodied." He strokes my jacket. "You've got your security blanket. Let me keep all the parts together. On the outside, at least."

Disembodied, that hand would be a symbol from Magritte: a castle on a rock, floating over the ocean; a green apple without a tree.

Alone, I'd know it anywhere.

Running Dreams

Barnes is running with the football. The sun strikes his white pants, making them shine like satin. The dog runs beside him, scattering autumn leaves, close to Barnes's ankles. By the time they get from the far end of the field to where Audrey and I are sitting, the dog has run ahead and tried to trip him three times, but Barnes gives him the football anyway. Barnes stops suddenly, holds the football out as delicately as a hostess offering a demitasse cup, and drops it. The dog, whose name is Bruno, snaps up the football—it is a small sponge rubber model, a toy—and runs off with it. Barnes, who is still panting, sits on the edge of Audrey's chaise, lifts her foot, and begins to rub her toes through her sock.

"I forgot to tell you that your accountant called when you were chopping wood this morning," she says. "He called to tell you the name of the contractor who put in his neighbor's pool. I didn't know you knew accountants socially."

"I knew his neighbors," Barnes says. "They're different neighbors now. The people I knew were named Matt and Zera Cartwright. Zera was always calling me to ask for Librium. They moved to Kentucky. The accountant kept in touch with them."

"There's so much about your life I don't know," Audrey says. She pulls off her sock and turns her foot in his hand. The toenails are painted red. The nails on her big toes are perfectly oval. Her heels have the soft skin and roundness of a baby's foot, which is miraculous to me, because I know she used to wear high heels to work every day in New York. It also amazes me that there are people who still paint their toenails when summer is over.

Predictably, Bruno is trying to bury the football. I once saw Bruno dig a hole for an inner tube, so the football will only be a minute's trouble. Early in the summer, Barnes came back to the house late at night—he is a surgeon—and gave the dog his black bag. If Audrey hadn't been less drunk than the rest of us, and able to rescue it, that would have been buried, too.

"Why do we have to build a pool?" Audrey says. "All that horrible construction noise. What if some kid drowns in it? I'm going to wake up every morning and go to the window and expect to see some little body—"

"You knew how materialistic I was when you married me. You knew that after I got a house in the country I'd want a pool, didn't you?" Barnes kisses her knee. "Audrey can't swim, Lynn," he says to me. "Audrey hates to learn new things."

We already know she can't swim. She's Martin's sister, and I've known her for seven years. Martin and I live together—or did until a few months ago, when I moved. Barnes has known her almost all her life, and they've been married for six months now. They were married in the living room of this house, while it was still being built, with Elvis Presley on the stereo singing "As Long as I Have You." Holly carried a bouquet of cobra lilies. Then I sang "Some Day Soon"—Audrey's favorite Judy Collins song. The dog was there, and a visiting Afghan. The stonemason forgot that he wasn't supposed to work that day and came just as the ceremony was about to begin, and decided to stay. He turned out to know how to foxtrot, so we were all glad he'd stayed. We had champagne and danced, and Martin and I fixed crêpes.

"What if we just tore the cover off that David Hockney book," Audrey says now. "The one of the man floating face down in a pool, that makes him look like he's been pressed under glass? We could hang it from the tree over there, instead of wind chimes. I don't want a swimming pool."

Barnes puts her foot down. She lifts the other one and puts it in his hand.

"We can get you a raft and you can float around, and I can rub your feet," he says.

"You're never here. You work all the time," Audrey says.

"When the people come to put in the pool, you can hold up your David Hockney picture and repel them."

"What if they don't understand that, Barnes? I can imagine that just causing a lot of confusion."

"Then you lose," he says. "If you show them the picture and they go ahead and put in the pool anyway, then either it's not a real cross or they're not real vampires." He pats her ankle. "But no fair explaining to them," he says. "It has to be as serious as charades."

Martin tells me things that Barnes has told him. In the beginning, Martin didn't want his sister to marry him, but Barnes was also his best friend and Martin didn't want to betray Barnes's confidences to him, so he asked me what I thought. Telling me mattered less than telling her, and I had impressed him long ago with my ability to keep a secret by not telling him his mother had a mastectomy the summer he went to Italy. He only found out when she died, two years later, and then he found out accidentally. "She didn't want you to know," I said. "How could you keep that a secret?" he said. He loves me and hates me for things like that. He loves me because I'm the kind of person people come to. It's an attribute he wishes he had, because he's a teacher. He teaches history in a private school. One time, when we were walking through Chelsea late at night, a nicely dressed old lady leaned over her gate and handed me a can of green beans and a can opener and said, "Please." On the subway, a man handed me a letter and said, "You don't have to say anything, but please read this paragraph. I just want somebody else to see it before I rip it up." Most of these things have to do with love, in some odd way. The green beans did not have to do with love.

Martin and I are walking in the woods. The poison ivy is turning a bright autumnal red, so it's easy to recognize. As we go deeper into the woods we see a tree house, with a ladder made of four boards nailed to the tree trunk. There are empty beer bottles around the tree, but I miss the most remarkable thing in the scene until Martin points it out: a white balloon wedged high above the tree house, where a thin branch forks. He throws some stones and finally bounces one off the balloon, but it doesn't break it or set it free. "Maybe I can lure it down," he says, and he picks up an empty Michelob bottle, holds it close to his lips, and taps his fingers on the glass as if he were playing a horn while he blows a slow stream of air across the top. It makes an eerie, hollow sound, and I'm glad when he stops and drops the bottle. He's capable of surprising me as much as I surprise him. We lived together for years. A month ago, he came to the apartment I was subletting late one night, after two weeks of not returning my phone calls at work and keeping his phone pulled at home—came over and hit the buzzer and was standing there smiling when I looked out the window. He walked up the four flights, came in still smiling, and said, "I'm going to do something you're really going to like." I was ready to hit him if he tried to touch me, but he took me lightly by the wrist, so that I knew that was the only part of my body he'd touch, and sat down and pulled me into the chair with him, and whistled the harp break to "Isn't She Lovely." I had never heard him whistle before. I had no idea he knew the song. He whistled the long, complex interlude perfectly, and then sat there, silently, his lips warm against the top of my hair.

Martin pushes aside a low-hanging branch, so I can walk by. "You know what Barnes told me this morning?" he says. "He sees his regular shrink on Monday mornings, but a few weeks ago he started seeing a young woman shrink on Tuesdays and not telling either of them about the other. Then he said he was thinking about giving both of them up and buying a camera."

"I don't get it."

"He does that—he starts to say one thing, and then he adds some non sequitur. I don't know if he wants me to question him or just let him talk."

"Ask."

"You wouldn't ask."

"I'd probably ask," I say.

We're walking on leaves, through bright-green fern. From far away now, he tosses another stone, but it misses the branch; it doesn't go near the balloon.

"You know what it is?" Martin says. "He never *seems* vague or random about anything. He graduated first in his class from medical school. All summer, the bastard hit a home run every time he was up at bat. He's got that charming, self-deprecating way of saying things—the way he was talking about the swimming pool. So when he seems to be opening up to me, it would be unsophisticated for me to ask what going to two shrinks and giving up both of them and buying a camera is all about."

"Maybe he talks to you because you don't ask him questions."

Martin is tossing an acorn in the air. He pockets it, and squeezes my hand.

"I wanted to make love to you last night," he says, "but I knew she'd be walking through the living room all night."

She did. She got up every few hours and tiptoed past the foldout bed and went into the bathroom and stayed there, silently, for so long that I'd drift back to sleep and not realize she'd come out until I heard her walking back in again. Audrey has had two miscarriages in the year she's been with Barnes. Audrey, who swore she'd never leave the city, never have children, who hung out with poets and painters, married the first respectable man she ever dated—her brother's best friend as well—got pregnant, and grieved when she lost the first baby, grieved when she lost the second.

"Audrey will be all right," I say, and push my fingers through his.

"We're the ones I'm worried about," he says. "Thinking about them stops me from talking about us." He puts his arm around me as we walk. Our skin is sweaty—we have on too many clothes. We trample ferns I'd avoid if I were walking alone. With his head pressed against my shoulder, he says, "I need for you to talk to me. I'm out of my league with you people. I don't know what you're thinking, and I think you must be hating me."

"I told you what I thought months ago. You said you needed time to think. What more can I do besides move so you have time to think?"

He is standing in front of me, touching the buttons of his wool shirt that I wear as a jacket, then brushing my hair behind my shoulders.

"You went, just like that," he says. "You won't tell me what your life is like."

He moves his face toward mine, and I think he's going to kiss me, but he only closes his eyes, puts his forehead against mine. "You know all my secrets," he whispers, "and when we're apart I feel like they've died inside you."

At dinner, we've all had too much to drink. I study Martin's face across the table and wonder what secrets he had in mind. That he's afraid of driving over bridges? Afraid of gas stoves? That he can't tell a Bordeaux from a Burgundy?

Barnes has explained, by drawing a picture on a napkin, how a triple-bypass operation is done. Audrey accidentally knocks over Barnes's glass, and the drawing of the heart blurs under the spilled water. Martin says, "That's a penis, Doctor." Then he scribbles on my napkin, drips water on it, and says, "That is also a penis." He is pretending to be taking a Rorschach test.

Barnes takes another napkin from the pile in the middle of the table and draws a penis. "What's that?" he says to Martin.

"That's a mushroom," Martin says.

"You're quite astute," Barnes says. "I think you should go into medicine when you get over your crisis."

Martin wads up a napkin and drops it in the puddle running across the table from Barnes's napkin. "Did you ever have a crisis in *your* life?" he says to him, mopping up.

"Not that you observed. There were a few weeks when I thought I was going to be second in my class in med school."

"Aren't you embarrassed to be such an overachiever?" Martin says, shaking his head in amazement.

"I don't think about it one way or another. It was expected of me. When I was in high school, I got stropped by my old man for every grade that wasn't an A."

"Is that true?" Audrey says. "Your father beat you?"

"It's true," Barnes says. "There are a lot of things you don't know about me." He pours himself some more wine. "I can't stand pain," he says. "That's part of why I went into medicine. Because I think about it all the time anyway, and doing what I do I can be grateful every day that it's somebody else's suffering. When I was a resident, I'd go to see the patient after surgery and leave the room and puke. Nurses puke sometimes. You hardly ever see a doctor puke."

"Did you let anybody comfort you then?" Audrey says. "You don't let anybody comfort you now."

"I don't know if that's true," Barnes says. He takes a drink of wine, raising the glass with such composure that I wouldn't know he was drunk if he wasn't looking into the goblet at the same time he was drinking. He puts the glass back on the table. "It's easier for me to talk to men," he says. "Men will only go so far, and women are so single-minded about soothing you. I've always thought that once I started letting down I might lose my energy permanently. Stay here and float in a swimming pool all day. Read. Drink. Not keep going."

"Barnes," Audrey says, "this is awful." She pushes her bangs back with one hand.

"Christ," Barnes says, leaning over and taking her hand from her face. "I sound like some character out of D. H. Lawrence. I don't know what I'm talking about." He gets up. "I'm going to get the other pizza out of the oven."

On the way into the kitchen, he hits his leg on the coffee table. Geodes rattle on the glass tabletop. On the table, in a wicker tray, there are blue stones, polished amethysts, inky-black pebbles from a stream, marbles with clouds of color like smoke trapped inside. The house is full of things to touch—silk flowers you have to put a finger on to see if they're real, snow domes to shake, Audrey's tarot cards. Audrey is looking at Martin now with the same bewildered look that she gets when she lays out the tarot cards and studies them. Martin takes her hand. He is still holding her hand when Barnes comes back, and only lets go when Barnes begins to lower the pizza to the center of the table.

"I'm sorry," Barnes says. "It's not a good time to be talking about my problems, is it?"

"Why not?" Martin says. "Everybody's been their usual witty and clever self all weekend. It's all right to talk about real things."

"Well, I don't want to make a fool of myself anymore," Barnes says, cutting the pizza into squares. "Why don't you talk about what it's like to have lived with Lynn for so many years and then suddenly she's famous." Barnes puts a piece of pizza on my plate. He serves a piece to Martin. Audrey holds her fingers above her plate. For a drunken minute, I don't realize she's saying she doesn't want more food—her fingers are hovering lightly, the way they do when she picks up a tarot card.

"Last Monday I put in an all-nighter," Barnes says to me. "Matty Klein was with me. We were riding down Park Avenue afterwards, and your song came on the radio. We were both so amazed. Not at what we'd just pulled off in five hours of surgery but that there we were in the back of a cab with the sun coming up and you were singing on the radio. I'm still used to the way you were singing with Audrey in the kitchen a while ago—the way you just sing, and she sings along. Then I realized in the cab that that wasn't private anymore." He takes another drink of wine. "Am I making any sense?" he says.

"It makes perfect sense," Martin says. "Try to explain that to her."

"It's not private," I say. "Other things are private, but that's just me singing a song."

Barnes pushes his chair back from the table. "I'll tell you what I never get over," he says. "That I can take my hands out of somebody's body, wash them, get in a cab, go home, and hardly wait to get into bed with Audrey to touch her, because that's so mysterious. In spite of what I do, I haven't found out anything."

"Is this leading up to your saying again that you don't know why I've had two miscarriages?" Audrey says.

"No, I wasn't thinking about that at all," Barnes says.

"I'll tell you what *I* thought it was about," Martin says. "*I* thought that Barnes wanted me to tell everybody why I've freaked out now that Lynn's famous. It doesn't seem very . . . timely of me to be pulling out now."

"When did I say that what I wanted was to be famous?" I say.

"I can't do it," Audrey says. "It's too hard to pretend to be involved in what other people are talking about when all I can think about are the miscarriages."

She is the first to cry, though any of us might have been.

Bruno, the dog, has shifting loyalties. Because Martin threw the football for him after dinner, he has settled by our bed in the living room. His sleep is deep, and fitful: paws flapping, hard breaths, a tiny, high-pitched yelp once as he exhales. Martin says that he is having running dreams. I close my eyes and try to imagine Bruno's dream, but I end up thinking about all the things he probably doesn't dream about: the blue sky, or the hardness of the field when the ground gets cold. Or, if he noticed those things, they wouldn't seem sad.

"If I loved somebody else, would that make it easier?" Martin says.

"Do you?" I say.

"No. I've thought that that would be a way out, though. That way you could think I was just somebody you'd misjudged."

"Everybody's changing so suddenly," I say. "Do you realize that? All of a sudden Barnes wants to open up to us, and you want to be left alone, and Audrey wants to forget about the life she had in the city and live in this quiet place and have children."

"What about you?" he says.

"Would it make sense to you that I've stopped crying and feeling panicky because I'm in love with somebody else?"

"I'll bet that's true," he says. I feel him stroking the dog. This is what he does to try to quiet him without waking him up—gently rubbing his side with his foot. "Is it true?" he says.

"No. I'd like to hurt you by having it be true, though."

He reaches for the quilt folded at the foot of the bed and pulls it over the blanket.

"That isn't like you," he says.

He stops stroking the dog and turns toward me. "I feel so locked in," he says. "I feel like we've got to come out here every weekend. I feel it's inevitable that there's a 'we.' I feel guilty for feeling bad, because Barnes's father beat him up, and my sister lost two babies, and you've been putting it all on the line, and I don't feel like I'm keeping up with you. You've all got more energy than I do."

"Martin—Barnes was dead-drunk, and Audrey was in tears, and before it was midnight I had to admit I was exhausted and go to bed."

"That's not what I mean," he says. "You don't understand what I mean."

We are silent, and I can hear the house moving in the wind. Barnes hasn't put up the storm windows yet. Air leaks in around the windows. I let Martin put his arm around me for the warmth, and I slide lower in the bed so that my shoulders are under the blanket and quilt.

"What I meant is that I'm not entitled to this," Martin says. "With what he goes through at the hospital, he's entitled to get blasted on Saturday night. She's got every right to cry. Your head's full of music all the time, and that wears you down, even if you aren't writing or playing." He whispers, even more quietly, "What did you think when he said that about his father beating him?"

"I wasn't listening to him any more than you two were. You know me. You know I'm always looking for a reason why it was all right that my father died when I was five. I was thinking maybe it would have turned out awful if he had lived. Maybe I would have hated him for something."

Martin moves his head closer to mine. "Let me go," he says, "and I'm going to be as unmovable as that balloon in the tree."

Bruno whimpers in his sleep, and Martin moves his foot up and down Bruno's body, half to soothe himself, half to soothe the dog.

I didn't know my father was dying. I knew that something was wrong, but I didn't know what dying was. I've always known simple things: how to read the letter a stranger hands me and nod, how to do someone a favor when they don't have my strength. I remember that my father was bending over—stooped with pain, I now realize—and that he was winter-pale, though he died before cold weather came. I remember standing with him in a room that seemed immense to me at the time, in sunlight as intense as the explosion from a flashbulb. If someone had taken that photograph, it would have been a picture of a little girl and her father about to go on a walk. I held my hands out to him, and he pushed the fingers of the gloves tightly down each of my fingers, patiently, pretending to have all the time in the world, saying, "This is the way we get ready for winter."

Afloat

Annie brings a hand-delivered letter to her father. They stand together on the deck that extends far over the grassy lawn that slopes to the lake, and he reads and she looks off at the water. When she was a little girl she would stand on the metal table pushed to the front of the deck and read the letters aloud to her father. If he sat, she sat. Later, she read them over his shoulder. Now she is sixteen, and she gives him the letter and stares at the trees or the water or the boat bobbing at the end of the dock. It has probably never occurred to her that she does not have to be there when he reads them.

Dear Jerome,

Last week the bottom fell out of the birdhouse you hung in the tree the summer Annie was three. Or something gnawed at it and the bottom came out. I don't know. I put the wood under one of the big clay pots full of pansies, just to keep it for old times' sake. (I've given up the fountain pen for a felt-tip. I'm really not a romantic.) I send to you for a month our daughter. She still wears bangs, to cover that little nick in her forehead from the time she fell out of the swing. The swing survived until last summer when—or maybe I told you in last year's letter—Marcy Smith came by with her "friend" Hamilton, and they were so taken by it that I gave it to them, leaving the ropes dangling. I mean that I gave them the old green swing seat, with the decals of roses even uglier than the scraggly ones we grew. Tell her to pull her bangs back and show the world her beautiful widow's peak. She now drinks spritzers. For the first two weeks she's gone I'll be in Ogunquit with Zack. He is younger than you, but no one will ever duplicate the effect of your slow smile. Have a good summer together. I will be thinking of you at unexpected times (unexpected to me, of course).

Love,
Anita

He hands the letter on to me, and then pours club soda and Chablis into a tall glass for Annie and fills his own glass with wine alone. He hesitates while I read, and I know he's wondering whether the letter will disturb me— whether I'll want club soda or wine. "Soda," I say. Jerome and Anita have been divorced for ten years.

In these first few days of Annie's visit, things aren't going very well. My friends think that it's just about everybody's summer story. Rachel's summers are spent with her ex-husband, and with his daughter by his second marriage, the daughter's boyfriend, and the boyfriend's best friend. The golden retriever isn't there this summer, because last summer he drowned. No one knows how. Jean is letting her optometrist, with whom she once had an affair, stay in her house in the Hamptons on weekends. She stays in town, because she is in love with a chef. Hazel's the exception. She teaches summer school, and when it ends she and her husband and their son go to Block Island for two weeks, to the house they always rent. Her husband has his job back, after a year in A.A. I study her life and wonder how it works. Of the three best friends I have, she blushes the most easily, is the worst dressed, is the least politically informed, and prefers AM rock stations to FM classical music. Our common denominator is that none of us was married in a church and all of us worried about the results of the blood test we had before we could get a marriage license. But there are so many differences. Say their names to me and what comes to mind is that Rachel cried when she heard Dylan's *Self Portrait* album, because, to her, that meant that everything was over; Jean fought off a man in a supermarket parking lot who was intent on raping her, and still has nightmares about the arugula she was going to the store to get; Hazel can recite Yeats's "The Circus Animals' Desertion" and bring tears to your eyes.

Sitting on the deck, I try to explain to Annie that there *should* be solidarity between women, but that when you look for a common bond you're really looking for a common denominator, and you can't do that with women. Annie puts down *My Mother/My Self* and looks out at the water.

Jerome and I, wondering when she will ever want to swim, go about our days as usual. She's gone biking with him, so there's no hostility. She has always sat at the foot of the bed while Jerome was showering at night and talked nonsense with me while she twisted the ends of her hair, and she still does. At her age, it isn't important that she's not in love, and she was once before anyway. When she pours for herself, it's sixty-forty white wine and club soda. Annie—the baby pushed in a swing. The bottom fell out of the birdhouse. Anita really knows how to hit below the belt.

Jerome is sulky at the end of the week, floating in the Whaler.

"Do you ever think that Anita's thinking of you?" I ask.

"Telepathy, you mean?" he says. He has a good tan. A scab by his elbow. Somehow, he's hurt himself. His wet hair is drying in curly strands. He hasn't had a haircut since we came to the summer house.

"No. Do you ever wonder if she just might be thinking about you?"

"I don't think about her," he says.

"You read the letter Annie brings you every year."

"I'm curious."

"Just curious for that one brief minute?"

Yes, he nods. "Notice that I'm always the one that opens the junk mail, too," he says.

According to Jerome, he and Anita gradually drifted apart. Or, at times when he blames himself, he says it's because he was still a child when he married her. He married her the week of his twentieth birthday. He says that his childhood wounds still weren't healed; Anita was Mama, she was the person he always felt he had to prove himself to—the stuff any psychiatrist will run down for you, he says now, trailing his hand in the water. "It's like there was a time in your life when you believed in paste," he says. "Think how embarrassed you'd be to go buy paste today. Now it's rubber cement. Or at least Elmer's glue. When I was young I just didn't know things."

I never had any doubt when things ended with my first husband. We knew things were wrong; we were going to a counselor and either biting our tongues or arguing because we'd loosened them with too much alcohol, trying to pretend that it didn't matter that I couldn't have a baby. One weekend Dan and I went to Saratoga, early in the spring, to visit friends. It was all a little too sun-dappled. Too *House Beautiful*, the way the sun, in the early morning, shone through the lace curtains and paled the walls to polka dots of light. The redwood picnic table on the stone-covered patio was as bright in the sunlight as if it had been waxed. We were drinking iced tea, all four of us out in the yard early in the morning, amazed at what a perfect day it was, how fast the garden was growing, how huge the heads of the peonies were. Then some people stopped by, with their little girl—people new to Saratoga, who really had no friends there yet. The little girl was named Alison, and she took a liking to Dan—came up to him without hesitation, the way a puppy that's been chastised will instantly choose someone in the room to cower by or a bee will zero in on one member of a group. She came innocently, the way a child would come, fascinated by . . . by his curly hair? The way the sunlight reflected off the rims of his glasses? The wedding ring on his hand as he rested his arm on the picnic table? And then, as the rest of us talked there was a squealing game, with the child suddenly climbing from the ground to his lap, some whispering, some laughing, and then the child, held around her middle, raised above his head, parallel to the ground. The game went on and on with cries of "Again!" and "Higher!" until the child was shrill and Dan complained of numb arms, and for a second I looked away from the conversation the rest of us were having and I saw her raised above him, smiling down, and Dan both frowning and amused—that little smile at the edge of his lips—and the child's mouth, wide with delight, her long blond hair flopped forward. He was keeping her raised off the ground, and she was hoping that it would never end, and in that second I knew that for Dan and me it was over.

We took a big bunch of pink peonies back to the city with us, stuck in a glass jar with water in the bottom that I held wedged between my feet. I had on a skirt, and the flowers flopped as we went over the bumpy road and the sensation I felt was amazing: it wasn't a tickle, but a pain. When he stopped for gas I went into the bathroom and cried and washed my face and dried it on one of those brown paper towels that smell more strongly than any perfume. I combed my hair. When I was sure I looked fine I came back to the car and sat down, putting one foot on each side of the jar. He started to drive out of the gas station, and then he just drifted to a stop. It was still sunny. Late afternoon. We sat there with the sun heating us and other cars pulling around our car, and he said, "You are impossible. You are so emotional. After a perfect day, what have you been crying about?" Then there were tears, and since I said nothing, eventually he started to drive: out into the merging lane, then onto the highway, speeding all the way back to New York in silence. It was already over. The only other thing I remember about that day is that down by Thirty-fourth Street we saw the same man who had been there the week before, selling roses guaranteed to smell sweet and to be everlasting. There he was, in the same place, his roses on a stand behind him.

We swim, and gradually work our way back to the gunwale of the Whaler: six hands, white-knuckled, holding the rim. I slide along, hand over hand, then move so that my body touches Jerome's from behind. With my arms around his chest, I kiss his neck. He turns and smiles and kisses me. Then I kick away and go to where Annie is holding on to the boat, her cheek on her hands, staring at her father. I swim up to her, push her wet bangs to one side, and kiss her forehead. She looks aggravated, and turns her head away. Just as quickly, she turns it back. "Am I interrupting you two getting it on out here?" she says.

"I kissed both of you," I say, between them again, feeling the weightlessness of my legs dangling as I hold on.

She continues to stare at me. "Girls kissing girls is so dumb," she says. "It's like the world's full of stupid hostesses who graduated from Sweet Briar."

Jerome looks at her silently for a long time.

"I guess your mother's not very demonstrative," he says.

"Were you ever?" she says. "Did you love Anita when you had me?"

"Of course I did," he says. "Didn't you know that?"

"It doesn't matter what I know," she says, as angry and petulant as a child. "How come you don't feed me birdseed?" she says. "How come you don't feed the carrier pigeon?"

He pauses until he understands what she is talking about. "The letters just go one way," he says.

"Do you have too much *dignity* to answer them, or is it too risky to reveal anything?"

"Honey," he says, lowering his voice, "I don't have anything to say."

"That you loved her and now you don't?" she says. "That's what isn't worth saying?"

He's brought his knees up to his chin. The scab by his elbow is pale when he clasps his arm around his knees.

"Well, I think that's bullshit," she says. She looks at me. "And I think you're bullshit, too. You don't care about the bond between women. You just care about hanging on to him. When you kissed me, it was patronizing."

There are tears now. Tears that are ironic, because there is so much water everywhere. Today she's angry and alone, and I float between them knowing exactly how each one feels and, like the little girl Alison suspended above Dan's head, knowing that desire that can be more overwhelming than love—the desire, for one brief minute, simply to get off the earth.

Girl Talk

Barbara is in her chaise. Something is wrong with the pool—everything is wrong with the pool—so it has not been filled with water. The green-painted bottom is speckled with goldenrod and geranium petals. The neighbor's cat sits licking a paw under the shade of the little mimosa tree planted in one of the raised boxes at one corner of the pool.

"Take a picture of that," Barbara says, putting her hand on top of her husband Sven's wrist. He is her fourth husband. They have been married for two years. She speaks to him exactly the way she spoke to her third husband. "Take a picture of a kitty licking its paw, Sven."

"I don't have my camera," he says.

"You usually always have it with you," she says. She lights an Indonesian cigarette—a *kretek*—waves out the match and drops it in a little green dish full of cherry pits. She turns to me and says, "If he'd had his camera last Friday, he could have photographed the car that hit the what-do-you-call-it—the concrete thing that goes down the middle of the highway. They were washing up the blood."

Sven gets up. He slips into his white thongs and flaps down the flagstone walk to the kitchen. He goes in and closes the door.

"How is your job, Oliver?" Barbara asks. Oliver is Barbara's son, but she hardly ever sees him.

"Air-conditioned," Oliver says. "They've finally got the air-conditioning up to a decent level in the building this summer."

"How is *your* job?" Barbara says to me.

I look at her, at Oliver.

"What job are you thinking of, Mother?" he says.

"Oh—painting wicker white, or something. Painting the walls yellow. If you'd had amniocentesis, you could paint them blue or pink."

"We're leaving up the wallpaper," Oliver says. "Why would a thirty-year-old woman have amniocentesis?"

"I hate wicker," I say. "Wicker is for Easter baskets."

Barbara stretches. "Notice the way it goes?" she says. "I ask a simple question, he answers for you, as if you're helpless now that you're pregnant, and that gives you time to think and zing back some snappy reply."

"I think you're the Queen of Snappiness," Oliver says to her.

"Like the Emperor of Ice Cream?" She puts down her Dutch detective novel. "I never did understand Wallace Stevens," she says. "Do any of you?"

Sven has come back with his camera and is focusing. The cat has walked away, but he wasn't focusing on the cat anyway; it's a group shot: Barbara in her tiny white bikini, Oliver in cut-off jeans, with the white raggedy strings trailing down his tan legs, and me in my shorts and baggy embroidered top that my huge stomach bulges hard against.

"Smile," Sven says. "Do I really have to say smile?"

This is the weekend of Barbara's sixtieth birthday, and Oliver's half brother Craig has also come for the occasion. He has given her an early present: a pink T-shirt that says "60." Oliver and I brought Godivas and a hair comb with a silk lily glued to it. Sven will give her a card and some orchids, flown in from some unimaginably far-off place, and a check. She will express shock at the check and not show anyone the amount, though she will pass around his birthday card. At dinner, the orchids will be in a vase, and Sven will tell some anecdote about a shoot he once went on in some faraway country.

Craig has brought two women with him, unexpectedly. They are tall, blond, silent, and look like twins but are not. Their clothes are permeated with marijuana. When they were introduced, one was wearing a Sony Walkman and the other had a tortoiseshell hair ornament in the shape of a turtle.

Now it is getting dark and we are all having spritzers. I have had too many spritzers. I feel that everyone is looking at everyone else's naked feet. The twins who are not twins have baby toes that curl under, so you can see the plum-colored polish on only four toes. Craig has square toenails and calluses on his heels which come from playing tennis. Oliver's long, tan feet are rubbing my legs. The dryness of his soles feels wonderful as he rubs his feet up and down the sticky sweat that has dried on my calves. Barbara has long toenails, painted bronze. Sven's big toes are oblong and shapeless, the way balloons look when you first begin to blow them up. My toenails aren't polished, because I can hardly bend over. I look at Oliver's feet and mine and try to imagine a composite baby foot. As Sven pours, it is the first time I realize that my drink is gone and I have been crunching ice.

In our bedroom, Oliver cups his hands around my hard stomach as I lie on my side facing away from him and kisses my hair from underneath, slowly moving down my spine to where his lips rest on one hipbone.

"My glass of ice water just made a ring on the night table," he says. He takes a sip of water. I hear him sigh and put the glass back on the table.

"I want to get married," I mumble into the pillow. "I don't want to end up bitter, like Barbara."

He snorts. "She's bitter because she kept getting married, and when the last one died he left almost everything to Craig. She's bored with Sven, now that his pictures aren't selling anymore."

"Oliver," I say, and am surprised at how helpless I sound. "You sounded like your mother just then. At least talk sense to me."

Oliver slides his cheek to my buttock. "Remember the first time you rubbed my back and it felt so good that I started laughing?" Oliver says. "And you didn't know why I was doing it and you got insulted? And the time you got drunk and sang along with Eddie Fisher on 'Wish You Were Here' and you were so good I laughed until I got the hiccups?" He rolls over. "We're married," he says. He slides his cheek to the hollow of my back. "Let me tell you what happened on the crosstown bus last week," he goes on. "A messenger got on. Twenty or so. Carrying a pile of envelopes. Started talking CB chatter to the baby on the lap of a woman sitting next to him. The woman and the baby got off at Madison, and between there and Third he started addressing the bus in general. He said, 'Everybody's heard of pie in the sky. They say Smokey in the Sky. Smokey the Bear's what they call the cops. But you know what I say? I say Bear in the Air. It's like "Lucy in the Sky with Diamonds"—LSD. LSD is acid.' He had on running shoes and jeans and a white button-down shirt with a tie hanging around his neck."

"Why did you tell me that story?" I say.

"*Anybody* can get it together to do something perfunctory. The minute that messenger got off the bus he tied that tie and delivered that crap he was carrying." He turns again, sighs. "I can't talk about marriage in this crazy house. Let's walk on the beach."

"It's so late," I say. "It must be after midnight. I'm exhausted from sitting all day, drinking and doing nothing."

"I'll tell you the truth," he whispers. "I can't stand to hear Barbara and Sven making love."

I listen, wondering if he's putting me on. "That's mice running through the walls," I say.

Sunday afternoon, and Barbara and I are walking the beach, a little tipsy after our picnic lunch. I wonder what she'd think if I told her that her son and I are not married. She gives the impression that what she hasn't lived through she has imagined. And much of what she says comes true. She said the pool would crack; she warned Craig that the girls weren't to be trusted, and, sure enough, this morning they were gone, taking with them the huge silver bowl she keeps lemons and limes in, a silver meat platter with coiled-serpent handles, and four silver ladles—almost as if they'd planned some bizarre tea party for themselves. He'd met them, he said, at Odeon, in the city. That was his explanation. Craig is the only person I know who gets up in the morning, brushes his teeth, and takes a Valium blue. Now we have left him playing a game called Public Assistance with Sven, at the side of the pool. Oliver was still upstairs sleeping when I came down at eleven. "I'll marry you," he said sleepily as I climbed out of bed. "I had a dream that I didn't and we were always unhappy."

I am in the middle of rambling on to Barbara, telling her that Oliver's dreams amaze me. They seem to be about states of feeling; they don't have any symbols in them, or even moments. He wakes up and his dreams have summarized things. I want to blurt out, "We lied to you, years ago. We said we got married, and we didn't. We had a fight and a flat tire and it rained, and we checked into an inn and just never got married."

"My first husband, Cadby, collected butterflies," she says. "I could never understand that. He'd stand by a little window in our bedroom—we had a basement apartment in Cambridge, just before the war—and he'd hold the butterflies in the frames to the light, as if the way the light struck them told him something their wings wouldn't have if they'd flown by." She looks out to the ocean. "Not that there were butterflies flying around Cambridge," she says. "I just realized that."

I laugh.

"Not what you were talking about at all?" she says.

"I don't know," I say. "Lately I catch myself talking just to distract myself. Nothing seems real but my body, and my body is *so heavy*."

She smiles at me. She has long auburn hair, streaked with white, and curly bangs that blow every which way, like the tide foaming into pools.

Both sons, she has just told me, were accidents. "Now I'm too old, and for the first time I'd like to do it again. I envy men for being able to conceive children late in life. You know that picture of Picasso and his son, Claude?

Robert Capa took it. It's in Sven's darkroom—the postcard of it, tacked up. They're on the beach, and the child is being held forward, bigger than its father, rubbing an eye. Being held by Picasso, simply smiling and rubbing an eye."

"What wine was that we drank?" I say, tracing a heart in the sand with my big toe.

"La Vieille Ferme blanc," she says. "Nothing special." She picks up a shell—a small mussel shell, black outside, opalescent inside. She drops it carefully into one cup of her tiny bikini top. In her house are ferns, in baskets on the floor, and all around them on top of the soil sit little treasures: bits of glass, broken jewelry, shells, gold twine. One of the most beautiful is an asparagus fern that now cascades over a huge circle of exposed flashbulbs stuck in the earth; each summer I gently lift the branches and peek, the way I used to go to my grandmother's summer house and open her closet to see if the faint pencil markings of the heights of her grandchildren were still there.

"You love him?" she says.

In five years, it is the first time we have ever really talked.

Yes, I nod.

"I've had four husbands. I'm sure you know that—that's my claim to fame, and ridicule, forever. But the first died, quite young. Hodgkin's disease. There's a seventy-percent cure now, I believe, for Hodgkin's disease. The second one left me for a lady cardiologist. You knew Harold. And now you know Sven." She puts another shell in her bikini, centering it over her nipple. "Actually, I only had two chances out of four. Sven would like a little baby he could hold in front of his face on the beach, but I'm too old. The body of a thirty-year-old, and I'm too old."

I kick sand, look at the ocean. I feel too full, too woozy, but I'm getting desperate to walk, to move faster.

"Do you think Oliver and Craig will ever like each other?" I say.

She shrugs. "Oh—I don't want to talk about them. It's my birthday, and I want to talk girl talk. Maybe I'll never talk to you this way again."

"Why?" I say.

"I've always had . . . *feelings* about things. Sven made fun of me when I said at Christmas that the pool would crack. I knew both times I was pregnant I'd have boys. I so much didn't want a second child, but now I'm glad I had him. He's more intelligent than Craig. On my deathbed, Craig will probably bring some woman to the house who'll steal the covers." She bends and picks up a shiny stone, throws it into the water. "I didn't love my first husband," she says.

"Why didn't you?"

"His spirit was dying. His spirit was dying before he got sick and died." She runs her hand across her bare stomach. "People your age don't talk that way, do they? We fought, and I left him, and that was in the days when young ladies did not leave young men. I got an apartment in New York, and for so many weeks I was all right—my mother sent all the nice ladies she knew over to amuse me, and it was such a relief not to have to cope. That was also in the days when young men didn't cry, and he'd put his head on my chest and cry about things I couldn't understand. Look at me now, with this body. I'm embarrassed by the irony of it—the dry pool, the useless body. It's too obvious even to talk about it. I sound like T. S. Eliot, with his bank-clerk self-pity, don't I?" She is staring at the ocean. "When I thought everything was in order—I even had a new beau—I was trying to hang a picture one morning: a painting of a field of little trees, with a doe walking through. I had it positioned where I thought it should go, and I held it to the wall and backed up, but I couldn't quite tell, because I couldn't back up enough. I didn't have any husband to hold it to the wall. I dropped it and broke the glass and cried." She pushes her hair back, twines the rubber band she has worn on her wrist around her hair again. Through her bikini I can see the outline of the shells. Her hands hang at her sides. "We've come too far," she says. "Aren't you exhausted?"

We are almost up to the Davises' house. That means that we've walked about three miles, and through my heaviness I feel a sort of light-headedness. I'm thinking, I'm tired but it doesn't matter. Being married doesn't matter. Knowing how to talk about things matters. I sink down in the sand, like a novice with a revelation. Barbara looks concerned; then, a little drunkenly, I watch her face change. She's decided that I'm just responding, taking a rest. A seagull dives, gets what it wants. We sit next to each other facing the water, her flat tan stomach facing the ocean like a mirror.

It is night, and we are still outdoors, beside the pool. Sven's face has a flickery, shadowed look, like a jack-o'-lantern's. A citronella candle burns on the white metal table beside his chair.

"He decided not to call the police," Sven says. "I agree. Since those two young ladies obviously did not *want* your crappy silver, they're saddled with sort of pirates' treasure, and, as we all know, pirate ships sink."

"You're going to wait?" Barbara says to Craig. "How will you get all our silver back?"

Craig is tossing a tennis ball up and down. It disappears into the darkness, then slaps into his hands again. "You know what?" he says. "One night I'll run into them at Odeon. That's the thing—nothing is ever the end."

"Well, this is my *birthday*, and I hope we don't have to talk about things ending." Barbara is wearing her pink T-shirt, which seems to have shrunk in the wash. Her small breasts are visible beneath it. She has on white pedal pushers and has kicked off her black patent-leather sandals.

"Happy birthday," Sven says, and takes her hand.

I reach out and take Oliver's hand. The first time I met his family I cried. I slept on their foldout sofa and drank champagne and watched *The Lady Vanishes* on TV, and during the night he crept downstairs to hold me, and I was crying. I had short hair then. I can remember his hand closing around it, crushing it. Now it hangs long and thin, and he moves it gently, pushing it aside. I can't remember the last time I cried. When I first met her, Barbara surprised me because she was so sharp-tongued. Now I have learned that it is their dull lives that make people begin to say cutting things.

I look over my shoulder at the beach at night—sand bleached white by the light of the moon, foamy waves silently washing ashore, a hollow sound from the wind all over, like the echo of a conch shell held against the ear. The roar in my head is all from pain. All day, the baby has been kicking and kicking, and now I know that the heaviness I felt earlier, the disquiet, must be labor. It's almost a full month early—labor coupled with danger. I keep my hands away from my stomach, as if it might quiet itself. Sven opens a bottle of club soda and it gushes into the tall glass pitcher that sits on the table between his chair and Barbara's. He begins to unscrew the cork in a bottle of white wine. Inside me, once, making my stomach pulse, the baby turns over. I concentrate, desperately, on the first thing I see. I focus on Sven's fingers and count them, as though my baby were born and now I have to look for perfection. There is every possibility that my baby will be loved and cared for and will grow up to be like any of these people. Another contraction, and I reach out for Oliver's hand but stop in time and stroke it, don't squeeze.

I am really at some out-of-the-way beach house, with a man I am not married to and people I do not love, in labor.

Sven squeezes a lemon into the pitcher. Smoky drops fall into the soda and wine. I smile, the first to hold out my glass. Pain is relative.

Like Glass

In the picture, only the man is looking at the camera. The baby in the chair, out on the lawn, is looking in another direction, not at his father. His father has a grip on a collie—trying, no doubt, to make the dog turn its head toward the lens. The dog looks away, no space separating its snout from the white border. I wonder why, in those days, photographs had borders that looked as if they had been cut with pinking shears.

The collie is dead. The man with a pompadour of curly brown hair and with large, sloping shoulders was alive, the last time I heard. The baby grew up and became my husband and now is no longer married to me. I am trying to follow his line of vision in the picture. Obviously, he'd had enough of paying attention to his father or to the dog that day. It is a picture of a baby gazing into the distance.

I have a lot of distinct memories of things that happened while I was married, but lately I've been thinking about two things that are similar, although they have nothing in common. We lived on the top floor of a brownstone. When we decided to separate and I moved out, Paul changed the lock on the door. When I came back to take my things, there was no way to get them. I went away and thought about it until I didn't feel angry anymore. By then it was winter, and cold leaked in my windows. I had my daughter, and other things, to think about. In the cold, though, walking around the apartment in a sweater most people would have thought thick enough to wear outside, or huddling on the sofa under an old red-and-brown afghan, I would start feeling romantic about my husband.

One afternoon—it was February 13, the day before Valentine's Day—I had a couple of drinks and put on my long green coat with a huge hood that made me look like a monk and went to the window and saw that the snow had melted on the sidewalk: I could get away with wearing my comfortable rubber-soled sandals with thick wool socks. So I went out and stopped at Sheridan Square to buy *Hamlet* and flipped through until I found what I was looking for. Then I went to our old building and buzzed Larry. He lives in the basement—what is called a garden apartment. He opened the door and unlocked the high black iron gate. My husband had always said that Larry looked and acted like Loretta Young; he was always exuberant, he had puffy hair and crinkly eyes, and he didn't look as if he belonged to either sex. Larry was surprised to see me. I can be charming when I want to be, so I acted slightly bumbly and apologetic and smiled to let him know that what I was asking was a silly thing: could I stand in his garden for a minute and call out a poem to my husband? I saw Larry looking at my hands, moving in the pockets of my coat. The page torn from *Hamlet* was in one pocket, the rest of the book in the other. Larry laughed. How could my husband hear me, he asked. It was February. There were storm windows. But he let me in, and I walked down his long, narrow hallway, through the back room that he used as an office, to the door that led out to the back garden. I pushed open the door, and his gray poodle came yapping up to my ankles. It looked like a cactus, with maple leaves stuck in its coat.

I picked up a little stone—Larry had small rocks bordering his walkway, all touching, as if they were a chain. I threw the stone at my husband's fourth-floor bedroom window, and hit it—*tonk!*—on the very first try. Blurrily, I watched the look of puzzlement on Larry's face. My real attention was on my husband's face, when it appeared at the window, full of rage, then wonder. I looked at the torn-out page and recited, liltingly, Ophelia's song: "'Tomorrow is Saint Valentine's day / All in the morning betime, / And I a maid at your window, / To be your Valentine.'"

"Are you *insane*?" Paul called down to me. It was a shout, really, but his voice hung thin in the air. It floated down.

"I did it," Larry said, coming out, shivering, cowering as he looked up to the fourth floor. "I let her in."

I could smell jasmine when the wind blew. I had put on too much perfume. Even if he did take me in, he'd back off; he'd never let me be his valentine. What he noticed, of course, when he'd come downstairs to lead me out of the garden, seconds later, was the Scotch on my breath.

"This is all wrong," I said, as he pulled me by the hand past Larry, who stood holding his barking poodle in the hallway. "I only had two Scotches," I said. "I just realized when the wind blew that I smell like a flower garden."

"You bet it's all wrong," he said, squeezing my hand so hard it almost broke. Then he shook off my hand and walked up the steps, went in and slammed the door behind him. I watched a hairline crack leap across all four panes of glass at the top of the door.

The other thing happened in happier times, when we were visiting my sister, Karin, on Twenty-third Street. It was the first time we had met Dan, the man she was engaged to, and we had brought a bottle of champagne. We drank her wine first, and ate her cheese and told stories and heard stories and smoked a joint, and sometime after midnight my husband went to the refrigerator and got out our wine—Spanish champagne, in a black bottle. He pointed the bottle away from him, and we all squinted, silently watching. At the same instant that the cork popped, as we were all saying "Hooray!" or "That does it!"—whatever we were saying—we heard glass raining down, and Paul suddenly crouched, and then we looked above him to see a hole in the skylight, and through the hole black sky.

I've just told these stories to my daughter, Eliza, who is six. She used to like stories to end with a moral, like fairy tales, but now she thinks that's kid's stuff. She still wants to know what stories mean, but now she wants me to tell her. The point of the two stories—well, I don't know what the point is, I'm always telling her. That he broke the glass by mistake, and that the cork broke the glass by a miracle. The point is that broken glass is broken glass.

"That's a joke ending," she says. "It's dumb." She frowns.

I cop out, too tired to think, and then tell her another part of the story to distract her: Uncle Dan and Aunt Karin told the superintendent that the hole must have come from something that fell from above. He knew they were lying—nothing was above them—but what could he say? He asked them whether they thought perhaps meteorites shrank to the size of gumballs falling through New York's polluted air. He hated not only his tenants but the whole city.

She watches me digress. She reaches for the cologne on her night table and lifts her long blond hair, and I spray her neck. She takes the bottle and sprays her wrists, rubs them together, holds out her wrists for me to smell. I make a silly face and pretend to be dazed by such a wonderful smell. I stroke her hair until she is silent, and tiptoe out, still moving as if I'm walking through broken glass.

Once a week, for a couple of hours, I read to a man named Norman, who is blind. In the year I've been doing it, he and I have sort of become friends. He usually greets me with something like "So what's new with your life?" He sits behind his desk and I sit beside it, in a chair. This is the way a teacher and pupil should sit, and I've fallen into the pattern of letting him ask.

He gets up to open the window. It's always too hot in his little office. His movements are exaggerated, like a bird's: the quickly cocked head, the way he grips the edge of his desk when he's bored. He grips the edge, releases his hold, grabs again, like a parrot shifting on its bar. Norman has never seen a bird. He has an eight-year-old daughter, who likes to describe things to him, although she is a prankster and sometimes deliberately lies, he has told me. He buys her things from the joke shop on the corner of the street where he works. He takes home little pills that will make drinks bubble over, buzzers to conceal in the palm of your hand, little black plastic flies to freeze in ice cubes, rubber eyeglass rims attached to a fat nose and a bushy mustache. "Daddy, now I'm wearing my big nose," she says. "Daddy, I put a black fly in your ice cube, so spit it out if it sinks in your drink, all right?" My daughter and I have gone to two dinners at their house. My daughter thinks that his daughter is a little weird. The last time we visited, when the girls were playing and Norman was washing dishes, his wife showed me the hallway she had just wallpapered. It took her forever to decide on the wallpaper, she told me. We stood there, dwarfed by wallpaper imprinted with the trunks of shiny silver trees that her husband would never see.

What's new with me? My divorce is final.

My husband remembers the circumstances of the photograph. I told him it was impossible—he was an infant. No, he was a child when the picture was taken, he said—he just looked small because he was slumped in the chair. He remembers it all distinctly. Rufus the dog was there, and his father, and he was looking slightly upward because that was where his mother was, holding the camera. I was amazed that I had made a mystery of something that had such a simple answer. It is a picture of a baby looking at its mother. For the millionth time he asks why must I make myself morose, why call in the middle of the night.

Eliza is asleep. I sit on the edge of her bed in the half-darkness, tempting fate, fidgeting with a paperweight with bursts of red color inside, tossing it in the air. One false move and she will wake up. One mistake and glass shatters. I like the smoothness of it, the heaviness as it slaps into my palm over and over.

Today when I went to Norman, he was sitting on his window ledge, with his arms crossed over his chest. He had been uptown at a meeting that morning, where a man had come up to him and said, "Be grateful for the cane. Everybody who doesn't take hold of something has something take hold of them." Norman tells me this, and we are both silent. Does he want me to tell him, the way Eliza wants me to summarize stories, what I think it means? Since Norman and I are adults, I answer my silent question with another question: What do you do with a shard of sorrow?

Desire

Bryce was sitting at the kitchen table in his father's house, cutting out a picture of Times Square. It was a picture from a coloring book, but Bryce wasn't interested in coloring; he just wanted to cut out pictures so he could see what they looked like outside the book. This drawing was of people crossing the street between the Sheraton-Astor and F. W. Woolworth. There were also other buildings, but these were the ones the people seemed to be moving between. The picture was round; it was supposed to look as if it had been drawn on a bottle cap. Bryce had a hard time getting the scissors around the edge of the cap, because they were blunt-tipped. At home, at his mother's house in Vermont, he had real scissors and he was allowed to taste anything, including alcohol, and his half sister Maddy was a lot more fun than Bill Monteforte, who lived next door to his father here in Pennsylvania and who never had time to play. But he had missed his father, and he had been the one who called to invite himself to this house for his spring vacation.

His father, B.B., was standing in the doorway now, complaining because Bryce was so quiet and so glum. "It took quite a few polite letters to your mother to get her to let loose of you for a week," B.B. said. "You get here and you go into a slump. It would be a real problem if you had to do anything important, like go up to bat with the bases loaded and two outs."

"Mom's new neighbor is the father of a guy that plays for the Redskins," Bryce said.

The scissors slipped. Since he'd ruined it, Bryce now cut on the diagonal, severing half the people in Times Square from the other half. He looked out the window and saw a squirrel stealing seed from the bird feeder. The gray birds were so tiny anyway, it didn't look as if they needed anything to eat.

"Are we going to that auction tonight, or what?" Bryce said.

"Maybe. It depends on whether Rona gets over her headache."

B.B. sprinkled little blue and white crystals of dishwasher soap into the machine and closed it. He pushed two buttons and listened carefully.

"Remember now," he said, "I don't want you getting excited at the auction if you see something you want. You put your hand up, and that's a *bid*. You have to really, really want something and then ask me before you put your hand up. You can't shoot your hand up. Imagine that you're a soldier down in the trenches and there's a war going on."

"I don't even care about the dumb auction," Bryce said.

"What if there was a Turkish prayer rug you wanted and it had the most beautiful muted colors you'd ever seen in your life?" B.B. sat down in the chair across from Bryce. The back of the chair was in the shape of an upside-down triangle. The seat was a right-side-up triangle. The triangles were covered with aqua plastic. B.B. shifted on the chair. Bryce could see that he wanted an answer.

"Or we'll play Let's Pretend," B.B. said. "Let's pretend a lion is coming at you and there's a tree with a cheetah in it and up ahead of you it's just low dry grass. Would you climb the tree, or start running?"

"Neither," Bryce said.

"Come on. You've either got to run or *something*. There's known dangers and unknown dangers. What would you do?"

"People can't tell what they'd do in a situation like that," Bryce said.

"No?"

"What's a cheetah?" Bryce said. "Are you sure they get in trees?"

B.B. frowned. He had a drink in his hand. He pushed the ice cube to the bottom and they both watched it bob up. Bryce leaned over and reached into the drink and gave it a push, too.

"No licking that finger," B.B. said.

Bryce wiped a wet streak across the red down vest he wore in the house.

"Is that my boy? 'Don't lick your finger,' he takes the finger and wipes it on his clothes. Now he can try to remember what he learned in school from the *Book of Knowledge* about cheetahs."

"What *Book of Knowledge*?"

His father got up and kissed the top of his head. The radio went on upstairs, and then water began to run in the tub up there.

"She must be getting ready for action," B.B. said. "Why does she have to take a bath the minute I turn on the dishwasher? The dishwasher's been acting crazy." B.B. sighed. "Keep those hands on the table," he said. "It's good practice for the auction."

Bryce moved the two half circles of Times Square so that they overlapped. He folded his hands over them and watched the squirrel scare a bird away from the feeder. The sky was the color of ash, with little bursts of white where the sun had been.

"I'm the same as dead," Rona said.

"You're not the same as dead," B.B. said. "You've put five pounds back on. You lost twenty pounds in that hospital, and you didn't weigh enough to start with. You wouldn't eat anything they brought you. You took an intravenous needle out of your arm. I can tell you, you were nuts, and I didn't have much fun talking to that doctor who looked like Tonto who operated on you and thought you needed a shrink. It's water over the dam. Get in the bath."

Rona was holding on to the sink. She started to laugh. She had on tiny green-and-white striped underpants. Her long white nightgown was hung around her neck, the way athletes drape towels around themselves in locker rooms.

"What's funny?" he said.

"You said, 'It's water over the—' Oh, you know what you said. I'm running water in the tub, and—"

"Yeah," B.B. said, closing the toilet seat and sitting down. He picked up a Batman comic and flipped through. It was wet from moisture. He hated the feel of it.

The radio was on the top of the toilet tank, and now the Andrews Sisters were singing "Hold Tight." Their voices were as smooth as toffee. He wanted to pull them apart, to hear distinct voices through the perfect harmony.

He watched her get into the bath. There was a worm of a scar, dull red, to the left of her jutting hipbone, where they had removed her appendix. One doctor had thought it was an ectopic pregnancy. Another was sure it was a ruptured ovary. A third doctor—her surgeon—insisted it was her appendix, and they got it just in time. The tip had ruptured.

Rona slid low in the bathtub. "If you can't trust your body not to go wrong, what can you trust?" she said.

"Everybody gets sick," he said. "It's not your body trying to do you in. The mind's only one place: in your head. Look, didn't Lyndon Johnson have an appendectomy? Remember how upset people were that he pulled up his shirt to show the scar?"

"They were upset because he pulled his dog's ears," she said.

She had a bath toy he had bought for her. It was a fish with a happy smile. You wound it with a key and then it raced around the tub spouting water through its mouth.

He could hear Bryce talking quietly downstairs. Another call to Maddy, no doubt. When the boy was in Vermont, he was on the phone all the time, telling B.B. how much he missed him; when he was here in Pennsylvania, he missed his family in Vermont. The phone bill was going to be astronomical. Bryce kept calling Maddy, and Rona's mother kept calling from New York; Rona never wanted to take the calls because she always ended up in an argument if she wasn't prepared with something to talk about, so she made B.B. say she was asleep, or in the tub, or that a soufflé was in the last stages. Then she'd call her mother back, when she'd gathered her thoughts.

"Would you like to go to that auction tonight?" he said to Rona.

"An auction? What for?"

"I don't know. There's nothing on TV and the kid's never been to an auction."

"The kid's never smoked grass," she said, soaping her arm.

"Neither do you anymore. Why would you bring that up?"

"You can look at his rosy cheeks and sad-clown eyes and know he never has."

"Right," he said, throwing the comic book back on the tile. "*Right.* My kid's not a pothead. *I was talking about going to an auction.* Would you also like to tell me that elephants don't fly?"

She laughed and slipped lower in the tub, until the water reached her chin. With her hair pinned to the top of her head and the foam of bubbles covering her neck, she looked like a lady in Edwardian times. The fish was in a frenzy, cutting through the suds. She moved a shoulder to accommodate it, shifted her knees, tipped her head back.

"There were flying elephants in those books that used to be all over the house when he visited," she said. "I'm so glad he's eight now. All those *crazy* books."

"You were stoned all the time," he said. "Everything looked funny to you." Though he hadn't gotten stoned with her, sometimes things had seemed peculiar to him, too. There was the night his friends Shelby and Charles had given a dramatic reading of a book of Bryce's called *Bertram and the Ticklish Rhinoceros.* Rona's mother had sent her a loofah for Christmas that year. It was before you saw loofahs all over the place. Vaguely, he could remember six people crammed into the bathroom, cheering as the floating loofah expanded in water.

"What do you say about the auction?" he said. "Can you keep your hands still? That's what I told him was essential—hands in lap."

"Come here," she said, "I'll show you what I can do with my hands."

The auction was in a barn heated with two wood stoves—one in front, one in back. There were also a few electric heaters up and down the aisles. When B.B. and Rona and Bryce came in the back door of the barn, a man in a black-and-red lumberman's jacket closed it behind them, blowing cigar smoke in their faces. A woman and a man and two teenagers were arguing about a big cardboard box. Apparently one of the boys had put it too close to the small heater. The other boy was defending him, and the man, whose face was bright red, looked as if he was about to strike the woman. Someone else kicked the box away while they argued. B.B. looked in. There were six or eight puppies inside, mostly black, squirming.

"Dad, are they in the auction?" Bryce said.

"I can't stand the smoke," Rona said. "I'll wait for you in the car."

"Don't be stupid. You'll freeze," B.B. said. He reached out and touched the tips of her hair. She had on a red angora hat, pulled over her forehead, which made her look extremely pretty but also about ten years old. A child's hat and no makeup. The tips of her hair were still wet from the bathwater. Touching her hair, he was sorry that he had walked out of the bathroom when she said that about her hands.

They got three seats together near the back.

"Dad, I can't see," Bryce said.

"The damn Andrews Sisters," B.B. said. "I can't get their spooky voices out of my head."

Bryce got up. B.B. saw, for the first time, that the metal folding chair his son had been sitting in had "PAM LOVES DAVID FOREVER AND FOR ALL TIME" written on it with Magic Marker. He took off his scarf and folded it over the writing. He looked over his shoulder, sure that Bryce would be at the stand where they sold hot dogs and soft drinks. He wasn't; he was still inspecting the puppies. One of the boys said something to him, and his son answered. B.B. got up immediately and went over to join them. Bryce was reaching into his pocket.

"What are you doing?" B.B. said.

"Picking up a puppy," Bryce said. He said it as he lifted the animal. The dog turned and rooted its snout in Bryce's armpit, its eyes closed. With his free hand, Bryce handed the boy some money.

"What are you *doing*?" B.B. said.

"Dime a feel," the boy said. Then, in a different tone, he said, "Week or so, they start eating food."

"I never heard of anything like that," B.B. said. The loofah popped up in his mind, expanded. Their drunken incredulity. The time, as a boy, he had watched a neighbor drown a litter of kittens in a washtub. He must have been younger than Bryce when that happened. And the burial: B.B. and the neighbor's son and another boy who was an exchange student had attended the funeral for the drowned kittens. The man's wife came out of the house, with the mother cat in one arm, and reached in her pocket and took out little American flags on toothpicks and handed them to each of the boys and then went back in the house. Her husband had dug a hole and was shoveling dirt back in. First he had put the kittens in a shoebox coffin, which he placed carefully in the hole he had dug near an abelia bush. Then he shoveled the dirt back in. B.B. couldn't remember the name of the man's son now, or the Oriental exchange student's name. The flags were what they used to give you in your sundae at the ice-cream parlor next to the bank.

"You can hold him through the auction for a quarter," the boy said to Bryce.

"You have to give the dog back," B.B. said to his son.

Bryce looked as if he was about to cry. If he insisted on having one of the dogs, B.B. had no idea what he would do. It was what Robin, his ex-wife, deserved, but she'd probably take the dog to the pound.

"Put it down," he whispered, as quietly as he could. The room was so noisy now that he doubted that the teenage boy could hear him. He thought he had a good chance of Bryce's leaving the puppy if there was no third party involved.

To his surprise, Bryce handed over the puppy, and the teenager lowered it into the box. A little girl about three or four had come to the rim of the box and was looking down.

"I bet you don't have a dime, do you, cutie?" the boy said to the girl.

B.B. reached in his pocket and took out a dollar bill, folded it, and put it on the cement floor in front of where the boy crouched. He took Bryce's hand, and they walked to their seats without looking back.

"It's just a bunch of junk," Rona said. "Can we leave if it doesn't get interesting?"

They bought a lamp at the auction. It had a nice base, and as soon as they found another lampshade it would be just right for the bedside table. Now it had a cardboard shade on it, imprinted with a cracked, fading bouquet.

"What's the matter with you?" Rona said. They were back in their bedroom.

"Actually," B.B. said, holding on to the window ledge, "I feel very out of control."

"What does that mean?"

She put *From Julia Child's Kitchen* on the night table, picked up her comb, and grabbed a clump of her hair. She combed through the snaggled ends, slowly.

"Do you think he has a good time here?" he said.

"Sure. He asked to come, didn't he? You could look at his face and see that he enjoyed the auction."

"Maybe he just does what he's told."

"What's the matter with you?" she said. "Come over here."

He sat on the bed. He had stripped down to his undershorts, and there were goose bumps all over his body. A bird was making a noise outside, screaming as if it were being killed. It stopped abruptly. The goose bumps slowly went away. Whenever he turned up the thermostat he always knew he was going to be sorry along about 5 a.m., when it got too hot in the room, but he was too tired to get up and go turn it down. She said that was why they got headaches. He reached across her now for the Excedrin. He put the bottle back on top of the cookbook and gagged down two of them.

"What's he doing?" he said to her. "I don't hear him."

"If you made him go to bed, the way other fathers do, you'd know he was in bed. Then you'd just have to wonder if he was reading under the covers with a flashlight or—"

"Don't say it," he said.

"I wasn't going to say that."

"What were you going to say?"

"I was going to say that he might have taken more Godivas out of the box my mother sent me. I've eaten two. He's eaten a whole row."

"He left a mint and a cream in that row. I ate them," B.B. said.

He got up and pulled on a thermal shirt. He looked out the window and saw tree branches blowing. *The Old Farmer's Almanac* predicted snow at the end of the week. He hoped it didn't snow then; it would make it difficult taking Bryce back to Vermont. There were two miles of unplowed road leading to Robin's house.

He went downstairs. The oval table Bryce sat at was where the dining room curved out. Window seats were built around it. When they rented the house, it was the one piece of furniture left in it that neither of them disliked, so they had kept it. Bryce was sitting in an oak chair, and his forehead was on his arm. In front of him was the coloring book and a box of crayons and a glass vase with different-colored felt-tip pens stuck in it, falling this way and that, the way a bunch of flowers would. There was a pile of white paper. The scissors. B.B. assumed, until he was within a few feet of him, that Bryce was asleep. Then Bryce lifted his head.

"What are you doing?" B.B. said.

"I took the dishes out of the dishwasher and it worked," Bryce said. "I put them on the counter."

"That was very nice of you. It looks like my craziness about the dishwasher has impressed every member of my family."

"What was it that happened before?" Bryce said.

Bryce had circles under his eyes. B.B. had read once that that was a sign of kidney disease. If you bruised easily, leukemia. Or, of course, you could just take a wrong step and break a leg. The dishwasher had backed up, and all the filthy water had come pouring out in the morning when B.B. opened the door—dirtier water than the food-smeared dishes would account for.

"It was a mess," B.B. said vaguely. "Is that a picture?"

It was part picture, part letter, B.B. realized when Bryce clamped his hands over his printing in the middle.

"You don't have to show me."

"How come?" Bryce said.

"I don't read other people's mail."

"You did in Burlington," Bryce said.

"Bryce—that was when your mother cut out on us. That was a letter for her sister. She'd set it up with her to come stay with us, but her sister's as much a space cadet as Robin. Your mother was gone two days. The police were looking for her. What was I supposed to do when I found the letter?"

Robin's letter to her sister said that she did not love B.B. Also, that she did not love Bryce, because he looked like his father. The way she expressed it was: "Let spitting images spit together." She had gone off with the cook at the natural-food restaurant. The note to her sister—whom she had apparently called as well—was written on the back of one of the restaurant's flyers, announcing the menu for the week the cook ran away. Tears streaming down his cheeks, he had stood in the spare bedroom—whatever had made him go in there?—and read the names of desserts: "Tofu-Peach Whip!" "Granola Raspberry Pie!" "Macadamia Bars!"

"It's make-believe anyway," his son said, and wadded up the piece of paper. B.B. saw a big sunflower turn in on itself. A fir tree go under.

"Oh," he said, reaching out impulsively. He smoothed out the paper, making it as flat as he could. The ripply tree sprang up almost straight. Crinkled birds flew through the sky. B.B. read:

> When I'm B.B.'s age I can be with you allways.
> We can live in a house like the Vt. house only not in Vt. no sno.
> We can get married and have a dog.

"Who is this to?" B.B. said, frowning at the piece of paper.

"Maddy," Bryce said.

B.B. was conscious, for the first time, how cold the floorboards were underneath his feet. The air was cold, too. Last winter he had weather-stripped the windows, and this winter he hadn't. Now he put a finger against a pane of glass in the dining-room window. It could have been an ice cube, his finger numbed so quickly.

"Maddy is your stepsister," B.B. said. "You're never going to be able to marry Maddy."

His son stared at him.

"You understand?" B.B. said.

Bryce pushed his chair back. "Maddy's not ever going to have her hair cut again," he said. He was crying. "She's going to be Madeline and I'm going to live with only her and have a hundred dogs."

B.B. reached out to dry his son's tears, or at least to touch them, but Bryce sprang up. She was wrong: Robin was so wrong. Bryce was the image of her, not him—the image of Robin saying, "Leave me alone."

He went upstairs. Rather, he went to the stairs and started to climb, thinking of Rona lying in bed in the bedroom, and somewhere not half-way to the top, adrenaline surged through his body. Things began to go out of focus, then to pulsate. He reached for the railing just in time to steady himself. In a few seconds the first awful feeling passed, and he continued to climb, pretending, as he had all his life, that this rush was the same as desire.

Moving Water

My brother's wife, Corky, is in the wicker chair in my bedroom tweezing her eyebrows, my magnifying mirror an inch from the tip of her nose. When I first met Corky, she was a student at Hunter; she wore long Indian dresses and high heels and had long hair. Now she wears running shoes and baggy slacks, has a sort of bowl haircut, and goes by her nickname instead of Charlotte. Plucking her eyebrows and being pregnant are two of her new self-improvement plans, along with taking driving lessons. She has come into the city from Morristown to spend the weekend, while Archie—new husband, my brother—is away on business. She is sitting by the telephone, waiting for her call to the obstetrician to be returned. Archie, on the phone last night, insisted that Corky check out whether it was all right for her to continue with her aerobic dance classes. Her end of the conversation was a long protest about his trying to make her into a neurotic now that she was pregnant. She gave me the phone and asked me to reason with him, but I stayed out of it. He and I discussed the progress of the wisteria. The wisteria in the back garden has leafed out and shot up four stories to my roof, where it cascades over the low brick railing and has worked its way through the skylight. In the morning, I find crumpled leaves and small purple flowers scattered over my sheet.

I'm stretched out on the bed, printing a letter to my grandmother. My grandmother can't read my writing, but she is insulted when I type. She calls my typed letters "business letters." I have a piece of lined paper underneath my writing paper so that I will remember to print large enough. As my letters go on, they tend to look as if they'd been put through a funnel. I reread my last sentence: "AS SOON AS THE WISTERIA GROWS, THOUSANDS OF TINY ANTS CLIMB UP AND COME IN THROUGH THE SCREENS." It seems not just distressing but alarming, put in such large, blocky letters.

The phone rings, and Corky pounces on it.

"I feel so silly asking this, but my husband . . . Oh, the nurse . . . But I don't have any bleeding! . . . Is this because you think I'm *old*?"

I ink out my last line and print instead, "ISN'T IT AMAZING THAT A HUGE WISTERIA VINE IS THRIVING RIGHT HERE IN NEW YORK CITY?"

I go into the living room. The view out of the tall windows is of the projects the next street over. Below me, in the back, are gardens, with high walls dividing them. Next door, two actors stand at opposite ends of their garden, each reading aloud from an identical book.

"'What if it tempt you toward the flood, my lord, or to the dreadful summit of the cliff . . .'"

"Again!" the actor from the far end of the garden hollers.

"'What if it tempt you . . .'"

"Oh, yeah. 'It waves me still. Go on, I'll follow thee.'"

As I'm watching, trying to block out Corky's mounting hysteria, I see a kid of about ten, who has hauled himself up so that he can see over the fence of the adjacent garden. He throws something—a stone or a bottle cap—and screams, "Get back where you belong, faggots!," drops to the ground, and runs toward his back door. Then I hear the ice-cream truck come down the street, playing its carrousel music. As my grandmother recently wrote me (with a fountain pen, flawlessly executing the Palmer method), "Sandy darling, everyone in New York's always worked up."

"All right, I'll do it your way," Corky is saying, as I go back to the bedroom and sit on the bed. She sounds like some brave actress in a nineteen-forties movie. This notion is reinforced by her bottom lip, quivering.

Two o'clock in the morning, and Corky and I are the last people in the restaurant except for Wyatt, my longtime friend. He's just shaken some vegetables around in a pan and brought them to the table, along with a bottle of pepper vodka. A truck rattles by. Corky and I share the last slice of lemon meringue pie. Wyatt's key ring is on the table: four keys to the restaurant, so he can set the alarms before he leaves.

"This place is pretty crazy," he says, picking up a snow pea. "I thought that nothing could be worse than teaching fifth-grade grammar. But knowing all the rhymes on the jukebox is probably worse than teaching grammar." He takes a joint out of his shirt pocket. "You know what happened tonight? My father's accountant came in here with a guy. They had on T-shirts with swirls of pink and blue and green—it would have been good protective coloration in a basket of Easter eggs. The accountant almost died when he saw me. Then, Tuesday night, my old Hackensack heartthrob, Dorie Vesco, came in. I saw her sitting at the bar. She was all tied up. She had on one of those blouses that lace up the front and those shoes with strings that you wrap around your ankles. The guy she was with was a real jerk. Dorie Vesco and I recognized each other at the same instant, and when I hugged her the guy said, 'This some kind of a setup?'" He laughs. "Wyatt and the cat," he says, rubbing his foot over an orange cat that has just darted under the table. "She's been around here longer'n me. Longer than anybody. Cat can't set alarms, Wyatt can."

We are in what used to be Jason's favorite restaurant. I used to live with Jason; now we're apart. After Wyatt took a job as a waiter here, though, Jason stopped coming. "Honey, it's just too odd," Jason said to me one night. "I don't feel comfortable being waited on by the same person I always call when I have a question about the correct use of apostrophes."

When we go out, Wyatt hands Corky the keys to the car. I open the back door, muttering about what a bad idea this is, because she has only had three driving lessons so far. She no more than pulls away from the curb than a cop car comes up alongside us and stops for the red light. I catch one cop's eye and look away. Our car is angled strangely through two lanes. No cars are in back of us or around us. Next, one of the cops catches Corky's eye. "You know what?" he calls over. "If you were a red Toyota with six guys inside, we'd have found what we're looking for." Then the cop in the driver's seat leans forward and hollers, "Now he'll tell you that if you twinkled you'd be the North Star, and we could follow you so we don't get lost."

The light changes and the cop car takes off, no siren, at about sixty miles an hour.

"Still nothing behind us," Wyatt says, patting Corky's leg. "First rule of driving: Many other dangerous people are driving at the same time you are, and you must drive defensively."

"Did you think you'd marry Jason?" Corky says.

I never lived in a dorm when I was in college, but Corky did. Lights-out is still a signal to her to start talking.

"We almost got married," I say. "I told you about that. The summer he bought the house in Garrison. We were as stupid as everybody else who's breaking up. We kept finding something to do that interested us, so we could pretend that we were interested in each other."

"What about you and Wyatt?"

"I've always thought that he loved somebody else. We had quite a talk about that years ago, and he said I was wrong. Then again, he never mentioned Dorie Vesco until tonight."

"Archie told me a week before our wedding that he'd been engaged twice before." She lights a cigarette. "Which was the one who flushed his credit card down the toilet?"

"Sally."

"And Sondra's the one who swallowed the ring?"

"A citrine with diamonds. Our grandmother's. When Archie took her to the emergency room and she filled out the form, she said that she'd swallowed a bone."

"She had to be nuts not to level with the people in the emergency room," Corky says.

I roll over to see Corky's face in the half-dark. She has unrolled the futon sofa into a mat on the bedroom floor, where she will sleep tonight.

"You know the rest of that story, don't you?" I say. "The next day, he got a book about training puppies. He took it home and showed her the part where they say not to worry if your dog swallows a rock unless it chokes. A joke, but when they went to couples therapy she kept bringing up the dog book."

Looking back, I can see how Jason liked to manipulate me. He relied on being a Southern boy when he wanted something. He talked about the house he wanted to buy as our opportunity to "live life on the plantation." Even before we went to look at the property in Garrison, he was planning the afternoon croquet games we were going to play there; we'd play croquet and drink mint juleps, he announced. When Jason really wanted something, he began by making it into some kind of fantasy—the more exaggerated and ridiculous the better. He said that made it easier to cope with whatever problems came up later. We had lived together in the city for more than a year, and he was restless and wanted a place in the country. So he bought the big yellow house up the Hudson in Garrison and he took a leave of absence from his job and spent a month that autumn painting it white. I glazed windows and helped him sand the floors, and by the time the house started to shape up I loved it more than Jason did. In the mornings, I had coffee and watched the sparrows and the squirrel fighting over the birdseed in the hanging feeder outside the kitchen. I began to wait, in the late afternoon, for the sky to get pale and the sun to set. Jason took to sleeping late and reading magazines and watching the evening news. When he went back to the law firm where he worked in New York, I stayed on. Wyatt visited. Jason called and said that he couldn't come up for a couple of weekends because he had so much paperwork. The next weekend, Corky and my brother drove up, and just before they left she took me by the arm in the driveway and walked me around to the back of their car. "I'd say that if you want to keep Jason you ought to get back to the city," she said. But by then I wanted to believe what Jason said he believed when he bought the house: that New York City was a battle, that it was important to escape to a place where you didn't always have to be on guard, that it was important to remember that it was a green world. Late in November, when I did leave the house at last and took the train back to New York, I walked into our apartment and felt like a stranger. He was still at the office. I wandered around, a little surprised that my things were still there—a pair of my sandals under the chair in the bedroom where I always kicked them. Walking around the bedroom verified what I hadn't been able to admit in Garrison: that it really was over between us. Seeing my things there didn't make me feel at home; it made me realize that it had always been Jason's apartment. He had hung up the Audubon prints his parents had given us for Christmas; I'd never liked them—they were like prints on the walls of some country inn—and here they were, out in plain view. They were on the north wall, which he had always insisted be left empty because pictures would spoil the beauty of the bricks. When Jason came home from work, we made drinks and went up to the roof and talked. It was clear that we wouldn't stay together, but he seemed to take it as a foregone conclusion. When I walked over to where he stood by the railing, it surprised me to see that he had tears in his eyes.

"Why be upset?" I said. "It's not your fault. We both feel the same way."

"When are you going to stop taking everything so casually?" he said. "As if you didn't matter. You're one of the nicest people I've ever known, and you made a really bad choice about me, way back. I feel guilty that I lived with you and let you assume that I loved you."

"You did love me," I said.

"Honey, I'm telling you the truth," he said sadly. "Don't forget what good Southern manners I have. You used to make fun of that. I *wanted* to love you. I acted as if I loved you."

When I left, I walked to the restaurant and sat at the bar, waiting for Wyatt to get off work. Jason didn't love me the time he said that on Saturday nights he never wanted to go out but only wanted to listen to Keith Jarrett's "The Mourning of a Star" and make love? Not when I read him Firbank's *The Flower Beneath the Foot* and he laughed until he had to cover his face and then wipe tears away with the palms of his hands? Not at Thanksgiving, when we were doing the dishes and he kept putting his arm around my waist and raising my soapy hand out of the water to waltz me out of the kitchen?

I saw Jason one more time after that night—when I went there on a Sunday afternoon in February, after I'd moved. I wanted us to be friends. I climbed to the fourth floor, certain, for the millionth time, that the ancient stairs were going to cave in. I sat in one of the canvas director's chairs and let him pour me a cup of coffee from the Melitta coffeepot. It was my pot, and I'd forgotten to pack it. Jason didn't offer to give it back. He told me about the Garrison house; he had put it up for sale, and a television producer and his wife had made an offer. They were negotiating. As we talked, my eye caught the bright-pink spine of the Firbank book on the topmost bookshelf across the room. Maybe he was harboring secret grudges. Maybe there were things I had taken home with me inadvertently. He got all the Keith Jarrett records. My down vest. The Firbank. Before I moved, he had helped me by separating my books and records from his and putting mine in cartons. I didn't unpack for weeks, so it took a while to realize how many were missing. If he'd done it deliberately, one other thing he did threw me off: at the bottom of one of the cartons of books he had put his gray corduroy shirt, which I had always pulled over my nightgown on cold winter mornings.

This weekend Corky told me, in the bedroom, that since Jason and I broke up I had begun to shut myself off from everyone—she was trying to be supportive, she said, and I wouldn't even talk about my anger or my sadness. I told her that I thought about it a lot—that when people weren't in love they had a lot of time to think; that's why there weren't very many surprises, or the surprises didn't have the same intensity they had when you were in love. What happened when I'd been waiting for her to come to my apartment the day before, for example: A bee flew into the bedroom, bumped against the skylight, buzzing. I dismissed my other options right away: hiding under the blanket all day; rolling the *Times* into a club and trying to kill it. I decided to do nothing, and when it flew lower, out of the skylight, it did the last thing I would have predicted—it flew in a straight line to the inch-wide crack in the screen, almost filled in by the lush vines that covered the building, and disappeared through the leaves. I waited for it to be perverse and fly back in, but it didn't. Then I got up and tore the leaves away from the screen and put masking tape over the crack where the screen had separated from the frame.

It's logical that everyone wants to be in love. Then, for a while, life isn't taken up with the tedium of thinking everything through, talking things through. It's nice to be able to notice small objects or small moments, to point them out and to have someone eager to pretend that there's more to them than it seems. Jason was very good at that—at convincing me that somehow, because we were together, what we saw took on an importance beyond itself. The last autumn we were together, we drove over to Cold Spring, late one afternoon. We drove to the far side of the railroad tracks, past the gazebo, to the edge of the paved area where cars park at the edge of the Hudson. How could he have tried to convince me, later, that he didn't love me? We were young lovers then, getting out of the car and throwing stale bread to the black ducks on the river. We sat on a bench, looking at the high cliffs across the water and tightening our hold on each other's waist as we imagined, I suppose, the voyage we'd have to take to get there, and the climb to the top. Or maybe we squeezed each other tighter because we were safe where we were: no boat, no possibility we'd swim, no reason to make such an effort anyway. It was October, and the wind was so strong that it nearly knocked us off the bench; tears came to my eyes long before Jason whispered to me to look: such strong wind—it made it seem that the water was being blown downstream, instead of flowing.

Coney Island

Drew is sitting at the kitchen table in his friend Chester's apartment in Arlington. It's a bright day, and the sun shining through the kitchen curtains, patterned with chickens, gives the chickens an advantage they don't have in real life; backlit, they're luminous. Beautiful.

Drew has been at Chester's for a couple of hours. The light is sharp now, in late afternoon. Between them, on the table, the bottle of Jack Daniel's is half empty. Chester pours another half inch into his glass, wipes the bottle neck with his thumb, licks it. He twirls the cap back on the bottle, like people who replace the cork after they've poured a glass of wine. Chester likes wine; his wife, Holly, converted him, but he knows better than to offer wine to Drew. Holly is in the hospital now, and will be there overnight; his tests for infertility were negative, and now the doctors are doing some kind of minor exploratory surgery on her. Maybe he would have gotten loaded today even if Drew hadn't shown up.

Drew is tapping the salt and pepper shakers together. The shakers are in the shape of penguins. What a sense of humor his friends Ches and Holly have! One penguin looks like a penguin, and the other has on a vest and top hat. Probably they were manufactured as jokes.

Chester's radio needs new batteries. He holds it in his right hand and shakes it with the motion he'd use to shake a cocktail shaker. Earlier, he thought about shaking up some Manhattans, but Drew said he preferred his bourbon straight.

Today, Drew drove across the mountains from Waynesboro to come to his nephew's christening in Arlington. The party afterward was at his mother's. Before the party he had pruned some bushes, fixed the basement door so it wouldn't stick. Afterward, when everyone had gone and his mother was in the bathroom, he used the phone and called his old girlfriend, Charlotte. That was unexpected, even to Drew. The month before, Charlotte married a man who managed a trendy hardware store in some mall outside of Arlington. Drew's mother cut the wedding announcement out of the paper and sent it to him at work, with "Personal" written on the envelope. Now when he has this affair with Charlotte, his secretary will know. What else would a secretary think about a boss getting a letter marked "Personal"?

It's less than an hour until Drew will go to meet Charlotte for a drink. Charlotte Coole, now Charlotte Raybill. Charlotte Coole Raybill, for all Drew knows. Chester has agreed to go along, so that if they're seen people may at least assume it's just some friends having a drink for old times' sake. Everybody knows everybody else's business. A cousin of Drew's, Howard, had a long affair with a married woman when he lived in New York. It lasted four years. They always met in Grand Central. For years, people hurried around them. Children were tugged past. Religious fanatics held out pamphlets. It was so likely that they'd see somebody one of them knew that of course they never did, and, to their knowledge, nobody ever saw them. They drank at Windows on the World. Who would ever find them there? Howard had a way of telling the story for laughs—the two of them holding each other beside the gate of the Mount Kisco local, kissing until their mouths felt burned, and then, downtown, sitting beside the floor-to-ceiling windows that overlooked Ellis Island, the Statue of Liberty. When Drew was a little boy, he went to New York with his family. They climbed up the statue, and for years he still believed what his father told him—that he'd climbed into the thumb. Howard's lover divorced her husband but married someone else. Howard got bitter and took it out on everybody. Once, he told Drew and Chester that they were nowhere, that they'd never examined anything for a moment in their lives. What did Howard know, Drew thinks. Howard used to look out high windows and he ended up in another skyscraper, in a shrink's office, with the blinds closed.

Drew says, "Charlotte's elbows were pointy, like a hard lemon. I used to hold on to her elbows when I made love to her. What a thing to be sitting here remembering."

"Drew, she's meeting you for a drink," Chester says sadly. "She's not going to leave her husband."

Chester taps the radio lightly on the table, the way he'd tap a cigarette out of a pack. Drew and Chester don't smoke. They haven't smoked since college. Drew met Charlotte and fell in love with her when he was a sophomore in college. "She's a *kid*," Howard had said to him back then, in one of those late-night fraternity-house rap sessions. Howard always took a fatherly tone, although he was only two years ahead of them. "Let's call Howard," Drew says now. "Ask him what he thinks about Holly." Howard is a surgeon in Seattle. They track him down sometimes at the hospital, or through his answering service, late at night. A couple of times, drunk, they disguised their voices and gave garbled panicky accounts of what they thought Howard would recognize as a heart attack or a ruptured appendix.

"I met the doctor Holly's been going to," Chester says. He points at the kitchen ceiling. "If *that* God Almighty and her God Almighty gynecologist think there's no reason why she can't have a baby, I'm just going to wait this one out."

"I just thought we might call him," Drew says. He takes off his shoes.

"No point calling about this," Chester says. Chester pours himself another drink. He rubs his hair back off his forehead, and that feels good. He does it again, then once again.

"Call the hospital and see how she made out," Drew says.

"I'm her husband and you think I wasn't *there*? I saw her. They wheeled her out and she said that she didn't care if she never had a kid—that she couldn't stand to feel like ice. That was the, you know . . . anesthetic. I held her feet in my hands for an hour. She was asleep and the nurse told me to go home. In the morning, when Dr. High and Mighty shows up, I guess we'll know something. How come you're so full of advice?"

"I didn't give any advice. I said to call her," Drew says.

Drew holds the bottle against his forehead for a second, then puts it back on the table. "I'm hungry," he says. "I ought to do everything before I see Charlotte, shouldn't I? Eat so there'll be time to talk. Drink and get sober. Do it all beforehand."

"How come you decided to call Charlotte today?" Chester says.

"My nephew—"

"I mean why call *Charlotte*? Why call her?"

This time, Drew fiddles with the radio, and a station comes in, faintly. They both listen, surprised. It's still only October, and the man is talking about the number of shopping days left until Christmas. Drew moves the dial and loses the station. He can't get it back. He shoves the radio across the table. A penguin tips over. It rests there, with its pointed face on the radio.

"I'll have another drink and stand her up," Drew says.

"Oh, I can do it for you," Chester says, and sets the penguin upright.

"Aren't you a million laughs," Drew says. "*Charlotte*—not the penguin. Charlotte, Charlotte—Charlotte who isn't going to leave her husband. Does that get her name into the conversation enough?"

"I don't want to go with you," Chester says. "I don't see the point of it."

He rubs his hands across his forehead again. He cups one hand over his eyes and doesn't say anything else.

Drew puts his hand over his glass. The gesture of a person refusing a refill, but no one's offering. He looks at his hands.

Chester reaches in his shirt pocket. If the missing laundry receipt isn't there or in his wallet, where is it? It has to be somewhere, in some pocket. He puts his index finger in the neck of the bottle. He wiggles it. There is a little pile of salt where the penguin tipped over. Chester pushes the salt into a line, pretends to be holding a straw in his fingers, touches the imaginary straw to the inch of salt, closes off one nostril, inhales with the other as he moves the straw up the line. He smiles more widely.

"Be glad you don't have that problem," Drew says.

"I am," Chester says. "I tell you, I'm glad I don't even remember being gassed when I had my tonsils out when I was a kid. Holly was so cold and sleepy. But not nice sleep—more like she'd been hit."

"She's O.K.," Drew says.

"How do you know?" Chester says. Then he's surprised by how harsh his voice sounds. He smiles. "Sneaking around to see her, the way you make arrangements to see Charlotte?" he says.

"You've got to be kidding," Drew says. "What a sick thing to say."

"I was kidding."

"And no matter what I said now, I couldn't win, could I? If I made out like I'd be crazy to be interested in Holly, you'd be insulted, right?"

"I don't want to talk about this," Chester says. "You go see Charlotte. I'll sit here and have a drink. What do you want me for?"

"I told her you were coming," Drew says. He takes a sip of his drink. "I was thinking about that time we went to Coney Island," he says.

"You told me," Chester says. "You mean years ago, right?"

"I told you about shooting the rifle?"

"Coney Island," Chester sighs. "Have some dogs at Nathan's, ride that Cyclone or whatever it's called, pop a few shots and win your girl a prize . . ."

"I told you?"

"Go ahead and tell me," Chester says.

Chester pours two drinks. After Drew's drink is poured, Drew puts his hand over the glass again.

"You've got about five minutes to tell me, by the way, unless you're really going to stand her up," Chester says.

"Maybe she'll stand *me* up."

"She won't stand you up."

"O.K.," Drew says. "Charlotte and I went to Coney Island. Got on those rides that tilt you every which way, and what do you call that thing with the glass sides that goes up the pole so you can look out—"

"I've never been to Coney Island," Chester says.

"I was showing her my style," Drew says. "The best part was later. This guy in the shooting gallery clips the cardboard card with the star on it to the string, sends it down to the end of the line, and I start blasting. Did it three or four times, and there was always some tiny part of the blue left. The pinpoint of the tip of one triangle. The middle of the target was this blue star. I was such a great shot that I was trying to win by shooting out the star, and the guy finally said to me, "Man, you're trying to blast that star away. What you do is shoot *around* it, and the star falls out." Drew looks at Chester through the circle of his thumb and first finger, drops his hand to the table. "What you're supposed to do is go around it, like slipping a knife around a cake pan to get the cake out." Drew takes a sip of his drink. He says, "My father never taught me anything."

Chester gets up, drinks the last of his bourbon, puts the glass in the sink. He looks around his kitchen as if it were unfamiliar. At one time, it was. Holly had it painted pastel green while he was at work. Now it's pearl-colored. Her skin was the color of the kitchen walls when they wheeled her out of the recovery room. He put his hands on her feet, for some reason, before she was even able to speak and tell him that she was cold. Sometimes in the winter when they're in bed, he reaches down and gets her feet and tucks them under his legs. Drew met Holly before he did, fifteen years ago. He went out with her once, and he didn't even kiss her. Now, when he comes to dinner every month or so, he kisses her forehead when he comes and when he goes. "I'm persuading her," Drew sometimes says—or something like that—when he leaves. "Fifteen years, and I'm still giving her every opportunity." Holly always blushes. She likes Drew. She thinks that he drinks too much but that nobody's perfect. Holly's way of thinking about things has started to creep into Chester's speech. A minute ago, wasn't he talking about God Almighty? Holly's the one who seriously believes in God Almighty.

Drew stands beside Chester at the kitchen sink and splashes water on his face. He's tan and he looks good. Hair a little shaggy. There's some white in his sideburns. He wipes his face on the dish towel and swirls water in his mouth, spits it out. He pours a glass of water and drinks a few sips. The five minutes were up ten minutes ago. They go out to the hall and get the keys off the table. They're on a Jaguar key chain. Chester's car is a '68 Pontiac.

"Who's driving the Indian?" Chester says.

Drew reaches for the keys. In the elevator, he sees coronas around the lighted buttons with the floor numbers on them and tosses the keys back to

Chester. Chester almost misses them because his mind is elsewhere. He has to remember to wash the glasses; he promised Holly he'd fix the leaking faucet. He'll have one drink at the bar, say hello to Charlotte, and do some work around the apartment later. The elevator is going frustratingly slow. If they can have a child and if it's a girl, Holly wants to name it for a flower: Rose or Lily or Margy—is that what she thought up? Short for Marigold.

Drew is thinking about what he can say to Charlotte. They were together for two years. There was a world between them. How do people make small talk when they've shared a world? And if you say something real, it always seems too sudden. There are a lot of things he'd like to know, questions he could probably shoot out like gunfire. She really loved him, and she married somebody else? She got tired of trying to convince him that she loved him? She read in some magazine that people who've had an unhappy childhood, the way he did, stay screwed up? He remembers his father: instead of walking him through museums and taking trips to see statues and to eat in dim taverns with pewter plates, places that had been standing since the nineteenth century, he could have done something practical, like teach him to shoot. Just put your arms outside the kid's, move his fingers where they should go, line up the rifle and show him how to sight, tell him how to keep the gun steady, if that isn't already obvious.

Drew slides into the car, bangs his knee on the side of the door as he pulls it shut. In another second, Chester has opened the driver's door and gotten in. But he doesn't start the car.

"You know, friendship's really what it's all about, isn't it?" Chester says, clamping his hand on Drew's shoulder.

Drew looks over at him, and Chester looks sad. Drew wonders if Chester is worried about Holly. Or is he just drunk? But that has to wait for a second. What Drew has just realized is that what felt like panic all day is really excitement. A drink with Charlotte—after all this time, he's seeing her again. What he wants to say to Chester is so difficult that he can't bring himself to look him in the eye.

"Ches," Drew says, looking through the windshield, rubbing his hand over his mouth, then resting it on his chin. "Ches—have you ever been in love?"

Television

Billy called early in the week to tell me he'd found out that Friday was Atley's birthday. Atley had been Billy's lawyer first, and then Billy recommended him to me. He became my lawyer when I called Billy after my car fell into a hole in the car wash. Atley gave me a free five minutes in his office so that I could understand that small claims court would be best. Billy had the idea that we should take Atley to lunch on his birthday. I said to him, "What are we going to do with Atley at lunch?" and he said that we'd think of something. I was all for getting some out-of-work ballerina to run into the restaurant with Mylar balloons, but Billy said no, we'd just think of something. He picked the restaurant, and when Friday came we were still thinking when the three of us met there and sat down, and because we were all a little uptight the first thing we thought of, of course, was having some drinks. Then Atley got to telling the story about his cousin who'd won a goldfish in a brandy snifter; he got so attached to the fish that he went out and got it an aquarium, but then he decided that the fish didn't look happy in the aquarium. Atley told his cousin that the brandy glass had magnified the fish and that's what made it look happy, but the cousin wouldn't believe it, so the cousin had a couple of drinks that night and decided to lower the brandy glass into the aquarium. He dug around in the pebbles and then piled them up around the base of the glass to anchor it, and the fish eventually started swimming around and around outside the top of the submerged glass in the same contented way, Atley said, that people in a hot tub sit there and hold their hands next to where the jets of water rush in.

The waiter came and told us the specials, and Billy and I both started smiling and looking away, because we knew that it was Atley's birthday and we were going to have to do something pretty soon. If we'd known the fish story beforehand, we could have gotten a fish as a gag present. The waiter probably thought we were laughing at him and hated us for it; he had to stand there and say "Côtelette Plus Ça Change" or whatever the specialty was, when actually he wanted to be John Travolta in *Saturday Night Fever*. He had the pelvis for it.

Billy said, when he was eating his shrimp, "My parents had a New Year's Eve party the last time I visited them, and some woman got ripped and took my father's shoe and sock off and painted his toenails." At this point I cracked up, and the waiter, who was removing my plate, looked at me as if I was dispensable. "That's not it, that's not the punch line!" Billy said. Atley held his hand up in cop-stopping-traffic style, and Billy made a fist and hit it. Then he said, "The punch line is, a week later my father was reading the paper at breakfast and my mother said, 'What if I get some nail-polish remover and fix your toes?' and my father said, 'Don't do it.' She was *scared* to do it!"

"I had such a happy childhood," I said. "We always rented a beach house during the summer, and my mother and father had one of each of our baby shoes bronzed—my sister's and mine—and my parents danced in the living room a lot. My father said the only way he'd have a TV was if he could think of it as a giant radio, so when they finally bought one he'd be watching and my mother would come into the room and he'd get up and take her in his arms and start humming and dancing. They'd dance while Kate Smith talked or whatever, or while Gale Storm made her *My Little Margie* noise."

Atley squinted and leaned against the table. "Come on, come on, come on—what do two people who have money do all day?" he whispered. That was when Billy kissed me, which made it look as if what we did was make love all day, which couldn't have been farther from the truth. In the back of my mind I thought that maybe it was part of some act Billy was putting on because he'd already figured out what to do about the birthday. The waiter was opening a bottle of champagne, which I guess Billy had ordered. I knew very few facts about Billy's ex. One was that she really liked champagne. Another was that she had been in Alateen. Her father had been a big drunk. He'd thrown her mother out a window once. She'd gone back to him but not until she'd taken him to court.

"I'll tell you something," Atley said. "I shocked the hell out of one of our summer interns. I took him aside in the office and I told him, 'You know what lawyers are? Barnacles on a log. The legal system is like one big, heavy log floating downstream, and there's nothing you can do about it. Remember every time one of those judges lifts a gavel that it's just a log with a handle.'"

The cork took off right across the restaurant. We all looked. It landed near the pastry cart. The waiter said, "It flew through my fingers," and looked at his hand, as surprised as if he'd been casually counting his fingers and found that he had seven of them. We were all sorry for the waiter because he was so shocked. He stared at his hand so long that we looked away. Billy kissed me again. I thought it might be a gesture to break the silence.

The waiter poured champagne into Atley's glass first; he did it quickly and his hand was shaking so much that the foam started to rise fast. Atley held up his hand to indicate that he should stop pouring. Billy punched Atley's hand again.

"You son of a gun," Billy said. "Do you think we don't know it's your birthday? Did you think we didn't know that?"

Atley turned a little red. "How did you know that?" he said.

Billy raised his glass and we all raised ours and clinked them, above the pepper mill.

Atley was quite red.

"Son of a gun," Billy said. I smiled, too. The waiter looked and saw that we had drained our glasses, and looked surprised again. He quickly came back to pour champagne, but Billy had beaten him to it. In a few minutes, the waiter came back and put three brandy snifters with a little ripple of brandy in them on the table. We must have looked perplexed, and the waiter certainly did. "From the gentleman across the room," the waiter said. We turned around. Billy and I didn't recognize anybody, but some man was grinning like mad. He lifted his lobster off his plate and pointed it at Atley. Atley smiled and mouthed, "Thank you."

"One of the best cytologists in the world," Atley said. "A client."

When I looked away, the man was still holding his lobster and moving it so that it looked as if it were swimming through air.

"The gentleman told me to bring the brandy now," the waiter said, and went away.

"Do you think it would be crude to tell him we're going to leave him a big tip?" Billy said.

"Are we?" I said.

"Oh, I'll leave the tip. I'll leave the tip," Atley said.

The waiter, who seemed always to be around our table, heard the word "tip" and looked surprised again. Billy picked up on this and smiled at him. "We're not going anywhere," he said.

It was surprising how fast we ate, though, and in a little while, since none of us wanted coffee, the waiter was back with the bill. It was in one of those folders—a leather book, with the restaurant's initials embossed on the front. It reminded me of my Aunt Jean's trivet collection, and I said so. Aunt Jean knew somebody who would cast trivets for her, to her specifications. She had an initialed trivet. She had a Rolls-Royce trivet—those classy intertwined *Rs*. This had us laughing. I was the only one who hadn't touched the brandy. When Billy put his credit card in a slot in the book, Atley said, "Thank you." I did too, and Billy put his hand over mine and kissed me again. He'd kissed me so many times that by now I was a little embarrassed, so to cover up for that I touched my forehead to his after the kiss so that it would seem like a routine of ours to Atley. It was either that or say, "What are you doing?"

Atley wanted to have his chauffeur drop us, but out on the street Billy took my hand and said that we wanted to walk. "This nice weather's not going to hold up," he said. Atley and I realized at the same moment that two young girls were in the back of the limousine.

"Who are they?" Atley said to the chauffeur.

The chauffeur was holding the door open and we could see that the girls were sitting as far back in the seat as they could, like people backed up against a wall who are hoping not to be hurt.

"What could I do?" the chauffeur said. "They were lit. They hopped in. I was just trying to chase them out."

"Lit?" Atley said.

"Tipsy," the chauffeur said.

"Why don't you proceed to get them out?" Atley said.

"Come on, girls," the chauffeur said. "You get out, now. You heard what he said."

One got out and the other one, who didn't have on as many clothes, took longer and made eye contact with the chauffeur.

"There you go," the chauffeur said, extending his elbow, but she ignored it and climbed out by herself. Both of them looked back over their shoulders as they walked away.

"Why do I put up with this?" Atley said to the chauffeur. His face was red again. I didn't want Atley to be upset and his birthday lunch to be spoiled, so I pecked him on the cheek and smiled. It is certainly true that if women ran the country they would never send their sons to war. Atley hesitated a minute, kissed me back, then smiled. Billy kissed me, and for a second I was confused, thinking he might have intended to send me off with Atley. Then he and Atley shook hands and we both said, "Happy birthday," and Atley bent over and got into the back of the limousine. When the chauffeur closed the door, you couldn't see that it was Atley in there, because the glass was tinted. As the chauffeur was getting into the front seat, the back door opened and Atley leaned forward.

"I can tell you one thing. I was surprised that somebody remembered my birthday," he said. "You know what I was just thinking apropos of your story about your mother and father dancing to the television? I was thinking that sometimes you go along in the same way so long that you forget how one little interlude of something different can change everything." He was grinning at Billy. "She's too young to remember those radio shows," he said. "*Life of Riley* and things like that." He looked at me. "When they wanted to let you know that time was passing, there'd be a few bars of music, and then they'd be talking about something else." Atley's foot, in a black sock and a shiny black oxford, was dangling out the door. The chauffeur pulled his door shut. Then Atley closed his door too, and the limo drove away. Before we had turned to leave, though, the car stopped and backed up to us again. Atley rolled down his window. He stuck his head out. "'Oh, Mr. Atley,'" he said in falsetto, "'wherever are you going?'" He whistled a few notes. Then, in a booming, gruff voice, he said, "'Why, Atley, back at work after your *surprise birthday lunch*?'" He rolled up the window. The chauffeur drove away.

Billy thought this was nice weather? It was March in New York, and there hadn't been any sun for three days. The wind was blowing so hard that an end of my scarf flew up over my face. Billy put his arm around my waist and we watched the limousine make it through a yellow light and swerve to avoid a car that had suddenly stopped to back into a parking space.

"Billy," I said, "why did you keep kissing me all through lunch?"

"We've known each other quite a while," he said, "and I realized today that I'd fallen in love with you."

This surprised me so much that as well as moving away from him I also went back in my mind to the safety and security of childhood. "You make a trade," my mother had said to me once. "You give up to get. I want a TV? Why, then, I let him make me dance every time I come into the room. I'll bet you think women are always fine dancers and men always try to avoid dancing? Your father would go out dancing every night of the week if he could." As Billy and I walked down the street, I suddenly thought how strange it was that we'd never gone dancing.

My mother had said all that to me in the living room, when Ricky was at his wit's end with Lucy on television and my father was at work. I sympathized with her at once. I liked being with my mother and thinking about something serious that I hadn't thought about before. But when I was alone—or maybe this only happened as I got older—puzzling things out held no fascination for me. The rug in the room where my mother and I talked was patterned with pink cabbage-size roses. Years later, I'd have nightmares that a huge trellis had collapsed and disappeared and I'd suddenly found the roses, two-dimensional, on the ground.

Lofty

_____

Kate could think of nothing but how she had cheated when she and Philip lived in this house. She had put little daubs of glue on the back of peeling wallpaper and pushed it back into place; she had stuffed the big aqua urns at the back door with rags—they were deep enough to hold twenty pounds of earth—and then poured a foot of soil on top. The pansies, pounded deep into the urns by summer rain, had shot up and cascaded over the rims anyway.

The house belonged to Philip's Great-Aunt Beatrice, and she had come in person every month for the rent check, but all Kate's worrying about their tenancy had been for nothing. The woman rarely looked closely at anything; in fact, in winter she often kept her car running in the driveway while she made the call, and wouldn't even come inside for coffee. In the summer she stayed a few minutes to cut roses or peonies to take back to the city. She was a tall old lady, who wore flowered dresses, and by the time she headed for her ancient Cadillac she herself often looked like a gigantic flower in motion, refracted through a kaleidoscope.

In retrospect, Kate realized that the house must have looked perfectly presentable. When she and Philip first moved in and were in love with each other, they were in love with the place, and when they were no longer in love the house seemed to sink in sympathy. The sagging front step made her sad; a shutter fell from the second story one night, frightening them into each other's arms.

When the two of them decided to part, they agreed that it was silly not to stay on until the lease was up at the end of summer. Philip's young daughter was visiting just then, and she was having a wonderful time. The house was three stories high—there was certainly room enough to avoid each other. He was being transferred to Germany by his firm in September. Kate planned to move to New York, and this way she could take her time looking for a place. Wadding newspaper to stuff into the urns for another summer, she had been shocked at how tightly she crushed it—as if by directing her energy into her hands she could fight back tears.

Today, ten years later, Kate was back at the house. Philip's daughter, Monica, was eighteen now, and a friend of Monica's was renting the house. Today was Monica's engagement party. Kate sat in a lawn chair. The lawn was nicely mowed. The ugly urns were gone, and a fuchsia plant hung from the lamppost beside the back door. A fuzz of green spread over a part of the lawn plot that had been newly plowed for a garden. The big maple tree that encroached on the kitchen had grown huge; she wondered if any light could penetrate that room now.

She knew that the spike in the maple tree would still be there. It had been there, mysteriously in place, when they first moved in. She walked up to the tree and put her hand on it. It was rusted, but still the height to allow a person to get a foot up, so that he could pull himself up into the nearest overhead branches.

Before the party, Philip had sent Monica a note that Monica showed to Kate with a sneer. He said that he was not going to attend the celebration of a mistake; she was too young to marry, and he would have nothing to do with the event. Kate thought that his not being there had less to do with his daughter and more to do with Kate and him. Either he still loved her or else he hated her. She closed her hand around the spike in the tree.

"Climb up so I can look up your skirt," her husband said.

And then he was surprised when she did.

Ignoring the finger she'd scraped on the bark pulling herself up, she stood on the first high branch and reached behind to tug her skirt free, laughing and letting the skirt drift away from her body. She went one branch higher, carefully, and leaned out to look down. She turned and leaned against a higher branch, facing him, and raised her skirt.

"O.K.," he said, laughing, too. "Be careful."

She realized that she had never looked down on him before—not out of a window, not in any situation she could think of. She was twelve or fifteen feet off the ground. She went one branch higher. She looked down again and saw him move closer to the tree, as quickly as a magnet. He was smaller.

"Birds used to peck birdseed from a seeded bell that dangled from there," she said, pointing to the branch her husband could almost touch. "This tree used to be filled with birds in the morning. They were so loud that you could hear them over the bacon sputtering."

"Come down," he said.

She felt a little frightened when she saw how small his raised hand was. Her body felt light, and she held on tighter.

"Sweetheart," he said.

A young man in a white jacket was coming toward her husband, carrying two drinks. "Whoa, up there!" he called. She smiled down. In a second, a little girl began to run toward the man. She was about two years old, and not steady on her feet where the lawn began to slope and the tree's roots pushed out of the ground. The man quickly handed the drinks to her husband and turned to swoop up the child as she stumbled. Kate, braced for the child's cry, exhaled when nothing happened.

"There used to be a tree house," Kate said. "We hung paper lanterns from it when we had a party."

"I know," her husband said. He was still reaching up, a drink in each hand. The man standing with him frowned. He reclaimed his drink and began to edge away, talking to the little girl. Her husband put his drink on the grass.

"Up in the tree!" the little girl squealed. She turned to look over her shoulder.

"That's right," the man said. "Somebody's up in the tree."

The glass at her husband's feet had tipped over.

"We didn't," Kate said. "I made it up."

He said, "Shall I come up and get you?" He touched his hand to the spike. Or else she thought he did; she couldn't lean far enough forward to see.

"You're so nice to me," she said.

He moved back and stretched up his arms.

She had never been daring when she was young, and she wanted to stand her ground now. It made her giddy to realize how odd a thought that was— the contradiction between "standing your ground" and being balanced in a tree. There could have been a tree house. And who else but she and Philip would have lived in such a place and not had lawn parties? She didn't think Monica was wrong about getting married; her fiancé was charming and silly and energetic. Her own husband was very charming—demonstrative only in private, surprised by her pranks to such an extent that she often thought he subtly encouraged her to act up because he admired people who could do such things. He was modest. It wasn't like him to say, "Climb up so I can look up your skirt."

"I'll fly," she said.

He dropped his hands to his sides. "A walk in the woods," he said.

At the back of the lawn, where the lawn tapered into the woods, the man and his daughter were crouched, looking at something in the grass. Kate could hear piano music coming from inside the house.

"A drive," her husband said. "We'll walk out on the celebration for a few minutes."

She shook her head no. Then her ribs felt like a tourniquet, and she decided to start down before she was in more pain. She was embarrassed that there was nothing courageous about her careful, gingerly descent. She felt the sweat above her lip and noticed, for the first time, a streak of blood along the side of her hand—the cut on her finger that had now stopped bleeding. She put her finger to her lips, and the salty taste brought tears to her eyes. She put her feet on the ground and faced her husband, then made the dramatic gesture of raising her arms and fanning them open for a second, as wide as a trellis, before they closed around him.

One Day

Henry was twenty, and for almost fifteen years of his life he had understood that he didn't like his older brother, Gerald. His father, Carl, didn't care that Henry didn't get along with Gerald, but his mother, who thought the boys would grow into affection for each other, now asked more often what was wrong. Whenever Henry admitted that he disliked Gerald, his mother said, "Life is too short not to love your brother." On this particular visit, Henry had told her that he didn't actually dislike Gerald—he was indifferent. "This is no time to be indifferent," she had said. Gerald was in the process of getting divorced. He had been married to a woman named Cora. Probably the nicest thing Henry could remember about her was that she had once praised him excessively and convincingly for changing a tire. The most embarrassing thing happened the time he shared a canoe with her on a water ride at an amusement park; thrown against her as the canoe turned and tilted, he had twice reached out reflexively to steady himself and made the mistake of grabbing her breast instead of her arm.

Henry and Gerald had just arrived, separately, at their parents' house in Wilton. Gerald was already stretched out on a chaise, with his shirt off, drinking a gin-and-tonic, getting a tan. After Henry had done a little work around the yard, he reverted, as always, to being childish: he was drinking Coke and putting together a jigsaw puzzle.

It was Carl's birthday. Henry had given his father a pair of swimming trunks patterned with a mishmash of hibiscus, hummingbirds, and something that looked like brown bananas. His mother had bought his father more weights for his barbell. Earlier in the day, two boxes had been delivered from the store. After the delivery boy lowered them to the kitchen floor, he had shaken his hands and then examined his palms. "God help me," he said.

"Henry, darling," his mother, Verna, said now. She had come out of the house and stood in front of the picnic table, where he was assembling a puzzle that would be a pizza all the way when he finished. She put a mug of iced tea next to him on the table. There were no glasses in the house—only mugs. He had never asked why. When she said "Henry, darling," it meant that she was announcing her presence in case he wanted to talk. He didn't. He pushed two pieces together. An anchovy overlapped a piece of green pepper.

"Thank you for trimming the hedge," she said.

"You're welcome," he said.

"I think that Gerald is more upset about the divorce than he lets on. A friend of Daddy's called Gerald this morning to play golf, and he wouldn't."

Henry nodded. More to get away from Verna than to commiserate with his brother, he got up and walked across the lawn to where Gerald lay stretched out on the chaise, eyes closed. Gerald was only twenty-seven, but he looked older. There was a little roll of fat around the belt line of his khaki jeans. Henry knew that Gerald knew that he was standing there. Gerald didn't open his eyes. An ant was running around the rim of Gerald's gin-and-tonic. Henry brushed it in.

"Feel like going down to the driving range and hitting a couple of buckets?" Henry said.

"You know what I feel like?" Gerald said. "I feel like going to bed with somebody who's beautiful and eighteen years old and who doesn't ask a million questions."

"You care if it's a girl?" Henry said.

"Ha, ha," Gerald said.

"What questions?" Henry said.

"About everything I ever did or thought before I got into bed with her, and what I'm going to act like and what I'm going to think the minute I stand up."

Henry sat on the grass, pulled a blade, and chewed on the end. Then he tossed it away and walked down the sloping lawn to where his mother stood, shaking insecticide onto rose leaves.

"He's pretty sad," Henry said. "But he's been thinking about things. He says he's going to church on Sunday."

"Church?" his mother said.

The sun shone through the green visor his mother was wearing. Her face was yellow.

Henry went back onto the porch to get out of the sun. Through the front screen he saw the newly cut grass, the level privet hedge that bordered the front lawn. In front of the walk, the street was empty. He tried to imagine Sally's rusty beige Ford parked there.

No one in the family approved of Sally, the woman he loved. She had been his graphic-design teacher. She was thirty-three, divorced, and had an eight-year-old daughter named Laurel, who wasn't at all charming; the girl wore thick glasses and usually stood behind, or right alongside, her mother. The child's skin, in full sun, was as pale as sand. She often had rashes and mosquito bites that she scratched until they got scabs. Henry and Sally had become lovers a few months ago, and recently he had been staying with her at the loft she was subletting in SoHo. This week, she and Laurel had gone to visit her sister in Providence, but they were coming back for Carl's birthday party, and in the morning the three of them would drive back to New York.

Henry looked out the other side of the porch. Gerald had gotten up and, with his gin-and-tonic mug in one hand, was fanning water out of a garden hose onto the roses.

"*No!*" Verna screamed, coming around the side of the house from the garden with a basket of freshly picked vegetables in one hand.

"Didn't you see the white powder? For the *aphids*, Gerald. Don't—"

Gerald turned the hose on Verna.

"Gerald!" she shrieked.

"How come you call him Henry darling and I'm just Gerald?" he said. "Showing preference damages children."

"You're insane," Verna said, running toward the porch, cucumbers and lettuce spilling out of the basket.

Gerald was laughing loudly. Verna ran onto the porch, dropped the basket, and stomped into the kitchen. Henry considered going inside to find out if she still wanted him to love his brother. Gerald trained the hose on one chaise after another. Then he aimed it at the roses again, no longer laughing. His face had the rigidity of a soldier pointing a rifle. Henry watched until Gerald dropped the hose and headed for the spigot outside the porch to turn off the water.

"You're losing it, darling," Henry said.

Sally's daughter, Laurel, was too shy to stand up with the rest of the group for a birthday toast. She was half under the picnic table, petting a neighbor's cat.

"To me!" Carl said heartily, raising a thermos cap full of champagne.

Gerald had given him the thermos for his birthday. Carl was also wearing the swimming trunks, with knee-high black socks and black cordovans. "To the birthday boy at the end of his forty-ninth year, and"—he turned toward Sally—"to new friends." He raised the cup higher. "To the sailboat I'm buying," he said.

"What sailboat?" Verna said.

"A white one," he said.

"You're going to buy a *sailboat*?" Verna said.

"A white one," he said.

"Telephone!" Gerald said, running down the lawn toward the house.

"Why not a sailboat?" Carl said. "Business was very good this year, considering. No one asks me how business is. It's fine, thank you." He raised his cup. He had still not had a drink of champagne. Sally sipped her champagne. Henry's mug was empty. He walked over to the table, knocking the box top with the pieces of puzzle onto the lawn with his elbow as he took the bottle out of the cooler and poured. Champagne foamed out of his mug. He held it away from him, then licked his wrist.

"Excuse me," Sally whispered to Henry. "I'm going to the bathroom." She handed him her empty mug. Head down, she walked down the hill toward the house.

Carl, sitting on a chaise now, said, "I was really expecting a new sand wedge for my birthday."

Verna sat on the bench by the picnic table. "Perhaps when Gerald gets back we should have the cake," she said.

"I'll get the cake," Henry said, and walked toward the house. Laurel caught his eye and ran to his side when he opened the porch door. She was still holding the cat. It jumped out of her arms and ran under a bush. He wished she'd stayed with the others; he thought that Sally had gone to the bathroom because his family had made her uncomfortable, and he wanted to talk to her.

"Where's Mommy?" Laurel said.

"In the bathroom," he said, pointing.

"Anything. Anything, if only you'll have me back," Gerald was saying on the telephone. "Counseling—hell, I'd have electroshock therapy. Anything. *Anything.*"

Henry stood in the hallway, looking at his brother. Gerald looked at him and smiled. "Wrong number," he said, and hung up.

"Mommy, the cat likes it here," Laurel said, skipping to the bathroom door. "It didn't go home or anything."

The birthday cake was on the kitchen table, sitting on top of a paper doily on top of a footed cake stand—a tall chocolate cake, with "Happy Birthday" written in loopy white icing. A packet of candles and a book of matches lay beside it, ready for the occasion. Henry tapped out some candles and began to press the little wicks upright, stiffening them between his thumb and forefinger.

"Mommy, that cat has a real short tail," Laurel said.

The telephone rang, and Henry picked it up.

"Gerald?" a woman said.

"No. This is Henry."

"Henry—it's Cora. Is Gerald there?"

"Did you just call?" he said.

"Yes."

"I think he's had a few drinks. Maybe you ought to call back later."

"I should have known better. I'm at the emergency room, waiting to have a broken ankle set. I fell off a damned stone wall. I called to see if he had that card with the insurance-policy number on it."

"Do you want me to go get him?" Henry said.

"No," she said. "I just remembered that even on the rare occasions when I can communicate with him it's never worth the price." She hung up.

Laurel walked on her heels through the kitchen, calling over her shoulder, "Mommy said I could play with the cat." Henry heard the door slam. He continued to push wicks upright. Then he arranged the candles in two concentric circles. Sally had been in the bathroom too long. He went to the bathroom door.

"Sally," he said.

"What?" she said.

"After we have the cake, let's leave, O.K.?"

"This is the way families turn out," she said.

"No, it isn't," he said.

"Rick got remarried this week. To that woman with the kid that we ran into on Sixth Avenue. Laurel hates the kid. She's going to have to spend July with them."

He put his fingertips to the door. "It's only June," he said.

Sally laughed.

"Sally," he said.

"I don't know how to act around your parents," she said. "I'm not doing anything right."

"You do more things right than anybody I can think of," he said.

She sniffled. She had been crying. "What if I was really going to the bathroom? It would be embarrassing, with you standing right up against the door."

"Nothing's changed between us," he said. "This is one day. My father's in a bad mood. My brother's nuts. I told you about my brother."

"I have to pee," she said. "Please get away from the door."

Laurel was sitting on a chair in the kitchen, facing the table and the cake. "I wish I could have that cat," she said.

Out the window Henry saw his father and brother wrestling. Verna was still on the bench, sipping champagne. The cat, standing by a tree, seemed to be watching what was going on. Henry saw Verna's face turn stony; she put her mug on the table and smacked her hands. The cat ran away, taking high leaps like a rabbit moving through tall grass. He picked up more candles and poked them into the inner circle of the cake.

"I'm not afraid of matches," Laurel said.

The birthday cake had gotten her attention. She swung her feet back and forth, eyes riveted on it. Her barrette had slipped; it was clamped below her ear, holding only a few strands of hair. Laurel picked up the book of matches. "Light one and give it to me," she said.

He struck a match and held it out to her. For a second, her fingers touched his. They were so thin that it didn't seem she could hold anything heavier than a match. He watched her, intent on seeing that she didn't burn her fingers—so intent that the whole ring was aflame and the match blown out before he realized the problem. The inner circle of candles was unlit, and now there was no way to light them. She knew it, too. "What should I do?" she said softly.

"Hurry up," he said, putting his hand on her back, tilting her forward. "Blow them out. Start again."

Laurel took a deep breath and blew out half the candles. She sucked in her breath and blew again. The others went out, and a little blue cloud rose above the cake. When the candles didn't flare up again—when he saw that this time they weren't those joke candles that somehow reignite themselves after a few seconds—he crouched and put his arm around Laurel. Outside, the light had almost disappeared. No one was coming toward the house yet, but things wouldn't stay the way they were much longer.

Heaven on a Summer Night

Will stood in the kitchen doorway. He seemed to Mrs. Camp to be a little tipsy. It was a hot night, but that alone wouldn't account for his shirt, which was not only rumpled but hanging outside his shorts. Pens, a pack of cigarettes, and what looked like the tip of a handkerchief protruded from the breast pocket. Will tapped his fingertips on the pens. Perhaps he was not tapping them nervously but touching them because they were there, the way Mrs. Camp's mother used to run her fingers over the rosary beads she always kept in her apron pocket. Will asked Mrs. Camp if she would cut the lemon pound cake she had baked for the morning. She thought that the best thing to do when a person had had too much to drink was to humor him, so she did. Everyone had little weaknesses, to be sure, but Will and his sister had grown up to be good people. She had known them since they were toddlers, back when she had first come to work for the Wildes here in Charlottesville. Will was her favorite, then and now, although Kate probably loved her more. Will was nineteen now, and Kate twenty. On the wall, above the sink, was a framed poem that Kate had written and illustrated when she was in the fifth grade:

> *Like is a cookie*
> *Love is a cake*
>
> *Like is a puddle*
> *Love is a lake*

Years later, Will told her that Kate hadn't made up the poem at all. It was something she had learned in school.

Mrs. Camp turned toward Will, who was sitting at the table. "When does school start?" she said.

"There's a fly!" he said, dropping the slice of cake back onto his plate.

"What?" Mrs. Camp said. She had been at the sink, rinsing glasses before loading them into the dishwasher. She left the water running. The steam rose and thinned out as it floated toward the ceiling. "It's a raisin," she said. "You got me all worried about a raisin."

He plucked some more raisins out of the pound cake and then took another bite.

"If you don't want to talk about school, that's one thing, but that doesn't mean you should holler out that there's a fly in the food," Mrs. Camp said.

A year ago, Will had almost flunked out of college, in his sophomore year. His father had talked to the dean by long distance, and Will was allowed to continue. Now, in the summer, Mr. Wilde had hired Will a tutor in mathematics. Mornings and early afternoons, when Will was not being tutored or doing math problems, he painted houses with his friend Anthony Scoresso. Scoreboard and Will were going to drive to Martha's Vineyard to paint a house there at the end of August. The house was unoccupied, and although she was a little hesitant about doing such a thing, Mrs. Camp was going to accept Will's invitation to go with the boys and stay in the house for the week they were painting it. Scoreboard loved her cooking. She had never been to the Vineyard.

Now that they were older, Will and Kate included Mrs. Camp in many things. They had always told her everything. That was the difference between being who she was and being a parent—they knew that they could tell her anything. She never met one of their friends without hearing what Will or Kate called the Truth. That handsome blond boy, Neal, who told the long story about hitchhiking to the West Coast, Will told her later, was such a great storyteller because he was on speed. The girl called Natasha who got the grant to study in Italy had actually been married *and* divorced when she was eighteen, and her parents never even knew it. Rita, whom Mrs. Camp had known since first grade, now slept with a man as old as her father, for money. It pleased Kate and Will when a worried look came over Mrs. Camp's face as she heard these stories. Years ago, when she told them once that she liked that old song by the Beatles, "Lucy in the Sky with Diamonds," Will announced gleefully that the Beatles were singing about a drug.

Kate's car pulled into the driveway as Mrs. Camp was rinsing the last of the dishes. Kate drove a little white Toyota that made a gentle sound, like rain, as the tires rolled over the gravel. Will got up and pulled open the screen door for his sister on his way to the liquor cabinet. He poured some gin into a glass and walked to the refrigerator and added tonic water but no ice. In this sort of situation, Mrs. Camp's mother would have advised keeping quiet and saying a prayer. Mrs. Camp's husband—he was off on a fishing trip on the Chesapeake somewhere—would never advise her to pray, of course. Lately, if she asked him for advice about almost anything, his reply was "Get off my back." She noticed that Will noticed that she was looking at him. He grinned at her and put down his drink so that he could tuck in his shirt. As he raised the shirt, she had a glimpse of his long, tan back and thought of the times she had held him naked as a baby—all the times she had bathed him, all the hours she had held the hose on him in the backyard. Nowadays, he and Scoreboard sometimes stopped by the house at lunchtime. With their sun-browned bodies flecked with paint, they sat at the table on the porch in their skimpy shorts, waiting for her to bring them lunch. They hardly wore any more clothes than Will had worn as a baby.

Kate came into the kitchen and dropped her canvas tote bag on the counter. She had been away to see her boyfriend. Mrs. Camp knew that men were always going to fascinate Kate, the way her tropical fish had fascinated her many summers earlier. Mrs. Camp felt that most men moved in slow motion, and that that was what attracted women. It hypnotized them. This was not the way men at work were. On the job, construction workers sat up straight and drove tractors over piles of dirt and banged through potholes big enough to sink a bicycle, but at home, where the women she knew most often saw their men, they spent their time stretched out in big chairs, or standing by barbecue grills, languidly turning a hamburger as the meat charred.

Kate had circles under her eyes. Her long brown hair was pulled back into a bun at the nape of her neck. She had spent the weekend, as she had every weekend this summer, with her boyfriend, Frank Crane, at his condominium at Ocean City. He was studying for the bar exam. Mrs. Camp asked Kate how his studying was going, but Kate simply shook her head impatiently. Will, at the refrigerator, found a lime and held it up for them to see, very pleased. He cut off a side, squeezed lime juice into his drink, then put the lime back in the refrigerator, cut side down, on top of the butter-box lid. He hated to wrap anything in wax paper: Mrs. Camp knew that.

"Frank did the strangest thing last night," Kate said, sitting down and slipping her feet out of her sandals. "Maybe it wasn't strange. Maybe I shouldn't say."

"That'll be the day," Will said.

"What happened?" Mrs. Camp said. She thought that Frank was too moody and self-absorbed, and she thought that this was another story that was going to prove her right. Kate looked sulky—or maybe just more tired than Mrs. Camp had noticed at first. Mrs. Camp took a bottle of soda water out of the refrigerator and put it on the table, along with the lime and a knife. She put two glasses on the table and sat down across from Kate. "Perrier?" she said. Kate and Will liked her to call everything by its proper name, unless they had given it a nickname themselves. Secretly, she thought of it as bubble water.

"I was in his bedroom last night, reading, with the sheet pulled up," Kate said. "His bathroom is across the hall from the bedroom. He went to take a shower, and when he came out of the bathroom I turned back the sheet on his side of the bed. He just stood there, in the doorway. We'd had a kind of fight about that friend of his, Zack. The three of us had gone out to dinner that night, and Zack kept giving the waitress a hard time about nothing. Sassing a waitress because a dab of ice cream was on the saucer when she brought it. Frank knew I was disgusted. Before he took his shower, he went into a big thing about how I wasn't responsible for his friends' actions, and said that if Zack had acted as bad as I said he did he'd only embarrassed himself."

"If Frank passes the bar exam this time around, you won't have anything to worry about," Will said. "He'll act nice again."

Kate poured a glass of Perrier. "I haven't told the story yet," she said.

"Oh," Will said.

"I thought everything between us was fine. When he stopped in the doorway, I put the magazine down and smiled. Then he said, 'Kate—will you do something for me?'" Kate looked at Mrs. Camp, then dropped her eyes. "We were going to bed, you know," she said. "I thought things would be better after a while." Kate looked up. Mrs. Camp nodded and looked down. "Anyway," Kate went on, "he looked so serious. He said, 'Will you do something for me?' and I said, 'Sure. What?' and he said, 'I just don't know. Can you think of something to cheer me up?'"

Will was sipping his drink, and he spilled a little when he started laughing. Kate frowned.

"You take everything so seriously," Will said. "He was being funny."

"No, he wasn't," Kate said softly.

"What did you do?" Mrs. Camp said.

"He came over to the bed and sat down, finally. I knew he felt awful about something. I thought he'd tell me what was the matter. When he didn't say anything, I hugged him. Then I told him a story. I can't imagine what possessed me. I told him about Daddy teaching me to drive. How he was afraid to be in the passenger seat with me at the wheel, so he pretended I needed practice getting into the garage. Remember how he stood in the driveway and made me pull in and pull out and pull in again? I never had any trouble getting into the garage in the first place." She took another sip of Perrier. "I don't know what made me tell him that," she said.

"He was kidding. You said something funny, too, and that was that," Will said.

Kate got up and put her glass in the sink. It was clear, when she spoke again, that she was talking only to Mrs. Camp. "Then I rubbed his shoulders," she said. "Actually, I only rubbed them for a minute, and then I rubbed the top of his head. He likes to have his head rubbed, but he gets embarrassed if I start out there."

Kate had gone upstairs to bed. *Serpico* was on television, and Mrs. Camp watched with Will for a while, then decided that it was time for her to go home. Here it was August 25th already, and if she started addressing Christmas cards tonight she would have a four-month jump on Christmas. She always bought cards the day after Christmas and put them away for the following year.

Mrs. Camp's car was a 1977 Volvo station wagon. Mr. and Mrs. Wilde had given it to her in May, for her birthday. She loved it. It was the newest car she had ever driven. It was dark, shiny green—a color only velvet could be, the color she imagined Robin Hood's jacket must have been. Mr. Wilde had told her that he was not leaving her anything when he died but that he wanted to be nice to her when he was above ground. A strange way to put it. Mrs. Wilde gave her a dozen pink Depression-glass wine goblets at the same time they gave her the car. There wasn't one nick in any of the rims; the glasses were all as smooth as sea-washed stones.

As she drove, Mrs. Camp wondered if Will had been serious when he said to Kate that Frank was joking. She was sure that Will slept with girls. (Will was not there to rephrase her thoughts. He always referred to young girls as women.) He must have understood that general anxiety or dread Frank had been feeling, and he must also have known that having sex wouldn't diminish it. It was also possible that Will was only trying to appear uninterested because Kate's frank talk embarrassed him. "Frank talk" was a pun. Those children had taught her so much. She still felt a little sorry that they had always had to go to stuffy schools that gave them too much homework. She even felt sorry that they had missed the best days of television by being born too late: no *Omnibus*, no *My Little Margie*, no *Our Miss Brooks*. The reruns of *I Love Lucy* meant nothing to them. They thought Eddie Fisher's loud tenor voice was funny, and shook their heads in disbelief when Lawrence

Welk, looking away from the camera, told folks how nice the song was that had just been sung. Will and Kate had always found so many things absurd and funny. As children, they were as united in their giggling as they were now in their harsh dismissals of people they didn't care for. But maybe this gave them an advantage over someone like her mother, who always held her tongue, because laughter allowed them to dismiss things; the things were forgotten by the time they ran out of breath.

In the living room, Mr. Camp was asleep in front of the television. *Serpico* was on. She didn't remember the movie exactly, but she would be surprised if Al Pacino ever got out of his dilemma. She dropped her handbag in a chair and looked at her husband. It was the first time she had seen him in almost two weeks. Since his brother retired from the government and moved to a house on the Chesapeake, Mr. Camp hardly came home at all. Tonight, many cigarettes had been stubbed out in the ashtray on the table beside his chair. He had on blue Bermuda shorts and a lighter blue knit shirt, white socks, and tennis shoes. His feet were splayed on the footstool. When they were young, he had told her that the world was theirs, and, considering the world her mother envisioned for her—the convent—he'd been right. He had taught her, all in one summer, how to drive, smoke, and have sex. Later, he taught her how to crack crabs and how to dance a rumba.

It was eight o'clock, and outside the light was as blue-gray as fish scales. She went into the kitchen, tiptoeing. She went to the refrigerator and opened the door to the freezer. She knew what she would find, and of course it was there: bluefish, foil-wrapped, neatly stacked to within an inch of the top of the freezer. He had made room for all of them by removing the spaghetti sauce. She closed the door and pulled open the refrigerator door. There were the two containers. The next night, she would make up a big batch of spaghetti. The night after that, they would start eating the fish he'd caught. She opened the freezer door and looked again. The shining rectangles rose up like steep silver steps. The white air blowing off the ice, surrounding them and drifting out, made her squint. It might have been clouds, billowing through heaven. If she could shrink to a fraction of her size, she could walk into the cold, close the door, and start to climb.

She was tired. It was as simple as that. This life she loved so much had been lived, all along, with the greatest effort. She closed the door again. To hold herself still, she held her breath.

Times

It was almost Christmas, and Cammy and Peter were visiting her parents in Cambridge. Late in the afternoon on the second day of their visit, Cammy followed Peter upstairs when he went to take a shower. She wanted a break from trying to make conversation with her mother and father.

"Why is it that I always feel guilty when we're not at my parents' house at Christmas?" he said.

"Call them," she said.

"That makes me feel worse," he said.

He was looking in the mirror and rubbing his chin, though he had shaved just a few hours ago. Every afternoon, she knew, he felt for a trace of beard but didn't shave again if he found it. "They probably don't even notice we're not there," he said. "Who'd have time, with my sister and her *au pair* and her three kids and her cat and her dog and her rabbit."

"Gerbil," Cammy said. She sat at the foot of the bed while he undressed. Every year was the same; they offered to visit his parents in Kentucky, and his mother hinted that there was not enough room. The year before, he had said that they'd bring sleeping bags. His mother had said that she thought it was silly to have her family sprawled on the floor, and that they should visit at a more convenient time. Several days ago, before Cammy and Peter left New York for Boston, they had got presents in the mail from his parents. Each of them had been sent a Christmas stocking with a fake-fur top. Cammy's stocking contained makeup. Peter's was full of joke presents—a hand buzzer, soap that turned black when you washed your hands, a key chain with a dried yellow fish hanging from it. Peter's stocking had had a hundred-dollar bill folded in the toe. In the toe of her stocking, Cammy found cuticle scissors.

While Peter showered, she wandered around her old room; when they arrived, they had been tired from the long drive, and she went to sleep with no more interest in her surroundings than she would have had in an anonymous motel room. Now she saw that her mother had got rid of most of the junk that used to be here, but she had also added things—her high-school yearbook, a Limoges dish with her Girl Scout ring in it—so that the room looked like a shrine. Years ago, Cammy had rolled little curls of Scotch Tape and stuck them to the backs of pictures of boyfriends or would-be boyfriends and then pushed the snapshots against the mirror to form the shape of a heart. Only two photos remained on the mirror now, both of Michael Grizetti, who had been her steady in her last year of high school. When her mother had moved them and put them neatly under the frame of the mirror, top left and right, she must have discovered the secret. Cammy pulled the larger picture out and turned it over. The hidden snapshot was still glued to the back: Grizzly with his pelvis thrust forward, thumbs pointing at his crotch, and the message "Nil desperandum x x x x x x x x x x" written on the snapshot across his chest. It all seemed so harmless now. He was the first person Cammy had slept with, and most of what she remembered now was what happened after they had sex. They went into New York, with fake IDs and fifty dollars Grizzly borrowed from his brother. She could still remember how the shag carpet tickled the soles of her feet when she went to the window of their hotel in the morning and pulled open the heavy curtains and looked across a distance so short that she thought she could reach out and touch the adjacent building, so close and so high that she couldn't see the sky; there had been no way to tell what kind of day it was. Now she noticed that there was a little haze over Michael Grizetti's top lip in the photograph. It was dust, not a mustache.

Peter came out of the bathroom. Over the years, he had gotten his hair cut closer and closer, so that now when she touched his head the curls were too tight to spring up at her touch. His head looked a little like a cantaloupe—a ridiculous idea, which would be useful just the same; she and her friends always said amusing things about their husbands when they wrote each other. She saved the more flattering images of him as things to say to him after making love. Her high-school English teacher would have approved. The teacher loved to invent little rhymes for the class:

> *Your conversation can be terrific;*
> *Just remember: be specific*

Peter's damp towel flew past her and landed on the bed. As usual, he discarded it as if he had just finished it off in a fight. The week before, he had been in Barbados on a retreat with his company, and he was still very tan. There was a wide band of white skin where he had worn his swimming trunks. In the dim afternoon light he looked like a piece of Marimekko fabric.

He pulled on sweatpants, tied the drawstring, and lit a cigarette with the fancy lighter she had bought him for Christmas. She had given it to him early. It was a metal tube with a piece of rawhide attached to the bottom. When the string was pulled, an outer sleeve of metal rose over the top, to protect the flame. Peter loved it, but she was a little sorry after she gave it to him; there had been something dramatic about huddling in doorways with him, using her body to help him block the wind while he struck matches to light a cigarette. She took two steps toward him now and gave him a hug, putting her hands under his armpits. They were damp. She believed it was a truth that no man ever dried himself thoroughly after showering. He kissed across her forehead, then stopped and pushed his chin between her eyebrows. She couldn't respond; she had told him the night before that she didn't understand how anyone could make love in their parents' house. He shook his head, almost amused, and tucked a thermal shirt into the sweatpants, then pulled on a sweater. "I don't care if it *is* snowing," he said. He was going running.

They walked downstairs. Her father, a retired cardiologist, was on his slant board in the living room, arms raised to heaven, holding the *Wall Street Journal*. "How do you reconcile smoking a pack a day, and then going running?" her father said.

"To tell you the truth," Peter said, "I don't run for my health. It clears my mind. I run because it gives me a high."

"Well, do you think mental health is separate from the health of the body?"

"Oh, Stan," Cammy's mother said, coming into the living room, "no one is trying to argue with you about medicine."

"I wasn't talking about *medicine*," he said.

"People just talk loosely," her mother said.

"I'd never argue that point," her father said.

Cammy found these visits more and more impossible. As a child she had been told what to do and think, and then when she got married her parents had backed off entirely, so that in the first year of her marriage she found herself in the odd position of advising her mother and father. Then, at some point, they had managed to turn the tables again, and now all of them were back to "Go." They argued with each other and made pronouncements instead of having conversations.

She decided to go running with Peter and pulled her parka off a hanger in the closet. She was still having trouble zipping it outside, and Peter helped by pulling the material down tightly in front. It only made her feel more helpless. He saw her expression and nuzzled her hair. "What do you expect from them?" he said, as the zipper went up. She thought, He asks questions he knows I won't bother to answer.

Snow was falling. They were walking through a Christmas-card scene that she hadn't believed in in years; she half expected carolers around the corner. When Peter turned left, she guessed that they were heading for the park on Mass. Avenue. They passed a huge white clapboard house with real candles glowing in all the windows. "Some place," Peter said. "Look at that wreath." The wreath that hung on the front door was so thick that it was convex; it looked as if someone had uprooted a big boxwood and cut a hole in the center. Peter made a snowball and threw it, almost getting a bull's-eye.

"Are you crazy?" she said, grabbing at his hand. "What are you going to do if they open the door?"

"Listen," he said, "if they lived in New York the wreath would be stolen. This way, everybody can enjoy throwing snowballs at it."

On the corner, a man stood staring down at a small brown dog wearing a plaid coat. The blond man standing next to him said, "I told you so. She may be blind, but she still loves it out in the snow." The other man patted the shivering dog, and they continued on their walk.

Christmas in Cambridge. Soon it would be Christmas Eve, time to open the gifts. As usual, she and Peter would be given something practical (stocks), and something frivolous (glasses too fragile for the dishwasher). Then there would be one personal present for each of them: probably a piece of gold jewelry for Cammy and a silk tie for Peter. Cammy occasionally wore one of the ties when she dressed like a nineteen-forties businessman. Peter thought the ties were slightly effeminate—he never liked them. The year before, when her parents gave her a lapis ring, he had pulled it off her finger to examine it on Christmas night, in bed, then pushed it on his little finger and wiggled it, making a Clara Bow mouth and pretending to be gay. He had been trying to show her how ridiculous he would look wearing a wedding ring. They had been married three years then, and some part of her was still so sentimental that she asked him from time to time if he wouldn't reconsider and wear a wedding ring. It wasn't that she thought a ring would be any sort of guarantee. They had lived together for two years before they suddenly decided to get married, but before the wedding they had agreed that it was naive to expect a lifetime of fidelity. If either one became interested in someone else, they would handle the situation in whatever way they felt best, but there would be no flaunting of the other person, and they wouldn't talk about it.

A couple of months before the last trip to her parents'—Christmas a year ago—Peter had waked her up one night to tell her about a young woman he had had a brief affair with. He described his feelings about being with the woman—how much he liked it when she put her hand over his when they sat at a table in a restaurant; the time she had dissipated some anger of his by suddenly putting her lips to the deepening lines in his forehead, to kiss his frown away. Then Peter had wept onto Cammy's pillow. She could still remember his face—the only time she had ever seen him cry—and how red and swollen it was, as if it had been burned. "Is this discreet enough for you?" he had said. "Do you want to push this pillow into my face so not even the *neighbors* can hear?" She didn't care what the neighbors thought, because she didn't even know the neighbors. She had not comforted him or touched the pillow. She had not been dramatic and gone out to sleep on the sofa. After he went to work in the morning, she had several cups of coffee and then went out to try to cheer herself up. She bought flowers at an expensive flower shop on Greenwich Avenue, pointing to individual blossoms for the florist to remove one by one, choosing with great care. Then she went home, trimmed the stems, and put them in little bottles—just a few stalks in each, all flowers and no greens. By evening, when Peter was about to come home, she realized that he would see them and know that she had been depressed, so she bunched them all together again and put them in a vase in the dining room. Looking at them, she suddenly understood how ironic it was that all during the past summer, when she was falling more deeply in love with Peter, he was having a flirtation and then an affair with someone else. Cammy had begun to be comfortable with how subtly attuned to each other they were, and she had been deluded. It made her embarrassed to remember how close she felt to Peter late one fall afternoon on Bleecker Street, when Peter stopped to light a cigarette. Something had made her poke him in the ribs. She didn't often act childish, and she could see that he was taken aback, and that made her laugh and poke him again. Every time he thought she'd finished and tried to light another match, she managed to take him by surprise and tickle him again; she even got through the barrier he'd made with his elbows pointed into his stomach. "What *is* this?" he said. "The American Cancer Society sent you to torture me?" People were looking—who said people don't notice things in New York?—and Peter was backing away, then doubling up, with the cigarette unlit in his mouth, admitting that he couldn't control her. When she moved toward him to hug him and end the game, he didn't believe it was over; he turned sideways, one hand extended to ward her off, clumsily trying to thumb up a flame with his right hand. This was the opposite of the night she had sex with Michael Grizetti: she could remember all of this moment—the smiling fat woman walking by, talking to herself, the buzzing sound of the neon sign outside the restaurant, Peter's stainless-steel watchband sparkling under the streetlight, the *de-de-de-deeeeeh* of a car horn in the distance. "Time!" he had shouted, backing away. Then, at a safe distance, he crossed his fingers above his head, like a child.

Now Peter slapped her bottom. "I'm going to run," he said. He took off into the park, his running shoes kicking up clods of snow. She watched him go. He was tall and broad-shouldered, and his short leather jacket came just to his waist, so that he looked like an adolescent in ill-fitting clothes. She had on cowboy boots instead of running shoes. Why did she hold it against him that she had decided at the last minute to go with him and that she was wearing the wrong shoes? Did she expect him to throw down his cape?

She probably would not have thought of a cape at all, except that his scarf flew off as he ran, and he didn't notice. She turned into the park to get it. The snow was falling in smaller flakes now; it was going to stay. Maybe it was the realization that even icier weather was still to come that suddenly made her nearly numb with cold. The desire to be in the sun was almost a hot spot between her ribs; something actually burned inside her. Like everyone she knew, she had grown up watching Porky Pig and Heckle and Jeckle on Saturday mornings—cartoons in which the good guys got what they wanted and no consequences were permanent. Now she wanted one of those small tornadoes that whipped through cartoons, transporting objects and characters with miraculous speed from one place to another. She wanted to believe again in the magic power of the wind.

They went back to the house. Music was playing loudly on the radio, and her father was hollering to her mother, "First we get that damned 'Drummer Boy' dirge, and now they've got the Andrews Sisters singing 'Boogie Woogie Bugle Boy.' What the hell does *that* have to do with Christmas? Isn't that song from the Second World War? What are they doing playing that stuff at Christmas? Probably some disc jockey that's high. Everybody's high all the time. The guy who filled my gas tank this morning was high. The kid they put on to deliver mail's got eyes like a pinwheel and walks like he might step on a land mine. What about 'White Christmas'? Do they think that Bing Crosby spent his whole life playing golf?"

Peter came up behind Cammy as she was hanging his scarf on a peg on the back of the kitchen door. He helped her out of her coat and hung it over the scarf.

"Look at this," Cammy's mother said proudly, from the kitchen.

They walked into the room where her mother stood and looked down. While they were out, she had finished making the annual *bûche de Noël:* a fat, perfect cylinder of a log, with chocolate icing stroked into the texture of tree bark. A small green-and-white wreath had been pumped out of a pastry tube to decorate one end, and there was an open jar of raspberry jam that her mother must have used to make the bow.

"It was worth my effort," her mother said. "You two look like children seeing their presents on Christmas morning."

Cammy smiled. What her mother had just said was what gave her the idea of touching the Yule log—what made her grin and begin to wiggle her finger lightly through a ridge, widening it slightly, giving the bark at least one imperfection. Once her finger touched it, it was difficult to stop—though she knew she had to let the wild upsweep of the tornado she might create stay an image in her mind. The consolation, naturally, was what would happen when she raised her finger. Slowly—while Peter and her mother stared—she lifted her hand, still smiling, and began to suck the chocolate off her finger.

In the White Night

"Don't think about a cow," Matt Brinkley said. "Don't think about a river, don't think about a car, don't think about snow. . . ."

Matt was standing in the doorway, hollering after his guests. His wife, Gaye, gripped his arm and tried to tug him back into the house. The party was over. Carol and Vernon turned to wave goodbye, calling back their thanks, whispering to each other to be careful. The steps were slick with snow; an icy snow had been falling for hours, frozen granules mixed in with lighter stuff, and the instant they moved out from under the protection of the Brinkleys' porch the cold froze the smiles on their faces. The swirls of snow blowing against Carol's skin reminded her—an odd thing to remember on a night like this—of the way sand blew up at the beach, and the scratchy pain it caused.

"Don't think about an apple!" Matt hollered. Vernon turned his head, but he was left smiling at a closed door.

In the small, bright areas under the streetlights, there seemed for a second to be some logic to all the swirling snow. If time itself could only freeze, the snowflakes could become the lacy filigree of a valentine. Carol frowned. Why had Matt conjured up the image of an apple? Now she saw an apple where there was no apple, suspended in midair, transforming the scene in front of her into a silly surrealist painting.

It was going to snow all night. They had heard that on the radio, driving to the Brinkleys'. The Don't-Think-About-Whatever game had started as a joke, something long in the telling and startling to Vernon, to judge by his expression as Matt went on and on. When Carol crossed the room near midnight to tell Vernon that they should leave, Matt had quickly whispered the rest of his joke or story—whatever he was saying—into Vernon's ear, all in a rush. They looked like two children, the one whispering madly and the other with his head bent, but something about the inclination of Vernon's head let you know that if you bent low enough to see, there would be a big, wide grin on his face. Vernon and Carol's daughter, Sharon, and Matt and Gaye's daughter, Becky, had sat side by side, or kneecap to kneecap, and whispered that way when they were children—a privacy so rushed that it obliterated anything else. Carol, remembering that scene now, could not think of what passed between Sharon and Becky without thinking of sexual intimacy. Becky, it turned out, had given the Brinkleys a lot of trouble. She had run away from home when she was thirteen, and, in a family-counseling session years later, her parents found out that she had had an abortion at fifteen. More recently, she had flunked out of college. Now she was working in a bank in Boston and taking a night-school course in poetry. Poetry or pottery? The apple that reappeared as the windshield wipers slushed snow off the glass metamorphosed for Carol into a red bowl, then again became an apple, which grew rounder as the car came to a stop at the intersection.

She had been weary all day. Anxiety always made her tired. She knew the party would be small (the Brinkleys' friend Mr. Graham had just had his book accepted for publication, and of course much of the evening would be spent talking about that); she had feared that it was going to be a strain for all of them. The Brinkleys had just returned from the Midwest, where they had gone for Gaye's father's funeral. It didn't seem a time to carry through with plans for a party. Carol imagined that not canceling it had been Matt's idea, not Gaye's. She turned toward Vernon now and asked how the Brinkleys had seemed to him. Fine, he said at once. Before he spoke, she knew how he would answer. If people did not argue in front of their friends, they were not having problems; if they did not stumble into walls, they were not drunk. Vernon tried hard to think positively, but he was never impervious to real pain. His reflex was to turn aside something serious with a joke, but he was just as quick to wipe the smile off his face and suddenly put his arm around a person's shoulder. Unlike Matt, he was a warm person, but when people unexpectedly showed him affection it embarrassed him. The same counselor the Brinkleys had seen had told Carol—Vernon refused to see the man, and she found that she did not want to continue without him—that it was possible that Vernon felt uncomfortable with expressions of kindness because he blamed himself for Sharon's death: he couldn't save her, and when people were kind to him now he felt it was undeserved. But Vernon was the last person who should be punished. She remembered him in the hospital, pretending to misunderstand Sharon when she asked for her barrette, on her bedside table, and picking it up and clipping the little yellow duck into the hair above his own ear. He kept trying to tickle a smile out of her—touching some stuffed animal's button nose to the tip of her nose and then tapping it on her earlobe. At the moment when Sharon died, Vernon had been sitting on her bed (Carol was backed up against the door, for some reason), surrounded by a battlefield of pastel animals.

They passed safely through the last intersection before their house. The car didn't skid until they turned onto their street. Carol's heart thumped hard, once, in the second when she felt the car becoming light, but they came out of the skid easily. He had been driving carefully, and she said nothing, wanting to appear casual about the moment. She asked if Matt had mentioned Becky. No, Vernon said, and he hadn't wanted to bring up a sore subject.

Gaye and Matt had been married for twenty-five years; Carol and Vernon had been married twenty-two. Sometimes Vernon said, quite sincerely, that Matt and Gaye were their alter egos who absorbed and enacted crises, saving the two of them from having to experience such chaos. It frightened Carol to think that some part of him believed that. Who could really believe that there was some way to find protection in this world—or someone who could offer it? What happened happened at random, and one horrible thing hardly precluded the possibility of others happening next. There had been that fancy internist who hospitalized Vernon later in the same spring when Sharon died, and who looked up at him while drawing blood and observed almost off-handedly that it would be an unbearable irony if Vernon also had leukemia. When the test results came back, they showed that Vernon had mononucleosis. There was the time when the Christmas tree caught fire, and she rushed toward the flames, clapping her hands like cymbals, and Vernon pulled her away just in time, before the whole tree became a torch, and she with it. When Hobo, their dog, had to be put to sleep during their vacation in Maine, that awful woman veterinarian, with her cold green eyes, issued the casual death sentence with one manicured hand on the quivering dog's fur and called him "Bobo," as though their dog were like some circus clown.

"Are you crying?" Vernon said. They were inside their house now, in the hallway, and he had just turned toward her, holding out a pink padded coat hanger.

"No," she said. "The wind out there is fierce." She slipped her jacket onto the hanger he held out and went into the downstairs bathroom, where she buried her face in a towel. Eventually, she looked at herself in the mirror. She had pressed the towel hard against her eyes, and for a few seconds she had to blink herself into focus. She was reminded of the kind of camera they had had when Sharon was young. There were two images when you looked through the finder, and you had to make the adjustment yourself so that one superimposed itself upon the other and the figure suddenly leaped into clarity. She patted the towel to her eyes again and held her breath. If she couldn't stop crying, Vernon would make love to her. When she was very sad, he sensed that his instinctive optimism wouldn't work; he became tongue-tied, and when he couldn't talk he would reach for her. Through the years, he had knocked over wineglasses shooting his hand across the table to grab hers. She had found herself suddenly hugged from behind in the bathroom; he would even follow her in there if he suspected that she was going to cry— walk in to grab her without even having bothered to knock.

She opened the door now and turned toward the hall staircase, and then realized—felt it before she saw it, really—that the light was on in the living room.

Vernon lay stretched out on the sofa with his legs crossed; one foot was planted on the floor and his top foot dangled in the air. Even when he was exhausted, he was always careful not to let his shoes touch the sofa. He was very tall, and couldn't stretch out on the sofa without resting his head on the arm. For some reason, he had not hung up her jacket. It was spread like a tent over his head and shoulders, rising and falling with his breathing. She stood still long enough to be sure that he was really asleep, and then came into the room. The sofa was too narrow to curl up on with him. She didn't want to wake him. Neither did she want to go to bed alone. She went back to the hall closet and took out his overcoat—the long, elegant camel's-hair coat he had not worn tonight because he thought it might snow. She slipped off her shoes and went quietly over to where he lay and stretched out on the floor beside the sofa, pulling the big blanket of the coat up high, until the collar touched her lips. Then she drew her legs up into the warmth.

Such odd things happened. Very few days were like the ones before. Here they were, in their own house with four bedrooms, ready to sleep in this peculiar double-decker fashion, in the largest, coldest room of all. What would anyone think?

She knew the answer to that question, of course. A person who didn't know them would mistake this for a drunken collapse, but anyone who was a friend would understand exactly. In time, both of them had learned to stop passing judgment on how they coped with the inevitable sadness that set in, always unexpectedly but so real that it was met with the instant acceptance one gave to a snowfall. In the white night world outside, their daughter might be drifting past like an angel, and she would see this tableau, for the second that she hovered, as a necessary small adjustment.

Summer People

The first weekend at their summer house in Vermont, Jo, Tom, and Byron went out for pizza. Afterward, Tom decided that he wanted to go dancing at a roadside bar. Byron had come with his father and Jo grudgingly, enthusiastic about the pizza but fearing that it would be a longer night than he wanted. "They have Pac-Man here," Tom said to his son, as he swung the car into the bar parking strip, and for a couple of seconds it was obvious that Byron was debating whether or not to go in with them. "Nah," he said. "I don't want to hang out with a bunch of drunks while you two dance."

Byron had his sleeping bag with him in the car. The sleeping bag and a pile of comic books were his constant companions. He was using the rolled-up bag as a headrest. Now he turned and punched it flatter, making it more a pillow, and then stretched out to emphasize that he wouldn't go in with them.

"Maybe we should just go home," Jo said, as Tom pulled open the door to the bar.

"What for?"

"Byron—"

"Oh, Byron's overindulged," Tom said, putting his hand on her shoulder and pushing her forward with his fingertips.

Byron was Tom's son from his first marriage. It was the second summer that he was spending with them on vacation in Vermont. He'd been allowed to decide, and he had chosen to come with them. In the school year he lived with his mother in Philadelphia. This year he was suddenly square and sturdy, like the Japanese robots he collected—compact, complicated robots, capable of doing useful but frequently unnecessary tasks, like a Swiss Army knife. It was difficult for Tom to realize that his son was ten years old now. The child he conjured up when he closed his eyes at night was always an infant, the tangled hair still as smooth as peach fuzz, with the scars and bruises of summer erased, so that Byron was again a sleek, seal-like baby.

The band's instruments were piled on the stage. Here and there, amps rose out of tangled wire like trees growing from the forest's tangled floor. A pretty young woman with a blond pompadour was on the dance floor, shaking her puff of hair and smiling at her partner, with her Sony earphones clamped on, so that she heard her own music while the band took a break and the jukebox played. The man stood there shuffling, making almost no attempt to dance. Tom recognized them as the couple who had outbid him on a chain saw he wanted at an auction he had gone to earlier in the day.

On the jukebox, Dolly Parton was doing the speaking part of "I Will Always Love You." Green bottles of Rolling Rock, scattered across the bar top, had the odd configuration of misplaced bowling pins. Dolly Parton's sadness was coupled with great sincerity. The interlude over, she began to sing again, with greater feeling. "I'm not kidding you," a man wearing an orange football jersey said, squeezing the biceps of the burly man who sat next to him. "I says to him, 'I don't understand your question. What is tuna fish *like*? It's tuna fish.'" The burly man's face contorted with laughter.

There was a neon sign behind the bar, with shining bubbles moving through a bottle of Miller. When Tom was with his first wife, back when Byron was about three years old, he had taken the lights off the Christmas tree one year while needles rained down on the bedsheet snowbank they had mounded around the tree stand. He had never seen a tree dry out so fast. He remembered snapping off branches, then going to get a garbage bag to put them in. He snapped off branch after branch, stuffing them inside, feeling clever that he had figured out a way to get the dried-out tree down four flights of stairs without needles dropping everywhere. Byron came out of the back room while this was going on, saw the limbs disappearing into the black bag, and began to cry. His wife never let him forget all the wrong things he had said and done to Byron. He was still not entirely sure what Byron had been upset about that day, but he had made it worse by getting angry and saying that the tree was only a tree, not a member of the family.

The bartender passed by, clutching beer bottles by their necks as if they were birds he had shot. Tom tried to get his eye, but he was gone, involved in some story being told at the far end of the bar. "Let's dance," Tom said, and Jo moved into his arms. They walked to the dance floor and slow-danced to an old Dylan song. The harmonica cut through the air like a party blower, shrilly unrolling.

When they left and went back to the car, Byron pretended to be asleep. If he had really been sleeping, he would have stirred when they opened and closed the car doors. He was lying on his back, eyes squeezed shut a little too tightly, enclosed in the padded blue chrysalis of the sleeping bag.

The next morning, Tom worked in the garden, moving from row to row as he planted tomato seedlings and marigolds. He had a two-month vacation because he was changing jobs, and he was determined to stay ahead of things in the garden this year. It was a very carefully planned bed, more like a well-woven rug than like a vegetable patch. Jo was on the porch, reading *Moll Flanders* and watching him.

He was flattered but also slightly worried that she wanted to make love every night. The month before, on her thirty-fourth birthday, they had drunk a bottle of Dom Pérignon and she had asked him if he was still sure he didn't want to have a child with her. He told her that he didn't, and reminded her that they had agreed on that before they got married. He had thought, from the look on her face, that she was about to argue with him—she was a teacher and she loved debate—but she dropped the subject, saying, "You might change your mind someday." Since then she had begun to tease him. "Change your mind?" she would whisper, curling up next to him on the sofa and unbuttoning his shirt. She even wanted to make love in the living room. He was afraid Byron would wake up and come downstairs for some reason, so he would turn off the television and go upstairs with her. "What *is* this?" he asked once lightly, hoping it wouldn't provoke her into a discussion of whether he had changed his mind about having a child.

"I always feel this way about you," she said. "Do you think I like it the rest of the time, when teaching takes all my energy?"

On another evening, she whispered something else that surprised him—something he didn't want to pursue. She said that it made her feel old to realize that having friends she could stay up all night talking to was a thing of the past. "Do you remember that from college?" she said. "All those people who took themselves so seriously that everything they felt was a fact."

He was glad that she had fallen asleep without really wanting an answer. Byron puzzled him less these days and Jo puzzled him more. He looked up at the sky now: bright blue, with clouds trailing out thinly, so that the ends looked as if kite strings were attached. He was rinsing his hands with the garden hose at the side of the house when a car came up the driveway and coasted to a stop. He turned off the water and shook his hands, walking forward to investigate.

A man in his forties was getting out of the car—clean-cut, pudgy. He reached back into the car for a briefcase, then straightened up. "I'm Ed Rickman!" he called. "How are you today?"

Tom nodded. A salesman, and he was trapped. He wiped his hands on his jeans.

"To get right to the point, there are only two roads in this whole part of the world I really love, and this is one of them," Rickman said. "You're one of the new people—hell, everybody who didn't crash up against Plymouth Rock is new in New England, right? I tried to buy this acreage years ago, and the farmer who owned it wouldn't sell. Made an offer way back then, when money meant something, and the man wouldn't sell. You own all these acres now?"

"Two," Tom said.

"Hell," Ed Rickman said. "You'd be crazy not to be happy here, right?" He looked over Tom's shoulder. "Have a garden?" Rickman said.

"Out back," Tom said.

"You'd be crazy not to have a garden," Rickman said.

Rickman walked past Tom and across the lawn. Tom wanted the visitor to be the one to back off, but Rickman took his time, squinting and slowly staring about the place. Tom was reminded of the way so many people perused box lots at the auction—the cartons they wouldn't let you root around in because the good things thrown on top covered a boxful of junk.

"I never knew this place was up for grabs," Rickman said. "I was given to understand the house and land were an eight-acre parcel, and not for sale."

"I guess two of them were," Tom said.

Rickman ran his tongue over his teeth a few times. One of his front teeth was discolored—almost black.

"Get this from the farmer himself?" he said.

"Real-estate agent, three years ago. Advertised in the paper."

Rickman looked surprised. He looked down at his Top-Siders. He sighed deeply and looked at the house. "I guess my timing was bad," he said. "That or a question of style. These New Englanders are kind of like dogs. Slow to move. Sniff around before they decide what they think." He held his briefcase in front of his body. He slapped it a couple of times. It reminded Tom of a beer drinker patting his belly.

"Everything changes," Rickman said. "Not so hard to imagine that one day this'll all be skyscrapers. Condominiums or what have you." He looked at the sky. "Don't worry," he said. "I'm not a developer. I don't even have a card to leave with you in case you ever change your mind. In my experience, the only people who change their minds are women. There was a time when you could state that view without having somebody jump all over you, too."

Rickman held out his hand. Tom shook it.

"Just a lovely place you got here," Rickman said. "Thank you for your time."

"Sure," Tom said.

Rickman walked away, swinging the briefcase. His trousers were too big; they wrinkled across the seat like an opening accordion. When he got to the car, he looked back and smiled. Then he threw the briefcase onto the passenger seat—not a toss but a throw—got in, slammed the door, and drove away.

Tom walked around to the back of the house. On the porch, Jo was still reading. There was a pile of paperbacks on the small wicker stool beside her chair. It made him a little angry to think that she had been happily reading while he had wasted so much time with Ed Rickman.

"Some crazy guy pulled up and wanted to buy the house," he said.

"Tell him we'd sell for a million?" she said.

"I wouldn't," he said.

Jo looked up. He turned and went into the kitchen. Byron had left the top off a jar, and a fly had died in the peanut butter. Tom opened the refrigerator and looked over the possibilities.

Later that same week, Tom discovered that Rickman had been talking to Byron. The boy said he had been walking down the road just then, returning from fishing, when a car rolled up alongside him and a man pointed to the house and asked him if he lived there.

Byron was in a bad mood. He hadn't caught anything. He propped his rod beside the porch door and started into the house, but Tom stopped him. "Then what?" Tom said.

"He had this black tooth," Byron said, tapping his own front tooth. "He said he had a house around here, and a kid my age who needed somebody to hang out with. He asked if he could bring this dumb kid over, and I said no, because I wouldn't be around after today."

Byron sounded so self-assured that Tom did a double take, wondering where Byron was going.

"I don't want to meet some creepy kid," Byron said. "If the guy comes and asks you, say no—O.K.?"

"Then what did he say?"

"Talked about some part of the river where it was good fishing. Where the river curved, or something. It's no big deal. I've met a lot of guys like him."

"What do you mean?" Tom said.

"Guys that talk just to talk," Byron said. "Why are you making a big deal out of it?"

"Byron, the guy's nuts," Tom said. "I don't want you to talk to him anymore. If you see him around here again, run and get me."

"Right," Byron said. "Should I scream, too?"

Tom shivered. The image of Byron screaming frightened him, and for a few seconds he let himself believe that he should call the police. But if he called, what would he say—that someone had asked if his house was for sale and later asked Byron if he'd play with his son?

Tom pulled out a cigarette and lit it. He'd drive across town to see the farmer who'd owned the land, he decided, and find out what he knew about Rickman. He didn't remember exactly how to get to the farmer's house, and he couldn't remember his name. The real-estate agent had pointed out the place, at the top of a hill, the summer he showed Tom the property, so he could call him and find out. But first he was going to make sure that Jo got home safely from the grocery store.

The phone rang, and Byron turned to pick it up.

"Hello?" Byron said. Byron frowned. He avoided Tom's eyes. Then, just when Tom felt sure that it was Rickman, Byron said, "Nothing much." A long pause. "Yeah, sure," he said. "I'm thinking about ornithology."

It was Byron's mother.

The real-estate agent remembered him. Tom told him about Rickman. *"De de de de, De de de de,"* the agent sang—the notes of the theme music from *The Twilight Zone.* The agent laughed. He told him the farmer whose land he had bought was named Albright. He didn't have the man's telephone number, but was sure it was in the directory. It was.

Tom got in the car and drove to the farm. A young woman working in a flower garden stood up and held her trowel up like a torch when his car pulled into the drive. Then she looked surprised that he was a stranger. He introduced himself. She said her name. It turned out she was Mr. Albright's niece, who had come with her family to watch the place while her aunt and uncle were in New Zealand. She didn't know anything about the sale of the land; no, nobody else had come around asking. Tom described Rickman anyway. No, she said, she hadn't seen anyone who looked like that. Over on a side lawn, two Irish setters were barking madly at them. A man—he must have been the woman's husband—was holding them by their collars. The dogs were going wild, and the young woman obviously wanted to end the conversation. Tom didn't think about leaving her his telephone number until it was too late, when he was driving away.

That night, he went to another auction, and when he came back to the car one of the back tires was flat. He opened the trunk to get the spare, glad that he had gone to the auction alone, glad that the field was lit up and people were walking around. A little girl about his son's age came by with her parents. She held a one-armed doll over her head and skipped forward. "I don't feel cheated. Why should you feel cheated? I bought the whole box for two dollars and I got two metal sieves out of it," the woman said to the man. He had on a baseball cap and a black tank top and cutoffs, and sandals with soles that curved at the heel and toe like a canoe. He stalked ahead of the woman, box under one arm, and grabbed his dancing daughter by the elbow. "Watch my dolly!" she screamed, as he pulled her along. "That doll's not worth five cents," the man said. Tom averted his eyes. He was sweating more than he should, going through the easy maneuvers of changing a tire. There was even a breeze.

They floated the tire in a pan of water at the gas station the next morning, looking for the puncture. Nothing was embedded in the tire; whatever had made the hole wasn't there. As one big bubble after another rose to the surface, Tom felt a clutch in his throat, as if he himself might be drowning.

He could think of no good reason to tell the officer at the police barracks why Ed Rickman would have singled him out. Maybe Rickman *had* wanted to build a house on that particular site. The policeman made a fist and rested his mouth against it, his lips in the gully between thumb and finger. Until Tom said that, the policeman had seemed concerned—even a little inter-ested. Then his expression changed. Tom hurried to say that of course he didn't believe that explanation, because something funny was going on. The cop shook his head. Did that mean no, of course not, or no, he did believe it?

Tom described Rickman, mentioning the discolored tooth. The cop wrote this information down on a small white pad. He drew crosshatches on a corner. The cop did not seem quite as certain as Tom that no one could have a grudge against him or anyone in his family. He asked where they lived in New York, where they worked.

When Tom walked out into the sunlight, he felt a little faint. Of course he had understood, even before the cop said it, that there was nothing the police could do at this point. "Frankly," the cop had said, "it's not likely that we're going to be able to keep a good eye out, in that you're on a dead-end road. Not a *route*," the cop said. "Not a *major thoroughfare*." It seemed to be some joke the cop was having with himself.

Driving home, Tom realized that he could give anyone who asked a detailed description of the cop. He had studied every mark on the cop's face—the little scar (chicken pox?) over one eyebrow, the aquiline nose that narrowed at the tip almost to the shape of a tack. He did not intend to alarm Jo or Byron by telling them where he had been.

Byron had gone fishing again. Jo wanted to make love while Byron was out. Tom knew he couldn't.

A week passed. Almost two weeks. He and Jo and Byron sat in lawn chairs watching the lightning bugs blink. Byron said he had his eye on one in particular, and he went "*Beep-beep, beep-beep*" as it blinked. They ate raw peas Jo had gathered in a bowl. He and Jo had a glass of wine. The neighbors' M.G. passed by. This summer, the neighbors sometimes tapped the horn as they passed. A bird swooped low across the lawn—perhaps a female cardinal. It was a surprise seeing a bird in the twilight like that. It dove into the grass, more like a seagull than a cardinal. It rose up, fluttering, with something in its beak. Jo put her glass on the little table, smiled, and clapped softly.

The bird Byron found dead in the morning was a grackle, not a cardinal. It was lying about ten feet from the picture window, but until Tom examined the bird's body carefully, he did not decide that probably it had just smacked into the glass by accident.

At Rusty's, at the end of summer, Tom ran into the cop again. They were both carrying white paper bags with straws sticking out of them. Grease was starting to seep through the bags. Rickman had never reappeared, and Tom felt some embarrassment about having gone to see the cop. He tried not to focus on the tip of the cop's nose.

"Running into a nut like that, I guess it makes getting back to the city look good," the cop said.

He's thinking *summer people*, Tom decided.

"You have a nice year, now," the cop said. "Tell your wife I sure do envy her her retirement."

"Her retirement?" Tom said.

The cop looked at the blacktop. "I admit, the way you described that guy I thought he might be sent by somebody who had a grudge against you or your wife," he said. "Then at the fire-department picnic I got to talking to your neighbor—that Mrs. Hewett—and I asked her if she'd seen anybody strange poking around before you got there. Hadn't. We got to talking. She said you were in the advertising business, and there was no way of knowing what gripes some lunatic might have with that, if he happened to know. Maybe you walked on somebody's territory, so to speak, and he wanted to get even. And your wife being a schoolteacher, you can't realize how upset some parents get when Johnny doesn't bring home the A's. You never can tell. Mrs. Hewett said she'd been a schoolteacher for a few months herself, before she got married, and she never regretted the day she quit. Said your wife was real happy about her own decision, too." The cop nodded in agreement with this.

Tom tried to hide his surprise. Somehow, the fact that he didn't know that Jo had ever exchanged a word with a neighbor, Karen Hewett, privately made the rest of the story believable. They hardly knew the woman. But why would Jo quit? His credibility with the cop must have been good after all. He could tell from the way the cop studied his face that he realized he had been telling Tom something he didn't know.

When the cop left, Tom sat on the hot front hood of his car, took the hamburgers out of the bag, and ate them. He pulled the straw out of the big container of Coke and took off the plastic top. He drank from the cup, and when the Coke was gone he continued to sit there, sucking ice. Back during the winter, Jo had several times brought up the idea of having a baby, but she hadn't mentioned it for weeks now. He wondered if she had decided to get pregnant in spite of his objections. But even if she had, why would she quit her job before she was sure there was a reason for it?

A teenage girl with short hair and triangle-shaped earrings walked by, averting her eyes as if she knew he'd stare after her. He didn't; only the earrings that caught the light like mirrors interested him. In a convertible facing him, across the lot, a boy and girl were eating their sandwiches in the front seat while a golden retriever in the back moved his head between theirs, looking from left to right and right to left with the regularity of a dummy talking to a ventriloquist. A man holding his toddler's hand walked by and smiled. Another car pulled in, with Hall and Oates going on the radio. The driver turned off the ignition, cutting off the music, and got out. A woman got out the other side. As they walked past, the woman said to the man, "I don't see why we've got to eat exactly at nine, twelve, and six." "Hey, it's twelve-fifteen," the man said. Tom dropped his cup into the paper bag, along with his hamburger wrappers and the napkins he hadn't used. He carried the soggy bag over to the trash can. A few bees lifted slightly higher as he stuffed his trash in. Walking back to the car, he realized that he had absolutely no idea what to do. At some point he would have to ask Jo what was going on.

When he pulled up, Byron was sitting on the front step, cleaning fish over a newspaper. Four trout, one of them very large. Byron had had a good day.

Tom walked through the house but couldn't find Jo. He held his breath when he opened the closet door; it was unlikely that she would be in there, naked, two days in a row. She liked to play tricks on him.

He came back downstairs, and saw, through the kitchen window, that Jo was sitting outside. A woman was with her. He walked out. Paper plates and beer bottles were on the grass beside their chairs.

"Hi, honey," she said.

"Hi," the woman said. It was Karen Hewett.

"Hi," he said to both of them. He had never seen Karen Hewett up close. She was tanner than he realized. The biggest difference, though, was her hair. When he had seen her, it had always been long and windblown, but today she had it pulled back in a clip.

"Get all your errands done?" Jo said.

It couldn't have been a more ordinary conversation. It couldn't have been a more ordinary summer day.

The night before they closed up the house, Tom and Jo lay stretched out on the bed. Jo was finishing *Tom Jones*. Tom was enjoying the cool breeze coming through the window, thinking that when he was in New York he forgot the Vermont house; at least, he forgot it except for the times he looked up from the street he was on and saw the sky, and its emptiness made him remember stars. It was the sky he loved in the country—the sky more than the house. If he hadn't thought it would seem dramatic, he would have gotten out of bed now and stood at the window for a long time. Earlier in the evening, Jo had asked why he was so moody. He had told her that he didn't feel like leaving. "Then let's stay," she said. It was his opening to say something about her job in the fall. He had hoped she would say something, but he hesitated, and she had only put her arms around him and rubbed her cheek against his chest. All summer, she had seduced him—sometimes with passion, sometimes so subtly he didn't realize what was happening until she put her hand up under his T-shirt or kissed him on the lips.

Now it was the end of August. Jo's sister in Connecticut was graduating from nursing school in Hartford, and Jo had asked Tom to stop there so they could do something with her sister to celebrate. Her sister lived in a one-bedroom apartment, but it would be easy to find a motel. The following day, they would take Byron home to Philadelphia and then backtrack to New York.

In the car the next morning, Tom felt Byron's gaze on his back and wondered if he had overheard their lovemaking the night before. It was very hot by noontime. There was so much haze on the mountains that their peaks were invisible. The mountains gradually sloped until suddenly, before Tom realized it, they were driving on flat highway. Late that afternoon they found a motel. He and Byron swam in the pool, and Jo, although she was just about to see her, talked to her sister for half an hour on the phone.

By the time Jo's sister turned up at the motel, Tom had shaved and showered. Byron was watching television. He wanted to stay in the room and watch the movie instead of having dinner with them. He said he wasn't hungry. Tom insisted that he come and eat dinner. "I can get something out of the machine," Byron said.

"You're not going to eat potato chips for dinner," Tom said. "Get off the bed—come on."

Byron gave Tom a look that was quite similar to the look an outlaw in the movie was giving the sheriff who had just kicked his gun out of reach.

"You didn't stay glued to the set in Vermont all summer and miss those glorious days, did you?" Jo's sister said.

"I fished," Byron said.

"He caught four trout one day," Tom said, spreading his arms and looking from the palm of one hand to the palm of the other.

They all had dinner together in the motel restaurant, and later, while they drank their coffee, Byron dropped quarters into the machine in the corridor, playing game after game of Space Invaders.

Jo and her sister went into the bar next to the restaurant for a nightcap. Tom let them go alone, figuring that they probably wanted some private time together. Byron followed him up to the room and turned on the television. An hour later, Jo and her sister were still in the bar. Tom sat on the balcony. Long before his usual bedtime, Byron turned off the television.

"Good night," Tom called into the room, hoping Byron would call him in.

"Night," Byron said.

Tom sat in silence for a minute. He was out of cigarettes and felt like a beer. He went into the room. Byron was lying in his sleeping bag, unzipped, on top of one of the beds.

"I'm going to drive down to that 7-Eleven," Tom said. "Want me to bring you anything?"

"No, thanks," Byron said.

"Want to come along?"

"No," Byron said.

He picked up the keys to the car and the room key and went out. He wasn't sure whether Byron was still sulking because he had made him go to dinner or whether he didn't want to go back to his mother's. Perhaps he was just tired.

Tom bought two Heinekens and a pack of Kools. The cashier was obviously stoned; he had bloodshot eyes and he stuffed a wad of napkins into the bag before he pushed it across the counter to Tom.

Back at the motel, he opened the door quietly. Byron didn't move. Tom put out one of the two lights Byron had left on and slid open the glass door to the balcony.

Two people kissed on the pathway outside, passing the pool on the way to their room. People were talking in the room below—muted, but it sounded like an argument. The lights were suddenly turned off at the pool. Tom pushed his heels against the railing and tipped his chair back. He could hear the cars on the highway. He felt sad about something, and realized that he felt quite alone. He finished a beer and lit a cigarette. Byron hadn't been very communicative. Of course, he couldn't expect a ten-year-old boy to throw his arms around him the way he had when he was a baby. And Jo—in spite of her ardor, his memory of her, all summer, was of her sitting with her nose in some eighteenth-century novel. He thought about all the things they had done in July and August, trying to convince himself that they had done a lot and had fun. Dancing a couple of times, auctions, the day on the borrowed raft, four—no, five—movies, fishing with Byron, badminton, the fireworks and the sparerib dinner outside the Town Hall on the Fourth.

Maybe what his ex-wife always said was true: he didn't connect with people. Jo never said such a thing, though. And Byron chose to spend the summer with them.

He drank the other beer and felt its effect. It had been a long drive. Byron probably didn't want to go back to Philadelphia. He himself wasn't too eager to begin his new job. He suddenly remembered his secretary when he confided in her that he'd gotten the big offer—her surprise, the way she hid her thumbs-up behind the palm of her other hand, in a mock gesture of secrecy. "Where are you going to go from there?" she had said. He'd miss her. She was funny and pretty and enthusiastic—no slouch herself. He'd miss laughing with her, miss being flattered because she thought that he was such a competent character.

He missed Jo. It wasn't because she was off at the bar. If she came back this instant, something would still be missing. He couldn't imagine caring for anyone more than he cared for her, but he wasn't sure that he was still in love with her. He was fiddling, there in the dark. He had reached into the paper bag and begun to wrinkle up little bits of napkin, rolling the paper between thumb and finger so that it formed tiny balls. When he had a palmful, he got up and tossed them over the railing. When he sat down again, he closed his eyes and began what would be months of remembering Vermont: the garden, the neon green of new peas, the lumpy lawn, the pine trees and the smell of them at night—and then suddenly Rickman was there, rumpled and strange, but his presence was only slightly startling. He was just a man who'd dropped in on a summer day. "You'd be crazy not to be happy here," Rickman was saying. All that was quite believable now—the way, when seen in the odd context of a home movie, even the craziest relative can suddenly look amiable.

He wondered if Jo was pregnant. Could that be what she and her sister were talking about all this time in the bar? For a second, he wanted them all to be transformed into characters in one of those novels she had read all summer. That way, the uncertainty would end. Henry Fielding would simply step in and predict the future. The author could tell him what it would be like, what would happen, if he had to try, another time, to love somebody.

The woman who had been arguing with the man was quiet. Crickets chirped, and a television hummed faintly. Below him, near the pool, a man who worked at the motel had rolled a table onto its side. He whistled while he made an adjustment to the white metal pole that would hold an umbrella the next day.

Janus

The bowl was perfect. Perhaps it was not what you'd select if you faced a shelf of bowls, and not the sort of thing that would inevitably attract a lot of attention at a crafts fair, yet it had real presence. It was as predictably admired as a mutt who has no reason to suspect he might be funny. Just such a dog, in fact, was often brought out (and in) along with the bowl.

Andrea was a real-estate agent, and when she thought that some prospective buyers might be dog lovers, she would drop off her dog at the same time she placed the bowl in the house that was up for sale. She would put a dish of water in the kitchen for Mondo, take his squeaking plastic frog out of her purse and drop it on the floor. He would pounce delightedly, just as he did every day at home, batting around his favorite toy. The bowl usually sat on a coffee table, though recently she had displayed it on top of a pine blanket chest and on a lacquered table. It was once placed on a cherry table beneath a Bonnard still life, where it held its own.

Everyone who has purchased a house or who has wanted to sell a house must be familiar with some of the tricks used to convince a buyer that the house is quite special: a fire in the fireplace in early evening; jonquils in a pitcher on the kitchen counter, where no one ordinarily has space to put flowers; perhaps the slight aroma of spring, made by a single drop of scent vaporizing from a lamp bulb.

The wonderful thing about the bowl, Andrea thought, was that it was both subtle and noticeable—a paradox of a bowl. Its glaze was the color of cream and seemed to glow no matter what light it was placed in. There were a few bits of color in it—tiny geometric flashes—and some of these were tinged with flecks of silver. They were as mysterious as cells seen under a microscope; it was difficult not to study them, because they shimmered, flashing for a split second, and then resumed their shape. Something about the colors and their random placement suggested motion. People who liked country furniture always commented on the bowl, but then it turned out that people who felt comfortable with Biedermeier loved it just as much. But the bowl was not at all ostentatious, or even so noticeable that anyone would suspect that it had been put in place deliberately. They might notice the height of the ceiling on first entering a room, and only when their eye moved down from that, or away from the refraction of sunlight on a pale wall, would they see the bowl. Then they would go immediately to it and comment. Yet they always faltered when they tried to say something. Perhaps it was because they were in the house for a serious reason, not to notice some object.

Once Andrea got a call from a woman who had not put in an offer on a house she had shown her. That bowl, she said—would it be possible to find out where the owners had bought that beautiful bowl? Andrea pretended that she did not know what the woman was referring to. A bowl, somewhere in the house? Oh, on a table under the window. Yes, she would ask, of course. She let a couple of days pass, then called back to say that the bowl had been a present and the people did not know where it had been purchased.

When the bowl was not being taken from house to house, it sat on Andrea's coffee table at home. She didn't keep it carefully wrapped (although she transported it that way, in a box); she kept it on the table, because she liked to see it. It was large enough so that it didn't seem fragile or particularly vulnerable if anyone sideswiped the table or Mondo blundered into it at play. She had asked her husband to please not drop his house key in it. It was meant to be empty.

When her husband first noticed the bowl, he had peered into it and smiled briefly. He always urged her to buy things she liked. In recent years, both of them had acquired many things to make up for all the lean years when they were graduate students, but now that they had been comfortable for quite a while, the pleasure of new possessions dwindled. Her husband had pronounced the bowl "pretty," and he had turned away without picking it up to examine it. He had no more interest in the bowl than she had in his new Leica.

She was sure that the bowl brought her luck. Bids were often put in on houses where she had displayed the bowl. Sometimes the owners, who were always asked to be away or to step outside when the house was being shown, didn't even know that the bowl had been in their house. Once—she could not imagine how—she left it behind, and then she was so afraid that something might have happened to it that she rushed back to the house and sighed with relief when the woman owner opened the door. The bowl, Andrea explained—she had purchased a bowl and set it on the chest for safekeeping while she toured the house with the prospective buyers, and she . . . She felt like rushing past the frowning woman and seizing her bowl. The owner stepped aside, and it was only when Andrea ran to the chest that the lady glanced at her a little strangely. In the few seconds before Andrea picked up the bowl, she realized that the owner must have just seen that it had been perfectly placed, that the sunlight struck the bluer part of it. Her pitcher had been moved to the far side of the chest, and the bowl predominated. All the way home, Andrea wondered how she could have left the bowl behind. It was like leaving a friend at an outing—just walking off. Sometimes there were stories in the paper about families forgetting a child somewhere and driving to the next city. Andrea had only gone a mile down the road before she remembered.

In time, she dreamed of the bowl. Twice, in a waking dream—early in the morning, between sleep and a last nap before rising—she had a clear vision of it. It came into sharp focus and startled her for a moment—the same bowl she looked at every day.

She had a very profitable year selling real estate. Word spread, and she had more clients than she felt comfortable with. She had the foolish thought that if only the bowl were an animate object she could thank it. There were times when she wanted to talk to her husband about the bowl. He was a stockbroker, and sometimes told people that he was fortunate to be married to a woman who had such a fine aesthetic sense and yet could also function in the real world. They were a lot alike, really—they had agreed on that. They were both quiet people—reflective, slow to make value judgments, but almost intractable once they had come to a conclusion. They both liked details, but while ironies attracted her, he was more impatient and dismissive when matters became many-sided or unclear. They both knew this, and it was the kind of thing they could talk about when they were alone in the car together, coming home from a party or after a weekend with friends. But she never talked to him about the bowl. When they were at dinner, exchanging their news of the day, or while they lay in bed at night listening to the stereo and murmuring sleepy disconnections, she was often tempted to come right out and say that she thought that the bowl in the living room, the cream-colored bowl, was responsible for her success. But she didn't say it. She couldn't begin to explain it. Sometimes in the morning, she would look at him and feel guilty that she had such a constant secret.

Could it be that she had some deeper connection with the bowl—a relationship of some kind? She corrected her thinking: how could she imagine such a thing, when she was a human being and it was a bowl? It was ridiculous. Just think of how people lived together and loved each other . . . But was that always so clear, always a relationship? She was confused by these thoughts, but they remained in her mind. There was something within her now, something real, that she never talked about.

The bowl was a mystery, even to her. It was frustrating, because her involvement with the bowl contained a steady sense of unrequited good fortune; it would have been easier to respond if some sort of demand were made in return. But that only happened in fairy tales. The bowl was just a bowl. She did not believe that for one second. What she believed was that it was something she loved.

In the past, she had sometimes talked to her husband about a new property she was about to buy or sell—confiding some clever strategy she had devised to persuade owners who seemed ready to sell. Now she stopped doing that, for all her strategies involved the bowl. She became more deliberate with the bowl, and more possessive. She put it in houses only when no one was there, and removed it when she left the house. Instead of just moving a pitcher or a dish, she would remove all the other objects from a table. She had to force herself to handle them carefully, because she didn't really care about them. She just wanted them out of sight.

She wondered how the situation would end. As with a lover, there was no exact scenario of how matters would come to a close. Anxiety became the operative force. It would be irrelevant if the lover rushed into someone else's arms, or wrote her a note and departed to another city. The horror was the possibility of the disappearance. That was what mattered.

She would get up at night and look at the bowl. It never occurred to her that she might break it. She washed and dried it without anxiety, and she moved it often, from coffee table to mahogany corner table or wherever, without fearing an accident. It was clear that she would not be the one who would do anything to the bowl. The bowl was only handled by her, set safely on one surface or another; it was not very likely that anyone would break it. A bowl was a poor conductor of electricity: it would not be hit by lightning. Yet the idea of damage persisted. She did not think beyond that—to what her life would be without the bowl. She only continued to fear that some accident would happen. Why not, in a world where people set plants where they did not belong, so that visitors touring a house would be fooled into thinking that dark corners got sunlight—a world full of tricks?

She had first seen the bowl several years earlier, at a crafts fair she had visited half in secret, with her lover. He had urged her to buy the bowl. She didn't *need* any more things, she told him. But she had been drawn to the bowl, and they had lingered near it. Then she went on to the next booth, and he came up behind her, tapping the rim against her shoulder as she ran her fingers over a wood carving. "You're still insisting that I buy that?" she said. "No," he said. "I bought it for you." He had bought her other things before this—things she liked more, at first—the child's ebony-and-turquoise ring that fitted her little finger; the wooden box, long and thin, beautifully dove-tailed, that she used to hold paper clips; the soft gray sweater with a pouch pocket. It was his idea that when he could not be there to hold her hand she could hold her own—clasp her hands inside the lone pocket that stretched across the front. But in time she became more attached to the bowl than to any of his other presents. She tried to talk herself out of it. She owned other things that were more striking or valuable. It wasn't an object whose beauty jumped out at you; a lot of people must have passed it by before the two of them saw it that day.

Her lover had said that she was always too slow to know what she really loved. Why continue with her life the way it was? Why be two-faced, he asked her. He had made the first move toward her. When she would not decide in his favor, would not change her life and come to him, he asked her what made her think she could have it both ways. And then he made the last move and left. It was a decision meant to break her will, to shatter her intransigent ideas about honoring previous commitments.

Time passed. Alone in the living room at night, she often looked at the bowl sitting on the table, still and safe, unilluminated. In its way, it was perfect: the world cut in half, deep and smoothly empty. Near the rim, even in dim light, the eye moved toward one small flash of blue, a vanishing point on the horizon.

Skeletons

Usually she was the artist. Today she was the model. She had on sweatpants—both she and Garrett wore medium, although his sweatpants fit her better than they did him, because she did not have his long legs—and a Chinese jacket, plum-colored, patterned with blue octagons, edged in silver thread, that seemed to float among the lavender flowers that were as big as the palm of a hand raised for the high-five. A *frog*, Nancy thought; that was what the piece was called—the near-knot she fingered, the little fastener she never closed.

It was late Saturday afternoon, and, as usual, Nancy Niles was spending the day with Garrett. She had met him in a drawing class she took at night. During the week, he worked in an artists' supply store, but he had the weekends off. Until recently, when the weather turned cold, they had often taken long walks on Saturday or Sunday, and sometimes Kyle Brown—an undergraduate at the University of Pennsylvania, who was the other tenant in the rooming house Garrett lived in, in a run-down neighborhood twenty minutes from the campus—had walked with them. It was Kyle who had told Garrett about the empty room in the house. His first week in Philadelphia, Garrett had been in line to pay his check at a coffee shop when the cashier asked Kyle for a penny, which he didn't have. Then she looked behind Kyle to Garrett and said, "Well, would *you* have a penny?" Leaving, Kyle and Garrett struck up the conversation that had led to Garrett's moving into the house. And now the cashier's question had become a running joke. Just that morning, Garrett was outside the bathroom, and when Kyle came out, wrapped in his towel, he asked, "Well, got a penny *now*?"

It was easy to amuse Kyle, and he had a lovely smile, Nancy thought. He once told her that he was the first member of his family to leave Utah to go to college. It had strained relations with his parents, but they couldn't argue with Kyle's insistence that the English department at Penn was excellent. The landlady's married daughter had gone to Penn, and Kyle felt sure that had been the deciding factor in his getting the room. That and the fact that when the landlady told him where the nearest Episcopal church was, he told her that he was a Mormon. "At least you have *some* religion," she said. When she interviewed Garrett and described the neighborhood and told him where the Episcopal church was, Kyle had already tipped him; Garrett flipped open a notebook and wrote down the address.

Now, as Garrett and Nancy sat talking as he sketched (Garrett cared so much about drawing that Nancy was sure that he was happy that the weather had turned, so he had an excuse to stay indoors), Kyle was frying chicken downstairs. A few minutes earlier, he had looked in on them and stayed to talk. He complained that he was tired of being known as "the Mormon" to the landlady. Not condescendingly, that he could see—she just said it the way a person might use the Latin name for a plant instead of its common one. He showed them a telephone message from his father she had written down, with "Mormon" printed at the top.

Kyle Brown lived on hydroponic tomatoes, Shake 'n Bake chicken, and Pepperidge Farm rolls. On Saturdays, Garrett and Nancy ate with him. They contributed apple cider—smoky, with a smell you could taste; the last pressing of the season—and sometimes turnovers from the corner bakery. Above the sputtering chicken Nancy could hear Kyle singing now, in his strong baritone: "The truth is, I *nev*-er left you . . ."

"Sit still," Garrett said, looking up from his sketchbook. "Don't you know your role in life?"

Nancy cupped her hands below her breasts, turned her head to the side, and pursed her lips.

"Don't do that," he said, throwing the crayon stub. "Don't put yourself down, even as a joke."

"Oh, don't analyze everything so seriously," she said, hopping off the window seat and picking up the conté crayon. She threw it back to him. He caught it one-handed. He was the second person she had ever slept with. The other one, much to her embarrassment now, had been a deliberate experiment.

"Tell your shrink that your actions don't mean anything," he said.

"You hate it that I go to a shrink," she said, watching him bend over the sketchbook again. "Half the world sees a shrink. What are you worried about—that somebody might know something about me you don't know?"

He raised his eyebrows, as he often did when he was concentrating on something in a drawing. "I know a few things he doesn't know," he said.

"It's not a competition," she said.

"*Everything* is a competition. At some very serious, very deep level, every single thing—"

"You already made that joke," she said, sighing.

He stopped drawing and looked over at her in a different way. "I know," he said. "I shouldn't have taken it back. I really do believe that's what exists. One person jockeying for position, another person dodging."

"I can't tell when you're kidding. Now you're kidding, right?"

"No. I'm serious. I just took it back this morning because I could tell I was scaring you."

"Oh. Now are you going to tell me that you're in competition with me?"

"Why do you think I'm kidding?" he said. "It would *kill* me if you got a better grade in any course than I got. And you're so good. When you draw, you make strokes that look as if they were put on the paper with a feather. I'd take your technique away from you if I could. It's just that I know I can't, so I bite my tongue. Really. I envy you so much my heart races. I could never share a studio with you. I wouldn't be able to be in the same room with somebody who can be so patient and so exact at the same time. Compared to you, I might as well be wearing a catcher's mitt when I draw."

Nancy pulled her knees up to her chest and rested her cheek against one of them. She started to laugh.

"Really," he said.

"O.K.—*really*," she said, going poker-faced. "I know, darling Garrett. You really do mean it."

"I do," he said.

She stood up. "Then we don't have to share a studio," she said. "But you can't take it back that you said you wanted to marry me." She rubbed her hands through her hair and let one hand linger to massage her neck. Her body was cold from sitting on the window seat. Clasping her legs, she had realized that the thigh muscles ached.

"Maybe all that envy and anxiety has to be burnt away with constant passion," she said. "I mean—I really, *really* mean that." She smiled. "Really," she said. "Maybe you just want to give in to it—like scratching a mosquito bite until it's so sore you cry."

They were within seconds of touching each other, but just at the moment when she was about to step toward him they heard the old oak stairs creaking beneath Kyle's feet.

"This will come as no surprise to you," Kyle said, standing in the doorway, "but I'm checking to make sure that you know you're invited to dinner. I provide the chicken, sliced tomatoes, and bread—right? You bring dessert and something to drink."

Even in her disappointment, Nancy could smile at him. Of course he knew that he had stumbled into something. Probably he wanted to turn and run back down the stairs. It wasn't easy to be the younger extra person in a threesome. When she raised her head, Garrett caught her eye, and in that moment they both knew how embarrassed Kyle must be. His need for them was never masked as well as he thought. The two of them, clearly lovers, were forgoing candlelight and deliberately bumped knees and the intimacy of holding glasses to each other's lips in order to have dinner with him. Kyle had once told Nancy, on one of their late-fall walks, that one of his worst fears had always been that someone might be able to read his mind. It was clear to her that he had fantasies about them. At the time, Nancy had tried to pass it off lightly; she told him that when she was drawing she always sensed the model's bones and muscles, and what she did was stroke a soft surface over them until a body took form.

Kyle wanted to stay close to them—meant to stay close—but time passed, and after they all had moved several times he lost track of them. He knew nothing of Nancy Niles's life, had no idea that in October, 1985, she was out trick-or-treating with Garrett and their two-year-old child, Fraser, who was dressed up as a goblin for his first real Halloween. A plastic orange pumpkin, lit by batteries, bobbed in front of her as she walked a few steps ahead of them. She was dressed in a skeleton costume, but she might have been an angel, beaming salvation into the depths of the mines. Where she lived—their part of Providence, Rhode Island—was as grim and dark as an underground labyrinth.

It was ironic that men thought she could lead the way for them, because Nancy had realized all along that she had little sense of direction. She felt isolated, angry at herself for not pursuing her career as an artist, for no longer being in love. It would have surprised her to know that in a moment of crisis, late that night, in Warrenton, Virginia, when leaves, like shadows on an X ray, suddenly flew up and obscured his vision and his car went into a skid, Kyle Brown would see her again, in a vision. *Nancy Niles!* he thought, in that instant of fear and shock. There she was, for a split second—her face, ghostly pale under the gas-station lights, metamorphosed into brightness. In a flash, she was again the embodiment of beauty to him. As his car spun in a widening circle and then came to rest with its back wheels on an embankment, Nancy Niles the skeleton was walking slowly down the sidewalk. Leaves flew past her like footsteps, quickly descending the stairs.

Where You'll Find Me

Friends keep calling my broken arm a broken wing. It's the left arm, now folded against my chest and kept in place with a blue scarf sling that is knotted behind my neck, and it weighs too much ever to have been winglike. The accident happened when I ran for a bus. I tried to stop it from pulling away by shaking my shopping bags like maracas in the air, and that's when I slipped on the ice and went down.

So I took the train from New York City to Saratoga yesterday, instead of driving. I had the perfect excuse not to go to Saratoga to visit my brother at all, but once I had geared up for it I decided to go through with the trip and avoid guilt. It isn't Howard I mind but his wife's two children—a girl of eleven and a boy of three. Becky either pays no attention to her brother Todd or else she tortures him. Last winter she used to taunt him by stalking around the house on his heels, clomping close behind him wherever he went, which made him run and scream at the same time. Kate did not intervene until both children became hysterical and we could no longer shout over their voices. "I think I like it that they're physical," she said. "Maybe if they enact some of their hostility like this, they won't grow up with the habit of getting what they want by playing mind games with other people." It seems to me that they will not ever grow up but will burn out like meteors.

Howard has finally found what he wants: the opposite of domestic tranquility. For six years, he lived in Oregon with a pale, passive woman. On the rebound, he married an even paler pre-med student named Francine. That marriage lasted less than a year, and then, on a blind date in Los Angeles, he met Kate, whose husband was away on a business trip to Denmark just then. In no time, Kate and her daughter and infant son moved in with him, to the studio apartment in Laguna Beach he was sharing with a screenwriter. The two men had been working on a script about Medgar Evers, but when Kate and the children moved in they switched to writing a screenplay about what happens when a man meets a married woman with two children on a blind date and the three of them move in with him and his friend. Then Howard's collaborator got engaged and moved out, and the screenplay was abandoned. Howard accepted a last-minute invitation to teach writing at an upstate college in New York, and within a week they were all ensconced in a drafty Victorian house in Saratoga. Kate's husband had begun divorce proceedings before she moved in with Howard, but eventually he agreed not to sue for custody of Becky and Todd in exchange for child-support payments that were less than half of what his lawyer thought he would have to pay. Now he sends the children enormous stuffed animals that they have little or no interest in, with notes that say, "Put this in Mom's zoo." A stuffed toy every month or so—giraffes, a life-size German shepherd, an overstuffed standing bear—and, every time, the same note.

The bear stands in one corner of the kitchen, and people have gotten in the habit of pinning notes to it—reminders to buy milk or get the oil changed in the car. Wraparound sunglasses have been added. Scarves and jackets are sometimes draped on its arms. Sometimes the stuffed German shepherd is brought over and propped up with its paws placed on the bear's haunch, imploring it.

Right now, I'm in the kitchen with the bear. I've just turned up the thermostat—the first one up in the morning is supposed to do that—and am dunking a tea bag in a mug of hot water. For some reason, it's impossible for me to make tea with loose tea and the tea ball unless I have help. The only tea bag I could find was Emperor's Choice.

I sit in one of the kitchen chairs to drink the tea. The chair seems to stick to me, even though I have on thermal long johns and a long flannel nightgown. The chairs are plastic, very nineteen-fifties, patterned with shapes that look sometimes geometric, sometimes almost human. Little things like malformed hands reach out toward triangles and squares. I asked. Howard and Kate got the kitchen set at an auction, for thirty dollars. They thought it was funny. The house itself is not funny. It has four fireplaces, wide-board floors, and high, dusty ceilings. They bought it with his share of an inheritance that came to us when our grandfather died. Kate's contribution to restoring the house has been transforming the baseboards into faux marbre. How effective this is has to do with how stoned she is when she starts. Sometimes the baseboards look like clotted versions of the kitchen-chair pattern, instead of marble. Kate considers what she calls "parenting" to be a full-time job. When they first moved to Saratoga, she used to give piano lessons. Now she ignores the children and paints the baseboards.

And who am I to stand in judgment? I am a thirty-eight-year-old woman, out of a job, on tenuous enough footing with her sometime lover that she can imagine crashing emotionally as easily as she did on the ice. It may be true, as my lover, Frank, says, that having money is not good for the soul. Money that is given to you, that is. He is a lawyer who also has money, but it is money he earned and parlayed into more money by investing in real estate. An herb farm is part of this real estate. Boxes of herbs keep turning up at Frank's office—herbs in foil, herbs in plastic bags, dried herbs wrapped in cones of newspaper. He crumbles them over omelets, roasts, vegetables. He is opposed to salt. He insists herbs are more healthful.

And who am I to claim to love a man when I am skeptical even about his use of herbs? I am embarrassed to be unemployed. I am insecure enough to stay with someone because of the look that sometimes comes into his eyes when he makes love to me. I am a person who secretly shakes on salt in the kitchen, then comes out with her plate, smiling, as basil is crumbled over the tomatoes.

Sometimes, in our bed, his fingers smell of rosemary or tarragon. Strong smells. Sour smells. Whatever Shakespeare says, or whatever is written in *Culpeper's Complete Herbal*, I cannot imagine that herbs have anything to do with love. But many brides-to-be come to the herb farm and buy branches of herbs to stick in their bouquets. They anoint their wrists with herbal extracts, to smell mysterious. They believe that herbs bring them luck. These days, they want tubs of rosemary in their houses, not ficus trees. "I got in right on the cusp of the new world," Frank says. He isn't kidding.

For the Christmas party tonight, there are cherry tomatoes halved and stuffed with peaks of cheese, mushrooms stuffed with puréed tomatoes, tomatoes stuffed with chopped mushrooms, and mushrooms stuffed with cheese. Kate is laughing in the kitchen. "No one's going to notice," she mutters. "No one's going to say anything."

"Why don't we put out some nuts?" Howard says.

"Nuts are so conventional. This is funny," Kate says, squirting more soft cheese out of a pastry tube.

"Last year we had mistletoe and mulled cider."

"Last year we lost our sense of humor. What happened that we got all hyped up? We even ran out on Christmas Eve to cut a tree—"

"The kids," Howard says.

"That's right," she says. "The kids were crying. They were feeling competitive with the other kids, or something."

"Becky was crying. Todd was too young to cry about that," Howard says.

"Why are we talking about tears?" Kate says. "We can talk about tears when it's not the season to be jolly. Everybody's going to come in tonight and love the wreaths on the picture hooks and think this food is so *festive*."

"We invited a new Indian guy from the Philosophy Department," Howard says. "American Indian—not an Indian from India."

"If we want, we can watch the tapes of *Jewel in the Crown*," Kate says.

"I'm feeling really depressed," Howard says, backing up to the counter and sliding down until he rests on his elbows. His tennis shoes are wet. He never takes off his wet shoes, and he never gets colds.

"Try one of those mushrooms," Kate says. "They'll be better when they're cooked, though."

"What's wrong with me?" Howard says. It's almost the first time he's looked at me since I arrived. I've been trying not to register my boredom and my frustration with Kate's prattle.

"Maybe we should get a tree," I say.

"I don't think it's Christmas that's making me feel this way," Howard says.

"Well, snap out of it," Kate says. "You can open one of your presents early, if you want to."

"No, no," Howard says, "it isn't Christmas." He hands a plate to Kate, who has begun to stack the dishwasher. "I've been worrying that you're in a lot of pain and you just aren't saying so," he says to me.

"It's just uncomfortable," I say.

"I know, but do you keep going over what happened, in your mind? When you fell, or in the emergency room, or anything?"

"I had a dream last night about the ballerinas at Victoria Pool," I say. "It was like Victoria Pool was a stage set instead of a real place, and tall, thin ballerinas kept parading in and twirling and pirouetting. I was envying their being able to touch their fingertips together over their heads."

Howard opens the top level of the dishwasher and Kate begins to hand him the rinsed glasses.

"You just told a little story," Howard says. "You didn't really answer the question."

"I don't keep going over it in my mind," I say.

"So you're repressing it," he says.

"Mom," Becky says, walking into the kitchen, "is it O.K. if Deirdre comes to the party tonight if her dad doesn't drive here to pick her up this weekend?"

"I thought her father was in the hospital," Kate says.

"Yeah, he was. But he got out. He called and said that it was going to snow up north, though, so he wasn't sure if he could come."

"Of course she can come," Kate says.

"And you know what?" Becky says.

"Say hello to people when you come into a room," Kate says. "At least make eye contact or smile or something."

"I'm not Miss America on the runway, Mom. I'm just walking into the kitchen."

"You have to acknowledge people's existence," Kate says. "Haven't we talked about this?"

"Oh, hel-*lo*," Becky says, curtsying by pulling out the sides of an imaginary skirt. She has on purple sweatpants. She turns toward me and pulls the fabric away from her hipbones. "Oh, hello, as if we've never met," she says.

"Your aunt here doesn't want to be in the middle of this," Howard says. "She's got enough trouble."

"Get back on track," Kate says to Becky. "What did you want to say to me?"

"You know what you do, Mom?" Becky says. "You make an issue of something and then it's like when I speak it's a big thing. Everybody's listening to me."

Kate closes the door to the dishwasher.

"Did you want to speak to me privately?" she says.

"Nooo," Becky says, sitting in the chair across from me and sighing. "I was just going to say—and now it's a big deal—I was going to say that Deirdre just found out that that guy she was writing all year is in *prison*. He was in prison all the time, but she didn't know what the P.O. box meant."

"What's she going to do?" Howard says.

"She's going to write and ask him all about prison," Becky says.

"That's good," Howard says. "That cheers me up to hear that. The guy probably agonized about whether to tell her or not. He probably thought she'd hot-potato him."

"Lots of decent people go to prison," Becky says.

"That's ridiculous," Kate says. "You can't generalize about convicts any more than you can generalize about the rest of humanity."

"So?" Becky says. "If somebody in the rest of humanity had something to hide, he'd hide it, too, wouldn't he?"

"Let's go get a tree," Howard says. "We'll get a tree."

"Somebody got hit on the highway carrying a tree home," Becky says. "Really."

"You really do have your ear to the ground in this town," Kate says. "You kids could be the town crier. I know everything before the paper comes."

"It happened yesterday," Becky says.

"Christ," Howard says. "We're talking about crying, we're talking about death." He is leaning against the counter again.

"We are not," Kate says, walking in front of him to open the refrigerator door. She puts a plate of stuffed tomatoes inside. "In your typical fashion, you've singled out two observations out of a lot that have been made, and—"

"I woke up thinking about Dennis Bidou last night," Howard says to me. "Remember Dennis Bidou, who used to taunt you? Dad put me up to having it out with him, and he backed down after that. But I was always afraid he'd come after me. I went around for years pretending not to cringe when he came near me. And then, you know, one time I was out on a date and we ran out of gas, and as I was walking to get a can of gas a car pulled up alongside me and Dennis Bidou leaned out the window. He was surprised that it was me and I was surprised that it was him. He asked me what happened and I said I ran out of gas. He said, 'Tough shit, I guess,' but a girl was driving and she gave him a hard time. She stopped the car and insisted that I get in the back and they'd take me to the gas station. He didn't say one word to me the whole way there. I remembered the way he looked in the car when I found out he was killed in Nam—the back of his head on that ramrod-straight body, and a black collar or some dark-colored collar pulled up to his hairline." Howard makes a horizontal motion with four fingers, thumb folded under, in the air beside his ear.

"Now you're trying to depress everybody," Kate says.

"I'm willing to cheer up. I'm going to cheer up before tonight. I'm going up to that Lions Club lot on Main Street and get a tree. Anybody coming with me?"

"I'm going over to Deirdre's," Becky says.

"I'll come with you, if you think my advice is needed," I say.

"For fun," Howard says, bouncing on his toes. "For fun—not advice."

He gets my red winter coat out of the closet, and I back into it, putting in my good arm. Then he takes a diaper pin off the lapel and pins the other side of the coat to the top of my shoulder, easing the pin through my sweater. Then he puts Kate's poncho over my head. This is the system, because I am always cold. Actually, Kate devised the system. I stand there while Howard puts on his leather jacket. I feel like a bird with a cloth draped over its cage for the night. This makes me feel sorry for myself, and then I *do* think of my arm as a broken wing, and suddenly everything seems so sad that I feel my eyes well up with tears. I sniff a couple of times. And Howard faced down Dennis Bidou, for my sake! My brother! But he really did it because my father told him to. Whatever my father told him to do he did. He drew the line only at smothering my father in the hospital when he asked him to. That is the only time I know of that he ignored my father's wishes.

"Get one that's tall enough," Kate says. "And don't get one of those trees that look like a cactus. Get one with long needles that swoops."

"Swoops?" Howard says, turning in the hallway.

"Something with some fluidity," she says, bending her knees and making a sweeping motion with her arm. "You know—something beautiful."

Before the guests arrive, a neighbor woman has brought Todd back from his play group and he is ready for bed, and the tree has been decorated with a few dozen Christmas balls and some stars cut out of typing paper, with paper-clip hangers stuck through one point. The smaller animals in the stuffed-toy menagerie—certainly not the bear—are under the tree, approximating the animals at the manger. The manger is a roasting pan, with a green dinosaur inside.

"How many of these people who're coming do I know?" I say.

"You know . . . you know . . ." Howard is gnawing his lip. He takes another sip of wine, looks puzzled. "Well, you know Koenig," he says. "Koenig got married. You'll like his wife. They're coming separately, because he's coming straight from work. You know the Miners. You know—you'll really like Lightfoot, the new guy in the Philosophy Department. Don't rush to tell him that you're tied up with somebody. He's a nice guy, and he deserves a chance."

"I don't think I'm tied up with anybody," I say.

"Have a drink—you'll feel better," Howard says. "Honest to God. I was getting depressed this afternoon. When the light starts to sink so early, I never can figure out what I'm responding to. I gray over, like the afternoon, you know?"

"O.K., I'll have a drink," I say.

"The very fat man who's coming is in A.A.," Howard says, taking a glass off the bookshelf and pouring some wine into it. "These were just washed yesterday," he says. He hands me the glass of wine. "The fat guy's name is Dwight Kule. The Jansons, who are also coming, introduced us to him. He's a bachelor. Used to live in the Apple. Mystery man. Nobody knows. He's got a computer terminal in his house that's hooked up to some mysterious office in New York. Tells funny jokes. They come at him all day over the computer."

"Who are the Jansons?"

"You met her. The woman whose lover broke into the house and did caricatures of her and her husband all over the walls after she broke off with him. One amazing artist, from what I heard. You know about that, right?"

"No," I say, smiling. "What does she look like?"

"You met her at the races with us. Tall. Red hair."

"Oh, that woman. Why didn't you say so?"

"I told you about the lover, right?"

"I didn't know she had a lover."

"Well, fortunately she *had* told her husband, and they'd decided to patch it up, so when they came home and saw the walls—I mean, I get the idea that it was rather graphic. Not like stumbling upon hieroglyphics in a cave or something. Husband told it as a story on himself: going down to the paint store and buying the darkest can of blue paint they had to do the painting-over, because he wanted it done with—none of this three-coats stuff." Howard has another sip of wine. "You haven't met her husband," he says. "He's an anesthesiologist."

"What did her lover do?"

"He ran the music store. He left town."

"Where did he go?"

"Montpelier."

"How do you find all this stuff out?"

"Ask. Get told," Howard says. "Then he was cleaning his gun in Montpelier the other day, and it went off and he shot himself in the foot. Didn't do any real damage, though."

"It's hard to think of anything like that as poetic justice," I say. "So are the Jansons happy again?"

"I don't know. We don't see much of them," Howard says. "We're not really involved in any social whirl, you know. You only visit during the holidays, and that's when we give the annual party."

"Oh, hel-*lo*," Becky says, sweeping into the living room from the front door, bringing the cold and her girlfriend Deirdre in with her. Deirdre is giggling, head averted. "My friends! My wonderful friends!" Becky says, trotting past, hand waving madly. She stops in the doorway, and Deirdre collides with her. Deirdre puts her hand up to her mouth to muffle a yelp, then bolts past Becky into the kitchen.

"I can remember being that age," I say.

"I don't think I was ever that stupid," Howard says.

"A different thing happens with girls. Boys don't talk to each other all the time in quite the same intense way, do they? I mean, I can remember when it seemed that I never talked but that I was always *confiding* something."

"Confide something in me," Howard says, coming back from flipping the Bach on the stereo.

"Girls just talk that way to other girls," I say, realizing he's serious.

"Gidon Kremer," Howard says, clamping his hand over his heart. "God—tell me that isn't beautiful."

"How did you find out so much about classical music?" I say. "By asking and getting told?"

"In New York," he says. "Before I moved here. Before L.A., even. I just started buying records and asking around. Half the city is an unofficial guide to classical music. You can find out a lot in New York." He pours more wine into his glass. "Come on," he says. "Confide something in me."

In the kitchen, one of the girls turns on the radio, and rock and roll, played low, crosses paths with Bach's violin. The music goes lower still. Deirdre and Becky are laughing.

I take a drink, sigh, and nod at Howard. "When I was in San Francisco last June to see my friend Susan, I got in a night before I said I would, and she wasn't in town," I say. "I was going to surprise her, and she was the one who surprised me. It was no big deal. I was tired from the flight and by the time I got there I was happy to have the excuse to check into a hotel, because if she'd been there we'd have talked all night. Acting like Becky with Deirdre, right?"

Howard rolls his eyes and nods.

"So I went to a hotel and checked in and took a bath, and suddenly I got my second wind and I thought what the hell, why not go to the restaurant right next to the hotel—or in the hotel, I guess it was—and have a great dinner, since it was supposed to be such a great place."

"What restaurant?"

"L'Étoile."

"Yeah," he says. "What happened?"

"I'm telling you what happened. You have to be patient. Girls always know to be patient with other girls."

He nods yes again.

"They were very nice to me. It was about three-quarters full. They put me at a table, and the minute I sat down I looked up and there was a man on a banquette across the room from me. He was looking at me, and I was looking at him, and it was almost impossible not to keep eye contact. It just hit both of us, obviously. And almost on the other side of the curve of the banquette was a woman, who wasn't terribly attractive. She had on a wedding ring. He didn't. They were eating in silence. I had to force myself to look somewhere else, but when I did look up he'd look up, or he'd already be looking up. At some point he left the table. I saw that in my peripheral vision, when I had my head turned to hear a conversation on my right and I was chewing my food. Then after a while he paid the check and the two of them left. She walked ahead of him, and he didn't seem to be with her. I mean, he walked quite far behind her. But naturally he didn't turn his head. And after they left I thought, That's amazing. It was really like kinetic energy. Just wham. So I had coffee, and then I paid my check, and when I was leaving I was walking up the steep steps to the street and the waiter came up behind me and said, 'Excuse me. I don't know what I should do, but I didn't want to embarrass you in the restaurant. The gentleman left this for you on his way out.' And he handed me an envelope. I was pretty taken aback, but I just said, 'Thank you,' and continued up the steps, and when I got outside I looked around. He wasn't there, naturally. So I opened the envelope, and his business card was inside. He was one of the partners in a law firm. And underneath his name he had written, 'Who are you? Please call.'"

Howard is smiling.

"So I put it in my purse and I walked for a few blocks, and I thought, Well, what for, really? Some man in San Francisco? For what? A one-night stand? I went back to the hotel, and when I walked in the man behind the desk stood up and said, 'Excuse me. Were you just eating dinner?,' and I said, 'A few minutes ago,' and he said, 'Someone left this for you.' It was a hotel envelope. In the elevator on the way to my room, I opened it, and it was the same business card, with 'Please call' written on it."

"I hope you called," Howard says.

"I decided to sleep on it. And in the morning I decided not to. But I kept the card. And then at the end of August I was walking in the East Village, and a couple obviously from out of town were walking in front of me, and a punk kid got up off the stoop where he was sitting and said to them, 'Hey—I want my picture taken with you.' I went into a store, and when I came out the couple and the punk kid were all laughing together, holding these Polaroid snaps that another punk had taken. It was a joke, not a scam. The man gave the kid a dollar for one of the pictures, and they walked off, and the punk sat back down on the stoop. So I walked back to where he was sitting, and I said, 'Could you do me a real favor? Could I have my picture taken with you, too?'"

"What?" Howard says. The violin is soaring. He gets up and turns the music down a notch. He looks over his shoulder. "Yeah?" he says.

"The kid wanted to know why I wanted it, and I told him because it would upset my boyfriend. So he said yeah—his face lit up when I said that—but that he really would appreciate two bucks for more film. So I gave it to him, and then he put his arm around me and really mugged for the camera. He was like a human boa constrictor around my neck, and he did a Mick Jagger pout. I couldn't believe how well the picture came out. And that night, on the white part on the bottom I wrote, 'I'm somebody whose name you still don't know. Are you going to find me?' and I put it in an envelope and mailed it to him in San Francisco. I don't know why I did it. I mean, it doesn't seem like something I'd ever do, you know?"

"But how will he find you?" Howard says.

"I've still got his card," I say, shrugging my good shoulder toward my purse on the floor.

"You don't know what you're going to do?" Howard says.

"I haven't thought about it in months."

"How is that possible?"

"How is it possible that somebody can go into a restaurant and be hit by lightning and the other person is, too? It's like a bad movie or something."

"Of course it can happen," Howard says. "Seriously, what are you going to do?"

"Let some time pass. Maybe send him something he can follow up on if he still wants to."

"That's an amazing story," Howard says.

"Sometimes—well, I hadn't thought about it in a while, but at the end of summer, after I mailed the picture, I'd be walking along or doing whatever I was doing and this feeling would come over me that he was thinking about me."

Howard looks at me strangely. "He probably was," he says. "He doesn't know how to get in touch with you."

"You used to be a screenwriter. What should he do?"

"Couldn't he figure out from the background that it was the Village?"

"I'm not sure."

"If he could, he could put an ad in the *Voice*."

"I think it was just a car in the background."

"Then you've got to give him something else," Howard says.

"For what? You want your sister to have a one-night stand?"

"You make him sound awfully attractive," Howard says.

"Yeah, but what if he's a rat? It could be argued that he was just cocky, and that he was pretty sure that I'd respond. Don't you think?"

"I think you should get in touch with him. Do it in some amusing way if you want, but I wouldn't let him slip away."

"I never had him. And from the looks of it he has a wife."

"You don't know that."

"No," I say. "I guess I don't know."

"Do it," Howard says. "I think you need this," and when he speaks he whispers—just what a girl would do. He nods his head yes. "Do it," he whispers again. Then he turns his head abruptly, to see what I am staring at. It is Kate, wrapped in a towel after her bath, trailing the long cord of the extension phone with her.

"It's Frank," she whispers, her hand over the mouthpiece. "He says he's going to come to the party after all."

I look at her dumbly, surprised. I'd almost forgotten that Frank knew I was here. He's only been here once with me, and it was clear that he didn't like Howard and Kate. Why would he suddenly decide to come to the party?

She shrugs, hand still over the mouthpiece. "Come here," she whispers.

I get up and start toward the phone. "If it's not an awful imposition," she says, "maybe he could bring Deirdre's father with him. He lives just around the corner from you in the city."

"Deirdre's father?" I say.

"Here," she whispers. "He'll hang up."

"Hi, Frank," I say, talking into the phone. My voice sounds high, false.

"I miss you," Frank says. "I've got to get out of the city. I invited myself. I assume since it's an annual invitation it's all right, right?"

"Oh, of course," I say. "Can you just hold on for one second?"

"Sure," he says.

I cover the mouthpiece again. Kate is still standing next to me.

"I was talking to Deirdre's mother in the bathroom," Kate whispers. "She says that her ex-husband's not really able to drive yet, and that Deirdre has been crying all day. If he could just give him a lift, they could take the train back, but—"

"Frank? This is sort of crazy, and I don't quite understand the logistics, but I'm going to put Kate on. We need for you to do us a favor."

"Anything," he says. "As long as it's not about Mrs. Joan Wilde-Younge's revision of a revision of a revision of a spiteful will."

I hand the phone to Kate. "Frank?" she says. "You're about to make a new friend. Be very nice to him, because he just had his gallbladder out, and he's got about as much strength as seaweed. He lives on Seventy-ninth Street."

I am in the car with Howard, huddled in my coat and the poncho. We are on what seems like an ironic mission. We are going to the 7-Eleven to get ice. The moon is shining brightly, and patches of snow shine like stepping stones in the field on my side of the car. Howard puts on his directional signal suddenly and turns, and I look over my shoulder to make sure we're not going to be hit from behind.

"Sorry," he says. "My mind was wandering. Not that it's the best-marked road to begin with."

Miles Davis is on the tape deck—the very quiet kind of Miles Davis.

"We've got a second for a detour," he says.

"Why are we detouring?"

"Just for a second," Howard says.

"It's freezing," I say, dropping my chin to speak the words so my throat will warm up for a second. I raise my head. My clavicle is colder.

"What you said about kinetic energy made me think about doing this," Howard says. "You can confide in me and I can confide in you, right?"

"What are you talking about?"

"This," he says, turning onto property marked "No Trespassing." The road is quite rutted where he turns onto it, but as it begins to weave up the hill it smooths out a little. He is driving with both hands gripping the wheel hard, sitting forward in the seat as if the extra inch, plus the brights, will help him see more clearly. The road levels off, and to our right is a pond. It is not frozen, but ice clings to the sides, like scum in an aquarium. Howard clicks out the tape, and we sit there in the cold and silence. He turns off the ignition.

"There was a dog here last week," he says.

I look at him.

"Lots of dogs in the country, right?" he says.

"What are we doing here?" I say, drawing up my knees.

"I fell in love with somebody," he says.

I had been looking at the water, but when he spoke I turned and looked at him again.

"I didn't think she'd be here," he says quietly. "I didn't even really think that the dog would be here. I just felt drawn to the place, I guess—that's all. I wanted to see if I could get some of that feeling back if I came here. You'd get it back if you called that man, or wrote him. It was real. I could tell when you were talking to me that it was real."

"Howard, did you say that you fell in love with somebody? When?"

"A few weeks ago. The semester's over. She's graduating. She's gone in January. A graduate student—like that? A twenty-two-year-old kid. One of my pal Lightfoot's philosophy students." Howard lets go of the wheel. When he turned the ignition off, he had continued to grip the wheel. Now his hands are on his thighs. We both seem to be examining his hands. At least, I am looking at his hands so I do not stare into his face, and he has dropped his eyes.

"It was all pretty crazy," he says. "There was so much passion, so fast. Maybe I'm kidding myself, but I don't think I let on to her how much I cared. She saw that I cared, but she . . . she didn't know my heart kept stopping, you know? We drove out here one day and had a picnic in the car—it would have been your nightmare picnic, it was so cold—and a dog came wandering up to the car. Big dog. Right over there."

I look out my window, almost expecting that the dog may still be there.

"There were three freezing picnics. This dog turned up at the last one. She liked the dog—it looked like a mutt, with maybe a lot of golden retriever mixed in. I thought it was inviting trouble for us to open the car door, because it didn't look like a particularly friendly dog. But she was right and I was wrong. Her name is Robin, by the way. The minute she opened the door, the dog wagged its tail. We took a walk with it." He juts his chin forward. "Up that path there," he says. "We threw rocks for it. A sure crowd-pleaser with your average lost-in-the-woods American dog, right? I started kidding around, calling the dog Spot. When we were back at the car, Robin patted its head and closed the car door, and it backed off, looking very sad. Like we were really ruining its day, to leave. As I was pulling out, she rolled down the window and said, 'Goodbye, Rover,' and I swear its face came alive. I think his name really was Rover."

"What did you do?" I say.

"You mean about the dog, or about the two of us?"

I shake my head. I don't know which I mean.

"I backed out, and the dog let us go. It just stood there. I got to look at it in the rearview mirror until the road dipped and it was out of sight. Robin didn't look back."

"What are you going to do?"

"Get ice," he says, starting the ignition. "But that isn't what you meant, either, is it?"

He backs up, and as we swing around toward our own tire tracks I turn my head again, but there is no dog there, watching us in the moonlight.

Back at the house, as Howard goes in front of me up the flagstone pathway, I walk slower than I usually do in the cold, trying to give myself time to puzzle out what he makes me think of just then. It comes to me at the moment when my attention is diverted by a patch of ice I'm terrified of slipping on. He reminds me of that courthouse figure—I don't know what it's called—the statue of a blindfolded woman holding the scales of justice. Bag of ice in the left hand, bag of ice in the right—but there's no blindfold. The door is suddenly opened, and what Howard and I see before us is Koenig, his customary bandanna tied around his head, smiling welcome, and behind him, in the glare of the already begun party, the woman with red hair holding Todd, who clutches his green dinosaur in one hand and rubs his sleepy, crying face with the other. Todd makes a lunge—not really toward his father but toward wider spaces—and I'm conscious, all at once, of the cigarette smoke swirling and of the heat of the house, there in the entranceway, that turn the bitter-cold outdoor air silver as it comes flooding in. *Messiah*—Kate's choice of perfect music for the occasion—isn't playing; someone has put on Judy Garland, and we walk in just as she is singing, "That's where you'll find me." The words hang in the air like smoke.

"Hello, hello, hello, hello," Becky calls, dangling one kneesocked leg over the balcony as Deirdre covers her face and hides behind her. "To both of you, just because you're here, from me to you: a million—a trillion—hellos."

Home to Marie

My wife, Marie, has decided to give a party—a catered party—and invite old friends and also some new people and the neighbors on the left, the ones we speak to. Just before the caterer arrives there's a telephone call from Molly Vandergrift, to say that her daughter's temperature is a hundred and two, and that she and her husband won't be able to come, after all. I can see my wife's disappointment as she consoles Molly. And then, a few seconds after the call, Molly's husband's car peels out of the drive. My thought, when I hear a car streaking off, is always that a person is leaving home. My wife's explanation is more practical: he's going to get medicine.

My wife herself has left home two times in the three years we've been reconciled. Once she left in a rage, and another time she extended her visit to a friend's house in Wyoming from one week to six, and although she did not really say that she wasn't coming back, I couldn't get her to make a plane reservation, couldn't get her to say she missed me, let alone that she loved me. I've done wrong things. I've bought myself expensive new cars and passed off my old ones on her; I've lost money gambling; I've come home late for dinner a hundred times. But I never left my wife. She was the one who moved out the time we were going to get divorced. And after we reconciled she was the one who tore off in the car as a finale to a disagreement.

These things bubble up from time to time; some little thing will remind me of all the times she's left, or threatened to leave. Or she'll want something we can't afford and she'll look at me with what I call her stunned-rabbit eyes. For the most part, we try hard to be cheerful, though. She's been looking for work, I come straight home at the end of the day, and we've worked out the problem with the remote control for the TV: I give it to her for an hour, she gives it to me for an hour. We don't tend to watch more than two hours of TV a night.

Tonight there won't be any TV at all, because of the cocktail party. Right now, the caterer's car is double-parked in front of our house, and the caterer—a woman—is carrying things in, helped by a teenage boy who is probably her son. He's as glum as she is cheerful. My wife and she give each other an embrace, all smiles. She darts in and out, carrying trays.

My wife says, "I wonder if I should go out and help," and then answers by saying, "No—I hired her to do it." Then she's smiling to herself. "It's a shame the Vandergrifts can't come," she says. "We'll save something for them."

I ask if I should put some music on the stereo, but my wife says no, it'll be drowned out by the conversation. Either that or we'd have to crank it up so loud that it would bother the neighbors.

I stand in the front room and look at the caterer and the boy. He comes through the door holding one of the trays at arm's length, carefully, like a child with a sparkler that he's half afraid of. As I watch, Mrs. May, the neighbor we don't speak to (she called the police one night when we went to bed and mistakenly left the light burning on the front porch), comes by with her toy poodles, Annaclair and Esther. She pretends not to notice that a caterer is carrying party food into our house. She can look right through you and make you feel like a ghost. Even the dogs have cultivated this look.

My wife asks me which person I'm most looking forward to seeing. She knows that I like Steve Newhall more than anybody else, because he's such a cutup, but just to surprise her I say, "Oh—it'll be nice to see the Ryans. Hear about their trip to Greece."

She snorts. "The day you care about travel," she says.

She's as responsible for fights as I am. She gets that edge to her voice. I try to keep a civil tongue in tone as well as in speech. She never minds giving one of those cynical little snorts and saying something cutting, though. This time, I decide to ignore it—just ignore it.

At first I can't figure out how come my wife and the caterer are so huggy-kissy, but as they talk I remember that my wife met the caterer at a shower in Alexandria a few months ago. The two of them are shaking their heads over some woman—not anyone I've met, so she must be a friend of my wife's from back when she had her job—and saying that they've never heard of a doctor who let labor go on for over sixty hours. I find out, as the foil is pulled back from the deviled eggs, that the woman is fine now, and that she had her tubes tied before she left the table.

The boy goes back to the car without saying goodbye. I stand in the hallway and look out the door. He gets in the car and slams the door shut.

Behind him, the sun is setting. It's another one of those pink-to-orange sunsets that used to take my breath away. I move back from the door quickly, though, because I know the caterer is on her way out. Truth is, if I don't have to exchange amenities with her, all the better. I'm not good at thinking of things to say to people I don't know.

The caterer ducks her head into the room where I'm standing. She says, "You have a good party tonight. I think you're really going to like the fiery-hot bean dip." She smiles and—to my surprise—shrugs. The shrug seems to have no context.

My wife comes out of the kitchen, carrying a tray of sliced meat. I offer to carry platters with her, but she says she's fussy and she'd rather do it herself. That way, she'll know where she's placed everything. I wonder whether she couldn't just look at the table and see where she's put things, but when my wife is preparing for something it is not the time to ask questions. She'll snap and get in a bad mood. So I go out to the front porch and watch the sky darken.

The caterer honks as she pulls away, and for some reason—probably because he's sitting so straight—the boy reminds me of what happened when part of the highway into Washington was reserved for cars carrying at least three passengers: people around here started buying inflatable dolls and sitting them in the car. They put hats and coats on them.

"Mary Virushi and her husband are having a trial separation, but she's coming to the party with him anyway," my wife says from the doorway.

"Why'd you have to tell me that?" I say, turning away from the sunset and coming back into the house. "It'll just make me feel uncomfortable around them."

"Oh, you'll survive," she says. She often uses this expression. She hands me a stack of paper plates and asks me to divide it in thirds and place the stacks along the front of the table. She asks me to get the napkins out of the cabinet and put piles of them down the middle of the table, between the vases of daisies.

"Nobody's supposed to know about the Virushis," she says, carrying out a tray of vegetables. Fanned out around the bowl in the middle, their colors—orange and red and white—remind me of the sky and the way it looked a few minutes ago.

"Also," she says, "please don't make it a point to rush to refill Oren's glass every time it's empty. He's making an effort to cut back."

"You do it," I say. "If you know everything, you do everything."

"You always get nervous when we entertain," she says. She brushes past me. When she comes back, she says, "The caterer really did a beautiful job.

All I have to do is wash the platters and put them out on the porch tomorrow, and she'll take them away. Isn't that wonderful?" She kisses my shoulder. "Have to get dressed," she says. "Are you going to wear what you've got on?"

I have on white jeans and a blue knit shirt. I nod yes. Surprisingly, she doesn't argue. As she walks up the stairs, she says, "I can't imagine needing air-conditioning, but do what you think best."

I go back to the porch and stand there a minute. The sky is darker. I can see a firefly or two. One of the little boys in the neighborhood passes by on his bike, all shiny blue, with training wheels on the back. There are streamers on the handlebars. The cat that kills birds walks by. I've been known to fill a water pistol and squirt the cat when nobody's looking. I've also turned the hose on it. It walks on the edge of our lawn. I know just what it's thinking.

I go in and take a look at the table. Upstairs, water is running in the shower. I wonder if Marie will wear one of her sundresses. She has a handsome back, and she looks lovely in the dresses. In spite of what she says, I do travel—and I often like it. Five years ago, we went to Bermuda. I bought the sundresses for her there. She never changes size.

On the table, there's enough food to feed an army. Half a watermelon has been hollowed out and filled with melon balls and strawberries. I have a strawberry. There are what look like cheese balls, rolled in nuts, and several bowls of dip, with vegetables around some and crackers in a bowl next to the others. I spear a piece of pineapple wrapped in prosciutto. I drop the toothpick in my pocket and push the pieces closer together, so the one I took won't be missed. Before the caterer came, my wife put out the liquor on the deep window ledge. There are candles with matches, ready to light. She might be wrong about the music—at least, it might be nice to have some music playing just as the first few people show up—but why argue? I agree that since there's a nice breeze we don't need air-conditioning.

In a little while, Marie comes down. She does not have on a sundress. She is wearing a blue linen dress I've never been fond of, and she is carrying a suitcase. She is not smiling. She looks, suddenly, quite drawn. Her hair is damp, and pulled back in a clip. I blink, not quite believing it.

"There isn't any party," she says. "I'd like you to see what it's like, to have food prepared—even though you didn't prepare it—and then just to wait. To wait and wait. Maybe this way you'll see what that's like."

As fast as I think *You're kidding!* I also know the answer. She isn't kidding. But the marriage counselor—no marriage counselor would agree that what she's doing is all right.

"You couldn't possibly be so childish," I say.

But she's out the door, going down the walk. Moths fly into the house. One flies across my mouth, tickling my skin. "What are you going to say about this to Dr. Ford?" I say.

She turns. "Why don't you ask Dr. Ford over for cocktails?" she says. "Or do you think the sight of real life might be too much for him?"

"Are you quitting?" I say. But I've lost heart. I'm out of steam, nearly out of breath. I say it so quietly I'm not sure that she heard. "Are you ignoring me?" I holler. When she doesn't answer, I know she is. She gets in the car, starts it, and drives away.

For a minute I'm so stunned that I sink down in one of the porch chairs and just stare. The street is unusually quiet. The cicadas have started to send up their sound. As I sit there, trying to calm myself, the boy on the bike pedals slowly up the hill. The neighbor's poodles start barking. I hear her shushing them. Then the barking subsides.

What was Marie thinking of? I can't remember the last time I was late for dinner. It was years ago. Years.

Katrina Duvall comes by. "Mitch?" she says, raising her hand over her brow and looking at the porch.

"Yes?" I say.

"Have you gotten your paper the last couple of Sundays?"

"Yes," I call back.

"We stopped it when we went to Ocean City, and we can't get it started again," she says. "I knew I should have just asked you to take it in, but you know Jack." Jack is her son, who is slightly retarded. She either does everything to please Jack or says that she does. The implication is that he is a tyrant. I know very little about him except that he slurs his words and once, during a snowstorm, he helped me dig out my driveway.

"All right, then," she says, and walks away.

In the distance, I hear rock and roll. There is loud laughter in the Vandergrifts' house. Who is having such a good time, if the child is sick? I squint hard at the house, but where the windows are lit it's too bright to see in. A squeal, and more laughing. I get up and walk across the lawn. I knock on the door. Molly, breathless, answers.

"Hi," I say. "I know this is a silly question, but did my wife invite you for drinks tonight?"

"No," she says. She smooths her bangs off her forehead. Behind her, her daughter zooms by on a skateboard. "Take it easy!" Molly hollers. To me, she says, "They're coming to refinish the floors tomorrow. She's in heaven, being able to do that in the house."

"You didn't speak to Marie on the phone tonight?" I say.

"I haven't even seen her in a week. Is everything all right?" she says.

"It must have been somebody else she invited over," I say.

The little girl whizzes by again on the skateboard, doing wheelies.

"Jesus," Molly says, putting her hand over her mouth. "Michael went to Dulles to pick up his brother. You don't think Marie asked Michael and he forgot to tell me, do you?"

"No, no," I say. "I'm sure I'm mistaken."

Molly smiles her usual radiant smile, but I can tell I've made her nervous.

Back in my house, I turn the light down a notch and stand at the front window, looking up at the sky. No stars tonight. Maybe in the country, but not here. I look at the candles and figure what the hell. I strike a match to light them. They're in ornate, heavy silver candlesticks—a hand-me-down from my aunt, who lives in Baltimore. As the candles burn, I look at the window and see the flames, and myself, reflected. The breeze makes the wax bead and drip, though, so I watch the candles burn only a few seconds more, then blow them out. They smoke, but I don't lick my fingers and pinch the wicks. After looking again at the empty street, I sit in a chair and look at the table.

I'll show her, I think. I'll be gone when she gets back.

Then I think about having a few drinks and some food.

But time passes, and I don't leave and I don't get a drink. I haven't touched the table when I hear a car coast to a stop. The blinking lights get my attention. An ambulance, I think—I don't know how, but somehow she hurt herself, and for some reason the ambulance is here, and . . .

I spring up.

The caterer is standing at the door. She is frowning. Her shoulders are a little hunched. She has on a denim skirt, a tube top, and running shoes. Behind me, the house is entirely quiet. I see her peer around me, toward the light in the front room. Her puzzlement is obvious.

"It was all a joke," I say. "My wife's joke."

She frowns.

"There isn't any party," I say. "My wife went away."

"You're kidding," the caterer says.

Now I am looking past her, at her car, with the lights blinking. The boy is not in the front seat. "What are you doing here?" I ask.

"Oh," she says, dropping her eyes. "I actually—I thought that you might need help, that I'd pitch in for a while."

I frown.

"I know that sounds funny," she says, "but I'm new in this business and I'm trying to make a good impression." She is still not looking at me. "I used to work in the bursar's office at the community college," she says, "and I hated that. So I figured that if I could get enough work as a caterer . . ."

"Well, come in," I say, standing aside.

For some time, bugs have been flying into the house.

"Oh, no," she says. "I'm sorry there's trouble. I just thought . . ."

"Come have a drink," I say. "Really. Come in and have a drink."

She looks at her car. "Just a minute," she says. She goes down the walkway. She turns off the lights and locks the car. She comes back up the walk.

"My husband said I shouldn't butt in," she says. "He says that I try too hard to please and when you let people know you're eager you'll never get what you want."

"His philosophy aside," I say, "please come in and have a drink."

"I thought your wife seemed edgy," the caterer says. "I thought she was nervous about having such a big party. That she might be grateful for some help."

She hesitates, then steps in.

"Well," I say, throwing up my hands.

She laughs nervously. Then I laugh.

"Wine?" I say, pointing to the windowsill.

"That would be fine. Thank you," she says.

She sits, and I pour her a glass of wine and carry it to her.

"Oh, I could have gotten that. What am I—"

"Sit still," I say. "I've got to be the host for somebody, right?"

I pour myself a bourbon and take a few ice cubes out of the ice bucket with my fingers and drop them in the glass.

"Do you want to talk about it?" the caterer says.

"I don't know what to say," I say. I move the ice around in my glass with one finger.

"I came here from Colorado," she says. "This place seems odd to me. Uptight, or something." She clears her throat. "Maybe it's not," she says. "I mean, obviously you never know   "

"What's really going on with other people," I say, finishing the sentence for her. "Case in point," I say, raising my glass.

"Will she come back?" the caterer asks.

"I don't know," I say. "We've quarreled before, certainly." I take a sip of bourbon. "Of course, this wasn't a quarrel. It was sort of a prank on her part, I guess you'd say."

"It is sort of funny," the caterer says. "She told you all those people were invited and—"

I nod, cutting her off.

"Funny if it's not you, I mean," she says.

I take another sip of my drink. I look at the caterer. She is a thin young woman. It doesn't seem she could have any particular interest in food herself. She is actually quite pretty, in a plain way.

We sit in silence for a while. I can hear squeals from next door, and am sure she hears them too. From where I sit, I can see out the window. The lightning bugs make brief pinpoints of light. From where she sits, the caterer can only see me. She looks at me, at her drink, and back at me.

"I don't mean that this should matter very much to you," she says, "but I think it's good for me to see that things aren't necessarily what they seem. I mean, maybe this town is an okay place to be. I mean, as complicated as any other town. Maybe I just have it unfairly stereotyped." She takes another drink. "I didn't really want to leave Colorado," she says. "I was a ski instructor there. The man I live with—he's not really my husband—he and I were going to start a restaurant here, but it fell through. He's got a lot of friends in this area, and his son, so here we are. His son lives here with his mother—my friend's ex. I hardly know anybody."

I get the bottle and pour her another glass of wine. I take a last sip of my drink, rattle the ice cubes, and fill my own glass with wine. I put the bottle on the floor.

"I'm sorry I stumbled in on this. My being here must embarrass you," she says.

"Not true," I say, half meaning it. "I'm glad to see somebody."

She turns and looks over her shoulder. "Do you think your wife is going to come back?" she says.

"Can't say," I say.

She nods. "It's funny to be in a situation where you know something about somebody and they don't know anything about you, isn't it?"

"What do you mean? You just told me about Colorado, and the restaurant you were going to open."

"Yeah," she says, "but that's nothing personal. You know what I mean."

"Then go ahead and tell me something personal."

She blushes. "Oh, I didn't mean that."

"Why not?" I say. "This is a strange enough night already, isn't it? What if you tell me something personal?"

She gnaws at her cuticle. She might be younger than I thought. She has long, shiny hair. I try to picture her in a nylon jacket, on a ski slope. That makes the night seem hotter suddenly. It makes me realize that in a few months, though, we will be wearing down-filled jackets. Last November there was a big snow.

"The guy I live with is an illustrator," she says. "You've probably seen some of his stuff. He doesn't need money, he just wants to have it all. To draw. To have a restaurant. He's grabby. He usually figures it out to have what he wants, though." She takes a drink. "I feel funny saying this," she says. "I don't know why I started to tell you about us." Then she stops talking, smiling apologetically.

Instead of coaxing her, I get up and put some things on two plates, put one plate on a table by my chair, and hand the other plate to her. I pour her another glass of wine.

"He has a studio next to the ceramics factory," she says. "That big building with the black shutters. In the afternoon he calls me, and I take over a picnic basket and we eat lunch and make love."

I break a cracker in half with my thumb and first finger and eat it.

"That's not it, though," she says. "The thing is, it's always something like Wonder bread. It's real kinky. I trim off the crust and make bologna sandwiches with a lot of mayonnaise. Or I'll make Cheez Whiz sandwiches with Ritz crackers, or peanut-butter-and-marshmallow sandwiches. And we drink Kool-Aid or root beer or something like that. One time I cooked hot dogs and sliced them to go on crackers and squirted cheese around the circles. We had that and Dr Pepper. The thing is, the lunch has to be really disgusting."

"I got that," I say. "I guess I got it."

"Oh," she says, dropping her eyes. "I mean, I guess it's obvious. Of course you figured it out."

I wait to see if she's going to ask me to reveal something. But instead she gets up and pours the last of the wine into her glass and stands with her back to me, looking out the window.

I know that ceramics factory. It's not in a good part of town. There's a bar just down the street from it, and one night when I was coming out of the bar a kid jumped me. I remember how fast he came at me on his bike, and the screech of tires, as if the bike were a big car. Then he was all over me, half punching and half squeezing, as if my wallet would pop out of hiding like a clown's head spinning out of a jack-in-the-box. "It's in my back pocket," I said, and when I said that he jammed his hand into the pocket and then slugged me in the side, hard. "Stay down!" he said in sort of a whisper, and I lay there, curled on my side, putting my hand over my face so that if he thought about it later he wouldn't come back and make more trouble because I'd gotten a good look at him. My nose was bleeding. I only had about twenty bucks in my wallet, and I'd left my credit cards at home. Finally I got up and tried to walk. There was a light on in the ceramics factory, but I could tell from the stillness that nobody was there—it was just a light that had been left on. I put my hand on the building and tried to stand up straighter. There was a point when a terrible pain shot through me—such a sharp pain that I went down again. I took a few breaths, and it passed. Through the big glass window I saw ceramic shepherds and animals—figures that would be placed in crèches. They were unpainted—they hadn't been fired yet—and because they were all white and just about the same size, the donkeys and the Wise Men looked a lot alike. It was a week or so before Christmas, and I thought, Why aren't they finished? They're playing it too close; if they don't get at it and start painting, it's going to be too late. "Marie, Marie," I whispered, knowing I was in trouble. Then I walked as well as I could, got to my car, and went home to my wife.

Horatio's Trick

A few days before Christmas, the UPS truck stopped in front of Charlotte's house. Charlotte's ex-husband, Edward, had sent a package to her and a larger package to their son, Nicholas, who was nineteen. She opened hers immediately. It was the same present she had been sent the year before: a pound of chocolate-covered macadamia nuts, wrapped in silver striped paper, with a card that read "Merry Christmas from Edward Anderson and family." This time, Edward's wife had written the card; it wasn't his handwriting. Charlotte dumped the contents out onto the kitchen floor and played a game of marbles, pinging one nut into another and watching them roll in different directions. She'd had a few bourbons, not too many, while Nicholas was off at the gas station getting an oil change. Before she began the game of chocolate marbles, she pulled the kitchen door closed; otherwise, Horatio, the dog, would come running in at full tilt, as he always did when he heard any sound in the kitchen. Horatio was a newcomer to the house—a holiday visitor. He belonged to Nicholas's girlfriend, Andrea, who had flown to Florida for a Christmas visit with her parents, and since Nicholas was going to drive here for *his* Christmas, he had brought Horatio along, too.

Nicholas was a junior at Notre Dame. He had his father's wavy hair—Edward hated that kind of hair, which he called kinky—but not his blue eyes. Charlotte had always been sad about that. Nicholas had her eyes: ordinary brown eyes that she loved to look at, although she could not say why she found them so interesting. She had to remember not to look at him too long. Only that morning he had said at breakfast, "Charlotte, it's a little unnerving to roll out of bed and be stared at." He often called her Charlotte now. She had moved to Charlottesville six years ago, and although it was a very sociable town and she had met quite a few people (she had finally reached the point with most of them where they had stopped making jokes about a Charlotte coming to live in Charlottesville), she did not know anyone with a son Nicholas's age. Oddly enough, she knew two women about her age who were having babies. One of them seemed slightly abashed; the other was ecstatic. It was a scandal (people parodied themselves in Charlottesville by calling scandals—which they did not believe in—"*scandales*") that the ecstatic forty-one-year-old mother-to-be, a recent graduate of the University of Virginia Law School, was not married. Other gossip had it that she was forty-three.

Charlotte worked as a legal secretary for an old and prestigious law firm in town. She had left New York after she and Edward separated a dozen years ago, and had moved to Washington, where she enrolled in American University to resume her B.A. studies in preparation for entering law school. Nicholas went to Lafayette School, and was taken care of on the weekends by her parents, who lived in the Cleveland Park area, while Charlotte sequestered herself and studied almost around the clock. But there were problems: Nicholas had a hard time making friends in his new school; also, the bitterness between Charlotte and Edward seemed to escalate when there was actual distance between them, so Charlotte was constantly distracted by Edward's accusatory phone calls and his total lack of faith in her ability to get a degree. It had all been too much, and finally she decided to abandon her plans of becoming a lawyer and became a legal secretary instead. Edward began to make visits, taking the Metroliner from New York to Washington; one day he turned up with a dark-haired, dark-eyed young woman who wore a bit too much jewelry. Soon after that they were married. The "and family" part of the gift card referred to her daughter from a previous marriage. Charlotte had never met the child.

Charlotte looked out the back window. Horatio was in the yard, sniffing the wind. Nicholas had stopped on the way south and bought a stake and a chain to keep Horatio under control during the visit. Actually, the dog seemed happy enough, and wasn't very interested in the birds or the occasional cat that turned up in Charlotte's yard. Right now, Nicholas was upstairs, talking to Andrea on the phone. Someone throwing a life ring to a drowning child could not have been more energetic and more dedicated than Nicholas was to the girl.

Charlotte poured another bourbon, into which she plopped three ice cubes, and sat on the stool facing the counter, where she kept the telephone and pads of paper and bills to be paid and whatever odd button needed to be sewn back on. There were also two batteries there that were either dead or unused (she couldn't remember anymore) and paper clips (although she could not remember the last time she used a paper clip at home), a few corks, a little bottle of Visine, some loose aspirins, and a broken bracelet. There was a little implement called a lemon zester that she had bought from a door-to-door salesman. She suddenly picked it up and pretended to be conducting, because Nicholas had just put on Handel upstairs. He always played music to drown out his phone conversations.

"For the Lord God omni-potent . . ." She had forgotten to get back to the Tazewells about Father Curnan's birthday party. She had promised that she would find out whether Nicholas would come, and then call back. She had meant to ask Nicholas at breakfast but had forgotten. Now she suddenly saw that Horatio might be her salvation. Whenever he came indoors he ran through the house in an excited fashion, and if that happened to get Nicholas off the phone, who would blame her? She went outdoors and, shivering, quickly unhitched the dog and led him in. His fur was soft and cold. He was glad to see her, as usual. The minute they were inside, he bounded up the stairs. She stood at the bottom, listening to Horatio's panting outside Nicholas's door, and then, sure enough, the door banged open. Nicholas was at the top of the stairs, staring down. He did look as if he had been rescuing a drowning child: disheveled, with not an extra second to spare. "What's he doing inside?" he asked.

"It's cold out," she said. "Nicky, the Tazewells are having a dinner for Father Curnan's birthday tonight. Will you go with me?"

The sopranos soared in unison. She must have looked alarmed—surely he noticed that she had suddenly put both hands on the banister railing—and perhaps that was why he quickly nodded yes and turned away.

Back in the kitchen, with her boots off, Charlotte stroked the dog with one stockinged foot, and in response he shot up and went into his little routine, his famous trick. Almost complacently, he sat and extended his right paw. Then he rubbed his snout down that leg, put the paw back on the floor, and lifted and rubbed the left paw in the same fashion. He sneezed, turned twice in a circle to his left, and then came over to be patted. The trick meant nothing, of course, but it never failed as a crowd-pleaser. Sometimes Charlotte had even come into a room and found him doing it all by himself. "Okay, you're wonderful," she whispered to Horatio now, scratching his ears.

She heard Nicholas's footsteps on the stairs and called, "Where are you going?" It dismayed her that he kept to himself so much. He stayed upstairs most of the day studying, or he talked on the telephone. He already had on his coat and scarf. Instead of hanging them in the hall closet, he kept them up in his room. He kept everything there, as if he were forever on the point of packing up for some quick journey.

"Back to the garage," he said. "Don't get upset. It's no big thing. I asked them yesterday if they had time to line the rear brakes, and they said they could fit me in this afternoon."

"Why would that upset me?" she said.

"Because you'd think the car was unsafe. You've always got your images of disaster."

"What are you talking about?" she said. She was addressing Christmas cards, trying to convince herself that there might be some truth to Better late than never.

"When I had the broken thumb, you carried on as if I was a quadriplegic."

He was talking about the year before—a bicycling injury, when he'd skidded on some icy pavement. She shouldn't have flown out to Indiana, but she missed him and she hated the idea of his being hurt. College was the first time he had ever lived away from her. She hadn't made a scene—she had just gone there and called from a motel. (It was in the back of her mind, she had to admit now, that the trip might also be a chance for her to meet Andrea, the off-campus student who had begun to turn up in Nicholas's letters.) Nicholas was horrified that she'd come all that distance. He was fine, of course—he had a cast on his left hand was all—and he had said almost angrily that he couldn't tell her anything without eliciting a huge overreaction.

"You didn't forget the dinner, did you?" she said now.

He turned and looked at her. "We already talked about that," he said. "Seven o'clock—is that right?"

"Right," she said. She began to address another envelope, trying to pass it off.

"It will take approximately one hour at the garage," he said.

Then he left—the way his father so often had left—without saying good-bye.

She wrote a few more cards, then called the florist's to see whether they had been able to locate bird-of-paradise flowers in New York. She wanted to send them to Martine, her oldest friend, who had just returned from a vacation in Key West to the cold winds of the Upper East Side. Charlotte was happy to hear that someone had them, and that a dozen had gone out. "I thought we'd have good luck," the woman at the florist's said. "If we couldn't locate some paradise in New York, I don't know where paradise *could* be tracked down." She had a young voice—and after Charlotte hung up it occurred to her that she might have been the VanZells' daughter, who had just been hired by a florist in town after having been suspended from college because of some trouble with drugs. Charlotte clasped her hands and touched them to her lips, in one of her silent prayers to the Virgin: No drugs for Nicholas, ever. Protect my Nicholas from harm.

The Tazewells' sunken dining room was done in Chinese red, and against the far wall there was an enormous glass china press edged in brass, illuminated from within in a way that flooded the cut glass with light. The shelves were also glass, and their edges sparkled and gleamed with a prism-bright clarity. Charlotte was not surprised to see that Martin Smith, who ran the Jefferson Dreams catering service, was there himself to oversee things. People in Charlottesville followed through—even fun wasn't left totally to chance—and Charlotte liked that. Edith Stanton, the host's cousin, almost Charlotte's first friend when she had moved here to Charlottesville (she could remember their first lunch together, and Edith's considering gaze above the seafood salad: was this nice-looking new single woman who was working down at Burwell, McKee going to *fit in*?), was talking with Father Curnan. Charlotte looked hard at his face—the round, open face of an adolescent, except that there were deep lines around his eyes—and saw on it the look she called Bemused Monsignor. He could nod and smile and murmur his "not to be *believed*" as Edith went on in her breathless way (surely she was telling him again about her session in a bodybuilding shop for women out in Santa Barbara last summer), but his interest was feigned. Edith was not a Catholic, and she could not know the sort of complicated, surprising man Philip Curnan really was. He had told Charlotte once that after working his way through Cornell (his father had an auto-repair garage in upstate New York somewhere), he had ridden across the country on a Harley-Davidson, while searching his soul about his desire to enter the priesthood. Charlotte smiled now, remembering the confidence. Just last week he had told her that there were still times when he longed to get back on a motorcycle; his helmet was still on the top shelf in his bedroom closet.

A server passed by, and Charlotte finally got a drink. Surveying the room, she was pleased to see that Nicholas was talking to the McKays' daughter, Angela, home from Choate for Christmas. Charlotte thought of the day, a month before, when Angela's mother, Janet, had consulted with the head of Burwell, McKee about filing for legal separation from Chaz, her husband. Chaz, a lawyer himself, stood with his arm around his wife's waist, talking to a couple Charlotte didn't know. Perhaps Chaz still did not know that she had made inquiries about getting a divorce. M.L., the hostess, passed in her peach-colored gown, and Charlotte touched her shoulder and whispered,

"It's wonderful. Thank you for having us." M.L. gave her a hug and said, "I must be somewhere *else* if I didn't even say hello." As she moved away, Charlotte smelled her perfume—at night, M.L. always wore Joy—and heard the rustle of silk.

Martin VanZell came up to Charlotte and began talking to her about his arthritic knee. He tapped a bottle in his breast pocket. "All doctors dote on Advil," he said. "Ask any of them. Their eyes light up. You'd think it was Lourdes in a bottle. Pull off the top, take out the cotton, and worship. I'm not kidding you." He noticed that he seemed to have caught Father Curnan's attention. "Meaning no disrespect," he said.

"Who was being slighted?" Father Curnan said. "The pharmaceutical company?" His eyes met Charlotte's for a second, and he winked before he looked away. He speared a shrimp and ate it, waving away the napkin a server extended in her other hand.

Frankie Melkins suddenly swooped in front of Charlotte, kissing the air above her cheek. Frankie had been in a bad car accident last New Year's, and had returned to the Church after Father Curnan's hospital visits. That had been much talked about, as well as the fact that the case was settled out of court, which led people to believe that Frankie had got a lot of money. As Frankie and Martin began to compare painkiller stories, Charlotte drifted away and went to the side door, where someone had been knocking for quite some time. Oren and Billy! Oren could be such a devil. He gave drums to his nephews for Christmas and once threw rice during a party that wasn't at all like a wedding. The minute she opened the door, he gave her a bear hug.

"What on earth!" M.L. said, staring out the door after the two men had come in. "Why, I'll bet Frankie has left the cabdriver out there waiting." She began to wave her arms wildly, whistling to him. She turned to Charlotte. "Can you believe it?" she said. She looked beyond Charlotte to Frankie. "Frankie!" she called. "Were you going to leave your cabdriver out in the driveway all night? There's plenty of food. Tell him to come in and have something to eat."

Father Curnan stood talking to the host, Dan Tazewell. They were look-ing at the mantel, discussing a small drawing of a nude that was framed and propped there. She overheard Father Curnan lamenting the fact that the artist had recently left the art department at the university and gone back to New York to live. Charlotte accepted another drink from a server, then looked back at Father Curnan. He was scrutinizing the drawing. On her way to the bathroom, Charlotte heard Nicholas telling Angela McKay details about hand surgery, spreading his thumb and first finger wide. Angela looked at the space between his fingers as though staring at some fascinating thing squirming beneath a microscope. His hand? Had Nicholas had hand surgery?

One of the servers was coming out of the bathroom as Charlotte got to the door. She was glad it was empty, because she had had two drinks before she left the house and another at the party. She put her glass on the back of the sink before she used the toilet. What if she left the drink there? Would anybody notice and think things?

The bathroom was tiny, and the little casement window had been flipped open. Still, Charlotte could smell cigarette smoke. She reached up and pulled the window closed, hooked it, and rubbed her hand down her new black shirt. "*Wheet,*" she said, imitating the sound the silk made. "Someone's in there," she heard a voice say. She took a sip of her drink, then unhooked the window and pushed it out again. The sky was black—no stars visible across the small part of the sky she could see. There was a huge wind out there, like an animal loose in the trees. She turned and began to wash her hands. The spigot reminded her of a fountain she had seen years ago in Rome, when she was first married. It had bothered her that so many things there were exaggerated but not full-form: massive marble heads—lions and gargoyles, rippling manes, mythic beasts spewing water—but whole bodies were usually to be found only on the angels and cherubs. She dried her hands. That couldn't be true—that couldn't have been what all the fountains looked like. What am I doing thinking about fountains in Rome, she thought.

When she opened the door, she saw Martin VanZell in the dim hallway, his white face a ghostly contrast to his dark pin-striped suit. "Great party, huh?" he said. She had stopped outside the door, dead center. It took her a minute to realize that she was staring, and blocking his way. "It is every year," she heard herself saying, and then he passed by and she turned toward the noise of the party. A man whose wife ran one of the nurseries on Route 29 came over as she walked down the two steps into the room. "Charlotte, you just missed my wife here, losing track again. She was telling Father Curnan—hey, he's gone off again—she thought Chernobyl was this year. It was *last* year. It happened in the spring."

"Well, I believe you," his wife said, with a false smile. "Why were you bringing it up, Arthur?"

Nicholas came up to Charlotte just as the host rang a bell and everyone fell silent.

"It's not Santa. It's the annual ringing out of one year for Father Curnan and a ringing in of the new," the host said cheerfully. He rang the bell again.

"Because today he's our birthday boy again, and if he's going to keep getting older we're going to keep noticing it."

Father Curnan raised his glass, blushing. "Thank you all—" he began, but the host clanged the bell again, drowning him out. "Oh, no, you don't. You don't make us take time out from the party to hear a speech," the host said. "Time for that on Sunday, Philip, when you've got your captive audience. But happy birthday, Father Phil, and on with the ball!" People laughed and cheered.

Charlotte saw that someone's glass had made a white ring on the table-top between two mats that had been put there. Janet's husband came up and started to talk about the cost of malpractice insurance, and then Charlotte felt Nicholas's hand on her elbow. "It's late," he said. "We should go." She started to introduce him to Janet's husband, but Nicholas steered them away and into a bedroom where two temporary clothes racks stood bulging with coats and furs. More coats made a great mound on the bed. Then suddenly she and Nicholas were standing with M.L. at the courtyard door, saying goodbye as they struggled into their coats and scarves. It was not until the door closed that Charlotte realized that she had not said a single word to Father Curnan. She turned and looked back at the house.

"Come on," Nicholas said. "He didn't even notice."

"Did you speak to him?" Charlotte said.

"No," Nicholas said. "I have nothing to say to him." He was walking toward their car, at the foot of the drive. She looked up.

"I only asked," she said.

He was too far ahead of her to hear. He held open the car door, and she got inside. He crossed in front of the car, and she realized that for some reason he was upset.

"All right," he said, getting in and slamming his door. "You're wronged. You're always wronged. Would you like it if I left the engine running and we both went back in and said good night to Father Curnan? Because that would be entirely proper. I could bow and you could curtsy."

Charlotte wouldn't have thought that at that moment there was an emotion she could feel stronger than frustration. Wouldn't have thought it until she realized that what was smothering her was sadness. "No," she said quietly. "You're entirely right. He didn't even notice that we left."

The telephone rang twice, interrupting their Christmas Eve ceremony of tea and presents. Nicholas had been nice to her all day—even taking her out to lunch and trying to make her laugh by telling her stories about a professor of his who delivered all his lectures in the interrogative—because he knew he had jumped on her the night before, leaving the party. Each time the phone rang, Charlotte hoped it wasn't Andrea, because then he would drift away and be gone for ages. The first call was from Martine in New York, overjoyed by the flowers; the next was from M.L., to wish them a good Christmas and to say that she was sorry she had not really got to talk to them amid the confusion of the party.

Nicholas gave her a cashmere scarf and light-blue leather gloves. She gave him subscriptions to *Granta* and *Manhattan, inc.*, a heavy sweater with a hood, and a hundred-dollar check to get whatever else he wanted. His father gave him a paperweight that had belonged to his grandfather, and a wristwatch that would apparently function even when launched from a rocket pad. When Nicholas went into the kitchen to boil up more water, she slid over on the couch and glanced at the gift card. It said, "Love, Dad," in Edward's nearly illegible script. Nicholas returned and opened his last present, which was from Melissa, his stepsister. It was a cheap ballpoint pen with a picture of a woman inside. When you turned the pen upside down her clothes disappeared.

"How old is Melissa?" Charlotte asked.

"Twelve or thirteen," he said.

"Does she look like her mother?"

"Not much," Nicholas said. "But she's really her sister's kid, and I never saw her sister."

"Her sister's child?" Charlotte took a sip of her tea, which was laced with bourbon. She held it in her mouth a second before swallowing.

"Melissa's mother killed herself when Melissa was just a baby. I guess her father didn't want her. Anyway, he gave her up."

"Her sister killed herself?" Charlotte said. She could feel her eyes widening. Suddenly she remembered the night before, the open window in the bathroom, the black sky, wind smacking her in the face.

"Awful, huh?" Nicholas said, lifting the tea bag out of the mug and lowering it to the saucer. "Hey, did I shock you? How come you didn't know that? I thought you were the one with a sense for disaster."

"What do you mean? I don't expect disaster. I don't know anything at all about Melissa. Naturally—"

"I know you don't know anything about her," he said, cutting her off. "Look—don't get mad at me, but I'm going to say this, because I think you aren't aware of what you do. You don't ask anything, because you're afraid of what every answer might be. It makes people reluctant to talk to you. Nobody wants to tell you things."

She took another sip of tea, which had gone tepid. Specks of loose tea leaves had floated to the top. "People talk to me," she said.

"I know they do," he said. "I'm not criticizing you. I'm just telling you that if you give off those vibes people are going to back off."

"Who backs off?" she said.

"Charlotte, I don't know everything about your life. I'm just telling you that you've never asked one thing about Dad's family in—what is it? Eleven years. You don't even mention my stepmother by name, ever. Her name is Joan. You don't want to know things, that's all."

He kicked a ball of wrapping paper away from his foot. "Let's drop it," he said. "What I'm saying is that you're always worried. You always think something's going to happen."

She started to speak, but took another drink instead. Maybe all mothers seemed oppressive when their children were teenagers. Didn't everyone say that parents could hardly do anything right during those years? That was what Father Curnan said—that although we may always try to do our best, we can't always expect to succeed. She wished Father Curnan were here right now. The whole evening would be different.

"Don't start sulking," Nicholas said. "You've been pissed off at me since last night, because I wouldn't go over and glad-hand Father Curnan. I hardly know him. I went to the party with you because you wanted me to. I don't practice anymore. I'm not a Catholic anymore. I don't believe what Father Curnan believes. Just because twenty years ago he had some doubt in his life and sorted it out, you think he's a hero. I don't think he's a hero. I don't care what he decided. That's fine for him, but it doesn't have anything to do with me."

"I never mention your loss of faith," she said. "Never. We don't discuss it."

"You don't have to say anything. What's awful is that you let me know that I've scared you. It's like I deliberately did something to you."

"What would you have me do?" she said. "How good an actress do you think I can be? I *do* worry. You don't give me credit for trying."

"You don't give *me* credit," he said. "I don't get credit for putting up with Dad's crap because I came to Virginia to be with you instead of going to his house. If I go to a stupid party for some priest who condescends to me by letter and says he'll pray for my soul, I don't get credit from you for going because you wanted me there. It never occurs to you. Instead I get told that I didn't shake his hand on the way out. If I had told you that the car was driving funny before I got it fixed, you would have bitten your nails some more and refused to ride in it. I wish you'd stop being scared. I wish you'd just stop."

She put the mug on the table and looked at him. He's a grown man, she thought. Taller than his father. Nicholas shook his head and walked out of the room. She heard him stomp upstairs. In a few minutes, the music began. He was playing rock, not Christmas music, and her heart seemed to pick up the relentless beat of the bass. Nicholas had scored his point. She was just sitting there, scared to death.

The sound jolted through her dream: once, twice, again. And then it awakened her. When she opened her eyes, it took her a minute to realize that she was in the living room in a chair, not in bed, and that she had been dreaming. The loud music had become part of her dream. She was squinting. Light flooded part of the living room—a painful brightness as constant as the noise. Out of the area of light she saw the shapes of crumpled gift wrappings by the tree. She passed one hand over her forehead, attempting to soothe the pain. The dog looked up from across the room. He yawned and walked over to the footstool beside her, wagging his tail.

The noise continued. It was from outside. A high-pitched squeal resonated in her chest. It had been snowing earlier. It must have gone on snowing. Someone's car was stuck out there.

The dog padded with her to the front window. Beyond the huge oak tree in the front yard, there was a car at an odd angle, with its headlights aimed toward the house. A front and back wheel were up on the hill. Whoever was driving had missed the turn and skidded onto her property. There was a man bending over by the side of the car. Somebody else, in the driver's seat, gunned the engine and wheels spun again. "Wait for me to move! Wait till I'm out of the way, for Christ's sake," the man outside the car hollered. The wheels screamed again, drowning out the rest of what he said.

Charlotte got her coat from the hall closet and snapped on the outside light. She nudged the dog back inside, and went carefully down the front walkway. Snow seeped into one shoe.

"What's going on?" she called, clasping her hands across her chest.

"Nothin'," the man said, as if all this were the most normal thing in the world. "I'm trying to give us something to roll back on, so's we can get some traction."

She looked down and saw a large piece of flagstone from her wall jammed under one back wheel. Again the man raced the engine.

"He's gonna get it," the man said.

"Do you want me to call a tow truck?" she said, shivering.

There were no lights in any nearby windows. She could not believe that she was alone in this, that half the neighborhood was not awake.

"We got it! We got it!" the man said, crouching as the driver raced the engine again. The tire screamed on the flagstone, but the car did not move.

Suddenly she smelled something sweet—liquor on the man's breath. The man sprang up and banged on the car window. "Ease up, ease up, God damn it," he said. "Don't you know how to drive?"

The driver rolled down the window and began to curse. The other man hit his hand on the roof of the car. Again, the driver gassed it and tires spun and screamed.

For the first time, she felt frightened. The man began to tug at the door on the driver's side, and Charlotte turned away and walked quickly toward the house. This has got to stop, she thought. *It has got to stop.* She opened the door. Horatio was looking at her. It was as though he had been waiting and now he simply wanted an answer.

Above the screeching of tires, she heard her voice, speaking into the telephone, giving the police the information and her address. Then she stepped farther back into the dark kitchen, over on the left side, where she could not be seen through the front windows or through the glass panels that stretched to each side of the front door. She could hear both men yelling. Where was Nicholas? How could he still be asleep? She hoped that the dog wouldn't bark and wake him, now that he'd managed to sleep through so much. She took a glass out of the cabinet and started toward the shelf where she kept the bourbon, but then stopped, realizing that she might be seen. She pulled open the refrigerator door and found an opened bottle of wine. She pulled the cork out and filled the glass half full and took a long drink.

Someone knocked on the door. Could it be the police—so soon? How could they have come so quickly and silently? She wasn't sure until, long after the knocking stopped, she peered down the hallway and saw, through the narrow rectangle of glass, a police car with its revolving red and blue lights.

At almost the same instant, she touched something on her lapel and looked down, surprised. It was Santa: a small pin, in the shape of Santa's head, complete with a little red hat, pudgy cheeks, and a ripply white plastic beard. A tiny cord with a bell at the bottom dangled from it. Nicholas must have gone back to the store where they had seen it on his first day home. She had pointed it out on a tray of Christmas pins and ornaments. She told him she'd had the exact same pin—the Santa's head, with a bell—back when she was a girl. He must have gone back to the store later to buy it.

She tiptoed upstairs in the dark, and the dog followed. Nicholas was snoring in his bedroom. She went down the hall to her room, at the front of the house, and, without turning on the light, sat on her bed to look out the nearest window at the scene below. The man she had spoken to was emptying his pockets onto the hood of the police car. She saw the beam of the policeman's flashlight sweep up and down his body, watched while he unbuttoned his coat and pulled it open wide in response to something the policeman said. The other man was being led to the police car. She could hear his words—"my car, *it's my car, I tell you*"—but she couldn't make out whole sentences, couldn't figure out what the driver was objecting to so strongly. When both men were in the car, one of the policemen turned and began to walk toward the house. She got up quickly and went downstairs, one hand sliding along the slick banister; the dog came padding down behind her.

She opened the door just before the policeman knocked. Cold flooded the hallway. She saw steam coming out of the car's exhaust pipe. There was steam from her own breath, and the policeman's.

"Could I come in, ma'am?" he asked, and she stood back and then shut the door behind him, closing out the cold. The dog was on the landing.

"He's real good, or else he's not a guard dog to begin with," the policeman said. His cheeks were red. He was younger than she had thought at first.

"They were going to keep that racket up all night," she said.

"You did the right thing," he said. His head bent, he began to fill out a form on his clipboard. "I put down about fifty dollars of damage to your wall," he said.

She said nothing.

"It didn't do too much damage," the policeman said. "You can call in the morning and get a copy of this report if you need it."

"Thank you," she said.

He touched his cap. "Less fun than digging out Santa and his reindeer," he said, looking back at the car, tilted onto the lawn. "Have a good Christmas, ma'am," he said.

He turned and left, and she closed the door. With the click, she remembered everything. Earlier in the evening she had gone upstairs to tell Nicholas that she was sorry they had ended up in a quarrel on Christmas Eve. She had said she wanted him to come back downstairs. She had said it through the closed door, pleading with him, with her mouth close to the blank white panel of wood. When the door opened at last, and she saw Nicholas standing there in his pajamas, she had braced herself by touching her fingers to the door frame, shocked to realize that he was real, and that he was there. He was looking into her eyes—a person she had helped to create—and yet, when he wasn't present, seeing him in her mind would have been as strange as visualizing a Christmas ornament out of season.

Nicholas's hair was rumpled, and he looked at her with a tired, exasperated frown. "Charlotte," he said, "why didn't you come up hours ago? I went down and let the dog in. You've been out like a light half the night. Nobody's supposed to say that you drink. Nobody's supposed to see you. If you don't ask any questions, we're supposed to stop noticing you. Nobody's supposed to put you on the spot, are they? You only talk to Father Curnan, and he prays for you."

Downstairs in the dark hallway now, she shuddered, remembering how she had felt when he said that. She had gone back downstairs and huddled in the chair—all right, she had had too much to drink—but it was she who had woken up and been alert to squealing tires and people screaming, and Nicholas who had slept. Also, she thought, relief suddenly sweeping through her, he couldn't have been as angry as he seemed. He must have put the pin on her coat after the party—after their words in the car—or even when he had come downstairs to let Horatio in and had seen her asleep or passed out in the chair. He must have pinned it onto her lapel when the coat still hung in the closet, so she would find it there the next day. She had found it early, inadvertently, when she went out to investigate the car and the noise.

She looked at the dog. He was watching her, as usual.

"Are you real good, or not a guard dog to begin with?" she whispered. Then she pulled the cord. Santa's face lit up. She pulled the cord again, several times, smiling as the dog watched. Over her shoulder, she looked at the kitchen clock. It was three-fifty Christmas morning.

"Come on," she whispered, pulling the cord another time. "I've done my trick. Now you do yours."

Second Question

There we were, in the transfusion room at the end of the corridor at Bishopgate Hospital: Friday morning, the patients being dripped with blood or intravenous medicine so they could go home for the weekend. It was February, and the snow outside had turned the gritty gray of dirty plaster. Ned and I stood at the window, flanking a card table filled with desserts: doughnuts, cakes, pies, brownies, cookies. Some plastic forks and knives were piled in stacks, others dropped pick-up-sticks style between the paper plates. Ned surveyed the table and took a doughnut. In his chair, Richard was sleeping, chin dropped, breathing through his mouth. Half an hour into the transfusion, he always fell asleep. He was one of the few who did. A tall, redheaded man, probably in his mid-fifties, was hearing from a nurse about the hair loss he could expect. "Just remember, honey, Tina Turner wears a wig," she said.

Outside, bigger snowflakes fell, like wadded-up tissues heading for the trash. Which was what I had turned away from when I went to the window: the sight of a nurse holding a tissue for a young woman to blow her nose into. The woman was vomiting, with her nose running at the same time, but she refused to relinquish the aluminum bowl clamped under her thumbs. "Into the tissue, honey," the nurse was still saying, not at all distracted by her posturing colleague's excellent imitation of Tina Turner. I'd stopped listening, too, but I'd stuck on the phrase "Gonna break every rule."

Richard was dying of AIDS. Ned, his ex-lover and longtime business associate, found that instead of reading scripts, typing letters, and making phone calls, his new job description was to place organically grown vegetables in yin/yang positions inside a special steamer, below which we boiled Poland Spring water. A few months earlier, in that period before Richard's AZT had to be discontinued so that he could enter an experimental outpatient-treatment program at Bishopgate, Ned had always slept late. He couldn't call the West Coast before two in the afternoon, anyway—or maybe an hour earlier, if he had the unlisted number of an actor or of a director's car phone. All of the people Richard and Ned did business with worked longer hours than nine-to-fivers, and it was a standing joke among us that I was never busy—I had no real job, and when I did work I was paid much more than was reasonable. Ned joked with me a lot, an edge in his voice, because he was a little jealous of the sudden presence of a third person in Richard's apartment. Richard and I had met in New York when we were seated in adjacent chairs at a cheapo haircutter's on Eighth Avenue. He thought I was an actress in an Off Broadway play he'd seen the night before. I was not, but I'd seen the play. As we talked, we discovered that we often ate at the same restaurants in Chelsea. His face was familiar to me, as well. Then began years of our being neighbors—a concept more important to New Yorkers than to people living in a small town. The day we met, Richard took me home with him so I could shower.

That year, my landlord on West Twenty-seventh Street remained unconcerned that hot water rarely made it up to my top-floor apartment. After I met Richard it became a habit with me to put on my sweatsuit and jog to his apartment, three blocks east and one block over. Richard's own landlord, who lived in the other second-floor apartment, could never do enough for him, because Richard had introduced him to some movie stars and invited him to so many screenings. He would sizzle with fury over the abuse I had to endure, working himself up to what Richard (who made *café filtre* for the three of us) swore was a caffeine-induced sexual high, after which he'd race around doing building maintenance. Now, in the too-bright transfusion room, it was hard for me to believe that only a few months ago I'd been sitting in Richard's dining alcove, with the cluster of phones that rested on top of *Variety* landslides and formed the centerpiece of the long tavern table, sipping freshly ground Jamaica Blue Mountain as my white-gloved hands curved around the pleasant heat of a neon-colored coffee mug. The gloves allowed the lotion to sink in as long as possible. I make my living as a hand model. Every night, I rub on a mixture of Dal Raccolto olive oil with a dash of Kiehl's moisturizer and the liquid from two vitamin E capsules. It was Richard who gave me the nickname "Rac," for "Raccoon." My white, pulled-on paws protect me from scratches, broken nails, chapped skin. Forget the M.B.A.: as everyone knows, real money is made in strange ways in New York.

I turned away from the snowstorm. On a TV angled from a wall bracket above us, an orange-faced Phil Donahue glowed. He shifted from belligerence to incredulity as a man who repossessed cars explained his life philoso-phy. Hattie, the nicest nurse on the floor, stood beside me briefly, considering the array of pastry on our table as if it were a half-played chess game. Finally, she picked up one of the plastic knives, cut a brownie in half, and walked away without raising her eyes to look at the snow.

Taking the shuttle to Boston every weekend had finally convinced me that I was never going to develop any fondness for Beantown. To be fair about it, I didn't have much chance to see Boston as a place where anyone might be happy. Ned and I walked the path between the apartment (rented by the month) and the hospital. Once or twice I took a cab to the natural-food store, and one night, as irresponsible as the babysitters of every mother's nightmare, we had gone to a bar and then to the movies, while Richard slept a drug-induced sleep, with the starfish night-light Hattie had brought him from her honeymoon in Bermuda shining on the bedside table. In the bar, Ned had asked me what I'd do if time could stop: Richard wouldn't get any better and he wouldn't get any worse, and the days we'd gone through—with the crises, the circumlocutions, the gallows humor, the perplexity, the sud-den, all-too-clear medical knowledge—would simply persist. Winter, also, would persist: intermittent snow, strong winds, the harsh late-afternoon sun we couldn't stand without the filter of a curtain. I was never a speculative person, but Ned thrived on speculation. In fact, he had studied poetry at Stanford, years ago, where he had written a series of "What If" poems. Rich-ard, visiting California, answering questions onstage after one of the movies he'd produced had been screened, had suddenly found himself challenged by a student whose questions were complex and rhetorical. In the following fifteen years, they had been lovers, enemies, and finally best friends, associ-ated in work. They had gone from Stanford to New York, New York to Lon-don, then from Hampstead Heath back to West Twenty-eighth Street, with side trips to gamble in Aruba and to ski in Aspen at Christmas.

"You're breaking the rules," I said. "No what-ifs."

"What if we went outside and flowers were blooming, and there were a car—a convertible—and we drove to Plum Island," he went on. "Moon on the water. Big Dipper in the sky. Think about it. Visualize it and your nega-tive energy will be replaced by helpful, healing energy."

"Is there such a place as Plum Island or did you make it up?"

"It's famous. Banana Beach is there. Bands play at night in the Prune Pavilion."

"There is a Plum Island," the man next to me said. "It's up by Newbury-port. It's full of poison ivy in the summer, so you've got to be careful. I once got poison ivy in my lungs from some asshole who was burning the stuff with his leaves. Two weeks in the hospital, and me with a thousand-dollar deductible."

Ned and I looked at the man.

"Buy you a round," he said. "I just saved a bundle. The hotel I'm staying at gives you a rate equal to the temperature when you check in. It's a come-on. I've got a queen-size bed, an honor bar, and one of those showers you can adjust so it feels like needles shooting into you, all for sixteen dollars. I could live there cheaper than heating my house."

"Where you from?" Ned asked.

"Hope Valley, Rhode Island," the man said, his arm shooting in front of me to shake Ned's hand. "Harvey Milgrim," he said, nodding at my face. "Captain, United States Army Reserve."

"Harvey," Ned said, "I don't think you have any use for guys like me. I'm homosexual."

The man looked at me. I was surprised, too; it wasn't like Ned to talk about this with strangers. Circumstance had thrown me together with Ned; fate precipitated our unlikely bonding. Neither of us could think of life without Richard. Richard opened up to very few people, but when he did he made it a point to be indispensable.

"He's kidding," I said. It seemed the easiest thing to say.

"Dangerous joke," Harvey Milgrim said.

"He's depressed because I'm leaving him," I said.

"Well, now, I wouldn't rush into a thing like that," Harvey said. "I'm Bud on draft. What are you two?"

The bartender walked over the minute the conversation shifted to alcohol.

"Stoli straight up," Ned said.

"Vodka tonic," I said.

"Switch me to Jim Beam," Harvey said. He rolled his hand with the quick motion of someone shaking dice. "Couple of rocks on the side."

"Harvey," Ned said, "my world's coming apart. My ex-lover is also my boss, and his white-blood-cell count is sinking too low for him to stay alive. The program he's in at Bishopgate is his last chance. He's a Friday-afternoon vampire. They pump blood into him so he has enough energy to take part in an experimental study and keep his outpatient status, but do you know how helpful that is? Imagine he's driving the Indy. He's in the lead. He screeches in for gas, and what does the pit crew do but blow him a kiss? The other cars are still out there, whipping past. He starts to yell, because they're supposed to fill the car with gas, but the guys are nuts or something. They just blow air kisses."

Harvey looked at Ned's hand, the fingers fanned open, deep Vs of space between them. Then Ned slowly curled them in, kissing his fingernails as they came to rest on his bottom lip.

The bartender put the drinks down, one-two-three. He scooped a few ice cubes into a glass and put the glass beside Harvey's shot glass of bourbon. Harvey frowned, looking from glass to glass without saying anything. Then he threw down the shot of bourbon and picked up the other glass, lifted one ice cube out, and slowly sucked it. He did not look at us or speak to us again.

The night after Ned and I snuck off to the bar, Richard started to hyperventilate. In a minute his pajamas were soaked, his teeth chattering. It was morning, 4 a.m. He was holding on to the door frame, his feet in close, his body curved away, like someone windsurfing. Ned woke up groggily from his sleeping bag on the floor at the foot of Richard's bed. I was on the foldout sofa in the living room, again awakened by the slightest sound. Before I'd fallen asleep, I'd gone into the kitchen to get a drink of water, and a mouse had run under the refrigerator. It startled me, but then tears sprang to my eyes because if Richard knew there were mice—mice polluting the environment he was trying to purify with air ionizers, and humidifiers that misted the room with mineral water—he'd make us move. The idea of gathering up the piles of holistic-health books, the pamphlets on meditation, the countless jars of vitamins and chelated minerals and organically grown grains, the eye of God that hung over the stove, the passages he'd made Ned transcribe from Bernie Siegel and tape to the refrigerator—we'd already moved twice, neither time for any good reason. Something couldn't just scurry in and make us pack it all up again, could it? And where was there left to go anymore? He was too sick to be in a hotel, and I knew there was no other apartment anywhere near the hospital. We would have to persuade him that the mouse existed only in his head. We'd tell him he was hallucinating; we'd talk him out of it, in the same way we patiently tried to soothe him by explaining that the terror he was experiencing was only a nightmare. He was not in a plane that had crashed in the jungle; he was tangled in sheets, not weighed down with concrete.

When I got to the bedroom, Ned was trying to pry Richard's fingers off the door frame. He was having no luck, and looked at me with an expression that had become familiar: fear, with an undercurrent of intense fatigue.

Richard's robe dangled from his bony shoulders. He was so wet that I thought at first he might have blundered into the shower. He looked in my direction but didn't register my presence. Then he sagged against Ned, who began to walk him slowly in the direction of the bed.

"It's cold," Richard said. "Why isn't there any heat?"

"We keep the thermostat at eighty," Ned said wearily. "You just need to get under the covers."

"Is that Hattie over there?"

"It's me," I said. "Ned is trying to get you into the bed."

"Rac," Richard said vaguely. He said to Ned, "Is that my bed?"

"That's your bed," Ned said. "You'll be warm if you get into bed, Richard."

I came up beside Richard and patted his back, and walked around and sat on the edge of the bed, trying to coax him forward. Ned was right: it was dizzyingly hot in the apartment. I got up and turned back the covers, smoothing the contour sheet. Ned kept Richard's hand, but turned to face him as he took one step backward, closer to the bed. The two of us panto-mimed our pleasure at the bed's desirability. Richard began to walk toward it, licking his lips.

"I'll get you some water," I said.

"Water," Richard said. "I thought we were on a ship. I thought the bath-room was an inside cabin with no window. I can't be where there's no way to see the sky."

Ned was punching depth back into Richard's pillows. Then he made a fist and punched the center of the bed. "All aboard the S.S. *Fucking A*," he said.

It got a fake laugh out of me as I turned into the kitchen, but Richard only began to whisper urgently about the claustrophobia he'd experienced in the bathroom. Finally he did get back in his bed and immediately fell asleep. Half an hour later, still well before dawn, Ned repeated Richard's whisperings to me as if they were his own. Though Ned and I were very dif-ferent people, our ability to imagine Richard's suffering united us. We were sitting in wooden chairs we'd pulled away from the dining-room table to put by the window so Ned could smoke. His cigarette smoke curled out the window.

"Ever been to Mardi Gras?" he said.

"New Orleans," I said, "but never Mardi Gras."

"They use strings of beads for barter," he said. "People stand up on the balconies in the French Quarter—women as well as men, sometimes—and they holler down for people in the crowd to flash 'em: you give them a thrill, they toss down their beads. The more you show, the more you win. Then you can walk around with all your necklaces and everybody will know you're real foxy. *Real* cool. You do a bump-and-grind, you can get the good ole boys—the men, that is—and the transvestites all whistling together and throwing down the long necklaces. The real long ones are the ones every-body wants. They're like having a five-carat-diamond ring." He opened the window another few inches so he could stub out his cigarette. One-fingered, he flicked it to the ground. Then he lowered the window, not quite pushing it shut. This wasn't one of Ned's wild stories; I was sure what he'd just told me was true. Sometimes I thought Ned told me certain stories to titillate me, or perhaps to put me down in some way: to remind me that I was straight and he was gay.

"You know what I did one time?" I said suddenly, deciding to see if I could shock him for once. "When I was having that affair with Harry? One night we were in his apartment—his wife was off in Israel—and he was cooking dinner, and I was going through her jewelry box. There was a pearl necklace in there. I couldn't figure out how to open the clasp, but finally I realized I could just drop it over my head carefully. When Harry hollered for me, I had all my clothes off and was lying on the rug, in the dark, with my arms at my side. Finally he came after me. He put on the light and saw me, and then he started laughing and sort of dove onto me, and the pearl necklace broke. He raised up and said, 'What have I done?' and I said, 'Harry, it's your wife's necklace.' He didn't even know she had it. She must not have worn it. So he started cursing, crawling around to pick up the pearls, and I thought, No, if he has it restrung at least I'm going to make sure it won't be the same length."

Ned and I turned our heads to see Richard, his robe neatly knotted in front, kneesocks pulled on, his hair slicked back.

"What are you two talking about?" he said.

"Hey, Richard," Ned said, not managing to disguise his surprise.

"I don't smell cigarette smoke, do I?" Richard said.

"It's coming from below," I said, closing the window.

"We weren't talking about you," Ned said. His voice was both kind and wary.

"I didn't say you were," Richard said. He looked at me. "May I be included?"

"I was telling him about Harry," I said. "The story about the pearls." More and more, it seemed, we were relying on stories.

"I never liked him," Richard said. He waved a hand toward Ned. "Open that a crack, will you? It's too hot in here."

"You already know the story," I said to Richard, anxious to include him. "You tell Ned the punch line."

Richard looked at Ned. "She ate them," he said. "When he wasn't looking she ate as many as she could."

"I didn't want them to fit anymore if she tried to put them over her head," I said. "I wanted her to know something had happened."

Richard shook his head, but fondly: a little gesture he gave to indicate that I was interchangeable with some gifted, troublesome child he never had.

"One time, when I was on vacation with Sander, I picked up a trick in Puerto Rico," Ned said. "We were going at it at this big estate where the guy's employer lived, and suddenly the guy, the employer, hears something and starts up the stairs. So I ran into the closet—"

"He played football in college," Richard said.

I smiled, but I had already heard this story. Ned had told it at a party one night long ago, when he was drunk. It was one of the stories he liked best, because he appeared a little wild in it and a little cagey, and because somebody got his comeuppance. His stories were not all that different from those stories boys had often confided in me back in my college days— stories about dates and sexual conquests, told with ellipses to spare my delicate feelings.

"So I grabbed whatever was hanging behind me—just grabbed down a wad of clothes—and as the guy comes into the room, I throw open the door and spring," Ned was saying. "Buck naked, I start out running, and here's my bad luck: I slam right into him and knock him out. Like it's a cartoon or something. I know he's out cold, but I'm too terrified to think straight, so I keep on running. Turns out what I've grabbed is a white pleated shirt and a thing like a—what do you call those jackets the Japanese wear? Comes halfway down my thighs, thank God."

"These are the things he thanks God for," Richard said to me.

Ned got up, growing more animated. "It's *all* like a cartoon. There's a dog in the yard that sets out after me, but the thing is on a *chain*. He reaches the end of the chain and just rises up in the air, baring his teeth, but he can't go anywhere. So I stand right there, inches in front of the dog, and put on the shirt and tie the jacket around me, and then I stroll over to the gate and slip the latch, and about a quarter of a mile later I'm outside some hotel. I go in and go to the men's room to clean up, and that's the first time I realize I've got a broken nose."

Although I had heard the story before, this was the first mention of Ned's broken nose. For a few seconds he seemed to lose steam, as if he himself were tired of the story, but then he started up again, revitalized.

"And here's the rest of my good luck: I come out and the guy on the desk is a fag. I tell him I've run into a problem and will he please call my boyfriend at the hotel where we're staying, because I don't even have a coin to use the pay phone. So he looks up the number of the hotel, and he dials it and hands me the phone. They connect me with Sander, who is sound asleep, but he snaps to right away, screaming, 'Another night on the town with a prettyboy? Suddenly the bars close and Ned realizes his wallet's back at the hotel? And do you think I'm going to come get you, just because you and some pickup don't have money to pay the bill'?"

Eyes wide, Ned turned first to me, then to Richard, playing to a full house. "While he was ranting, I had time to think. I said, 'Wait a minute, Sander. You mean they didn't get anything? You mean I left my wallet at the hotel?'" Ned sank into his chair. "Can you believe it? I'd actually left my fuckin' wallet in our room, so all I had to do was pretend to Sander that I'd gotten mugged—sons of bitches made me strip and ran off with my pants. Then I told him that the guy at the hotel gave me the kimono to put on." He clicked his fingers. "That's what they're called: 'kimonos.'"

"He didn't ask why a kimono?" Richard said wearily. He ran his hand over the stubble of his beard. His feet were tucked beside him on the sofa.

"Sure. And I tell him it's because there's a Japanese restaurant in the hotel, and if you want to wear kimonos and sit on the floor Japanese style, they let you. And the bellboy thought they'd never miss a kimono."

"He believed you?" Richard said.

"Sander? He grew up in L.A. and spent the rest of his life in New York. He knew you had to believe everything. He drives me back to the hotel saying how great it is that the scum that jumped me didn't get any money. The sun's coming up, and we're riding along in the rental car, and he's holding my hand." Ned locked his thumbs together. "Sander and I are like *that* again."

In the silence, the room seemed to shrink around us. Sander died in 1985.

"I'm starting to feel cold," Richard said. "It comes up my body like somebody's rubbing ice up my spine."

I got up and sat beside him, half hugging him, half massaging his back.

"There's that damn baby again," Richard said. "If that's their first baby, I'll bet they never have another one."

Ned and I exchanged looks. The only sound, except for an intermittent hiss of steam from the radiator, was the humming of the refrigerator.

"What happened to your paws, Rac?" Richard said to me.

I looked at my hands, thumbs pressing into the muscles below his shoulders. For the first time in as long as I could remember, I'd forgotten to put on the lotion and the gloves before going to sleep. I was also reflexively doing something I'd trained myself not to do years ago. My insurance contract said I couldn't use my hands that way: no cutting with a knife, no washing dishes, no making the bed, no polishing the furniture. But I kept pressing my thumbs in Richard's back, rubbing them back and forth. Even after Ned

dropped the heavy blanket over Richard's trembling shoulders, I kept pressing some resistance to his hopeless dilemma deep into the bony ladder of
Richard's spine.

"It's crazy to hate a baby for crying," Richard said, "but I really hate that
baby."

Ned spread a blanket over Richard's lap, then tucked it around his legs.
He sat on the floor and bent one arm around Richard's blanketed shins.
"Richard," he said quietly, "there's no baby. We've gone through the building floor by floor, to humor you. That noise you get in your ears when your
blood pressure starts to drop must sound to you like a baby crying."

"Okay," Richard said, shivering harder. "There's no baby. Thank you for
telling me. You promised you'd always tell me the truth."

Ned looked up. "Truth? From the guy who just told the Puerto Rico
story?"

"Or maybe you're hearing something in the pipes, Richard," I said.
"Sometimes the radiators make noise."

Richard nodded hard, in agreement. But he didn't quite hear me. That
was what Ned and I had found out about people who were dying: their
minds always raced past whatever was being said, and still the pain went
faster, leapfrogging ahead.

Two days later, Richard was admitted to the hospital with a high fever, and
went into a coma from which he never awoke. His brother flew to Boston
that night, to be with him. His godson, Jerry, came, too, getting there in
time to go with us in the cab. The experimental treatment hadn't worked.
Of course, we still had no way of knowing—we'll never know—whether
Richard had been given the polysyllabic medicine we'd come to call "the
real stuff," or whether he'd been part of the control group. We didn't know
whether the priest from Hartford was getting the real stuff, either, though
it was rumored among us that his flushed face was a good sign. And what
about the young veterinarian who always had something optimistic to say
when we ran into each other in the transfusion room? Like Clark Kent, with
his secret "S" beneath his shirt, the vet wore a T-shirt with a photograph
reproduced on the front, a snapshot of him hugging his Border collie on the
day the dog took a blue ribbon. He told me he wore it every Friday for good
luck, as he sat in oncology getting the I.V. drip that sometimes gave him the
strength to go to a restaurant with a friend that night.

Ned and I, exhausted from another all-nighter, took the presence of
Richard's brother and godson as an excuse to leave the hospital and go get
a cup of coffee. I felt light-headed, though, and asked Ned to wait for me in

the lobby while I went to the bathroom. I thought some cold water on my face might revive me.

There were two teenage girls in the bathroom. As they talked, it turned out they were sisters and had just visited their mother, who was in the oncology ward down the hall. Their boyfriends were coming to pick them up, and there was a sense of excitement in the air as one sister teased her hair into a sort of plume, and the other took off her torn stockings and threw them away, then rolled her knee-length skirt up to make it a micromini. "Come on, Mare," her sister, standing at the mirror, said, though she was taking her time fixing her own hair. Mare reached into her cosmetic bag and took out a little box. She opened it and began to quickly streak a brush over the rectangle of color inside. Then, to my amazement, she began to swirl the brush over both knees, to make them blush. As I washed and dried my face, a fog of hair spray filtered down. The girl at the mirror fanned the air, put the hair spray back in her purse, then picked up a tube of lipstick, opened it, and parted her lips. As Mare straightened up after one last swipe at her knees, she knocked her sister's arm, so that the lipstick shot slightly above her top lip.

"Jesus! You feeb!" the girl said shrilly. "Look what you made me *do*."

"Meet you at the car," her sister said, grabbing the lipstick and tossing it into her makeup bag. She dropped the bag in her purse and almost skipped out, calling back, "Soap and water's good for that!"

"What a bitch," I said, more to myself than to the girl who remained.

"Our mother's dying, and she doesn't care," the girl said. Tears began to well up in her eyes.

"Let me help you get it off," I said, feeling more light-headed than I had when I'd come in. I felt as if I were sleepwalking.

The girl faced me, mascara smudged in half-moons beneath her eyes, her nose bright red, one side of her lip more pointed than the other. From the look in her eyes, I was just a person who happened to be in the room. The way I had happened to be in the room in New York the day Richard came out of the bathroom, one shirtsleeve rolled up, frowning, saying, "What do you think this rash is on my arm?"

"I'm all right," the girl said, wiping her eyes. "It's not your problem."

"I'd say she does care," I said. "People get very anxious in hospitals. I came in to throw some water on my face because I was feeling a little faint."

"Do you feel better now?" she said.

"Yes," I said.

"We're not the ones who are dying," she said.

It was a disembodied voice that came from some faraway, perplexing place, and it disturbed me so deeply that I needed to hold her for a moment—which I did, tapping my forehead lightly against hers and slipping my fingers through hers to give her a squeeze before I walked out the door.

Ned had gone outside and was leaning against a lamppost. He pointed the glowing tip of his cigarette to the right, asking silently if I wanted to go to the coffee shop down the block. I nodded, and we fell into step.

"I don't think this is a walk we're going to be taking too many more times," he said. "The doctor stopped to talk, on his way out. He's run out of anything optimistic to say. He also took a cigarette out of my fingers and crushed it under his heel, told me I shouldn't smoke. I'm not crazy about doctors, but there's still something about that one that I like. Hard to imagine I'd ever warm up to a guy with tassels on his shoes."

It was freezing cold. At the coffee shop, hot air from the electric heater over the door smacked us in the face as we headed for our familiar seats at the counter. Just the fact that it wasn't the hospital made it somehow pleasant, though it was only a block and a half away. Some of the doctors and nurses went there, and of course people like us—patients' friends and relatives. Ned nodded when the waitress asked if we both wanted coffee.

"Winter in Boston," Ned said. "Never knew there was anything worse than winter where I grew up, but I think this is worse."

"Where did you grow up?"

"Kearney, Nebraska. Right down Route Eighty, about halfway between Lincoln and the Wyoming border."

"What was it like, growing up in Nebraska?"

"I screwed boys," he said.

It was either the first thing that popped into his head, or he was trying to make me laugh.

"You know what the first thing fags always ask each other is, don't you?" he said.

I shook my head no, braced for a joke.

"It's gotten so the second thing is 'Have you been tested?' But the first thing is still always 'When did you know?'"

"Okay," I said. "Second question."

"No," he said, looking straight at me. "It can't happen to me."

"Be serious," I said. "That's not a serious answer."

He cupped his hand over mine. "How the hell do you think I got out of Kearney, Nebraska?" he said. "Yeah, I had a football scholarship, but I had to hitchhike to California—never been to another state but Wyoming—hitched with whatever I had in a laundry bag. And if a truck driver put a hand on my knee, you don't think I knew that was a small price to pay for a ride? Because luck was with me. I always knew that. Just the way luck shaped those pretty hands of yours. Luck's always been with me, and luck's with you. It's as good as anything else we have to hang on to."

He lifted his hand from mine, and yes, there it was: the perfect hand, with smooth skin, tapered fingers, and nails curved and shining under the gloss of a French manicure. There was a small, dark smudge across one knuckle. I licked the middle finger of the other hand to see if I could gently rub it away, that smudge of mascara that must have passed from the hand of the girl in the bathroom to my hand when our fingers interwove as we awkwardly embraced. The girl I had been watching, all the time Ned and I sat talking. She was there in the coffee shop with us—I'd seen them come in, the two sisters and their boyfriends—her hair neatly combed, her eyes sparkling, her makeup perfectly stroked on. Though her sister tried to get their attention, both boys hung on her every word.

Zalla

Recently, I had reason to think about Thomas Kurbell—Little Thomas, as the family always called him. Little Thomas fooled the older members of the family for a while because he was so polite as a child—almost obsequious—and because his father, Thomas Sr., had been a genuinely nice man. Ours was an urban family, based in Philadelphia and Washington, D.C., and Little Thomas's father's death reinforced every bit of paranoia everyone had about life in the country. No matter that he actually died of complications of pneumonia, which he had contracted in the hospital as he was lying in traction, recovering from a broken leg, shattered ankle, and patched-together pelvis, suffered after falling from a hay wagon. Legend had it that he'd died instantly from the fall, and this was always invoked as a cautionary warning to any youngster in the family who took an interest in skiing or sailing or even hiking. For the sake of storytelling, Thomas Sr.'s death often dovetailed into the long-ago death of his cousin Pete, who had been struck by lightning when he got out to investigate a backup on the Brooklyn Bridge: wham! With Thomas still sliding out of the hay wagon, there was a sudden bolt of electricity, and Pete, moved to New York City, was struck dead, lit up for such a quick second it seemed somebody was just taking a picture with a flash. I suppose it's true in many families that some things get to be lumped together for effect, and others to obscure some issue. I was thirty years old before I got the chronology of the two deaths correct. It's just the way people in our family tell stories: it wasn't done to mislead Little Thomas.

Little Thomas was a sneaky child. He'd sneak around for no good reason, padding through the house in his socks, sometimes scaring his mother and his sister Lilly when they turned a corner and found him standing there like a statue. His mother always said Little Thomas had no radar. No instinct for avoiding people and things. His going around in his socks made things worse, because if you were frightened and yelped he would become frightened, too, and burst into tears or topple something from a table in his fright. But he wouldn't wear shoes in the house—to get even with his mother, he said, for making him wear boots to school on days when it wasn't even raining, only damp—and no amount of pleading or punishment could make him change his ways. As he got older, he deliberately frightened his sister from time to time, because he loved to see her jump, but most of the scares with his mother were unintentional, he later maintained.

Little Thomas's mother was named Etta Sue. She was five years older than my mother, Alice Dawn Rose. There was a brother in between, who had died of rheumatic fever. Though Etta Sue married a man named Thomas Kurbell, she maintained that Little Thomas was named not for him but for her dead brother, Thomas Wyatt. Little Thomas's middle name was Nathaniel. "She put that name in because she wanted to include everybody, even the milkman," Thomas Sr. used to say. Apparently, the milkman was a subject of fond kidding between them: she really did like the milkman, and he became a family friend. He'd push open the back door, come in, and wipe off the milk bottles before putting them on the top shelf of the refrigerator, and then pour himself some tea and sit and talk to whoever happened to be in the kitchen—Thomas Sr.; my mother, on a visit; me. He was Nat the Milkman. One time when I wasn't there, Little Thomas jumped out of the broom closet and startled Nat the Milkman, and Nat grabbed him and flipped him over, holding him upside down by his ankles for a good long while. This was the reason Little Thomas hated him.

As well as slipping around in his stocking feet, Little Thomas was quiet and rarely could be coaxed into a conversation. He was quiet and troubled—that much the family would finally allow, though they refused to admit that there were any *real* problems. It was said he was troubled because he'd had to wear glasses as a child. Or because his father was so personable that he'd presented his son with a hard act to follow. Later, Little Thomas's asthma was blamed, and then his guilt over the fact that Punkin Puppy, the family's russet-colored mutt, had to be given away because of Little Thomas's allergies. Growing up, I heard these things over and over. The reasons were like a mantra, or like the stages of grief being explained—the steps from denial to acceptance. By the time he was a teenager, it was no longer a question just of his being troubled but of his actively troubling others. Garden hoses were turned on in the neighbors' gardens late at night, washing their flowers away in great landslides of mud; brown bags filled with dog excrement were set burning on some neighbor's porch, so whoever opened the door would be ankle deep in dog shit when he stomped out the flames. Things got worse, and then Little Thomas was sent away to a special school.

Yesterday I visited my mother in her new apartment in Alexandria. She was afraid of crime in downtown Washington and thought she should relocate. Her nurse-companion came with her, a kindhearted woman named Zalla, who attended the school of nursing at American University two nights a week and every summer. When she got her nursing degree, Zalla intended to return to her home, Belize, where she was going to work in a hospital. The hospital was still under construction. Building had to be stopped when the architect was accused of embezzling; then the hurricane struck. But Zalla had faith that the hospital would be completed, that she would eventually graduate from nursing school, and that—though this went unsaid—she would not be with my mother forever. My mother has emphysema and diabetes, and needs someone with her. Zalla cooks and washes and does any number of things no one expects her to do, and during the day she's never off her feet. At night she watches James Bond movies over and over on my mother's VCR. My mother sits in the TV room with her, rereading Dickens. She says the James Bond movies provide wonderful soundtracks for the stories: Carly Simon singing "Nobody Does It Better" in *The Spy Who Loved Me* as my mother's reading about Mr. Pickwick.

Anyway, what happened was in no way Zalla's fault, but she was tortured by guilt. Days after the incident I'm going to tell about, which I heard of when I visited, Zalla was still upset.

That Monday, my mother had checked into Sibley Hospital for a day of tests. In the afternoon, there was a knock on the door and Zalla looked out of the peephole and saw Little Thomas. She'd met him several times through the years, so of course she let him in. He said he was there to return some dishes my mother had let him borrow when he was setting up housekeeping. He also wanted to say goodbye, because he was moving out of the apartment he'd been sharing with other people in Landover, Maryland, and was headed down to the Florida Keys to tend bar. Then he worked the conversation around to asking Zalla for a loan: fifty dollars, which he'd send back as soon as he got to Key West and opened a bank account and deposited some checks. She had thirty-some dollars and gave him everything she had, minus the bus fare she needed to get to Sibley Hospital that evening. He asked for a sheet of paper so he could write a goodbye note to my mother, and Zalla found him a notepad. He sat at the kitchen table, writing. It didn't occur to her to stand over him. She unpacked the dishes and loaded them into the dishwasher, and then tidied up in the TV room. He wrote and wrote. He was writing my mother a nasty note, telling her that through therapy he had come to realize that the family perpetuated harmful myths, and that no one had ever chosen to "come clean" about his father's death, because his father had actually died of pneumonia, not from the fall off a wagon. He told her how horrifying it had been to see his father slipping away in the hospital, and he blamed her and Etta Sue for always discussing Cousin Pete's last moments when they talked about his father's death. "Fact is, lightning impressed you more than simple pneumonia," he wrote. He also thought they should have talked more to him about his father's accomplishments. He thought they should have told about his father's love for him. He made no mention of his sister Lilly, from whom he was estranged. He folded the note and put it under the saltshaker, and then he mixed himself a cup of instant cocoa and left, taking the mug he was drinking from.

Zalla was nervous. She thought he might have been drinking, though his breath didn't smell of alcohol. He'd gone to the bathroom while he was there, so Zalla went into the bathroom to make sure everything was all right. It was, but she still had an uneasy feeling. It wasn't until that evening, when she left for the hospital to escort my mother home, that she saw the black felt-pen graffiti on the wall in the downstairs hallway: stick people with corkscrew hair like Martians' antennae, and a quickly scrawled SCREW YOU BLOWING THIS JOINT. She was horrified, and at first she thought she'd keep quiet about Little Thomas's visit—just pretend it was all a mystery—but she knew that was wrong and she'd have to make a full disclosure.

By the time I heard the story, Zalla and my mother had agreed he was probably drunk—or, worse, on drugs—and that he was a coward to pretend to confront my mother, when all he did was write a note. He also hadn't had the nerve to face his own mother, who was still living on Twentieth Street, and tell her that he was moving away. Zalla kept quiet about the thirty dollars, but the next morning she confessed that, too. In with the dishes he'd brought back were several strange, gold-bordered plates my mother had not given him; neither she nor Zalla knew exactly what to make of that. Both feared, irrationally, that someone would now come for the plates. They seemed to understand, though, that Little Thomas was gone and wouldn't be heard from for some time, if ever. Zalla remained afraid of him, in the abstract. She said he'd crept around like a burglar. That gave my mother and me a good laugh, because he'd been sneaky all his life. Good that he spared Mother's bathroom wall, I joked: bad enough that they'd had to call the management to apologize and to arrange to have the hallway repainted.

While Zalla watched *Goldfinger*, my mother led me into her bedroom and told me one of the Dark Secrets she'd never before revealed. It turned out she had always feared Little Thomas would do something really awful, because he had done something very bad as a child. My mother had been furious, but she had never told on him, because she was embarrassed at her own fury, and also because she felt that Little Thomas's demons tortured him enough.

She asked whether I remembered the silhouettes. I did remember them, vaguely, though I had to be reminded that they'd once hung on a satin ribbon in Etta Sue's living room. I remembered them from later on, when they'd hung below the light above the bed in my mother's bedroom, attached to the same ribbon. There had also been one of Lilly, as a baby, and another of Punkin Puppy, in separate frames. The three framed silhouettes on the ribbon had been of Thomas Sr., Etta Sue, and the man who, Etta Sue told my mother, had cut the silhouettes. Etta Sue explained this somewhat humorous fact by saying that the silhouette cutter was going to throw his self-portrait away—he probably did it the way secretaries practice their typing, or something—and that she had rescued it from the trash. Little Thomas had destroyed *his* silhouette before it got into the frame, and though Etta Sue always meant to have another one cut, Little Thomas wouldn't sit still a second time. My mother shook her head. She said that she supposed the silhouette cutter's self-portrait was sort of like Alfred Hitchcock's including himself in his own films, though that wasn't a good comparison, because Etta Sue had hung it up, not the man himself.

When Etta Sue was forced to move out of her house and into the Twentieth Street apartment after Thomas Sr.'s death, she had to discard many things. The furniture my mother could understand, but parting with so many personal possessions had seemed to her a mistake. When the ribbon with the framed silhouettes went into the trash, my mother grabbed it out and said she would keep it for Etta Sue until she felt better. And Etta Sue had given her the strangest look. First shocked, then sad, my mother thought. And in all the years my mother had the silhouettes hung in her bedroom, Etta Sue never mentioned them, although she did eventually ask for Thomas Sr.'s shaving mug back, and for the framed picture of herself and her husband taken at a Chinese restaurant on their first anniversary.

But the point of the story, my mother said, was this: One weekend a few months after Thomas Sr.'s death, she was taking care of Little Thomas and Lilly, and Little Thomas had gone into the bedroom while all the rest of us were in the backyard and he had taken the silhouettes out of the frames and cut the noses off. Then he slipped them all back into their frames and rehung them. It was days before my mother noticed—everyone with his or her nose chopped off, plus Punkin Puppy, earless.

She hurried right over to Little Thomas's school and waited for him to get out. He walked home, but that day he didn't go anywhere before she confronted him. By her own account, she grabbed the tip of his nose and squeezed it, asking him how he thought he'd like being without his nose. Then she grabbed his ears and asked him if he thought he might like to spend the rest of his life not hearing, too. She crouched and made him look her in the eye and tell her why he'd done it. It was amazing that someone didn't notice her making such a scene and come over, she said. Little Thomas gasped when she pulled him around and shook him by his shoulders, but he never cried.

He had done it, he told her, because the faces in the frames were miniature black ghosts, there to haunt people. He disfigured them because they were ghost monsters with special powers of sneaking inside people. If he got rid of the black ghosts, cut them up a little, they would become white ghosts, with no special power.

My mother was so horrified she couldn't stand. He had given a quite specific, terribly upsetting answer, and she had no idea what response to make, because if he really thought those things he was mad. That would make it the first incidence of real madness in the family. She was 90 percent sure he was telling her what he really believed, but she also thought there was some small chance he might be having her on. She stayed there quite a while, weak in the knees, staring into his face, looking for more information.

"You think I'd care if I didn't have a nose?" he said. "*I* wouldn't care if I didn't have a nose or a mouth or eyes. I wish the sperm had never gone into the egg. I wouldn't mind if there was no me, and you wouldn't either."

My mother remembered being surprised that he knew about sex—that he knew such words as "sperm" and "egg." She didn't remember what she said to him next, but it had something to do with how she understood that he was very upset that his father was dead and had disappeared, but that he mustn't confuse that with thinking his father didn't love him.

Little Thomas broke away from her. "You stupid fool," he said. She remembered that distinctly: "You stupid fool."

After Little Thomas's father's death, my mother now suddenly reminded me, someone courted Etta Sue for a bit, but eventually faded away. In retrospect, my mother said, she thought it might quite possibly have been ("Now, don't laugh," she said) the milkman. Because, come to think of it, why else—unless she was a little embarrassed—would Etta Sue refuse to let anyone in the family know whom she was seeing? Also, Nat the Milkman had been a Sunday painter, so perhaps he had also cut silhouettes.

"Say nothing of this to Zalla," my mother said. It was something she had begun to say increasingly, as an afterthought, in recent years—or perhaps as an end to each of her stories, not as an afterthought, really.

I kissed her cheek and gave her hand a squeeze, turning off her bedside lamp with my free hand. It was early evening and dark. We were in autumn, the season when Thomas Sr. had slipped from high atop the mounded hay—slipped in slow motion, compared to the way his cousin Pete had been struck by lightning.

That was the past. I imagined the future: the graffiti figures that had already disappeared in the downstairs hallway, whited out by a paint roller. Then I thought about the hospital in Belize, to which for all intents and purposes that paint roller could travel like a comet, to whiten the drywall that had at long last been installed in the corridors of the new hospital. Zalla would be standing there, her starched white nurse's uniform contrasting with her dark skin, and in a blink my mother would be dead, quite unexpectedly—gone from her white-sheeted bed to the darkness, as Zalla paused in her busy day to remember us, a nice American family.

The Women of This World

The dinner was going to be good. Dale had pureed leeks and salsify to add to the pumpkin in the food processor—a tablespoon or so of sweet vermouth might give it a little zing—and as baby-girl pink streaked through the gray-blue sky over the field, she dropped a CD into the player and listened matter-of-factly to Lou Reed singing matter-of-factly, "I'm just a gift to the women of this world."

By now her husband, Nelson, would be on his way back from Logan, bringing his stepfather, Jerome, and Jerome's girlfriend, Brenda—who had taken the shuttle from New York, after much debate about plane versus train versus driving—for the annual (did three years in a row make something annual?) pre-Thanksgiving dinner. They could have come on Thanksgiving, but Didi, Jerome's ex (and Nelson's mother), was coming that day, and there was no love lost between them. Brenda didn't like big gatherings, anyway. Brenda was much younger than Jerome. She used to nap half the afternoon—because she was shy, Jerome said—but lately her occupation had become glamorous and she had quit teaching gym at the middle school to work as a personal trainer, and suddenly she was communicative, energized, radiant—if that wasn't a cliché for women in love.

Dale turned on the food processor and felt relieved as the ingredients liquified. It wasn't that the food processor hadn't always worked—when she placed the blade in the bottom correctly, that is—but that she feared it wouldn't work. She always ran through a scenario in which she'd have to scoop everything out and dump it in the old Waring blender that had come with the rented house in Maine and that didn't always work. With blenders so cheap, she amazed herself by not simply buying a new one.

Nelson was forever indebted to Jerome for appearing on the scene when he was five years old, and staying until he was sixteen. Jerome had seen to it that Nelson was spared going to Groton, and had taught him to play every known sport—at least every ordinary sport. But would Nelson have wanted to learn, say, archery?

Nelson wanted to learn everything, though he didn't want to do everything. He was happy to have quit teaching and wanted to do very little. He liked to know about things, though. That way, he could talk about them. Her cruel nickname for him was No-Firsthand-Knowledge Nelson. It got tedious sometimes: people writing down the names of books from which Nelson had gotten his often esoteric information. People calling after the party was over, having looked up some strange assertion of Nelson's in their kid's *Encyclopedia Britannica* and discovered that he was essentially right, but not entirely. They often left these quibbles and refutations on the answering machine: "Dick here. Listen, you weren't exactly right about Mercury. It's because Hermes means 'mediator' in Greek, so there *is* an element of logic to his taking the souls of the dead to the underworld"; "Nelson? This is Pauline. Listen, Rushdie did write the introduction to that Glen Baxter book. I can bring it next time and show you. He really does write introductions all the time. Well, thanks to you both for a great evening. My sister really appreciated Dale's copying that recipe for her—though no one can make butterflied lamb like Dale, I told her. Anyway. Okay. Bye. Thanks again."

Jerome and Brenda would be twenty or thirty minutes away, assuming the plane landed on time, which you could never assume if you knew anything about Logan. Still: Dale could manage a quick shower, if not a bath, and she should probably change into a dress because it seemed a little oblivious to have people over when you were wearing sweats, even if you did have a cashmere sweater pulled over them. Maybe a bra under the sweater. A pair of corduroys, instead of the supercomfortable sweats. And shoes . . . definitely some sort of shoes.

Nelson called from the cell phone. "Need anything?" he said. She could hear Terry Gross's well-modulated, entirely reasonable voice on the radio. Only Nelson and Terry and her guest were talking in the car: the passengers were silent, in case Dale had forgotten some necessary ingredient. Yes, pink peppercorns. Try finding them on 95 North. And, of course, they weren't really peppercorns; they were only called peppercorns because they looked like black peppercorns. Or: purple oregano. An entirely different flavor from green.

"Not a thing," she said. She had changed into black corduroy pants and a white shirt. Keeping it clean would preoccupy her, give her some way to stay a little detached from everyone. She was shy, too. Though she wore bad-girl black boots.

"Brenda wants to see the Wedding Cake House. I thought we'd swing by. Would that mess up your timing?"

"I didn't cook anything," Dale said.

Silence, then. Unkind of her, to set his mind scrambling for alternatives.

"Kidding," she said.

She had toured the Wedding Cake House soon after they moved to the area. It was in Kennebunkport, a huge yellow-and-white creation, with Gothic spires like pointed phalluses. Legend had it that it had been built by a sea captain for his bride, to remind her of their wedding night when he left for sea.

"We'll be back around four."

Someone else was talking to Terry Gross in a deep, earnest voice.

"See you soon," Nelson said. "Hon?" he said.

"Bye," Dale said. She picked up two bottles of red wine from the wine rack near the phone. A little too close to the heat grate, so no wine was kept on the last four shelves. Not a problem in summer, but a minor inconvenience come cold weather. She remembered that Brenda had been delighted with a Fumé Blanc she'd served last time, and bought the same bottle for her again. Jerome, of course, because of his years in Paris, would have the Saint-Émilion. Nelson had taken to sipping Jameson's lately. Still, she'd chilled several bottles of white, because he was unpredictable. On the top rack lay the bottle of Opus One an appreciative student from the photography workshop she'd taught had given her. Two nights later, she planned to serve it to the doctor who had diagnosed both her hypoglycemia and her Ménière's disease, which meant, ironically, that she could no longer drink. If she did, she'd risk more attacks of the sickening vertigo that had plagued her and gone misdiagnosed for years, leaving her sweaty and trembling and so weak she'd often have to stay in bed the day after the attack. "Like taking acid and getting swept up in a tidal wave," she had said to the otolaryngologist. The woman had looked at her with surprise, as if she'd been gathering strawberries and suddenly come upon a watermelon. "Quite a vivid description," the doctor had said. "My husband is a writer. He sometimes stops me dead in my tracks the same way."

"Is he Brian McCambry?" Dale had asked.

"Yes," the doctor said. Again, she seemed surprised.

Nelson had been the one who speculated that Dr. Anna McCambry might be the wife of Brian McCambry. Dale, herself, had read only a few pieces by McCambry, though Nelson—as she told the doctor—had read her many others.

"I'll pass on the compliment," the doctor said. "Now back to the real world."

What a strange way to announce the transition, Dale had thought, though her symptoms sometimes were the real world for her, crowding out any other concerns. What was more real than telescoping vision, things blurring and swarming you, so that you had no depth perception, no ability to stand? The doctor talked to her about alterations in her diet. Prescribed diuretics. Said so many things so fast that Dale had to call the nurse later that afternoon, to be reminded what several of them had been. The doctor had overheard the call. "Bring your husband and come for drinks and I'll go over this with you while they talk," the doctor had said. " 'Drinks' in your case means seltzer."

"Thanks," Dale said. No doctor had ever asked to see her out of the office.

She opened the Fumé Blanc but left the bottle of Saint-Émilion corked. How did she know? Maybe Jerome would decide to go directly to the white French burgundy. What hadn't seemed fussy and precious before did now, a little: people and their wine preferences. Still, she indulged the vegetarians in their restrictions, knew better than to prepare veal for anyone, unless she was sure it wouldn't result in a tirade. Her friend Andy liked still water, her photography student Nance preferred Perrier. Dale's mind was full of people's preferences and quirks, their mystical beliefs and food taboos, their ways of demonstrating their independence and their dependency at table. The little tests: would there happen to be sea salt? Was there a way to adjust the pepper grinder to grind a little more coarsely? A call for chutney. That one had really put her over the top. There was Stonewall Kitchen Roasted Onion and Garlic Jam already on the table. She had sent Nelson for the chutney, since Paul was more his friend than hers.

She went into the downstairs bathroom and brushed her hair, gathering it back in a ponytail. She took off the white shirt and changed back into her cashmere sweater, giving it a tug she knew she shouldn't give it to make sure it fell just right. She looked at her boots and wished it was still summer; she'd be more comfortable barefoot, but it wasn't summer, and her feet would freeze. She remembered that Julia Roberts had been barefoot when she married Lyle Lovett. Julia Roberts and Lyle Lovett: not as strange as Michael Jackson and Lisa Marie Presley.

Brenda came in first, shaking her thick mane of prematurely white hair. She was full of enthusiasm about the trip to the Wedding Cake House. It was *amazing, beautiful,* somehow sort of *weird*—a little creepy, some woman living inside her wedding cake like the old woman who lived in a shoe. Then Brenda began apologizing: she had insisted they drive down the longest dirt road in history, to get a basket of apples. Nelson put the basket down on the kitchen island, which Dale would soon need every inch of to do the final dinner preparations. She could no longer eat apples, or anything excessively sweet. She was sick of explaining to people what she couldn't eat, and why. In fact, she had started to say she was diabetic, since everyone seemed to know that that meant you couldn't eat sugar. There was also the possibility that the apples might be Brenda and Jerome's, to take back to New York, so she said, "Nice," rather than "Thank you."

The real owners of the house obviously must have loved to cook. The kitchen was well laid out, with the exception of the dishwasher being to the left of the sink. Dale had become so adept at using her left hand to load the dishwasher that she thought it might be amusing to be both diabetic and left-handed. By the time she left the house, she might be an entirely different person.

"It's great to see you. Did you get my note? You didn't go to a lot of trouble, did you?" Jerome said, squeezing Dale, then letting go.

Brenda was still in a dither. "We didn't mess you up, did we?" she said.

"Not at all," Dale said.

"I shouldn't ask, but I've been cooped up in the plane, and then in the car. Would there be time to take a walk? A quick walk?"

"Sure," Dale said. She had just put the roast in the oven to bake. There was plenty of time.

"Would you mind if Nelson and I take a look at that wiring problem? I'm much better when there's natural light," Jerome said.

"Oh, he's on his kick again about how he can't see or hear!" Brenda said. She added, as if they didn't know, "He's *sixty-four.*"

"What wiring problem?" Dale said. She wanted to be barefoot. She wanted to be Julia Roberts, with a big, dazzling smile. Instead, she could feel the skin between her eyebrows tightening. *Wiring problem?* The way Brenda talked got into her brain; in her presence, she started thinking in concerned italics.

"I was trying to hook up speakers in the upstairs hallway. I can get one of them going but not the other. Might be a bad speaker," Nelson said.

Nelson had spent a good portion of his book advance on new sound equipment. His compromise with Dale was: when guests arrived, there would be no music. So far, the day had consisted of bluegrass, Dylan's first electric album, Japanese ceremonial music, an hour or so of *La Bohème,* and

Astor Piazzolla. Dale had listened to the weather report and one cut from a Lou Reed CD that she imagined might be Jerome's theme song. She was fond of Jerome, but he did think he was God's gift to women.

"You'll come on a walk with me, won't you?" Brenda said. She was wearing shoes that would have been inappropriate for a walk, if she hadn't been Brenda: brown pointy-toed boots with three-inch heels. This year's hip look, while Dale's had become the generic. Brenda had shrink-wrapped herself into a black leather skirt, worn over patterned pantyhose. On top was a sweater with a stretched-out turtleneck that Dale thought must be one of Jerome's. He had kept his collection of French handknit sweaters for twenty-some years.

"Just down the road?" Dale said, gesturing to the dirt road that went past the collapsed greenhouse behind the garage. She liked the road. You could usually see deer this time of the evening. Also, because of the way the road dipped, it seemed like you were walking right into the sky, which had now turned Hudson River School radiant. Dale's friend Janet Lebow was the only year-rounder at the end of the road. When the nasty summer people left, taking their Dobermans and their shiny four-wheel drives with them, Janet was happy not only to let Dale walk the No Trespassing/ Danger/Posted/Keep Out road; Janet usually sent her dog, Tyrone (who was afraid of the summer dogs), out to exercise with Dale. Janet was divorced, fifty going on twenty-five, devoted to tabloids, late-night movies, astrological forecasts, and "fun" temporary tattoos of things like unicorns leaping over rainbows. She was not a stupid woman, only childish and a little too upbeat, traumatized by her ex-husband's verbal abuse. Janet shuddered when she mentioned her ex-husband's name and rarely talked about the marriage. Tyrone was a smart golden retriever–black lab mix. When he wasn't in the tributary to the York River, he was wriggling in the field, trying to shed fleas. The dog and the kitchen were the two things Dale felt sure she would miss most when they had to vacate the house. They had it through the following summer, when the philosophy professor and his wife would return from their year in Munich. By then, Nelson's book would supposedly be finished. Dale knew she was not going to enjoy the home stretch. Nelson had written other books, which inevitably made him morose because of the enormousness of the task. Then the music selections would really become eclectic.

Dale reached into the flour bin of the Hoosier cabinet and took out her secret stash of doughnut holes, which she bought on Saturdays at the Portsmouth Farmers' Market. She did not eat doughnut holes: they were exclusively for Tyrone, who thought Dale had invented the best game of fetch imaginable. He would race for the doughnut hole, sniff through the field for it, throw it in the air so Dale could see he'd gotten it, then gulp it down in one swallow. She had taken to applauding. Lately, she had started to add "Good dog, Tyrone" to the applause.

"Is that *cigarettes*?" Brenda whispered to Dale, though Nelson and Jerome were already walking up the stairs.

"Doughnut holes," Dale whispered back. "You'll see." She plunged what remained of them, in their plastic bag, into the deep pocket of her coat.

"I keep peanut M&M's in my lingerie drawer," Brenda said. "And Jerome—you know, he doesn't think I know he still drinks Pernod."

"It's for a dog," Dale said.

"Pernod?" Brenda asked.

"No. Doughnut holes."

"What do you mean?"

"Come on," Dale said. "You'll see."

At dinner—during which Dale could sense Brenda's respect for her, both as a cook and as a crazy woman (she'd sent three doughnut holes up in the air at the same time, like the last moments of the Fourth of July fireworks)—they discussed the brass sundial Dale had placed atop autumn leaves in the center of the table. Nelson informed everyone that the piece sticking up was called the gnomon.

"No mon is an island," Jerome said. Jerome very much enjoyed wordplay and imitating dialects. Dialect from de islands was currently his favorite. He and Brenda had recently vacationed in Montego Bay.

"And this is the shadow," Nelson said, pointing, ignoring Jerome's silly contribution. "This is the plate, this the hour line, this the dial, or diagram."

"You are a born teacher," Brenda said.

"I broke that habit," Nelson said. He had. He had resigned when the theorists outnumbered what he called "the sane art historians." Worried that his ex-colleagues would resent his work with Roman coins, he was fond of stressing that he was not a numismatist. Dale had left with him, retaining only two loyal students who drove hours each week to work with her in the darkroom.

"Groton or no Groton, he had such an interest in knowledge that we had nothing to worry about with Nelson. I wore her down, and I was right to have done it," Jerome said. The time would never come when Jerome would not want to be thanked, one more time, for having saved Nelson—as they both thought of it—from the clutches of Groton.

"Which I thank you for," Nelson said.

"And, if I'd been around at your birth, I could have stopped her from naming you for a sea captain," Jerome said.

"Oh, Nelson is a *lovely* name," Brenda said.

"Of course, if I'd been around at your birth, people might have suspected something funny was going on," Jerome said.

"I thought you met Didi in Paris, when Nelson was five or six," Brenda said.

"He was four. He was five when we got married."

Didi had gone to Paris to study painting. Actually, she had gone to have an affair with her Theosophy instructor. That hadn't had a happy ending, though Didi had met Jerome at Les Deux Magots. No snail-like dawdling; by her own admission, she had struck with the speed of a snake.

"I didn't understand what you meant then, when you said 'If I'd been around,'" Brenda said.

"I was just saying if. If things had been otherwise. Other than what they were. If."

"But I think you implied that you knew Didi when she gave birth. Didn't he?" Brenda said.

"Brenda, you were a child when all this happened. You need not be jealous," Jerome said.

"I know I should let this drop, Jerome, but it seemed sort of strange to suggest you might have been there," Brenda said. "Am I being too literal-minded again?"

"Yes," Nelson said.

"Well, no, I mean, sometimes I feel like something is being said between the lines and because I'm a newcomer I don't quite get it."

"I've lived with you for six years, Brenda," Jerome said. He said it with finality, as if she would do well to drop the subject, if she wanted to live with him another six seconds.

Brenda said nothing. Dale gestured to the soup tureen, beside the sundial. Also on the table was a silver bowl of freshly snipped chives and a little Chinese dish, enameled inside, that Dale had found for a quarter at a tag sale. People in the area did not value anything they were selling that was smaller than a beachball. The Chinese dish was an antique. Inside, there was a pyramid of unsweetened whipped cream.

"Fabulous. Fabulous soup," Jerome said. "So when are you going to let me bankroll your restaurant?"

He'd wanted Dale to open a restaurant in New York for years. Jerome had all the money in the world, inherited when his parents died and left him half the state of Rhode Island. Since Jerome was a part-time stockbroker, he'd managed to invest it wisely. Back in the days before Dale showed her photographs at a gallery on Newbury Street, in Boston, it had been more difficult to dismiss Jerome's ideas.

"So how's the photography coming?" he said, when she didn't answer. Brenda was still eating her soup, not looking up.

"I've got some interesting stuff I've been working on," Dale said. "The woman down the road . . ." She gestured into the dark. Only a tiny blinking light from the bridge to Portsmouth could be seen, far in the distance. "There's one woman who lives there year-round—heating with a woodstove—and I've taken photographs. . . . Well, it always sounds so stupid, talking about what you're photographing. It's like paraphrasing a book," she said, hoping to elicit Nelson's sympathy.

"Just the general idea," Jerome said.

"Well, she does astrological charts for people, and they're really quite beautiful. And she has amazing hands, like Georgia O'Keeffe's. I've photographed her hands as she makes marks on the parchment paper. Hands say so much about a person, because you can't change your hands."

The longer she talked, the more stupid she felt.

"Have you had your chart done?" Jerome said. The stiffness of disapproval registered in his voice.

"No," Dale said.

"I had my chart done once," Brenda said. "I have it somewhere. It was apparently very unusual, because all my moons were in one house."

Jerome looked at her. "Didi believed in astrology," he said. "She thought we were mismatched because she was a Libra and I was a Scorpio. This apparently gave her license to have an affair with a policeman."

"I'm not Didi," Brenda said flatly. She had evidently decided not to let Jerome relegate her to silence. Dale was proud of her for that.

"Will you carve the roast?" Dale said to Nelson. "I'll get the vegetables out of the oven."

She felt a little bad about leaving Brenda alone at the table with Jerome, but Nelson was much better at carving than she was. She stood and began collecting soup bowls.

"Does that woman with the earmuffs still see you?" Dale said to Brenda as she picked up her bowl. Very offhanded. As if the conversation had been going fine. It would give Brenda the excuse to rise and follow her into the kitchen, if she wanted to. But Brenda didn't do that. She said, "Yeah. I've gotten to like her a little better, but her worrying about losing body heat through her ears—you've got to wonder."

"All the world is exercising," Jerome said. "Brenda has more requests for her services than she can keep up with. The gym stays open until ten at night now on Thursdays. Do you two exercise?"

"There's an Exercycle in the downstairs bedroom. Sometimes I do it while I'm watching CNN," Nelson said.

Jerome gave his little half nod again. "And you?" he said to Dale. "Still doing the fifty situps? You're looking wonderful, I must say."

"She can't," Nelson said, answering for her. "The Ménière's thing. It screws up her inner ear if she does that sort of repetitive activity."

"Oh, I forgot," Brenda said. "How are you feeling, Dale?"

"Fine," she said. Things were better. The problem would never go away unless, of course, it spontaneously went away. Things had been so bad because the hypoglycemia complicated the problem, and that was pretty much under control, but she didn't want to talk about it.

"Remind me of what you can't eat," Jerome said. "Not that we wouldn't be too intimidated to have you to dinner anyway. Better to reciprocate at a restaurant in the city."

"You don't have to reciprocate," Dale said. "I like to cook."

"I wouldn't be intimidated," Brenda said.

"You wouldn't," he said. "I stand corrected."

"It can be a problem, when you're really good at something, no one will even try to do that thing for you," Brenda said. "There's a girl at work who gives the best massage in the world, and nobody will touch her because she's the best. The other day, I rubbed just her shoulders, and she almost swooned."

"Taking up massage also?" Jerome said.

"What do you mean, also?" Brenda said. "This is about the fact that you don't like me working late on Thursdays, isn't it? I might remind you that if a client calls, whatever time it is, it's nothing for you to be on the phone for an hour."

"No fighting!" Nelson said.

"We're not fighting," Jerome said.

"Well, you've been *trying* to provoke a fight with me," Brenda said.

"Then it was unconscious. I apologize," Jerome said.

"Oh, honey," Brenda said, getting up, putting her napkin on the table. She went around the table and hugged Jerome.

"She likes me again," Jerome said.

"We all like you," Nelson said. "I, personally, think you saved my life."

"That goes too far," Jerome said. "I just wasn't one of those stereotypically disinterested stepfathers. I considered it a real bonus that I could help raise you."

"If only you'd taught me more about electrical problems," Nelson said.

"It's toggled together, but it should hold until I get my hands on a soldering gun," Jerome said. "But seriously—Dale—what do they think the prognosis is about this thing you have?"

Roasted vegetables cascaded into the bowl. Dale put the Pyrex dish carefully in the sink and opened the drawer, looking for a serving spoon. "I'm fine," she said.

"It's complicated," Nelson said. "She eats nothing but walnuts and cheese sticks for breakfast. You think she looks good? Will she still, if she loses another fifteen pounds?"

"Cheese is full of calories," Dale said. It was going to be impossible not to talk about it until everyone else's anxiety was alleviated. She lowered her voice. "Come on, Nelson," she said. "It's boring to talk about."

"Cheese? What's with the cheese?" Jerome said.

"Honey, you are *cross-examining* her," Brenda said.

"So—here is some fresh applesauce, and here are the vegetables—I'll put them by you, Jerome—and Nelson's got the roast," Dale said, going back to her chair. The chairs were Danish Modern, with a geometric quilted pattern on the seats. Apparently, the professor and his wife had also had a sabbatical in Denmark.

"Oh, you already had apples. I knew you would," Brenda said.

"She won't touch the applesauce. Pure sugar," Nelson said.

"Nelson," Dale said, "please stop talking about it." She asked, "Does anyone want water?"

"I think, if you don't mind, I'll have that Mâcon-Lugny Les Charmes Nelson told me you laid in," Jerome said.

"Absolutely," Dale said, getting up. Nelson walked around her with the platter.

"She has some wine called Opus One for the doctor, who's coming to dinner—when is it, Thursday?" Nelson said. "We were supposed to go there for drinks, but Dale countered with dinner. Talk about being grateful."

"What year?" Jerome said.

"It was a present," Dale said. "From a student who's married to a wine importer, so I suspect it's good."

Nelson held the platter for Brenda to serve herself.

"Has it been properly stored?" Jerome said. "That could be an excellent wine. We can only hope nothing happened to it."

Dale looked at him. As interested as he'd ostensibly been in her health, the concern about the wine was far greater. She had thought, to begin with, that being so solicitous had actually been Jerome's way of pointing out her vulnerability. Poor Dale, who might have to be stretched out on the floor any second. It fit with his concept of women.

Nelson moved to Jerome's side. He was holding the bottle. "Nineteen eighty-five," he said.

"You know, that is a very elegant wine indeed. Let me see that," Jerome said. Jerome cradled the bottle against his chest. He looked down at it, smiling. "May I, as the person who once saved your husband's life, ask what would you think about my opening this to go with dinner?" he said.

"Jerome!" Brenda said. "Give that back to Nelson."

Nelson looked at Dale, with an expression somewhere between perplexity and pleading. It was just a bottle of wine. She had no reason to think the doctor or her husband were wine connoisseurs. There was the bottle of Saint-Émilion, but it would have seemed churlish to mention it now. "Absolutely," Dale said. She pushed her chair back and went to the cupboard and took out their own stemmed glasses with a wide bowl which they had brought with them, along with her duvet and the collection of cooking magazines.

Dale put a glass at everyone's place. Jerome was smiling. "We can only hope," he said.

Brenda was looking at Dale, but Dale did not meet her eyes. She was determined to let them all see that she was unconcerned. Jerome was usually so polite.

"Tell me," he said, wine bottle clamped between his legs, turning the corkscrew. "Surely you aren't going to decline one small glass of this, Dale?"

"I can't drink," she said.

"Then what is that glass for?" he said.

"Perrier," she said, pronouncing the word very distinctly.

Jerome looked attentively at the bottle as he slowly withdrew the cork. He picked up the bottle slowly and sniffed. Then he put his white linen napkin over his finger and worked it around the top, inside the bottle. That was the first time it became clear to her that he was doing what he was doing out of anger. She picked up her fork and speared a piece of eggplant.

"You've fallen quiet, Dale," he said. "Is everything all right?"

"Yes," she said, trying to sound mildly surprised.

"It's just that you're so quiet," he persisted.

Brenda seemed about to speak, but said nothing. Dale managed a shrug. "I hope there are enough spices on the vegetables," she said. "I roasted them without salt. Would anyone like salt?"

Of course, since they had all now turned their attention to Dale, whatever she said sounded false and shallow.

"I appreciate your laying in Mâcon-Lugny for me," Jerome went on. "In most cases, white would go well with pork roast. But an '85 Opus One—that, of course, is completely divine." Jerome sniffed the bottle. It might have been snuff, he inhaled so deeply. Then he sat the bottle on the table, near the sundial. "Let it breathe for a moment," he said. He turned his chair at an angle, feigning closeness with Dale.

Dale picked up a piece of carrot with her fingers and bit into it. She said nothing.

"You had Didi to dinner last month with some friends of yours, I hear," he said.

Who had told him, since he and Didi didn't speak? Nelson, obviously. Why?

"Yes," Dale said.

Jerome took a bite of meat and a bite of vegetable. He reached for the applesauce and ladled some on his plate. He said nothing about the food.

"I understand you've made a portrait of her," he said.

Brenda was chewing slowly. She knew, and Dale knew, that Jerome was warming up to something. In fact, Dale herself didn't much like Didi—in part because they seemed to have little in common. On top of that, Didi condescended by acting as if Dale was the sophisticate, and she—the world traveler—just a poor old lady. Dale had thought that photographing her—in spite of the momentary imbalance of power—might ultimately get the two of them on a more even footing.

Jerome said: "I'd be curious to see it."

"No," Dale said.

"No? Why ever not?" Jerome said.

"You don't like your ex-wife," she said. "There's no reason to look at a picture of her."

"Listen to her!" Jerome said, jutting his chin in Nelson's direction.

"Jerome—what's wrong?" Nelson said quietly.

"What's wrong? There's something wrong about my request to see a photograph? I have a curiosity about what Didi looks like. We were married for years, you'll remember."

"I don't want to see it," Brenda said.

"You don't have to. If you don't want any of the wine, you don't have to have that, either." Jerome twirled the bottle. As the label revolved in front of him, he picked up the bottle and poured. A thin stream of wine went into the glass.

"I don't quite see how not wanting to look at a photograph of your ex means I don't want wine," Brenda said.

"You prefer white. Isn't that so?" Jerome said.

"Usually. But you made this wine sound very good."

"It's good, but not great," Jerome said, inhaling. He had not yet taken a sip. He swirled the wine in his glass, then put the glass to his lips and slowly tilted it back. "Mmm," he said. He nodded. "Quite good, but not perfect," he said. He cut a piece of roast.

Nelson kept his eyes on Dale, who was intent upon not looking at Brenda. Brenda was doing worse than anyone else with Jerome's behavior. "May I talk to you in the kitchen?" Brenda said to Jerome.

"Oh, just take me to task right here. In the great tradition of Didi, who never lowered her voice or avoided any confrontation."

"I'm not Didi," Brenda said. "What I want to know is whether you're acting this way because you're pissed off I have a job I enjoy and that means I'm not there to answer your every whim, or whether there's some real bone you have to pick with Dale."

"Forget it," Nelson said. "Come on. Dale has made this wonderful meal."

"Don't tell me what not to say to Jerome," Brenda said.

"Let's take another walk and cool off," Dale said to Brenda. "Maybe they'd like to talk. Maybe we could use some air."

"All right," Brenda said, surprising Dale. She had thought Brenda would dig her heels in, but she seemed relieved by the suggestion. She got up and walked through the kitchen and into the hallway where the coats were hung. In the dark, she put on Dale's jacket instead of her own. Dale noticed, but since they wore the same size, she put on Brenda's without comment. Outside, Brenda realized her error when she plunged her hand in the pocket and felt the doughnut holes. "Oh, this is yours," she said, and began to unzip the jacket.

"We wear the same size. Keep it on," Dale said. Brenda looked at her, making sure she meant it. Then she took her fingers off the zipper. As they walked, Brenda began apologizing for Jerome. She said she'd only been guessing, back at the house. She didn't really know what he was so angry about, though she assumed they knew that he was more fond of them than his own children—these being the daughter he'd had between Didi and Brenda, and the son whose mother was married to someone else. "He had a couple of beers on the plane. They took a bottle upstairs when they went to fix the wiring, too. Maybe he just had too much to drink," Brenda said.

"It doesn't matter," Dale said. She pointed at the Portsmouth light. "I like that," she said. "In the evening I like the colorful sky, but at night I like that one little light almost as much."

Dale tried to see her watch, but couldn't read it. "Too late to round up

Tyrone," she said. She knew that it was, even without being able to see the time. In the distance, wind rustled the willows. They were walking where the path turned and narrowed, between the divided field. It was Dale and Nelson's responsibility, as renters, to have the fields plowed so the scrub wouldn't take over. In the distance, you could hear the white noise of cars on the highway. That, and the wind rustling, disguised the sound of tires until a black car with its headlights off was almost upon them. Brenda clutched Dale's arm as she jumped in fear, moving so quickly into the grass in her high-heeled boots that she lost her balance and fell, toppling both of them. "Oh, shit, my ankle," she said. "Oh, no." Both were sprawled in the field, the hoarfrost on the grass crunching like wintery quicksand as they struggled to stand. A car without headlights? And after nearly sideswiping them, it accelerated. The big shadow of the car moved quickly away, crunching stones more loudly as it receded than it had on the approach.

Brenda had turned her ankle. Dale helped her up, dusting wetness from her own jacket on Brenda's back, wanting to delay the moment when Brenda would say she couldn't walk. "Some God-damned maniac," Dale said. "Can you put pressure on it? How does it feel?"

"It hurts, but I don't think it's broken," Brenda said.

Dale looked into the distance, Brenda's hand still on her shoulder. "Shit," Brenda said again. "I'd better take these things off and walk home in my tights. You know, if I didn't know better, I'd say that was Jerome, zeroing in for the kill."

Kill. With a worse chill than the night air explained, she had realized that the car must have been speeding away from Janet's house. That they would have to go on—she, at least, would have to go on—and see what had happened.

"It's something bad—" Dale began.

"I know," Brenda said, crying now. "But the worst thing is that I'm pregnant, and I don't dare tell him, he's been so shitty lately. It's like he hates me. I feel like he'd like it if my ankle was broken."

"No," Dale said, hearing what Brenda said, but not quite hearing it. "Something at the house down there. Janet's house."

Brenda's hand seized Dale's shoulder. "Oh, my God," she said.

"Wait here," Dale said.

"No! I'm coming with you," Brenda told her.

"I've got a very bad feeling," Dale said.

"We don't know," Brenda said. "It could have been kids—drunk, playing a game with the lights out." From the tenuous way she spoke, it was clear she didn't believe herself.

Slowly, helping her to walk, Brenda's boots in one of her hands, the other around Brenda's waist, the two of them walked until the little house came in sight. "Not exactly a wedding cake," Brenda said, squinting at what was hardly more than a clapboard shack. There was one light on, which was an ambiguous sign: it could be good, or it could mean nothing at all.

The front door slightly ajar was the worst possible sign. Dale surprised herself by having the courage to push it open. Inside, the wood fire had burned out. A cushion was on the floor. A mug lay near it, in a puddle of whatever had been inside. The house was horribly, eerily silent. It was rare that Dale found herself surrounded by silence.

"Janet?" Dale said. "It's Dale. Janet?"

She was on the kitchen floor. They saw her when Dale turned on the light. Janet was breathing shallowly, a small trickle of blood congealed at one side of her mouth. Dale's impulse was to gather Janet in her arms, but she knew she should not move her head. "Janet? Everything's going to be okay," she heard herself say dully. She meant to be emphatic, but instead her voice was monotonic. Her ears had begun to close—the warning that she would soon have an attack of vertigo. But why? She had drunk no wine; she had eaten no sugar. Panic attacks had been ruled out when Ménière's had been ruled in. "You must learn the power of positive thinking," she heard the doctor saying to her. "I know it sounds ridiculous, but it works. I'm not a mystical person. It's more like biofeedback. Say to yourself, 'This will not happen to me.'"

The room was quivering, as if the walls themselves were vibrating because of some tremor in the earth. Dale repeated the words, silently. She could see Janet's chest rising and falling. Her breathing did not seem to be labored, though whoever had been there had tried to strangle her with a piece of rope. From the color of her face, it was obvious she had been deprived of oxygen. Her long fingers were balled into fists. Blood oozed from a cut on her arm. An ankh cross dangled from one end of the rope. *The Dictionary of Symbols* lay on the floor, a blood-smudged chart beside it. Beside that, torn from the wall, was a photograph Dale had taken of Janet's hand holding the fine pearwood brush she used to draw symbols. The photograph had been ripped so that the brush was broken in half. Remembering, suddenly, what she must do, Dale went to the wall phone and dialed 911. "Someone is unconscious at the end of Harmony Lane," she said. It was difficult to tell how loud, or soft, her words were. Harmony Lane—was that what she had just said? What ridiculous place was that? Some fake street in some ridiculous Walt Disney development? But no—they hadn't gone there. They had rented a house in Maine, that was where they were. She squinted against the star shining through the kitchen window, like a bright dart aimed at her eye. It was not a star, though. It was the light from Portsmouth.

The woman who answered told Dale to stay calm. She insisted she stay where she was. It was as if all this was about Dale—not Janet, but Dale, standing in Janet's kitchen. For a second the voice of the woman at 911 got confused with the voice of the doctor saying, This will not happen to me.

There was a shriek of sirens. They sounded far, far away, yet distinct: background music that portended trouble. Dale was so stunned that, instead of hanging up, she stood with the phone in her hand, imagining she'd hung up. She had seen Janet two days before. Three? They had talked about squash. The squash Janet would appreciate Dale's buying for her at the Farmers' Market. "This is her neighbor, Dale," she said, in what she thought was an answer to the question the woman was asking, faintly, on the opposite end of the phone. Why didn't the woman ask about Janet? "We saw a car," she heard herself say, though her mouth was not near enough for the 911 operator to hear.

That was the moment when Tyrone burst out from underneath the two-seat sofa, charging so quickly he overshot Dale and knocked Brenda down. She screamed with fear long after she might have realized it was only a dog. Tyrone was as afraid as they were; everything was made worse by Brenda's high-pitched scream.

"Oh, God, I'm so sorry," Brenda said, apologizing to the cowering dog, its back legs shaking so pathetically, Dale could not see how he remained upright. "Oh, God, here," Brenda said, inching closer, reaching in the jacket pocket with trembling hands for a doughnut hole and holding it out to the dog, who did not approach but stood shakily leaning into Dale's leg. No one looked at Janet's body. Wind rattled the glass, but the louder sound was that of sirens. Dale saw Brenda cock her head and turn, as if she could see the sound. Brenda turned back and threw the doughnut hole to the dog, missing by a mile.

"It's okay," Dale said, moving her leg astride the dog and edging the doughnut hole toward him with the toe of her boot. It was a powdered-sugar doughnut hole that left a streak of white on the floorboards. By Janet's hand had been a streak—no: a puddle, not a streak—of blood. Dale did not look in that direction; she was so afraid Janet might have stopped breathing.

Dale looked across the room at Brenda. Brenda, dejectedly, was about to throw another doughnut hole. Dale watched as she tossed it slowly, repeating Dale's words: "It's okay." Then she took a step forward and said to Dale: "Make him forgive me. Make him like me again."

Dale was stroking Tyrone's head. Tyrone had become her dog. Brenda and Jerome's child, she thought, would become Brenda's child. All of Jerome's women had wanted babies, and he had bitterly resented every one: the son born to the married woman in France, whose husband believed the child to be his; the daughter born as his marriage to his second wife was disintegrating. Nelson had been the only one he wanted. Well—if you had what you already considered the perfect child, maybe that made sense. Nelson was intellectually curious, smart, obedient, favoring his stepfather over his mother, a loyal child.

Nelson and Jerome would be at the table, finishing dinner, Nelson having found a way to excuse Jerome, Jerome's passive aggression subsiding into agreeableness—as if, by the two women's disappearing, any problem automatically disappeared, too. Without them, Nelson and Jerome could move on to the salad course. Drink the entire bottle of Opus One. Nelson would probably have brought down the photograph of Didi, her face deeply lined by years of having kept up with Jerome in his drinking, as well as other bad decisions she had made, and of course from the years at Saint-Tropez, enjoying too much sun.

Too much sun. Too much son. Jerome would like to play with that.

Though what Jerome was talking about, having already told Nelson he was seriously considering separating from Brenda, was the story of Baron Philippe de Rothschild: the Baron, being a clever businessman, and, more important, a visionary, realized that much might be gained by joining forces with the California winegrower, Robert Mondavi. Mondavi was invited to the Baron's, where both men dined on fabulous food and drank great wine. It was a social evening: business was not discussed. It was not until the next morning that the Baron—by this point, Mondavi genuinely admired him, for his taste, elegance, and good manners—summoned Mondavi to his bedside, like a character in a fairy tale. The possibility of combining their efforts was discussed, and of sharing the profits fifty-fifty. Mondavi suggested producing only one wine, which would be similar to a great Bordeaux. Did he say this tentatively? The Baron agreed. Would he have said the same? The wine would be made in California, where the Baron's winemaker would visit. Mondavi, flattered, was thrilled as well. His name linked to that of Baron Philippe de Rothschild! The Baron also triumphed, realizing that embracing his would-be adversary would lead both men to profit. Nothing remained except the ceremonial drinking of a hundred-year-old Mouton, followed by a very cold Château d'Yquem: a perfect deal; a perfect meal—it even rhymed, as Jerome pointed out. A brilliant label was designed, providing the perfect finishing touch.

The talk back at the house was about perfection. In a perfect world, all wines would be perfect. Ditto marriages. All books brilliant (a toast was drunk). Superior music (again, glasses were raised) would be listened to, keenly. In that fairy tale, which was not Dale's, and which was not Brenda's, either, no woman would lie badly wounded on her kitchen floor.

Brenda crossed the room and stood at Dale's side. "Doughnut hole," she said quietly, looking down, then picked it up, at the end of its trail of powdered sugar, as if plucking a shooting star from the darkness.

This time, Tyrone showed interest. Dale picked up the other two. The dog was definitely interested. There was no dirt on the doughnut holes that Dale and Brenda could see, as they examined them closely.

"Why not?" Dale said, giving voice to what Brenda was thinking. They could pretend to be people at a cocktail party, eating pleasant tidbits.

But sirens pierced the night.

They signified a problem for someone, Nelson knew. Another problem, Jerome also thought.

The sound overwhelmed Bartók on the stereo. The sirens were shrill and constant: a sound you might say was annoyingly like a woman's voice—if one could still say such things, but of course one could not.

Then the crescendo of noise, demanding their attention.

One man preceded the other out of the house. That door, too, was left open to the wind.

A police car, a second police car, an ambulance, a fire engine—the full militia leading the way.

To what? The two words were like a heartbeat: *to what, to what.*

Down a dirt road in a country far from France.

Down a narrow road across from a rented house.

The meal left behind, one or the other having remembered to extinguish the candles.

That Last Odd Day in L.A.

Keller went back and forth about going into Cambridge to see Lynn, his daughter, for Thanksgiving. If he went in November, he'd miss his niece and nephew, who made the trip back East only in December, for Christmas. They probably could have got away from their jobs and returned for both holidays, but they never did. The family had gathered for Thanksgiving at his daughter's ever since she moved into her own apartment, which was going on six years now; Christmas dinner was at Keller's sister's house, in Arlington. His daughter's apartment was near Porter Square. She had once lived there with Ray Ceruto, before she decided she was too good for a car mechanic. A nice man, a hard worker, a gentleman—so naturally she chose instead to live in serial monogamy with men Keller found it almost impossible to get along with. Oh, but they had white-collar jobs and white-collar aspirations: with her current boyfriend, she had recently flown to England for all of three days in order to see the white cliffs of Dover. If there had been bluebirds, they had gone unmentioned.

Years ago, Keller's wife, Sue Anne, had moved back to Roanoke, Virginia, where she now rented a "mother-in-law apartment" from a woman she had gone to school with back in the days when she and Keller were courting. Sue Anne joked that she herself had become a sort of ideal mother-in-law, gardening and taking care of the pets when her friends went away. She was happy to have returned to gardening. During the almost twenty years that she and Keller had been together, their little house in the Boston suburbs, shaded by trees, had allowed for the growth of almost nothing but springtime bulbs, and even those had to be planted in raised beds because the soil was of such poor quality. Eventually, the squirrels discovered the beds. Sue Anne's breakdown had had to do with the squirrels.

424 ◆ ANN BEATTIE

So: call his daughter, or do the more important thing and call his neighbor and travel agent, Sigrid, at Pleasure Travel, to apologize for their recent, rather uneventful dinner at the local Chinese restaurant, which had been interrupted by a thunderstorm grand enough to announce the presence of Charlton Heston, which had reminded Keller that he'd left his windows open. He probably should not have refused to have the food packed to go. But when he'd thought of having her to his house to eat the dinner—his house was a complete mess—or of going to her house and having to deal with her son's sour disdain, it had seemed easier just to bolt down his food.

A few days after the ill-fated dinner, he had bought six raffle tickets and sent them to her, in the hope that a winning number would provide a bicycle for her son, though he obviously hadn't given her a winning ticket, or she would have called. Her son's expensive bicycle had been taken at knifepoint, in a neighborhood he had promised his mother he would not ride through.

Two or three weeks before, Sigrid and Keller had driven into Boston to see a show at the MFA and afterward had gone to a coffee shop where he had clumsily, stupidly, splashed a cup of tea onto her when he was jostled by a mother with a stroller the size of an infantry vehicle. He had brought dish towels to the door of the ladies' room for Sigrid to dry herself off with, and he had even—rather gallantly, some might have said—thought to bite the end off his daily vitamin-E capsule from the little packet of multivitamins he carried in his shirt pocket and urged her to scrape the goop from the tip of his finger and spread it on the burn. She maintained that she had not been burned. Later, on the way to the car, they had got into a tiff when he said that it wasn't necessary for her to pretend that everything was fine, that he liked women who spoke honestly. "It could not have been all right that I scalded you, Sigrid," he'd told her.

"Well, I just don't see the need to criticize you over an *accident*, Keller," she had replied. Everyone called him by his last name. He had been born Joseph Francis, but neither Joe nor Joseph nor Frank nor Francis fit.

"It was clumsy of me, and I wasn't quick enough to help," he said.

"You were fine," she said. "It would have brought you more pleasure if I'd cried, or if I'd become irrational, wouldn't it? There's some part of you that's always on guard, because the other person is sure to become *irrational.*"

"You know a little something about my wife's personality," he said.

Sigrid had lived next door before, during, and after Sue Anne's departure. "So everyone's your wife?" she said. "Is that what you think?"

"No," he said. "I'm apologizing. I didn't do enough for my wife, either. Apparently I didn't act soon enough or effectively enough or—"

"You're always looking for forgiveness!" she said. "I don't forgive you or not forgive you. How about that? I don't know enough about the situation, but I doubt that you're entirely to blame for the way things turned out."

"I'm sorry," he said. "Some people say I'm too closemouthed and I don't give anyone a chance to know me, and others—such as you or my daughter—maintain that I'm self-critical as a ploy to keep their attention focused on me."

"I didn't say any such thing! Don't put words in my mouth. I said that my getting tea dumped on my back by accident and the no doubt very complicated relationship you had with your wife really don't—"

"It was certainly too complicated for me," Keller said quietly.

"Stop whispering. If we're going to have a discussion, at least let me hear what you're saying."

"I wasn't whispering," Keller said. "That was just the wheezing of an old man out of steam."

"Now it's your age! I should pity you for your advanced age! What age are you, exactly, since you refer to it so often?"

"You're too young to count that high." He smiled. "You're a young, attractive, successful woman. People are happy to see you walk into the room. When they look up and see me, they see an old man, and they avert their eyes. When I walk into the travel agency, they all but duck into the kneeholes of their desks. That's how we got acquainted, as you recall, since calling on one's neighbors is not the American Way. Only your radiant face met mine with a smile. Everybody else was pretending I wasn't there."

"Listen: Are you sure this is where we parked the car?"

"I'm not sure of anything. That's why I had you drive."

"I drove because your optometrist put drops in to dilate your pupils shortly before we left," she said.

"But I'm fine now. At least, my usual imperfect vision has returned. I can drive back," he said, pointing to her silver Avalon. "Too noble a vehicle for me, to be sure, but driving would be the least I could do, after ruining your day."

"Why are you saying that?" she said. "Because you're pleased to think that some little problem has the ability to ruin my day? You are being *impossible*, Keller. And don't whisper that that's exactly what your wife would say. Except that she's a fellow human being occupying planet Earth, I don't *care* about your wife."

She took her key ring out of her pocket and tossed the keys to him.

He was glad he caught them, because she sent them higher into the air than necessary. But he did catch them, and he did remember to step in front of her to hold open her door as he pushed the button to unlock the car.

Coming around the back, he saw the PETA bumper sticker her husband had adorned the car with shortly before leaving her for a years-younger Buddhist vegan animal-rights activist.

At least he had worked his way into his craziness slowly, subscribing first to *Smithsonian* magazine and only later to newsletters with pictures of starved, manacled horses and pawless animals with startled eyes—material she was embarrassed to have delivered to the house. In the year before he left, he had worked at the animal-rescue league on weekends. When she told him he was becoming obsessed with the plight of animals at the expense of their marriage and their son, he'd rolled up one of his publications and slapped his palm with it over and over, protesting vehemently, like someone scolding a bad dog. As she recalled, he had somehow turned the conversation to the continued illegal importation of elephant tusks into Asia.

"You always want to get into a fight," she said, when she finally spoke again, as Keller wound his way out of Boston. "It makes it difficult to be with you."

"I know it's difficult. I'm sorry."

"Come over and we can watch some *Perry Mason* reruns," she said. "It's on every night at eleven."

"I don't stay up that late," he said. "I'm an old man."

Keller spoke to his daughter on the phone—the first time the phone had rung in days—and listened patiently while she set forth her conditions, living her life in the imperative. In advance of their speaking, she wanted him to know that she would hang up if he asked when she intended to break up with Addison (Addison!) Page. Also, as he well knew, she did not want to be questioned about her mother, even though, yes, they were in phone contact. She also did not want to hear any criticism of her glamorous life, based on her recently having spent three days in England with her spendthrift boyfriend, and also, yes, she had got her flu shot.

"This being November, would it be possible to ask who you're going to vote for?"

"No," she said. "Even if you were voting for the same candidate, you'd find some way to make fun of me."

"What if I said, 'Close your eyes and imagine either an elephant or a donkey'?"

"If I close my eyes, I see ... I see a horse's ass, and it's you," she said. "May I continue?"

He snorted. She had a quick wit, his daughter. She had got that from him, not from his wife, who neither made jokes nor understood them. In the distant past, his wife had found an entirely humorless psychiatrist who had summoned Keller and urged him to speak to Sue Anne directly, not in figurative language or through allusions or—God forbid—with humor. "What should I do if I'm just chomping at the bit to tell a racist joke?" he had asked. The idea was of course ludicrous; he had never made a racist joke in his life. But of course the psychiatrist missed his tone. "You anticipate the necessity of telling racist jokes to your wife?" he had said, pausing to scribble something on his pad. "Only if one came up in a dream or something," Keller had deadpanned.

"I thought you were going to continue, Lynn," he said. "Which I mean as an observation, not as a reproach," he hurried to add.

"Keller," she said (since her teenage years, she had called him Keller), "I need to know whether you're coming to Thanksgiving."

"Because you would get a turkey weighing six or seven ounces more?"

"In fact, I thought about cooking a ham this year, because Addison prefers ham. It's just a simple request, Keller: that you let me know whether or not you plan to come. Thanksgiving is three weeks away."

"I've come up against Amy Vanderbilt's timetable for accepting a social invitation at Thanksgiving?" he said.

She sighed deeply. "I would like you to come, whether you believe that or not, but since the twins aren't coming from L.A., and since Addison's sister invited us to her house, I thought I might not cook this year, if you didn't intend to come."

"Oh, by all means don't cook for me. I'll mind my manners and call fifty-one weeks from today and we'll set this up for next year," he said. "A turkey potpie from the grocery store is good enough for me."

"And the next night you could be your usual frugal self and eat the leftover packaging," she said.

"Horses don't eat cardboard. You're thinking of mice," he said.

"I stand corrected," she said, echoing the sentence he often said to her. "But let me ask you another thing. Addison's sister lives in Portsmouth, New Hampshire, and she issued a personal invitation for you to join us at her house for dinner. Would you like to have Thanksgiving there?"

"How could she issue a personal invitation if she's never met me?" he said.

"Stop it," his daughter said. "Just answer."

He thought about it. Not about whether he would go but about the holiday itself. The revisionist thinking on Thanksgiving was that it commemorated the subjugation of the Native Americans (formerly the Indians). Not as bad a holiday as Columbus Day, but still.

"I take it your silence means that you prefer to be far from the maddening crowd," she said.

"That title is much misquoted," he said. "Hardy's novel is *Far from the Madding Crowd*, which has an entirely different connotation, *madding* meaning 'frenzied.' There's quite a difference between *frenzied* and *annoying*. Consider, for instance, your mother's personality versus mine."

"You are *incredibly* annoying," Lynn said. "If I didn't know that you cared for me, I couldn't bring myself to pick up the phone and let myself in for your mockery, over and over."

"I thought it was because you pitied me."

He heard the click, and there was silence. He replaced the phone in its cradle, which made him think of another cradle—Lynn's—with the decal of the cow jumping over the moon on the headboard and blue and pink beads (the cradle manufacturer having hedged his bets) on the rails. He could remember spinning the beads and watching Lynn sleep. The cradle was now in the downstairs hallway, used to store papers and magazines for recycling. Over the years, some of the decal had peeled away, so that on last inspection only a torso with two legs was successfully making the jump over the brightly smiling moon.

He bought a frozen turkey potpie and, as a treat to himself (it was not true that he constantly denied himself happiness, as Lynn said—one could not deny what was rarely to be found), a new radio whose FM quality was excellent—though what did he know, with his imperfect hearing? As he ate Thanksgiving dinner (two nights before Thanksgiving, but why stand on formality?—a choice of Dinty Moore beef stew or Lean Cuisine vegetable lasagna remained for the day of thanks itself), he listened with pleasure to Respighi's *Pini di Roma*. He and Sue Anne had almost gone to Rome on their honeymoon, but instead they had gone to Paris. His wife had just finished her second semester of college, in which she had declared herself an art history major. They had gone to the Louvre and to the Jeu de Paume and on the last day of the trip he had bought her a little watercolor of Venice she kept admiring, in a rather elaborate frame that probably accounted for the gouache's high price—it was a gouache, not a watercolor, as she always corrected him. They both wanted three children, preferably a son followed by either another son or a daughter, though if their second child was a son, then of course they would devoutly wish their last to be a daughter. He remembered with bemusement the way they had prattled on, strolling by the Seine, earnestly discussing those things that were most out of their control: Life's Important Matters.

Sue Anne conceived only once, and although they (she, to be honest) had vaguely considered adoption, Lynn remained their only child. Lacking brothers and sisters, she had been fortunate to grow up among relatives, because Keller's sister had given birth to twins a year or so after Lynn was born, and in those days the two families lived only half an hour apart and saw each other almost every weekend. Now Sue Anne and his sister Carolynne (now merely Carol), who lived in Arlington with her doctor husband (or who lived apart from him—he was forbidden to inquire about the status of their union), had not spoken for months, and the twins, Richard and Rita, who worked as stockbrokers and had never married—smart!— and shared a house in the Hollywood Hills, were more at ease with him than his own daughter was. For years Keller had promised to visit the twins, and the previous summer, Richard had called his bluff and sent him a ticket to Los Angeles. Richard and Rita had picked Keller up at LAX in a BMW convertible and taken him to a sushi restaurant where at periodic intervals laser images on the wall blinked on and off like sexually animated hieroglyphics dry-humping to a recording of "Walk Like an Egyptian." The next morning, the twins had taken him to a museum that had been created as a satire of museums, with descriptions of the bizarre exhibits that were so tongue-in-cheek he was sure the majority of people there thought that they were touring an actual museum. That night, they turned on the lights in their pool and provided him with bathing trunks (how would he have thought to pack such a thing?—he never thought of a visit to sprawling Los Angeles as a visit to a *beach*), and on Sunday they had eaten their lunch of fresh pineapple and prosciutto poolside, drinking prosecco instead of mineral water (the only beverages in the house, except for extraordinarily good red wine, as far as he could tell), and in the late afternoon they had been joined by a beautiful blonde woman who had apparently been, or might still be, Jack Nicholson's lover. Then he went with Rita and Richard to a screening (a shoot-'em-up none of them wanted to see, though the twins felt they must, because the cinematographer was their longtime client), and on Monday they had sent a car to the house so Keller wouldn't get lost trying to find his way around the freeways. It transported him to a lunch with the twins at a restaurant built around a beautiful terraced garden, after which he'd been dropped off to take the MGM tour and then picked up by the same driver—a dropout from Hollywood High who was working on a screenplay.

It was good they had bought him a ticket for only a brief visit, because if he'd stayed longer he might never have gone home. Though who would have cared if he hadn't? His wife didn't care where he lived, as long as she lived in the opposite direction. His daughter might be relieved that he had moved away. He lived where he lived for no apparent reason—at least, no reason apparent to him. He had no friends, unless you called Don Kim a friend—Don, with whom he played handball on Mondays and Thursdays. And his accountant, Ralph Bazzorocco. He supposed Bazzorocco was his friend, though with the exception of a couple of golf games each spring and the annual buffet dinner he and Bazzorocco's other clients were invited to every April 16—and except for Bazzorocco's calling to wish him a happy birthday, and "Famiglia Bazzorocco" (as the gift card always read) sending him an enormous box of biscotti and Baci at Christmas . . . oh, he didn't know. Probably that was what friendship was, he thought, a little ashamed of himself. He had gone to the hospital to visit Bazzorocco's son after the boy injured his pelvis and lost his spleen playing football. He'd driven Bazzorocco's weeping wife home in the rain so she could shower and change her clothes, then driven her, still weeping, back to the hospital. Okay: he had friends. But would any of them care if he lived in Los Angeles? Don Kim could easily find another partner (perhaps a younger man more worthy as a competitor); Bazzorocco could remain his accountant via the miracle of modern technology. In any case, Keller had returned to the North Shore.

Though not before that last odd day in L.A. He had said, though he hadn't planned to say it (Lynn was not correct in believing that everything that escaped his lips was premeditated), that he'd like to spend his last day lounging around the house. So they wouldn't feel too sorry for him, he even asked if he could open a bottle of Merlot—whatever they recommended, of course—and raid their refrigerator for lunch. After all, the refrigerator contained a tub of mascarpone instead of cottage cheese, and the fruit drawer was stocked with organic plums rather than puckered supermarket grapes. Richard wasn't so keen on the idea, but Rita said that of course that was fine. It was *Keller's* vacation, she stressed. They'd make a reservation at a restaurant out at the beach that night, and if he felt rested enough to eat out, fine; if not, they'd cancel the reservation and Richard would cook his famous chicken breasts marinated in Vidalia-onion sauce.

When Keller woke up, the house was empty. He made coffee (at home, he drank instant) and wandered out through the open doors to the patio as it brewed. He surveyed the hillside, admired the lantana growing from Mexican pottery urns flanking one side of the pool. Some magazine had been rained on—it must have rained during the night; he hadn't heard it, but then, he'd fallen asleep with earphones on, listening to Brahms. He walked toward the magazine—as offensive as litter along the highway, this copy of *Vogue* deteriorating on the green tiles—then drew back, startled. There was a small possum: a baby possum, all snout and pale narrow body, clawing the water, trying futilely to scramble up the edge of the pool. He looked around quickly for the pool net. The night before, it had been leaning against the sliding glass door, but it was no longer there. He went quickly to the side of the house, then ran to the opposite side, all the while acutely aware that the drowning possum was in desperate need of rescue. No pool net. He went into the kitchen, which was now suffused with the odor of coffee, and threw open door after door looking for a pot. He finally found a bucket containing cleaning supplies, quickly removed them, then ran back to the pool, where he dipped the bucket in, missing, frightening the poor creature and adding to its problems by making it go under. He recoiled in fear, then realized that the emotion he felt was not fear but self-loathing. Introspection was not his favorite mode, but no matter: he dipped again, leaning farther over this time, accepting the ludicrous prospect of his falling in, though the second time he managed to scoop up the possum—it was only a tiny thing—and lift it out of the water. The bucket was full, because he had dipped deep, and much to his dismay, when he saw the possum curled up at the bottom, he knew immediately that it was already dead. The possum had drowned. He set the bucket down and crouched on the tile beside it before he had a second, most welcome epiphany and realized almost with a laugh that it wasn't dead: it was playing possum. Though if he didn't get it out of the bucket, it really would drown. He jumped up, turned the bucket on its side, and stood back as water and possum flowed out. The water dispersed. The possum lay still. That must be because he was watching it, he decided, although he once more considered the grim possibility that it was dead.

He stood still. Then he thought to walk back into the house, far away from it. It was dead; it wasn't. Time passed. Then, finally, as he stood unmoving, the possum twitched and waddled off—the flicker of life in its body resonated in Keller's own heart—and then the event was over. He continued to stand there, cognizant of how much he had loathed himself just moments before. Then he went out to retrieve the bucket. As he grasped the handle, tears welled up in his eyes. What the hell! He cried at the sink as he rinsed the bucket.

He dried his eyes on the crook of his arm and washed the bucket thoroughly, much longer than necessary, then dried it with a towel. He put the Comet, the Windex, and the rag and the brush back inside and returned the bucket to its place under the sink and tried to remember what he had planned to do that day, and again he was overwhelmed. The image that popped into his mind was of Jack Nicholson's girlfriend, the blonde in the bikini with the denim shirt thrown over it. He thought . . . what? That he was going to get together with Jack Nicholson's girlfriend? Whose last name he didn't even know?

But that *had* been what he was thinking. No way to act on it, but yes—that was what he had been thinking, all along.

The water had run off, though the tiles still glistened. No sign, of course, of the possum. It was doubtless off assimilating its important life lesson. On a little redwood table was a waterproof radio that he turned on, finding the classical station, adjusting the volume. Then he unbuckled his belt and unzipped his fly, stepped out of his pants and underpants, and took off his shirt. Carrying the radio, he walked to the deep end of the pool, placed the radio on the rim, and dove in. He swam underwater for a while, and then, as his head broke the surface, he had the distinct feeling that he was being watched. He looked back at the house, then looked slowly around the pool area. The fence that walled it off from the neighbors was at least ten feet high. Behind the pool, the terrace was filled with bushes and fruit trees and pink and white irises—Keller was crazy: he was alone in a private compound; no one was there. He went under the water again, refreshed by its silky coolness, and breaststroked to the far end, where he came up for air, then used his feet to push off the side of the pool so he could float on his back. When he reached the end, he pulled himself out, then saw, in the corner of his eye, who was watching him. High up on the terrace, a deer was looking down. The second their eyes met, the deer was gone, but in that second it had come clear to him—on this day of endless revelations—that the deer had been casting a beneficent look, as if in thanks. He had felt that: that a deer was acknowledging and thanking him. He was flabbergasted at the odd workings of his brain. How could a grown man—a grown man without any religious beliefs, a father who, in what now seemed like a different lifetime, had accompanied his little daughter to *Bambi* and whispered, as every parent does, "It's only a movie," when Bambi's mother was killed . . . how could a man with such knowledge of the world, whose most meaningful accomplishment in as long as he could remember had been to fish an animal out of a swimming pool—how could such a man feel unequivocally that a deer had appeared to bless him?

But he knew it had.

As it turned out, the blessing hadn't exactly changed his life, though why should one expect so much of blessings, just because they were blessings?

Something that *had* profoundly changed his life had been Richard's urging him, several years before, to take a chance, take a gamble, trust him, because the word he was about to speak was going to change his life. "Plastics?" he'd said, but Richard was too young: he hadn't seen the movie. No, the word had been *Microsoft*. Keller had been in a strange frame of mind that day (one month earlier, to the day, his father had killed himself). At that point, he had hated his job so much, had stopped telling half-truths and finally admitted to Sue Anne that their marriage had become a dead end, that he assumed he was indulging the self-destructiveness his wife and daughter always maintained was the core of his being when he turned over almost everything he had to his nephew to invest in a company whose very name suggested smallness and insubstantiality. But, as it turned out, Richard had blessed him, as had the deer, now. The blonde had not, but then, very few men, very few indeed, would ever be lucky enough to have such a woman give them her benediction.

"You're *fun!*" Rita laughed, dropping him off at LAX. On the way, he had taken off his white T-shirt and raised it in the air, saying, "I hereby surrender to the madness that is the City of Angels." It had long been Rita's opinion that no one in the family understood her uncle; that all of them were so defensive that they were intimidated by his erudition and willfully misunderstood his sense of humor. Richard was working late, but he had sent, by way of his sister (she ran back to the car, having almost forgotten the treat in the glove compartment), a tin of white-chocolate brownies to eat on the plane, along with a note Keller would later read that thanked him for having set an example when he and Rita were kids, for not unthinkingly going with the flow, and for his wry pronouncements in a family where, Richard said, everyone else was "afraid of his own shadow." "Come back soon," Richard had written. "We miss you."

Back home, on the telephone, his daughter had greeted him with a warning: "I don't want to hear about my cousins who are happy and successful, which are synonymous, in your mind, with being rich. Spare me details of their life and just tell me what you did. I'd like to hear about your trip without feeling diminished by my insignificance in the face of my cousins' perfection."

"I can leave them out of it entirely," he said. "I can say, quite honestly, that the most significant moment of my trip happened not in their company but in the meeting of my eyes with the eyes of a deer that looked at me with indescribable kindness and understanding."

Lynn snorted. "This was on the freeway, I suppose? It was on its way to be an extra in a remake of *The Deer Hunter*?"

He had understood, then, the urge she so often felt when speaking to

him—the urge to hang up on a person who had not even tried to understand one word you had said.

"How was your Thanksgiving?" Sigrid asked. Keller was sitting across from
her at the travel agency, arranging to buy Don Kim's stepdaughter a ticket to
Germany so she could pay a final visit to her dying friend. The girl was dying
of ALS. The details were too terrible to think about. Jennifer had known
her for eleven of her seventeen years, and now the girl was dying. Don Kim
barely made it from paycheck to paycheck. It had been necessary to tell Don
that he had what he called "a considerable windfall from the eighties stock
market" in order to persuade him that in offering to buy Jennifer a ticket, he
was not making a gesture he could not afford. He had had to work hard to
persuade him. He had to insist on it several times, and swear that in no way
had he thought Don had been hinting (which was true). The only worry was
how Jennifer would handle such a trip, but they had both agreed she was a
very mature girl.

"Very nice," Keller replied. In fact, that day he had eaten canned stew
and listened to Albinoni (probably some depressed DJ who hadn't wanted
to work Thanksgiving night). He had made a fire in the fireplace and caught
up on his reading of *The Economist*. He felt a great distance between himself and Sigrid. He said, trying not to sound too perfunctorily polite, "And
yours?"

"I was actually . . ." She dropped her eyes. "You know, my ex-husband has
Brad for a week at Thanksgiving and I have him for Christmas. He's such a
big boy now, I don't know why he doesn't put his foot down, but he doesn't.
If I knew then what I know now, I'd never have let him go, no matter what
rights the court gave that lunatic. You know what he did before Thanksgiving? I guess you must not have read the paper. They recruited Brad to liberate
turkeys. They got arrested. His father thinks that's fine: traumatizing Brad,
letting him get hauled into custody. And the worst of it is, Brad's scared to
death, but he doesn't dare *not* go along, and then he has to pretend to me
that he thinks it was a great idea, that I'm an indifferent—" She searched for
the word. "That I'm subhuman because I eat dead animals."

Keller had no idea what to say. Lately, things didn't seem funny enough
to play off of. Everything just seemed weird and sad. Sigrid's ex-husband had
taken their son to liberate turkeys. How could you extemporize about that?

"She could go Boston, London, Frankfurt on British Air," Sigrid said, as
if she hadn't expected him to reply. "It would be somewhere around seven
hundred and fifty." She hit the keyboard again. "Seven eighty-nine plus
taxes," she said. "She'd be flying out at six p.m. Eastern Standard, she'd get

there in the morning." Her fingers stopped moving on the keyboard. She looked at him.

"Can I use your phone to make sure that's a schedule that's good for her?" he said. He knew that Sigrid wondered who Jennifer Kim was. He had spoken of her as "my friend, Jennifer Kim."

"Of course," she said. She pushed a button and handed him the phone. He had written the Kims' telephone number on a little piece of paper and slipped it in his shirt pocket. He was aware that she was staring at him as he dialed. The phone rang three times, and then he got the answering machine. "Keller here," he said. "We've got the itinerary, but I want to check it with Jennifer. I'm going to put my travel agent on," he said. "She'll give you the times, and maybe you can call her to confirm it. Okay?" He handed the phone to Sigrid. She took it, all business. "Sigrid Crane of Pleasure Travel, Ms. Kim," she said. "I have a British Airways flight that departs Logan at six zero zero p.m., arrival into Frankfurt by way of London nine five five a.m. My direct line is—"

He looked at the poster of Bali framed on the wall. A view of water. Two people entwined in a hammock. Pink flowers in the foreground.

"Well," she said, hanging up. "I'll expect to hear from her. I assume I should let you know if anything changes?"

He cocked his head. "What doesn't?" he said. "You'd be busy every second of the day if you did that."

She looked at him, expressionless. "The ticket price," she said. "Or shall I issue it regardless?"

"Regardless." (Now, there was a word he didn't use often!) "Thanks." He stood.

"Say hello to my colleagues hiding under their desks on your way out," she said.

In the doorway, he stopped. "What did they do with the turkeys?" he said.

"They took them by truck to a farm in Vermont where they thought they wouldn't be killed," she said. "You can read about it in yesterday's paper. Everybody's out on bail. Since it's a first offense, my son might be able to avoid having a record. I've hired a lawyer."

"I'm sorry," he said.

"Thank you," she said.

He nodded. Unless she had two such garments, she was wearing the same gray sweater he had spilled tea on. It occurred to him that, outside his family, she was the only woman he spoke to. The woman at the post office, women he encountered when running errands, the UPS deliveryperson, who he personally thought might be a hermaphrodite, but in terms of real female acquaintances, Sigrid was the only one. He should have said more to her about the situation with her ex-husband and son, though he could not imagine what he would have said. He also could not get a mental picture, humorous or otherwise, of liberated turkeys, walking around some frozen field in—where had she said? Vermont.

She took an incoming call. He glanced back at the poster, at Sigrid sitting there in her gray sweater, noticing for the first time that she wore a necklace dangling a silver cross. Her high cheekbones, accentuated by her head tipped forward, were her best feature; her worst feature was her eyes, a bit too close together, so that she always seemed slightly perplexed. He raised his hand to indicate goodbye, in case she might be looking, then realized from what he heard Sigrid saying that the person on the other end must be Don Kim's stepdaughter; Sigrid was reciting the Boston-to-Frankfurt schedule, tapping her pen as she spoke. He hesitated, then went back and sat down, though Sigrid had not invited him back. He sat there while Jennifer Kim told Sigrid the whole sad story—what else could the girl have been saying to her for so long? Sigrid's eyes were almost crossed when she finally glanced up at him, then put her fingers on the keyboard and began to enter information. "I might stop by tonight," he said quietly, rising. She nodded, talking into the telephone headset while typing quickly.

Exiting, he thought of a song Groucho Marx had sung in some movie which had the lyrics "Did you ever have the feeling that you wanted to go, and still you had the feeling that you wanted to stay?" He had a sudden mental image of Groucho with his cigar clamped in his teeth (or perhaps it had been Jimmy Durante who sang the song?), and then Groucho's face evaporated and only the cigar remained, like a moment in *Alice in Wonderland*. And then—although Keller had quit smoking years before, when his father died—he stopped at a convenience store and bought a pack of cigarettes and smoked one, driving home, listening to some odd space-age music. He drove through Dunkin' Donuts and got two plain doughnuts to have with coffee as he watched the evening news, remembering the many times Sue Anne had criticized him for eating food without a plate, as if dropped crumbs were proof that your life was about to go out of control.

In his driveway, he saw that his trash can had been knocked over, the plastic bag inside split open, the lid halfway across the yard. He looked out the car window at the rind of a melon, then at the bloody Kleenex he'd held to his chin when he'd nicked himself shaving—he had taken to shaving before turning in, to save time in the morning, now that his beard no longer grew so heavily—as well as issues of *The Economist* that a better citizen would have bundled together for recycling. He turned off the ignition and stepped out of the car, into the wind, to deal with the mess.

As he gathered it up, he felt as if someone were watching him. He looked up at the house. Soon after Sue Anne left, he had taken down not only the curtains but the blinds as well, liking clear, empty windows that people could go ahead and stare into, if such ordinary life was what they found fascinating. A car passed by—a blue van new to this road, though in the past few weeks he'd seen it often—as he was picking up a mealy apple. Maybe a private detective stalking him, he thought. Someone his wife had hired, to see whether another woman was living in the house. He snatched up the last of the garbage and stuffed it in the can, intending to come out later to rebag it. He wanted to get out of the wind. He planned to eat one of the doughnuts before the six o'clock news.

Sigrid's son was sitting with his back against the storm door, his knees drawn in tight to his chest, smoking a cigarette. Keller was startled to see him, but did his best to appear unfazed, stopping on the walkway to extract a cigarette of his own from the pack in his pocket. "Can I trouble you for a light?" he said to the boy.

It seemed to work. Brad looked taken aback that Keller wasn't more taken aback. So much so that he held out the lighter with a trembling hand. Keller towered above him. The boy was thin and short (time would take care of one, if not the other); Keller was just over six feet, with broad shoulders and fifteen or twenty pounds more than he should have been carrying, which happened to him every winter. He said to the boy, "Is this a social call, or did I miss a business appointment?"

The boy hesitated. He missed the humor. He mumbled, "Social."

Keller hid his smile. "Allow me," he said, stepping forward. The boy scrambled up and stepped aside so Keller could open the door. Keller sensed a second's hesitation, though Brad followed him in.

It was cold inside. Keller turned the heat down to fifty-five when he left the house. The boy wrapped his arms around his shoulders. The stub of the cigarette was clasped between his second and third fingers. There was a leather bracelet on his wrist, as well as the spike of some tattoo.

"To what do I owe the pleasure?" Keller said.

"Do you . . ." The boy was preoccupied, looking around the room.

"Have an ashtray? I use cups for that," Keller said, handing him the mug from which he'd drunk his morning coffee. He had run out of milk, so he'd had it black. And damn—he had yet again forgotten to get milk. The boy stubbed out his cigarette in the mug without taking it in his hands. Keller set it back on the table, tapping off the ash from his own cigarette. He gestured to a chair, which the boy walked to and sat down.

"Do you, like, work or anything?" the boy blurted out.

"I'm the idle rich," Keller said. "In fact, I just paid a visit to your mother, to get a ticket to Germany. For a friend, not for me," he added. "That being the only thing on my agenda today, besides reading *The Wall Street Journal*"—he had not heard about the boy's arrest because he never read the local paper, but he'd hesitated to say that to Sigrid—"and once again forgetting to bring home milk."

Keller sat on the sofa.

"Would you not tell my mother I came here?" the boy said.

"Okay," Keller said. He waited.

"Were you ever friends with my dad?" the boy asked.

"No, though once we both donated blood on the same day, some years ago, and sat in adjacent chairs." It was true. For some reason, he had never told Sigrid about it. Not that there was very much to say.

The boy looked puzzled, as if he didn't understand the words Keller had spoken.

"My dad said you worked together," the boy said.

"Why would I lie?" Keller said, leaving open the question: Why would your father?

Again, the boy looked puzzled. Keller said, "I taught at the college."

"I was at my dad's over Thanksgiving, and he said you worked the same territory."

In spite of himself, Keller smiled. "That's an expression," Keller said. "Like 'I cover the waterfront.'"

"Cover what?" the boy said.

"If he said we 'worked the same territory,' he must have meant that we were up to the same thing. A notion I don't understand, though I do suppose it's what he meant."

The boy looked at his feet. "Why did you buy me the raffle tickets?" he said.

What was Keller supposed to tell him? That he'd done it as an oblique form of apology to his mother for something that hadn't happened, and that he therefore didn't really need to apologize for? The world had changed: here sat someone who'd never heard the expression "worked the same territory." But what, exactly, had been Brad's father's context? He supposed he could ask, though he knew in advance Brad would have no idea what he meant by context.

"I understand Thanksgiving was a pretty bad time for you," Keller said. He added, unnecessarily (though he had no tolerance for people who added things unnecessarily), "Your mother told me."

"Yeah," the boy said.

They sat in silence.

"Why is it you came to see me?" Keller asked.

"Because I thought you were a friend," the boy surprised him by answering.

Keller's eyes betrayed him. He felt his eyebrows rise slightly.

"Because you gave me *six* raffle tickets," the boy said.

Clearly, the boy had no concept of one's being emphatic by varying the expected numbers: one rose instead of a dozen; six chances instead of just one.

Keller got up and retrieved the bag of doughnuts from the hall table. The grease had seeped through and left a glistening smudge on the wood, which he wiped with the ball of his hand. He carried the bag to Brad and lowered it so he could see in. Close up, the boy smelled slightly sour. His hair was dirty. He was sitting with his shoulders hunched. Keller moved the bag forward an inch. The boy shook his head no. Keller folded the top, set the bag on the rug. He walked back to where he'd been sitting.

"If you'd buy me a bike, I'd work next summer and pay you back," Brad blurted out. "I need another bike to get to some places I got to go."

Keller decided against unscrambling the syntax and regarded him. The tattoo seemed to depict a spike with something bulbous at the tip. A small skull, he decided, for no good reason except that these days skulls seemed to be a popular image. There was a pimple on Brad's chin. Miraculously, even to a person who did not believe in miracles, Keller had gone through his own adolescence without ever having a pimple. His daughter had not had similar good luck. She had once refused to go to school because of her bad complexion, and he had made her cry when he'd tried to tease her out of being self-conscious. "Come on," he'd said to her. "You're not Dr. Johnson, with scrofula." His wife, as well as his daughter, had then burst into tears. The following day, Sue Anne had made an appointment for Lynn with a dermatologist.

"Would this be kept secret from your mother?"

"Yeah," the boy said. He wasn't emphatic, though; he narrowed his eyes to see if Keller would agree.

He asked, "Where will you tell her you got the bike?"

"I'll say from my dad."

Keller nodded. "That's not something she might ask him about?" he said.

The boy put his thumb to his mouth and bit the cuticle. "I don't know," he said.

"You wouldn't want to tell her it was in exchange for doing yard work for me next summer?"

"Yeah," the boy said, sitting up straighter. "Yeah, sure, I can do that. I *will*."

It occurred to Keller that Molly Bloom couldn't have pronounced the word *will* more emphatically. "We might even say that I ran into you and suggested it," Keller said.

"Say you ran into me at Scotty's," the boy said. It was an ice cream store. If that was what the boy wanted him to say, he would. He looked at the bag of doughnuts, expecting that in his newfound happiness the boy would soon reach in. He smiled. He waited for Brad to move toward the bag.

"I threw your trash can over," Brad said.

Keller's smile faded. "What?" he said.

"I was mad when I came here. I thought you were some nutcase friend of my dad's. I know you've been dating my mom."

Keller cocked his head. "So you knocked over my trash can, in preparation for asking me to give you money for a bike?"

"My dad said you were a sleazebag who was dating Mom. You and Mom went to Boston."

Keller had been called many things. Many, many things. But sleazebag had not been among them. It was unexpected, but it stopped just short of amusing him. "And if I *had been* dating Sigrid?" he said. "That would mean you should come over and dump out my trash?"

"I never thought you'd lend me money," Brad mumbled. His thumb was at his mouth again. "I didn't . . . why would I think you'd give me that kind of money, just because you bought twelve bucks' worth of raffle tickets?"

"I'm not following the logic here," Keller said. "If I'm the enemy, why, exactly, did you come to see me?"

"Because I didn't know. I don't know what my father's getting at half the time. My dad's a major nutcase, in case you don't know that. Somebody ought to round him up in one of his burlap bags and let him loose far away from here so he can go live with his precious turkeys."

"I can understand your frustration," Keller said. "I'm afraid that with all the world's problems, setting turkeys free doesn't seem an important priority to me."

"Why? Because you had a dad that was a nutcase?"

"I'm not understanding," Keller said.

"You said you understood the way I feel. Is it because you had a dad that was nuts, too?"

Keller thought about it. In retrospect, it was clear that his father's withdrawal, the year preceding his death, had been because of depression, not old age. He said, "He was quite a nice man. Hardworking. Religious. Very generous, even though he didn't have much money. He and my mother had a happy marriage." To his surprise, that sounded right: for years, in revising his father's history, he had assumed that everything had been a façade, but now that he, himself, was older, he tended to think that people's unhappiness was rarely caused by anyone else, or alleviated by anyone else.

"I came here and threw over your trash and ripped up a bush you just planted," Brad said.

The boy was full of surprises.

"I'll replant it," Brad said. He seemed, suddenly, to be on the verge of tears. "The bush by the side of the house," he said tremulously. "There was new dirt around it."

Indeed. Just the bush Keller thought. On a recent morning, after a rain, he had dug up the azalea and replanted it where it would get more sun. It was the first thing he could remember moving in years. He did almost nothing in the yard—had not worked in it, really, since Sue Anne left.

"Yes, I think you'll need to do that," he said.

"What if I don't?" the boy said shrilly. His voice had changed entirely.

Keller frowned, taken aback at the sudden turnaround.

"What if I do like I came to do?" the boy said.

Suddenly there was a gun pointed at Keller. A pistol. Pointed right at him, in his living room. And, as suddenly, he was flying through the air before his mind even named the object. It went off as he tackled the boy, wresting the gun from his hand. "You're both fucking nutcases, and you were, too, dating that bitch!" Brad screamed. In that way, because of so much screaming, Keller knew that he had not killed the boy.

The bullet had passed through Keller's forearm. A "clean wound," as the doctor in the emergency room would later say, his expression betraying no awareness of the irony inherent in such a description. With an amazing surge of strength, Keller had pinned the boy to the rug with his good arm as the other bled onto the doughnut bag, and then the struggle was over and Keller did not know what to do. It had seemed they might stay that way forever, with him pinning the boy down, one or the other of them—both of them?—screaming. He somehow used his wounded arm as well as his good arm to pull Brad up and clench him to his side as he dragged the suddenly deadweight, sobbing boy to the telephone and dialed 911. Later, he would learn that he had broken two of the boy's ribs, and that the bullet had missed hitting the bone in his own forearm by fractions of an inch, though the wound required half a dozen surprisingly painful sutures to close.

Keller awaited Sigrid's arrival in the emergency room with dread. His world had already been stood on its head long ago, and he'd developed some fancy acrobatics to stay upright, but Sigrid was just a beginner. He remembered that he had thought about going to her house that very night. It might have been the night he stayed. Everything might have been very different, but it was not. And this thought: If his wife held him accountable for misjudging the importance of their daughter's blemishes, might Sigrid think that, somehow, the violent way things had turned out had been his fault? Among the many things he had been called had been provocative. It was his daughter's favorite word for him. She no longer even tried to find original words to express his shortcomings: he was *provocative*. Even she would not buy the sleazebag epithet. No: he was *provocative*.

In the brightly lit room, they insisted he remain on a gurney. Fluid from a bag was dripping into his arm. Sigrid—there was Sigrid!—wept and wept. Her lawyer accompanied her: a young man with bright blue eyes and a brow too wrinkled for his years, who seemed too rattled to be in charge of anything. Did he hover the way he did because he was kind, or was there a little something more between him and Sigrid? Keller's not having got involved with Sigrid hadn't spared her any pain, he saw. Once again, he had been instrumental in a woman's abject misery.

Trauma was a strange thing, because you could be unaware of its presence, like diseased cells lurking in your body (a natural enough thought in a hospital) or like bulbs that would break the soil's surface only when stirred in their depths by the penetrating warmth of the sun.

Keller remembered the sun—no, the moon—of Lynn's cradle. The cradle meant to hold three babies that held only one. He had suggested that Sue Anne, depressed after the birth, return to school, get her degree in art history, teach. He had had a notion of her having colleagues. Friends. Because he was not a very good friend to have. Oh, *sometimes*, sure. It had been a nice gesture to buy a plane ticket for someone who needed to visit a dying friend. How ironic it was, his arranging for that ticket the same day he, himself, might have died.

Sigrid was wearing the gray sweater, the necklace with the cross. Her son had blown apart her world. And Keller was not going to be any help: he would not even consider trying to help her put it together again. All the king's horses, and all the king's men . . . even Robert Penn Warren couldn't put Sigrid together again.

Keller had tried that before: good intentions; good suggestions; and his wife had screamed that whatever she did, it was *never enough, never enough*, well, maybe it would be enough if she showed him what strength she possessed—what strength he hadn't depleted with his sarcasm and his comic asides and his endless equivocating—by throwing the lamp on the floor, his typewriter against the wall (the dent was still there), the TV out the window. These thoughts were explained to him later, because he had not been home when she exhibited her significant strength. The squirrels had eaten every bulb. There was not going to be one tulip that would bloom that spring. He suspected otherwise—of course the squirrels had not dug up *every* bulb—but she was in no state of mind to argue with. Besides, there were rules, and his role in the marriage was not to be moderate, it was to be *provocative*. His daughter had said so.

And there she was, his daughter, rushing to his side, accompanied by a nurse: the same person who had once been shown to him swaddled in a pink blanket, now grown almost as tall as he, her face wrinkled then, her face wrinkled now.

"Don't squint," he said. "Put your glasses on. You'll still be pretty."

He stood quickly to show her he was fine, which made the nurse and a doctor who rushed to his side very angry. He said, "I don't have health insurance. I demand to be discharged. The gun got discharged, so it's only fair that I be discharged also."

The nurse said something he couldn't hear. The effort of standing had left him light-headed. Across the room, Sigrid appeared in duplicate and went out of focus. Lynn was negating what he'd just said, informing everyone in a strident voice that of course he had health insurance. The doctor had quite firmly moved him back to his gurney, and now many hands were buckling straps over his chest and legs.

"Mr. Keller," the nurse said, "you lost quite a bit of blood before you got here, and we need you to lie down."

"As opposed to up?" he said.

The doctor, who was walking away, turned. "Keller," he said, "this isn't *ER*, where we'd do anything for you, and the nurse isn't your straight man."

"Clearly not," he said quickly. "She's a woman, we assume."

The doctor's expression did not change. "I knew a wiseass like you in med school," he said. "He couldn't do the work, so he developed a comedy routine and made a big joke of flunking out. In the end, I became a doctor and he's still talking to himself." He walked away.

Keller was ready with a quick retort, heard it inside his head, but his lips couldn't form the words. What his nearest and dearest had always wished for was now coming true: his terrible talent with words was for the moment suspended. Truly, he was too tired to speak.

The phrase *nearest and dearest* carried him back in time and reminded him of the deer. The deer that had disappeared in the Hollywood Hills. His own guardian angel, appropriately enough a little mangy, with hooves rooting it to the ground, instead of gossamer wings to carry it aloft. And his eyes closed.

When he opened them, Keller saw that his daughter was looking down at him, and nodding slowly, a tentative smile quivering like a parenthesis at the sides of her mouth, a parenthesis he thought might contain the information that, yes, once he had been able to reassure her easily, as she, in believing, had reassured him.

In appreciation, he attempted his best Jack Nicholson smile.

Find and Replace

True story: my father died in a hospice on Christmas Day, while a clown dressed in big black boots and a beard was down the hall doing his clown-as-Santa act for the amusement of a man my father had befriended, who was dying of ALS. I wasn't there; I was in Paris to report on how traveling art was being uncrated—a job I got through my cousin Jasper, who works for a New York City ad agency more enchanted with consultants than Julia Child is with chickens. For years, Jasper's sending work my way has allowed me to keep going while I write the Great American I Won't Say Its Name.

I'm superstitious. For example, I thought that even though my father was doing well, the minute I left the country he would die. Which he did.

On a globally warmed July day, I flew into Fort Myers and picked up a rental car and set off for my mother's to observe (her terminology) the occasion of my father's death, six months after the event. It was actually seven months later, but because I was in Toronto checking out sites for an HBO movie, and there was no way I could make it on June 25, my mother thought the most respectful thing to do would be to wait until the same day, one month later. I don't ask my mother a lot of questions; when I can, I simply try to keep the peace by doing what she asks. As mothers go, she's not demanding. Most requests are simple and have to do with her notions of propriety, which often center on the writing of notes. I have friends who are so worried about their parents that they see them every weekend, I have friends who phone home every day, friends who cut their parents' lawn because no one can be found to do it. With my mother, it's more a question of: Will I please send Mrs. Fawnes a condolence card because of her dog's death, or, Will I be so kind as to call a florist near me in New York and ask for an arrangement to be delivered on the birthday of a friend of my mother's, because ordering flowers when a person isn't familiar with the florist can be a disastrous experience. I don't buy flowers, even from Korean markets, but I asked around, and apparently the bouquet that arrived at the friend's door was a great success.

My mother has a million friends. She keeps the greeting-card industry in business. She would probably send greetings on Groundhog Day, if the cards existed. Also, no one ever seems to disappear from her life (with the notable exception of my father). She still exchanges notes with a maid who cleaned her room at the Swift House Inn fifteen years ago—and my parents were only there for the weekend.

I know I should be grateful that she is such a friendly person. Many of my friends bemoan the fact that their parents get into altercations with everybody, or that they won't socialize at all.

So: I flew from New York to Fort Myers, took the shuttle to the rental-car place, got in the car and was gratified that the air-conditioning started to blow the second I turned on the ignition, and leaned back, closed my eyes, and counted backward, in French, from thirty, in order to unwind before I began to drive. I then put on loud music, adjusted the bass, and set off, feeling around on the steering wheel to see if there was cruise control, because if I got one more ticket my insurance was going to be canceled. Or maybe I could get my mother to write a nice note pleading my case.

Anyway, all the preliminaries to my story are nothing but that: the almost inevitable five minutes of hard rain midway through the trip; the beautiful bridge; the damned trucks expelling herculean farts. I drove to Venice, singing along with Mick Jagger about beasts of burden. When I got to my mother's street, which is, it seems, the only quarter-mile-long stretch of America watched directly by God, through the eyes of a Florida police-man in a radar-equipped car, I set the cruise control for twenty and coasted to her driveway.

Hot as it was, my mother was outside, sitting in a lawn chair flanked by pots of red geraniums. Seeing my mother always puts me into a state of confusion. Whenever I first see her, I become disoriented.

"Ann!" she said. "Oh, are you exhausted? Was the flight terrible?"

It's the subtext that depresses me: the assumption that to arrive any-where you have to pass through hell. In fact, you do. I had been on a USAir flight, seated in the last seat in the last row, and every time suitcases thudded into the baggage compartment my spine reverberated painfully. My travel-ing companions had been an obese woman with a squirming baby and her teenage son, whose ears she squeezed when he wouldn't settle down, pro-ducing shrieks and enough flailing to topple my cup of apple juice. I just sat there silently, and I could feel that I was being too quiet and bringing everyone down.

My mother's face was still quite pink. Shortly before my father's death, after she had a little skin cancer removed from above her lip, she went to the dermatologist for microdermabrasion. She was wearing the requisite hat with a wide brim and Ari Onassis sunglasses. She had on her uniform: shorts covered with a flap, so that it looked as if she were wearing a skirt, and a T-shirt embellished with sequins. Today's featured a lion with glittering black ears and, for all I knew, a correctly colored nose. Its eyes, which you might think would be sequins, were painted on. Blue.

"Love you," I said, hugging her. I had learned not to answer her questions. "Were you sitting out here in the sun waiting for me?"

She had learned, as well, not to answer mine. "We can have lemonade," she said. "Paul Newman. And that man's marinara sauce—I never cook it myself anymore."

The surprise came almost immediately, just after she pressed a pile of papers into my hands: thank-you notes from friends she wanted me to read; a letter she didn't understand regarding a magazine subscription that was about to expire; an ad she'd gotten about a vacuum cleaner she wanted my advice about buying; two tickets to a Broadway play she'd bought ten years before that she and my father had never used (what was being asked of me?); and—most interesting, at the bottom of the pile—a letter from Drake Dreodadus, her neighbor, asking her to move in with him. "Go for the vacuum instead," I said, trying to laugh it off.

"I've already made my response," she said. "And you may be very surprised to know what I said."

Drake Dreodadus had spoken at my father's memorial service. Before that, I had met him only once, when he was going over my parents' lawn with a metal detector. But no: as my mother reminded me, I'd had a conversation with him in the drugstore, one time when she and I stopped in to buy medicine for my father. He was a pharmacist.

"The only surprising thing would be if you'd responded in the affirmative," I said.

"'Responded in the affirmative!' Listen to *you*."

"Mom," I said, "tell me this is not something you'd give a second of thought to."

"Several *days* of thought," she said. "I decided that it would be a good idea, because we're very compatible."

"Mom," I said, "you're joking, right?"

"You'll like him when you get to know him," she said.

"Wait a minute," I said. "This is someone you hardly know—or am I being naive?"

"Oh, Ann, at my age you don't necessarily want to know someone extremely well. You want to be compatible, but you can't let yourself get all involved in the dramas that have already played out—all those accounts of everyone's youth. You just want to be—you want to come to the point where you're compatible."

I was sitting in my father's chair. The doilies on the armrests that slid around and drove him crazy were gone. I looked at the darker fabric, where they had been. Give me a sign, Dad, I was thinking, looking at the shiny fabric as if it were a crystal ball. I was clutching my glass, which was sweating. "Mom—you can't be serious," I said.

She winked.

"Mom—"

"I'm going to live in his house, which is on the street perpendicular to Palm Avenue. You know, one of the big houses they built at first, before the zoning people got after them and they put up these little cookie-cutter numbers."

"You're moving in with him?" I said, incredulous. "But you've got to keep this house. You are keeping it, aren't you? If it doesn't work out."

"Your father thought he was a fine man," she said. "They used to be in a Wednesday-night poker game, I guess you know. If your father had lived, Drake was going to teach him how to e-mail."

"With a, with—you don't have a computer," I said stupidly.

"Oh, Ann, I wonder about you sometimes. As if your father and I couldn't have driven to Circuit City, bought a computer—and he could have e-mailed you! He was excited about it."

"Well, I don't—" I seemed unable to finish any thought. I started again. "This could be a big mistake," I said. "He only lives one block away. Is it really necessary to move in with him?"

"Was it necessary for you to live with Richard Klingham in Vermont?"

I had no idea what to say. I had been staring at her. I dropped my eyes a bit and saw the blue eyes of the lion. I dropped them to the floor. New rug. When had she bought a new rug? Before or after she made her plans?

"When did he ask you about this?" I said.

"About a week ago," she said.

"He did this by mail? He just wrote you a note?"

"If we'd had a computer, he could have e-mailed!" she said.

"Mom, are you being entirely serious about this?" I said. "What, exactly—"

"What, *exactly*, what *one single thing*, what *absolutely* compelling reason did you have for living with Richard Klingham?"

"Why do you keep saying his last name?" I said.

"Most of the old ladies I know, their daughters would be delighted if their mothers remembered a boyfriend's first name, let alone a last name," she said. "Senile old biddies. Really. I get sick of them myself. I see why it drives the children crazy. But I don't want to get off on that. I want to tell you that we're going to live in his house for a while, but are thinking seriously of moving to Tucson. He's very close to his son, who's a builder there. They speak *every single day* on the phone, *and* they e-mail," she said. She was never reproachful; I decided that she was just being emphatic.

Just a short time before, I had relaxed, counting *trois, deux, un*. Singing with Mick Jagger. Inching slowly toward my mother's house.

"But this shouldn't intrude on a day meant to respect the memory of your father," she said, almost whispering. "I want you to know, though, and I really mean it: I feel that your father would be pleased that I'm compatible with Drake. I feel it deep in my heart." She thumped the lion's face. "He would give this his blessing, if he could," she said.

"Is he around?" I said.

"Listen to you, disrespecting the memory of your father by joking about his not being among us!" she said. "That is in the poorest taste, Ann."

I said, "I meant Drake."

"Oh," she said. "I see. Yes. Yes, he is. But right now he's at a matinee. We thought that you and I should talk about this privately."

"I assume he'll be joining us for dinner tonight?"

"Actually, he's meeting some old friends in Sarasota. A dinner that was set up before he knew you were coming. You know, it's a wonderful testament to a person when they retain old friends. Drake has an active social life with old friends."

"Well, it's just perfect for him, then. He can have his social life, and you and he can be compatible."

"You've got a sarcastic streak—you always had it," my mother said. "You might ask yourself why you've had fallings-out with so many friends."

"So this is an occasion to criticize me? I understand, by the way, that you were also criticizing me when you implied that you didn't understand my relationship with Richard—or perhaps the reason I ended it? The reason I ended it was because he and an eighteen-year-old student of his became Scientologists and asked me if I wanted to come in the van with them to Santa Monica. He dropped his cat off at the animal shelter before they set out, so I guess I wasn't the only one to get shafted."

"Oh!" she said. "I didn't know!"

"You didn't know because I never told you."

"Oh, was it *horrible* for you? Did you have any *idea*?"

She was right, of course: I had left too many friends behind. I told myself it was because I traveled so much, because my life was so chaotic. But, really, maybe I should have sent a few more cards myself. Also, maybe I should have picked up on Richard's philandering. Everybody else in town knew.

"I thought we could have some Paul Newman's and then maybe when we had dessert we could light those little devotional lights and have a moment's silence, remembering your father."

"Fine," I said.

"We'll need to go to the drugstore to get candles," she said. "They burned out the night Drake and I had champagne and toasted our future." She stood. She put on her hat. "I can drive," she said.

I straggled behind her like a little kid in a cartoon. I could imagine myself kicking dirt. Some man she hardly knew. It was the last thing I'd expected. "So give me the scenario," I said. "He wrote you a note and you wrote back, and then he came for champagne?"

"Oh, all right, so it hasn't been a great romance," my mother said. "But a person gets tired of all the highs and lows. You get to the point where you need things to be a little easier. In fact, I didn't write him a note. I thought about it for three days, then I just knocked on his door."

The candles were cinnamon-scented and made my throat feel constricted. She lit them at the beginning of the meal, and by the end she seemed to have forgotten about talking about my father. She mentioned a book she'd been reading about Arizona. She offered to show me some pictures, but they, too, were forgotten. We watched a movie on TV about a dying ballerina. As she died, she imagined herself doing a pas de deux with an obviously gay actor. We ate M&M's, which my mother has always maintained are not really candy, and went to bed early. I slept on the foldout sofa. She made me wear one of her nightgowns, saying that Drake might knock on the door in the morning. I traveled light: toothbrush, but nothing to sleep in. Drake did not knock the next morning, but he did put a note under the door saying that he had car problems and would be at the repair shop. My mother seemed very sad. "Maybe you'd want to write him a teeny little note before you go?" she said.

"What could I possibly say?"

"Well, you think up dialogue for characters, don't you? What would you imagine yourself saying?" She put her hands to her lips. "Never mind," she said. "If you do write, I'd appreciate it if you'd at least give me a sense of what you said."

"Mom," I said, "please give him my best wishes. I don't want to write him a note."

She said, "He's DrDrake@aol.com, if you want to e-mail."

I nodded. Best just to nod. I thought that I might have reached the point she'd talked about, where you have an overwhelming desire for things to be simple.

We hugged, and I kissed her well-moisturized cheek. She came out to the front lawn to wave as I pulled away.

On the way back to the airport, there was a sudden, brief shower that forced me to the shoulder of the road, during which time I thought that there were obvious advantages in having a priest to call on. I felt that my mother needed someone halfway between a lawyer and a psychiatrist, and that a priest would be perfect. I conjured up a poker-faced Robert De Niro in clerical garb as Cyndi Lauper sang about girls who just wanted to have fun.

But I wasn't getting away as fast as I hoped. Back at the car-rental lot, my credit card was declined. "It might be my handheld," the young man said to me, to cover either my embarrassment or his. "Do you have another card, or would you please try inside?"

I didn't know why there was trouble with the card. It was AmEx, which I always pay immediately, not wanting to forfeit Membership Rewards points by paying late. I was slightly worried. Only one woman was in front of me in line, and after two people behind the counter got out of their huddle, both turned to me. I chose the young man.

"There was some problem processing my credit card outside," I said.

The man took the card and swiped it. "No problem now," he said. "It is my pleasure to inform you that today we can offer you an upgrade to a Ford Mustang for only an additional seven dollars a day."

"I'm returning a car," I said. "The machine outside wouldn't process my card."

"Thank you for bringing that to my attention," the young man said. He was wearing a badge that said "Trainee" above his name. His name, written smaller, was Jim Brown. He had a kind face and a bad haircut. "Your charges stay on American Express, then?"

An older man walked over to him. "What's up?" he said.

"The lady's card was declined, but I ran it through and it was fine," he said.

The older man looked at me. It was cooler inside, but still, I felt as if I were melting. "She's returning, not renting?" the man said, as if I weren't there.

"Yes, sir," Jim Brown said.

This was getting tedious. I reached for the receipt.

"What was that about the Mustang?" the man said.

"I mistakenly thought—"

"I mentioned to him how much I like Mustangs," I said.

Jim Brown frowned.

"In fact, how tempted I am to rent one right now."

Both the older man and Jim Brown looked at me suspiciously.

"Ma'am, you're returning your Mazda, right?" Jim Brown said, examining the receipt.

"I am, but now I think I'd like to rent a Mustang."

"Write up a Mustang, nine dollars extra," the older man said.

"I quoted her seven," Jim Brown said.

"Let me see." The man punched a few keys on the keyboard. "Seven," he said, and walked away.

Jim Brown and I both watched him go. Jim Brown leaned a little forward, and said in a low voice, "Were you trying to help me out?"

"No, not at all. Just thought having a Mustang for a day might be fun. Maybe a convertible."

"The special only applies to the regular Mustang," he said.

"It's only money," I said.

He hit a key, looked at the monitor.

"One day, returning tomorrow?" he said.

"Right," I said. "Do I have a choice about the color?"

He had a crooked front tooth. That and the bad haircut were distracting. He had lovely eyes, and his hair was a nice color, like a fawn's, but the tooth and the jagged bangs got your attention instead of his attributes.

"There's a red and two white," he said. "You don't have a job you've got to get back to?"

I said, "I'll take the red."

He looked at me.

"I'm freelance," I said.

He smiled. "Impulsive, too," he said.

I nodded. "The perks of being self-employed."

"At what?" he said. "Not that it's any of my business."

"Jim, any help needed?" the older man said, coming up behind him.

In response, Jim looked down and began to hit keys. It increased his schoolboyish quality: he bit his bottom lip, concentrating. The printer began to print out.

"I used to get in trouble for being impulsive," he said. "Then I got diagnosed with ADD. My grandmother said, 'See, I told you he couldn't help it.' That was what she kept saying to my mom: 'Couldn't help it.'" He nodded vigorously. His bangs flopped on his forehead. Outside, they would have stuck to his skin, but inside it was air-conditioned.

His mentioning ADD reminded me of the ALS patient—the man I'd never met. I had a clearer image of a big-footed, bulbous-nosed clown. If I breathed deeply, I could still detect the taste of cinnamon in my throat. I declined every option of coverage, initialing beside every X. He looked at my scribbled initials. "What kind of writing?" he said. "Mysteries?"

"No. Stuff that really happens."

"Don't people get mad?" he said.

The older man was looming over the woman at the far end of the counter. They were trying not to be too obvious about watching us. Their heads were close together as they whispered.

"People don't recognize themselves. And, in case they might, you just program the computer to replace one name with another. So, in the final version, every time the word *Mom* comes up it's replaced with *Aunt Begonia* or something."

He creased the papers, putting them in a folder. "A-eight," he said. "Out the door, right, all the way down against the fence."

"Thanks," I said. "And thanks for the good suggestion."

"No problem," he said. He seemed to be waiting for something. At the exit, I looked over my shoulder; sure enough, he was looking at me. So was the older man, and so was the woman he'd been talking to. I ignored them. "You wouldn't program your computer to replace *Mustang convertible* with one of those creepy Geo Metros, would you?"

"No, ma'am," he said, smiling. "I don't know how to do that."

"Easy to learn," I said. I gave him my best smile and walked out to the parking lot, where the heat rising from the asphalt made me feel like my feet were sliding over a well-oiled griddle. The key was in the car. It didn't look like the old Mustang at all. The red was very bright and a little unpleasant, at least on such a hot day. The top was already down. I turned the key and saw that the car had less than five hundred miles on it. The seat was comfortable enough. I adjusted the mirror, pulled on my seat belt, and drove to the exit, with no desire to turn on the radio. "That's a beauty," the man in the kiosk said, inspecting the folder and handing it back.

"Just got it on impulse," I said.

"That's the best way," he said. He gave a half salute as I drove off.

And then it hit me: the grim reality that I had to talk sense to her, I had to do whatever it took, including insulting her great good friend Drake, so he wouldn't clean her out financially, devastate her emotionally, take advantage, dominate her—who knew what he had in mind? He'd avoided me on purpose—he didn't want to hear what I'd say. What did he think? That her busy daughter would conveniently disappear on schedule, or that she might be such a liberal that their plans sounded intriguing? Or maybe he thought she was a pushover, like her mother. Who knew what men like that thought.

The cop who pulled me over for speeding turned on the siren when I didn't come screeching to a halt. He was frowning deeply, I saw in the rearview mirror, as he approached the car.

"My mother's dying," I said.

"License and registration," he said, looking at me with those reflective sunglasses cops love so much. I could see a little tiny me, like a smudge on the lens. I had been speeding, overcome with worry. After all, it was a terrible situation. The easiest way to express it had been to say that my mother was dying. Replace *lost her mind* with *dying*.

"Mustang convertible," the cop said. "Funny car to rent if your mother's dying."

"I used to have a Mustang," I said, choking back tears. I was telling the truth, too. When I moved from Vermont, I'd left it behind in a friend's barn, and over the winter the roof had fallen in. There was extensive damage, though the frame had rusted out anyway. "My father bought it for me in 1968, as a bribe to stay in college."

The cop worked his lips until he came up with an entirely different expression. I saw myself reflected, wavering slightly. The cop touched his sunglasses. He snorted. "Okay," he said, stepping back. "I'm going to give you a warning and let you go, urging you to respect your life and the life of others by *driving at the posted speed*."

"Thank you," I said sincerely.

He touched the sunglasses again. Handed me the warning. How lucky I was. How very, very lucky.

It was not until he returned to his car and sped away that I looked at the piece of paper. He had not checked any of the boxes. Instead, he had written his phone number. Well, I thought, if I kill Drake, the number might come in handy.

I also played a little game of my own: replace *Richard Klingham* with *Jim Brown*.

He was probably twenty-five, maybe thirty years younger than me. Which would be as reprehensible, almost, as Richard's picking up the teenager.

Back over the bridge, taking the first Venice exit, driving past the always closed House of Orchids, dismayed at the ever-lengthening strip mall.

My mother, again in the lawn chair, reading the newspaper, but now not bothering to look up as cars passed. I could remember her face vividly from years before, when my father and I had turned in to our driveway in Washington in an aqua Mustang convertible. She had been so shocked. Just shocked. She must have been thinking of the expense. Maybe also of the danger.

My mother seemed less timid now. Obviously, she, too, could be quite impulsive. I was just about to tap the horn when my mother stood and took a minute to steady herself before heading toward the house. Why was she bent over, walking so slowly? Had she been pretending to be spry earlier, or had I just not noticed? Then the door opened, and a man—it was Drake, that was who it was—stood on the threshold, extending a hand and waiting, not going down the steps, just waiting. He stood ramrod straight, but, even driving slowly, I got only a glimpse of him: this man who was not my father, with his big hand extended, and my mother lifting her hand like a lady ascending an elegant, carpeted staircase, instead of three concrete steps.

There was nothing I could say. It had all been decided. There was not a word I could say that would stop either one of them.

I turned left just before the street dead-ended, not wanting to risk passing by a second time. I realized that there was someone waiting to hear from me: possibly two people—the kid *and* the cop—if not three (my mother, who was probably hoping for an apology for my dire warnings about Drake). I could have made a phone call, had the evening go another way entirely, but everyone will understand why I decided otherwise.

You can't help understanding. First, because it is the truth, and second, because everyone knows the way things change. They always do, even in a very short time. Back in Fort Myers, the transaction was all business: another shift was at work at the rental agency, and there was only the perfunctory question as I opened the door and got out about whether everything was all right with the car.

The Rabbit Hole
as Likely Explanation

My mother does not remember being invited to my first wedding. This comes up in conversation when I pick her up from the lab, where blood has been drawn to see how she's doing on her medication. She's sitting in an orange plastic chair, giving the man next to her advice I'm not sure he asked for about how to fill out forms on a clipboard. Apparently, before I arrived, she told him that she had not been invited to either of my weddings.

"I don't know why you sent me to have my blood drawn," she says.

"The doctor asked me to make an appointment. I did not send you."

"Well, you were late. I sat there waiting and waiting."

"You showed up an hour before your appointment, Ma. That's why you were there so long. I arrived fifteen minutes after the nurse called me." It's my authoritative but cajoling voice. One tone negates the other and nothing much gets communicated.

"You sound like Perry Mason," she says.

"Ma, there's a person trying to get around you."

"Well, I'm very sorry if I'm holding anyone up. They can just honk and get into the other lane."

A woman hurries around my mother in the hospital corridor, narrowly missing an oncoming wheelchair brigade: four chairs, taking up most of the hallway.

"She drives a sports car, that one," my mother says. "You can always tell. But look at the size of her. How does she fit in the car?"

I decide to ignore her. She has on dangling hoop earrings, and there's a scratch on her forehead and a Band-Aid on her cheekbone. Her face looks a little like an obstacle course. "Who is going to get our car for us?" she asks.

"Who do you think? Sit in the lobby, and I'll turn in to the driveway."

"A car makes you think about the future all the time, doesn't it?" she says. "You have to do all that imagining: how you'll get out of the garage and into your lane and how you'll deal with all the traffic, and then one time, remember, just as you got to the driveway a man and a woman stood smack in the center, arguing, and they wouldn't move so you could pull in."

"My life is a delight," I say.

"I don't think your new job agrees with you. You're such a beautiful seamstress—a real, old-fashioned talent—and what do you do but work on computers and leave that lovely house in the country and drive into this . . . this crap five days a week."

"Thank you, Ma, for expressing even more eloquently than I—"

"Did you finish those swordfish costumes?"

"Starfish. I was tired, and I watched TV last night. Now, if you sit in that chair over there you'll see me pull in. It's windy. I don't want you standing outside."

"You always have some reason why I can't be outside. You're afraid of the bees, aren't you? After that bee stung your toe when you were raking, you got desperate about yellow jackets—that's what they're called. You shouldn't have had on sandals when you were raking. Wear your hiking boots when you rake leaves, if you can't find another husband to do it for you."

"Please stop lecturing me and—"

"Get your car! What's the worst that can happen? I have to stand up for a few minutes? It's not like I'm one of those guards outside Buckingham Palace who has to look straight ahead until he loses consciousness."

"Okay. You can stand here and I'll pull in."

"What car do you have?"

"The same car I always have."

"If I don't come out, come in for me."

"Well, of course, Ma. But why wouldn't you come out?"

"SUVs can block your view. They drive right up, like they own the curb. They've got those tinted windows like Liz Taylor might be inside, or a gangster. That lovely man from Brunei—why did I say that? I must have been thinking of the Sultan of Brunei. Anyway, that man I was talking to said that in New York City he was getting out of a cab at a hotel at the same exact moment that Elizabeth Taylor got out of a limousine. He said she just kept handing little dogs out the door to everybody. The doorman. The bellhop. Her hairdresser had one under each arm. But they weren't hers—they were his own dogs! He didn't have a free hand to help Elizabeth Taylor. So that desperate man—"

"Ma, we've got to get going."

"I'll come with you."

"You hate elevators. The last time we tried that, you wouldn't walk—"

"Well, the stairs didn't kill me, did they?"

"I wasn't parked five flights up. Look, just stand by the window and—"

"I know what's happening. You're telling me over and over!"

I raise my hands and drop them. "See you soon," I say.

"Is it the green car? The black car that I always think is green?"

"Yes, Ma. My only car."

"Well, you don't have to say it like that. I hope you never know what it's like to have small confusions about things. I understand that your car is black. It's when it's in strong sun that it looks a little green."

"Back in five," I say, and enter the revolving door. A man ahead of me, with both arms in casts, pushes on the glass with his forehead. We're out in a few seconds. Then he turns and looks at me, his face crimson.

"I didn't know if I pushed, whether it might make the door go too fast," I say.

"I figured there was an explanation," he says dully, and walks away.

The fat woman who passed us in the hallway is waiting on the sidewalk for the light to change, chatting on her cell phone. When the light blinks green, she moves forward with her head turned to the side, as if the phone clamped to her ear were leading her. She has on an ill-fitting blazer and one of those long skirts that everybody wears, with sensible shoes and a teeny purse dangling over her shoulder. "Right behind you," my mother says distinctly, catching up with me halfway to the opposite curb.

"Ma, there's an elevator."

"You do enough things for your mother! It's desperate of you to do this on your lunch hour. Does picking me up mean you won't get any food? Now that you can see I'm fine, you could send me home in a cab."

"No, no, it's no problem. But last night you asked me to drop you at the hairdresser. Wasn't that where you wanted to go?"

"Oh, I don't think that's today."

"Yes. The appointment is in fifteen minutes. With Eloise."

"I wouldn't want to be named for somebody who caused a commotion at the Plaza. Would you?"

"No. Ma, why don't you wait by the ticket booth, and when I drive—"

"You're full of ideas! Why won't you just let me go to the car with you?"

"In an elevator? You're going to get in an elevator? All right. Fine with me."

"It isn't one of those glass ones, is it?"

"It does have one glass wall."

"I'll be like those other women, then. The ones who've hit the glass ceiling."

"Here we are."

"It has a funny smell. I'll sit in a chair and wait for you."

"Ma, that's back across the street. You're here now. I can introduce you to the guy over there in the booth, who collects the money. Or you can just take a deep breath and ride up with me. Okay?"

A man inside the elevator, wearing a suit, holds the door open. "Thank you," I say. "Ma?"

"I like your suggestion about going to that chapel," she says. "Pick me up there."

The man continues to hold the door with his shoulder, his eyes cast down.

"Not a chapel, a booth. Right there? That's where you'll be?"

"Yes. Over there with that man."

"You see the man—" I step off the elevator and the doors close behind me.

"I did see him. He said that his son was getting married in Las Vegas. And I said, 'I never got to go to my daughter's weddings.' And he said, 'How many weddings did she have?' and of course I answered honestly. So he said, 'How did that make you feel?' and I said that a dog was at one of them."

"That was the wedding you came to. My first wedding. You don't remember putting a bow on Ebeneezer's neck? It was your idea." I take her arm and guide her toward the elevator.

"Yes, I took it off a beautiful floral display that was meant to be inside the church, but you and that man wouldn't go inside. There was no flat place to stand. If you were a woman wearing heels, there was no place to stand anywhere, and it was going to rain."

"It was a sunny day."

"I don't remember that. Did Grandma make your dress?"

"No. She offered, but I wore a dress we bought in London."

"That was just desperate. It must have broken her heart."

"Her arthritis was so bad she could hardly hold a pen, let alone a needle."

"You must have broken her heart."

"Well, Ma, this isn't getting us to the car. What's the plan?"

"The Marshall Plan."

"What?"

"The Marshall Plan. People of my generation don't scoff at that."

"Ma, maybe we'd better give standing by the booth another try. You don't even have to speak to the man. Will you do it?"

"Do you have some objection if I get on the elevator with you?"

"No, but this time if you say you're going to do it you have to do it. We can't have people holding doors open all day. People need to get where they're going."

"Listen to the things you say! They're so obvious, I don't know why you say them."

She is looking through her purse. Just below the top of her head, I can see her scalp through her hair. "Ma," I say.

"Yes, yes, coming," she says. "I thought I might have the card with that hairstylist's name."

"It's Eloise."

"Thank you, dear. Why didn't you say so before?"

I call my brother, Tim. "She's worse," I say. "If you want to visit her while she's still more or less with it, I'd suggest you book a flight."

"You don't know," he says. "The fight for tenure. How much rides on this one article."

"Tim. As your sister. I'm not talking about your problems, I'm—"

"She's been going downhill for some time. And God bless you for taking care of her! She's a wonderful woman. And I give you all the credit. You're a patient person."

"Tim. She's losing it by the day. If you care—if you care, see her now."

"Let's be honest: I don't have deep feelings, and I wasn't her favorite. That was the problem with René: Did I have any deep feelings? I mean, kudos! Kudos to you! Do you have any understanding of why Mom and Dad got together? He was a recluse, and she was such a party animal. She never understood a person turning to books for serious study, did she? Did she? Maybe I'd be the last to know."

"Tim, I suggest you visit before Christmas."

"That sounds more than a little ominous. May I say that? You call when I've just gotten home from a day I couldn't paraphrase, and you tell me—as you have so many times—that she's about to die, or lose her marbles entirely, and then you say—"

"Take care, Tim," I say, and hang up.

I drive to my mother's apartment to kill time while she gets her hair done, and go into the living room and see that the plants need watering. Two are new arrivals, plants that friends brought her when she was in the hospital, having her foot operated on: a kalanchoe and a miniature chrysanthemum. I rinse out the mug she probably had her morning coffee in and fill it under the faucet. I douse the plants, refilling the mug twice. My brother is rethinking Wordsworth at a university in Ohio, and for years I have been back in this small town in Virginia where we grew up, looking out for our mother. Kudos, as he would say.

"Okay," the doctor says. "We've known the time was coming. It will be much better if she's in an environment where her needs are met. I'm only talking about assisted living. If it will help, I'm happy to meet with her and explain that things have reached a point where she needs a more comprehensive support system."

"She'll say no."

"Regardless," he says. "You and I know that if there was a fire she wouldn't be capable of processing the necessity of getting out. Does she eat dinner? We can't say for sure that she eats, now, can we? She needs to maintain her caloric intake. We want to allow her to avail herself of resources structured so that she can best meet her own needs."

"She'll say no," I say again.

"May I suggest that you let Tim operate as a support system?"

"Forget him. He's already been denied tenure twice."

"Be that as it may, if your brother knows she's not eating—"

"Do you know she's not eating?"

"Let's say she's not eating," he says. "It's a slippery slope."

"Pretending that I have my brother as a 'support system' has no basis in reality. You want me to admit that she's thin? Okay. She's thin."

"Please grant my point, without—"

"Why? Because you're a doctor? Because you're pissed off that she misbehaved at some cashier's stand in a parking lot?"

"You told me she pulled the fire alarm," he says. "She's out of control! Face it."

"I'm not sure," I say, my voice quivering.

"I am. I've known you forever. I remember your mother making chocolate-chip cookies, my father always going to your house to see if she'd made the damned cookies. I know how difficult it is when a parent isn't able to take care of himself. My father lived in my house, and Donna took care of him in a way I can never thank her enough for, until he . . . well, until he died."

"Tim wants me to move her to a cheap nursing home in Ohio."

"Out of the question."

"Right. She hasn't come to the point where she needs to go to Ohio. On the other hand, we should put her in the slammer here."

"The slammer. We can't have a serious discussion if you pretend we're talking to each other in a comic strip."

I bring my knees to my forehead, clasp my legs, and press the kneecaps hard into my eyes.

"I understand from Dr. Milrus that you're having a difficult time," the therapist says. Her office is windowless, the chairs cheerfully mismatched. "Why don't you fill me in?"

"Well, my mother had a stroke a year ago. It did something. . . . Not that she didn't have some confusions before, but after the stroke she thought my brother was ten years old. She still sometimes says things about him that I can't make any sense of, unless I remember that she often, really quite often, thinks he's still ten. She also believes that I'm sixty. I mean, she thinks I'm only fourteen years younger than she is! And, to her, that's proof that my father had another family. Our family was an afterthought, my father had had another family, and I'm a child of the first marriage. I'm sixty years old, whereas she herself was only seventy-four when she had the stroke and fell over on the golf course."

The therapist nods.

"In any case, my brother is forty-four—about to be forty-five—and lately it's all she'll talk about."

"Your brother's age?"

"No, the revelation. That they—you know, the other wife and children—existed. She thinks the shock made her fall down at the fourth tee."

"Were your parents happily married?"

"I've shown her my baby album and said, 'If I was some other family's child, then what is this?' And she says, 'More of your father's chicanery.' That is the exact word she uses. The thing is, I am not sixty. I'll be fifty-one next week."

"It's difficult, having someone dependent upon us, isn't it?"

"Well, yes. But that's because she causes herself so much pain by thinking that my father had a previous family."

"How do you think you can best care for your mother?"

"She pities me! She really does! She says she's met every one of them: a son and a daughter, and a woman, a wife, who looks very much like her, which seems to make her sad. Well, I guess it would make her sad. Of course it's fiction, but I've given up trying to tell her that, because in a way I think it's symbolically important. It's necessary to her that she think what she thinks, but I'm just so tired of what she thinks. Do you know what I mean?"

"Tell me about yourself," the therapist says. "You live alone?"

"Me? Well, at this point I'm divorced, after I made the mistake of not marrying my boyfriend, Vic, and married an old friend instead. Vic and I talked about getting married, but I was having a lot of trouble taking care of my mother, and I could never give him enough attention. When we broke up, Vic devoted all his time to his secretary's dog, Banderas. If Vic was grieving, he did it while he was at the dog park."

"And you work at Cosmos Computer, it says here?"

"I do. They're really very family-oriented. They understand absolutely that I have to take time off to do things for my mother. I used to work at an interior-design store, and I still sew. I've just finished some starfish costumes for a friend's third-grade class."

"Jack Milrus thinks your mother might benefit from being in assisted living."

"I know, but he doesn't know—he really doesn't know—what it's like to approach my mother about anything."

"What is the worst thing that might happen if you did approach your mother?"

"The worst thing? My mother turns any subject to the other family, and whatever I want is just caught up in the whirlwind of complexity of this thing I won't acknowledge, which is my father's previous life, and, you know, she omits my brother from any discussion because she thinks he's a ten-year-old child."

"You feel frustrated."

"Is there any other way to feel?"

"You could say to yourself, 'My mother has had a stroke and has certain confusions that I can't do anything about.'"

"You don't understand. It is absolutely necessary that I acknowledge this other family. If I don't, I've lost all credibility."

The therapist shifts in her seat. "May I make a suggestion?" she says. "This is your mother's problem, not yours. You understand something that your mother, whose brain has been affected by a stroke, cannot understand. Just as you would guide a child, who does not know how to function in the world, you are now in a position where—whatever your mother believes—you must nevertheless do what is best for her."

"You need a vacation," Jack Milrus says. "If I weren't on call this weekend, I'd suggest that you and Donna and I go up to Washington and see that show at the Corcoran where all the figures walk out of the paintings."

"I'm sorry I keep bothering you with this. I know I have to make a decision. It's just that when I went back to look at the Oaks and that woman had mashed an éclair into her face—"

"It's funny. Just look at it as funny. Kids make a mess. Old people make a mess. Some old biddy pushed her nose into a pastry."

"Right," I say, draining my gin-and-tonic. We are in his backyard. Inside, Donna is making her famous osso buco. "You know, I wanted to ask you something. Sometimes she says 'desperate.' She uses the word when you wouldn't expect to hear it."

"Strokes," he says.

"But is she trying to say what she feels?"

"Does it come out like a hiccup or something?" He pulls up a weed.

"No, she just says it, instead of another word."

He looks at the long taproot of the dandelion he's twisted up. "The South," he says. "These things have a horribly long growing season." He drops it in a wheelbarrow filled with limp things raked up from the yard. "I am desperate to banish dandelions," he says.

"No, she wouldn't use it like that. She'd say something like, 'Oh, it was desperate of you to ask me to dinner.'"

"It certainly was. You weren't paying any attention to me on the telephone."

"Just about ready!" Donna calls out the kitchen window. Jack raises a hand in acknowledgment. He says, "Donna's debating whether to tell you that she saw Vic and Banderas having a fight near the dog park. Vic was knocking Banderas on the snout with a baseball cap, Donna says, and Banderas had squared off and was showing teeth. Groceries all over the street."

"I'm amazed. I thought Banderas could do no wrong."

"Well, things change."

In the yard next door, the neighbor's strange son faces the street lamp and, excruciatingly slowly, begins his many evening sun salutations.

Cora, my brother's friend, calls me at midnight. I am awake, watching *Igby Goes Down* on the VCR. Susan Sarandon, as the dying mother, is a wonder. Three friends sent me the tape for my birthday. The only other time such a thing has happened was years ago, when four friends sent me *Play It as It Lays* by Joan Didion.

"Tim thinks that he and I should do our share and have Mom here for a vacation, which we could do in November, when the college has a reading break," Cora says. "I would move into Tim's condominium, if it wouldn't offend Mom."

"That's nice of you," I say. "But you know that she thinks Tim is ten years old? I'm not sure that she'd be willing to fly to Ohio to have a ten-year-old take care of her."

"What?"

"Tim hasn't told you about this? He wrote her a letter, recently, and she saved it to show me how good his penmanship was."

"Well, when she gets here she'll see that he's a grown-up."

"She might think it's a Tim impostor, or something. She'll talk to you constantly about our father's first family."

"I still have some Ativan from when a root canal had to be redone," Cora says.

"Okay, look—I'm not trying to discourage you. But I'm also not convinced that she can make the trip alone. Would Tim consider driving here to pick her up?"

"Gee. My nephew is eleven, and he's been back and forth to the West Coast several times."

"I don't think this is a case of packing snacks in her backpack and giving her a puzzle book for the plane," I say.

"Oh, I am not trying to infantilize your mother. Quite the opposite: I think that if she suspects there's doubt about whether she can do it on her own she might not rise to the occasion, but if we just . . ."

"People never finish their sentences anymore," I say.

"Oh, gosh, I can finish," Cora says. "I mean, I was saying that she'll take care of herself if we assume that she *can* take care of herself."

"Would a baby take care of itself if we assumed that it could?"

"Oh, my goodness!" Cora says. "Look what time it is! I thought it was nine o'clock! Is it after midnight?"

"Twelve-fifteen."

"My watch stopped! I'm looking at the kitchen clock and it says twelve-ten."

I have met Cora twice: once she weighed almost two hundred pounds, and the other time she'd been on Atkins and weighed a hundred and forty. *Brides* magazine was in the car when she picked me up at the airport. During the last year, however, her dreams have not been fulfilled.

"Many apologies," Cora says.

"Listen," I say. "I was awake. No need to apologize. But I don't feel that we've settled anything."

"I'm going to have Tim call you tomorrow, and I am really sorry!"

"Cora, I didn't mean anything personal when I said that people don't finish sentences anymore. I don't finish my own."

"You take care, now!" she says, and hangs up.

"She's where?"

"Right here in my office. She was on a bench in Lee Park. Someone saw her talking to a woman who was drunk—a street person—just before the cops arrived. The woman was throwing bottles she'd gotten out of a restaurant's recycling at the statue. Your mother said she was keeping score. The woman was winning, the statue losing. The woman had blood all over her face, so eventually somebody called the cops."

"Blood all over her face?"

"She'd cut her fingers picking up glass after she threw it. It was the other woman who was bloody."

"Oh, God, my mother's okay?"

"Yes, but we need to act. I've called the Oaks. They can't do anything today, but tomorrow they can put her in a semiprivate for three nights, which they aren't allowed to do, but never mind. Believe me: once she's in there, they'll find a place."

"I'll be right there."

"Hold on," he says. "We need to have a plan. I don't want her at your place: I want her hospitalized tonight, and I want an MRI. Tomorrow morning, if there's no problem, you can take her to the Oaks."

"What's the point of scaring her to death? Why does she have to be in a hospital?"

"She's very confused. It won't be any help if you don't get to sleep tonight."

"I feel like we should—"

"You feel like you should protect your mother, but that's not really possible, is it? She was picked up in Lee Park. Fortunately, she had my business card and her beautician's card clipped to a shopping list that contains—it's right in front of me—items such as Easter eggs and arsenic."

"Arsenic? Was she going to poison herself?"

There is a moment of silence. "Let's say she was," he says, "for the sake of argument. Now, come and pick her up, and we can get things rolling."

Tim and Cora were getting married by a justice of the peace at approximately the same time that "Mom" was tracking bottles in Lee Park; they converge on the hospital room with Donna Milrus, who whispers apologetically that her husband is "playing doctor" and avoiding visiting hours.

Cora's wedding bouquet is in my mother's water pitcher. Tim cracks his knuckles and clears his throat repeatedly. "They got upset that I'd been sitting in the park. Can you imagine?" my mother says suddenly to the assembled company. "Do you think we're going to have many more of these desperate fall days?"

The next morning, only Tim and I are there to get her into his rental car and take her to the Oaks. Our mother sits in front, her purse on her lap, occasionally saying something irrational, which I finally figure out is the result of her reading vanity license plates aloud.

From the back seat, I look at the town like a visitor. There's much too much traffic. People's faces inside their cars surprise me: no one over the age of twenty seems to have a neutral, let alone happy, expression. Men with jutting jaws and women squinting hard pass by. I find myself wondering why more of them don't wear sunglasses, and whether that might not help. My thoughts drift: the Gucci sunglasses I lost in London; the time I dressed as a skeleton for Halloween. In childhood, I appeared on Halloween as Felix the Cat, as Jiminy Cricket (I still have the cane, which I often pull out of the closet, mistaking it for an umbrella), and as a tomato.

"You know," my mother says to my brother, "your father had an entire family before he met us. He never mentioned them, either. Wasn't that cruel? If we'd met them, we might have liked them, and vice versa. Your sister gets upset if I say that's the case, but everything you read now suggests that it's better if the families meet. You have a ten-year-old brother from that first family. You're too old to be jealous of a child, aren't you? So there's no reason why you wouldn't get along."

"Mom," he says breathlessly.

"Your sister tells me every time we see each other that she's fifty-one. She's preoccupied with age. Being around an old person can do that. I'm old, but I forget to think about myself that way. Your sister is in the back seat right now thinking about mortality, mark my words."

My brother's knuckles are white on the wheel.

"Are we going to the hairdresser?" she says suddenly. She taps the back of her neck. Her fingers move up until they encounter small curls. When Tim realizes that I'm not going to answer, he says, "Your hair looks lovely, Mom. Don't worry about it."

"Well, I always like to be punctual when I have an appointment," she says.

I think how strange it is that I was never dressed up as Cleopatra, or as a ballerina. What was wrong with me that I wanted to be a tomato?

"Ma, on Halloween, was I ever dressed as a girl?"

In the mirror, my brother's eyes dart to mine. For a second, I remember Vic's eyes as he checked my reactions in the rearview mirror, those times I had my mother sit up front so the two of them could converse more easily.

"Well," my mother says, "I think one year you thought about being a nurse, but Joanne Willoughby was going to be a nurse. I was in the grocery store, and there was Mrs. Willoughby, fingering the costume we'd thought about the night before. It was wrong of me not to be more decisive. I think that's what made you impulsive as a grown-up."

"You think I'm impulsive? I think of myself as somebody who never does anything unexpected."

"I wouldn't say that," my mother says. "Look at that man you married when you didn't even really know him. The first husband. And then you married that man you knew way back in high school. It makes me wonder if you didn't inherit some of your father's fickle tendencies."

"Let's not fight," my brother says.

"What do you think other mothers would say if I told them both my children got married without inviting me to their weddings? I think some of them would think that must say something about me. Maybe it was my inadequacy that made your father consider us second-best. Tim, men tell other men things. Did your father tell you about the other family?"

Tim tightens his grip on the wheel. He doesn't answer. Our mother pats his arm. She says, "Tim wanted to be Edgar Bergen one year. Do you remember? But your father pointed out that we'd have to buy one of those expensive Charlie McCarthy dolls, and he wasn't about to do that. Little did we know, he had a whole other family to support."

Everyone at the Oaks is referred to formally as "Mrs." You can tell when the nurses really like someone, because they refer to her by the less formal "Miz."

Miz Banks is my mother's roommate. She has a tuft of pure white hair that makes her look like an exotic bird. She is ninety-nine.

"Today is Halloween, I understand," my mother says. "Are we going to have a party?"

The nurse smiles. "Whether or not it's a special occasion, we always have a lovely midday meal," she says. "And we hope the family will join us."

"It's suppertime?" Miz Banks says.

"No, ma'am, it's only ten a.m. right now," the nurse says loudly. "But we'll come get you for the midday meal, as we always do."

"Oh, God," Tim says. "What do we do now?"

The nurse frowns. "Excuse me?" she says.

"I thought Dr. Milrus was going to be here," he says. He looks around the room, as if Jack Milrus might be hiding somewhere. Not possible, unless he's wedged himself behind the desk that is sitting at an odd angle in the corner. The nurse follows his gaze and says, "Miz Banks's nephew has feng-shuied her part of the room."

Nearest the door—in our part of the room—there is white wicker furniture. Three pink bears teeter on a mobile hung from an air vent in the ceiling. On a bulletin board is a color picture of a baby with one tooth, grinning. Our mother has settled into a yellow chair and looks quite small. She eyes everyone, and says nothing.

"Would this be a convenient time to sign some papers?" the nurse asks. It is the second time that she has mentioned this—both times to my brother, not me.

"Oh, my God," he says. "How can this be happening?" He is not doing very well.

"Let's step outside and let the ladies get to know each other," the nurse says. She takes his arm and leads him through the door. "We don't want to be negative," I hear her say.

I sit on my mother's bed. My mother looks at me blankly. It is as if she doesn't recognize me in this context. She says, finally, "Whose Greek fisherman's cap is that?"

She is pointing to the Sony Walkman that I placed on the bed, along with an overnight bag and some magazines.

"That's a machine that plays music, Ma."

"No, it isn't," she says. "It's a Greek fisherman's cap."

I pick it up and hold it out to her. I press "play," and music can be heard through the dangling earphones. We both look at it as if it were the most curious thing in the world. I adjust the volume to low and put the earphones on her head. She closes her eyes. Finally, she says, "Is this the beginning of the Halloween party?"

"I threw you off, talking about Halloween," I say. "Today's just a day in early November."

"Thanksgiving is next," she says, opening her eyes.

"I suppose it is," I say. I notice that Miz Banks's head has fallen forward.

"Is that thing over there the turkey?" my mother says, pointing.

"It's your roommate."

"I was joking," she says.

I realize that I am clenching my hands only when I unclench them. I try to smile, but I can't hold up the corners of my mouth.

My mother arranges the earphones around her neck as if they were a stethoscope. "If I'd let you be what you wanted that time, maybe I'd have my own private nurse now. Maybe I wasn't so smart, after all."

"This is just temporary," I lie.

"Well, I don't want to go to my grave thinking you blame me for things that were out of my control. It's perfectly possible that your father was a bigamist. My mother told me not to marry him."

"Gramma told you not to marry Daddy?"

"She was a smart old fox. She sniffed him out."

"But he never did what you accuse him of. He came home from the war and married you, and you had us. Maybe we confused you by growing up so fast or something. I don't want to make you mad by mentioning my age, but maybe all those years that we were a family, so long ago, were like one long Halloween: we were costumed as children, and then we outgrew the costumes and we were grown."

She looks at me. "That's an interesting way to put it," she says.

"And the other family—maybe it's like the mixup between the man dreaming he's a butterfly, or the butterfly dreaming he's a man. Maybe you were confused after your stroke, or it came to you in a dream and it seemed real, the way dreams sometimes linger. Maybe you couldn't understand how we'd all aged, so you invented us again as young people. And for some reason Tim got frozen in time. You said the other wife looked like you. Well, maybe she *was* you."

"I don't know," my mother says slowly. "I think your father was just attracted to the same type of woman."

"But nobody ever met these people. There's no marriage license. He was married to you for almost fifty years. Don't you see that what I'm saying is a more likely explanation?"

"You really do remind me of that detective, Desperate Mason. You get an idea, and your eyes get big, just the way his do. I feel like you're about to lean into the witness stand."

Jack Milrus, a towel around his neck, stands in the doorway. "In a million years, you'll never guess why I'm late," he says. "A wheel came off a truck and knocked my car off the road, into a pond. I had to get out through the window and wade back to the highway."

A nurse comes up behind him with more towels and some dry clothes.

"Maybe it's just raining out, but it feels to him like he was in a pond," my mother says, winking at me.

"You understand!" I say.

"Everybody has his little embellishments," my mother says. "There wouldn't be any books to read to children and there would be precious few to read to adults if storytellers weren't allowed a few embellishments."

"Ma! That is absolutely true."

"Excuse me while I step into the bathroom and change my clothes."

"Humor him," my mother whispers to me behind her hand. "When he comes out, he'll think he's a doctor, but you and I will know that Jack is only hoping to go to medical school."

You think you understand the problem you're facing, only to find out there is another, totally unexpected problem.

There is much consternation and confusion among the nurses when Tim disappears and has not reappeared after nearly an hour. Jack Milrus weighs in: Tim is immature and irresponsible, he says. Quite possibly a much more severe problem than anyone suspected. My mother suggests slyly that Tim decided to fall down a rabbit hole and have an adventure. She says, "The rabbit hole's a more likely explanation," smiling smugly.

Stretched out in bed, her tennis shoes neatly arranged on the floor, my mother says, "He always ran away from difficult situations. Look at you and Jack, with those astonished expressions on your faces! Mr. Mason will find him," she adds. Then she closes her eyes.

"You see?" Jack Milrus whispers, guiding me out of the room. "She's adjusted beautifully. And it's hardly a terrible place, is it?" He answers his own question: "No, it isn't."

"What happened to the truck?" I ask.

"Driver apologized. Stood on the shoulder talking on his cell phone. Three cop cars were there in about three seconds. I got away by pointing to my MD plates."

"Did Tim tell you he just got married?"

"I heard that. During visiting hours, his wife took Donna aside to give her the happy news and to say that we weren't to slight him in any way, because he was ready, willing, and able—that was the way she said it to Donna—to assume responsibility for his mother's well-being. She also went to the hospital this morning just after you left and caused a commotion because they'd thrown away her wedding bouquet."

The phone call the next morning comes as a surprise. Like a telemarketer, Tim seems to be reading from a script: "Our relationship may be strained beyond redemption. When I went to the nurses' desk and saw that you had included personal information about me on a form you had apparently already filled out elsewhere, in collusion with your doctor friend, I realized that you were yet again condescending to me and subjecting me to humiliation. I was very hurt that you had written both of our names as 'Person to be notified in an emergency,' but then undercut that by affixing a Post-it note saying, 'Call me first. He's hard to find.' How would you know? How would you know what my teaching schedule is when you have never expressed the slightest interest? How do you know when I leave my house in the morning and when I return at night? You've always wanted to come first. It is also my personal opinion that you okayed the throwing out of my wife's nosegay, which was on loan to Mom. So go ahead and okay everything. Have her euthanized, if that's what you want to do, and see if I care. Do you realize that you barely took an insincere second to congratulate me and my wife? If you have no respect for me, I nevertheless expect a modicum of respect for my wife."

Of course, he does not know that I'm joking when I respond, "No, thanks. I'm very happy with my AT&T service."

When he slams down the phone, I consider returning to bed and curling into a fetal position, though at the same time I realize that I cannot miss one more day of work. I walk into the bathroom, wearing Vic's old bathrobe, which I hang on the back of the door. I shower and brush my teeth. I call the Oaks, to see if my mother slept through the night. She did, and is playing bingo. I dress quickly, comb my hair, pick up my purse and keys, and open the front door. A FedEx letter leans against the railing, with Cora's name and return address on it. I take a step back, walk inside, and open it. There is a sealed envelope with my name on it. I stare at it.

The phone rings. It is Mariah Roberts, 2003 Virginia Teacher of the Year for Grade Three, calling to say that she is embarrassed but it has been pointed out to her that children dressed as starfish and sea horses, dancing in front of dangling nets, represent species that are endangered, and often "collected" or otherwise "preyed upon," and that she wants to reimburse me for materials, but she most certainly does not want me to sew starfish costumes. I look across the bedroom, to the pointy costumes piled on a chair, only the top one still awaiting its zipper. They suddenly look sad—deflated, more than slightly absurd. I can't think what to say, and am surprised to realize that I'm too choked up to speak. "Not to worry," I finally say. "Is the whole performance canceled?" "It's being reconceived," she says. "We want sea life that is empowered." "Barracuda?" I say. "I'll run that by them," she says.

When we hang up, I continue to examine the sealed envelope. Then I pick up the phone and dial. To my surprise, Vic answers on the second ring.

"Hey, I've been thinking about you," he says. "Really. I was going to call and see how you were doing. How's your mother?"

"Fine," I say. "There's something that's been bothering me. Can I ask you a quick question?"

"Shoot."

"Donna Milrus said she saw you and Banderas having a fight."

"Yeah," he says warily.

"It's none of my business, but what caused it?"

"Jumped on the car and his claws scratched the paint."

"You said he was the best-trained dog in the world."

"I know it. He always waits for me to open the door, but that day, you tell me. He jumped up and clawed the hell out of the car. If he'd been scared by something, I might have made an allowance. But there was nobody. And then as soon as I swatted him, who gets out of her Lexus but Donna Milrus, and suddenly the grocery bag slips out of my hands and splits open . . . all this stuff rolling toward her, and she points the toe of one of those expensive shoes she wears and stops an orange."

"I can't believe that about you and Banderas. It shakes up all my assumptions."

"That's what happened," he says.

"Thanks for the information."

"Hey, wait. I really was getting ready to call you. I was going to say maybe we could get together and take your mother to the Italian place for dinner."

"That's nice," I say, "but I don't think so."

There is a moment's silence.

"Bye, Vic," I say.

"Wait," he says quickly. "You really called about the dog?"

"Uh-huh. You talked about him a lot, you know. He was a big part of our lives."

"There was and is absolutely nothing between me and my secretary, if that's what you think," he says. "She's dating a guy who works in Baltimore. I've got this dream that she'll marry him and leave the dog behind, because he's got cats."

"I hope for your sake that happens. I've got to go to work."

"How about coffee?" he says.

"Sure," I say. "We'll talk again."

"What's wrong with coffee right now?"

"Don't you have a job?"

"I thought we were going to be friends. Wasn't that your idea? Ditch me because I'm ten years younger than you, because you're such an ageist, but we can still be great friends, you can even marry some guy and we'll still be friends, but you never call, and when you do it's with some question about a dog you took a dislike to before you ever met him, because you're a jealous woman. The same way you can like somebody's kid, and not like them, I like the dog."

"You love the dog."

"Okay, so I'm a little leery about that word. Can I come over for coffee tonight, if you don't have time now?"

"Only if you agree in advance to do me a favor."

"I agree to do you a favor."

"Don't you want to know what it is?"

"No."

"It calls on one of your little-used skills."

"Sex?"

"No, not sex. Paper cutting."

"What do you want me to cut up that you can't cut up?"

"A letter from my sister-in-law."

"You don't have a sister-in-law. Wait: Your brother got married? I'm amazed. I thought he didn't much care for women."

"You think Tim is gay?"

"I didn't say that. I always thought of the guy as a misanthrope. I'm just saying I'm surprised. Why don't you rip up the letter yourself?"

"Vic, don't be obtuse. I want you to do one of those cutout things with it. I want you to take what I'm completely sure is something terrible and transform it. You know—that thing your grandmother taught you."

"Oh," he says. "You mean, like the fence and the arbor with the vine?"

"Well, I don't know. It doesn't have to be that."

"I haven't practiced in a while," he says. "Did you have something particular in mind?"

"I haven't read it," I say. "But I think I know what it says. So how about a skeleton with something driven through its heart?"

"I'm afraid my grandmother's interest was landscape."

"I bet you could do it."

"Sailboat riding on waves?"

"My idea is better."

"But out of my field of expertise."

"Tell me the truth," I say. "I can handle it. Did you buy groceries to cook that woman dinner?"

"No," he says. "Also, remember that you dumped me, and then for a finale you married some jerk, so I'd be entitled to do anything I wanted.

Then you call and want me to make a corpse with a stake through its heart because you don't like your new sister-in-law, either. Ask yourself: Am I so normal myself?"

Banderas nearly topples me, then immediately begins sniffing, dragging the afghan off the sofa. He rolls on a corner as if it were carrion, snorting as he rises and charges toward the bedroom.

"That's the letter?" Vic says, snatching the envelope from the center of the table. He rips it open. "Dear Sister-in-law," he reads, holding the paper above his head as I run toward him. He looks so different with his stubbly beard, and I realize with a pang that I don't recognize the shirt he's wearing. He starts again: "Dear Sister-in-law." He whirls sideways, the paper clutched tightly in his hand. "I know that Tim will be speaking to you, but I wanted to personally send you this note. I think that families have differences, but everyone's viewpoint is important. I would very much like—" He whirls again, and this time Banderas runs into the fray, rising up on his back legs as if he, too, wanted the letter.

"Let the dog eat it! Let him eat the thing if you have to read it out loud!" I say.

"—to invite you for Thanksgiving dinner, and also to offer you some of our frequent-flier miles, if that might be helpful, parenthesis, though it may be a blackout period, end paren."

Vic looks at me. "Aren't you embarrassed at your reaction to this woman? Aren't you?"

The dog leaps into the afghan and rolls again, catching a claw in the weave. Vic and I stand facing each other. I am panting, too shocked to speak.

"Please excuse Tim for disappearing when I came to the door of the Oaks. I was there to see if I could help. He said my face provoked a realization of his newfound strength." Vic sighs. He says, "Just what I was afraid of—some New Ager as crazy as your brother. 'I'm sure you understand that I was happy to know that I could be helpful to Tim in this trying time. We must all put the past behind us and celebrate our personal Thanksgiving, parenthesis, our wedding, end paren, and I am sure that everything can be put right when we get together. Fondly, your sister-in-law, Cora.'"

There are tears in my eyes. The afghan is going to need major repair. Vic has brought his best friend into my house to destroy it, and all he will do is hold the piece of paper above his head, as if he'd just won a trophy.

"I practiced this afternoon," he says finally, lowering his arm. "I can do either a train coming through the mountains or a garland of roses with a butterfly on top."

"Great," I say, sitting on the floor, fighting back tears. "The butterfly can be dreaming it's a man, or the man can be dreaming he's . . ." I change my mind about what I was going to say: "Or the man can be dreaming he's desperate."

Vic doesn't hear me; he's busy trying to get Banderas to drop a starfish costume he's capering with.

"Why do you think it would work?" I say to Vic. "We were never right for each other. I'm in my fifties. It would be my third marriage."

Carefully, he creases the letter a second, then a third time. He lifts the scissors out of their small plastic container, fumbling awkwardly with his big fingers. He frowns in concentration and begins to cut. Eventually, from the positive cuttings, I figure out that he's decided on the train motif. Cutting air away to expose a puff of steam, he says, "Let's take it slow, then. You could invite me to go with you to Thanksgiving."

Coping Stones

Cahill—Dr. Cahill to those who knew him in his small town in Maine—had decided that his screened porch should be relocated. Wouldn't it be better to winterize the current porch, adding a door at the far end which would lead to a new, smaller porch, perpendicular to the original? That way, he could walk out of the kitchen in the winter with his cup of freshly brewed coffee and his vitamin drink (those mornings when he went to the trouble to make it) and enjoy the late-blooming flowers on an enclosed, heated porch. In the summer, he could set up a makeshift desk—probably just the card table—and not have to worry that rain would ruin his paperwork. There was so much paperwork! His wife, Barbara, used to manage most of it, but she'd been dead for more than eight years, and, except for what his accountant did and the occasional question he asked his tenant, Matt, he dealt with it all himself now, and not a bit of it had anything to do with medicine.

Matt lived in Cahill's renovated barn. Thirty-two years old, he had already suffered a divorce (at twenty-four) and the death of his second wife, who'd been knocked out of her kayak by a low-hanging branch and drowned, in Canada. Several times during the past year, Cahill had noticed Matt coming home with a woman, but he'd also noticed that the woman—or women—almost always left the same night. Once, he had been lured into playing a game of croquet with Matt and a woman named Leora, but usually he avoided contact when Matt had company; he felt that Matt became sour and withdrawn when women were around, as if he were still suffering through adolescence. But Matt—Matt was his preoccupation. Cahill had the sense to extend fewer dinner invitations to his tenant and friend than he wanted to, because the man needed his freedom. If Barbara were alive, and if Matt's wife had not died, Matt would no doubt have been living somewhere else, and Cahill would have had more interesting things to think about. It was just that his world had shrunk since he'd retired.

Right now, Cahill was talking to a man Matt had nicknamed You Know What I Mean, a tall, perpetually windblown-looking carpenter whom Cahill had recently advised to have what he felt sure was a skin cancer removed from the side of his nose. His real name was Roadie Petruski, and, as Roadie tried to smooth down his electrified hair, Cahill listened to his beliefs concerning pressure-treated wood: "You know yourself, Doc, these things leach into the environment. Before you know it, your lungs are Swiss cheese, you know what I mean? This genetically engineered corn, the Europeans don't want nothing to do with it. But us? We always got optimism. You probably read about rat kidneys shutting down when they was fed the stuff? I read it in one of those doctor's-office magazines—meaning no disrespect. My advice is always to seal up pressure-treated boards with the best sealant available, and even then you don't want to walk on it without shoes, you know what I mean?"

"Whatever you think best in terms of flooring, Roadie," Cahill said.

"Not up to me! Always up to the customer!"

"Well, I certainly agree with what you've informed me of, so let us proceed as you suggest."

"That's the thing, Doc. That's the direction you want to go."

In the distance, a cardinal twittered on a tree branch. If Cahill had had his binoculars, he would have raised them—he loved cardinals—but they were on the back porch. The same back porch that was going to be transformed into a heated room off the kitchen. Matt must be at home, Cahill thought: he could faintly hear Mick Jagger singing. The bird, too, must have heard the music, because it swooped away, dipping down for just a second to check out the goings-on on the porch.

A man he and Matt had dubbed You Got No Choice had visited a few days earlier. He'd come from town hall to inform Cahill that a wall on his property was in need of maintenance, and that, as the owner of the property on which the wall stood, surrounding a four-headstone cemetery dating back to the eighteen-hundreds, Cahill was responsible for repairs; he had no choice. There had been a lot of freezing during the winter, the man explained, and spring had been unusually wet. Such things accelerated deterioration. Cahill was told that he must keep "vegetation" six feet from the wall in all directions (he had no choice) and that no mortar could be used in rebuilding it. "I took a look just now, Doc, and from what I can tell it's pretty much just a matter of replacing some of them coping stones along the top," the man said, moving one hand up and down to indicate peaks and gulleys. "And—just to remind you—it's all gotta be done by hand." He handed Cahill a Post-it note with "URGNT fx g-yard wall 7/16" written on it in pencil, and then nodded while backing away, as though he were taking leave of the Queen of England. If Cahill hadn't known better, he would have thought he was being made fun of. The man climbed into his truck and drove away, music blaring. Tchaikovsky's notes bit the air like muriatic acid.

Following the encounter, Cahill proceeded directly to Matt's, where he knocked and entered to find him starting a new painting of a fruit bowl. Matt's still lifes were distinguished by the unconventional objects he included—plastic rhinos, a single beaded earring, a Princess Di figurine lying on its side. Cahill was gratified not to see a beer bottle on Matt's table. The daytime drinking was new, and not a good sign. The painting class—of course it was harmless, and no doubt interesting, but did he imagine that solitary painting was a way of rejoining the world? In his opinion, Matt had got entirely too large a payment from his wife's life-insurance company. Cahill had a millionaire living in his barn and functioning variously as his repairman, class clown, snow-removal guy, and sometime chauffeur. But he liked Matt, relied on him. The cliché would probably be that Matt was the son he never had, but then his daughter, Joyce, was enough like a son: in spite of his dire warnings, for years she'd taken steroids and lifted weights. The year her mother died, she had come East and chopped down the dead trees on his property and sawed and stacked them for firewood. She had size-11 feet encased in men's work boots, and a tattoo on her arm of the nation's flag, below which lurked a spiny lizard with a tongue unfurled to capture an insect. It seemed likely that Matt had a nickname for Joyce, too, but he'd had the good manners to keep quiet about it.

Cahill examined Matt's odd painting and pronounced it "coming along." He grumbled briefly about the visit from You Got No Choice, which provoked—as Cahill knew it would—negative generalizations about the self-righteousness of New Englanders.

On his way back to the house, Cahill went to inspect the graveyard. He had not noticed that the wall there was in need of repair, nor had he thought that anyone would tell him that fixing it was his responsibility. In the plot lay two children, one aged three, the other eleven months, the cuts in their stones mostly filled with moss. Their mother had died at twenty-three, the father at seventy-one—a good age to have attained. No headstone indicated another marriage. Pink and white phlox grew nearby, and sometimes—rarely, but sometimes—Cahill would cut a few stalks and put them in one of his late wife's crystal vases to commemorate her domesticity.

That afternoon, Napoleon, the neighbor's basset hound, paid a visit and was rewarded—though Cahill knew it was wrong—with one saltine. Cahill flipped through a copy of *Science News* and, finally, an hour or so later, walked the basset hound to the road, picking him up for the dangerous crossing, then down four houses, where he saw that Breezy's car was gone and the back gate unlatched. He led the dog into the backyard and firmly shut the gate.

A week or so after You Got No Choice stopped by, a letter arrived from Code Enforcement informing "Property Owner Cahill" that he was in violation of an assemblage of hyphenated numbers. He was so angry that he could hardly focus on what it said. You Got No Choice had told him that he had thirty days in which to make repairs. Nevertheless, after he made a cup of tea and stopped fuming, he put on his work clothes and stalked into the yard. He took his tool kit with him, though he didn't know why; it seemed the sort of job best done with one's hands. He saw that his tool kit contained work gloves, so he put them on and set about replacing the rocks that had fallen. Some were missing, but where had they gone? Matt must have moved them to mow and stacked them somewhere. But he'd already interrupted Matt once that morning, so he decided to find the few rocks he needed elsewhere. He took off the gloves and dropped them back in the tool kit. As he did, a wasp came out of nowhere, like a stealth bomber, and stung him. He yanked his hand sideways in pain, wincing and squeezing his wrist. In the house, he made a paste of baking soda and water in a teacup and smeared it on, then swallowed an antihistamine, just in case.

When the Benadryl kicked in, he went upstairs to lie down, and he was surprised when he woke up hours later. He went into the bathroom and undressed, turned on the shower, and stepped in, grasping the shower bar. What would his wife have said of this latest mishap? That he had somehow invited the wasp? Barbara had had many good qualities, but charity toward him when he was hurt was not among them. He thought that perhaps it had frightened her, to know that he was human. She had said many times, only half-jokingly, that she'd married a man she thought could take good care of her.

He dried off with his favorite towel, threw it over the shower door, and went downstairs, where he made another cup of tea. His wrist was tender but no longer painful. Napoleon was standing silently at the porch door. The dog was going to be killed crossing Route 91. Didn't Breezy care? He opened the door, and the basset hound bounded in, something clamped in his teeth. It was a dead chipmunk. Napoleon dropped it, with its bitten bloody neck, at Cahill's feet and looked up expectantly.

"Maybe the doctor could work it in around five o'clock," Cahill said, staring down at the creature. "But the doctor is a very busy man, you know."

The dog knew none of these words. Cahill relented. "Good boy," he said to the dog, who wagged his tail furiously and nosed the chipmunk, then looked up for further approval. This would have set his wife screaming. Cahill patted the dog's head, keeping it from the dead thing, then picked the chipmunk up by its tail and dropped it in the trash. This meant that he would have to take the trash out immediately, but no matter. He washed his hands. All those years of careful washing, using the brush, scrubbing under nonexistent fingernails—oh, his precious hands. Now a minuscule rim of fingernail protruded on a few of his fingers, and this brought him a certain sense of pride. He'd never tell anyone anything so ridiculous, but there it was: he liked having fingernails. "We are two very impressive gentlemen, aren't we?" he said to the dog. The interrogative always made the dog's tail wag frantically. "But maybe it's time to be getting home—what do you say?" He looked at the list of phone numbers taped to his refrigerator, then welled up with sudden anger: he'd call Breezy, and she could walk over and get her dog this time. Enough of the escort service. He dialed her number. Above the phone was hung a copy of an etching he had always loved, and had kept above his desk in the private part of his office: "Abraham's Sacrifice," by Rembrandt, the angel's hands so exquisitely, so lightly placed. "Breezy?" he said, when he heard her voice. "I've got Napoleon over here and I think it's time for him to come home, if you'd be so kind."

"I am sorry. Did he run away again?" Breezy asked. "Ever since I started taking classes up in Orono, there's no keeping him in the yard. But the other thing is, he just loves you. It's hard to keep him behind the fence."

"I noticed that. He's going to be hit by a car, Breezy, and you're never going to forgive yourself. You've got to do something about that gate latch."

He looked at the dog, sniffing the trash can. It was too tall for him to get his snout in.

"Absolutely," she said. "I'm going to speak to Ed at the hardware store about how to fix the latch. Tomorrow."

"They're open till nine tonight," he said.

"Morty, you do not hint subtly!" she exclaimed. "I'm overwhelmed tonight, if you must know, with Father having misplaced his glasses and his teeth, and he's got a terrible cold, so he's in a foul mood. The practical nurse didn't show up today, either."

"A lot of part-timers in that profession," he said. "Doesn't make for reliability."

"Well, Morty, that may be true, but what alternative do I have? If dear Barbara were still alive, I could at least get a hug."

Breezy had been his wife's best friend. She had received endless sympathy from Barbara—especially concerning her father's move into her house. Breezy was one of the reasons that Barbara had wanted to spend what turned out to be the last winter of her life in Maine.

After they hung up, Breezy did not appear for so long that he suspected she might not be coming at all. The dog lay curled next to him in the living room, as Cahill read a book called *How Buildings Learn,* his feet stretched out on the footstool. Finally, she arrived.

"Morty, I hope I didn't cause you pain by mentioning Barbara," she blurted, instead of saying hello. The dog rose and shook himself, ambling toward her. She bent and stroked his side. "You ran away again," she said. "Did Napoleon run away again?"

"Exile to Elba next time," Cahill said.

"I've been to the hardware store. Ed was off tonight, but I left a note saying I came in and that it was an emergency. We are going to solve this problem, aren't we?" she said in baby talk to the dog. Then she turned to Cahill. "Morty, I feel sometimes that when I say something you aren't . . . I don't know . . . that you don't approve of what I'm saying. I don't want a gold star for going to the hardware store, but I did go there as you suggested."

"I'm afraid the dog is going to be hit by a car, Breezy," he said, with the firm sympathy of a doctor giving a bad diagnosis. He heard his voice pitched a bit too low, and softened. "Just a long day," he said, standing. Breezy—she'd got her nickname because she loved to talk—was clearly hoping to be asked to stay for a cup of tea. But it had been a bad day—the officious letter, the wasp—and he realized that he'd had nothing to eat since breakfast. He patted Breezy's shoulder as if she were a patient he was steering gently out the door. At the front stoop, she turned to face him and said, "I know you miss her very much, Morty. I do, too, every day of my life," and then she was gone, down the steps, curving with the path into the night, Napoleon—so named because the dog did not like to chew on bones, though he liked to tear the bones apart (the sole original thing he'd ever known Breezy's father to come up with)—trotting along on his leash without a backward glance.

Cahill went into the kitchen and took a potpie from the freezer, placed it on a cookie sheet, and set the oven for four-fifty. Though the oven had not reached the correct temperature, he put his dinner in anyway. Then came another knock at the front door: most certainly Breezy, back for some reason.

Cahill went to the door and opened it. A young woman was standing there.

"Dr. Cahill?" she said. "Excuse me for knocking so late. I'm Audrey Comstock. I live in Portsmouth."

"Yes?" he said.

"May I come in? I'm a friend of Matt's."

"Enter," he said, gesturing toward the living room. She walked in and looked around. She did not sit, nor did he motion toward a chair. Patients were that way: some would remain standing forever if you did not formally offer them a seat. "What can I do for you?" he said.

"Get him to marry me," she said.

"Excuse me?"

"He doesn't think he can leave here. You," she amended. "Leave you."

"I know nothing about this," he said.

"We've been seeing each other for more than a year. We met at a painting group in Portsmouth. At Christmas, he all but proposed."

"Oh?" he said. At Christmas, Matt had prepared a goose and cooked parsnips from the root cellar. They had eaten the meal with some Stonewall Kitchen condiment—a sort of jelly with garlic. Was he to believe that all that time Matt had been in love but had never mentioned the person's name? Of course, anything was possible. A patient having a physical would say that nothing was bothering him, and only when he'd taken off his shirt would Cahill see that he was broken out in shingles, or had cut himself badly and wasn't properly healing.

"I'm not sure why you're here," he said. She was an unpleasant-looking woman—in her early twenties, he thought. Her beak of a nose, crammed too tightly between her small eyes, made it difficult to look at her with a neutral expression.

She said, "I wanted to tell you that you wouldn't be losing a son; you'd be gaining a daughter."

"My child is grown and gone," he said. "I am looking for neither."

She looked at him blankly for a moment. "He doesn't feel like he can leave," she said again.

"I assure you he can," Cahill said.

"We have our art work in common," she said, as if he'd asked for further explanation.

He looked at her.

"Matt and me," she said finally.

"This matter is entirely between you and Matt," he said. "You don't have to persuade me of anything."

"He respects you. You're like a father figure to him. It's just that he doesn't think he can leave you."

"You've said that many times," Cahill said. "I've explained that he can leave."

"He loves me," she said. "He said he'd take care of me."

"Well," he said, "perhaps you can work things out. When people are meant to be together, such things have been known to happen."

"You're trying to get rid of me," she said in a trembling voice. "You don't think I'm good enough."

"Please do me the favor of not attempting to read my mind," he said. "I was about to eat a late dinner when you knocked, and now it's time to do that, if you'll excuse me."

She stamped her foot. The woman was ridiculous; he would have to get a peephole and not let such people in.

"Can I see?" she said plaintively.

Cahill stared at her. "See what?" he said.

"Just once, can I find out if somebody's trying to get rid of me or if you're really eating dinner?"

He almost expressed his surprise, but checked his reaction. He leveled his eyes on her, wondering whether she wasn't shamed by her own childishness. Of course, such people rarely were. "By all means," he said. "The kitchen door is right there."

Surely she would not really go in, but no—of course she would. Like an obese patient advised to diet who would proceed immediately to the nearest vending machine for a candy bar. There she went, to view his potpie. She would be seeing that, and the landslide of mostly unread newspapers that needed to be thrown out, a few days' worth of dirty dishes in the sink. He had not yet carried out the trash, so perhaps even the dead chipmunk had begun to smell.

"That's all you're eating?" she said, returning to the room. In a gentler tone of voice, she said, "I could cook for you. Make extra when I cook for Matt and me."

"I assume Matt doesn't know you're here?" he said.

She shrugged. "I can't find him," she said. "I thought maybe he was here."

He gestured toward the front door. "When you find him, you can discuss with him these generous impulses," he said. "I wish you good night."

She started to say something. He could almost sense the second when she decided against it and turned to leave. He followed her out the door and stood on the stoop. No lights were on in the barn. The stars shone brightly, and there was a faint, wind-chime-tinged breeze. Breezy's house was the only one he could see that was lit. Matt's car was not in the driveway. Audrey waved sadly, overacting, the poor child cast out into the night. He did not return the wave.

Damn the woman! There was nothing he liked less than getting caught up in other people's soap operas. He wrote a quick note on the pad by the phone and walked over to stick it to Matt's front door. "Met your friend Audrey," the note said. "Stop by when you get back."

The next morning, when he answered his front door he saw not Matt but Deirdre Rambell, who worked as a secretary at town hall and had heard about what she called, with hushed sincerity, the situation. "Deirdre, it's a few rocks that I've already put back," he said. "The town is making a mountain out of a molehill."

"Oh, it's the Historical Society, you know. The volunteers go around checking, and they really care. For my own part, I've always felt the dead have souls that cannot be at peace when they sense any lack of respect."

"Souls sense respect?" he said. He realized with slight embarrassment that although he was wearing chinos, he still had on his pajama top.

"Indeed they do," she said.

"Then let me inform you, Deirdre, that at this point I have replaced all but a couple of the six or seven stones necessary to give the souls their deserved respect. Let me also ask you this: Do you happen to really know or care anything about the people buried on this property? About their lives, I mean—as people, rather than as souls?"

Nothing in his tone registered with her. "Aren't they Moultons?" she said. "Fine people, among the first settlers."

"Onward!" she exclaimed when she finally drove away.

Yes, he thought, that sort of woman always feels that she's making progress.

You Got No Choice appeared next, apologizing for what he called the "slipup" at town hall. "That lamebrained letter was embarrassing," he said, rolling his eyes. "I just found out, Doc, and came right over to apologize."

"You, and the rest of the town, will be relieved to know that, as infirm as I am, the wall has been repaired, and now all is well with the world."

"Excellent, Doc!" He tugged the brim of his cap.

"You wouldn't have seen Matt's van anywhere around town, would you?" Cahill said. "I haven't seen him in a while."

"Are you kidding?" You Got No Choice said.

"Kidding?"

"You don't know?"

"Know what?" Cahill said.

"Up in Warren," he said warily, as if Cahill might be having him on. "It's been all over the papers."

You Got No Choice saw the answer in Cahill's expression. "Doc—they got him on some molesting-a-minor thing, or something. I didn't want to bring up a sore subject. I know he was like a son to you. You get rounded up by the cops, you got no choice—you go where the Man says you go, right? Don't mean you're guilty."

Cahill put his hand out to brace himself on the door frame. His mind was racing, but it moved neither backward nor forward. It raced like a car on a lift, with someone inside gunning the engine.

"Sorry to drop a bomb on you. Articles have been in the paper every day, as far's I know."

"It's impossible," Cahill said, having recovered enough to speak, though he could hardly hear his own voice.

"Say what?"

"Why wouldn't he have called me? Why wouldn't police have come to the barn, why—"

"There you go," You Got No Choice said. "Fishy, huh? You got a point; it's odd if they haven't made no search."

Cahill almost tripped on the rug in the entryway on his way back into the house. He walked toward the kitchen and the pile of papers, which he wanted to look through immediately, and not at all. "Real life," as his wife would have said. He sank into a kitchen chair and brushed the newspapers onto the floor, putting his head in his hands. The phone rang, and he got up and walked numbly toward it. Matt? Calling to say what? "This is Joyce," his daughter said.

"Joyce, my dear, this is not a time I can talk," he said, but another voice intruded. "And this is Tara," a younger, more high-pitched voice sing-alonged, and he realized he'd been talking to a recording. He heard chimes, and the first unmistakable notes of the wedding march. His daughter's voice said, "We're sending this recording on the happiest day of our lives to announce that at one o'clock July 20, 2005, we were joined together in a commitment cere-mony, blessed by Mother Goddess Devi, and we are now officially Joyce"—the squeaky voice broke in—"and Tara." "Forever!" the voices shouted in unison. Next, he recognized the familiar strident voice of his daughter: "Don't be put out that you weren't invited," she said. "Our ceremony consisted of only Mother Devi, Tara's brother who lives next door—who did a bee-yoo-tee-ful Sufi dance—and our little girl Fluffy Sunshine, with a collar of bells and white pansies." Tara broke in: "When you get this message, we'll be in the air to Hawaii." "Peace and love to you, and may you recognize the happiness we have experienced today," his daughter said. Bells clanged merrily; over their ringing, he heard them giggling, voices overlapping: "*Inshallah.* G-g-g-goodbye, folks!"

He put his head in his hands again, pushing his fingertips against his eyelids until he felt pain.

He went to the barn in the dark, shining the flashlight in front of him. It had rained, and tiny frogs leaped across the dirt road like tiddlywinks. In front of him grew the rhododendrons that Matt had been so delighted to have found in some nursery's compost heap: two of them, with electric-lavender flowers, grown large beside the door. The ink on Cahill's Post-it note had run into one black smear. He knocked, though it was obvious that the place was deserted. He had read enough in the paper to make him sick.

An oversized T-shirt was draped over an oak ladder-back chair. Matt had glued the chair's leg for him some months back, and somehow it had remained in the barn. On the kitchen table were a few shiny copper pennies, and a *Little Mermaid* key ring. Cahill felt revulsion. He was also afraid that the police might zoom in on the barn and find him there, snooping. He understood sadly and too late about the toys that Matt had taken pride in rescuing from the dump. They were to lure children, of course. The tag-sale Barbies on the bathroom shelf, stripped of clothes and bracketing the can of shaving cream, the bathroom glass, and the electric razor that Cahill had given Matt for his birthday—he saw the dolls as the bait they were. How could he have been so obtuse?

He sat in his old chair and surveyed the room. It resonated with silence. This had once been his wife's dance studio, the place where she practiced— only for the love of it; she'd been too old to seriously dance ballet. This had been her private place, where she watched tapes of Nureyev dancing and no doubt imagined herself being lifted high by his strong hands; where she wore tights and one of Cahill's old white shirts long beyond the time when she would have appeared coquettish in such attire. But now he had to accept the fact that the barn had been desecrated, inhabited for years by a person he'd misjudged, toward whom his wife would have felt the greatest contempt. A slight smell of sweat hung in the air—at least, the kitchen had that odor. He got up and opened the refrigerator—not expecting a Jeffrey Dahmer banquet but checking nonetheless. A bottle of cheap champagne lay on its side, and a couple of packs of moldy cheese, unsealed. Yellow celery lay in a brownish puddle in the drawer. The opened cans he didn't peer into. He took out the one can of Coke, pulled back the top, and drank it, hoping it would settle his stomach. It was not exactly reassuring that the police hadn't come. Hadn't they made Matt tell them where he lived? He saw an old calendar held with a magnet to the side of the refrigerator: Shirley Temple as a child, sniffing a yellow daisy. Oh, the banality of it. The sad predictability of people's intense yet ultimately unoriginal desires. "You're so superior?" his wife used to chide. Well, yes, he was. At least to some. He took another sip and put the can aside. Well: there were no lollipops. No pictures of little girls naked on the computer, because Matt did not own a computer. A back-to-basics child molester.

It might be, Cahill thought, that the space itself was cursed. There was the time, during its reconstruction, when the carpenter—a strong-bodied, red-haired woman named Elsie—had flirted with him, the strap of her sweaty tank top fallen from one shoulder, and he had questioned her with his eyes, and she had answered in the affirmative. He had moved toward her and gently slipped down the other strap, intending only a kiss to such peach-perfect breasts, when, with the timing of a bad movie, Deirdre Rambell had walked into the barn, carrying the sandwiches and drinks his wife had sent out on a tray. It was funny now—or, if not funny, he still took pleasure in having shocked Deirdre, that holier-than-thou woman. There had been no chance in the world that she would ever report what she'd seen to Barbara. He could still hear the glasses rattling on the tray.

He called the police from Matt's phone—a rotary dial, another of Matt's Salvation Army finds. That was what Cahill thought Matt had been doing: going here and there, collecting trivia as a way of getting over his wife's death. The policeman who answered on the eighth ring—eighth!—seemed none too interested in what he was saying until he raised his voice. "That child molester you've got up there in Warren," he said. "You might want to come over to his house and check through it. This is his landlord calling." Already, he had retreated from the notion of friendship. "I can't understand why you haven't been here before now," he added. The Coke rose up his throat, the acid rush subsiding sickly. He looked at a pencil sketch of trees in an open sketchbook on the counter. A rather lovely little depiction. Well, he thought, nobody does what they do all the time. Another person came on the phone and took down his name and address. When the police appeared, about fifteen minutes later—local police first—he found out three things: that Matt had given an address in Syracuse, though he claimed he'd been living out of his van; and that there *was* an address in Syracuse—the address of his second wife, who was not dead at all. The third thing he found out, but not until they were leaving, was that Matt had got into an altercation with a man in the holding cell and had been stabbed with a homemade shiv.

A few weeks later, Cahill received a note from You Got No Choice, whom he now resolved to think of, more charitably, as Bill: "My boss is breathing down my neck and even though these are rough times and you have my heartfelt condolences, Doc, the wall around the grave still hasn't been fixed to come up to code. I'd be glad to drop by this weekend and have at it with some stone." It was nice of Bill to offer to pitch in, but the letter only strengthened Cahill's resolve to fix the wall himself.

Which he set out to do, after eating a grilled-cheese sandwich for lunch. Protein and carbohydrates were good together, midday. Bad eating had contributed to his wife's untimely death; she'd been diabetic and sometimes wouldn't eat anything for an entire day, calling him a nag. She "felt sick," yes, but it was a vicious circle: feel sick, don't eat; don't eat, feel sick.

He walked to the side of the house where the soil was mixed with chips of old brick and rocks. Nothing much would grow in the shady area, but it was a good place to harvest rocks. He piled them into a discarded one-gallon plastic flowerpot. After some digging, he had what he hoped was enough, and set off with the pot pressed to his ribs, his other hand grasping the handle of his toolbox. Hi ho, hi ho. He wondered if Matt would expect him to get in touch. Hear his side of things. Offer help—if not as a doctor, then as a friend? Whatever Matt expected, Cahill could not bring himself to make an attempt to contact him—at least, not at this point in time.

The barn wasn't roped off, though he supposed it wasn't really a crime scene. So many men had come in unmarked cars lately: anybody could have been rummaging around inside, after a while. What was he supposed to do, run out every time he saw another car and ask to see identification?

Cahill turned to see Napoleon bounding across the lawn, foolish ears flapping like luffing sails. The dog tipped sideways as he came close, rudderless with friendliness. "Come to see the old man?" he said. In answer, Napoleon snapped at a bug. "Cross the busy road for the billionth time, tempting fate?" He rubbed the dog beneath his ears. "Let's let her come after you if and when she gets lonely, yeah," Cahill said, continuing to scratch. While he stacked rocks, he kept an eye on the dog, who was nosing at the edge of the woods.

The wall repair took longer than he'd anticipated, and he had to get the shovel and dig up one quite large stone from beside the porch, but finally he stood back and admired his handiwork. "There you go, Bill, my friend," he said aloud, saluting the air. "Your job done, my job done." He cleaned some fallen leaves and bits of stick out of the area, stepping carefully around the wall. What had they died of, these four? In those days, people could die from an infected tooth. Dying young was to be expected: young, then, had another meaning.

By the time his daughter had graduated from high school, he hadn't loved her or his wife for some time. His fingertips scratching beneath Napoleon's ears now communicated more sincerity than all the kisses he'd planted formally on the cheeks of his wife and daughter. His wife knew that he'd done things automatically, without feeling. "Reading your rhymes like they make order of things," she'd sneered, as, in her last days, he sat beside her bed reading poems by Yeats, or D. H. Lawrence, poems that rarely rhymed. It was clear where his daughter got her mocking ability. She'd pattern-stepped into bitterness, too. She'd complained about being named for a man (James Joyce), especially for a man whose own daughter had ended up a madwoman. But what ultra-feminine name had she wished they'd given her, what other rose would have gone better with her scuffed work boots and her black-framed glasses? He had no wand of malice; age alone had turned his wife into a failed ballerina, while genetic signals had resulted in her diabetes. He had determined nothing about his daughter's future by naming her Joyce; it was her own doing that made her what she was. He'd provided well for them, even after he'd stopped loving them. You could will yourself to stop (as he'd done upon hearing the revelations about Matt), or you could stop slowly, point the blades of your skates inward, so to speak, so that coming to a halt was done gracefully, sometimes unnoticed by you or by others. He thought of some lines from Byron:

> . . . I seek no sympathies, nor need;
> The thorns which I have reap'd are of the tree
> I planted: they have torn me, and I bleed:
> I should have known what fruit would spring from such a seed.

There it was! The thorns and bloodshed were a bit of a cliché, but look at the poet's real passion. To know something about oneself—that was what caused that pleasurable ache which put one in another state entirely. Too much time was lost trying to figure out other people.

There had been nights in recent years when he had sat awake, a tumbler in his hand filled with chilly Perrier (as a young man, he would have had a glass of brandy), reading to Matt. What did it mean that someone who appreciated poetry also appreciated, sexually, children? Oh, he supposed he knew that humans were "complicated," that they clung to exteriors, that they instinctively turned away from the illustrations in *Gray's Anatomy,* which offered factual information about their inner selves; why did people have no interest in the real coherence of their inner workings, the rhythms of the muscles, the—all right—poetry of the vascular system? He knew that these were the thoughts of a peculiar old man, marginalized and dismissed for years, acerbically pronounced upon by his daughter. Guileless children told the truth? They did, but not so well as poets.

On his way back to the house, he picked up the day's mail. He found in the pile a newsletter from the A.A.R.P., a packet of coupons, a letter from a local charity, and—he almost dropped the flyer—a grainy photocopied picture:

"MISSING PERSON," it read, and gave her age as sixteen. Last seen in Portsmouth, New Hampshire. He remembered Audrey standing at his door. But could this be the same girl, if she was only sixteen? He held the page farther away, squinting. Audrey's eyes followed him as if he held a hologram. He wandered into the living room, debating whether to call the police yet again. Audrey's having been a friend of Matt's, her visit . . . all of it would be of interest to them. It was his obligation to call—he really should—but for the moment he thought that, actually, no one had done much for him lately, except to hassle him about rebuilding a pointless wall around a graveyard. It also occurred to him that he did not want to be the one to put another nail in Matt's coffin, so to speak: Matt's friendship with the disturbed teenage girl could not possibly help his cause, whatever had or had not gone on between the two of them. Cahill decided that he could use a shower and a nap.

This many years after her death, he was still using his wife's Dove soap. Yellowed packages of it were stacked here and there, even in canisters in the pantry. You discovered people's secret stashes when they died. The little, unknown things filled them in, as if they hadn't had quite enough dimension in life. Or perhaps those discoveries took them farther away, dried-out cigarettes and hidden half-pints reminding you that everyone was little known.

He turned on the fan and curled onto the bed, and when he awoke it was evening, and he was in a cold sweat. Sounds he'd been making had awoken him, and he struggled up so suddenly from a dream that he knocked his arm against the light. It was a dream, it had been a dream, but it had been so shockingly real. He went into the bathroom and splashed water on his face, but the water only intensified his already palpable dread. He all but ran down the stairs and across the lawn to the graveyard. He had dreamed that Audrey was buried there. Just hours earlier he'd seen that the ground was undisturbed, yet he had gone to sleep and smelled the newly dug soil, felt its graininess beneath his fingernails, stared wide-eyed at the fallen gravestones.

His horrific vision—the only one he'd ever had—turned out to have some validity, though it was wrong in the specifics. There was no sign of digging, but there were scratch marks in the soil, and the smallest of the gravestones was leaning toward the ground. But no: the ground had not been dug in. In the center of the plot—he could not stop a wry smile: dead center—was a pile of dog shit, immense in size. A mound of it. Napoleon!

Some of Cahill's earlier handiwork had been toppled yet again, and he realized with embarrassment that his efforts had been slapdash.

He went back to the house and found Roadie standing in the hallway inside the screen door, holding his cap in one hand and a clipboard in the other. "Roadie," Cahill said.

"Yes, sir," Roadie said, replacing his cap on his head. It said "SHERYL CROW."

Cahill blurted, "Neighbor's dog just took a huge crap in my backyard. Really annoying."

"Dog's gotta do what a dog's gotta do," Roadie said.

"Right," he said.

Roadie cleared his voice. "Doc, I've talked to two people I respect, who've advised two different approaches to your porch situation. One thinks sliding thermal doors, and, for my personal opinion, it's more money but that's what I'd be inclined to go with."

"Then that sounds fine with me, Roadie," Cahill said.

"Approach No. 2, Doc, for full disclosure, this comes from Hank, down at Elbriddle's. He thinks . . ."

He let Roadie drone on. As a younger man, he might have studied the figures longer, asked more questions, but if it was Roadie's opinion that the first option was the best, he was inclined to go along.

"Awful about your friend," Roadie said suddenly, with no segue. "My wife said, 'Don't you be bringing that up, it's none of your business, and how do you think the doctor feels? Don't tell me that no-good didn't hoodwink him, because the doctor wouldn't have a tenant but what he thought he was an honorable man—'"

Roadie stopped, seeing that Cahill was numbed by this sudden outpouring. Roadie cleared his throat again—a nervous habit. He said, "Men like that ain't much liked by other men. Way I've always heard it, you'd get more sympathy from the jailbirds if you killed your mother than if you've fooled with a child. I've got Hannahlee and Junior, as you know. Any pervert touched a hair on their head, I'd be on 'em in one second flat. How do you suppose a guy like that seemed so regular?"

Silence. Finally, Cahill spoke. "Roadie," he said, "do you think I should undertake such a project at all, given my age? Do you think I'll last the winter to enjoy it?"

Roadie's tongue darted over his lips. "Well, Doc, you'd know the answer better than me. You in bad health?"

"No," Cahill said.

"Well, I ain't here to build if you think your money should best be used elsewhere, but a closed-in porch with a real one down at the end? That's something I'd spring for if I had the money."

For Roadie, this was tactful—turning the subject from death to money. Roadie made a fist and pounded a black ant racing across the table. "Something my wife said, she said, 'Roadie, you go over there and express some human kindness to the doctor. That's a man's done a lot for a lot of people, and, if he had a moment of misjudgment, you tell me who hasn't.' She says, 'Come to think of it, I guess time's proven me a fool for marrying somebody like you, needs this much instruction before he goes to see somebody who lost his wife and his friend!'"

"She thinks herself a fool for marrying you?" Cahill said.

"You met Gloria Sue. Turns out she married me thinking I was going to build the Taj Mahal, or something. Where'd she get that? Nothing I ever told her."

"Do you love her?" Cahill said.

Roadie looked up, surprised. "Well, I don't know," he said slowly.

"I stopped loving my wife," Cahill said. "First, I thought I was just overloaded with all her minor annoyances—snoring, refusing to take her diabetes medicine, the way she ignored the phone every time it rang. Half the time it turned out to be her sister."

Roadie looked sideways, kicking some grass off his boot. "That right?" he said. He took a deep breath. "Well, these plans here, Doc—you want to give me a deposit, I'll run down and get some things Monday morning?"

"No," Cahill said. He waited for Roadie's face to register surprise, which it did immediately. "But I will," he said, "because it seems like closing in the porch is betting against death. Today I feel like that would be a good idea."

"You do?" Roadie said nervously.

Cahill clasped his hands. "Roadie," he said, "how often do men speak frankly? I think some of the things we've just been talking about . . . We've spoken frankly to each other."

Roadie nodded silently.

"One more thing," Cahill said. "I've never been a mystical person, but things change as you age. You'll find that out. Some things—people, even—disappear, then something else comes in to replace them." Cahill paused. "Life is like having a garden, Roadie, because inevitably the time comes when the deer eat everything, or you don't mulch and the soil gets exhausted. Right away, the weeds are in there. So I suppose what I'm getting at is that, well, tending your garden seems to me now like a young man's game. When you don't have the inclination or the energy or the . . . optimism to tend it anymore, the weeds rush in." He looked Roadie square in the eyes.

He barely knew what he had said himself. He said, "The moment you stop loving something, the moment you're inattentive, the wrong things and the wrong people take over."

"That's one of the best ways of puttin' it I ever heard," Roadie said. "I'll go back to talk to Gloria Sue, try to tell her what we discussed. There's no way I'm gonna be able to put it like you did, though."

"Express it in your own way," Cahill said. "It seems to me you love her if you're going home to talk to her."

He went to the beach, a place he'd gone only once or twice, quite early in the season, and unfolded a chair and looked at the water.

He'd never called the police in response to the flyer. He'd never spoken a word to Breezy about what the dog had done in the graveyard. He tried to think philosophically: Audrey and Matt had been involved in whatever way they'd chosen—two losers, in any case, who were no good for each other; the dog was just a dog. People projected onto dogs, so they found themselves surprised when dogs acted like dogs instead of people.

What did not change? Change was part of the natural process.

Coming to terms with what Matt had done, though, was difficult. It wasn't a matter of Matt's having been like his son, as Audrey had suggested, but, rather, that Matt seemed at times like a source of . . . what? Guidance? Ironic, thinking of what Matt might have guided him toward. But of course parents didn't tell their secrets to their children, just as the children withheld theirs from their parents.

"I didn't do it! I didn't do it!" little Joyce had cried, hand stained red, lipsticked J's all over the bathroom mirror, the bath tiles, even the toilet lid.

"You never really got involved," his wife had said, when she was still able to discuss his shortcomings. "If you don't get involved, you don't have to take responsibility. That was the way you always operated as a parent. As if you were the éminence grise, as if your family was just too much pressure. The aloof doctor."

The sadness of family life. The erosion of love until only a little rim was left, and that, too, eventually crumbled. *Rationalization:* he had been no worse a father than many. No worse than a mediocre husband. That old saying about not being able to pick your family until you married and had your own . . . People rarely remarked upon the fact that time passed, and you kept picking friends who were closer to you than family members; dogs you'd come to prefer to people. The next "family" in the line of succession could be a goldfish in a bowl, he supposed.

In front of him, a little boy in a wetsuit played with a fishing rod that dangled no lure, casting it all wrong, the way he'd learned to throw a soft-ball. His mother and father sat on a blanket, their attention focused on each other.

As the sky turned that indescribable silvery tone it often attained in late summer in Maine, Cahill rubbed his face and was surprised that his skin was still hot from the sun. A real Mainer would have worn his baseball cap. He slid a bit lower in his chair, and some time later was startled awake by squawking gulls. The charcoal-gray sky was flatlining a thin horizontal line of pale pink; the breeze had a bite to it. The couple and their child had gone, a bucket with a broken handle and a pile of shells left behind. He stood and folded the chair, scooping up his shoes with his other hand.

He drove home, appreciating what a pretty town this was, how the residents kept their houses in such good repair. Back home, he stashed the chair in the garage, where the garter snake who'd lived there contentedly for years slithered away behind piles of tied-up newspapers. His wife's plastic planters dangled from a beam, the few dried stems that remained deteriorating into dust. As he started up the walkway, he saw something suddenly dart past a bush at the side of the house, startling him so that he teetered for balance on the edge of the bricks. It was Napoleon, panting, big ears flapping.

"You listen here," he said to the dog, grabbing his collar. "You desecrated a graveyard, you—" He stopped, automatically rephrasing, in case he might not be understood. "You shit in the graveyard and knocked down the new wall!" he yelled. "You come with me."

He was dragging the dog across the lawn, though the animal dug down, clawing as if to score music, trying to stop the forward rush. The dog yelped as Cahill dragged him all the way to the wall, which was now even more caved in, though thankfully there was no more shit inside the enclosure. "Bad dog! Bad dog!" he said, jerking the collar. The dog risked further pain to turn his neck to look up at him, and what Cahill saw was fear. Fear and incomprehension. The sad squeaky sound went infinitely sharp, and Cahill realized he'd been intending to push the dog's nose against a pile of shit that was not his. It had been left by a much larger animal. Of course it had. Look at the size of the dog, and look at the pile of shit.

Instantly, he loosened his hold on the collar but stopped short of releasing it entirely, because of course the dog—any sane creature—would immediately run away.

"I'm sorry," he said, bending and putting his lips close to the dog's head, the smell of grass and dog mixed with a hint of . . . could it be lavender? "I'm sorry," he said staunchly, as if someone might overhear. Then, leaning in even closer, he risked letting go of the collar, whispering, "I misunderstood."

The Confidence Decoy

Francis would be driving his Lexus back from Maine. His wife, Bernadine, had left early that morning, taking their cat, Simple Man, home to Connecticut with her. Their son, Sheldon, had promised to be home to help out when the moving truck arrived, but that was before he'd got a phone call from his girlfriend, saying that she would be flying into J.F.K. that afternoon. So he was gone—when was Sheldon not outta there?—though the moving men were perfectly capable of unloading furniture without anyone's help. What had Bernadine imagined—that Sheldon would have ideas about decorating, about what should go where?

Francis's aunt had died, and, since he was one of only two surviving relatives and the other, Uncle Lewis, was in an assisted-living facility in California, the emptying of her summer house had fallen to Francis. Uncle Lewis had asked for the pie safe and for the bench in the entryway, nothing else, maybe an Oriental rug, if the colors were still good and it wasn't very big. Francis had rolled up the small Tabriz, which he tied with string and put in the bottom of the pie safe.

A few days earlier, Sheldon had taken his father aside to ask his advice: should he become engaged to his girlfriend now, or get the first year, or even the first two years, of law school behind him first? Sheldon and Lucy had already discussed marriage, and she seemed in no hurry, but he hadn't liked her going off to teach English in Japan with no engagement ring on her finger. Francis thought Lucy a nice young woman, pretty, neither shy nor aggressive, but, really, despite the many occasions on which they'd interacted, he could not get much of a sense of her. She'd twice been involved in car accidents in the past year, both times when she was driving, but that didn't necessarily mean anything—three times would have been more definitive. The biggest clue Francis had got about Lucy had come one morning after she'd spent the night, when she'd come down to breakfast late, wearing a T-shirt and jeans, and trailing her underpants in one leg of the jeans. Bernadine had whispered to her, and Lucy had turned bright-red and snatched up the underpants, stuffing them down the front of her jeans. She'd had no sense of humor about it at all. Well, he couldn't imagine having come downstairs at the Streetmans' (what would it be—forty-some years ago?) after sleeping with Bern, because no such thing would ever have happened. They would have had him arrested. But this was a different age, and he had no objection to Lucy's sleeping with Sheldon in their house. They put their cups and saucers in the sink, and were extremely quiet. The TV in Sheldon's bedroom never went on, as Bern had pointed out.

Bernadine said that she liked Lucy, but Francis thought she might like her only moderately. For a woman who'd wanted a daughter, Bern was quite skeptical of other people's daughters, though her skepticism about Lucy took the form of mentioning little oddities and quickly adding, "Nothing wrong with that, of course." One of the things that there was nothing wrong with was Lucy's inability to cook—her ineptitude extending even to lettuce-washing, to not understanding what a salad spinner was. She recoiled from the blender and the toaster as if they might become animated without her touching them. She drank a lot of tea, so she could boil water. But why did she resist when Bern tried to explain how other things were done in the kitchen?

Then Bern had begun finding banana peels in strange places: thrown behind a flowering bush in the garden, or pushed into a vase. "Fortunately none in the linen closet yet," Bern said wryly. She had found two or three folded inside empty toilet-paper rolls in the trash; she'd found another buried in the little trash can that held lint from the dryer.

"What do you think?" she asked Francis. "Is it some kind of eating disorder? Some comment on something or other?"

"She's realized we're monkeys," he said, curling his fingers and scratching his ribs, puckering his lips.

"It isn't funny to me, Francis, it's upsetting. I've never known anyone to stash banana peels."

"How do you know it isn't Sheldon?"

"Have you ever once known him to bring any food whatsoever into this house? He doesn't even come in eating a candy bar. I've never once seen him with a cup of takeout coffee. He's so lazy he relies entirely on the groceries I bring home."

Francis put down his newspaper and looked over the top of his glasses. "Maybe it's a mating ritual," he said, but she'd already left the room.

Now Francis stood in the hallway of his aunt's house, wondering if it would be worth it to take out the ceiling fixture and replace it with something less expensive and less unique before the real-estate agent came back. This required outguessing the people who would eventually tour the house: would they be inclined to like everything, once they'd seen such a splendid light fixture, or would they breeze past, the men concerned about the basement, the women interested in the kitchen? He was contemplating calling Bern to ask her opinion when he saw the Burwell Boys Moving truck turn in to the driveway, sending gravel flying into the peony beds. A hollyhock went flying like a spear. Low-hanging tree limbs snapped off.

Two men wearing chinos and dark-brown T-shirts hopped out. "Mr. Field? How do you do, Mr. Field?" the burlier of the two said. "Moving day, Mr. Field," the other man said, retrieving a clipboard from the passenger seat. He had a couple of feathers in his shirt pocket. "I'm Jim Montgomery. My partner here is Don O'Rourke."

"Don," the partner echoed. "We want to do a good job here, make sure you got no reason to remember us."

Both men came forward to shake Francis's hand. Jim plucked a pen from between the feathers in his pocket. "Just need your John Hancock on the line, then we can get started."

Francis signed their forms, then led the movers inside. "My aunt's summer house," he explained, giving them a quick tour. He'd supposed that everyone in the area knew that his aunt was dead, though, of course, he had no reason to suspect that she would have met these particular men.

"Aunt didn't have tons of furniture," Jim said. "She an older lady?"

"Ninety," Francis said.

Don let out a low whistle. "Make it to ninety, then a couple of crooks come in and load everything out."

Jim crouched to examine a side table, then looked at Francis. "You tagged the pieces we load last?"

"They're both in the hallway. The pie safe and the hall seat." The movers had told Bern that they would be unloading these pieces to another moving company, which would transport them to California.

"We'll get started, then," Jim said. He turned to Don. "What that remark was about us being crooks, I won't ask."

"We took those six-packs of water from behind the 7-Eleven," Don said.

He grinned at Francis. "Go to auctions, get things and distress 'em, bang 'em up and make 'em old."

Francis nodded, trying to indicate that, whatever they'd done, he did not intend to pass judgment. (It didn't much matter to him.) His wife had arranged for the moving men, who had been recommended—wasn't that what she'd said?—by the real-estate agent.

Jim and Don began issuing orders to each other, pulling furniture into the center of the room, moving quickly. Francis turned, pretending to have something to do upstairs. Over his shoulder he noticed something small on the floor and went back to see what it was, as the two men carried the Sheridan sofa out the door. It was Jim's feather. He put it on the chair cushion, where Jim would be sure to notice it, and returned to the stairs. He went up three steps, four . . . then stopped. Through the window, he saw the broken limb of a tree dangling over the front windshield of the moving truck. On the stairs, a dust ball grazed his foot, stirred up by the small breeze coming through the door. His aunt had lived to be ninety, and he was sixty-six. His son was twenty-four, which, he quickly computed, was the difference in age between his aunt and him. The computation meant nothing.

Francis had practiced law for years, and he did not think his son was at all suited to the vocation. But what was he suited to? He'd been a solid B-plus student, but he'd done very well on his law boards, and he had two very good letters of recommendation, plus one that Bern had helped him get from their congressman. Sheldon played tennis and golf, if that mattered. Lawyers were always disparaged and joked about; probably passion was not a prerequisite quality. Still, he imagined the worst: that Sheldon might get engaged to Lucy just to keep her from other men; that, yes, Lucy did have an eating disorder, and, even if she didn't, being sneaky was a problem; Sheldon would begin law school then quit—Francis was entirely sure that that was the way things would go—and then he and Lucy would rethink things, though it would be too late if they were already married, or if she was pregnant. She was pregnant. That was why she was eating the bananas, he realized, standing on his aunt's stairs, the moving men coming and going, oblivious to him. She was coming back—Lucy was coming back from Tokyo early, because she was pregnant. He and Bern would be grandparents. Sheldon would be overwhelmed with responsibility. His life would be nothing but takeout coffee. He wouldn't have time to study if he wanted to. He would be in a relationship with a woman who did not love him, and whom he did not love.

"That feather," Francis said, standing (how had he got there?) in the living room. Jim and Don were sweating. The clipboard was on a table. Both feathers were in Jim's pocket. The pen lay on the clipboard.

"Yeah?" Jim said, patting his pocket.

"What is it from?"

"From? From a bird. I picked it up because I didn't recognize it, and around here I know the birds. After the hurricane, we lost a lot, then this spring we got some others that hadn't come around before. Big bird, obviously. I've got a book at home. I'm gonna check it."

"Do you hunt?" Francis asked. He was giving in to his nervousness, making idle conversation.

"Sure," Jim said slowly. "Hunt, fish. Only go after deer with bow and arrow, though. You wouldn't be one of those people who get upset because a guy wants to eat, would ya?"

"No, no. I was just curious. Because of your interest in birds. Whether you also hunted, I mean."

"Know what else he does?" Don interrupted. "Famous for his carving."

"Oh?" was all Francis could think to say.

"Decoys," Jim said quietly, almost shyly.

"People collect 'em," Don said. "Real artistry involved. He apprenticed himself to his grandfather. His grandfather's things are in that museum in Hartford, Connecticut. You must have been there."

"The Wadsworth Atheneum," Francis said. "It's not that close to where I live."

"Well, when you go there, you look for Roy Jay Bluefield's decoys. They're beautiful things, and my friend here is the bearer of the flame."

"I'd like to see your work," Francis said.

"You would?" Jim said. "I live in a workshop that would about fit in the living room of this house. Wife put me out three years ago. You would be interested in seeing decoys?" he said again, as if he didn't quite believe it.

Francis nodded.

"Tell you what," Jim said. "You go upstairs, like you were doin', and in an hour we'll be outta here. We can swing by my place on our way to Connecticut, if you were serious."

"Oh, I was very serious. Most serious," Francis added. That was right: he had been going up the stairs, and suddenly time had gone into a warp, and now it was much later. At this moment, if the plane had landed on time, Lucy might be telling Sheldon the news. That was how your life could change: someone would tell you something.

The moving men resumed giving each other orders, furniture was lifted and shifted into other positions, then something was selected and carried down the steps to the driveway, where the big truck sat. Francis thought again about calling his wife, but realized that she would still be driving home and wouldn't answer the cell phone. She would probably stop for groceries, which she bought most days, though they both had light appetites. Their son was taller and heavier and ate more than they did, though he was big-boned, rather than heavy. Six feet; a nice-looking boy, with thick wavy hair and those square glasses that all the young people wore unapologetically now. The novel he'd worked on in college had become a novella, then had been abandoned entirely, except for sections he obsessed over and had used to apply to various M.F.A. programs, not one of which admitted him. Good or bad, Francis had no idea; Sheldon would show his writing to no one. An entire year had passed after he finished college, during which he'd lived in their attic and—a bit histrionically, Francis thought—started and abandoned a second novel. Then he had moved out and worked for a year or so with a college friend, doing ordering for the friend's father's company, even taking a trip to London. Then—how exactly had it happened?—he had let his lease expire and had moved back into the house, forgoing the attic for his old bedroom, which he repainted charcoal gray. On the weekends Lucy often joined him there.

What did they plan to do? Have the baby and live in the house?

Francis had climbed to the second floor, where his wife had packed his aunt's clothes into boxes to be donated to charity. There was toile de Jouy wallpaper in his aunt's bedroom. Near the end, his aunt, on high doses of painkiller, had thought she was stretched on a divan surrounded by a party of French aristocrats, the women dressed in feathery bonnets and carrying parasols, the men on horseback, all awaiting her cue to open celebratory bottles of champagne. Aristocrats, in a nine-by-twelve bedroom on the second floor of a house in rural Maine. Who knew what she'd made of them all being pastel blue? Perhaps that they were cold.

His aunt had died of pancreatic cancer less than two months after she was given the diagnosis. When she called them with the bad news, he and Bern had driven out to the house and cried and cried, unable to think of anything optimistic to say. His aunt had pressed jewelry on his wife, though Bern was a no-nonsense sort of woman who usually wore nothing but her wedding ring and a Timex. His aunt had told them her sensible plan for what she called "home help." She had asked him, as a complete non sequitur, to change the light bulbs in the hallway, but instead of doing this immediately they had talked more—Bern, in her strong way, had been very upset. And then he had left that night, forgetting to do the one little thing his aunt had asked of him. He had not remembered until almost the day she died.

There was a faint odor of ammonia in every room, and he thought that might be what he'd been squinting against. Bern had opened all the blinds;

it made the house look more spacious, the real-estate agent had told her. So where had his aunt's spirit gone, he wondered; had it lingered for a moment in the pastel confusion, then permeated the window—nicely beveled old glass—to alight briefly in the now smashed tree? If so, she'd had a safe landing, leaving well before the moving van pulled in.

Francis never knew what was the proper amount to tip moving men. It had probably become more than he could imagine, if the average tip in a nice restaurant was at least twenty percent, no matter how indifferent the service. He wondered if his seeing the decoys meant that he must buy one; if so, what would they cost, and shouldn't he tip the men before he got to Jim's workroom, because otherwise the price of purchase might be confused with the tip. Or, if he tipped generously in advance (whatever generously meant), might the decoy have a more reasonable price?

He backed the Lexus out to follow the moving truck down the drive. Jim drove faster than Francis expected, but he kept up, patting his pocket to make sure that his cell phone was there. They drove for a while, then turned down a rutted road where someone had put a red-and-black cone to indicate a deep pothole. The houses here were smaller than the ones on the main road. With all that he had to do, what was he doing going into the woods with two men to see decoys? It was the sort of thing that could turn out badly, though his instincts told him it would not. Still, he could imagine being in court, asking the defendant with a hint of skepticism in his voice, "You followed these two strangers to one of their houses?"

When the road forked, the truck slowed and Jim put down his window, pointing to the right with his thumb. Francis hesitated. The truck continued to the left, bumping onto a field. He thought he understood and took the right fork, stopping in front of a little clapboard house that stood alone, with no trees in front and only a half-dead bush in the side yard. It was, indeed, very small. Again he heard himself in the courtroom: "And with no hesitation you got out of your car?"

He got out. Don and Jim were walking toward him. He could tell from their faces that there was nothing to fear. Don was holding a can of seltzer. Jim—who looked much larger beside his tiny house—had a set of keys in his hand, though he used none of them to open the unlocked door.

"Used to live in a Victorian over in Milo," Jim said. "Wife comes home one day, says she's seen to it I can't come within ten feet of her. For nothing! Never laid a hand on a woman in my life. You can march into the police station, if you're a woman, and just get an order to have a guy gone from your personal space, like it hadn't been his space, too."

"Bitch," Don said, under his breath.

"Do you have children?" Francis asked.

"Children?" Jim said, somewhat puzzled. "Yeah, we had a kid that had a lot of problems that we couldn't take care of at home. One of those things," he said.

Don averted his eyes and toed a dandelion that had gone to seed.

"I'm sorry," Francis said.

Don said, "I got one wife, no kids, a bulldog, and half my life stacked up in some storage place by her brother's, since we had to downsize when the balloon came due. Downsized into my brother-in-law's garage! You know what I mean?"

He did, actually. "Yes," he said.

Jim tossed the big key ring on the worktable, which took up most of the room. There was a single bed pushed in the corner with a cat lying on it that looked something like Simple Man. The cat raised its head, then curled onto its side to continue its nap. There was a brown refrigerator in the corner opposite the bed, and a sink hung on the wall. The toilet sat next to the sink. He saw no sign of a shower.

"Sit," Don said, pulling out a canvas director's chair. Francis counted seven such chairs, most of them similar to the first, but avoided the one that sagged badly.

"Could you use a beer?" Jim said.

"That would be nice," Francis said. He told himself, I can't call my wife, because how would I explain where I am? He reached for the can of Coors, which was icy cold. He could not think of the last time he'd had a beer, rather than a Scotch-on-the-rocks. He raised the can, as they all did, in silent toast to whatever they were toasting.

It did not look as though Jim had done any work on the table recently. There were piles of newspapers, dishes, something that looked like part of a saddle. In a glass, there were some feathers. Francis wished that he could see some wood chips. The table looked too low to carve on—you would stand to carve, wouldn't you? He saw with relief that there were a few tools, but the one he focused on looked rusty. "O.K., let me get 'em out," Jim said, kneeling.

He lifted a box from under the table, opened the lid, and unwrapped a white towel inside. The box itself was beautifully made, with the word "Mallard" burned into the wood on the underside of the lid. Jim removed a duck and put it on the table.

"Un-fucking-believable," Don said, shaking his head.

Jim took a step back, cleared his throat, and said, rather formally, "Some would do it different, but I use black eyes on the mallards. Ten millimeter," he added. Francis stood with his can of beer, looking down. He wondered if he was supposed to touch it. It was quite convincing, and really beautiful. He moved forward tentatively, and, as he did, Don said, "Let me get that Coors outta your way," sweeping the can out of Francis's hand.

Francis held the decoy at a distance where he could see it clearly without putting on his reading glasses. Jim was pulling out other boxes. "Got one more to go, then I ship 'em off. Guy from Austin, Texas. He got himself an art gallery as a 'ship to' address, so maybe it doesn't matter if he's got no real idea what he's doing," Jim said. "Guy wants nothing but mallards, O.K., but if you're going to set out decoys, then, yeah, you can have mallard, mallard, mallard, mallard—lots of 'em. But you throw in one of these—" He set another box on the table, and unwrapped a beach towel. "This is your egret. You put all the mallards out there, but if you're going hunting you need something like this egret, for a confidence decoy."

Francis had never heard the term, but he understood. In any case, the egret was a real piece of art.

"Yeah, like things are just nice and casual," Don said. "An egret happens to be standing around, you know? Could be something else. A crow. Got to mix it up a little bit, so the ducks don't get suspicious. 'Hey, look down there, quite a flock of 'em, even an egret wandered in. Let's go down and see if we can join the party.'" Don put his beer and Francis's on the table. "Bang!" he said loudly.

"That's the idea," Jim said.

"How many of these did you make for the man in Texas?" Francis said. He was amazed at the detail. He stared at the black eye, and it seemed to stare back, the way it reflected light.

"Just over a dozen. If he's a hunter, which I doubt from the way he talked and looked, maybe he's been having bad luck. That'll change when he gets this confidence decoy. Might have overdone it just a bit, carving an egret, but what the hey. You know, if you've got 'em in fields, most of them will be eating, but then there's always one at least that acts as a sentry head. You think about all that while you're working. About how the whole flock's gotta look."

"Well, the detail is just incredible. You say you learned this from your grandfather?"

"Learned a couple of things on my own, I guess. Went to some shows, got some ideas."

"I do the naming," Don said. "I've got a kit. I'm enrolling in a course in special writing at night school, come fall."

"Calligraphy," Jim said. "We're a team."

"I wonder if you would be offended if someone who didn't hunt wanted a mallard just as a beautiful piece of handwork to put on his desk?" Francis asked.

Jim shrugged. "All the same to me," he said.

"May I ask what they cost?"

"Two twenty-five," Jim said. "Cost of eyes just went through the roof."

"They're worth every penny," Francis said. "They—I'm sure they do the job, but just as something to look at and contemplate . . ." He trailed off. "Would you have time to make one for me?"

"This is what I do," Jim said. "Sure."

"Well, may I give you a down payment? That, and of course I wanted to tip you, because the way you drive, you're sure to get to my house in Connecticut before I do!" Without waiting for a response, he reached into his back pocket. His finger slid through. His wallet was not there. He quickly patted his jacket pocket. Only the cell phone was inside. Then he jerked the chair back and felt shock reddening his face. He almost ran out to see if the wallet was on the ground, but tried to remember that nothing would be gained by being in a rush, by being sloppy. He walked back to the car, sensing both of them conferring silently behind him, searching too. The wallet had been full of cash, because he'd known that he would need to tip them. How would he drive without a license? He would have to notify the bank, American Express, too many places to remember.

"Bad break," Jim said, holding a can of beer toward Francis. "Worth going back to the house to look? It would be, wouldn't it?"

"This is hardly your problem," he said.

"Terrible feeling," Jim said. "I got my wallet picked at a Sox game in Boston, summer before last. Caused me no end of trouble. You think it might be back at your aunt's place?"

"It couldn't be. I mean, it could, but I would have noticed. It was empty up there."

"Let's leave the truck here and go in your car," Jim said. "Maybe it'll turn up."

"It's no use," Francis said. "I can envision where I was standing, and I know it wasn't there."

"You don't know," Don persisted. "C'mon, back we go. We'll impress you with our fast drivin'."

It was getting dark. Francis felt terrible, as if he'd lost a friend. He had lost his wallet only once before—left it behind in a hotel room, actually, and it had been returned to him empty. He tried to tell himself that twice in sixty-six years wasn't so bad, but both times had happened in the past year.

He closed his eyes to envision the second-floor room in which he'd been standing. It was something he'd trained himself to do as a lawyer, to reimagine something. Something concrete, not something abstract, like an idea.

"You prayin' or something?" Jim said and held out his hand for Francis's keys. Francis shrugged and handed them to him. At least he hadn't lost his keys.

Jim drove as if they were being chased, taking a shortcut he'd had to avoid with the truck. When they pulled in to the drive and got out, Jim began to pace the lawn, in the last of the waning light, leaving Francis and Don to go inside. Francis began looking through the first floor, feeling utterly defeated. Then he heard someone bolting up the stairs. "We got gold!" Don shouted almost immediately. "Hunt's off."

It was unbelievable; what concluded that way, so easily, so well? He couldn't believe what he heard, and stood with his head turned toward Don's voice, perplexed, allowing only the slightest tingle of relief to pass through his clenched stomach.

"What's this? Is this a wallet?" Don said, stepping off the last step into the hallway.

In that second, Francis, who had never been paranoid, realized that the wallet had been missing because Don had taken it. Hidden it somewhere. He had meant to go back later to get it. But then why had he insisted that they all come back there? Why had he produced the wallet so suspiciously soon? Why would Don do such a thing?

"Holy shit!" Jim said, giving Don a quick slap on the back when he and Francis emerged from the house. "He found it! Just like that, he found it! See?"

It was the moment when Francis, too, should have thrown his arms around Don. But he knew Don had taken the wallet. O.K.: maybe it had fallen out of his pocket, but then Don had noticed it on the floor and either pocketed it or put it somewhere where he could get it later. As sure as Francis had an instinct for anything, he knew that the man preening in front of him had both taken, and returned, the wallet. Because he wants to be the big man in his friend's eyes, Francis thought. His more talented friend, whom he wanted to impress. Don was like those firemen who set fires so they can be heroes when they extinguish them.

"Where exactly did you find it?" Francis asked when they were back in the car, not turning to look at Don.

"On the shelf in the hallway," Don answered. "Sitting right there."

Francis searched his mind, but could not remember having gone near that shelf.

Zooming again through the dark back roads, Jim seemed energized. In the back seat, Don fell silent. The silence was deafening, but Francis thought it would be rude to put on the radio when he wasn't the driver. He would almost certainly not select the sort of music Don and Jim would like. Fidgeting, he took the wallet from his breast pocket and tilted it toward him: it was accordioned-out with money. "I think I should give you the two hundred and twenty-five dollars now, rather than just a deposit. Will that be all right?" he said.

"Hey, I don't turn down an offer like that," Jim said.

"But then, separate from that, I want to thank you for working so quickly and getting everything out of there so well—I mean both of you, of course," he rushed to add. An image of the broken tree limbs sprang into his mind. He blinked. "I'm much older than you two," he said, "so will you permit me an awkwardness?"

"What's that?" Jim said.

"I've never really known exactly how to tip, when furniture is moved. Never in my life. Is there some—"

"Like you'd tip a whore," Don said.

"Excuse me?" Francis said.

"He's kidding," Jim said, disgusted.

"No, I'm not. Don't you tip whores? They name a price, and you've got to pay it, but, if you really like what they did, don't you give them a big tip and go to them again?"

"At my age, I'm not sure I'll have any more moving jobs for you, unless it's moving us into the old-age home," Francis said.

"You never went to a whore, did you?" Don said.

"Shut up," Jim said.

"I'm not bragging," Don said. "I never did it in Kuwait. I did it once in Las Vegas, and once in the Combat Zone, when one almost pulled me outta my car. She was terrible, but the one in Vegas had red hair."

"I've been to Vegas," Francis said. "But you're right—not for anyone's services. I was with Hugh Hefner, who had to fly there to pick up the sister of that month's Playmate, to help Miss November, or whoever she was, get her twin into rehab. They were only seventeen, lying that they were eighteen."

"What?" Jim said. "You're puttin' us on."

"No," Francis said, with the dismissive tone of someone telling the truth. "No, I was advising Hugh Hefner about a legal matter I'm still not free to disclose. We talked business on the plane, because we thought a trial might be coming up soon. I found him to be a gentleman. This was long before he went everywhere in pajamas."

They rode in silence for a moment. Then Jim said, "So did it work out O.K. with the sister?"

"She completed rehab but died in a skiing accident," Francis said. He could feel it as if it were yesterday: Hefner's broken voice on the phone, going straight into his ear.

"You wouldn't have struck me as the sort of guy who hung out with Hugh Hefner," Don said.

"I was a lawyer," Francis said. "Lawyers meet all kinds of people." He let the comment hang in the air. What he still did not know was how one calculated a tip. He decided to delay payment until the furniture was unloaded, which might have been the way to do it, in the first place.

By the time they got on the road with the truck, it was after ten o'clock. They drove for a while, and then Francis blinked his lights several times; eventually, Jim responded by pulling to the side of the road. It was late and Francis was tired. He asked Jim if they could check into a motel. The two detours had cost them several hours, and Francis was having trouble staying awake. He was worried for Jim, as well, and insisted on paying for their room. Jim thought it over for a second. "Sure," he said.

Half an hour later, as they registered for two rooms at a Hampton Inn, Francis handed Jim a folded-up wad of money. "For the decoy," he said solemnly, as the night clerk handed them their key cards. Don had fallen asleep in the truck but stumbled out, groggily, when he realized where they were. He stood outside the door on the passenger side, blinking, his hair matted. He looked young, and helpless, and for a second Francis felt sympathy for him—he'd acted impulsively, then regretted what he'd done, because he wasn't a bad guy, after all. Tough lives, both of them had. Fighting in the Gulf War. Having a damaged child.

Jim said that he would wake Francis early if he was sure he wanted to follow the truck. Why did he want to follow them? But Francis insisted that he did, and then Jim and Don hopped back in the truck to drive to a faraway but well-lit area that the clerk had said was for large vehicles. They went their separate ways without saying good night.

"Bern?" he said, sitting on the side of his bed.

"God! I thought you'd never call!" she said. "Where are you?"

"A Hampton Inn," he said. "Has everything gone to hell?"

"It's terrible," she said. "Lucy's mother calling, like a woman possessed, forgetting it's three hours later on the East Coast, and poor Lucy at wit's end, trying to calm her. And Francis, it is unbelievable to me, but Sheldon is no help whatsoever. He went out for a walk! A walk! If I were Lucy, I'd never speak to him again."

The non-smoking room smelled of cigarette smoke. Did it come as a surprise to him that people did not follow rules, when unobserved? He pinched the tip of his nose between thumb and finger, let go, but the itching continued. He rubbed his nose. "What is her mother so upset about?" he said.

"The crash landing! What do you think she's upset about? Three people died."

Francis let his mouth drop open. "Crash landing? The plane crashed?"

"You heard it on the radio, didn't you? Somewhere?"

"No," he said.

"You didn't? Then what did you mean by asking—"

"I thought there was trouble between them," he said.

"I just assumed you'd heard. They almost didn't let the passengers who survived leave the airport. The investigators are coming to our house, Francis, at the crack of dawn. Something about someone on the plane telling his seatmate it was going to happen. Francis, go turn on the television."

Francis didn't move. He took in what she'd said with dumb shock.

"And Francis," she said, "I do not have the slightest idea how we raised a son who could not reach out and comfort poor Lucy—who stalked off, instead, to take a walk."

"Maybe he lives in his own head, like his father."

"This is not the time to reproach me for criticizing you, Francis. Whether you do or do not live in your own little world, in the larger world, poor Lucy was two seats behind someone who died."

"Horrible," he murmured. "He's still on his walk? Would it help if I spoke to Lucy, do you think?"

"I've given her an Ambien, poor thing. Her mother is hysterical about the U.S. government and wants to give us all a civics lesson, dragging in the war in Iraq. She's a terrible woman."

"Lucy's asleep upstairs?" he said. He suddenly felt quite exhausted himself.

"Yes, of course. What did you think—that I'd have her stretch out on the sofa?" His wife's voice broke.

"We're coming home first thing in the morning," he said.

"Who is 'we'?"

"The moving men. There was some confusion about my wallet and we were delayed. I thought it best to put us all up at a motel. We'll set out first thing in the morning."

"What do you mean, 'confusion'?"

"One of them took my damned wallet, then felt remorse and returned it. But do not breathe a word of this to either of them, do you understand? I want to remain cordial and simply conclude this move."

She sniffed. "I suppose it's very late, and I might not be understanding you," she said. "You have the wallet, you and the moving men will be on your way. All right. But tell me, Francis—what do I say to our son about his behavior, when he returns?"

"That he's an insensitive asshole, I guess."

"I don't think I should cross him," she said quietly. "He got very angry when Lucy's mother upset her, as if that was Lucy's doing."

"Get some sleep," he said.

"We've raised an immature idiot," she said.

He nodded, but of course she could not see him. "Sleep," he repeated.

"He has a screw missing," she said.

"See you tomorrow, early," he said.

"You have your wallet? That all worked out all right, did it?"

"It worked out," he said.

She said, "For God's sake, turn on the television."

At the Continental-breakfast buffet, he saw Jim sitting alone at a circular table. Jim had piled two Danish pastries onto a napkin—for Don, Francis was sure. A cup of coffee sat on the table, with a lid on the cup. "Didn't hear the news until this morning," Jim said. "Seems like plane stuff happens a lot more than it ought to."

"Do they know what caused it?" Francis asked.

Jim looked at him. He seemed more tired than he had when they checked in. He had circles under his eyes, dark, like a raccoon's. "They tell us what they want us to hear," he said.

"Your friend Don," Francis said, pulling back a plastic chair. "He obviously looks up to you."

"He wanted the two of us to spring my son and take care of him, you know that? Go on welfare and take care of him." Jim shook his head. "He's somethin'," he said.

"Would that not be at all possible?" Francis said.

"No, it wouldn't," Jim said. "You'd know that in one second."

"He miscalculated, then. He obviously looks up to you," Francis said again.

"Yeah, well, it's no 'Brokeback Mountain,'" Jim said, taking a big bite of his bagel.

Francis tried again: "I think he might do things—say things, maybe—to impress you."

"Scare me, is more like it. My son's a pretzel," he said. "Not one doctor, ever, thought anybody could take care of him anywhere but in an institution." He got up. "Ten minutes, out front," he said.

Francis stood to get some coffee. "I hope I didn't offend you by asking whether Don's idea might have some viability," he said.

"No, it's just that Don's not my kid and sometimes it feels like he is." Jim started for the door, shaking his head. Then he turned back. "If he pressured you into saying you wanted one of the decoys and you don't, no hard feelings."

"He didn't do that. I want one very much. You do beautiful work. You're a real artist," Francis said.

Jim nodded slowly. "My grandfather was better, back twenty years ago, but I stick with it, and every now and then I learn something."

"The price is very reasonable," Francis said.

"If I have more money or less money things are about the same, I notice."

"You didn't feel you had to quote me a low price, for any reason?" Francis asked.

Jim looked at him.

"You know, it might be a little tense at my house. My son's girlfriend was on that plane. That's bad enough, but she's also pregnant, and he doesn't want to marry her."

A look of concern flickered over Jim's face. "You're full of surprises today," he said. He seemed to be debating continuing on his way or staying rooted to the spot. "Tell him not to," he said. "If he'll listen to your advice."

"I wanted to prepare you, because there might be a bit of tension in the air," Francis said.

"We'll just carry the furniture in. Leave," Jim said. "We're just the moving men."

"My wife sometimes deals with her anxiety by remaining rather aloof."

Jim nodded. "Not lookin' to make friends with your wife," he said.

"Five minutes?" Francis said.

"About," Jim said, turning and walking across the breakfast area's chaotic carpeting, which looked like shards from a broken kaleidoscope, the wild colors dusted with crumbs.

"Your friend Don," Francis said, coming up behind Jim. "Is he like a bad kid, sometimes? Does the wrong thing?"

"That's shit-shootin' sure," Jim said. "But what can you do?"

"I don't know what to do about my son," Francis said. "Like you said—he's my son. He isn't very likely to listen to me."

Jim nodded. "Worth a try to stop him from marrying somebody he doesn't want to marry," he said. "Life doesn't hold a lot of happy surprises."

"That's exactly what I think," Francis said.

"Friends, family, they get you every time," Jim said.

With that, Francis felt sure that Jim had known about Don and the wallet, or at least he'd known that Don was capable of having hidden the dropped wallet so that he could return for it later. Otherwise, what would they have been talking about? Friends and family?

Francis took a deep breath and entered the oppressively gray-walled bedroom where Lucy lay facing the window. She had told his wife that she and Sheldon had been writing and talking to each other, and that they had decided to separate, but at the last minute she'd e-mailed him from Japan and asked him to come to the airport. Then she had done a very bad thing: she had insisted, when she was finally allowed to leave J.F.K., that he wouldn't have cared if she had died. She wanted it both ways: to break up with him, and also to have him love her. Lucy told Francis that Sheldon had pointed that out, calmly but coldly, and when she would not let up he had stalked out of the house. So it hadn't been as simple as Bern had reported.

Still, he knew there was more. She did not look pregnant, but maybe she just wasn't showing yet. Or maybe she had done something about it.

"Lucy," he said, sitting down on the bed, "when I practiced law, I was often successful because I followed my instincts. I used to clear my head by closing my eyes and letting my mind drift until I admitted to myself what I knew. Lucy?"

"You and your wife have been very good to me. I don't know why your son holds you at a distance, but when I was here I was imitating him, for no good reason. I guess I was wary, because I've always been overwhelmed by my parents. My mother, in particular."

"Before we get off track," he said. "Because my mind does wander and I do get off track when I shouldn't. I quit practicing law before other people noticed that—good to quit when you're still on top. But my mind wandered somewhere recently and it came to me that you were pregnant."

She rolled toward him and stared, wide-eyed. Perhaps it was the background—the gray walls—that made her look unusually pale. "How could you know that?" she whispered.

"Do you want to know? Because of the bananas," he said. "Though it was Bern who noticed the banana skins."

"Oh my God," Lucy said. She rolled away, facing the window again.

"But she didn't put it together," he said. "I didn't either, at first. Maybe if you'd left out empty jars of marshmallow cream and pizza boxes, it would have been easier."

"Just bananas," she said.

He nodded.

"You know, and you hate me," she said.

"Hate you? Bern and I like you. It's our son whose behavior—even if you were mixed up, jet-lagged, scared to death . . . still. He should have been more understanding."

"Where is he?"

"I'm not clairvoyant," he said. "Sometimes I close my eyes and things come to me, but most times they don't."

"What are you going to do?" she said.

"Me? Would it be O.K. to ask what you're going to do?" He looked at her long, thin legs. Her flat belly. "Or what you've done?"

She sprang up suddenly. She said, "I'm afraid to tell him. I don't know if I missed him because I wanted to convince myself that I loved him, or whether I really do. My mother will kill me. She put me on birth-control pills when I was thirteen."

"You returned early because you have to deal with this," he said.

She nodded.

"He'll come back, and you two have to talk it over."

"Does your wife know?" she said.

"No."

"You didn't tell your wife?"

"I thought I was right, but I wasn't sure," he said. "In fact, if I'd been wrong, it would have taken me down a peg. It would have made me wonder whether something else I'd just recently figured out might not have been wrong, too."

"What might have been wrong?" she said.

"Oh, that someone stole my wallet, then decided to look like a hero by finding it."

"You knew the person who took it?" she asked. "Did you tell him that you knew?"

"Why would you assume it was a man?" he said.

"What?"

It wasn't the time to play with her, she was in a bad way—she didn't realize that he was trying to tease her into examining her assumptions. He said, "No, because I couldn't prove it. But I more or less told his best friend, the one he wanted to impress, that I'd realized what was going on."

He put his hands on his knees, getting ready to stand. She shifted her weight onto her hip, following him with her eyes. "Do you know what I should do?" she asked, as he stood. "I don't have a lot of time."

He thought about it. "I'd think you'd want to talk this over with Sheldon, as soon as he shows up."

"Nothing tells you that he won't show up?"

He smiled. He'd impressed her too easily, when usually he understood very little. Common sense told him that his son—his lazy, spoiled son— would return to the family home, if only because there was nowhere else for him to go. Even now, he could sense Sheldon watching, the way ducks circled decoys, waiting for some instinctive sense that everything looked right, that it was safe to move in; fooled by the sentry heads (that would be Bern, sitting in her chair with her embroidery, her head cocked in semi-disbelief at the way her life was turning out). The mallards would look harmonious, feeding as they bobbed on the water, much the way lawyers struck a pose to suggest how effortlessly they kept themselves afloat. Then the eye would travel to the oddly lovely egret, who just happened to have landed in his bed, having drifted in after a long flight. Francis smiled at his own conjecturing: who was really the writer in the family, he wondered. His son would keep himself apart a bit longer, making his calculations: Things in place? Feeding time? The most ordinary of things going on? The egret would verify the ordinary by interjecting something different. But then—to extend the metaphor— his son would be wrong, and he would fall into a trap, though not a deadly one: nothing worse than domesticity, nothing he couldn't escape. Francis thought that he, himself, might have left long before, when he first realized that he'd married a good woman, but not a woman he would die for, and that their only child was deeply flawed. Did he regret having stayed? No. He had never believed in the idea of perfection. Nor did he believe that he was owed a reward for staying: Jim's mallard would merely represent the receipt of something he had paid for.

It did not ever arrive, with or without its white towel, with or without its burnished coffin, and he did not pursue it. In two days' time, though, his son returned home.

About the Author

Ann Beattie has been included in four O. Henry Award collections and in John Updike's *Best American Short Stories of the Century*. In 2000, she received the PEN/Malamud Award for achievement in the short story form. In 2005, she received the Rea Award for the Short Story. She and her husband, Lincoln Perry, live in Key West, Florida, and Charlottesville, Virginia, where she is Edgar Allan Poe Professor of Literature and Creative Writing at the University of Virginia.